MILAN
The Houses of Visconti & Sforza

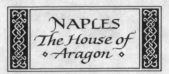

NAPLES
The House of Aragon

Gian Galeazzo Visconti
(B. 1351 – D. 1402)
DUKE OF MILAN
(1395–1402)

Filippo Maria Visconti
(B. 1389 – D. 1447)
DUKE OF MILAN
(1412–1447)

Valentina Visconti
(B. 1366 – D. 1408)
m.
Louis de Valois
DUC D'ORLÉANS

Alfonso I
(B. 1385 – D. 1458)
FIRST ARAGONESE
KING OF NAPLES
(1442–1458)

Bianca Maria Visconti
(ILLEG., B. 1424 – D. 1468)
DUCHESS OF MILAN
m.

Ferrante I
(B. 1424)

Francesco Sforza
(B. 1401 – D. 1...)
DUKE OF M...
(1450–14...)

Galeazzo Mar...
(B. 1444, assass...
DUKE OF ...
(1466...
m.
Bona of ...
(B. 14...
DUCHESS ...
(1468...

...onora
...agon
...155)
...HESS
...RARA
...n.
...d'Este
...FERRARA
...73)

Gian Galea...
(B. 14...
DUKE OF ...
(147...
m.
Isabella ...
(14...

...Aragon
...MILAN
...Sforza
...LAN

Frances...
(B. 1...
COUNT O...

DUCHESS
OF MILAN

DUCHESS
OF MILAN

MICHAEL ENNIS

VIKING

VIKING
Published by the Penguin Group
Viking Penguin, a division of Penguin Books USA Inc.,
375 Hudson Street, New York, New York 10014, U.S.A.
Penguin Books Ltd, 27 Wrights Lane, London W8 5TZ, England
Penguin Books Australia Ltd, Ringwood, Victoria, Australia
Penguin Books Canada Ltd, 10 Alcorn Avenue, Suite 300,
Toronto, Ontario, Canada M4V 3B2
Penguin Books (N.Z.) Ltd, 182–190 Wairau Road, Auckland 10, New Zealand

Penguin Books Ltd, Registered Offices:
Harmondsworth, Middlesex, England

First published in 1992 by Viking Penguin,
a division of Penguin Books USA Inc.

1   3   5   7   9   10   8   6   4   2

LIBRARY OF CONGRESS CATALOGING IN PUBLICATION DATA
Ennis, Michael.
Duchess of Milan / Michael Ennis.
p.   cm.
ISBN 0-670-83783-0
1. Isabella, d'Aragona, Duchess of Milan, consort of Gian Galeazzo
Sforza, 1470–1524—Fiction.   2. Beatrice, consort of Lodovico Sforza
il Moro, Duke of Milan, 1475–1497—Fiction.   3. Milan (Italy)–
—History—To 1535—Fiction.   I. Title.
PS3555.N63D83   1992
813'.54—dc20   91–26983

Printed in the United States of America
Set in Bembo
Designed by Katy Riegel
Endpapers by Anita Karl and James Kemp.

TO ELLEN AND ARIELLE

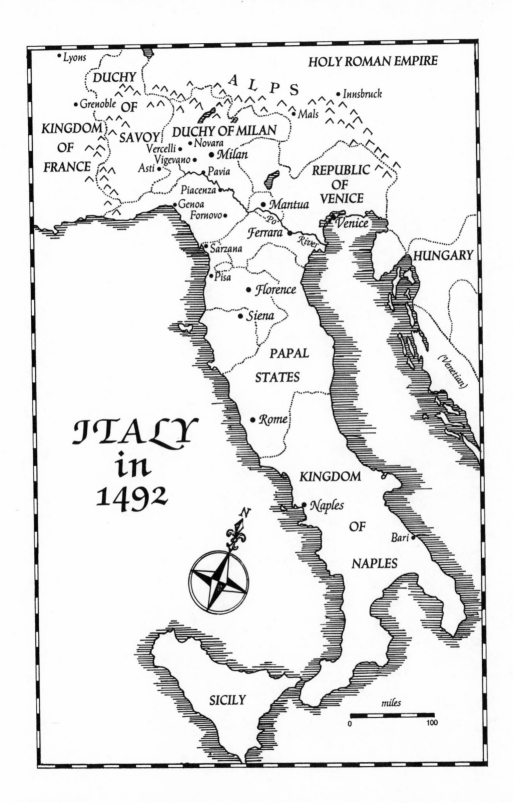

HOLY ROMAN EMPIRE

• Lyons

DUCHY

A L P S

• Innsbruck

• Grenoble OF

• Mals

KINGDOM

SAVOY DUCHY OF MILAN

OF

Vercelli • • Novara

REPUBLIC

FRANCE

Vigevano • • Milan

OF

Asti •

• Pavia

VENICE

Piacenza

• Genoa

• Mantua

Fornovo •

Po

• Venice

Ferrara

River

HUNGARY

• Sarzana

• Pisa

• Florence

• Siena

PAPAL

(Venetian)

STATES

ITALY
in
1492

• Rome

KINGDOM

N

• Naples

OF

• Bari

NAPLES

SICILY

miles

0   100

PREFACE

All histories are fiction. Poets were the first historians, and until relatively recent times the job was left to professional apologists, liars, and storytellers. Today's practitioners simply apply modern academic prejudices to this timeless legacy of slander, cover-ups, and geopolitical public relations. With that caution in mind, *Duchess of Milan* is a work of fiction that claims to be unusually faithful to history. The characters and events in this novel, all of whom actually lived and all of which actually took place, have been re-created as accurately as possible from letters, paintings, archives, and on-site research. The resulting drama represents a novelist's answers to questions that have kept historians guessing—and writing their own fictions—for five hundred years.

The last decade of the fifteenth century was one of the most fateful junctures in the history of the world—but not because a Genoese sea captain named Cristoforo Colombo made landfall on a few Caribbean islands in 1492. Mariners bumping into uncharted islands, whether off the Atlantic coast of Africa or slightly farther to the west, were rather ordinary news events for late-fifteenth-century cosmopolites. To the people who actually lived at the time of the discovery of the Americas it was Renaissance Italy, in the full flush of its commercial might and cultural splendor, that represented the most astonishing new world. And it was in Italy in the 1490s that history would be irrevocably fractured and re-aligned, set in a pattern that has determined the fate of nations, in the new world as well as the old, far into our own century.

At the epicenter of this historic upheaval was the relationship between two young women: Isabella of Aragon, the twenty-year-old wife of Gian Galeazzo Sforza, the Duke of Milan; and Beatrice d'Este, the teenage bride of Lodovico Sforza, known as "Il Moro," Duke of Bari, regent for the Duke of Milan, and the most im-portant man of a momentous time. But during that crucial decade, no man shook the earth quite like the passions of Beatrice and Isabella. Before their hearts were spent, they had changed the world forever.

DUCHESS
OF MILAN

CAST OF CHARACTERS

Principal Characters

ALFONSO OF ARAGON (b.1448), DUKE OF CALABRIA: Father of Isabella of Aragon; son of Ferrante and heir to the Kingdom of Naples.

BEATRICE D'ESTE (b.1475), DUCHESS OF BARI: Wife of Lodovico Sforza, "Il Moro"; first cousin of Isabella of Aragon.

BONA OF SAVOY (b.1448), DUCHESS MOTHER OF MILAN: Mother of Gian Galeazzo Sforza, the Duke of Milan; aunt to King Charles VIII of France.

CECILIA GALLERANI (b.1465), Il Moro's mistress.

CHARLES VIII (b.1470), KING OF FRANCE: Nephew of Bona of Savoy; first cousin of the Duke of Milan.

ELEONORA D'ESTE (b.1455), DUCHESS OF FERRARA: Beatrice's mother; daughter of Ferrante of Aragon.

ERCOLE D'ESTE (b.1431), DUKE OF FERRARA: Beatrice's father.

FERRANTE OF ARAGON (b.1424), KING OF NAPLES: Beatrice's maternal grandfather; Isabella of Aragon's paternal grandfather.

GALEAZZO DI SANSEVERINO, referred to as **GALEAZZ** (b.1461): Captain General of the Armies of Milan.

GIAN GALEAZZO SFORZA, referred to as **GIAN** or **GIAN GALEAZZO** (b.1469), DUKE OF MILAN: Husband of Isabella of Aragon; nephew of Il Moro.

ISABELLA OF ARAGON (b.1471), DUCHESS OF MILAN: First cousin of Beatrice; daughter of Alfonso.

ISABELLA D'ESTE, referred to as **THE MARQUESA** or **BEL** (b.1474), MARQUESA OF MANTUA: Beatrice's sister; wife of Francesco Gonzaga, Captain General of the Armies of Venice.

LODOVICO SFORZA, known as **IL MORO** (b.1451), DUKE OF BARI and regent for the Duke of Milan: Beatrice's husband; uncle to Gian Galeazzo Sforza, the Duke of Milan.

A genealogical chart showing the ruling houses of Italy and France in 1491 appears on the endpapers of this book.

Supporting Characters

Ambrogio da Rosate: Chief physician and astrologer at the Court of Milan.

Anne de Beaujeu: Sister of King Charles VIII, and his regent; *de facto* ruler of France.

Antonello di Sanseverino: Exiled Prince of Salerno; uncle of Galeazzo di Sanseverino; adviser to Charles VIII.

Bernard Stuart d'Aubigny: Adviser to King Charles VIII; head of French embassy to Milan in 1491.

Bernardino da Corte: Assistant castellan of Porta Giovia and Il Moro's chief of security.

Bianca Sforza (b.1480): Illegitimate daughter of Il Moro.

Bianca Maria Sforza (b.1473): Sister of the Duke of Milan; daughter of Bona of Savoy; later, wife of Emperor Maximilian.

Count Carlo Belgioioso: Milanese ambassador to France.

Francesco Gonzaga: Marquis of Mantua; Captain General of the Armies of Venice; husband of Isabella d'Este.

Francesco Sforza (b.1490): Count of Pavia and heir to the Duchy of Milan. Son of Isabella of Aragon and Gian Galeazzo Sforza.

Giacomo Trotti: Ferrarese ambassador to Milan.

Girolamo da Tuttavilla: Senior diplomat at the Court of Milan.

Guillaume de Briconnet: Bishop of St. Malo, later Cardinal. Principal adviser to King Charles VIII.

Leonardo da Vinci: Engineer and painter at the Court of Milan; employed by Il Moro beginning 1482.

Louis de Valois, referred to as **Louis Duc d'Orléans**: Duke of Orleans; cousin of Charles VIII and First Prince of the Blood. Claimant to the Duchy of Milan by virtue of descent from Valentina Visconti.

Maximilian: Archduke of Austria; later, Holy Roman Emperor (referred to as **German Emperor**).

Polissena Romei: Matron of honor to Beatrice d'Este.

Vincenzo Calmeta: Beatrice's secretary; poet.

Deceased

Bianca Maria Sforza, née Visconti (b.1424, d.1468): Il Moro's mother; wife of Francesco Sforza; illegitimate daughter of Filippo Maria Visconti (see below).

Filippo Maria Visconti (b.1389, d.1447): Last Duke of Milan representing the House of Visconti, which had ruled in Milan since 1277.

Francesco Sforza (b.1401, d.1466): Il Moro's father; first Sforza Duke of Milan (1450–1466). A famed *condottiere*—mercenary commander—employed by the Visconti, he was wedded to Filippo Maria Visconti's illegitimate daughter Bianca Maria, and claimed the title of Duke of Milan when Filippo Maria died without a legitimate heir.

Galeazzo Maria Sforza (b.1444, assassinated 1476): Eldest son of Francesco Sforza; Duke of Milan from 1466 until his death. Il Moro's brother; husband of Bona of Savoy and father of Gian Galeazzo Sforza, the Duke of Milan.

PROLOGUE

Milan, December 1490

"Massage the soft parts." The voice of Messer Ambrogio da Rosate, chief physician and astrologer at the Court of Milan, soughed mysteriously from his dotage-slackened lips.

The Duchess of Milan could not hear this whispered prescription, even though she was seated in the birthing chair directly beneath Messer Ambrogio's watery gaze. But she observed the physician motioning silently with the tips of his fingers and the midwife reaching for her like a taloned Harpy materializing from the black haze of her pain and fear. In that moment the Duchess detected the first glimmer of the light, and she told herself that she must fly toward it.

"Get away from me, *puttana!* If you touch me there again I will kick you in yours!" the Duchess heard herself scream, though only distantly. She believed that it was not her muffled voice but the light, an abstract golden fog in which she could float, that somehow had made the midwife recoil. The Duchess pulled back the fine woolen chemise draped over her upper thighs. She placed her fingers to her distended, searingly numb "soft parts" and felt her baby's smooth wet skull. "He's coming! *Al nome d'Iddio Gesù,* he's coming!" She arched her back, and the push was so powerful

5

that she imagined the light sucking her insides out. She groaned as if possessed, then shrieked: "Get your back against the chair, you dribbling bitch!"

The midwife, joined by one of the Duchess's ladies-in-waiting, scurried to brace the heavy oak birthing chair. Messer Ambrogio motioned for his assistant to lift the Duchess's chemise, and he crouched to peer between her legs. His wiry eyebrows arched with alarm, and he moved swiftly to the door, trailing his long velvet cape. He stepped into the hallway and confronted the chamberlain posted by the door. "The witnesses." Messer Ambrogio gasped for a reinforcing breath. "Bring the witnesses in again. I am certain that this time the Duchess will give birth."

Within a few minutes a half-dozen men, all of them ranking clerics in heavy damask cassocks or officers of state in embroidered silk tunics and bright woolen hose, stood peering at the bloody head emerging from beneath the hem of the Duchess's chemise. Messer Ambrogio motioned for his assistant to pull up the hem again so that the witnesses could irrefutably testify to the infant's authenticity. The Duchess glared far beyond the gentlemen's pontifical nods, her gray-green eyes lit from within.

The head popped out. Perspiration streaked the Duchess's cheeks, and her neck corded. The midwife palmed the head and began to tug. The Duchess showed her teeth and snarled, "Don't pull him, *cacapensieri.*" The midwife cradled the head passively, and the Duchess returned to her reverie. The shoulders emerged, and with two slippery, rhythmic surges, the baby slid into the midwife's hands. As the midwife raised the glistening arrival, the witnesses observed the sex and began to murmur gravely.

The Duchess peered through the golden nimbus that framed her vision. Her baby's bloated claret scrotum seemed as intensely hued as a polished gemstone. A river of emotion ran through her, and she conjured an image: Dame Fortune, drifting beside her in a robe woven of light, smiling at her, a smile more brilliant than the sun, and handing her her baby. Her son. The next Duke of Milan.

The midwife began to lower the bawling infant to the porcelain tub of tepid water set beside the birthing chair. The Duchess reached out swiftly and snatched him away. "I made him," she snapped, her upper lip curled. She wiped the cheesy white vernix from his face with the hem of her chemise. He stopped crying, and sputtered and coughed. The Duchess looked up at the witnesses. "You've seen my son. Get out." The gentlemen murmured again, bowed, and exited.

Messer Ambrogio's assistant ligatured and cut the umbilical cord while the child was still in the Duchess's arms. When the Duchess convulsed to pass the afterbirth, the midwife reached for the baby. "Don't touch him!" The midwife, her beefy face flushed, drew back. After a moment the placenta oozed out and slapped the floor. Messer Ambrogio's assistant scooped the discarded pulp into a silver dish. "Take what is yours and leave me," the Duchess said. Messer Ambrogio whispered to the midwife, bowed, and led his helper from the room.

"Help me out of my chemise." The Duchess's voice was suddenly calmer, almost seductive, as if she were urging a lover. The midwife and the lady-in-waiting guided the sweat-and-blood-sodden garment over the Duchess's head. The Duchess kneaded a nipple, then stroked her baby's cheek; the infant opened his eyes, and his head wobbled as he searched for the pap.

"Your Highness . . . ," the midwife protested. Her eyes widened as she studied the almost blasphemous vision of the Duchess of Milan: a naked madonna, seated in a chair that resembled an instrument of torture, legs splayed to reveal her bloodied genitals, suckling her child with the weary ecstasy of a woman exhausted by lovemaking. "Your Highness, you have had an extremely difficult birth. . . ."

The Duchess heard nothing except a huge rushing of wind and light, carrying her away. "My son," she whispered as she fingered his hot, sticky head. "*Gesù*, I have made a son."

· PART ·

ONE

C H A P T E R

1

Letter of ISABELLA D'ESTE DA GONZAGA, Marquesa of Mantua, to her sister-in-law ELISABETTA GONZAGA, Duchess of Urbino. Pavia, 19 January 1491

My dearest and most desperately missed companion,

My sister Beatrice is no longer a virgin! After three postponements, Father's threats, and not least our journey in the most execrable conditions (I thought I was going to have to sleep with my sister's horrid old matron of honor Polissena, she was so cold—and I was so cold I would have been happy to do so!), it has finally happened. The wedding was three days ago, here in Pavia, as Il Moro must avoid any suggestion that he considers himself the Duke of Milan. I can now tell you with certainty that despite the name by which he is known—and all the jests with which we have plagued poor Beatrice—Il Moro is not a Moor or any other sort of *negre!* His hair is black, his skin fair, and the regal fashion in which he carries himself reminds me of the statue of a Roman emperor they have here. But he appears younger than I had expected, given his age (one year shy of forty) and how important everyone (himself included!) believes him to be. Beatrice is terrified of him! Fortunately he spent most of their time

11

together attending to me. We arrived Sunday afternoon after journeying by water from Piacenza (there is ice along the banks of all the rivers, and the canals are frozen entirely in the mornings) and were allowed a day to thaw before the ceremony. Il Moro showed us about the *castello* here, and I can now verify that everything they say about his wealth is true. The silver, the majolica, the paintings, the jewels, the glassware, the tapestries, the books— there is a *Chanson de Roland* with a pearl-and-gold binding, done God knows where (I don't believe there is even a shop in Flanders that could do it), that has got to be worth over twenty thousand ducats. *Per mia fe!* It occurs to me while I am writing you this that you don't know about the necklace Il Moro sent Beatrice (it arrived after I left last summer—a peace offering to Father, who is not here regardless). Fifteen large pearls set in gold flowers, with a ruby pendant surrounded by pearls and emeralds. Two hundred thousand ducats!

Despite her new wealth, Beatrice was bedded in the usual barbaric fashion. Everyone came in the room with their noise-makers, jerking the strings up and down like drooling peasants masturbating and making a clamor like a cloud of shrieking locusts. Fortunately Beatrice's tears did not come until the next morning, by which time her husband was already back in Milan. I am not exaggerating! He cannot have been alone with her for more than a half hour. He showed the sheet, with a single spot where he might have spit (though Beatrice later confirmed that he achieved penetration), and rode off while it was still dark. Mama insists that he is merely anxious to see that everything goes well when we arrive in Milan. I am of the belief that Mama is keeping a secret—I know you have already guessed.

Tomorrow we will depart by canal for Milan, and we expect to complete our journey on Sunday morning. The Duchess of Milan is going to receive us at a church near the docks, after which we will join Il Moro and the Duke of Milan and all proceed through Milan in suitable panoply. Do you know that the Duchess of Milan is our cousin? In fact she and Beatrice grew up together in Naples. We visited there when we were little girls, and Mama left Beatrice behind with grandfather—she was there for eight years. Mama is already worried that the Duchess of Milan will regard Beatrice as a rival—everyone here believes that Il Moro intends to make himself Duke of Milan. As if he isn't already in all but name! The Duke of Milan (we have not met him yet) is said to do nothing but chase after stags and drink like a friar, while Il Moro runs the state like a Florentine bank—you do not see him without a secretary at his elbow. But the Duke of Milan should be more secure now that he has provided his heir. The *puttino* is six weeks old— I am choking with envy this very moment just thinking about their good fortune. I got my out-of-ordinaries three weeks ago and will have no happiness until I am reunited with my husband and can try again.

It seems a thousand years since I have enjoyed your kisses and caresses. I am hoping you are in better health since your last letter.

Your most adored, most special friend,

Isabella d'Este da Gonzaga, by her own hand

Milan, 21 January 1491

"Eels." Polissena Romei, matron of honor to Beatrice d'Este, the newly wed Duchess of Bari, rapidly bobbed her seemingly bald head like an irate infant buzzard; her wizened forehead had been plucked for so many years in that long-discarded fashion that her hairline had given up and was now lost inside her black velour widow's hood. Polissena's fiercely indignant eyes remained fixed on Beatrice and the Marquesa of Mantua, who stood behind her sister, fastidiously straightening the ribbons encasing the bride's thick, waist-length braid. Polissena venomously addressed Beatrice's mother. "Your Highness, the Duchess and the Marquesa have been eating pickled eels, and now the Duchess is obstructed. I warned the Duchess in Pavia that she was eating too many, but of course her sister the Marquesa encouraged her to devour enough for a grown man. The Duchess thinks that she can eat so richly at supper and then, simply because she plays tennis afterward, will not suffer from an obstruction of her bowels. The Duchess of Bari now suffers chronically from obstruction."

"*Che chiacchiera,*" the Marquesa snapped, her tone suited to the vulgarity of the expression: what horseshit. She was sixteen years old and already one of Italy's most celebrated beauties: full, erotic lips, an exquisite milk-and-rose complexion, a figure that tended to voluptuousness, and, as her crowning glory, an extravagant halo of pearl-laced blond curls. She wore an enormous puffy coat called a *cioppa,* made entirely of black sable, along with a matching muff fashioned from a whole skin; there was a curious correspondence between the dead sable's belligerent, strangely animate stare and the Marquesa's lively dark eyes.

Undeterred by the Marquesa's lack of contrition, Polissena swiveled her palsied head as if she intended to admonish the entire wedding party gathered on the dockside piazza. At the perimeter, several hundred Ferrarese gentlemen, sheathed in black steel ceremonial armor, had already mounted and were arranging themselves into contingents beneath silk banners. Within this mounted cordon, order had yet to be imposed. Ferrarese noblewomen, wrapped in brocade-and-fur *cioppe,* gems and pearls sparkling like ice in their hair, chattered at their secretaries and chamberlains; chaplains in their cassocks, pressed into emergency service, joined the tailors and maidservants in making last-minute adjustments to the ladies' coiffures and couture. A dozen ducal singers assembled around two sheets of music while grooms saddled their caparisoned horses. Beatrice's uncle, Cardinal Sigismondo d'Este, sipped a sugared liqueur from a silver cup; a priest picked lint from the Cardinal's red velvet cape. A dwarf in a miniature suit of black armor scooted through the crowd, swishing past women's hems and barking nonsensical commands.

Eleonora d'Este, the Duchess of Ferrara, flipped a pudgy hand at her chief of protocol. "Messer Niccolò! Move them along now! The Duchess of Milan is waiting on us!" She turned, propped her palms on well-padded hips, and confronted her newly wed daughter.

Ignoring her mother's cue, Beatrice continued to stare at the cobbled pavement. A woman's tragedy might have been read in the subtle quiver of her mouth, but Beatrice's small, upturned nose and the exposed white teeth that seemed to wedge her lips slightly open made her every expression childish and somehow trivial. She was fifteen years old, and it was hard to say if her puffy cheeks were those of a very young woman on the verge of obesity or an adolescent who might someday shed her baby fat and become a rather attractive woman.

"You had a good cry this morning," Eleonora said, "such a good cry that I cannot imagine that you could have any more tears. Every bride has such tears. But now you must remember that your husband, as his nephew's regent, has responsibility for the people of Milan, and so do you. If their initial perception is that you are of a weak and hysterical nature, you will never gain their confidence. And someday your life, your husband's life, and the freedom of your people may depend on that confidence. So today I know you will not cry."

Polissena began to nod vehemently at Beatrice. "Listen to your sainted mother—"

"Polissena," the Marquesa interjected, "if we hear one more time how Mama stood on the garden loggia to rally the city, with Father on his deathbed and the plague in the city and the Venetian army camped in the park, I believe that I shall start crying more hysterically than Beatrice did this morning."

"If it hadn't been for your sainted mother's courage in standing before her people, the city would have fallen. I pray every night to thank the Holy Mother that I was delivered from the Venetians. To think of rape at the hands of those Greek savages they employ. It is a tribute to your mother's strength that you girls have never had to worry about such horrors as we have seen." Polissena's head bobbed furiously.

"Polissena, if the Venetian mercenaries had been confronted with the prospect of savaging your virtue as the reward for their victory, they would have turned their pikes upon themselves. In any event, as my husband the Marquis is now the Captain General of the Armies of Venice, I think we can rest assured that the age of such outrages has ended."

Eleonora scarcely heard the inevitable battle between Polissena and Isabella, the war with Venice being nine hard years behind her and her mind on more pressing issues, of which there were already too many. She had dreamed just before awakening this morning; such dreams were considered to be prophetic. Fortunately, she supposed, she had forgotten this one, but she had awakened with a foreboding nonetheless. A dark dream, shrouded in black drapes . . . Nonsense. Her girls would bury her, as it was supposed to be.

But things were not right here. Eleonora looked north past the city wall, a massive ring of russet brick. The seemingly endless skyline offered the grand sweep of Milan's history: ice-white marble domes in the current *all'antica* style; gray medieval battlements with toothlike merlons; thousand-year-old brick bell towers with salmon-hued tile roofs; stately rows of weather-stained ancient Corinthian columns, a reminder of the era when Milan had contested with Rome itself for control of the Roman Empire. Milan was five times as big as Ferrara, its vast dominions a hundredfold as wealthy. But Milan was no different from Ferrara, Eleonora reminded herself. It was not so much a state as a single house, a house dependent on the custodianship of one ducal family for its well-being, its very survival. And there was trouble in this house.

Eleonora made a final adjustment of the pearl-tasseled satin headband that intersected the part in the middle of her daughter's high, obstinate brow. "It is very gracious of your cousin to make the gesture of welcoming you," Eleonora said. "It is important for you and the Duchess of Milan to be friends. I have already told you how delicate your relationship may be. . . ."

She had become Dante's Beatrice, wandering in the gardens of the Earthly Paradise, certain that none of them could find her here. Everywhere she looked were the most extraordinary trees and flowers: cypresses made of jade, irises with amethyst petals, apples like huge rubies. Everything made music; the blossoms sang a lyric soprano chorus, the trees hummed like pipe organs. Her canary, Gia, who must have followed her from Ferrara, flew into her hand. The brook at her feet was as clear as liquid sky, and Gia told her that if she drank from it she would forget everything that had happened. She stooped and cupped her hands.

Mama's voice entered the garden like a cold wind. The petals of the singing flowers trembled in the bitter gust, and Gia flapped his wings and looked at Beatrice fearfully. They listened, horrified, as Mama's voice rose to a howling cyclone and the trees screamed, their gilded limbs shattering. The brook turned to dark and putrid

DUCHESS OF MILAN   17

ice. Gia flew into the storm and vanished, and stinging black sleet
filled her eyes with tears. . . .

Beatrice's brother Alfonso materialized out of the ruins of her
imagination, no longer a pimply-faced thirteen-year-old but an
ember-eyed Charon come to dispatch her to eternal woe. He lifted
her carelessly onto her horse, and she hooked her lifeless thigh
over the pommel of the sidesaddle. Cold air rushed under her
velvet skirts. She had not been warm for two weeks, and yes, she
had eaten too many eels; she only wished she had eaten enough
eels to kill herself. Her throat ached from suppressing her sobs all
morning. "Ride tall," her mother commanded, demonstrating the
correct posture by drawing up her fleshy chin and thrusting out
her massive bosom. "Remember that you are an Este."

The church was only two blocks away. A guard of Milanese
gentlemen waited in the recessed portal; the sun reached in and
reflected off their armor, lighting them like big lanterns. At the
base of the steps, Messer Niccolò helped Beatrice from her horse.
The cavernous stone nave of the church was nearly as cold as the
outside; it smelled of fresh paint and the must of the bodies buried
beneath the floor. Hundreds of candles blazed from the altar and
the aisle chapels, illuminating choirs of colored stucco angels and
brilliant new frescoes of ancient martyrdoms. The Duchess of
Milan's ladies, bundled in their *cioppe*, waited in front of the altar.
Beatrice had not seen her cousin in five years, but she recognized
Isabella of Aragon's tall, broad-shouldered, head-slightly-down-
cast posture at once. The memories flashed by in precise detail,
like miniature paintings from a book of hours. Isabella with a
leopard—they let her have her own leopard—on a leash with a
diamond collar. Isabella in a gown of black Spanish silk, the only
girl with pearls in her hair. Isabella's extravagant bed, with a
striped satin canopy fringed with tassels and little gold balls, the
bed Beatrice had always dreamed of sitting on, holding hands with
her cousin and laughing. . . .

Beatrice escaped into one of the intricate little images. She was
so small that she couldn't see over the balcony but had to look
out from between the stone balustrades. The Bay of Naples, far
below her, glowed like a huge sapphire. Across the water was
Vesuvio, her magic volcano, a thin banner of mist streaming from
its broken cone. She wasn't frightened to be so high, but she was

afraid for her mother and sister and baby brother, because they had gone someplace where bad things had happened; she had gotten to stay with Grandfather, and he had given her a new doll with a complete bride's trousseau. The doll's white porcelain skin was as warm as the sun. Her name was Bella. Beatrice stood Bella beside her and told her about Vesuvio. Suddenly her cousin Ferrantino raced through the balcony, appearing and vanishing in a tattoo of frantic footsteps. Then she turned and saw Isabella. She was so tall that the sun seemed tangled in her hair. She carried a *palla* bat in one hand; the wooden club had been carved and painted with figures Beatrice could not quite make out. It was hard to see Isabella's face because the sun was behind her. She walked over, picked up Beatrice's new doll, set it on the broad, flat stone railing, and spread its white satin dress over stiff porcelain legs. . . .

"Beatrice, go to your cousin and offer her your hand," Eleonora hissed. Suddenly there was Isabella, lit by the candles framing the altar. Her chestnut hair was still parted in the middle and draped loosely over her shoulders in the Neapolitan fashion. But her face was fuller; her once awkwardly dominating nose, with its slender tip and long, masculine bridge, now had a striking elegance. A tight leather glove sheathed her hand; her clasp was cold, even through Beatrice's glove. Isabella's eyes, Beatrice thought, were the exact gray-green color and mysterious opalescence of the Bay of Naples before a storm.

The vision of Isabella vanished behind Eleonora's bulk. "I have hot spiced wine for the ladies," Isabella said after she had returned her aunt's embrace. Her throaty voice had a beautiful, sexual melancholy, as if pining for some absent lover.

A hand came into Beatrice's, a faint warmth like a small bird. The girl standing beside her was so haunted and beautiful that for a moment Beatrice thought she had invented her: china-white skin, lips as brilliant as berry juice, heavy black eyebrows, and feverish brown irises glowing within deep, shaded sockets.

"I am Bianca, Your Highness," the girl said in a high, fragile voice. Bianca could not have been older than ten or eleven. She tugged on Beatrice's hand and led her out of the circle of ladies.

The Marquesa drew Eleonora aside and whispered: "Mama, who is that girl with Beatrice?"

"That is Il Moro's bastard."

"*Per mia fe*, Mama. Does Beatrice know?"

"I told her this morning. She . . . accepted it."

"Mama." The Marquesa paused. "Mama, there is something else, isn't there? Something you have not told her."

Eleonora grasped the Marquesa's sable muff as if she intended to strangle the dead beast. "I will not permit—" A Milanese lady drifted within earshot, and Eleonora smiled graciously.

Bianca guided Beatrice to a chapel in the south transept. Shadows flickered over carved marble figures hoisting a huge white sarcophagus. "The man in there was formerly our Duke," Bianca said in a wondering voice. She looked up at Beatrice. "My bird died. I would have preferred that she be buried in a church, but of course that couldn't be. We buried her in a marble casket carved by Ser Domenico. Her name was Daria."

Having not spoken since the previous night, Beatrice was now convinced that only this enchanted child could hear her. "When my first parrot died, we wrapped him in black silk and lit candles around him and sent him down the Po"—the Po was the river that ran through Ferrara—"in a little galley that we had painted and gilded. Perhaps he is still floating far out in the sea on his beautiful ship."

"My mother is dead. I never saw her. I imagine that she was very beautiful."

Beatrice gave Bianca's hand a comforting squeeze. "I'm sorry about your mother."

"I imagine I already prefer you to the Duchess of Milan and certainly to Duchess Bona," Bianca chirped. Bona of Savoy was the Duke of Milan's widowed mother, the dowager Duchess of Milan.

Beatrice leaned over and gave Bianca a light kiss on her cheek. As she did, she glanced back at the ladies. Isabella was watching her. For a moment the Duchess of Milan's face was shadowed; then the candles washed her features with light. Beatrice remembered something about her cousin's eyes, the narrowing, the elongation at the corners. A twist of her lips, a way she had of looking amused and angry at once. The memory lured Beatrice across time, and she again confronted her cousin on that balcony high above the Bay of Naples, this time to see the end of it: Isabella smoothing the doll's dress, looking at her like that for a long moment. And then the *palla* bat blurred past and Bella's head exploded and her entire body flipped off the railing. Beatrice could see her falling, her white satin dress iridescent in the sun, the fragments of her head showering into the sea like a shattered snowball, and she could hear Isabella laughing. . . .

Beatrice blinked the present into focus. But her cousin was still looking at her, her bemused expression unchanged over all these years, as if she, too, remembered that day.

Satan did not raise Jesus to a high place and tempt Him with Milan, thought Cecilia Gallerani. Her high place was just beneath the brass cupola atop the soaring central tower of the Castello di Porta Giovia. The cold breeze that huffed through the streets below was, from this promontory, a biting wind. Behind her sprawled the Castello, as big as a good-size town, with moats like rivers, its massive wings engulfing vast courtyards, the rectangular severity relieved by white-columned arcades and gracefully arched window moldings of sun-pinked terra-cotta.

To the south and east lay the great wheel of Milan, rimmed by its cyclopean wall. The city's hub was the cathedral called the Duomo, the largest in Italy, its unfinished dome gaping, the rest a gleaming lace of sculpted marble, as sugary white and fantastic as a confectioner's creation. Cecilia guessed that the crowd packed into the piazza in front of the Duomo numbered a hundred thousand; they were shrouded in the white fog of their own exhalations. The day was so clear that she could see the blackbirds wheeling over the throng.

The wedding procession had already reached the piazza, and it paused in front of the Duomo while the guards cleared a broad path through the crowd. Il Moro was distinctly visible as a tiny figure in a pearl-white tunic flecked with gold; for a moment Cecilia thought she detected a pinpoint of light glancing from the grape-size diamond that always hung from his black velvet cap. Effortlessly, she conjured a life-size portrait from that distant miniature image. Il Moro's boyishly unlined skin was fair, his coloring otherwise dark—long, sable-hued bangs, shadowed, opaque eyes, heavy eyebrows—and this contrast emphasized the character of his face as deftly as an artist's chalk on a blank sheet of vellum. His nose, elegantly narrow from the front, strongly humped in profile—the nose of a Caesar—evoked experience and command; his small dark mouth, almost as delicate as a woman's, suggested sophistication and sensuality. These sharply sketched features could appear almost angelic from one angle and then hawklike, menacingly evil from another; all Il Moro had to do was turn his head slightly to make a complete transit of human nature.

As little as a year earlier, Cecilia had believed that she understood what was really there, between those apparent extremes. But now she was less certain. For her, Il Moro's eyes had always measured the true breadth of his character; usually guarded and impenetrable, they occasionally revealed shimmering glimpses of their brilliant depths. She would never forget the first time she had seen that inner radiance, a light she still believed destined to rise like a new sun over all Europe. But lately she wondered if Il Moro's incandescence hadn't blinded her to something hidden more deeply in his soul, a darkness inhabited by ghosts even he could not bring into the light.

Cecilia blinked, focusing again on the distant piazza. Alongside Il Moro rode the Duke of Milan, mounted on his white stallion, Neptune. When the crowd had been pushed aside, Neptune broke from the formation and trotted forward. The horse stilled again, then began a series of complicated dressage maneuvers, rearing back, forelegs churning in perfect circles, like a marvelous mechanical toy. An acclamation rose up from the crowd and drifted through the snapping wind. "Duca! Duca! Duca!"

The rest of the wedding party joined the Duke and proceeded across the piazza toward the Via degli Armorai, the broad, straight avenue, flanked by the arms factories for which it had been named, that ended directly beneath the central tower of the Castello. The factories, fronted with porticoes that faced the street, resembled large villas; the spires of the wooden cranes used to lift the immense foundry molds rose from open central courts. To celebrate Il Moro's marriage, both sides of the Via degli Armorai had been lined, for their entire length, with thousands of dummy warriors on wooden horses, all of them attired in real armor; the gold damascening of the polished steel plate flickered in the sun. At regular intervals the blunt snouts of bronze siege cannons jutted into the street.

The wedding party entered the armored cordon. Il Moro and the Duke of Milan rode side by side. The first fitful shouts, from the far end of the avenue, lost their meaning in the wind. Cecilia's hands jerked to her blanched face; for a moment she suspected an assassination attempt. But she quickly established the source of the still-faint calls. Crowded behind the wood-and-steel dummies, largely hidden within the shadowed porticoes, was the real army of the Via degli Armorai, tens of thousands of smiths and foundry workers, uniformed in dirty muslin shirts and soiled leather aprons.

The shouts cut through the wind, the muffled clamor beginning to harden and take shape, rhythmically, as if the armorers were hammering the two syllables on their anvils. "Mor-o. Mor-o. Mor-o."

Before the wedding party had passed the first factory, the oaths had raced the entire length of the avenue. Within moments the vast sprawl of Milan seemed to have a single voice. "Moro! Moro! Moro!" the armorers thundered again and again. "Moro! Moro! Moro!" The sound pounded away until it seemed that the oaths were actually echoing off the icy blue vault of the sky, as if the hammers of the Via degli Armorai were smashing that immaculate porcelain dome to bits, as if the name "Moro" were a challenge to heaven itself.

The harsh percussion wakened the baby sleeping in Cecilia's womb; tiny, indistinct limbs pummeled her belly. She slipped her hand inside her *cioppa* and pressed it against her swollen abdomen. "Don't be frightened, *anima mia*," she whispered against the gale from the streets. "That is your father's name you hear."

C H A P T E R

2

The Marquesa extended her arm and dismissively flipped her fingers at the view through the large arched window. The pool in the center of the arcaded court was still frozen. The neatly shaped topiaries and patterned hedges surrounding the pool also had an icy glimmer; garlands of tinsel and paper and ribbon streamers had been woven into the dead branches and arbors. In spite of the decorations, the topiaries, which in the spring would flesh out into fanciful shapes—lions, dragons, leaping dolphins—had a disquieting appearance without their leaves, as if they were ossified spirits. Beyond the skeletal foliage, at the far end of the courtyard, loomed a suitable backdrop: a windowless, three-story gray stone bastion.

"Appalling. They should have consulted Alberti's treatise on architecture before they built that monstrosity. What do they call it, the Rochetta? The Rock. How very poetic. Didn't Il Moro tell us that Duchess Mother Bona lives in there? Actually that is rather poetic. In the name of God, Mama, could you believe her this morning, standing beneath the gate of the Castello like Cerberus at the gate of Hell? I didn't know if she was going to kiss Beatrice or bite her. *Cacasangue*, Mama"—Eleonora looked up sharply in response to her daughter's profanity—"the woman has been widowed for fifteen years, and as I have heard, she hardly let the sheets get cold, and yet to look at her you would think her husband departed only yesterday. Black is such a becoming color for a young woman with my complexion, but the effect is quite spoiled when these old hags are everywhere with their widow's weeds. I get quite distressed at having to say, 'No, the Marquis is still with us,' whenever I wear black." The Marquesa paused for a heartbeat. "Mama, I think you had better tell Beatrice."

Eleonora, seated in a thick-ribbed, Venetian-style folding chair, continued to arrange colored glass jars of cosmetics on the lid of a wooden storage chest. She entirely ignored her daughter's abrupt suggestion.

The Marquesa smiled tartly and put her hands on her hips, in the manner of her mother. "Mama, doesn't it concern you that Il Moro seems curiously reluctant to sleep with Beatrice?"

Eleonora still didn't look up. Her voice had a tremolo of contrivance. "Beatrice's husband shows an admirable control over his passions. I cannot tell you how many grooms I have seen fall seriously ill in the midst of their wedding *feste* because they could not restrain their lust. The Duke of Milan was in peril of his life."

"Oh, Mama, everyone in Italy knows that it took the Duke of Milan the better part of a year to consummate the marriage. That is the kind of wedding *festa* certain to make the bride ill."

"Il Moro has assured me that he will attend to Beatrice. His astrologer is preparing a schedule."

"*Per mia fe*, Mama. I have never personally known a woman to have success with that method. As long as Il Moro continues to sleep with his mistress"—Eleonora's head involuntarily snapped up—"his astrologer is more likely to become pregnant than is Beatrice."

Eleonora's ringing soprano lowered at least an octave. "You are presuming something that simply is not true."

"Oh, Mama, you haven't lied to me successfully since I was eight, when you briefly convinced me that it was impossible for Signorina Anabella to be with child because she wasn't married and that she was going to the convent because she wanted Jesus to be her husband."

Eleonora picked up a silver-framed mirror and self-consciously tilted her head as if appraising her image. She glared at something else and said nothing.

"Mama. You can practically smell her perfume in the halls. I believe she even has a suite of apartments in this Castello. Those rooms that were blocked by scaffolding, which our host so graciously regretted he could not show us because they are under renovation: when we passed by those rooms I thought I observed you incline your head slightly to the right. It is a tic you have whenever you are anxious about something."

The room became as still as a tomb. The faint screech of a swift could be heard as it flitted past the big arched window overlooking the steel-blue moat. Eleonora examined the engraved frame of her mirror. Finally, still watching her fingers trace over the engraving, she said, "I don't believe that your sister is likely to be as observant. And I am certain I can depend on you to understand the necessity for discretion in this matter."

"You can depend on me for my discretion, but I don't believe you can depend on Beatrice to be so easily duped. You and Father have never realized how truly clever she is. I don't know if Maestro Guarino ever told you this, he was so fond of me—that reminds me, I must write him—but, Mama, there were days in our Latin tutorials when Beatrice recited better than I did." The Marquesa offered this information as gravely as if she had just revealed Beatrice's central role in the creation of the universe. "She will find out, and she will feel betrayed. You know how loyal she is, and nothing hurts her worse than betrayal."

"No. She is too preoccupied at the moment to go snooping for a mistress whose existence her husband and I have been very careful to conceal from her. No. Not now. She will find out later, of course, and there will be tears and recriminations. But they will pass. It will all pass. But if we tell her now, while we are still here, she will feel she has our strength on her side, and she will force the issue. And I cannot allow that to happen." Eleonora looked up again, toward something distant, visible only to her.

The Marquesa shook her head slightly, a gesture for her own benefit, not her mother's. "Mama, I am going to help Beatrice unpack her chests. You have my word that I won't tell her anything, even though she is going to hate me as much as she will you and Father when she finds out. You are wrong, Mama."

After the Marquesa had swished out of the room, Eleonora held the mirror before her face. The silvered image that stared back at her was one of heavy, almost vitreous white jowls framed by graying dark hair. The vivid sea-green irises were alien to her, someone else's eyes. She could not find her guilt in them.

Then, in a terrible instant, the girl behind those eyes materialized and mocked her. Eleonora could hear that girl laugh derisively, telling Cardinal Riario that she had wearied of his feast in her honor, and watch every man at the gold-and-silver-strewn banquet table strain to hear her childish complaints as if they had received miraculous clues to her ineffable soul. She contemptuously snorted back at the girl, who'd had no soul then, only a girl's dreams. Eleonora was now thirty-six; when she had married Duke Ercole d'Este, eighteen years previously, she had been the most famous beauty of her generation. Her nuptial journey from Naples to Ferrara had become virtually a religious event; in every town and village along the route manic throngs had come out to gawk at her as if she were an incarnation of the Virgin Mary. But this virgin had required the constitution of an ox to present Duke Ercole with six children in the first six years of her marriage, and she had been rewarded with a suitably bovine physique. Of her beauty only the luminous green irises remained, eyes she could no longer confront. Not because there was no soul behind them but because they still harbored a dream.

Light scampered in the ribbed ceiling vaults: cherry amber light from the massive stone fireplace, syrupy golden light from rows of candles arrayed along a carved wooden chest placed against the wall, illuminating a gilt-framed portrait, the ghost of this room —Galeazzo Maria Sforza, the previous Duke of Milan, dead to assassins' knives for fifteen years. Isabella was drawn as always, and always against her will, by the face of the father-in-law she had never known. In many ways Galeazzo Maria had looked so much like his son and heir, Gian Galeazzo. The thick neck and proud square jaw, the pretty, sensitive lips, the narrow shoulders and the almost effeminate pose of his gloved hand. But the nose and eyes were not Gian's, were not even human. The late Duke had been posed in profile, looking toward the picture frame, but nevertheless his small dark eyes seemed about to pivot and attack.

The nose was enormous, hawklike, a cruel beak modeled in mortal clay by a sculptor of infinite vision and insight, to warn mere men that the mind of a demon lived behind that high, effete forehead. But when that face had lived, by the time most men saw its terrible truth they were already lost.

"Who have you been with?"

The French-accented voice came screeching from the shadows. "And don't tell me you haven't, *puttana*. When you are this late it means one thing to me: You have stopped for the first greasy pair of hands that want to wander up your skirts. It is a scandal to everyone how you go about whither you will without a single lady-in-waiting to attend you. It sickens me to think of how many have touched you."

Isabella peered through the black gauze bed curtains and located the pale round face of Bona of Savoy, Duchess Mother of Milan; even through the shrouds, her mother-in-law's bulging eyes leered with owlish ferocity. "I am not late, Duchess Mother," Isabella said, her voice artificially high and taut. "Messer Ambrogio has added an ingredient to your draught that he says will ease the swelling in your feet."

"Poison!" Duchess Bona barked, but with a swift clawing motion she snatched the goblet and took the draught in three audible gulps. "I wouldn't need the attentions of Il Moro's sorcerer if I hadn't had to stand at the gate of the Castello all morning waiting on that Este brat. They took their time on the Via degli Armorai, to wallow in the treason of those filthy swine. I heard them! I heard them!" Duchess Bona snorted vilely. "She is short and will be as fat as her mother before she is your age. I do not believe that Il Moro even slept with her in Pavia." Bona's head swiveled to confront her daughter-in-law. "Any more than I believe that my baby Gian ever soiled himself in you. Not that that will stop her any more than it did you. You were both raised by the same *impicatti* in Naples and gave up your virtue to the same lechery, as even the devil is ashamed to witness. She'll steal your lovers. I can see in her eyes she is more clever than you. I told everyone the first day Satan sent you to us that you had no more sense than a donkey with a thistle under its tail."

"It is truly marvelous, Duchess Mother, how generous you are," Isabella said. "Whatever qualities you possess, you are will-

ing to credit to others in even greater abundance. You are the
most infamous slut I have ever known, and yet you think that
every other woman, even if she is an untouched maiden, has had
more lovers than a Roman streetwalker. You are the most foolish
woman I have ever known, and yet there is no one whom you
do not presume the greater fool and will proceed to lecture as if
you were a doctor at the University of Pavia. You are a very
astonishing creature, Duchess Mother."

As if she regarded Isabella's carefully cadenced assault as a
subtle form of flattery, Bona displayed a row of ragged black teeth,
the decayed corpse of the artificially winsome smile she had favored her suitors with three decades previously. "Yes, you will
soon come whining to me about that Este brat, with never the
thanks that I warned you."

"And you, who have done nothing to defend the rights of your
son's wife against Il Moro's mistress—a scrawny whore who believes in her diseased mind that her pimp lover is already Duke
of Milan and she his duchess—will be even less effective against
Il Moro's wife."

"As if God had given me the time to separate you spitting
bitches when every day I must prevent Il Moro from taking everything that belongs to Gian. Better that the Gallerani whore were
to send you and the Este brat home to the pit that spawned you
both. Her child could never challenge Gian."

"Challenge Gian? Challenge Gian? You disgusting old slut."
Isabella's voice rose to an incredulous pitch. "Gian has already
been defeated. It is my baby whom Il Moro now must challenge,
and Il Moro must have his own son to do that, he must be able
to offer Milan the promise of his own succession before the people
will allow him to depose Gian and declare himself their Duke.
And I will never give up, the way you did with Gian. I will defeat
Il Moro's son no matter which of the two bitches—his wife or
his whore—presents him with an heir."

"Your devil-sent spawn has no more right to be Duke of Milan
than the issue of a whore and a horse-comber. Which no doubt
he is."

Isabella stared down at her mother-in-law. When she spoke
her tone was measured, almost deliberately dull. "You don't think
we would have something to fear if Cecilia Gallerani were to give

birth to a male child, Duchess Mother? Particularly since Il Moro does not seem inclined to spend much time sowing his new bride's field."

"Birdbrain. I know the people of Milan like you never could. I was their Duchess. A real duchess. The people of Milan would never accept a bastard as their duke's heir." Bona's black teeth emerged again. "If he intended to make the Gallerani whore's bastard his heir, why did he need the Este brat?"

"Perhaps, Duchess Mother, Il Moro's marriage had something to do with the Duke of Ferrara's threats to turn Venice against Il Moro, now that the Duke of Ferrara's son-in-law is Captain General of the Venetian armies. And Il Moro finally agreed to honor the marriage contract in early August, which was most likely before his whore conceived, so he most certainly did not know about her pregnancy then. And even now, how can he be certain the child will be a son? Perhaps, Duchess Mother, Il Moro is like a man who enters two horses in a *palio* race. He doubles his odds. Then he will place the colors of his house on whichever mare crosses the finish first."

"Idiot. He has already tried to marry the Gallerani whore once before. Everyone was against it."

Isabella understood that by "everyone" her mother-in-law meant the leading Milanese nobles, who had the most to lose in the event of political instability. "And every week Il Moro coaxes one of them into his hand. You see how he has just given Count Borromeo a concession to manufacture silk in Mortara? A day will come when no one will care whether Il Moro's selection of a bride is agreeable to the Duke of Ferrara. And don't for a moment believe that the Pope would not annul Il Moro's marriage. For a proper price, His Holiness would sell Il Moro the virtue of Christ's own Mother. And what if Beatrice d'Este cannot conceive, Duchess Mother? You know that her sister has been married for a year, and she told me today that she still does not have any signs of a child."

Bona snorted. "The Duchess of Ferrara had a squalling brat every time her husband pinched her cheek. That is why she looks like a cow. Hah! The ones everybody calls *bellissima* as girls are the ones who most quickly become *grossa* as women." Bona's eyes contracted like two sphincters. "You had better pray to your devil that the Gallerani whore has a son and that Il Moro continues to believe she is his duchess and her bastard his heir. Because if Beatrice d'Este has a son, only my dear nephew the King of France will be able to save us."

"If your nephew crosses the Alps with his army," Isabella said wearily, as if repeating a self-evident proposition, "it will not only mean the end of Il Moro's obscene ambitions. It will be the end of Italy."

Bona grinned like a madwoman.

"So you are saying that the best thing for us to do would be to support Cecilia Gallerani against Beatrice d'Este?" Isabella asked, her tone conciliatory.

"Now you have found the speck of sense in your empty head. Better to have two hens fighting over the same cock. If you defeat Cecilia Gallerani, the Este brat will be the next Duchess of Milan."

"As usual you have given me a great deal to think about, Duchess Mother." Isabella nodded respectfully. "I am going to retire and consider what you have told me. Sleep well, Duchess Mother." Isabella collected the goblet, dropped the dark bed curtain like a shadow between herself and her mother-in-law, and turned to leave. But as she passed the portrait of the murdered Duke, she paused and met his eyes.

C H A P T E R

3

Extract of a letter of LEONARDO DA VINCI, engineer at the Court of Milan, to international traveler and raconteur BENEDETTO DEI. Milan, 22 January 1491

. . . nor is there quiet in which to pursue one's own studies, owing to the great clamor and commotion of the wedding *feste* within the Castello. Certainly the most egregious and noisome of these events is the wedding joust, which commenced in the great piazza of the Castello this morning and will continue for two more days. O tumult of iron and clash of steel! All of this antique martial cacophony is taking place beneath the windows of my studios, from early morning until late in the afternoon. And I arose before the sun to attire Messer Galeazzo di Sanseverino in a costume of my design, a Scythian warrior's garb of marvelous ingenuity and wondrous invention. I have also supervised the decorations of the great hall for the occasion of a ladies' ball this evening. You can imagine my vexation at having time for little else. . . .

Having seen the bride, I am convinced that the bust of her executed in marble by a certain Maestro Cristoforo Romano, which made no claims for her beauty, nevertheless represents a meretricious report. However, my dear Benedetto, do not labor under the perception that the Duke of Ferrara has been reduced to penury to provide this pitiable creature's dowry. On the contrary, I am told by authorities most reliable that the Duke of Ferrara has extorted through various means a profit on the merchandise he has sent to us. The prestige of the Este, the oldest ruling family in Italy, has been purchased in dear coin by the far more recently arrived Sforza, who are desperate for it. O Cities of the Earth! What thunderbolt of Jovian rage shall be hurled down upon us when misbegotten children are bought and sold for the purpose of binding together the affairs of men. . . .

. . . Benedetto, you must write to me immediately if you have details as to the French foundry techniques. I can only assume that they have arrived at a process for settling impurities out of the bronze, thereby overcoming the brittleness that has hitherto made heavy artillery too cumbersome for an army determined to rapidly encroach upon its foe. . . .

"Careful where you step," the Cardinal of Novara intimated, grasping his companion's elbow to help her negotiate the stuffed burlap bag lying on the wet stone floor. "Careful that you don't soil your *cioppa*." The Cardinal gestured with his torch and sent shadows darting along the black walls of the narrow passage; they were beneath the level of the moat, in what had formerly been the dungeons of the Castello di Porta Giovia. Another bag blocked the way. "Salt," offered the Cardinal as he and his guest crunched over the obstacle. "Except for a few rooms reserved for . . . unusual circumstances, that is all this is used for now. The storage of salt." The sale of salt, which was monopolized by the state of Milan, was an important form of revenue; the exorbitant price included a substantial tax. The Cardinal made three rapid, shallow exhalations, his habitual expression of mirth. "The estimable, late, and not widely lamented Duke Galeazzo Maria Sforza amused himself by bringing his subjects down here and nailing them into their coffins while they were still alive. He would then maintain a vigil until his guest was actually in need of a sarcophagus, listening to the desperate cries and the scratching, all the while describing in explicit detail how he had debauched the dying wretch's wife and sodomized his daughters. Then consider the late Duke's brother, our present Duke's regent, Il Moro, who has not executed anyone for a crime less than murder in five years but in that time has doubled the salt tax. I leave you to choose the greater tyrant."

"Only peasants and laborers pay the salt tax," Caterina da Borromeo, lady-in-waiting to the Duchess of Milan, ventured without a hint of irony. She was sixteen years old, and her father was one of the wealthiest noblemen in Milan.

"And no doubt the peasants and the laborers received their twelve coppers' worth of amusement at the joust this afternoon," the Cardinal remarked agreeably. He almost slipped, and muttered, "And no doubt we have each consumed a gold ducat's worth of wine." The Cardinal thrust his torch into an open doorway, plunging the dank stone passage into a terrifying blackness. He withdrew the torch. "Not what I was looking for."

After several more exploratory thrusts, the Cardinal found what he was looking for and pulled Caterina into a small room, barren except for a large circular wooden frame set in the center of the fungus-blackened floor. The Cardinal took two fresh tapers from his cloak, lit them with the torch, and set all three lights into the corroded iron rings nailed into the walls. The light revealed the Cardinal as a nearly bald man in his early thirties, with a swarthy complexion and a plump, indolent chin. He had been a cardinal for five years. The office had been purchased for him by his father, the leader of Novara's informal council of ruling nobility, in exchange for massive commercial concessions to Il Moro; the nobles had replaced the ceded revenues by raising their local taxes and had profited from their influence in Rome. The deal had been brokered by Il Moro's brother, Cardinal Ascanio Sforza.

"The wheel," the Cardinal said in a mocking tone that could not entirely disguise a certain unease. He gave the device a slow, groaning quarter turn. "I like to think of this wheel as an ancillary to Dame Fortune's far more prodigious mechanism. When this wheel spins, it can turn a saint into a heretic and a heretic into a saint." He looked at Caterina, his eyes swimming with a flagellant's desire. "Which would you rather be, my child: a heretic or a saint?"

Caterina's face seemed to waver in the torchlight, flickering between generations; her lips were lush with prepubescent innocence, but she had the hard cheekbones of a thirty-year-old. "I would like to confirm our understanding," she said in an assured woman's voice. "There are three benefices. The total income is two hundred ducats a year. They are to be assigned to my brother separately, so that he can sell one or two if the need arises."

The Cardinal nodded. "If your brother has your skill at mercantile transactions, my child, I am certain he will aggrandize these incomes in short time."

"He is an idiot who will gamble them away in a fortnight." Caterina's eyes had a glassy determination. "I won't take all my clothes off. It's too cold in here."

"I don't expect you to," the Cardinal whispered. "I am, after all, a prince of the Church." He withdrew several lengths of gold cord from his ermine-trimmed cloak. "I think you can stand comfortably on the rim. I won't be giving you a spin."

Caterina stood on the rim and leaned back against the angled frame of the wheel. The Cardinal gently spread her legs and arms and with the cords tied her wrists and ankles. "My delicious little martyr," he murmured reverently. "You are a far more felicitous vision of virtuous self-denial than one finds amid the obscene gore favored by these modern painters, who force one to count each droplet spurting from a saint's truncated neck. How very much more agreeable. I imagine you didn't know I was such a disciple of tradition, did you, my child?"

The Cardinal drew closer, and his fingers hovered over the hooks that fastened Caterina's *cioppa*. "May I peek?" he whispered. Caterina responded with a high-pitched giggle. The Cardinal unhooked the *cioppa* and spread the fur lapels gently aside. Caterina wore a gown in the currently fashionable style called a *camora;* the tight bodice had a deeply cut, rectangular neckline that revealed Caterina's prominent collarbones and an impressive amount of firm, high bosom. The Cardinal sighed admiringly. After a few moments' contemplation, his fingers delicately worked at the laces of the bodice; he then spread the bodice apart and slipped the underlying chemise off Caterina's shoulders and breasts. "Ah," he sharply exhaled. "Your nipples are hard." Caterina giggled again.

The Cardinal stepped back and drew up his floor-length velvet robes. He fumbled for a moment, then rocked his hips in a steady, swaying rhythm. Caterina smirked and teasingly pressed her erect nipples toward him.

The light in the room rippled and brightened. Suddenly Caterina's eyes were wide with fear, as if she were a real victim on the wheel. The Cardinal observed her response and stopped masturbating.

"You are a dedicated servant of God, Your Reverence. I can see that you practice your collegial duties even when absent from Rome."

The Cardinal let his robes fall, then turned and inclined his head in acknowledgment. The Duchess of Milan stood in the doorway like a condemned man's last vision. The Cardinal made the sign of the cross with wry urgency.

"Administer your sacraments elsewhere, Reverence. I have business with my lady-in-waiting." Isabella's voice was husky and calm.

The Cardinal shrugged, retrieved one of his torches, and left. The Duchess of Milan stepped in front of Caterina.

"I need you to perform for me as well. Tonight, at the ladies' ball in honor of the Duchess of Bari. The time has come to do away with Cecilia Gallerani."

Caterina snorted contemptuously. "You're mad."

"You are going to do it, little slut, or I will make known your business with the Cardinal."

"My father already knows," Caterina spit back. "He introduced me to the Cardinal. He needs a place for my idiot brother, Cesare."

"I wasn't referring to your father. I meant your lover."

Caterina thought to say: In your case that would be the same, but she decided she didn't want to die in this place. "Messer Bernardino doesn't care who else I sleep with," she offered in a sulking voice.

"I didn't mean him. Or Galeazz." Isabella's delicate lips scrolled a subtle smile. She came closer. "I saw you drinking in the grandstands at the joust. You must have been quite besotted to come down here with that pervert." Isabella was close enough to whisper in Caterina's ear. "You are really very pretty. The most lovely of all my ladies. I don't know why you waste yourself." Isabella touched her lips to Caterina's cheek. Caterina's head jerked slightly, and her solid breasts swayed.

Isabella's kisses moved down Caterina's neck, then along the slope of her bosom. Her tongue flicked at Caterina's nipple, raising a tight knot. Caterina shuddered. "You like it, don't you?" Isabella whispered hotly. Caterina hiccuped and circled her head, her eyes closed.

Isabella stood straight up. "But you like it better with Madonna Giulia, don't you?"

Caterina's eyes shot open. Giulia Landriano, a married woman in her late twenties, was also one of the Duchess's ladies-in-waiting—like Caterina from a prominent and ambitious Milanese family. "When I tell Giulia how you have betrayed her love, she will use her knife far more readily than any cuckold. Do you remember that serving girl who was stabbed during Holy Week the year last?" Isabella smiled at the terror in Caterina's eyes. "I am certain you know that she, too, committed the error of disappointing your Giulia."

Caterina broke down with a series of explosive dry sobs; finally the tears came. Isabella untied her and helped her from the wheel, then took her in her arms and began to stroke her hair maternally.

"Y-you might as well kill me now," Caterina whined with genuine pain. "Either way I am *finito*."

Isabella laughed. "I don't mean for you to assassinate Cecilia Gallerani, nor do I intend to. All I expect of you is to help me sharpen someone else's blade. Now, you are going to need an accomplice to assist you. Someone extremely facile in conversation." Isabella began to lace up the bodice of Caterina's *camora*. "Your friend Giulia has an agile tongue, does she not?"

The Sala della Palla was the largest room in the Castello di Porta Giovia. Used variously for state banquets, balls, and tennis matches, it was a three-story, ribbed-vaulted hall overlooked by a long balustraded mezzanine gallery. For the ladies' ball arches of woven ivy spanned the vaults, creating an enormous indoor arbor, beneath which were suspended wheel-shaped silver candelabra. Musicians in gold tunics, playing trombones and large woodwinds called *piffari*, clustered at one end of the chamber. Rows of pages in red-white-and-blue uniforms stood along the walls, holding up trumpet-shaped ceremonial torches. The torches illuminated a series of new frescoes depicting the manifold victories of Il Moro's father, the legendary *condottiere*—mercenary commander—Francesco Sforza: a sweeping martial pageant featuring dashing mounted knights, forests of lances, elegantly choreographed surrenders, and ornate victory dedications to the Virgin.

Beatrice stood on the open mezzanine gallery, surrounded by her mother, sister, ladies-in-waiting, and the Duchess of Milan and her attendants. She was screened from her cousin by the Duke of Milan's unmarried sister, Bianca Maria Sforza, an astonishingly beautiful and perpetually distracted seventeen-year-old; Bianca Maria was presently destroying the effect of her sublime dark features by childishly wagging her head in rhythm to the music. But she apparently had a sweet, innocent nature. She and Beatrice had discovered that they had been tutored by the same dance master, Maestro Lavagnolo.

The ducal ladies were in turn surrounded by perhaps two hundred Milanese noblewomen, ranging in age from reedy bejeweled adolescents to waddling bejeweled dowagers who could scarcely stand without younger relatives to prop them up. But most of the women were frightening in their hard, varnished beauty. Their faces, coated with glossy white ceruse and crimson rouge, seemed fashioned of wax; their cerused breasts, plumped up by the tight bodices of their *camore*, were of such consistent roundness that they might have been shaped in molds. Most of the younger women were blond—either natural or bleached with lemon juice—and virtually all of them wore their hair pulled back, parted in the middle, and entirely slicked down with gum arabic except for a fringe of delicate Venetian-style curls. They moved among one another in wary circling packs, busy scarlet lips dipping to curl-draped ears. Emerald chokers and pearl-beaded hair nets returned the light with piercing glints.

"You know what they say, Mama." The Marquesa whispered into her mother's ear, mirroring the pose of so many other couples in the gallery. "In no place save England or the Sultanate of Turkey is marriage held in lower regard than it is in Milan. They say that a Milanese husband, confronted with the inevitability of being cuckolded, prefers to serve as his wife's pimp and will deliver her to her lover's *palazzo* in his own carriage and kiss her goodbye on the doorstep, and anyone passing on the street will doff his hat in salute to this *étalage* of marital devotion. Then of course the cuckold will call on his own mistress.''

Beatrice could not bring herself to look at the women of Milan, but their liberally applied perfumes—scented with ambergris, cinnamon, myrtle, and aloe—and the pungency of the ivy and evergreen boughs gave the hall the cloying atmosphere of an overgrown garden on a sultry spring afternoon. The dancers whirling on the main floor below her were simple peasant girls costumed in red, white, and blue vests and skirts; their fervent Spanish-style *moresca* made up in sensual abandon for what it lacked in artistic precision. Beatrice peered over the marble balustrade and wished that she could leap to the floor and dance with them. There had been a time when she loved dancing more than anything, because there had been a time when she believed that one day she would be beautiful, that every time she rose on her toes in response to Maestro Lavagnolo's baton she would hasten the day when her heavy thighs would be drawn like hot blown glass into slender stems. But now when she danced she forgot entirely the liquid elegance that Maestro Lavagnolo had insisted on, and like these peasant girls she whirled and leapt in fierce staccato movements, punishing her short, muscular legs by forcing them to dance in a style to which they were more suited.

The music stopped and the dancers' skirts wilted; the girls turned in unison to the gallery and curtsied. "Beatrice," Eleonora whispered, "you must receive the ladies now."

Beatrice's entire body ached with fear. She forced herself to turn. The Duchess of Milan stared down at her, narrow nostrils flared slightly, the gray-green eyes set above her high cheekbones like cold Alpine lakes. With a strange wistfulness, Beatrice admitted to herself that she had no more chance to earn her imperiously beautiful cousin's friendship here in Milan than she had as a girl in Naples. But at least here she wouldn't make a fool of herself with clumsy, unrequited overtures. She stared back at Isabella. I hate you too, she silently offered as a reinforcing litany. I hate you too.

The eyes of the noblewomen of Milan were no warmer than Isabella's. Beatrice imagined them made of glass, the eyes of sinister dolls. At first she heard nothing when they greeted her. She saw the lacquered lips move and the metallic brocade *camore* crinkle into curtsies. She nodded to each supplicant, again and again. Each face was like a mask, not a real woman.

The woman who would not let go of Beatrice's hand was tall, with a sharp, aquiline nose; a pear-shaped diamond brooch perched just above her cleavage. She had been introduced as Giulia Landriano, one of the Duchess of Milan's senior ladies-in-waiting. ". . . delightful, were they not, Your Highness." The words began to enter Beatrice's consciousness and compose sentences. Giulia had been talking about the dancers. "So entirely fresh and simple and quaint. Delightful." Beatrice could not imagine that Giulia's acerbic eyes had ever found anything pleasing. "But then everything to do with Your Highness has been delightful. We so rarely see such *dolcezza* here." Beatrice, accustomed to the oblique speech of courtiers and diplomats, began to hear Giulia's subtext as well. *Dolcezza* was the code word: sweetness. Sweet, delightful, simple. What was really meant was that Beatrice and the Ferrarese were perceived, like the dancers, as provincial and vulgar. "You bring *dolcezza* to Milan, Your Highness."

The Marquesa took a half step toward her sister's antagonist. "And we rarely see such art as we have beheld here this evening, Madonna Giulia." The Marquesa's ripe lips contorted with sarcasm. "An art so expertly contrived that at first glance one is scarcely aware of the common substance beneath such extravagant ornament. Rather like pouring gilt syrup on stale pastries."

The surrounding conversation hesitated; the crowd contracted. Giulia inclined her head slightly, as if to signal that she had accepted the Marquesa's escalation of hostilities. "If one's tastes are limited to pastries, then one might indeed be overwhelmed by the ornament one sees here." Giulia conspicuously caressed the diamond-studded gold chain that draped her bosom; the gold links were an exquisitely detailed miniature garland. "Is Your Highness familiar with the work of Maestro Caradasso?" The Milanese goldsmith

Caradasso del Mundo was renowned throughout Europe. "Of course one must be able to pay for such skill in order to appreciate it. It is rather more dear than a confectioner's wares."

The Marquesa flushed at the allusion to the Este family's relatively modest means; more than a few of the ranking Milanese nobles were wealthier than the ruling family of Ferrara. She stroked the choker around her neck; the pearls were spaced with intricate gold rosettes. "I prefer the work of our own Enrico da Fidele. Maestro Enrico is that sort of artist who emphasizes subtlety over contrivance, assuming as he does that his patrons are able to complement his creations with their own charms."

Giulia nodded curtly at the Marquesa, then looked directly at Beatrice. From Beatrice's vantage the reflections of the torches gave the woman's pale irises a gold tint. "How charming that your sister has retained her native simplicity. But I can see that the Duchess of Bari already favors Milanese elegance." Giulia stepped closer and appraised the floriate gold links of the ruby pendant Il Moro had given Beatrice. "I immediately knew this as the work of our Caradasso. He did a piece with virtually identical pendants for Cecilia Gallerani."

Giulia had mentioned the name casually enough, but then she immediately pulled back as if startled by her own voice. Her eyes dilated with alarm. She made an abrupt curtsy. "Forgive me, Your Highness," she said urgently. "I . . ."

The conversation in the room fell away precipitously. The Marquesa snapped her head around, confronting her mother. Eleonora's jowls were slack, her eyes so intense they looked like emeralds.

Beatrice's forehead prickled, and then the cold realization rushed through her torso. She turned to her mother. "Mama?" she asked in a small, brittle voice. But she already knew. "Mama." This time the word was not a question but had not yet formed into an accusation. Beatrice turned back to Giulia. "Who is Cecilia Gallerani?"

Giulia curtsied again. "Your Highness . . ." Her mouth remained open, but she offered nothing else. The only sounds in the entire hall were scattered coughing and the collective shuffling of slippers and rustling of skirts.

For some reason Beatrice was drawn to the woman standing

next to Giulia. Beatrice had met her minutes earlier and remembered her as Caterina, one of Isabella's ladies-in-waiting. She was perhaps sixteen or seventeen, with large, almost perfectly hemispherical breasts encroaching on her collarbones. And she had started to cry, her bare shoulders jerking rhythmically, her sobs like shouts in the silence. Finally she screamed: "Why won't someone tell her! Tell her! It is so cruel!" Caterina's hands clutched in pathetic supplication. "I can't believe no one has told her!"

"Beatrice." Eleonora powerfully gripped Beatrice's arm, attempting to pull her back.

"Tell me what?" Beatrice called out, straining against her mother. "Tell me." She wrenched her arm from her mother's grip and seized Caterina's slender shoulders. "Tell me!"

Caterina looked to Giulia. Her sobs were as regular as hiccups. Eleonora grabbed Beatrice again.

"*Tell* me!"

Caterina vomited the words. "Cecilia Gallerani is your husband's mistress! She is going to have his baby! It is so horrible what everyone is doing to you!" She put her hands on her knees and keened dreadfully. Then her features went slack and she slumped to the floor.

Beatrice's instinct was to grasp something before she was sucked up into the sky like a feather in a cyclone. The scent-laden atmosphere was suddenly stifling. Her mother spun her around. A black penumbra began to close on her vision. She whirled away from her mother, and only her cousin's face was visible through the narrowing tunnel of light: Isabella with green cat's eyes, her lips sinuous with amusement. That was the last Beatrice saw before the dark circle closed.

C H A P T E R

4

"Mama, she is not going to sleep through the night, and she most certainly will refuse one of this Messer Ambrogio's draughts when she does awaken." The Marquesa paced the floor of the small sitting room that joined her temporary bedroom to her sister's antechamber; all these rooms would become part of Beatrice's permanent suite when the wedding party left. The sitting room was unfurnished except for several chairs and a cupboard enameled with elaborate heraldic motifs: lions, eagles, twining flowers, and the ubiquitous symbol of Milan's Sforza rulers, a looping, lurid blue viper with the flayed body of a man in its fangs.

"I warned you we should tell her. You will recall very distinctly that I raised the issue just yesterday. Mama, I am beside myself, I truly am. I simply hope she is not lying there plotting revenge on both of us right now. She is an expert at revenge. Do you remember what she did to Eugenia Casella? That was very clever. They had to shave Eugenia's head entirely. Her hair grew back another color too, and they never could make her a braid after that. . . ."

The Marquesa was interrupted by a crash echoing through Beatrice's *guardaroba*, a room ordinarily used for the display and storage of clothes and valuables, but which was now filled with wedding gifts. "Mama, I told you that Polissena was too aged to be of use here. I would sooner have a drunken centaur in my *guardaroba* handling my plates. . . ." The two quick crashes that followed were too harshly orchestrated to be accounted for by the palsied hands of an old woman. *"Per mia fe,* Mama . . ."

Eleonora came out of her chair with startling agility; three more crashes resounded before she reached the *guardaroba.* Porcelain shards littered the floor. What at first seemed a child darted along the wall and clutched for the sanctuary of Eleonora's skirts; it was Fritello, Beatrice's dwarf. In the fluttering lamplight Beatrice's face appeared almost indigo with rage. She had methodically removed from their wooden presses at least two dozen large majolica plates, intricately glazed with mythological and religious scenes, and arrayed them on top of several wooden storage chests. With a spasmodic, marionette motion she plucked up another plate, raised it overhead, and smashed it against the floor. Eleonora crunched across the remains of the wedding plates, grasped her daughter's rigid arms, and jerked her off the floor as if she were indeed a large puppet.

"Remember who you are and who you represent," Eleonora hissed. "You are not some child whose tantrums can be ignored. You are a symbol of the state, the mother of the state. . . ."

Beatrice's voice was so low and vicious that it visibly startled Eleonora. "You lied to me, Mama."

"I withheld from you the unpleasant truth that is the first great test of marriage, because I did not think you were ready to accept it like a woman and a duchess. And now I can see that I was correct. . . ."

"*You* see! *You* see! It is I who see, Mama! *I* see! *I* see! I see how you have piled lie on top of lie. I see that you tell me to behave like a duchess when you permit me to be disgraced in front of everyone." Beatrice paused and stammered wordlessly, considering an unthinkable oath. "I hate you, Mama!"

The slap cracked through the room, and Beatrice's head rolled drunkenly. "Never, ever say that to your mother. You could hate me for a thousand years and that could not add up to one instant of the love I have for the baby I carried in my womb. The baby I carried—" Eleonora stopped herself, but the moment came screaming out of time. Six-week-old Alfonso under one arm,

Beatrice wrapped around her neck, almost strangling her, Isabella's desperate little hand in hers, the children's shrieks in the dark stone passageway like all the souls trapped in Hell . . . And then, as always, she banished the memory of that failed coup with a quick, savage image: an executioner's sword flashing in the sun and the spout of blood from her nephew Niccolò's headless neck.

Beatrice's shoulders heaved, and she wrenched forward; the tears literally burst from her eyes. Eleonora wrapped her in her massive reassuring arms. "This will all change, baby," Eleonora whispered as she stroked her daughter's hair. "I promise you it will. He will love you more and her less with each day. I promise you. I have known the same tears you are tasting now, and I have seen how in time that bitterness can turn into the most indescribable sweetness." But Eleonora knew that she had not tasted this particular gall. She would never forget the look on Ercole's face at their first meeting, that proud, arrogant face seemingly carved from ice, those diamond-hard eyes. *Diamante*, the diamond, his people called him. Hard, brilliant, and cold. And yet when that face had beheld hers for the first time . . . That night, as he lay in her virgin arms, it had been his diamond-hard eyes that had wept with the fulfillment of his desire.

Beatrice sniffed loudly. "Mama, when is she going to have his baby?"

"That is no concern of yours. If the child lives, it will be a whore's bastard and nothing more. You are Il Moro's wife before the witness of God, and your son will be his heir."

"Mama, she is not just a whore. She lives here in this Castello in a suite of rooms, just like a wife. Those rooms we were told were under renovation."

Silence followed. "Mama . . . ," the Marquesa said threateningly.

"Isabella!" Eleonora snapped. "Close all the doors! Tell the guards that no one shall be admitted to the Duchess of Bari's suite until the Duchess of Ferrara instructs them otherwise. Then join me in your sister's bedchamber."

Eleonora sat on the bed and gestured for Beatrice to sit beside her. Beatrice refused. The Marquesa closed the bedchamber door behind her, walked warily by Beatrice, and then nervously smoothed her skirts as she sat beside her mother on the bed.

Eleonora's voice was lovely and unequivocal. "Beatrice, Cecilia Gallerani will continue to occupy her suite of rooms in this *castello*. Your father and I agreed to this as a condition of your marriage contract."

This betrayal clutched Beatrice's heart like a cold fist. Father knew? They all knew? They sold me as a concubine, to be little more than a greased whore in some filthy Moor's harem?

Eleonora knew from Beatrice's glazed silence how painful the blow had been. "Beatrice, Isabella, there is no moment in the arms of a man that will ever exceed the passion when your child first grasps for your breast. And yet it is a strange passion, because to fulfill it you must so often deny it. That denial begins when you turn your child from your aching teat and place him in the arms of his wet nurse. And it never stops. Do you remember, Isabella, when I first sent you beneath the rod of Maestro Guarino? You were only three years old, my first baby. Do you think I no longer cared for your little girl's chatter and to punish you condemned you to recite from Latin? God, the sound of your childish babble was to me worth all the orations of Cicero. I gave away my joy and your . . . childhood so that you would become a woman daunted by no intellect beneath the divine spheres. And what once caused both of us pain has come around to bring us both happiness."

"I know, Mama," the Marquesa said reverently.

"Beatrice, I loved you no less because you were not with us, and spared you no less the pain of being shaped into a woman who could proudly wear the crest of Este. Do you think that when you finally came home from Naples my heart did not beg me to hold your hand all day and all night, to walk with you the entire length of the Po, to tell you everything I could not say to you all those years you were away? When I gave you up to your tutors each day, I tore the fibers pulsing from my breast. I dread more than if I were a condemned man walking to the scaffold the moment two days hence when I must leave you here. You are my last girl. Do you know how terrible the silence of our *castello* will be without a girl's laughter ringing?"

For a moment Eleonora's eyes seemed haunted by the silence of her girls' empty rooms. Then she thrust out her massive brocaded bosom and sat stridently erect. "I know you girls do not like to hear stories about the war with Venice. You were little girls then and you cannot remember, and for that I am grateful. And God knows I am grateful that we have been at peace ever since. The reason we have enjoyed this concord is because your father, my father, Il Moro, and the Signory of Venice have all agreed that Italy will not survive another such war. The French have become too powerful, too ambitious. If we are divided by our own quarrels, the Frenchmen will bring their army over the mountains and destroy each of us one by one. But this peace we enjoy is a fragile and complex construction. It needs a strong foundation if it is to endure.

"We, the women of the house of Este, are that foundation. Through our blood and that of your children all Italy will be joined. Naples and Milan and Mantua and Ferrara. Isabella's husband is the Captain General of the Armies of Venice. Florence is an ally of such long standing with Milan that they are ours as long as Il Moro lives. The only great power of which we are in doubt is Rome, but when the Holy Father dies, and that will not be long"—Eleonora crossed herself—"your uncle Cardinal Sigismondo and Il Moro's brother Cardinal Ascanio will have the power to make the next Pope their servant. We three women are the base upon which the power of Italy will be raised. And yet the foundation we provide is like a tripod. If any one of us is taken away, the entire structure will topple. And from those ruins Italy will never rise again. Not in your lifetimes, not in your children's lifetimes."

Beatrice pursed her lips. She clearly understood the great mechanism of history her mother had described; she had grown up listening to the negotiations that had taken place at her grandfather's and her father's dining tables. "Mama, you say I am one leg of this tripod and that I must not be weak. How strong do I appear to be when my husband's whore is in all but name the Duchess of Bari?"

"Beatrice, we had to make a difficult choice. Your husband would not agree to the marriage otherwise, and we decided that no interest would be served if we broke the contract over this point."

"Then you will have to forfeit my dowry. Because I will not live in the same *castello* as my husband's whore."

"Beatrice, you do not know what difficulties we had in bringing this marriage—"

"I do not know, Mama?" Beatrice interrupted with sarcastic incredulity. "I was the one who waited each time he postponed the wedding, wondering what was wrong with me. I was there the night Il Moro's emissary came to withdraw the contract. I saw Father's face." She saw it again, his muscular jaw hardened with fury, his thin lips like a blade, his murderous black eyes. "Father made him marry me. I know that. If father now asks Il Moro to remove his whore from my lodgings, it will happen."

Eleonora listened to her daughter's defiant tone and studied her glaring face. Of all the children, Beatrice had been the least familiar with Ercole, yet she was the most like him. Like her sister, Isabella, Beatrice had Ercole's agile intellect and self-interested practicality, but unlike Bel or any of the four boys (would to God her boys had her girls' intellect), Beatrice also had an intensely emotional, irrational, often mystical aspect of her nature, the same paradox that made Ercole so difficult to fathom. More ominously, Eleonora reflected, Beatrice combined Bel's fiercely competitive nature with Ercole's recklessness. If Fortune were not capricious enough, Beatrice seemed determined to relentlessly taunt Her. That love of danger was what made Beatrice such a gifted rider; her horses sensed that she had no fear of being thrown, and respected her for it. But for a woman as close to the levers of fate as the Duchess of Bari might someday be, disregard for consequences was a curse. Perhaps, Eleonora sadly admitted to herself, that aspect of Beatrice's character underscored the importance of Cecilia Gallerani in this equation: estranged from her husband and his power, Beatrice would be relatively harmless. The real danger would arise if Il Moro ever came to love her.

"Beatrice," Eleonora said with ruthless finality, "your father will never insist that Il Moro remove Cecilia Gallerani from her rooms." She paused. "Because I will never counsel your father to make cause with you on this issue."

"I want to come home, Mama," Beatrice proclaimed.

Eleonora said nothing.

"I won't live here, Mama. I'm going to leave. I will take the jewels he has given me and go see my grandfather in Naples. Nonno will give me a town of my own. With a very stout wall."

In an instant Beatrice fled to those walls, ancient terra-cotta bastions covered with brilliant green ivy and iridescent butterflies; she stood atop a parapet, guarded by her dolls in their taffeta *camore* and her tropical birds with their huge enamel beaks, and when Il Moro, kneeling far below, begged her to return, her birds assaulted him with screeching invective.

Eleonora sighed inwardly, her feelings too complex to untangle: pain, guilt, empathy, relief that her daughter's obstinacy had degenerated into fantasy. She stood up and wrapped Beatrice in her arms and kissed her still-wet cheeks. "I know that you are going to remain here and represent us proudly, because you have always done what your father and I have asked of you," she said, stroking her daughter's hair. "Messer Ambrogio has prepared a draught for you. Drink it and you will sleep all night. You will see how much better everything looks when you are rested. These wedding *feste* tax everyone's nerves. There is no good reason for them to go on so long." Eleonora kissed Beatrice again, briefly met the eyes of the Marquesa, and moved slowly to the door.

"Mama, I am never going to let him touch me again. I will not even take his hand."

Eleonora didn't turn back to Beatrice; she did not want her daughter to see the wry etching of a smile on her sad, weary face.

A greyhound skidded across the marble floor and thudded into Isabella's knees; a second dog thrust its snout into her skirts. On the canopied bed, four bodies, naked flesh glazed with lamplight, were entwined in a sexual permutation that could not immediately be deciphered. A woman gasped sharply, and one of the dogs barked.

"I see you have guests."

Gian Galeazzo Sforza, Duke of Milan, had not looked up when his wife entered the room; now he ignored her comment. He leaned forward in his chair and flicked his tongue at the wine in his Murano glass goblet. His fine platinum-blond hair brushed at the ermine collar of his satin mantle. Gian's lustrous eyes struggled to fix on the naked couple silhouetted in front of the fireplace. The woman, somewhat heavyset, was on her knees, her head resting on her arms and her nipples grazing the sable throw rug; the man knelt behind her, his pelvis slapping her buttocks in a steady rhythm. Like Gian and the couples on the bed, the two lovers seemed oblivious of the Duchess of Milan, perhaps even of one another.

The goblet slipped from Gian's hands and fell to the Persian carpet; the stem snapped off.

"Go to bed, Gian." The Duchess appeared to regard the copulating couples as little more than furniture.

Gian's head shot up, and he looked at his wife, his sultry lips twisted with a sneer. There was a strange, wild beauty to him, at once fey and robust; his pallid skin was so delicate that it seemed translucent, but he had broad, angular cheeks and a powerful jaw.

"Go to bed. You are doubtless weary from the burdens of your title."

Gian sprang to his feet, swayed as if he would collapse backward, and with the same motion that righted his balance, milled his arm. His fist caught Isabella just under her ear and sent her reeling sideways. She fell to her knees. The couple dallying before the fireplace disengaged and pattered from the room.

Isabella leapt up and raced to the oil lamp set on the scrolled brass sconce beside the bed. The group on the bed began to unknot; a woman fumbled for her chemise. Isabella snatched the lamp and began to stalk her husband, thrusting the flaming wick like a knife. "*Cacapensieri.* I'll burn your *cazzo* off. For what use you have of it."

In a seemingly choreographed burst, the remaining guests, fleetingly recognizable as two women, one man, and a slender male adolescent, scurried out the door. Gian watched his companions depart, the clean planes of his jaw distinct. Then the resolution on his face vanished, as if the underlying bone and muscle had collapsed. A moment before, he had been a man. Now he was a boy. He stepped back.

Isabella threw the lamp into the fireplace. The glass globe popped, and the fire flared up. "Do you want to try tonight, Gian? Undo my laces."

After hesitating for a moment, Gian began to untie the laces that bound the bodice of his wife's *camora*, his elegant fingers making an art of his fumbling. Isabella slipped the dress over her head and pulled her silk chemise off. No trace of her recent pregnancy remained, except a slight fullness in her breasts. The black patch between her legs was a broad triangle against the perfect white of her thighs.

"You haven't tried in a long time, Gian." Isabella helped Gian remove his belt, tunic, and hose; his shirt concealed his genitals. She led him to the sable throw beside the fire.

For a half hour Isabella stroked, licked, panted, whimpered, squeezed, and grappled; nothing aroused her husband's flaccid desire. Finally she let Gian suckle her breast until he fell asleep.

CHAPTER

5

Smoke and sparks from the foundries along the Via degli Armorai poured into the low, slate-gray clouds. At the end of the boulevard, the unfinished roofline of the Duomo was a ghostly sketch against the glowering sky. Snow on the wind, her brother Alfonso had said; you can smell it. Beatrice realized she would even miss Alfonso.

"Mama, if it snows again I am going to perish. I am beside myself at the thought of going all the way to Pavia in this." The Marquesa looked up at the facade of the Castello di Porta Giovia; the enormous central tower seemed to poke the belly of the ugly, overladen sky. The noise of the retinue gathered in front of the Castello was considerable; Il Moro had added two hundred Milanese men-at-arms to the Ferrarese contingent. Horses snorted and whinnied, and car drivers shouted at their teams. The ladies attending the Marquesa and Eleonora huddled inside their fur-lined *cioppe* and looked about sullenly. Alfonso pressed a pimpled cheek to Beatrice's. He didn't look at her, but he said goodbye graciously.

The Marquesa pulled her hands out of her sable muff and took Beatrice's bare hands in hers. There were suddenly tears in her eyes. "Remember that you must hire a secretary as soon as you find someone suitable. You will no doubt be proffered some aging flatterer, but there are simply too many brilliant young men about today to settle for a toothless *vecchio* who has spent his life writing sonnets about horse races and wolf hunts. Now, as soon as your choir is entirely assembled, you must write me for the compositions *à la Flandre* that Girolamo da Sestola has collected for Father and me. And in any event you must write me once every week, *by your own hand* and to be dispatched by special messenger. I am dying at this moment; you know that, don't you?" The Marquesa engulfed Beatrice in her voluminous sable *cioppa* and kissed her four times on each cheek. "My dearest, most special sister," she said, and then she backed away and wiped at her nose with her sable muff.

"Messer Niccolò is giving the order to move along," Eleonora said as she took Beatrice's hands. Her eyes were so brilliantly green that Beatrice imagined they had the sun locked away inside them. If you think your sister is beautiful, she had always been told, you should have seen your mother when she was young. Beatrice could not really remember her mother before Naples, and when she had come home, Eleonora was already growing old and fat.

Eleonora glanced over Beatrice's head to the looming tower of the Castello. She reflexively plumped up the fur collar of Beatrice's *cioppa*. "Make certain you keep your fires burning during the day throughout April, even if the climate warms considerably. That will take the damp out of the walls. You do not want to become ill in the first months of your marriage, or you will not have the strength for your first baby. That is always the most taxing birth." She pressed Beatrice to her. "I will come back when you have your first baby. I promise you I will be here for that."

Beatrice stared numbly into her mother's shoulder. Her mind was so slow today; it was as if the snow on the wind had already fallen and blanketed her thoughts, encasing her in cottony silence. The thoughts that struggled through the drifts were strange ones, faces emerging suddenly from a blizzard. "Mama," she whispered, "when they cut the May branches this year, cut one for me." The annual ceremony on the first of May came back to her with painful vividness: almost the entire court galloping through the fragrant countryside, the men in armor, the wind in her ears, the sticky sap of the cut greens on her gloves. . . . She was certain they did not cut the May branches in Milan.

As Eleonora squeezed her tightly, Beatrice felt that she was closer to her mother than she had ever been before. Perhaps that was why she asked the forbidden question that lay beneath all her questions like an endlessly drawn-out *Kyrie Eleison* in a Mass. "Mama, why did you leave me in Naples?"

"Why would you ask that after all these years? And why now?" Eleonora released Beatrice and held her away from her. She looked at her daughter with wary eyes. "It is not so unusual for a child to grow up at another court. And your father had many enemies at the time. I knew you would be safe with your grandfather."

"But why did Isabella and Alfonso come back with you, and not me?"

"This is silly and inappropriate. You are the Duchess of Bari now, one of the most important women in Italy. Whatever your father and I did on your behalf as a child was to make you capable of the duties you now have as a woman," Eleonora said as she plumped up Beatrice's collar again. "You will understand when you have your own children. We always loved you as our daughter whether you were with us or not. And we always will. Now kiss me. Messer Niccolò is waiting."

"I love you, Mama," Beatrice said, kissing her mother's fleshy, almost lifelessly cold cheeks. But her mother simply turned and walked to her horse; she mounted with the ease of a woman half her age or girth.

Like an ebbing tide the retinue fell away, trumpets blowing, gloved hands waving and wind-flushed faces bravely smiling, banners snapping in the snow-scented wind. Soon the piazza was empty and only Polissena and several Castello guards remained alongside Beatrice. She was not aware of them, or of the first glassy grains of sleet. She watched until the Via degli Armorai had consumed even the banners of her mother's escort. Finally she turned and stared up at the gray walls of her new home. The three malevolent towers that faced the Via degli Armorai were the color of bruises against the grim sky. But Beatrice's trudging mind retreated from whatever future it apprehended within those stone walls. Instead her benumbed consciousness made a lonely pilgrimage back to childhood. And there, like the poet Dante staring up at the monstrous visage of Satan in the frozen center of Hell, she confronted the terrible central doubt of her existence: Had Mama left her in Naples because Mama had never loved her?

"Buongiorno, signore." Il Moro gestured at the empty chairs, upholstered in mulberry velour embroidered with gold Sforza vipers, then settled back in his own chair, similarly upholstered but with a massive curving back and thick scrolled and gilded legs and arms. Behind him, his three secretaries sat at their tall, slant-topped writing lecterns, their three quill pens already bobbing across sheets of parchment like birds engaged in some frantic mating ritual. A large Persian rug had been spread over the patterned marble floor; the walls had recently been painted with a pattern of red, white, and blue lozenges punctuated with rows of vivid blue Sforza vipers. Two enormous arched windows overlooked the ducal park, but the view was obscured by the shower of wet snowflakes.

The smaller of the two men who took their chairs opposite Il Moro was Count Carlo Belgioioso, the Milanese ambassador to France. Belgioioso was a sturdy-looking man in his early thirties, his youth and stout build well suited to the grueling routine of transalpine travel to which his job subjected him. The second man was the *condottiere* Galeazzo di Sanseverino, Captain General of the Armies of Milan. Messer Galeazz, as he was known, looked like Apollo as the ancients had carved him, all symmetry and grace, yet larger than life, his immaculately tailored embroidered tunic draped over preposterously expansive shoulders and chest. His features were Grecian as well, but sweeter, more boyish, the face the Florentine sculptor Donatello had given his lithe, adolescent David. He lounged with an athlete's insouciance, for a moment extending a muscular leg sheathed in azure woolen hose and massaging his hamstring.

Galeazz and the men he commanded were hired soldiers, as was customary in Italy. But Il Moro had secured a more enduring (if hardly less mercenary) allegiance by marrying Galeazz to his bastard daughter Bianca. Bianca had been only nine at the time of the marriage, but in a world where girls were routinely betrothed in childhood and scarcely pubescent brides became the seals on treaties, their fates cast for a lifetime for the sake of an alliance that might last a few months, the hasty liaison was regarded as good politics rather than a betrayal of innocence. And mercifully, Bianca's marriage was for the time being only political; no one expected her to consummate the marriage or even live with her husband until she was at least fifteen.

Il Moro lifted his arm to emphasize the sealed parchment packet he held in his hand; a large ruby cameo flashed from his third finger. He looked directly at Count Belgioioso. His irises were like bits of obsidian. "I have a letter for the King of France." Il Moro spoke in a low, careful voice, sonorous with self-assurance. "I am asking His Most Christian Majesty to invest the Duke of Milan with the privileges of the Duchy of Genoa."

Belgioioso had to exercise all of his diplomatic skills to avoid betraying his surprise. Galeazz's chair creaked as he sat straight up. Many of the Italian city-states technically were considered fiefdoms of either the King of France or the German Emperor, and although these anachronistic feudal relationships had little to do with real power in modern Italy, ritually reinvoking them could seal an alliance between an Italian state and the French or Germans. The great port of Genoa was the largest French fief among the cities under Milanese rule, so Il Moro was making a highly visible gesture of friendship.

"Your Highness . . . ," Belgioioso began, understanding that he was expected to offer his opinion.

"Speak candidly, *signor.*"

"Your Highness, I do not understand this initiative at all. You have virtually succeeded in uniting all Italy, and now you risk fracturing those alliances by pursuing a friendship with a state whose posture has become increasingly threatening. You know as well as I the advancements they have made in foundry techniques. Their bronze is of such quality that they are already capable of casting cannons light enough to be brought over the Alps, yet powerful enough to reduce masonry walls six *braccia* thick." Belgioioso paused and lowered his eyebrows for emphasis. "There are currently no fortifications in Italy with walls greater than six *braccia* in thickness. We should be sending Paris a signal of Italian unity, not an independent gesture of conciliation."

Il Moro's features betrayed nothing beyond their inherent complexity. He was thirty-nine years old, but his thick, glossy black bangs made him appear younger. Visiting ambassadors often credited his skill as a negotiator to the baffling imperturbability of his face, an impassivity that was all the more confusing because his features conveyed so many possibilities, from the ruthless line of his Roman nose to the gentleness of his subtle, almost feminine mouth. It was a dangerously ambiguous face, because in it even the most wary observer could find something to believe.

After a contemplative interval, Il Moro spoke. "Yes. I am of course aware of the progress their foundries are making. But they are at least three years away from designing carriages capable of safely transporting these cannons on steeply inclined mountain roads. Three years," he reiterated, his tone abstract and distant. His eyes sought Count Belgioioso again. "What do you think of Madame de Beaujeu's situation?" Madame de Beaujeu was the French King's older sister; for the previous eight years she had ruled France as her brother's regent.

"She is still very much in control. But her child is expected in May." Belgioioso speculatively spread his broad, thick hands. "She is slender. The birth may be difficult. If Madame were to be incapacitated, I think the more bellicose factions in Paris would seize the opportunity. All the more reason for caution on our part."

"You are a diplomat, Count Belgioioso, and a very good one, so I needn't instruct you in your craft. But you must remember that the first duty of the astute statesman is to persuade his adversaries that he intends to do one thing, and then do another." Il Moro extended the sealed packet to his ambassador. "Forgive me for sending you off in this weather. But trust me that we are due for a change. By the time you get to Asti, I believe we will have a thaw."

Belgioioso stood up, accepted the packet, bowed, and exited. Galeazz rose with the ambassador, but Il Moro asked him to stay. Galeazz took his chair again and leaned forward, his fingertips pressed together.

The secretaries' pens scratched, and the silent snow rushed past the windows. "Count Belgioioso is a very prudent man," Il Moro said, apparently prompting Galeazz to offer a rebuttal.

"Just as Madame de Beaujeu is a very prudent woman." Galeazz spoke with a florid, self-important diction; his pronunciation of the French name was flawless. "But I think we could benefit if certain factions were to gain ascendance in Paris. That the French intend to cross the Alps does not mean that their objective is to conquer us." Galeazz did not need to elaborate. The French army's alternative conquest had been clearly implied: Naples. The French had ruled Naples until a half century previously, when they had been ousted by the Spanish prince and military adventurer Alfonso of Aragon. The loss had not merely punished French pride; the annual revenues of Naples and its tributaries exceeded those of the entire Kingdom of France. The reconquest of Naples was a standing item on the agenda of any French monarch, but now a group of Italian noblemen, exiled by the current King of Naples, Ferrante of Aragon, had settled in Paris and begun a well-organized and well-funded campaign to stir up the hotheads at the French court. The leader of these Italian agitators was the exiled Prince of Salerno, Antonello di Sanseverino, who happened to be Galeazz's uncle.

"Boldness. That is what I admire most about you, Galeazz." Il Moro suddenly allowed himself a tight but genial smile. "When passion inspires you, you do not hesitate. Italy needs more men like you. But permit a more cautious head to consider what you have suggested. First of all, I am now tied more closely than ever to the house of Aragon." Alfonso of Aragon's blood still coursed through the ruling families of much of Italy: his son Ferrante was the King of Naples; his grandchildren included Eleonora d'Este, the Duchess of Ferrara, and Alfonso of Aragon, Duke of Calabria and heir to throne of Naples; his great-granddaughters included the Marquesa of Mantua, the Duchess of Milan, and Il Moro's new bride. "Secondly, you must remember that our illustrious Duchess Mother is the French King's aunt. And apparently King Charles is quite fond of Duchess Bona." Il Moro paused. "However, for the sake of argument, let us assume that I did wish to betray my family, and King Charles his. What would I profit by establishing the French in Naples?"

The question was deliberately disingenuous. While Il Moro

enjoyed a respectful if wary cordiality with the aging King Ferrante, Galeazz knew that Il Moro despised Ferrante's heir, Alfonso, the Duke of Calabria. Galeazz decided not to belabor this point but to advance to a more adventuresome theme; clearly he had been given an invitation. "Your Highness, you know that our illustrious Duke of Milan has no more faithful servant, yourself excepted, than the Captain General of his armies. But I am not blind or deaf. One need only accompany you through the streets to observe that the people of Milan regard you as their duke." Galeazz's features were so boyishly earnest that he looked ridiculous, David's humble head on Zeus's Olympian body. "I am worried that this popular acclamation may reach such a fever that our people will insist that you assume the title of Duke of Milan, and if we do not accede, Milan will be threatened with civil insurrection. I would not want to be put in the position of attacking the people of Milan simply to deny them this expression of devotion to the regent who governs them so capably." Galeazz shrugged, rolling his shoulders with a panther's menacing grace. "But of course if we acceded to this kind of public demand, the Kingdom of Naples would declare war on us. And Venice, in spite of our closer ties, would most likely join Naples against us. In that event only the French could provide the means of our deliverance."

All of this had been politely coded: Galeazz was suggesting that Il Moro seize the title of Duke of Milan without any urging from the streets.

Il Moro's eyes were impenetrable, unblinking. "I am instituting a new salt tax, so I should think the only acclamation I am likely to receive from our people in the coming months will be their demand that I resign as our illustrious Duke's regent."

Galeazz settled back in his chair. Il Moro abruptly rose and walked to one of the windows. The snow was falling so swiftly and thickly that it gave the Castello an eerie sense of silent motion, as if the sky were speeding past. "Galeazz, Fortune is a woman. To truly enjoy a woman's pleasure, a man must never force her. He must seduce her so that she offers herself, indeed even forces him. The more formidable the woman, the more painstaking and elaborate that seduction must be. And Fortune is the most formidable of all women. What does Dante tell us? 'No mortal knowledge can stay her spinning wheel. One nation triumphs, the other is vanquished, both in obedience to her decree.' "

He turned and faced Galeazz, his eyes no longer hard and distant but so open and luminous that Galeazz thought he could see the fires of ambition burning deep within.

"Galeazz, I am wooing Fortune. Not to hold her in my arms for an aching instant, as most men aspire, to smell her lingering and fading scent for the rest of a lifetime and beg her to pass my way again. I want to win Fortune, to win her adoration, to make her pause in her relentless caprice and submit wholly to me. I want to make Fortune my whore."

Il Moro's eyes burned for a heartbeat longer and then instantly went flat, and Galeazz could sense that the moment of intimacy had passed; he stood to take his leave. Il Moro scarcely seemed to notice Galeazz's departure. He settled in his chair and began reading from a pile of documents stacked on the small table beside him. But after a moment he was distracted by the motion at the door; a man trailing a velvet cape swept urgently into the room. Tall and gaunt, with a parturient-looking paunch and bristling eyebrows, the visitor resembled a comic Mephistopheles on an errand of fate.

"Messer Ambrogio." Il Moro respectfully rose to greet the court astrologer.

"Your Highness," Messer Ambrogio intoned with his strange, deeply sighing voice, "I believe you will find this evening propitious for the conception of a son."

"Look at me well! Indeed I am she, I am Beatrice.
By what effrontery have you climbed this mountain?
Did you not know that here man is happy?"

Beatrice looked up from her volume of Dante's *Purgatorio*, a gift from her mother. The pages, printed in Venice on fine goatskin parchment, had been bound in red damask by Dutch artisans; the corners and clasps were beaded with pearls and granulated gold. She envisioned herself as her namesake, confronting the poet as he completed his ascent of the mountain of Purgatory. Except that in her version Il Moro was the chastened penitent beholding the eternal beauty of the woman he had abandoned in this life, his heart suddenly turned as cold as the ice of the Alps at the realization that he had so grievously wronged her. Bitter tears of remorse coursed down his cheeks as he confessed that he had been enticed by the false allure of another woman. . . .

The fantasy failed to assuage Beatrice's queasy stomach. She closed the book and settled into the plump down pillow propped against the ornate plaster headboard. The flames in the fireplace opposite her bed illuminated the terra-cotta lions supporting the mantle, a wavering chiaroscuro that made them appear to lift their paws and nod their fierce heads. She reluctantly admitted to herself that she was not Dante's Beatrice, waiting to torment her errant lover with her divine beauty. She was someone now called the Duchess of Bari, waiting for her husband. In a parting warning, Mama had told her to expect him to call on her in her rooms once the wedding *feste* had concluded, and earlier in the evening Polissena had intimated that the visit would probably occur sooner rather than later.

She anxiously fingered the lace collar of her white wool chemise, hating the meaningless, mechanical act she was now forced to anticipate only because it represented her husband's right to invade at his whim her rooms, her body, her thoughts. She could hear the droning noisemakers called *cacarelle* that had serenaded her first time with him, see the grave, mineral-black eyes that had appeared to refuse her image as effectively as a mirror coated with lamp-black, smell the faint scent of perfume on his nightshirt. He had performed with more efficiency than brutality; it had been no more strange to have him inside her than to have him outside her, his thick chest pressed down on her, his hand pushing her buttocks upward. This is nothing like Tristan and Isolde, she had thought to herself the whole time, staring up at the dim gold ceiling coffers over her head, that insistent banal thought spinning endlessly to the accompaniment of the *cacarelle* in the hall. This is what it is really like.

But what it was really like was still worse. Cecilia Gallerani had not been present that first time. Cecilia Gallerani, for whom he had postponed the wedding twice and had finally tried to void the marriage contract, Cecilia Gallerani who had stolen all the magic incantations of his love, Cecilia Gallerani who had engineered her utter humiliation. Beatrice had already devised a thousand ingenious ways to avenge herself on Cecilia Gallerani, but Mama had warned her that Father would send her to a convent if she said or did anything. More importantly, her sister had also urged caution, advising Beatrice to wait, strengthen her own position at court, and acquire intelligence as to Cecilia Gallerani's weaknesses. Of course that was easy enough for her sister to say; Bel's husband had sent her love letters since he was ten years old. And while the stealth and calculation Bel had suggested appealed to one aspect of Beatrice's nature, so did the notion of doing something rash.

She studied the life-size porcelain doll sitting on the brightly painted wooden storage chest set at the end of her bed. The most truly dramatic thing she could do would be to do nothing. Nothing at all. She would not eat, she would not drink, she would not leave her bed. She would lie there, as unmoving as her doll, to wither and die even as they all stood beside her bed in a tragic chorus, begging her to live. She could see the great crowds weeping at her immense black bier, her pale face haloed with the light of a thousand candles, so beautiful in her eternal repose that Il Moro would clutch at his frozen heart in agony and remorse. . . .

Two rapid knocks at the door were followed by the entrance of Polissena. She crossed the room with short, furious steps, her wooden soles rapping the marble floor. "His Highness is coming." Polissena vehemently snatched the doll from the storage chest; porcelain legs swung as though kicking in protest. "You won't be needing her tonight," Polissena cawed. "You'll have proper company. Remember what your sainted mother told you, and we will be seeing more of the Duke of Bari. It means nothing that he wasn't taken with you the first time. It's something you must learn, like riding a horse. I've seen more than one man of His Highness's experience become so enamored of a girl your age that he wouldn't leave her alone." Polissena's head bobbed admonishingly. "You may think it is uncomfortable now, but you are strengthening your female parts so that your births won't be so difficult. The pain you pay tonight is a coin you won't be asked for later."

Clomping about the room, Polissena tucked Beatrice's doll and books into the storage chest, saw that the brass snuffer hung from the oil lamp on the wall, and made certain there was water in the majolica pitcher on the small table. Finally she returned to the bed and wrestled Beatrice's chemise over her head. Beatrice stiffly submitted but glared up at her tormentor. "You're his wife," Polissena explained. "If you're feeling modest, keep the covers pulled up." She smiled toothlessly. "But I can tell you that the sight of bare breasts will put His Highness about his business more quickly."

Polissena's slippers rapped out her exit; she left the door ajar. Beatrice pulled the covers up to her neck. She tasted the dry bitterness of fear, and her heart seemed to want to explode through her ears.

"His Highness the Duke of Bari," Polissena announced on her return. She curtsied with arthritic formality, then closed the door behind her.

"*Cara esposa*," Il Moro said grandly, as if he had an audience in attendance. He wore a cerulean-and-gold brocade tunic with blue hose; his hands cradled a parcel of gold-striped green velvet. He sat on the bed and unfolded a magnificently embroidered and tailored *camora*. "This cloth arrived from Genoa just two days ago. I don't believe I have ever seen such an exquisite *riccio sopra riccio*. I put our seamstresses to work so that I could present it to you tonight as a token of how very pleased I am at the marvelous compliments I am constantly receiving about you. Remarks, I hasten to add, I have conveyed to your father's ambassador—"

"Did your seamstresses also make a *camora* of this cloth for Cecilia Gallerani?" The words came almost automatically, like the Latin recitations Beatrice had memorized as a small child.

There was no perceptible change in Il Moro's expression. After a moment he turned his head very slightly toward Beatrice, making some minute adjustment in his opaque gaze. "My darling, I think you should understand about Madonna Cecilia. When a man waits as long as I have to marry, it is only natural that he amuse himself with—"

"She is having your baby."

"I am afraid that is an inescapable consequence of such amusements. I know that you have a half-brother and a half-sister. The honor your father and mother have shown both those children honors the house of Este." Ercole d'Este's two bastards had been raised alongside the legitimate children; Beatrice's half-sister Lucrezia was almost as dear to her as her sister Isabella. "I like to think that we Sforza will also show charity to those who carry our blood, even if they will never have the rights of those progeny born with God's sanction. Can you now see why I cannot turn Madonna Cecilia out of her rooms? After Cecilia's child is born, of course we will make other arrangements for her and her baby."

Beatrice's mind churned in debate. Her childish fantasies of vindication called out for a total rejection of this nonsense (as did some far more acute instinct that she was hardly aware she had); since he had failed to convince her that Cecilia didn't exist, he was now claiming that she was merely transient. But the young woman struggling to establish her marriage observed that everything he had just said was reasonable, consistent, even honorable. A skilled negotiating position perhaps, but what was marriage if not a negotiation? And there was something beneath his cool, detached demeanor that seemed charmingly earnest, that made her desperately want to believe him, almost as if in believing this she could hear the words she desperately wanted her lover to tell her. . . .

"*Carissima*," he said, and touched her cheek. He slid closer to her, and his thumb traced lightly across her jawline. His hair shimmered in the firelight. "*Carissima sposa*," he whispered in her ear. His lips were dry and soft on her cheek, like warm silk. Her head buzzed. He gently pressed her against the pillows and lay down beside her. His lips played softly at hers, and her head became so light that she imagined she was floating. "I'm afraid I rushed you the first time, *amatissima*," he murmured, stroking her collarbones, his fingers hot and smooth. And then the words. He whispered to her the words that she had always dreamed of hearing, words such as Tristan had told his Isolde and Petrarch had written his Laura, words that flowed through her mind like rivers of sparking molten gold. "*Amore, amore, amore . . .*"

His fingertip brushed her nipple, and a shiver rippled through her entire body as he reached beneath the covers and stroked her thigh. His tongue teased her ear. "I want you to have my son," he whispered hotly.

In the same way that she could detect a discordant note among a roomful of lyres and lutes, Beatrice heard the slight, but to her unmistakable, change in her husband's timbre. The realization, when it came to her, was like a cold gust rifling through the room: What he has just told me is his true desire. All the rest has been a lie.

He pressed impatiently against her sudden tension, his kiss so aggressive that for a moment she couldn't breathe. His full weight pinned her, and he drew the covers back and forced his hand into her crotch. She wrestled an arm loose and pushed at his jaw. He groped crudely at her genitals. She pressed her fingernails into his cheek and pulled.

Il Moro lurched back and frantically pressed his hand to his face. After a moment he took it away and examined his fingers. It was the first time Beatrice had ever seen a genuine expression on her husband's face. He stared at his fingertips as if they were covered with gore. But there was not even a drop of blood; Beatrice had only raised welts on his face.

"I warned your father that you were too immature for the duties expected of you." Il Moro stood and looked down at her. His chest swelled, followed by an audible exhalation through his nose. "All I am going to ask of you is that you make the proper appearance of a wife for the sake of your family and the people of Milan. If you can agree to that, we can forget this evening, and the prospect of its recurrence, entirely."

Beatrice felt as if she were choking on a cold stone. She quickly nodded assent, hoping he would leave before she started crying. She closed her eyes, and the welling tears spilled onto her cheeks. When she opened her eyes again he was gone.

"He's hungry, Your Highness." The wet nurse looked proudly into the glazed eyes of Francesco Sforza, the six-week-old heir to Milan. Francesco fed in greedy surges, his tiny mouth flattened against the dark areola, his jaw pulsing.

"I loved that," Isabella said. She sat on a simple wooden stool beside her baby and his nurse. "I wanted to keep doing it. But of course Messer Ambrogio and the Duchess Mother wouldn't hear of it."

"You've so much else to concern you, Your Highness. This one wears me out with all his feeding. He's going to be quite a man. Aren't you, *bello puttino*. It's a joy just to look down and see him, Your Highness, he's so pretty."

"I love to look at him too. I never get tired of watching him." Isabella looked up quickly. An old woman came into the nursery and curtsied before the Duchess.

"Your Highness," the old woman said, "Cecilia Gallerani is still occupying her rooms."

"I did not expect any change there," Isabella said idly.

The old woman worked her sunken mouth. "The Duke of Bari went to his wife's rooms last evening. He wasn't with her more than a few minutes."

Isabella took her baby and held him to her shoulder and patted his back. The windows behind her opened onto the Piazza d'Armi, the large central court of the Castello. The sun had broken through a thin layer of gray clouds. The field of glistening snow reflected such an intense light that from the old woman's vantage the Duchess of Milan was a dark silhouette surrounded by a glaring white halo.

"There is no way to make a man regret a wager he has yet to make. But now Il Moro has made his choice," Isabella said. "And Fortune enjoys no greater delight than when she mocks our choices."

TWO

CHAPTER

6

Château du Louvre, Paris, February 1491

"Tenez!"

The Prince of Salerno's overdone roast capon miraculously took flight, a wheeling, flat trajectory that ended in the middle of the King of France's bed. The charred, headless fowl, feet still attached and wings spread, lay on the red satin bedcloth like a curious heraldic emblem. Antonello di Sanseverino, the Prince of Salerno, looked down at his suddenly empty pewter dining platter and then with saturnine elegance turned his head toward the King of France. Antonello was almost seventy years old, with white hair swept back from a high forehead darkened by a lifetime in the sun of southern Italy. But his finely modeled features and bullish chest evidenced the hereditary disposition of the Sanseverino men to maintain their good looks and robust health to the end. At a Sanseverino funeral, it was said, the best-looking man present was always the corpse.

"When I say '*Tenez,*' it means I intend to put the ball into play, *monseigneur.* I do hope you haven't taken affront." His Most Christian Majesty Charles VIII of France held up his tennis racket and apologetically shrugged his shoulders, which would have been

virtually nonexistent if not for the copious padding of his pink
velvet coat.

"Well, Your Majesty, if you were aiming at my capon, you
can congratulate yourself on a very fine ball indeed."

Charles emitted a brief noise like an irate goose, which he might
have extended into the honking of an entire gaggle if he had found
Prince Antonello's jest truly amusing. The King walked toward
the bed, displaying spindly, childlike legs adorned with fashionable
nine-color hose, and feet enlarged to absurd proportions by the
latest style in French slippers, which featured enormous, scallop-
shaped splayed toes. A humped back echoed the contour of his
bulging stomach, his head was oversize, his huge eyes vague and
watery, his nose an enormous bony protrusion. His coarse red
beard grew up into his nostrils and down his neck but refused to
cover his pale cheeks and collapsing chin.

This collection of anatomical misfortunes sat on the edge of
his bed, joining his mistress of the week—a Parisian prostitute
wearing, as Antonello observed to himself, the kind of tastelessly
anachronistic costume that many Frenchwomen still favored:
sleeves as big as tents and linen headpieces that rose up like horns
and trailed wisps of silk tissue. Antonello glanced at the strumpet
long enough to see His Majesty's hand disappear into her billowing
skirts. The prostitute giggled, and Antonello looked out the window, motivated by boredom rather than modesty—the King had
already shown him pictures of the strumpet naked, in a pose that
invited intercourse *d'arrière;* His Most Christian Majesty kept several artists busy making such drawings of all his conquests.

A freight barge covered with dirty brown canvas drifted by
on the Seine, which was itself stained a dingy color by sewage
and the sullen sky. Across the river, dozens of jagged medieval
towers raked the mist, their copper spires, topped with crucifixes
and weathercocks, jutting like the lances of a vast army. Paris is
an ugly city, Antonello reflected, with an ugly climate, in an ugly
country peopled with filthy *oltramontani* barbarians who disdain
bathing as earnestly as they repudiate learning. The previous
month he had gone to Amboise with the King, and they had
encountered perhaps a thousand homeless peasants on the road,
pathetic wretches who owned nothing but brown canvas sacks to
cover their torsos and counted themselves lucky if they got a scrap

of brown bread twice a week. It had been raining that day, and the road was awash with mud the color of excrement, mud that covered the bare limbs of the peasants to match the filthy hue of their sackcloths, and they had all looked like walking *caca*, two-legged turds sloshing through the sewer that was France. . . . To be in Naples this day, Antonello mused, with the bay the color of Eleonora of Aragon's eyes and the lemon trees climbing the hills . . . I would give my soul to be in Naples this day.

Antonello stood up; he was so tall that the brass columns of the King's bed were level with his nose. "Your Majesty, it has just occurred to me that you have made the emblem of the German Emperor." He pointed to the charred capon, which indeed looked like a headless, distorted version of the black imperial eagle that was the symbol of the ancient Holy Roman Empire, now neither holy nor Roman and usually referred to simply as Germany.

"Remarkable." His Most Christian Majesty withdrew his arm from his mistress's skirts and sprang to his feet. He stood over the capon, his lips slack and his nose jutting, as if he were examining the talking head of a decapitated saint. "You see what it is I have made, my good Prince: I have created a portent! I verily have! It is indeed a portent! It will lead forth our Christian multitude against the heathen Turk, to free Constantinople from the Sultan's yoke! O Roland and Olivier, rise and live again, most Christian knights! The murdering paynim awaits our holy vengeance!" Charles whirled as if brandishing a sword, then stopped suddenly. "I'm not certain I want this to be my portent," he said. "It is, after all, *his* emblem." Charles was referring to Maximilian, Archduke of Austria and imminent heir to his ailing father's title of Holy Roman Emperor. As far as Charles was concerned, only the presence of Maximilian and his German hordes lurking at France's borders prevented him from leading the French army on the last great Crusade.

"I think what it means, Your Majesty, is that you will soon have the Germans on a spit."

"Yes. Of course. And then we shall be free for our Christian enterprise!" Charles searched frantically about the room—the floor was littered with tennis rackets, whips, swords, arrows, arquebuses—until he located one of his ponderous jousting lances. "We shall ride with all the great paladins of Christendom!" Charles shouted as he prepared his charge. He lunged at the bed and expertly speared the capon.

"Well, it appears you are already halfway to Constantinople, Your Majesty. But of course you must take Naples first. It will be your leaping-off point for the Turk strongholds. Would you like to see the maps?"

"The maps? Yes, yes, the maps."

With a casual motion of his massive arm, Antonello swept the pewter platter to the floor. He unrolled two parchments over the tabletop. One was a map of Naples, the other a more detailed plan of the Castel Nuovo, the city's enormous, impregnable seaside fortress. Antonello did not need to remind Charles of their mutual interest in the third great city of Europe, surpassed in size and wealth, if not in magnificence or sophistication, by only Venice and Milan. The French King had inherited his nation's half-century-old grudge against the house of Aragon, which had snatched Naples away from France, while Prince Antonello had a more recent score to settle with Ferrante of Aragon, the current King of Naples, who had driven Antonello into exile and confiscated his vast landholdings in southern Italy.

Charles made admiring hums over the invasion plans, and Antonello could not help but reflect that when His Most Christian Majesty stood over a campaign map, he was a titan of sorts. For the same taxes that had reduced France to a stinking sewer of a nation had built the most magnificent military machine in Europe: a standing army, available at a moment, its loyalty unquestioned—unlike the mercenary bands the Italian princes employed—a standing army of elite cavalry and trained infantry and, most important of all, cannons. The French could scarcely make edible bread, but they could cast cannons as if they commanded the forge of Vulcan. Cannons light enough to be brought over the Alps, yet powerful enough to bring down the walls of even the Castel Nuovo in Naples. Antonello believed that the French cannons would change the map of Europe. And he intended to be a beneficiary of those changes.

"*Monseigneurs.*" The voice was brisk and somewhat shrill. Charles dropped his jousting lance with a loud clang; the impaled capon carcass fell from the tip. Antonello hastily rolled up his maps.

The woman who breezed into the room with implacable authority was a bit taller than the King and dressed in the restrained new Italian style: a black silk dress with narrow sleeves and contrasting square-necked bodice in white velvet. Her hair was pulled back from her forehead to reveal a sharp widow's peak, then hidden by a black hoodlike cap hemmed with double rows of pearls. Her slender, sour face featured a rapier nose so sparely fleshed that it appeared to be bare bone; her full lips were shaped into a habitual pucker of anxiety. Despite her tailored dress, one would have had to look carefully to discern that she was in the sixth month of her pregnancy.

"Madame," Prince Antonello said. He stood and bowed deeply. Anne, Madame de Beaujeu, or simply "Madame," as she was known throughout France, scrutinized the *mis-en-scène* with cynical, piercing eyes. When her father, King Louis XI, died eight years previously, Madame had ruthlessly wrested from her own mother, Charlotte of Savoy, the title of regent to her then thirteen-year-old brother. Madame's prize had been the virtual corpse of a nation, and yet against all odds she had nursed France back to life, shuttling that splendid army (her father's only legacy of any real value) from one end of the country to another, bludgeoning one fractious feudal lord or rebellious province after another into obedience.

Madame dismissed Antonello with a quick redirection of her icy gaze; while his Naples "campaign" might inflame those idlers at court who read old-fashioned tales of chivalry and dreamed of grandiose conquests—her brother the King being the foremost example—it might also provide her leverage someday in negotiating with the Italians, so she tolerated Antonello's presence. "*Monseigneur*," she said to her brother, "I have a letter from Il Moro."

"Il Moro! Il Moro! Il Moro!" Charles whined; a large drop of mucus fell from his nose. "Truly! All I hear every day from the ambassadors is Il Moro. From the Venetian ambassador and the Roman ambassador and this gentleman from Naples, nothing but Il Moro! Even the English go on about him! Truly! Why must everything be Il Moro!"

"Because, *monseigneur*, Il Moro has succeeded in consummating his alliance with the house of Este in Ferrara and is now in a position to unite all Italy into a common polity. It is my concern to establish whether Il Moro will then bring Italy into an alliance with us against the Germans or join the Germans and oppose us." Madame whipped her head to confront Prince Antonello. "You are familiar with events at the court of Milan. How would you assess Il Moro's intentions, *monseigneur?*" Actually Madame knew everything that Antonello did, because although Antonello's nephew Galeazzo di Sanseverino was Captain General of the Armies of Milan, Madame had been intercepting all of Galeazz's letters to his uncle, none of which had revealed any state secrets. Still, there was the possibility that Galeazz used a code.

"When it comes to concealing his intentions, no man is more skilled than Il Moro." Antonello smiled sardonically.

Madame lifted her heavy, already high and inquisitive eyebrows. "Il Moro has written us to ask that my brother agree to the investiture of the Duke of Milan with the privileges of the Duchy of Genoa." Madame's puckered lips relaxed slightly, wryly. "Curious, is it not, Monseigneur Antonello, that when Il Moro asks a single question, a dozen answers are required? With this request Il Moro warns me that he could as easily turn to the German Emperor and ask for his nephew's formal investiture with the privileges of Milan, which is an imperial fief. Perhaps he intends to do so even if I agree. Or perhaps he sincerely desires our friendship and intends to solicit our help in crushing Naples should he wish to usurp his nephew. And with that done, then Il Moro might invite the German Emperor to invest *him* as the new Duke of Milan, turn all Italy against our army while it was still occupied in Naples, while at the same time the Germans marched into Paris. Or perhaps Il Moro merely intends to wage peace on Europe and use his considerable treasury to configure the map to his liking." She paused and her dour eyes flickered. "The real question is not to what extent Il Moro intends to deceive us but to what extent Il Moro wishes to deceive himself.

"*Monseigneur*, I intend to deliberate upon this matter at greater length," Madame said, snapping her gaze back to her bewildered brother. "When I have drafted a reply to Il Moro, I will of course expect you to sign it." With that Madame abruptly turned and exited the room.

His Most Christian Majesty retrieved his lance and desultorily poked at the capon carcass. Finally he looked up morosely at Prince Antonello. "Perhaps we can interest Il Moro in our Crusade," he mumbled, then shuffled back to his bed and placed his oversize head facedown in his mistress's lap.

CHAPTER

7

Extract of a letter of POLISSENA ROMEI, matron of honor to the Duchess of Bari, to ELEONORA D'ESTE, Duchess of Ferrara. Milan, 2 March 1491

. . . her husband accords her the utmost cordiality and good will, and no effort has been spared to provide her with amusements and pleasures. Today Messer Galeazz has taken her fishing to Cussago. . . . One does not hear the end of the accolades devoted to your daughter's horsemanship, Your Highness. . . .

Extract of a letter of GIACOMO TROTTI, Ferrarese ambassador to the Court of Milan, to ERCOLE D'ESTE, Duke of Ferrara. Milan, 10 March 1491

. . . on the occasions on which he visits the Gallerani woman in her rooms, he proceeds there as brazenly as if he were progressing to the Duomo on Easter Sunday. The situation is manageable at present, but I have grave concerns about what may ensue once the child is born. I suspect that Il Moro intends to have his bastard christened publicly and upon that occasion acknowledge the child as his own. The possibility also exists that your daughter will create an incident in the general view. While she at times appears melancholic, her eruptions of temper are sudden and violent. She has bruised poor Fritello, her dwarf. The company of Il Moro's daughter relieves her despondency, but the girl is too frail to ride or accompany Madonna Beatrice on her many excursions. The Duke and Duchess of Milan have been in Pavia since early February, but Madonna Beatrice is going there tomorrow. We can expect no cordiality in those relations, either. . . .

Il Moro has not had a response from the French. . . .

Pavia, 11 March 1491

The spires and cupola of the Certosa di Pavia rose above the trees, a tracery of pinkish brick cones and white marble columns against an incandescent blue sky. A poplar-lined road ran straight toward the huge Carthusian monastery, still under construction after a century of lavish spending. The road was the consistency of porridge, a reminder of a week of heavy rains.

Beatrice brushed at the skirt of her brocade *cioppa*, spotted with mud kicked up by her ladies' horses as they trotted past. Rid of their largely superfluous Duchess, the ten young women regrouped into a sauntering, gossiping, snickering band. Beatrice had come to regard her Milanese ladies-in-waiting as the most insufferable burden of matrimony. Though her ladies were the wives and daughters of the haughtiest and most powerful Milanese noblemen, they were often little more than extravagantly priced prostitutes sent to court to advance the family fortunes, exchanging their bodies for favors and offices. Not only did they not wait on Beatrice (she had a staff of pages and maidservants for that purpose); they openly displayed their contempt for the little *forestiera* Duchess whose husband would not even sleep with her. Beatrice was happy to be shunned; she had never felt more lonely than she did when surrounded by her ladies-in-waiting. Indeed the entire ritual surrounding her new status as Duchess of Bari was the most dreary and absurd routine she could imagine. The sole function of all these activities devoted to her amusement,

Beatrice realized, was simply to distract her from the baldly apparent fact that nobody at court really cared whether she was happy or not.

A chorus of throaty feminine laughter erupted behind her, followed by another shower of mud as the Duchess of Milan's ladies charged up ahead, brocaded torsos inclined forward, skirts billowing over their horses' rumps, plumed velvet caps tilted jauntily to one side. After spattering Beatrice, the Duchess of Milan's ladies proceeded to pass Beatrice's ladies and speckle them with mud. A contest ensued, the two groups of ladies beginning to trot as fast as the precarious footing and their awkward sidesaddle posture would permit.

Beatrice, her legs slung over her horse's left shoulder, looked to her right. The Duchess of Milan had come alongside. Isabella glared at her with sea-green malice, as if she blamed Beatrice for her own ladies' discourtesy. A spot of mud blemished her windrouged cheek.

The words Beatrice wanted to scream out loud boiled in her ears. I hate you too! I hate you too! I hate every one of you! Except for Bianca and Bianca Maria, I hate everyone in Milan! Without at first realizing what she was doing, she flourished her riding crop and whacked her horse's rump. The beast lurched into a gallop, but Beatrice, steadied by her powerful hands and sturdy legs, expertly stayed in the saddle. She quickly closed on her ladies, despite their speed. As she drew even with the last lady in the group, she swung her right arm in a vicious arc, catching the woman squarely across the collarbone and toppling her over the rump of her horse. Arms and legs akimbo, the lady splatted into the mud like a silk-plumaged bird shot from the sky.

Quickly perfecting the technique, Beatrice dumped two more of her ladies into the mud before the alarm was sounded. The Duchess of Milan's ladies looked back and began flailing with their riding crops to escape Beatrice's menacing charge. Beatrice pounded with her crop, gaining. She was surprised when a rider caught her from behind: Isabella, squinting into the wind.

Beatrice made an even more furious charge and caught up with Isabella just as they reached the twin files of the Duchess of Milan's ladies. The two duchesses instinctively divided the spoils, each thundering down a frantic row. Four more ladies joined their companions in the slop.

Leaving behind their squealing and squirming attendants, the duchesses continued to ride side by side down the road, speed increasing, crops slapping, their horses beginning to sweat. Beatrice's horse stumbled, and she felt he soon would either slip and topple into the mud or balk and throw her. But only a hand from heaven could have made her slow at that moment. The wind rushed past her ears, and her limbs throbbed with effort. The anger had become something else inside her, buoyant, tingling. In another moment she actually would be flying.

Isabella was the first to slow. Regretfully Beatrice gave her horse's reins a gentle pull, and the two beasts trotted alongside one another. Beatrice listened to her horse gasp and was suddenly aware how hard her own breath was coming, cold gulps of a glorious, liberating ether.

Isabella circled around and faced Beatrice. She had lost her cap in the chase, and her reddish-brown hair was a tangle of coppery, sun-spun gossamer. She nodded at Beatrice, who was as astonished as if a terra-cotta statue of the Virgin had suddenly winked at her.

"I have enjoyed riding with you, Your Highness," Isabella said.

Extract of a letter of LEONARDO DA VINCI, engineer at the Court of Milan, to international traveler and raconteur BENEDETTO DEI. Milan, 28 March 1491

. . . Knowing your proclivity and desire to remain informed of the events at our court, and to learn of whatever affiliations might bring their weight to bear upon said events, let me provide you with my observations of the Duchesses of Milan and Bari. Consider if you will, my dear Benedetto, the days and years which learned men such as Fra Pacioli and Maestro Vincenzo might have devoted to the study of true science and the marvelous schemes of nature, were not their good offices instead diverted to the education of the progeny of the ruling families of our Italian states. An intellect that might have divined the causes and devices of nature is to the contrary condemned to instruct a child scarcely unswaddled in the elocutions of Cicero or the lyrics of Virgil. In many cases these children will never acquire enough knowledge of the tongue of ancient Rome to even converse with the bones of this long-dead race, which lies moldering beneath our soil yet eternally lures men of science from the proper course of study, which is that of nature. And such children as have the intelligence to become learned in these ancient orations, what are they? These dreadful prodigies are induced at court gatherings to recite their mnemonics in an infelicitous child's soprano, to the marvel of all, and yet their discourse requires no more the faculty of divine reason than does the pealing bell of a mechanical clock as it announces the hours. O idolators of ancient texts! Think not that I deplore this profligacy and wastage because I am a man without letters, but instead know that I am one who labors ceaselessly in the true light.

Then consider, my dear Benedetto, how the Duchesses of Bari and Milan have employed the education in which so many learned men have squandered their resources. Not a day passes that these two young women are not mounted on the backs of swift steeds, invariably accompanied by a retinue one might more properly find in the train of an Oriental despot. Think that they avail themselves of our boundless parks and woodlands to study the infinite creations of nature? No, these duchesses race about in perpetual and unceasing competition, darting hither and thither like riders in a *palio*. And when their unfortunate beasts are wearied by these pursuits, said duchesses take up the dubious recreation of tennis, and having used up a barrel of balls, summon men versed in the most exquisite musical harmonies to accompany their dancing. And all the while scarce word of Latin nor language of living men is heard among said duchesses. If theirs is a friendship, or alternatively a rivalry in some equally peculiar manifestation, I cannot discern. . . .

CHAPTER

8

Milan, April 1491

"His Highness," the chamberlain announced in a reverent whisper, as though he had intruded in a holy place. He bowed fluidly and exited, his footsteps scarcely audible. The secretary seated next to Cecilia Gallerani's bed gathered up his pens and inkwell and left the room.

Il Moro walked directly to the large arched window facing the ducal park. The forest of pines, elms, and oaks was already dark, the twilight sky a deep satiny blue. The peaks of the Alps were a faintly rosy serrated band across the horizon. Il Moro stood for a long moment, his hands behind his back, clutching a folded parchment. A coinlike gold seal, attached to a purple cord, dangled from the document.

At length Il Moro turned and faced the bed. Brass columns supported a canopy of heavy gold cloth; the white satin bedspread was decorated with a white appliqué detailing some medieval romance. Cecilia was a similar study in white on white, wrapped in an ivory silk chemise, her pale face and hands almost phosphorescent in the fading light. Her laugh was airy, musical. "I think you have received your answer from the King of France, *amante*. Do you want to share it with me?"

Il Moro sat on the bed and handed Cecilia the parchment. Her gold-tinted gray eyes quickly roamed the text, then paused and retreated into some contemplative depth. "So they have agreed to the investiture. Fortune has given you a sign, *amante*."

"We have our beginning. Now we must wait," Il Moro said, lacing his fingers with Cecilia's.

Cecilia turned and kissed Il Moro. She had thin lips and a small subtle mouth, and for her kissing was not a preferred means of expression. But this kiss conveyed a curious urgency. And then she was gone, swinging her swollen belly to propel the rest of her still-slender body, rising with a quick, almost vehement effort. "I get up as often as I can," she said, preempting her lover's protest. "When Messer Ambrogio carries his first child, I will do every-thing he prescribes."

She walked to the gilt-framed painting hung on the wall op-posite the window. "Look how much I have changed." The portrait was ten years old; Cecilia had sat for Leonardo da Vinci only months after he arrived in Milan, having introduced himself with a ten-item memo boasting of his skills as a military engineer; only as the final item had Leonardo added, "I can do in painting whatever can be done, as well as any other master, whoever he may be." Cecilia considered Leonardo a very good painter; Il Moro was not so sure. He thought the portrait made Cecilia seem gaunt, hunchbacked, and querulous. Leonardo had placed an ermine in her arms, and she stroked the animal's gray velvet fur with her extraordinarily long, lithe fingers; Il Moro was weary of the jests that the ermine resembled him. Cecilia felt that the artist had captured her strength, foresight, and doubt. She knew she would have the painting when she no longer had Il Moro.

Peering at her image as if studying a sister from whom she had been separated for ten years, Cecilia said in appraisal, "I was sixteen years old when this was painted. I was not so lovely a girl as that the quality of being a girl made me lovely. And that I loved you. Every girl has that *grazia;* it is born within us. Nature gives it unequivocally and takes it back inexorably." She turned and smiled, a warm, sad smile that the brittle, coiled girl in the portrait could not have presented.

"I would like to stay with you tonight," Il Moro said, as though assuming she needed some validation of her charms.

"That is so dear of you, *amante*. But I would keep you up all night. I can't seem to get comfortable anymore." She placed her hands lightly on her belly.

"You're not having doubts about the baby?"

"Oh, no, *amante*. I cannot describe to you the joy this has brought me. Never think that."

"I had assumed my news would also bring you joy. Instead it seems to have been the source of your melancholy."

Cecilia smiled again, and her eyes glittered. She came back to the bed and took Il Moro's face in her hands, her elegant fingers framing his powerful jaw. "Your news brought me a very great joy. God, Lodovico, we are at the threshold of realizing the dream I have always held deepest in my soul. But perhaps dreams are like babies in the womb. To actually bring them into the world we must give them away. That is why at every birth there is a parting. Perhaps I was thinking of that."

"Glo-ri-a in ex-cel-sis De-o."

"Et in ter-ra pax ho-mi-ni-bus bo-nae vo-lun-ta-tis."

The alternating choruses of the ducal household choir drifted through the ancient basilica of Sant'Ambrogio. The singers' chiming polyphony was accompanied by a third chorus, a relentless buzz of conversation punctuated by occasional shouts of greeting, mischievous squeals, and the shrieks of a dozen or so pet monkeys, some freed from their leashes and clambering among the stalls like tiny costumed demons. The celebrants of this morning Mass included the Duchesses of Milan and Bari, their ladies-in-waiting and attendants, and various male courtiers, as well as the scores of prostitutes, gamblers, and sundry opportunists who had come to mingle with Milan's ranking dignitaries. Of the crowd of several hundred, probably less than two dozen actually knelt and listened to the service. The rest had organized into whispering cliques or dallying pairs; some courtiers simply wandered about, gazing at the aisle chapels or munching on a breakfast pastry while waiting to be importuned. The crypt beneath the altar was a favorite spot for assignations, as a customer could obtain a furtive sample of the merchandise before rendering full payment. But occasionally an entire transaction might be concluded right atop the white marble sarcophagus of Saint Ambrose, the great Milanese bishop who had founded the basilica over one thousand years previously.

"Look." Isabella nudged Beatrice. "Caterina and Giulia are negotiating with a *meretrice*. I cannot imagine what they have in mind. Perhaps to complete their *ménage* they intend to slip into the crypt and revive Saint Ambrose."

Beatrice smiled, feeling only a momentary anxiety at her cousin's irreverence. Isabella had clearly inherited the beliefs of her father, Alfonso, Duke of Calabria, who had never made even a pretense of attending Mass and had twice besieged the Pope in Rome. Raised in the laxity of Naples, Beatrice on her return to Ferrara had been disconcerted by her mother's quiet yet ardent piety and her father's almost fanatical mysticism. She had eventually arrived at a compromise, acknowledging God as a supernal version of a secular lord; one owed Him a cursory obedience in His own house, but otherwise did not need to give Him much thought.

An old woman suddenly appeared at Isabella's side; Beatrice recognized the *vecchia* as Lucia, one of the women who cared for Isabella's son, Francesco. Lucia's wool cape was spattered with rain; apparently she had just come from the Castello. Beatrice could discern nothing of Lucia's toothless gumming. After a moment Isabella hissed, "Are you certain?"

"We are leaving," Isabella said, whipping around and grabbing Beatrice's arm. Beatrice hesitated, and Isabella tugged her arm. "We must go now. Something has happened." Beatrice momentarily debated the conflicting claims of God and the Duchess of Milan, and as the Duchess of Milan had actually spoken to her, heeded her summons.

The small piazza in front of the church, framed by an arcade, was glazed with a misting rain. The clusters of gamblers, many of them young men who wore short jackets over waist-high hose that precisely detailed the contours of their buttocks, hadn't bothered to move their dice and tarot-card games into the covered porticoes; they simply spread blankets on the damp flagstones. A tooth-drawer had set up shop in one of the porticoes, attracting an eager crowd of onlookers, one of whom assisted by holding the patient's head. The tooth-drawer brandished his menacing iron tongs, and his audience tittered appreciatively.

Isabella drew a length of cheap black wool from her *cioppa* and ripped it in half. She handed a piece to Beatrice and wrapped the other over her head; a scarf was common rainwear in Naples, but among Milanese women it was not considered respectable attire. "Everyone will know we are *forestiere*," Isabella said. "You will never see a Milanese lady walking in the rain. They are afraid the faces they paint on every morning will wash away."

A terrifying howl came from the portico. The tooth-drawer held up his trophy for the admiring crowd: a bloody molar, still fixed in the tongs.

Beatrice and Isabella stepped out into the drizzle. A young gambler eyed them, clutched his padded codpiece, and called out, "Ho, madonna, you want some of this!"

"*Eh, cacastecchi!*" Isabella shouted back. "Your prick couldn't plug a keyhole!" She turned to Beatrice and said with disgust inflected with a certain satisfaction: "He thinks that because we are two well-dressed women out alone we must be *meretrice*."

The street that led to the Castello was lined with three- and four-story *palazzi;* the first story was usually an open arcade sheltering one or more shops: a perfume shop glittering with colored glass phials; a confectioner's shop displaying spun-sugar models of castles and dragons and knights on horseback; a potter's shop filled with majolica and sgraffito and ceramic hand warmers. A goldsmith ruled his portico from an enormous cushioned chair, his goblets and reliquaries and chased plates spread out before him as if he were a Turkish sultan displaying his treasure. Chains strung between the columns of the arcades kept livestock and large dogs out of the shops; cats and small dogs were captured by the shopkeepers' apprentices and periodically hurled back onto the street.

Dense gray clouds were massed on the eastern horizon, portending a heavier rain, and a strong wind carried a curious blend of scents: perfume, garbage, and human waste. *Bravi,* young thugs hired by the shopkeepers to police the street, lounged arrogantly against the columns, daggers stuck in the belts of their gaudy doublets. When similarly dressed young men loitered for a moment too long, the *bravi* urged them along with curses. They

smirked and leered when Beatrice and Isabella passed; if the presumed *meretrice* hadn't been so well dressed, they, too, would have
been shooed away, or perhaps requested to offer their wares in
trade for the privilege of peddling on this street.

Two four-wheel carriages with silk window shades were
parked in front of an expensive fabric shop. A half-dozen Milanese
ladies in fashionable *camore*, escorted by two guards, clustered
around the counter while the owner and his apprentices exhibited
lengths of *velluto allucciolato*, a silk velvet with tiny loops of silver
and gold thread woven into the weft. The shelves were crammed
with thick bolts of satin damask, Genoese samite and taffeta,
Rheims linen, sendal silk from China, tabi silk from Damascus,
a dozen different brocades, embroidered with patterns ranging
from doves to lions.

A young woman posted by the chain, vulgarly but expensively
overdressed in an orgy of multicolored striped velours, warily
eyed the approach of the two hooded *meretrice*. "*Forestiere* sluts,"
she muttered. "Why don't you go back to Rome or Germany or
wherever they wear towels over their heads. Stop spreading your
forestiera diseases among our men."

Isabella's fist shot up, making the "fig," the vulgar sign for
the sex act: thumb thrust between the first two fingers. "Any man
who sleeps with you already has a disease."

"Get off our street, or I'll have our boys sweep you off with
the rest of the trash."

"I want to shop for some *velluto controtagliato*," Isabella said to
Beatrice.

The woman motioned for the apprentice not to remove the
chain; Isabella gathered her skirts and stepped over it. Another
young woman, dressed similarly and bearing a family resemblance
to the first, emerged from behind the counter and blocked Isabella.
"Get out of our shop, *puttana*."

"You don't think my ducats are made of gold, eh?" Isabella
gestured at the Milanese ladies. "Ask them. Their husbands and
fathers are my best customers," she said, sneeringly assuming the
role. "Decent men like that don't cheat their whores with gilded
coppers, though perhaps the men you sleep with do."

The first woman turned on Beatrice. "You and your *put-*

tana friend are about to sleep with the jailer for free." She snatched up a broom and held it threateningly across her breast.

"*Cacapensieri,*" Beatrice snapped. "If you take one step toward me, that broomstick will be your next lover."

One of the guards advanced on Isabella. She glared at him for a moment, then stepped back over the chain. "We don't have time to settle with these little whores," she said to Beatrice. "You and I have business to settle with Milan's foremost slut." Before Beatrice could puzzle over this reference, Isabella began to kick street filth onto the shop's neatly swept marble floor. The guard stepped over the chain. Isabella grabbed Beatrice's hand and they dashed up the street.

After a block the duchesses looked back and saw that the guard had not continued his pursuit. Isabella clutched Beatrice's shoulders. Her breast heaved slightly and her gray-green eyes had that stormy opalescence. For the first time Beatrice could sense that those eyes were not merely looking at her but looking into her. "Your husband has obtained the consent of the King of France to invest my husband with the privileges of the Duchy of Genoa. Do you understand what that means?"

Exhilaration shivered down Beatrice's spine. So far in her unexpected friendship with Isabella she had been content with her largely mute role as tennis competitor or riding companion; just being near her cousin seemed to provide some of the self-assurance she so admired in Isabella, and just to be treated civilly by her had somehow redeemed all those childhood cruelties. But now Isabella was intimating a new sort of friendship, that of women rather than girls, a future of whispered conspiracies and adult intrigues.

"It means that my husband intends to make an accommodation with the French," Beatrice answered confidently.

"Do you know why he would do that?"

"He might wish to appease them. My mother says that France has always lusted after Italy. Or my husband might wish to hire the King of France in the fashion he has employed Messer Galeazz."

Isabella's elongated, catlike eyes widened slightly, startled by

Beatrice's acuity. "Then I think you also understand what use your husband might have for the French army. If he were to usurp my husband, my father would have *his* army at the gates of Milan within two weeks."

Beatrice felt a needle of fear whenever she recalled her uncle Alfonso, his swollen, dusky face almost blue with rage; he would slap or kick a servant for the slightest mistake. But Alfonso was indeed a great *condottiere;* she could still see the celebration of his victory over the Turks at Taranto, the fireworks shot from the boats out in the bay and the dark men in chains brought into the banquet hall. . . .

"But if the King of France were to attack Naples," Isabella went on, "my father could be prevented from protecting his grandson's birthright."

Not wanting her cousin to think even for an instant that she would collude in such a scheme, Beatrice blurted the first mollifying argument that came to her. "But your husband is the one who is being invested with the privileges of Genoa. Won't that strengthen him, not my husband?"

"That is not the opportunity that this investiture presents." Isabella sniffed dismissively. "What Fortune has given us is an opportunity to be rid of Cecilia Gallerani once and for all."

Beatrice's head jerked back. She no longer cared that Cecilia Gallerani had stolen the magic golden words she had once dreamed of hearing from a man. But Cecilia Gallerani had made her an object of ridicule, and for that Beatrice hated her so much that just the name was a white-hot blade in her stomach. She had simply never imagined that hatred of Cecilia Gallerani was something else she and Isabella shared.

"Why are you surprised?" Isabella asked sharply. "That arrogant, conniving bitch has disgraced my household far longer than she has yours." She gripped Beatrice's shoulders tightly, as if to emphasize their vehement alliance. "Fortune is the most capricious bitch of all. When she comes around, you must wrestle her to the ground, for she is not likely to pass your way again." Isabella's eyes narrowed fiercely. "Are you willing to wrestle with Fortune to be rid of Cecilia Gallerani?"

Beatrice nodded unhesitating assent. She would not risk an instant of Fortune's wrath to snatch her husband's love away from

Cecilia Gallerani. But to win her cousin's love, she had decided, she would pursue Fortune to the last circle of Hell.

"Come in, Messer Giacomo."

Giacomo Trotti, the Ferrarese ambassador to Milan, was a slender, balding man with meek, tired eyes and a nasty beak. Despite the invitation, he hesitated for a moment, seemingly daunted by the lamplit glitter of Il Moro's treasure vault. Bushel baskets full of gold ducats, stacked like olives at an oil press, took up much of the floor space; in one corner loose silver ducats had been piled halfway to the coffered ceiling. The walls were lined with credenzas displaying a staggering array of jeweled and gilded altarpieces, crucifixes, goblets, salvers, and vases; rows of wooden presses held hundreds of plates of embossed gold, chased silver, and intricately detailed majolica pottery.

Il Moro stood before one of the credenzas, peering at the miniature templelike architecture of a reliquary; the little doors, framed by solid-gold pilasters and arches, were ivory plaques decorated with scenes from the life of Christ. He turned to Trotti. His smile was wry, almost miserable, and immediately put Trotti at ease. Trotti knew that if Il Moro intended to take a serious negotiating position, his face would have been an implacable mask.

"Do you have any notion as to what this is about, Messer Giacomo?"

"I was informed by the Duchess of Bari that she wished me to be present, Your Highness." Actually Trotti had acceded to Beatrice's request with profound reservations. On the one hand, he considered the situation regarding Cecilia Gallerani a humiliation for Ferrara and welcomed the opportunity to register a protest. But Beatrice had refused to give Trotti any idea of what sort of protest she intended to make. He had warned her that a petulant outburst would only worsen matters, but given Beatrice's obstinacy and mercurial temperament, he could only expect the worst.

"Well, you must convey to the Duke and Duchess of Ferrara how earnestly I am endeavoring to ensure that their daughter is happy here. If you would like, I will have my chief secretary, Messer Bartolommeo, furnish you with a list of the *feste,* theatricals, and hunts we have staged for her amusement. And when I cannot look after Beatrice, I delegate Messer Galeazz to see that she is not neglected. If you wish, I can also ask Galeazz to dictate for your examination the considerable itinerary of outings upon which he has escorted her." Il Moro casually handed Trotti an enormous oblong ruby. "I have asked you and Beatrice to meet with me here because I intend to give her this, along with something of her own choosing. An agent who would not reveal his client has offered me two hundred thousand ducats for it," Il Moro said as Trotti examined the thumb-size stone. The sum was three times the annual revenues of Ferrara. "I thought that was rather low."

Trotti silently complimented Il Moro on the skill with which he had already stated his position: I have amply compensated the house of Este for our alliance and will continue to do so, as long as I am left to govern my household as I wish.

"Ah, here is my lovely wife."

Beatrice walked so stiffly in her tight, glistening brocade *camora* that she might have been a mechanical doll. Her hands were clasped in front of her to prevent them from shaking. Her head moved in abrupt, nervous gestures. Il Moro kissed her lightly on the cheek.

"Tante bellezza," Il Moro said. He turned to Trotti. "You may also tell the Duke and Duchess of Ferrara that their daughter becomes more beautiful each day she is with us. And of course she is already the most accomplished horsewoman in Milan. I am immensely proud and delighted with all of the marvelous things I am constantly told about her."

Silence followed. Il Moro smiled at Beatrice, so convincingly that she wanted to believe what he had said. But she knew too well the timbre of his lies. Trotti cleared his throat, prompting her to submit her agenda. Her stomach gave a terrorizing heave. She saw herself summoned home in disgrace, excoriated by her parents, then hustled along a darkened road to a convent. Once she had disappeared inside the silent, gloomy cloisters, she would never be seen again. . . .

Her voice wavered when she started to speak, but she forced herself on, thinking only that she could never face her cousin again if she did not say it. "I do not intend to accompany my lord husband to the investiture of the Duke of Milan with the privileges of the Duchy of Genoa, nor will I be present to receive the French ambassadors. I . . . I do not feel that I can represent my husband or the Este family as long as I am disgraced by the singular honor shown my husband's mistress. The ostentatious presence of Cecilia Gallerani in this *castello* makes a mockery of the marital bonds that unite the houses of Este and Sforza."

Trotti masked his reaction. He had to admire Beatrice's courage and credit her cleverness; she had identified the proper point of attack. Unfortunately she had vastly overestimated her own strength and underestimated that of her opponent. Il Moro could come up with a dozen expedients for dealing with his wife's refusal to attend the ceremonies. Still, Il Moro would suffer from any suspicions his wife's absence might arouse among the French envoys; Ferrara was the linchpin of Il Moro's united Italy. Trotti determined that disaster had been averted and that the proper course now was to force Il Moro into a concession that would at least allow Beatrice to make a dignified retreat.

"Your Highness," Trotti said delicately, "perhaps the time has come to find lodgings elsewhere for Madonna Cecilia." Trotti shrugged, indicating in diplomat's code that he meant temporary alternative lodgings, at least until after the investiture; he did not need to add that Il Moro could visit those lodgings as freely as he wished.

"The woman in question is currently in confinement, awaiting the imminent birth of her child." Il Moro's face was inscrutable, his black eyes like beads. "I scarcely think that removing her from her rooms at this time would reflect favorably on either the house of Sforza or that of Este. At the very least, the French envoys would be scandalized by our disregard for Christian charity."

Trotti cursed silently. Now he would have to back down as well, or call on Duke Ercole to help him win a minor concession. He wished he had never gotten involved in this child's business. . . .

"I believe that I, not the Duke of Bari, am responsible for what constitutes the charity of this household. I am its mistress."

Forgoing diplomatic decorum, Trotti wheeled to face the door. The Duchess of Milan advanced into the vault like a siege machine, her broad shoulders squared, elbows extended, fingers pressed lightly together at her slender, high waist. She wore a *camora* of Naples black satin, slit at the shoulders to reveal two white puffs of silk chemise. A thin black satin band bound her forehead, and a string of onyx beads circled her neck.

"I have informed my father's ambassador that the Duchess of Milan will also be absent from the ceremonies of investiture," Isabella said directly to Il Moro.

Trotti glanced between the two young duchesses with new respect. A moment ago Il Moro merely had been confronted with a disgruntled teenage bride; now he had an international incident in the making. Il Moro could never excuse the absence of both duchesses from the investiture and the accompanying round of theatricals and banquets; there was even some doubt that the Duke of Milan could survive a week of entertainments without his wife on hand to constantly supervise him. If Il Moro wanted the French to regard him as Italy's strongman, he would have to concede to these two girls.

Il Moro smiled amiably at Isabella. "I can understand how even a charitable act might be construed as offensive. Is it your wish as well, Your Highness, that Madonna Cecilia be asked to vacate her rooms in this *castello?*"

Isabella nodded curtly.

Il Moro held to the light a many-faceted diamond the size of a robin's egg, carefully examining the brilliant, prismatic refractions. "Then I will see that Madonna Cecilia is removed immediately to lodgings in the Palazzo del Verme."

Trotti struggled to conceal his outrage, at the same time acknowledging Il Moro's ruthless brilliance as a negotiator; Il Moro could be so casual and amiable that at times one forgot that he probably would soon be master of all Europe. The Palazzo del Verme was the largest private home in Milan. Vacant for a year, the huge medieval palace overlooking the Piazza del Duomo had been undergoing renovation recently after its purchase by a mysterious buyer. Now Trotti realized that Il Moro had intended all along to move Cecilia there, where he could flaunt their relationship while at the same time assuaging the criticism her presence in the Castello had aroused. He would thus satisfy the two people who mattered in this affair: Cecilia Gallerani and Duke Ercole d'Este. As for the two duchesses, they would have been wiser to—

"That will not entirely satisfy our requirements."

Alarmed by Beatrice's emphatic, entirely uncharacteristic tenor, Trotti thought for a moment he heard something of her father's voice—Duke Ercole's steely resolve, but also his brittle undertone of fanaticism. What could Beatrice possibly gain now . . . ?

"It could hardly be considered charitable," Beatrice went on, "to abandon Madonna Cecilia and her bastard without ensuring that they will be adequately provided for and shielded from scandal. We insist that your charity extend beyond the simple expedient of placing a roof over Madonna Cecilia's head."

Il Moro studied his wife curiously, as if he had never heard her speak before. Even the Duchess of Milan cocked her head quizzically. Trotti, deducing that Beatrice had not even discussed with the Duchess of Milan whatever she intended to propose now, listened with dreadful fascination.

"We insist that Madonna Cecilia be provided with a husband," Beatrice offered.

Il Moro's face went blank. He turned the prodigious diamond over and over in his long, graceful fingers, as though deeply entranced by the dazzling little spectral display he held in his hand.

Very good, Trotti thought, resisting his impulse to nod approvingly at Beatrice; as Trotti essentially considered himself an Este, he even experienced a surge of filial pride. The little Duchess has put an interesting ball into play, he reflected. Of course marriages of convenience were more common than love matches in Milan: a man might marry his mistress to his son in order to keep her close without arousing suspicion, or he might marry a maidservant he was boffing to one of his stableboys so that his wife couldn't throw her out of the house; the variations on the theme were endless. But Trotti wondered if Il Moro could deal so cynically with Cecilia. Certainly he would arrive at some clever invention, but at least Beatrice had made a request that Il Moro could not so glibly dismiss.

Deciding that the interests of Ferrara could only be served by his vigorously supporting Beatrice's initiative, Trotti added, "Ah, Your Highness, this really is a most humane and painless solution to a problem that I must say, with all respect, continues to cast a shadow over relations between Milan and Ferrara. I intend to dispatch by fast courier a letter to Duke Ercole, in which I will commend his daughter's good judgment, magnanimity, and Christian charity. I am certain Duke Ercole will find the Duchess of Bari's request as reasonable as do I."

Il Moro turned the diamond over once more; the huge gem caught the light and shimmered with rainbow hues. He said nothing.

CHAPTER

9

Cecilia Gallerani looked out across the moat. The park beyond was renascent with emerald-bright leaves; to the far north the Alps wrapped the horizon, a ragged ribbon of white satin beneath a sky of perfect cobalt blue.

"Count Bergamini has agreed to all my conditions," Il Moro said gently, standing two steps behind Cecilia. "He assures me that the marriage can only bring honor to his family and that he will accommodate us in any way he can. He has even agreed to pay for some of the renovations at the Palazzo del Verme. And I needn't tell you that he has given me his inviolate pledge that he will press no connubial demands of any sort—"

"And deprive me of such a marvelous adventure?" Cecilia turned and faced Il Moro. "After all, *amante*, you are the only man I have ever slept with. When I am bedded by my husband, I shall enjoy all the pleasures of adultery and yet have my sin sanctioned by the sacrament of marriage."

Il Moro shut his eyes. "What do you want me to do?"

"Truly, *amante*, you sometimes make me wonder if you ever really knew me." Cecilia paused and glanced at her portrait on the opposite wall. "Or is it that I have changed so much that I no longer know myself?" She shrugged her narrow shoulders as if the answer were of no consequence. "I want you to send the contracts to my father for his approval. I intend to marry Count Bergamini and live with him and my child in the Palazzo del Verme. I may or may not sleep with Count Bergamini, as I so desire. But in any event I will not cuckold him. That would be unworthy of you and of the love we have had."

"I can assure you that this will be only a temporary arrangement. After the investiture—"

"After the investiture there will be another occasion on which your wife can extort such concessions from you. And after that there will be another. . . ."

"Very well. I will tell you what you obviously insist on hearing." Il Moro paused and jutted his chin out. "I will not go through with the investiture. I will resign as regent to the Duke of Milan. We can go together to Bari." Bari was the tiny duchy in southern Italy that Il Moro had inherited at the death of one of his older brothers.

Cecilia's shoulders stiffened. "How much easier that would have been last summer."

"If I had known of this child last summer, I never would have submitted to Duke Ercole." Il Moro placed his hand on Cecilia's swollen belly. "I would have resigned then. I would have made you the Duchess of Bari."

"I believe that, *amante*, I truly do. And I would not have permitted you to resign." Cecilia's voice had a fluent stridency, like the notes of a savagely plucked lyre. "Don't you see, Lodovico, I never wanted to be the Duchess of Bari. The mistress of the Duke of Milan, yes, I have always wanted that, if only because I have wanted that more than anything for you. Duke of Milan, *amante*. Duke of Milan. You see, I know the truth that has guided you all along, the truth that you still cannot bring yourself to confess, my foolish, wonderful, lovely *fanciullo*. Do you know what that truth is? Do you know?" Il Moro said nothing; Cecilia reached up and gently touched his cheek. "The truth is, *amante*, that Beatrice can make you Duke of Milan and I cannot. With me you are a usurper with his whore and bastard. With Beatrice d'Este and her child, you are a dynasty. *Amante*, all along, even now, Beatrice has been my ally, not my enemy."

The expression on Il Moro's face was entirely self-absorbed, and remarkable; it was as though he were observing some fantastic apocalypse taking place inside his own head.

"Our choices can become cruel masters, can't they, *amante?*" There was no bitterness in the question, only a sense of shared remorse. Cecilia walked to the window again and looked out over the vivid landscape for several silent minutes. Il Moro remained lost within himself.

When Cecilia finally spoke, her voice was high and clear. "It is such a remarkable time we live in, isn't it, *amante?* We no longer wait on the gods or God; we move ahead faster than even the gods could have dreamed. There is something *al'nuovo*, something new, every day. A new style of painting, new architecture, new poetry, new music. New islands off Africa . . . there is not a year or two that goes by without some new land discovered. New crops, new machines . . . look at the things Leonardo has drawn. It is the age of new things, an age that endlessly reinvents itself, and what we hold today is gone tomorrow. We live in an age given to the moment. We no longer see life through the spectacles of death, a journey to eternal darkness, but as our moment in the light of reason."

Cecilia turned. "What makes passion and youth so wonderful is that they are so evanescent, that they slip away like light off a wave. You can only hold someone, truly hold him, for a moment of the moment that is your life. When that moment has ended, you cannot stand by the dark sea, calling it back. You can only cherish the memory. I will never see that light in your eyes again, *amante.* Long ago, before Beatrice ever came here, I knew that such a day would come. But every time I look into this baby's eyes I will remember that light and cherish it. My moment has passed. The next moment belongs to Beatrice. And to you."

Il Moro shook his head, and his throat pumped. Finally he said, "I cannot bear to think of you . . ."

"With another man?" Cecilia's face set like the features of a marble bust. "I would marry the devil if I thought it would make you Duke of Milan." She stared at him intently and then, without picking up her skirts, rushed to him and seized his arms in a painful grip. "Duke of Milan! Duke of Milan! It is yours to take, *amante!* Take it! Take it! Take it!"

Il Moro could not meet her eyes. His self-defense was mumbled, virtually automatic. "You know better than anyone what will need to happen before—"

With a stiff darting movement, Cecilia slapped him squarely on the cheek. "Galeazzo Maria is dead, Lodovico. Your brother is dead." Her voice had a lulling, narcotic inflection, as if she were reasoning with a child awakening from a nightmare. "I will have them pull the slab from his tomb and embrace the corpse myself if that is what it takes to prove it to you. He is bones and dust, like all the bones and dust he made of other men. His malignant spirit does not live on in that idiot boy. He will not rise from his grave and strangle you with his skeletal hands if you depose his pathetic son."

But such was the power of that corpse that it rose from the depths of Il Moro's eyes, a black glaze of terror over his dark irises. Perspiration beaded on his forehead and his heavy chest labored for quick shallow breaths.

"Lodovico!" Cecilia grasped his jaw. "Listen to me!" When she had finally taken his eyes back she lowered her voice to a whisper. "He is gone, Lodovico."

Il Moro swallowed and his breathing evened out. "You know my brother has left behind more than his evil spirit."

"Lodovico. Bona of Savoy in France is no different than Bona Sforza in Milan. A shriveled, feebleminded bag of wind who could not induce the French army to march around a dung heap, much less cross the Alps. The French army will come to Italy only at the invitation of Il Moro. You know that is true. As for the wife of your brother's son—"

"The Duchess of Milan has now made an agent of this . . . *Beatrice* of yours," Il Moro snapped, like a child angry over the death of a parent.

Cecilia could not help herself. She started to laugh, beautifully, a sound like bells and lyres, with only a hint of irony. "Beatrice is the wife *you* married, *amico*, not some disease *I* have given you."

Il Moro looked at Cecilia in wounded astonishment. And then he smiled, slowly, petulantly.

That weak, pained smile was proof to Cecilia that Il Moro could deal with the inevitable death of their love, and her heart lightened. "Lodovico, remember this. *Your* Beatrice has already proven that she is far too clever to be manipulated for long by that conniving, dishonest bitch. She will learn the truth herself, and it will be much more effective than if anyone attempts to warn her about her cousin. And when Beatrice turns against the Duchess of Milan, that will be your moment. Never forget that, Lodovico, because I will not always be available to remind you." Cecilia lifted her hands and clutched her fists solidly, as if she had found something substantial in the air to hold on to. "That will be the moment Fortune has given to you."

Extract of a letter of GIACOMO TROTTI, Ferrarese ambassador to the Court of Milan, to ERCOLE D'ESTE, Duke of Ferrara. Milan, 20 April 1491

My dear Highness and most illustrious lord Duke,

You will be relieved to know that yesterday Cecilia Gallerani was removed from her rooms in the Castello di Porta Giovia and has been installed in the Palazzo del Verme, awaiting the birth of her child. I have personally reviewed the marriage contracts, signed and sealed by Count Bergamini and Count Gallerani. And lest you think that Il Moro is temporizing until the investiture is done, let me assure you that he has displayed a grief so shamelessly theatrical that I can only assume it is authentic. For six days he has been closeted alone in his rooms, the shutters drawn by day, the lamps unlit at night. Those who have seen him describe a man so deep in mourning that he can scarcely bring himself to speak. I am certain we can expect his recovery in time to welcome the French envoys, who are due here, we are told, a week or so hence. . . .

During his self-imposed period of isolation, Il Moro had wandered his darkened rooms like a ghost, floating in the dense silence. He believed that the pain would never leave him, but that eventually his body would leave the pain.

After a while he had learned that he was in the company of other ghosts—his father and mother, Bianca's mother, his youngest brother, Ottaviano. At first merely fleeting presences, they had started to become as real as the body he was leaving behind. He could not explain himself to them, but for a time he had welcomed their distraction.

On the seventh day the door appeared—not a figurative portal, and not the shadowy outline of the double doors he had sealed seven days previously. This door was so real that he could smell the moldy oak, see the brass Sforza viper nailed to the blackened wood. And he knew that on the other side was his eldest brother, Galeazzo Maria, fully embodied, waiting for him.

His substance returned to him with an icy rush. He stood staring at the door, his feet numb and his heart thudding, and in a dreadful epiphany realized what Cecilia's absence really meant. She had been the guardian of the gate, the sentinel who kept his memories sealed inside. She alone had prevented him from opening the door and joining his brother on the other side.

Now he was free to go in, and the dark chasm of possibility yawned before him. His arms trembled and his cheek twitched, and for an instant he embraced the mad urge to do it, to complete the self-negation his grief demanded. Then he realized that simply crossing the forbidden threshold was not enough, that once inside he would have to look again into his brother's eyes. Only that elemental fear, stronger even than his fear of death, held him back.

He stared at the door for a moment longer. "I am not like you," he said in a cracking whisper. "I am not a monster."

Il Moro pressed his hands to his aching eyes. The door vanished. He went to the double doors of his bedchamber, instructed the chamberlain waiting outside to light all the lamps in his rooms, and sent for his secretaries.

Beatrice crept in the darkness, surrounded by the chill and must of damp stone, following the sobs and screams. Finally she found the place and peered through a tiny hole in the thick masonry, probably drilled there by a jealous husband or lover. She could see the room clearly, crowded with midwives and physicians. The woman who was screaming sat in the birthing chair. The heavy oaken chair rhythmically heaved off the floor with the force of her convulsions.

The birthing chair suddenly whirled to face Beatrice. She knew that the woman was Cecilia Gallerani, though she had never seen her before. Blood gushed from between Cecilia's legs, and she reached inside herself and pulled out a creature with blue, ropy limbs, the face of a doll, and a mangled skull. Her arms shot out and held the horrible thing right in front of Beatrice.

In an instant Cecilia had come through the wall. She stood beside Beatrice in a pool of her own blood; her eyes (but now they were Isabella's eyes) lit up the entire passageway. She pointed to Beatrice's navel, and suddenly Beatrice's abdomen inflated grotesquely. Beatrice felt a watery evacuation from between her legs and looked down in horror at the crimson torrent rushing out. Cecilia laughed, her head back, her teeth like fangs. "Mama!" Beatrice screamed. "Mama . . ."

Beatrice bolted upright in bed. She was intensely cold; the embers in the fireplace seemed impossibly far away, like a traveler's lantern viewed from a distant hill. She remembered the dream vividly. She wondered if she had actually screamed "Mama," and if anyone had heard.

She placed her hands to her belly. Was it possible that the seed had already been planted? Her sister had said that it took many attempts and that the stars were a very poor guide for success. Mama had said that it could happen the first time and that the stars were often reliable. The consensus among the kitchen maids in Ferrara, the principal source of sexual education in the Este household, had been that it was always possible unless you were having your monthly out-of-ordinaries, but no decent man would want you then. Beatrice had been regular as soon as she had started two years earlier, but since the negotiations over her marriage last summer she had only had a trickle once, and not on schedule. So how could she tell if . . . *it* was inside her now? She had started vomiting last summer too, even when she wasn't sick. So the only certain sign would be her weight. As long as she didn't gain weight . . .

A faint rattle of footsteps came from the sealed antechamber. Beatrice burrowed beneath the down coverlet and prayed for deliverance. After a long while she admitted to herself that she probably had imagined the sound. But her fear remained, a taste like blood in her mouth. The price of her victory over Cecilia Gallerani, she realized, had yet to be paid. One night, as inevitably as the endless cycling of Fortune's wheel, he would come.

CHAPTER

10

Vigevano, 28 April 1491

Leonardo da Vinci stood on the crest of the gradual rise and swept his arm out toward the Ticino River Valley, his gesture so elegant and important that he might have been a god sprinkling the land-scape with powdered sunlight. But what Leonardo actually had brought to the Ticino Valley was water. The evidence of that miracle was everywhere: in the vast silvery grid of canals traced across the countryside; in the finer web of glittering threads mark-ing the paths of the innumerable irrigation ditches. Nourished via sluices opened and shut in a complex orchestration, the hundreds of precisely squared fields created a patchwork of lustrous variety. Many lay entirely flooded, mirrors of the cloud-cobbled cerulean sky that had followed the morning rain; those fields where the heads of grass had begun to emerge above the flat sheets of water had an almost brocadelike, citron-hued iridescence. Others were thick, wind-rustled viridian carpets of wheat, barley, rice, and alfalfa. Some fields lay fallow, the dull, neutral beige of the soil belying its extraordinary fertility.

Bernard Stuart d'Aubigny, head of the French embassy to Milan and proxy for His Most Christian Majesty Charles VIII, came to Leonardo's side, accompanied by Il Moro and the interpreter on this excursion, Galeazzo di Sanseverino, Captain General of the Armies of Milan. D'Aubigny was in his early thirties, a medium-size man with a heavy red beard and bright blue eyes.

Leonardo's large, powerful hand flapped at the wrist in a kind of waving motion, as if he were indicating something beyond the horizon. Chin tilted up, flowing gray hair swept back from his high forehead, he appeared to be withstanding a cosmic gale. His high, musical voice added to the sense of wonder. After every two or three sentences Galeazz would translate Leonardo's words in his own poetic cadence.

". . . the Ticino River, two leagues distant. Along the banks I propose the construction of ten separate towns, each of these communities limited to precisely five thousand dwellings containing no more than thirty thousand inhabitants. Every privy would empty into an underground conduit that would then be carried by canal into the river and thence away into the sea. In addition, we would offer public privies to ensure that odious habits of public urination and defecation are discouraged. The chimney smoke that so deprives our cities of light and contaminates our every breath would be spirited away by a system of revolving cowls, operated by the convection of the fire beneath, that would propel the offending vapors high into the atmosphere—"

"Ah, yes, Maestro Leonardo, do forgive me," Il Moro interjected. "But we must move along if we are to tour Vigevano before dark." Vigevano was an ancient Roman city two dozen miles west of Milan, recently revived under Il Moro's aegis. "You will be most impressed at what we have done there," Il Moro told d'Aubigny. "We have taken the old Roman forum and redone it in the very latest *all'antica* style, and Maestro Donato Bramante, whose work you have seen in Milan and who is without peer at recalling the glories of the ancients, is building us a tower."

The party remounted and rode into the sun. Dozens of large buildings sprawled over the western horizon, red tile roofs flaming in the late afternoon light. A cylindrical brick creamery towering like the donjon of a French castle was the centerpiece of the complex. The road leading to the creamery was jammed with oxcarts loaded with clay urns. The visitors had already spent most of the afternoon touring the vast farm, called Sforzesca, Il Moro's personal experiment in advanced agricultural techniques.

D'Aubigny rode in silence, plucking thoughtfully at his beard. He had been prepared, at least in concept, for Milan. But finally to see it? Perhaps Paris had been the great city of Europe two or three centuries before, a golden age still manifest in the glorious glass-walled cathedrals like Notre Dame and Saint Chapelle. But while more than a hundred years of almost continuous war with the English had beaten down the provincial nobility and had vastly increased the relative strength of the French kings, the spirit and intellect of the French people had been crushed, a decline as evident in the capital city as it was in the ravished countryside. Idle, incestuous, frivolous, Paris had joined Babylon, Athens, Rome, Alexandria, Constantinople, that litany of toppled giants. Paris had been dying for two hundred years. It belonged to another time. And Milan would be the future. Paris was winding, cluttered, festering. Milan was clean, with broad, paved avenues, neat rows of shop arcades, and spacious *piazze*. In Milan d'Aubigny had seen a hospital as large as the Château du Louvre, built in the modern, reasoned, elegant Italian style. Anyone who needed treatment was accepted; there were beds for fifteen hundred patients, and d'Aubigny had been told of another such charity hospital, almost as large, elsewhere in the city. Just as profoundly affecting was the Milanese commitment to destruction. The Via degli Armorai, with its endless rows of clanging forges, had literally shaken d'Aubigny to the bones.

But after the wonders of Milan, d'Aubigny had expected to see a countryside strangled by tax collectors, the price France had paid with her dun, wasted fields and brutalized peasantry. Instead this, a city of agricultural commerce on a scale unheard-of elsewhere in Europe. D'Aubigny studied the rows of two-story stables marching along toward the northern horizon. The cattle and horses fed in their stalls, on rolled bales of hay stocked in the second-story lofts; d'Aubigny believed he had been shown more livestock here this single afternoon than he had seen cumulatively in France in five years. The workers were housed in rows of whitewashed, tile-roofed houses, and they wore neat linen tunics, clean white leggings, and ankle-high leather slippers; to d'Aubigny, accustomed as he was to the filthy rags and mud-crusted bare legs of the French peasantry, this was perhaps the greatest of the Milanese miracles.

And yet if one listened to Il Moro and his officers of state, this was only the beginning. Il Moro. Two days ago he had seemed just another wayfarer on the avenues of history, a name briefly shouted as its bearer journeyed from anonymity to oblivion. But now it was obvious that Il Moro was more than a mere pilgrim searching for the elusive shrine of fame. He was a builder of history's roads, a man who would determine his own route across the continents of time.

The party of sixty secretaries, diplomats, and men-at-arms headed north. The main road to Vigevano was muddy from the rain, and the afternoon wagon traffic had left deep ruts, slowing the horses to a cautious walk. D'Aubigny glanced over at Il Moro, regal yet insouciant, with his proud Caesar's nose and intense black eyes. Who are you? d'Aubigny wondered. You are the most skilled liar in Christendom, and yet every man wants to believe your words. You talk to us of nothing but peace, yet your arms factories all but bellow "War! War! War!" You say you are the humble servant of the Duke of Milan, and yet what you have shown me today is an ambition that would rule the world.

D'Aubigny let the reins fall and allowed his horse to pick its own path through the ruts and muck. Madame de Beaujeu would probably give birth before he returned to Paris, he reflected. He did not expect any collapse of Madame's authority during her confinement; Madame's husband, Pierre de Beaujeu, was certainly capable of controlling the various factions attempting to beguile the King in her absence. But the risks were still great. Madame was too old—thirty—to be having her first child; the birth, even if successful, could leave her health shattered. And even in the best of circumstances, motherhood would likely dull the razor edge of Madame's temperament. Over time, the war parties would gain their ascendance over a king all too eager to embark on a military adventure; they already had advanced their cause significantly in the last few months. But perhaps what was inevitable was not undesirable. D'Aubigny looked out over the flat, sparkling green checkerboard of irrigated fields. There was more to be won here than even the adventurers in Paris could imagine, the wealth and resources to build a French nation that would dominate the world for centuries.

As the highest-ranking courtier to hold both the King's friendship and Madame's confidence, d'Aubigny knew that his counsel might set in motion the millstones of destiny. But what would that counsel be? A dying France could be reborn on these verdant plains. And Italy could also be France's crypt.

"Ah, Messer Bernard Stuart, do look ahead." Il Moro pointed. "You can just see the spire of Maestro Bramante's tower."

The Alps, sharp-toothed and dusty purple, stretched across the entire horizon like the wall of some mythic city. Finally d'Aubigny distinguished the immense brass cross, diminished by distance to a tiny sun-gilded crucifix seemingly burned into the Alpine massif. Without thinking of it, d'Aubigny moved his hand quickly across his breast, sketching over his own flesh that blazing symbol of death, resurrection, and final judgment.

C H A P T E R

11

Milan, 30 April 1491

"Maria, don't hit it to Beatrice!" The ball popped up toward the cavernous vaults of the Sala della Palla and was lost for a moment in the shadows three stories above. Beatrice's billowing skirts concealed her furiously driving legs as she raced past Il Moro's daughter, Bianca. Her bare feet pounded to an abrupt halt, and she reached with her racket, just missing the window to her left. The ball pinged off the gut strings and streaked toward the Duke of Milan's sister Bianca Maria, who dove for the floor, escaping a painful encounter with the sphere of tightly compressed wool sheathed in hard leather. "Bianca Maria," Isabella fumed, "I told you not to hit it to Beatrice."

Bianca Maria remained flat on the floor and spread her arms and legs. "I didn't hit it to her. She wasn't there when I hit it." She rapped the floor with her racket. "Let's not play anymore. It doesn't matter who Beatrice's partner is—she will always win. She can run as fast as a man."

"Bianca Maria," Isabella said, exasperated, "a half hour ago you were complaining that there was no one to play tennis with at your mother's villa in Abbiategrasso."

"There *wasn't* anyone to play with in Abbiategrasso," Bianca

Maria asserted; apparently she assumed that her sister-in-law was commenting on her veracity rather than her attention span.

"What did you do in Abbiategrasso, Maria?" Bianca asked sweetly.

"Niente," Bianca Maria said, still on her back, her lips curled into an erotic sneer as she overenunciated the word. *"Niente, niente, niente.* There is never anything to do in Abbiategrasso." She sat up. "I want a hawk. If I had a hawk I could hunt herons with him. I would get him a gold hood with a peacock crest." Bianca Maria frowned, scrunched her skirts up between her legs, and looked out over her long, gorgeous limbs. "There's nothing to do here," she said definitively.

"If your mother finds you with your legs like that, you will have something to do." Isabella gave up on the tennis game and sat on the floor beside her sister-in-law.

Bianca Maria made silent fishlike motions with her mouth, miming her mother. "Ca-ca. Pu-pu." She peered out into the ether in search of further inspiration. "I really want a husband," she concluded as casually as if she had decided to order a breakfast pastry. She considered that option for a while, then smiled with radiant enthusiasm. "I want a monkey! Everyone has a monkey now. I would buy him a hat . . . and a flute . . . and a drum, and a mirror so that he could look at himself!"

Isabella put her arm around her sister-in-law's shoulder and kissed her on the cheek. "Tomorrow, after the investiture, we are all going to dine with the French ambassadors," she said patiently. "And there is going to be a theatrical after supper."

"Ca-ca. Pu-pu."

Beatrice forbade herself even to consider how she would survive an entire evening in the company of her husband. Owing to the hectic activity surrounding the arrival of the French ambassadors, she had seen Il Moro only four times since Cecilia's departure. The first time, his grief-dulled eyes had flinched from her. But subsequently he had stared directly at her, revealing no feeling at all, as if his own utterly blank features were a mirror that proved to her and anyone else who cared to look that his wife had ceased to exist.

"You girls!" The voice shrilled through the Sala della Palla. Bianca Maria immediately made a fish face. Duchess Mother Bona rattled across the floor, clapping her hands like a peasant woman shooing a hare out of her garden. "You girls! Are these the courtly manners you would have our visitors impute to our ladies!" She looked down at Isabella and Bianca Maria with goggle-eyed disgust. "In my day a young woman did not allow her rear end to touch anything but a mattress or a velvet cushion. Yet why do I wonder why my daughter tries to eat her meals on the floor and all of you spend more hours in the saddle than a state courier, when I see the example the Duchess of Milan sets for you? God should have given you girls to Gypsy families, and then you could have rested your backsides on the dirt all night and ridden bareback on a mule all day." Bona clapped her hands again. "Bianca Maria and Bianca are late for their Latin tutor."

Bianca Maria rose dutifully. Bianca looked pleadingly to Beatrice. Beatrice pressed her lips to Bianca's ear and whispered, "You know you must study your Latin, *carissima*. When you are done I will teach you a naughty song about an old woman and the young man who had to slice her tough old loins." Bianca's brilliant red cheeks suddenly inflated with suppressed laughter. Shortly after the assassination of Duke Galeazzo Maria, his widow had found solace with one of the young men who carved meat at the ducal table; Bona had quickly banished any of her husband's trusted advisers who dared object to the liaison. Eventually the meat carver had fled, taking with him most of Bona's jewels and leaving in his wake a leadership vacuum, eagerly filled by Il Moro.

With a flip of her fingers, Duchess Bona whisked the two girls on their way. Bianca happily kissed Beatrice on both cheeks and took Bianca Maria's hand. Bona remained for a moment, staring with undisguised malice at Isabella, who defiantly remained seated on the floor. She diverted her glare to Beatrice, as though to add: We know the real reason why these girls have become moral degenerates. Then Bona whirled about; as soon as her back was turned, Isabella shot her the fig.

"Can you imagine her?" Isabella said when the furious echoes of the Duchess Mother's footsteps had finally vanished. "I think we should write His Holiness and inform him that the Frenchmen have resurrected the Duchess Mother. Lucia says that the old *puttana* was in the kitchen for two hours this morning, telling the cooks just what a Frenchman will and won't eat and how he likes it prepared. She can't herself read two words of Latin and two weeks ago couldn't have cared if her daughter even spoke Italian, but now she is chasing down pupils for Maestro Vincenzo. The Duchess Mother does not have the sense to remember that she did not invite the Frenchmen to Milan. They are here to do Il Moro's bidding."

Beatrice worried her lower lip with her teeth. She hated the whole issue of the French and her husband's ambitions. All the arguments and speculation had become for her a maddeningly complex, black-walled labyrinth constantly diverting her from the shining objective at its center: her cousin's love. But she was afraid that if she ignored the matter, Isabella would imagine that she condoned her husband's schemes. "Do you really think he will ask the Frenchmen to attack Naples?" she asked morosely.

"He would be a fool if he did. The Frenchmen are just as interested in Milan as they are in Naples. The Duc d'Orléans claims that Milan is his because his great-grandmother was a Visconti." The Visconti had been the ruling dynasty of Milan prior to the Sforza. "And the Duc d'Orléans has such an influence on the King that Madame de Beaujeu has had to keep him locked up for the last four years. But the Orleanist faction in Paris is still powerful. That is another thing that both your husband and the Duchess Mother seem to forget." Isabella suddenly gathered up the tennis ball and with a mighty address sent it smashing against the far wall of the Sala della Palla. She turned, and Beatrice instinctively recoiled from the anger on her face; for a moment Beatrice could see Isabella's father. "Fools. All of them," Isabella said. "If the Frenchmen come over the mountains, there will be nothing left for anyone." She fanned the air with her racket. *"Niente."*

"Tell them you will have the woman later." Bernard Stuart d'Aubigny motioned his junior envoy, Jean Roux de Visque, to come away from the partially open door. In halting, crude Italian, de Visque said as much to someone beyond the door. Feminine laughter followed.

De Visque shut the door. "Italian women," he said appreciatively, shaking his shaggy head. "An Italian whore is as refined as a French duchess. And even their duchesses dress like whores. What is the name of that dress? Gamoora? You could go to a German butcher's shop and not find as much meat on display."

"You must remember that for His Majesty," d'Aubigny said, laughing. Then the amusement passed from his face as quickly as if he had stepped into shadow. "I have decided what I must tell Paris."

De Visque, too, instantly composed himself. He stepped closer. Trilling Italian could be heard on the other side of the outer door. D'Aubigny drew de Visque into the privy set in a corner of the room and shut the door behind them. The two men sat on the lacquered privy bench, on either side of the anatomically shaped lid. The walls were painted with red-white-and-blue Sforza crests.

D'Aubigny studied one of the Sforza vipers. "France is dying," he said flatly. "If a dying man is offered a medicine that may save him or may hasten his death, he is hardly at greater risk by taking it."

"Our thinking is in concert," de Visque said in a near whisper.

"It may mean opposing Madame."

De Visque stroked his short black beard and nodded.

"First, we must convince Paris to settle with the Germans. We can go nowhere with the Germans waiting for our army to depart, so that they can march into Paris."

"What if Il Moro intends to purchase the services of the German army?"

"All the more reason we must settle with the Germans. Next, we should advocate the release of Louis Duc d'Orléans from the tower at Bourges. Not only will Orléans inflame passions in Paris; he will give any Italian expedition a second objective: Milan. That is essential, because we cannot leave Milan at our back if we assault Naples."

"What about Duchess Mother Bona? She is His Majesty's aunt, and the Duke of Milan is His Majesty's cousin. Do you think His Majesty will sanction an attack on his family?"

"You forget that Orléans is also His Majesty's cousin. His

Majesty's favorite cousin. And I do not believe that His Majesty's Italian cousin will be the Duke of Milan once we cross the mountains. Indeed, we can count on Duchess Mother Bona to offer the pretext for our march on Milan. She will summon us to rescue her son from the uncle who is plotting to usurp him. Once we have succeeded, the Duchess Mother and her son will be expendable."

"And if the Venetians come to the assistance of Milan? Il Moro's wife is the sister-in-law of Venice's Captain General. We can hardly expect to defeat both Milan and Venice."

"I don't believe that Venice will ever trust Il Moro." D'Aubigny pursed his lips thoughtfully. "Still . . . I will ask for permission to speak with Il Moro's wife. Perhaps she will inadvertently reveal something. Yes, that is the fundamental weakness in our construction. We do not know what Venice will do."

"It occurs to me that Il Moro also has a fundamental weakness. We assume that his first objective is to become Duke of Milan. He can hardly expect to rule Europe if he cannot legally rule his own state. But as yet he has no heir. The people of Milan have not forgotten the three years of bloody chaos they suffered when the last Visconti duke died without legitimate issue. Now that the present duke has an heir, the people of Milan are unlikely to encourage a usurper who can't promise them the stability offered by a legitimate succession."

"I am certain Il Moro intends for his wife to present him an heir."

"A man can give his wife this"—de Visque made an obscene punching motion with his fist—"all he wants. But only God can give a man a son."

"Then we should ask God to withhold Il Moro's son until we have designed the carriages to get our cannons over the mountains. Because if Il Moro can produce an heir before we have the means to stop him, he will bury France."

De Visque rubbed his beard and stared numbly at the Sforza vipers on the wall; finally he seemed to banish the vision with a shake of his head. "Well," he said, "given the possibility that we may not return, I suppose I should avail myself of the opportunity to sleep with an Italian woman."

D'Aubigny smiled grimly and stood up. "And I must seduce Duchess Mother Bona."

"Get away, Hermes." The greyhound continued to sniff at Isabella's skirts, and she batted him on the snout.

"Shall I ask the chamberlain to have the dog removed, Your Highness?" Giovanna da Maino, one of the oldest ladies-in-waiting at court—and the only one resourceful enough to handle the Duchess Mother—looked solicitously at Isabella. Giovanna's weary, craggy-featured face, masculinized and soured by age, concealed good intentions if not a gentle demeanor; a gentle woman would not have survived in this court for forty years.

"Hermes is the worst-behaved dog Gian has ever had, and that is no small achievement," Isabella said, trying to keep the agitation out of her voice. She had been waiting in her mother-in-law's antechamber for at least half an hour while Bona was closeted with Gian and Bernard Stuart d'Aubigny. Though the wait was a deliberate insult, she felt a far more powerful sense of injury, a fear more desperate than any concern for herself. They were talking about her baby, Francesco, in there. Not simply in the sense that everything that concerned the future of Milan involved her son, but directly. She could feel their words like ice splinters driven straight through her being.

Hermes made a skidding, inexplicably frantic circuit of the room and then sniffed at Isabella's feet. The door to Bona's bedchamber opened, and Giovanna rushed inside. She returned a moment later and curtsied. "Your Highness, Her Highness will see you now."

The Duchess Mother was seated erect on her bed, wearing a black, high-necked dress of squarish proportions that made her face appear almost absurdly round, as if it had been drawn by one of the modern Florentine painters, an artist so obsessed with circles and spheres that he imposed his geometry on every living thing. But Bona's features had some hitherto unnoticed vestiges of beauty. Her skin, though too heavily cerused, looked tauter, and the eyes were alert and focused. Isabella was almost ready to concede that a man could have loved the old crone once, but then Bona smiled (Why? Isabella asked herself. Is she gloating?), and her black teeth destroyed the illusion.

Gian reclined on the bed next to his mother, propped up on one elbow. He fingered a goblet half full of red wine. His rugged jaw was angrily set, but rather than suggesting masculine resolve, the pose was boyishly petulant.

Dressed in a broad-shouldered, pinch-waisted French coat, Messer Bernard Stuart d'Aubigny stood a step away from the bed. The French envoy bowed deeply, clumsily flourished with his hand, and said "Your Highness" in virtually unrecognizable Italian. Isabella glanced at the candlelit portrait on the opposite wall. From her position, the evil, coal-black eyes of Galeazzo Maria Sforza stared directly at her.

Bona glared at Isabella with hatred so intense that it seemed her dead husband's malignant spirit was grinning out of her vacant round sockets. "I have asked Gian if he can swear before God, Messer Bernard Stuart, and myself that he has slept with you."

Spilling wine over the satin bedspread as he sprang up, Gian looked down at his wife for a moment, nostrils flared, then strutted past her. Isabella's eyes twitched slightly at the corners. Gian stopped, turned, and faced his wife again.

"You had better tell your mother and Messer Bernard Stuart the truth God already knows, Gian," Isabella said coldly.

Gian's pale forehead vividly crimsoned. "I am a man!" he shouted. "Of course I have screwed this bitch! Do you want to know the ways I have screwed her! I have screwed her like a dog! I have made her take all her clothes off and sit on my horse and screwed her on my horse's back!"

Isabella turned to the Duchess Mother with a demure, almost beatific smile.

Bona's hands trembled with rage. "He has let you foul him only because a *puttana* like you will not rest until she has had every stableboy—"

"I have never slept with the boys who carve the meat at my husband's table."

"*Puttana! Forestiera* filth! That you would insult the Duchess Mother in front of His Most Christian Majesty's ambassador! God cursed me the day he made your soul! You are cursed like the devils of Aragon who sowed your seed! You have fouled my boy, but your cursed spawn will never become Duke of Milan!"

Isabella took a step forward and towered over her diminutive mother-in-law. "You pathetic old *cacapensieri*. My Francesco is the only reason Il Moro is not already Duke of Milan. You have already given away what was Gian's."

"Swear to me, God, and Messer Bernard Stuart that you are the only one this whore has slept with," Bona demanded of her son.

Gian hurled his goblet against the wall. "Stop this, Mother," he whispered, his voice hissing from his corded throat.

"Don't you realize that Gian would kill with his own hands any man who even touched me?" Isabella shook her head contemptuously at Bona.

Bona slumped and contracted, her dress shriveling like a wilting black orchid. "Gian cannot kill your father," she offered without vehemence. "He was your first lover."

"Don't you see what you are doing, Duchess Mother?" Isabella smiled generously, her voice gentle, maternal. "In trying to separate Gian from his wife and son, you are playing into Il Moro's hands. You think that you can offer the Frenchmen Naples in exchange for their help in destroying Il Moro. But if the Frenchmen come over the mountains, they will not be satisfied with Naples. They will want Milan as well."

The black teeth suddenly appeared, and the black orchid revived. Bona's high-pitched voice sang with triumph. "Messer Bernard Stuart has this evening informed me that His Most Christian Majesty, my dear nephew Charles, guarantees with all the might of France the honors with which he is investing Gian tomorrow."

"He guarantees Genoa? After all, Gian is only being invested with Genoa. What about Milan? Milan is an imperial fief and can be guaranteed only by the German Emperor."

"Let me put it into language you can understand, *uccelliaccia*. His Most Christian Majesty will never allow Il Moro to become Duke of Milan. Never. Never. Never."

Isabella looked searchingly at Bona and then at d'Aubigny. She was certain that the French envoy understood scarcely any Italian, so whatever agreement—if indeed there had been any—arrived at between Bona and d'Aubigny could hardly be verified. She nodded slightly at d'Aubigny and continued to look at him as she spoke to Bona. "Thank you, Duchess Mother. Tell Messer Bernard Stuart that we are grateful for His Most Christian Majesty's assurances. And wish him a good night." Isabella walked over to Gian and lightly brushed the lank platinum hair from his forehead. "My beautiful husband," she whispered to him, and then looked once more at Bona sitting alone on her bed before she led Gian out of the room.

CHAPTER

12

Milan, 1 May 1491

The investiture of Gian Galeazzo Sforza, Duke of Milan, with the honors of the Duchy of Genoa took place out of doors, just in front of the central portal of the Duomo. Enameled wooden pillars and a canopy of deep vermilion damask, embroidered with doves, lions, Sforza vipers, and French fleurs-de-lis, created a temporary porch. Il Moro and Gian, dressed in identical floor-length *vestiti* of gold-flecked white Lyons brocade trimmed with black sable at the collars and cuffs, knelt before the Archbishop of Milan and Bernard Stuart d'Aubigny, who for the purposes of this ceremony was to be regarded as the King of France. A French clerk in a hastily fitted silk mantle stood beside Messer Bernard Stuart and examined the Diploma of Investiture, a richly illuminated parchment document; until this morning no one had taken into account that d'Aubigny, like most French noblemen, could not read Latin and would require a translator.

The women of the ducal families knelt on the steps of the Duomo, the long tails of their *cioppe* cascading over the white stone. Representatives of the noble families of Milan sat in rows of benches placed in front of the steps. In the piazza beyond, caps reverently removed, stood scores of thousands of ordinary Milanese, perhaps as many as had come for Il Moro's wedding procession. The crowd was so silent that out on the Via degli Armorai they could still hear the banners flapping from the unfinished roof of the Duomo, and the halting cadence of d'Aubigny's voice as he repeated what the clerk prompted him to say, sentence by sentence.

"How much longer do you think he will go on?" Isabella whispered. "You would think he is individually describing every house and shop in Genoa."

"Had I known that Messer Bernard Stuart could not read, I would have requested a mattress to sleep upon rather than a cushion to kneel on," Beatrice whispered in reply. She glanced at Bianca Maria, who knelt next to her on the steps. Curiously, Bianca Maria was attentively rapt with the endless ceremony, her soft, dreamy eyes as unwavering as the fierce stare of Duchess Mother Bona, who knelt like a wooden statue to her daughter's left.

Bona's eyes darted balefully to the two duchesses. She made a muffled strangling sound, apparently intended as an admonition to stop the whispering. The French ambassador lifted the ivory scepter, crested with a gold fleur-de-lis, high enough that the hushed crowd in the piazza could see it, placed it in Gian's hand, then draped a gem-encrusted sword and scabbard over Gian's shoulder. The two dukes and d'Aubigny proceeded solemnly to the front of the porch.

D'Aubigny planted himself resolutely between Gian and Il Moro. He clasped their hands, then raised them overhead. The dignitaries seated just in front of the steps stood in unison. At this signal the silent crowd erupted with vast exhalations of "Duca! Duca! Duca!" D'Aubigny grinned with genial satisfaction, his crooked teeth visible behind his thick red beard.

The first few choruses of "Moro!" came from isolated pockets of several dozen men, probably armorers who had prearranged this demonstration. At first their shouts were vague and distant amid the thunderous acclaim for the Duke of Milan. But the armorers hammered again and again, gaining new voices with each oath, and the shouts of "Duca" dwindled in concert. There was a moment of equilibrium as the two forces reached equal volume. Then the balance tilted with unearthly suddenness, and the cries of "Moro! Moro! Moro!" from a hundred thousand throats rolled over the Piazza del Duomo like a massive cannonade. D'Aubigny continued to hold the two dukes' hands high, but his jagged teeth were no longer visible.

"Now that all has turned out as we have both wished, brother, let us return to our native land!" a practiced thespian voice boomed through the vaults of the Sala della Palla.

Menaechmus of Epidamnus placed his arm around his long-lost twin, Menaechmus of Syracuse, and intoned, in an actor's swaggering baritone, "Brother, I'll do whatever you wish! I'll hold an auction and sell everything I have. In the meantime, let's go inside, brother!" Menaechmus of Epidamnus gestured at his "house," a small wooden building erected on the left side of the stage. Painted with faux stonework, the house had no wall facing the audience seated out in the Sala della Palla, giving an unobstructed view of the interior. Behind the house an elaborate perspective view had been painted on the stage flats, representing an ancient Adriatic seaport as imagined by Leonardo da Vinci. Illusionistic arcades receded toward a ceremonial arch, beyond which glimmered the azure waters of the harbor at Epidamnus and a glimpse of galleys floating at anchor. The set was so startlingly realistic that one could imagine the actors strolling beneath the arch and boarding one of the distant ships.

The Menaechmi twins ducked beneath the wooden lintel and entered the house; they were followed by Menaechmus of Syracuse's slave, Messenio, who darted after them with a buffoonish, arm-jerking agitation that drew weary titters of amusement from the audience.

"Do you know what I would like, sirs!" Messenio said in his usual importunate whine. "Allow me to be the auctioneer!"

"I give it to you." Menaechmus of Epidamnus bowed with a flourish.

Messenio rubbed his hands together greedily, then left the twins to their joyous reunion and ran back into the make-believe street. He stopped, dramatically considered an afterthought, and turned to face the audience. "Auction of the effects of Menaechmus, one week from today!" he began in a peddler's singsong. "We are selling slaves, household goods, land, buildings, everything! For sale! Whatever you want to give us we'll take, your price as long as it's your cash, if you want credit we'll give you our price! For sale! We're even offering one scarcely used wife, if there's anyone willing to bid." Messenio cupped his hand to his mouth and leaned toward the audience. "I can't believe that item would net a copper," he offered in sneering, *sotto voce* confidence, to the generous laughter of most of the men and many of the older women present. "Now, spectators"—he flourished his arm grandly—"goodbye, but first leave us with your loud applause!"

The red-and-blue damask curtain dropped in front of Messenio, tambourines rattled, shawms and lutes lilted, and red-and-blue-vested ducal singers added a choral finale. When the music ended, the several thousand spectators, seated on amphitheaterlike tiers of benches, stood and applauded, though less from enthusiasm for the rambling farce than from a desire to get their blood circulating again.

Beatrice, seated with the ducal party just in front of the stage, rose with a much more fervent desire: to escape Il Moro. Her stomach ached from the effort of control. She had been at his side throughout the endless state banquet, and then the interminable, misogynistic comedy (there had been one exquisitely embarrassing scene in which Menaechmus of Syracuse's father-in-law had ridiculed his own daughter for complaining about her husband's mistress).

Throughout the evening Il Moro had been courteous to his wife, though not with the mocking effusion he had displayed in the early days of their marriage; he had simply put on a proper, flawless show for the French envoys. But beneath her husband's smooth manner Beatrice sensed something new, something stirring behind the icy composure of his hate, something so terrifying that every casual contact with him, the merest touch of their elbows, jolted her. What did he want? What did he want with her?

". . . Your Highness?" Beatrice looked up to see Galeazzo di Sanseverino peering down at her like a troubled Apollo. Galeazz's head, wreathed in blond curls, was so far above her that it was uncomfortable to look up at him. She retrieved his question. He had asked her if she liked the theatrical.

Beatrice forced a smile, then noted with relief that her husband had disappeared. "I think Plautus is a bit silly, Galeazz. I suppose I cannot enjoy a theatrical when everyone in it is a fool. Would you want to go to a supper and find that everyone else seated at the table was a clown? You would quickly tire of it."

Galeazz studied Beatrice for a moment, his frosty blue eyes blinking in concentration. "I had better see to our guests. When His Most Christian Majesty's envoys leave, you and I will have a long ride and decide whether we prefer Terence to Plautus." He bowed elegantly and retreated to the side of Jean Roux de Visque. The two men began an animated conversation in French.

Isabella observed Beatrice standing alone and picked her way through the ducal party. As she passed Messer Galeazz he gestured expressively, and his elbow struck her sharply on the arm. He turned, his boyishly smooth cheeks flushed, and began profuse, bowing apologies. Isabella's eyes narrowed, and she did not wait for him to finish.

"Are you all right?" Isabella asked when she reached Beatrice. She put her hand on her cousin's forehead. "You might be sick. All this business of entertaining Frenchmen has gone on too long for anybody's health." She took Beatrice's hand. "I am going to offer my apologies to the Frenchmen and go to bed. I think you should do the same."

"I . . . I'm not allowed to leave yet," Beatrice said. "My husband has asked that I stay and speak with Messer Bernard Stuart d'Aubigny. I guess it is my turn to be inspected like a goose on the butcher's counter."

"You're right," Isabella whispered into Beatrice's ear. "I don't like these Frenchmen at all. They look at us like we're mares in a breeder's pen. And since they can't afford to buy, I presume they are only interested in stealing. If Messer Bernard Stuart asks to see your teeth, demonstrate their health by biting him right on the tip of his misshapen nose."

Beatrice laughed, and she and Isabella hugged and kissed good night. As she watched Isabella thread through the crowd, Beatrice sensed someone behind her. She turned. Her stomach cramped painfully.

"His Most Christian Majesty's envoy would like to speak with you now," Il Moro said in an uninflected voice. He placed his hand beneath Beatrice's elbow and ushered her to the side of Messer Bernard Stuart and his interpreter, a young, pox-scarred scholar from the university at Pavia. Il Moro excused himself and left Beatrice in the unfamiliar company of the two men. The first several exchanges concerned the theatrical and the scantily costumed dancers who had performed during the intermissions. Beatrice painstakingly explained to d'Aubigny how dance music progressed metrically, by sixths, from a slow *bassa danza* to the throbbing *moresca*.

Finally d'Aubigny focused on Beatrice. "You are so very pretty and youthful, Your Highness, and yet now that the Duchess of Milan has bid us good night, you are the queen of this great court. Is that not a very great responsibility?"

What you are trying to do is as plain as the crooked nose on your face, thought Beatrice. Do you really think I will let some freckled barbarian start something between my cousin and me? Beatrice looked directly into d'Aubigny's eyes. "You must forgive me, messer, but I would never presume myself queen of this court. I would be a poor substitute for my dearest cousin and even dearer friend, the Duchess of Milan."

After her response had been translated, Beatrice noticed that d'Aubigny's implacable demeanor was briefly disturbed by a twitter of his red-tipped eyebrows. She greatly enjoyed this little triumph and eagerly awaited his next question.

"Yes, I have been told that you and the Duchess of Milan have become fast companions. Are you also as close to your sister?"

"My sister is half my self." But why, Beatrice asked herself, is my relationship with my sister of interest to a Frenchman?

"She is certainly fortunate to have such a devoted sister. And of course one hears that her husband, the Marquis of Mantua, considers himself the most fortunate man in Christendom, to have such a splendid wife. Next to your own husband, of course."

"No, I am certain that even my dear husband would agree that the Marquis of Mantua is the most fortunate man in Christendom, Messer Bernard Stuart."

D'Aubigny looked down at the adolescent Duchess of Bari. Perhaps the French were not as adept as their hosts at the art of diplomatic deception, but they understood the art of romance. Il Moro's display of cordial regard for his wife had not fooled d'Aubigny; the little Duchess of Bari's surprisingly witty comment only confirmed what he already suspected. Could the Duchess of Bari, d'Aubigny wondered, be a sword in French hands?

"Only to avoid disagreeing with Your Highness would I agree that your sister's husband is more fortunate than the Duke of Bari. And surely the Marquis of Mantua cannot consider himself fortunate to have to spend so much time away from his wife, as I am certain must be required by his duties as Venice's Captain General. Even if that time is spent in a city as lovely as Venice. Have you ever visited there, Your Highness?"

Now Beatrice understood the objective of Messer Bernard Stuart's circumlocution. Venice. Of course. When Venice's Lion of Saint Mark roared, the whole world trembled. Even Il Moro regarded Venice with extremely wary respect. "Messer Bernard Stuart," Beatrice said impulsively, "what is it you wish to know about Venice?"

D'Aubigny almost choked with astonishment. Watching the flash of Beatrice's clever dark eyes, he realized where he had seen that kind of restless acuity once before: Madame de Beaujeu when she had been eighteen or twenty, before power had given a focus to her relentless energy and lancing intellect. This precocious child was clearly a blade that required careful handling. "I rather have a feeling that Your Highness knows more about Venice than Your Highness would consider it prudent to disclose," he told her, "so I will be prudent enough not to ask."

Beatrice was momentarily delighted that she had so easily bested Messer Bernard Stuart. Then she realized her mistake. She should have let him go on and found out what the Frenchmen were so desperate to learn about Venice. The next time she played this game she would remember that.

D'Aubigny retreated into the usual diplomatic prattle. After his vacuous series of observations on the beauty of Italian women, Beatrice lost interest and her eyes wandered. She noticed Bernardino da Corte, the assistant castellan of Porta Giovia and Il Moro's chief of security, standing at the left corner of the stage. Bernardino signaled with a finger to his lips. Il Moro quickly appeared at Bernardino's side, as if he had been expecting an urgent message. Bernardino whispered in Il Moro's ear. The message was brief,

and the messenger quickly departed. Il Moro stood staring into
the damask curtain with dull, lifeless eyes. A small muscle at the
base of his jaw ticked several times.

". . . you have convinced me," continued d'Aubigny via his
interpreter, "that you Italian women are the most remarkable creatures on earth. His Most Christian Majesty will be fascinated."
D'Aubigny bowed and took his leave.

Beatrice turned to find Il Moro at her side. His eyes were alive
again, obsidian black and roaming with manic ferocity. He took
her arm with a grip that brought tears to her eyes. "It is time for
the Duchess of Bari to wish all a good night," he said through
clenched teeth, his voice acid. "Bid one and all good night, Beatrice, and go to bed. But do not sleep, for the dream you will
have tonight will be my dream."

"Gian?" Isabella sat up and clutched the down coverlet over her
naked breasts. The glowing coals on the hearth cast an orange
sheen over the marble floor and filled the room with dark, vague
shapes. "Gian, I thought you weren't feeling well. Come here and
I will massage your temples."

A distinct shadow fell over the glossy orange of the floor.
Isabella drew in her breath. "I will call my guards," she said in a
low, quavering voice.

"For Francesco's sake you will not."

"Don't come closer. What do you want?"

"You know what I have always wanted. You can see how I
look at you, but you cannot know how my body is one flame
every time I think of you. That desire will never be quenched.
Never."

"Your sentiments are as artless as your words. Go away."

"I love you."

"You . . . love? You aren't capable even of loving yourself.
Only your reflection. What you see mirrored in all their faces.
Most of all his. And they love you only because they don't
know you."

The intruder followed his shadow to the side of the bed and

fell to his knees, dipping his head to the covers in supplication. "Please," he begged in a harsh, overly dramatic whisper, "please just take my hand in yours. Please, for the sake of our son."

"My son!" Isabella hissed. "My son! He will never be anyone's son but my son! I am his father and his mother. The instant I felt his life inside me I never wanted to touch you again. He is my son!"

The intruder slowly lifted his head and then struck out like a vengeful phantom, ripping the covers away and pinning Isabella beneath his huge, muscular form. She writhed in protest, wrestling her arms free to fight him off. Then her entire body convulsed as if struck by a thunderbolt. She frantically pulled off her assailant's hose and ripped open his linen shirt. Her hips pressed up greedily and her mouth assaulted his and her legs circled his back. She raked his hard buttocks with her fingernails, her body snapping again when he entered her. She pushed him back and made him sit up and prop her on his thighs. "Bite my breast!" she commanded in quick, hysterical breaths. She rocked and whimpered and grabbed his luxuriant blond hair with both hands and pulled so hard that his pale-blue eyes, luminous with pain, floated eerily out of the darkness.

The man soon reached his climax, and he moaned as if mortally wounded. At that moment Isabella finally gave him the offering he had really wanted, the proof that he existed to her: his name, only his name. She growled the name as his pumping thighs lifted her and she shoved her finger into his anus. He held her suspended, rigid with his release, and she shuddered at the vague surge of his semen deep inside her and felt it lift her toward the light. And then she was carried by her own effortless wings, wings as vast as the great golden canopy above her, and when she had gathered all the light, all the meaning in the universe into her enormous span, she gasped his name again. Finally to herself, alone, as she soared above an infinite horizon: Give me another baby, Galeazz.

But if your love for the Highest Sphere
turned upward your desire,
your breast would never know such a fear.

Beatrice closed her volume of Dante's *Purgatorio*. She had not really read anything beyond this page in all these hours, and now, as she had expected, he was here.

Il Moro staggered slightly. He had already removed his *vestito*. When he reached the side of the bed, he stripped off his doublet and hose with jerky motions and stood over her in his loose linen shirt. His chest rose and fell, and she could hear his rough exhalations. She had never before smelled wine on his breath, and the faint scent that reached her quickened her fear.

His voice came from deep in his chest. "Madonna Cecilia Gallerani gave birth to a healthy infant this evening." He paused, and a tic pulsed through his temple and cheek. "A son."

The words instantly sucked away her soul. She no longer had the will or energy even to turn her head from the infinite spite in her husband's eyes. God save me, she heard her reeling consciousness plead, but the words disappeared, a distant shout in a shrieking wind. No one, least of all God, was listening anymore.

He did not bother to snuff the lamp. He threw aside the covers and straddled her. He pulled her chemise up to her breasts and stripped his shirt off and pressed his heavy chest against her until she thought she would suffocate. The sour stench of wine made her gag. For a moment she resisted his hasty penetration, attempting with muscles she had been unaware she had to expel the thing pushing inside her. But he fought back savagely.

She began to fall, plunging into a terrible, lonely darkness, cast down by Mama and Father and everyone she had believed loved her, cast down by her powerlessness and humiliation. Her attacker was the only living presence in this dark universe, and in a delirium of pain and outrage she imagined that she could free herself only by crying out to him, begging him to stop. . . .

No. She would not let him take that last dignity from her. She bit her lip against the pain, forcing back her sobs. And then in a moment of beautiful clarity she saw that the pain was not her scourge but her salvation, that only when the soul had accepted suffering could it rise from the abyss and climb to redemption. I will suffer, but I will not let him hear me cry out, she told herself again and again. I will suffer, but I will not cry.

His moment came, but she did not know it. She only knew that the pain, her savior, was drawing back into the blazing heights from which it had descended, but it had left behind a residue of strength, a tempering of her soul. Il Moro glared down at her, shoulders and chest heaving, and she met his eyes with the diamond-hard will of her heart. I have defeated you, she thought with silent venom, and have stolen your victory. And when your baby begins to grow inside me, I will defeat it, and rob you of that victory as well.

C H A P T E R

13

Paris, June 1491

The cradle rocked noiselessly, the only sound a baby's fitful cough, a phantom presence in the darkness. "*Maman* is here," murmured Madame de Beaujeu. "*Maman* is here."

The door creaked, a soft cricket chirp. Slippers brushed across the floor. The light coming from the next room illuminated Madame's face. She was not happy about the intrusion.

The unwelcome visitor, a well-dressed lady-in-waiting, whispered next to Madame's ear. "Forgive me, Your Highness. It is very urgent. Madame's husband must speak with Madame at once."

Pierre de Beaujeu waited in the antechamber. He was a small man with a large nose, a deeply cleft chin, and warmly intelligent eyes.

"I think she is going to sleep for a while," Madame said, as if this news had precedence over any crisis. Her daughter, Suzanne, had been a tiny baby, and for the first three weeks it had seemed that her struggling lungs could not sustain her wrinkled little body. But in the past few days Suzanne had begun to gain weight, and her bluish tint had faded. Madame nevertheless maintained her unflagging vigil, still sleeping and eating beside her baby's cradle.

Pierre offered his wife a knowing smile. "She is strong like her mother. She wants to live. She will live. We can thank God for that." His mouth tightened. "Yesterday morning Bernard Stuart d'Aubigny arrived at Bourges and ordered, in your brother's name, that Louis be released from the tower. Louis was taken to Pont de Baragon, where he met your brother. I believe there is still time to arrest de Vesc and the Bishop of Mountabon before they can arrive there and rendezvous with Louis and your brother." Étienne de Vesc and the Bishop of Mountabon were the two most powerful Orleanists still allowed at court.

Madame's weary face revealed no reaction. Her menacing eyes, however, seemed to click through thousands of calculations. Then everything stopped, and she reached for Pierre's hands. "No, no," she said softly. "It is time. It is time." She brought her husband into her arms. "You and I are in no danger from this. With one hand God has given us Suzanne, and with the other He has set Louis free. If that is the bargain God wishes to strike, then we have been blessed that He is so generous." Madame placed her head on Pierre's shoulder. For the first time since she had been fifteen years old, she permitted herself to cry.

· PART ·

THREE

CHAPTER

14

Naples, 25 December 1491

"I want to know why we have been brought here." The request was uttered in a hoarse, desperate voice.

The guard smashed the butt of his knife against his questioner's nose. The prisoner collapsed into a motionless heap on the slimy stones; with his filthy cloak, tangled hair, and emaciated limbs, he looked like little more than a pile of rags and bones unearthed from a hasty grave.

The remaining prisoners, a disordered assembly of about thirty men, responded to the assault with whispered prayers. They already looked like specters of the dead: blanched, gaunt faces and puckered, toothless mouths. They had been brought to the isle of Ischia from Naples, six hours distant by boat, the previous evening, Christmas Eve. Some had anticipated freedom; perhaps their ransom by the French. But they had merely exchanged their dungeons in the notorious Castel Sant'Elmo for equally doleful accommodations in a desolate, ancient fortress.

Another prisoner summoned the strength and courage to ask: "Why are we here?"

The guard who had struck the first prisoner stepped forward, searching for the culprit. But his superior, a grave-looking man wrapped in a fine wool cape, held him back.

"You are guests of the house of Aragon," the man in the wool cape said casually. The irony was not entirely lost on his starvation-dulled audience. Most of these men were important Neapolitan nobles with a long history of opposition, sometimes violent, to the Aragonese rulers of Naples; many were the sons of noblemen who had actively supported French claims to Naples a generation previously. Five years before, Ferrante of Aragon, the King of Naples, had made peace with the rebellious nobles. To seal the accord, Ferrante had arranged the marriage of his niece to one of his principal opponents and had invited the rest of the rebels to a celebratory banquet in the great hall of the Castel Nuovo. (One prominent nobleman had declined the invitation. Antonello di Sanseverino, the Prince of Salerno, had responded with a note reading: "The old sparrow doesn't fly into a cage," and had then fled to Paris.) Shortly after the fourth course had been served, Ferrante had ordered the doors sealed; the guests had been summarily arrested and imprisoned, their property confiscated. The women and children had eventually been released, but the noblemen had spent the subsequent years in the lightless dungeons beneath the Castel Sant'Elmo. They had not been permitted any contact with the outside world. Many of their families already presumed them dead.

"God's robe," whispered one of the wraiths. "Today we will see Jesus." The infection of fear quickly spread among the prisoners; it made sense that they would be killed out here, where the bodies could be disposed of in secrecy. Anxious queries and desperate murmurs became a frantic, chaotic chorus. Several men repeated saints' names over and over. Finally one prisoner called out, "Let God witness that we asked you to provide us a priest!"

"Let the devil watch you die," the man in the wool cape answered. He turned and motioned one of the guards to open the low wooden door. A cold draft swept into the chamber, and the wind moaned through the hallway beyond. The man in the wool cape ducked his head beneath the lintel and disappeared. A moment later the noise of the wind rose to a tremulous shriek, as if a cyclone were raging outside.

Seemingly propelled by the tremendous gust, a crouching,

nearly naked figure came through the doorway. He stood erect, a towering black man wearing only a loincloth, his massive shoulders and arms glistening with rain. In one hand he carried a smith's hammer, the tapered end sharpened to a spike.

The chamber echoed with protests and prayers as the guards pushed back the cluster of prisoners. Two guards brought one man forward. The prisoner was tall, with a prominent nose that seemed half his virtually fleshless face. His feverish eyes frantically searched the black man's impassive features. In a movement so quick it did not seem real, the black man brought the spike end of the hammer smashing into the prisoner's face, then ripped it out again almost before the split-melon sound had registered. The grotesque puncture spurted blood, brilliant crimson against ghastly white skin, and the man fell like an empty sack.

The guards had to hold the second victim's long, stringy hair. He spit, missing the black man, and shouted: "Jesus curse the devils of Aragon until every bastard's son burns in hell! Jesus curse the whoreson Ferrante! Jesus curse Alfonso the—" The spike plunged into his eye socket.

Within minutes all of the prisoners lay in a heap of rags and skeletal limbs, splotched with darkening blood and the yellowish-gray serum that moments before had been memories and hope. The wind screamed. The man in the wool cape came back into the chamber and slipped up behind the executioner. The black man did not seem to hear, and he glared with astonishment when the man in the wool cape reached up and quickly and expertly cut his throat.

The gale came from the east in a steady roar, driving enormous spume-capped swells across the usually placid Bay of Naples. The waves rolled against the concrete harbor mole and slapped into the massive seafront flank of the Castel Nuovo. Alfonso of Aragon, Duke of Calabria, heir to the throne of Naples, stood at his window high above the water and watched the phosphorescing foam climb toward him. No one in Naples could remember such a storm. It had come up just after midnight, and now this Christmas midmorning was as dark as dusk.

"It is done," Alfonso whispered to himself. He turned away from the window. He wore nothing except two large rings, one of sapphires and diamonds set in gold, the other ruby-studded. His thighs were thick and solid, a necessary support for his expansive belly and heavily muscled shoulders. A cap of black curled hair fell over the nape of his neck and concealed all but a finger's width of his forehead. His rounded jowls were massive yet firm, suggestive of both indolence and brutish strength. But Alfonso's mouth was urbane, delicate, as if shaped by constant poetic utterances, and his painfully squinted eyes—a congenital deformity—made him appear as if he were always weeping.

"What do you think of them?" Alfonso addressed his question to a young, compactly fleshy woman with large, dark nipples and luxuriantly wavy black hair. She was sitting up in a canopied bed strewn with embroidered silk pillows, studying a sheaf of architectural renderings; several of the large drawings were detailed plans for an entire city laid out in a precise grid.

The woman looked up. "What is the word?" she asked rhetorically. "*Simmetria.* Everything is just alike. Too much *simmetria.*"

"That is the beauty of it. *Simmetria. Regola.* Do you think we can pass an ordinance that the people of Naples will no longer be permitted to empty their chamber pots into the streets? But if all the streets run in straight lines from the hills to the sea, every time it rains, the shit will be washed away."

"So that is what you tell your architects? Foremost, you must consider the shit?"

Alfonso's massive shoulders jerked slightly, a reflex of amusement. "*Belleza*, simply because you have proved to be an expert at your profession does not mean that you are ready to instruct these *maestri* in theirs."

"If I were as inventive at my work as these *maestri* are at theirs, I would be sleeping with peasants and footmen."

Alfonso knelt on the bed and presented his penis. "Let us see what sort of *invenzione* you have for this."

The woman laughed and stroked Alfonso's massive thigh. When Alfonso's penis began to stiffen, she looked up at him with challenging blue eyes and a wry smile.

She turned, startled. The double doors at the end of the room had rattled. Two men, one thin and sumptuously dressed, the other plump and attired with grotesque extravagance, walked casually into the bedchamber.

The thin man intoned, "Your Highness, His Majesty your father."

Alfonso signaled the woman with a slight motion of his head. She stacked the drawings neatly, got up, entirely naked, and sauntered toward the door, her plump buttocks twitching to her insouciant gait. She curtsied to the King of Naples and vanished through the doors. The thin man, who was the King's chamberlain, bowed and retreated, closing the doors behind him.

Ferrante of Aragon, the King of Naples, walked to the windows and looked out at the screaming sea. He was a mocking image of his son grown old: the once-muscular shoulders atrophied, the belly a swollen paunch, the jowls sagging until they almost swallowed his neck. The effete nature suggested by Alfonso's mouth was more pronounced in his father. Ferrante's gray hair ringed his face in painstakingly shaped curls, and he clasped pudgy white hands over his breast. His immense girth corseted in a pale-blue tunic embroidered with riotous floral patterns, his sloping shoulders wreathed with a massive necklace of gold fruit clusters, the King of Naples resembled a court buffoon's caricature of an aging homosexual. But there was also a measure of strength and intelligence absent from his son's more robust features. Ferrante's aggressive, chiseled nose seemed to spring from his forehead, flanked by wary, worldly, frighteningly alert green eyes. He turned from the window, and his eyes posed a question.

"I had them moved last night." Alfonso's voice was a deep bass, but his delivery was strangely quiet, almost a whisper. "I gave the order. Obviously we will not have word from Ischia for at least a day or two."

Ferrante nodded almost imperceptibly. Then his eyes indicated that the subject had changed. "Did you talk to Camillo?" Camillo de Scorziatis was a Neapolitan envoy who had just returned from Milan.

"Why?" Alfonso asked irritably, joining his father at the window. "He only confirms your opinions."

"Perhaps because my opinions are correct." Ferrante chuckled softly. "You know he says that your daughter and Beatrice have become *amice*. I thought that might happen. They were both such gifted children. So very special."

"And you imagine that the friendship between two girls will concern Il Moro? If Il Moro had his prick in God's Mother, She would not influence his policy. As it is, Beatrice is less of a wife to Il Moro than the Duke of Milan is a husband to my daughter."

Ferrante turned to his son, his lips subtly pursed. "I would say that is one of the advantages of the situation. Camillo says that Il Moro sleeps with her once a month, the date determined by his astrologer. Rather better that Beatrice and Il Moro are not so close and are so unlikely to produce an heir. Or you don't agree?"

"Perhaps you should pay more attention to what is happening in Paris and less to who is sleeping with whom in Milan." Alfonso swiveled his massive head and confronted his father. "They are coming. It is a question not of if but of when."

"They will come *if* they can get their cannons over the mountains, and *if* Il Moro invites them. They are as yet unable to accomplish the former, and I think the latter unlikely. The loudest commotion in Paris currently is the ranting of the Orleanists, who want to attack Milan, not Naples. Il Moro has the best ears in Europe. He hears those voices. He knows that his head is on the same block as ours."

"Il Moro's head is too big to share a block with anyone. He has betrayed us once. He will betray us again." Alfonso referred to the war with Venice eight years previously, when Il Moro had negotiated a separate peace, without even consulting his Neapolitan allies.

"That was a wise decision on his part. I did not like it any better than you did, but he did what was expedient. What was best for his state and his people. I put more trust in a clever scoundrel than in a honest fool. And Il Moro is too clever to let the French come over the mountains."

"And if he negotiates a secret agreement with the Venetians? He will not need to fear the French."

Ferrante looked to the sea and shook his head. "The Signory of Venice will permit Il Moro to unite all Italy, but the Signory will never permit Il Moro to become Duke of Milan," he said softly. "Il Moro's only real ally is a chimera, the same imaginary beast you are bent on pursuing. His strength is not in what he is capable of doing—though he is capable indeed—but in what other men fear he might do.''

An enormous gust blustered against the window. One of the panes cracked with an audible chink; a moment later it exploded into the room, and the cold rain howled through the opening. Both men stumbled back in alarm. Then the wind subsided to an eerie whistle, and Ferrante began to chuckle. But Alfonso of Aragon, the conqueror of the Turks at Taranto, the man who had twice marched his armies to the gates of Rome, stared at the shattered glass on the floor, his burly face a mask of horror.

C H A P T E R

15

Milan, April 1492

"*Elefante*, Francesco. Eh-lay-faahn-tay." Isabella pointed to the elephant. Chained by the foot to one of the pillars ringing the courtyard of Il Moro's menagerie, the beast passively swished its trunk across the straw-strewn flagstones.

Beatrice held Isabella's son, Francesco. The sixteen-month-old boy was still swaddled below the waist but wore a white silk shirt and a little jacket of gold-embroidered brocade. "*Elefante*," Beatrice said. "*Elefante*."

"Della," Francesco blurted somewhat peevishly.

A lion growled. Both duchesses started and turned to the cage directly behind them. The lion began to roar, so powerfully that they could smell its carrion-tainted breath a half-dozen paces away. Francesco screamed and began to cry hysterically, his face quickly reddening in vivid contrast to his fine, almost transparent hair. The elephant stomped and snorted, the caged tropical birds shrieked, and monkeys began to screech. The duchesses and Francesco's *vecchia*, Lucia, scurried across the courtyard and exited the menagerie through the gleaming white peristyle entrance.

Outside, Francesco continued to cry, his hearty protest obscuring even the racket from the menagerie. Isabella took him from Beatrice, kissed him fervently, and stroked his silky hair. When that failed to calm him she passed him to Lucia, who had no more success.

"He's tired," Isabella said. She signaled for the waiting coachmen to bring her carriage up. "Let Angela feed him," she told Lucia. "Then put him to bed." She kissed the still-squalling toddler and murmured to him, then assisted Lucia into the gilded belly of the four-wheeled *carrozza*. "Don't come back," she called up to the driver. "Her Highness and I are going to get horses."

The Duke of Milan's stables were a short walk from the menagerie. Surrounded by deep green pines, oaks, and elms, the stable complex resembled a large *palazzo* in the *all'antica* style; the ground floor was enclosed by an arcade of white marble columns and classical arches. The horse stalls were some of the finest accommodations in all Europe, regardless of resident species. Columns capped with intricately carved stone garlands supported the ribbed ceiling vaults, and superbly lifelike frescoes of horses decorated the walls; the Duke of Milan presumed that just as the human occupants of the Castello enjoyed pictures of their glorious ancestors, so his horses would be inspired by images of equine champions. The plumbing was the most advanced available: piped-in water in each stall, and a system of clay conduits to remove waste.

The uniformed grooms quickly saddled and bridled the duchesses' horses. Beatrice and Isabella rode north through the ducal park. The afternoon warmed, and they pushed their horses to a lather, the trees flying past in a green blur.

"Let's circle back toward the lake," Isabella said when they finally decided to cool their horses; Il Moro had built an artificial lake near the stables and menagerie. "We can unsaddle and water them there."

The landscaped park surrounding the lake was deserted except for a cluster of white swans at the north end; the workmen who had been installing a marble balustrade around the perimeter of the lake had apparently been sent elsewhere. The horses drank from the lake, and Beatrice and Isabella sipped from a tiered fountain of newly cut marble. They spread a saddle cloth on the grass and lay down side by side, squinting up at the sun. The horses slurped and snorted and flapped their manes.

Isabella turned her head to Beatrice. "In the sun I can see the red in your hair. I have it too. It's our Spanish blood. But I love the way yours is, so dark underneath, with this transparent red halo. So beautiful."

"I'm not beautiful, Eesh." Eesh was a childhood nickname the duchesses had revived, a toddler's Spanish pronunciation of Isabella's Latin monogram, IX. "You're beautiful."

"It would be nice to hear my husband say that. But I'm two legs short of earning that sort of compliment from him."

"Maybe Gian will change. Mama wrote me that marriage is like a lute. You mustn't be distressed if it does not play properly at first. Day by day you must adjust the strings to produce a harmony. At least that's what Mama says."

"Gian isn't a lute," Isabella said dryly. "He's a *cacarella*." With her fist she made an obscene masturbating motion. Beatrice shrieked with laughter, which provoked a similar outburst in her cousin. The duchesses crowed and cackled and wrapped their arms around one another.

When they had stopped laughing they remained in their embrace. Isabella looked intently into Beatrice's eyes. "Have you ever wondered how it would feel to be like this with a man?" she whispered. "I don't mean in bed, quickly proceeding to their objective, but like this. To hold someone close without wanting that, even if you did that later."

For a moment Beatrice couldn't imagine wanting anything more than the intimacy she was enjoying with Isabella. But of course she remembered. Those velvet, sultry nights at the Villa Belriguardo on the river Po, when she had stayed up and raptly listened to her half-sister Lucrezia fantasize about her husband-to-be, nights when her sister had read from her fiancé's letters, embellishing his ardent declarations of love with anticipatory visions of their lovemaking. A hundred nights, a thousand nights when Beatrice had read and reread all the great romances in the light of flickering oil lamps, memorizing the words of Rolando and Tristan and Petrarch and hearing them again in the darkness, feeling the warm hand of a gallant cavalier or an ardent poet in her own, and falling asleep with his words sparking like fireworks in her mind.

"Words," Beatrice whispered. "I want a man to tell me things."

"I only want a man to kiss me. Not like men kiss, but like this. . . ." Isabella's lips brushed Beatrice's, as softly as her own breath. The kisses moved in an infinitesimal procession from one corner of Beatrice's mouth to the other; there was never a sensation of pressure, only warmth and a perfect smoothness.

Beatrice's head buzzed, surprising and alarming her. But she was strangely disappointed when her cousin stopped.

"Oh, God," Isabella said. She groaned and let her head fall back. "Kissing Gian is like sticking your head in a wine barrel full of pickled eels." She turned to Beatrice. "I'll tell you what it's like sleeping with Gian if you'll tell what it is like with Il Moro."

The duchesses shrieked with laughter.

"I will go first," Isabella announced. "Gian cannot do anything if he hasn't had enough to drink, and he can't do anything if he's had too much to drink. At first he is most interested in my breasts, which I like. I love to have my breasts sucked. He likes to see me entirely naked, so there is always a lamp left lit or it is done during the day. If I can surprise him and not give him time to think about it, he can become very excited. One time I was able to persuade him when we were out riding. That's when I enjoy it the most, when Gian gets . . . excited."

Beatrice reminded herself that at least one of her childhood dreams had come true: perhaps she wasn't sitting beside Eesh on her bed, as she had dreamed in Naples, but here she was talking to her as intimately as a sister. "My husband drinks a little too," she said. "I can always smell it. But he never . . . It's like he is giving me one of Messer Ambrogio's medications. Once a month he sends word to expect him. He never talks, he lifts my chemise and lifts his shirt, and he proceeds. I know it will be over more quickly if I relax, so I think about things I like. I pretend I'm floating down the Po River on a summer afternoon, with the musicians playing, throwing petals in the water and counting them. It doesn't take very long."

"Do you ever enjoy it?"

"It doesn't feel bad anymore. I know he tries not to hurt me."

"Do you want a baby?"

The question startled Beatrice so much that she sat straight up. Isabella's pitch was wrong: disingenuous, dishonest. But Beatrice told herself that Isabella was only hiding an understandable con-

cern, a concern they both shared. If she were to give Il Moro an
heir, everything would change. If . . . The fear suddenly made
her queasy, and she fought the truth *she* was hiding. Her voice
was high and tentative. "Eesh . . . Eesh, weren't you afraid when
you had your baby?"

Isabella sat up, pulled the hem of her skirt to her knees, and
stroked her slender white legs. There was a strange movement of
her eyes; a narrowing, a flicker. But it passed. She shook her head.
"You would be frightened if you listened to all the *favole* the old
women tell you, how if you see a lizard on your windowsill the
day you conceive you will have a monster with a lizard's tail, and
how you must have learned this on Christmas Eve if you want
to stop hemorrhaging: 'On Christmas night Jesus was born, and
Christmas night he was lost. On Christmas night he recovered
again. Blood, stay in your vein, as Christ's blood stayed in his.'
As if you could remember to say that if you were bleeding to
death." Isabella's lips twisted sarcastically. "You know that when
you're a duchess you have to have witnesses present, don't you?
They show them in as soon as they get you in the birthing chair.
You are sitting there with all of them staring between your legs,
to make sure you don't cheat and pull some whore's newborn
infant out of the washing basin. Messer Ambrogio kept getting
me out of bed and sitting me in the birthing chair, even though
I could tell I wasn't close to ready. That tired me more than the
birth—getting up, sitting there for an hour, lying down when the
baby didn't come, getting up . . . on and on." Isabella shook her
head contemptuously. "Even if you weren't carrying a baby in
your belly, all that activity would tire you. Have you ever had a
fever so bad that even your bones ache? That's how I felt. As if
a poison were running through my veins. As if a hot cannonball
were inside me, pressing against my backbone. And when the
baby started to come, I believed I would look down and see my
bowels spilling out of me."

Isabella stopped, frowned, and made several silent words with
her mouth. "I saw this way out of the pain," she said at last. "A
light. I could fly in it. Toto"—Toto was little Francesco's pet
name for Beatrice and had been adopted by his mother—"it was
. . . I felt I had huge wings and could fly, and with each thrust of

my wings I rose away from all of them and yet at the same time pushed my baby into the light. And suddenly I was free, I was above all of them, floating in the light, and my baby was with me. And when I saw my baby's face for the first time I knew that he wasn't God's baby or his father's baby but that he was mine alone. My will, my strength, a strength that no one else could ever have, had given him life." Isabella clutched her legs tightly. "I can't wait to have another baby."

Beatrice stared off toward the lake; two of the swans drifted on the water like white marble statues set on a sheet of lapis lazuli. "Eesh, do you think there are things inside us that our whole being knows yet conceals from our minds, because we could not endure the knowledge and continue to live?"

"You mean a premonition? You'd better not talk like that. They are still burning witches out in the country. And in Florence too!"

"No, I'm serious, Eesh. I don't mean a vision such as a saint might have. I mean something the mind conceals, a . . . foresight that does not reach the eye. But it remains in our minds, like . . . like a painting waiting to be unveiled, and if we come too close to removing the drape from that picture, the rest of our being must warn us of the peril. Do you think that's possible?"

"Yes. I didn't mean to make sport of you. Yes. I think I understand what you are saying. You are talking about a profound intuition, one that . . ." Isabella's own intuition flew out at her like a cawing raven, and she fought it away. "It is a warning that was planted in your soul the day you came into the world, but you can't see the thing you fear, only sense it when you are near it."

"Eesh, do you remember when Giovanna . . . died?" Beatrice reached into the unfathomable depths of her fear. Giovanna had been one of the ladies-in-waiting who had attended their grandfather's second wife, also named Giovanna.

"You remember that? I was about ten then, and they wouldn't let me anywhere near her. But I heard the stories. How did you find out?"

"Eesh, I saw it. I promise you I am not imagining. I wasn't supposed to be there, but I knew where to hide." She had crawled into one of the narrow stone passages—built to facilitate escapes, spying, and clandestine liaisons—that laced the walls of the Castel Nuovo in Naples. "I saw them. . . . I saw them bring the baby out."

"*Al nome d'Iddio.* Was it really . . . like they said?"

Nausea and a feverish, vertiginous sensation swept through Beatrice as she continued. "Yes. I saw it, Eesh. They couldn't get its head through, so they had to . . . Eesh, I heard it." She heard it again, the wet crunching as the baby's skull, irrevocably wedged in the pelvis, was crushed with a surgeon's lance, in the hope that at least the mother might be saved. "The surgeon used a hook to bring the baby out. Its head was . . ." She could still vividly see the horrible thing they had pulled out of Giovanna, the tattered pulp of its skull and its limp, slimy limbs, like an octopus on a gaff. "Eesh, I saw Giovanna die too."

Now the images overwhelmed her, coming in rapid, nightmare sequence. Giovanna had seemed to get better for several days. Then infection had begun to spread throughout her body, a dreaded gas gangrene that had rotted her insides, swelling her grotesquely. "Eesh, she looked like a pigskin full of water. She kept getting bigger and bigger. She screamed so much." The screams again pained Beatrice, like a knife scraping her bones. "When she finally died, the pus gushed out of her mouth and nose, and then she swelled up even bigger. I couldn't believe she didn't burst."

"That is the kind of thing that might happen once in ten years." Isabella shook her head emphatically. "I remember one of the *vecchie* saying that Giovanna was so narrow in the hips it was a wonder she could even piss, much less pass a child."

Beatrice's dread was not assuaged. Her stomach cramped, and the feverish heat filled her like a hot gas; she imagined herself swelling like Giovanna, then exploding. The truth seemed to burst out of her. "Eesh, I know I will die if I have a baby. My baby is going to kill me. I know it as well as I know that if I cut my skin I will bleed."

Isabella reflexively crossed herself. "Toto, are you . . . ?"

"No. No, Eesh, I know I am not." Beatrice's cadence was frantic. "I don't ever want to be. I don't ever want to have his baby. Francesco is the only baby I ever want. I promise you,

Eesh." Beatrice shuddered with rapid sobs. She had the strange idea that she had just betrayed her mother. And that her mother deserved to be betrayed.

"Oh, darling," Isabella murmured, and folded Beatrice in her arms.

C H A P T E R

16

Letter of ISABELLA D'ESTE DA GONZAGA, Marquesa of Mantua, to ELEONORA D'ESTE, Duchess of Ferrara. Pavia, 1 August 1492

Most illustrious and beloved lady Mother,

I arrived safely in Pavia yesterday, where I was met at the docks by Beatrice and the Duchess of Milan and thereupon conducted through the city to the gates of the *castello*. There I was received by Il Moro and all the ambassadors who are here, and was heralded by two dozen trumpeters. You would not believe Beatrice and the Duchess of Milan! Were Roland and Olivier more devoted to one another? They have pet names and secret glances, and one virtually finishes the other's sentence. Together with the Duchess of Milan's *puttino*, they make a fine little family. Il Moro accords Beatrice the utmost respect and cordiality. And, Mama, Beatrice's *guardaroba* is nothing less than a spectacle! She has by my count sixty-three *camore*, and that is just here at the *castello* in Pavia—she says she has even more in Vigevano, not to mention Milan. I examined them, and I will swear on the Girdle of the

Virgin that none has been made of cloth that could be had for less than twenty ducats an arm-span! And I do not have time to account for all the books she has ordered. Now I know why one must wait so long to locate fine goatskin parchment in Venice! As to marital relations between Il Moro and Beatrice, I am not as yet certain. There are no signs of a baby, but that may indicate nothing—look how hard Francesco and I have tried. (I got my out-of-ordinaries last Thursday. When it happens I must force myself not to yield to despondency. I am not giving up on my *puttino*, Mama.) The Duchess of Milan likewise has nothing to show for her recent endeavors.

The news here is all of the election of the new Pope, said to be entirely due to the devices of Il Moro's brother Cardinal Ascanio, who it is said will be the new papal Vice-Chancellor. All of the ambassadors are here—Milan, Naples, Florence, and, as you know, Messer Giacomo, who begs that I send you his solicitations for your health. Of course the serious discussions will not begin until Father arrives. He is expected to join us this Thursday at Vigevano—we are all trembling with anticipation. I think everyone here, including Il Moro, realizes that an agreement must be reached if we are to keep the French on their side of the mountains.

We are hunting here tomorrow and will be in Vigevano on Wednesday. I am salivating at the prospect of seeing all the work Maestro Donato Bramante has done there.

As much joy as I feel in finally seeing my only sister again and in knowing that Father will soon be here, your absence is a shadow over my gayest moments.

Your adoring daughter and one who misses Your Highness,

Isabella d'Este da Gonzaga, by her own hand

Pavia, 2 August 1492

"I know they are getting closer." The Marquesa cocked her head slightly; with a jewel-studded peacock feather mounted on her blue velvet cap, she looked for a moment like an inquisitive tropical bird. "I can hear them." She pointed to the border of the dense poplar-and-pine wood, about an arrow-shot away across the sloping meadow. "The Duke of Milan's greyhounds are in there. Right there."

A dozen white canvas pavilions dotted the grassy rise, sheltering the hunting party from the daunting August sun; a gracefully arching pergola woven of fresh pine boughs provided shade for the Marquesa, the Duchesses of Milan and Bari, and a few of their ladies-in-waiting. The two duchesses squinted into the sunlight. Isabella shrugged her *camora*-bared, lightly sun-rouged shoulders, a gesture repeated an instant later by Beatrice. "We can't hear them yet," Beatrice said.

"Didn't I always have a better ear than you?" the Marquesa retorted.

"Yes, yes, you did," Beatrice said, wrapping her arms around her sister and kissing her neck and ear. "I will concede to your superiority in everything simply because I am so delighted you are here. But if your ear is truly so keen, I wish you would tell us what my husband and the ambassadors are discussing."

The Marquesa stared intently into the adjacent pavilion for a moment, as if she really could decipher the quiet buzzing of the group. In their short brocade hunting doublets and brilliantly colored hose, the four men—Il Moro, Giacomo Trotti, and the ambassadors from Naples and Florence—resembled *condottieri* discussing a campaign. Il Moro's dark eyes flashed among his audience, his hands moving in confident, didactic thrusts.

"I will tell you exactly what they are discussing," the Marquesa ventured. "With the King of France rapt at the foot of both the Duc d'Orléans and the Prince of Salerno, no one in Italy is safe anymore. I think it is a blessing that the French are making their intentions so obvious. If we show the *oltramontani* that we are united against them, they will stay home. Thank God that the new Pope is not a French sympathizer."

"*You* may thank God for the elevation of Cardinal Borgia, my dearest sister," Beatrice said, "but the new Pope is more likely to thank Cardinal Ascanio." The duchesses snorted sarcastically. It was widely rumored that the newly elected Alexander VI—formerly Cardinal Rodrigo Borgia—had secured his votes with lavish payments to Il Moro's brother.

"My little sister has become quite the student of statecraft. Or at least of the latest gossip from Rome. *Per mia fe!* Look!" The Marquesa pointed to the treeline.

A white-bellied doe loped from the thick underbrush at the edge of the woods, followed by a fawn. A moment later four or five greyhounds burst from the brush in pursuit. "Doe!" Isabella shouted frantically. "Call back the dogs!" As if by her command, two game wardens dashed from the woods on foot. Cracking their whips and shouting commands, they collared the greyhounds into a yapping circle. The doe and her fawn sprinted over a small hill to the east.

"There is the stag!" the Marquesa called out with high-pitched excitement. A large, powerful buck bounded along near the tree-line to the west, trailing a half-dozen tiring greyhounds and a rider on a thundering white stallion.

The ladies in the surrounding pavilions trilled a spontaneous chorus of recognition: "Galeazz! Galeazz!" Even the ambassadors turned from their discussion. Galeazz quickly overtook the dogs, drew even with the stag near the crest of the hill, aimed his lance—his riding was so fluid that his head and torso remained as still as an equestrian statue—and impaled the beast directly behind the shoulder. Rivulets of blood streamed over the stag's belly, and then it stumbled and fell. The ladies shrieked enthusiastically.

"You would think that Galeazz had just speared your ladies," the Marquesa told the duchesses, her lips puckered with wry eroticism. "Perhaps they are remembering when he did."

A game warden bellowed from the edge of the woods. "Boar!"

Beatrice clenched her fists and turned rapidly to either side, as if run by clockworks gone out of control. "We must get our horses. We must join the pursuit. We must! Eesh! Bel! We must go in there after the boar!" Beatrice called to the grooms to bring the horses. Then she suddenly wound down and looked to Isabella as if she had made some sort of gaffe. Isabella simply replied with a barely discernible shake of her head.

The red-white-and-blue-uniformed grooms brought up the la-dies' horses and began cinching the saddles. Il Moro glanced at the activity, abruptly interrupted his discussion, and strode to the pine-bough pergola. He looked among the three women, finally addressing the Marquesa. "I have long ago given up cautioning the Duchesses of Milan and Bari. There is simply no prevailing on them to observe their own welfare, much less the protocol required by their sex and station. They are so determined to do mayhem to themselves that most of the gentlemen of my court will not ride with them." Il Moro recited his complaint with a good-natured smile, but there was a peevish edge to his voice. "I realize that I have no influence whatever with the duchesses, but I pray that you will at least stay here and spare me your husband's wrath should anything happen to you."

"You may lift me to my horse, Your Highness," the Marquesa said; she followed her request with a saucy laugh.

"Then these gentlemen and I will go with you." Il Moro gestured to indicate the ambassadors and officers of state in the adjacent pavilions. But as soon as the duchesses and the Marquesa had been settled in their saddles, they galloped off, skirts billowing. The Marquesa lost her feathered cap and called out for someone to pick it up. The gentlemen hurriedly summoned their pages and grooms.

The woods swallowed up the three women. The underbrush, thick with ferns, vines, and lilies of the valley, slowed their horses to a walk. "Look," Beatrice whispered. Just ahead, two rows of huge oaks, branches joined high above, bowered a clearing. Slender shafts of sunlight streamed down from the dense canopy. The women reined their mounts and were momentarily silenced by the beauty of the enclosure. The brush nearby rustled.

"I think we should wait for the rest of the party," the Marquesa said.

"You two wait," Beatrice whispered. "I'm going inside." She nudged her horse with her riding crop and emerged into the grass-carpeted clearing. Silvery fragments of light mottled her brocade *camora*. "It's beautiful," she called out. "You must come in."

Isabella prodded her horse's flank and moved through the screen of trees. The Marquesa lagged behind, her chin lifted as she listened for something. Brush rattled.

"Beatrice!" Isabella screamed, so loud she wondered if she had ripped her throat. A massive, bristling, mud-brown creature erupted from the trees just to her right, as huge as a bull, its devil-red eyes focused on Beatrice.

Beatrice's horse reared frantically. She grimaced and pulled savagely on the reins and somehow stayed on her precarious perch, her legs flying straight out as if she were a marionette seated on its wooden rump. The boar came right under her legs, and its tusks ripped the hem of her voluminous skirt.

Other than the single detached observation that Beatrice was going to be killed, Isabella's mind was entirely empty, the scene before her playing in the slow, silent cadence of a dream: Beatrice's silk-sheathed arm rising again and again as she pounded her crop against the rump of her hysterical horse; the horse, wide-eyed, finally turning, its body now a shield for Beatrice's legs; the boar, far more agile, pivoting on its devilish hooves, ducking its head.

The boar charged beneath the horse's ribs, to the accompaniment of a sickening crack. And then it rose up instead of charging through, its massive shoulders lifting Beatrice and her horse entirely off the ground, like some grotesque, brute Hercules carrying them on its back. Beatrice is going to be killed, Isabella's mind reiterated.

"No!" Isabella screamed. She flailed with her crop, trying to force her frantic horse toward the boar in an effort to divert the attack. She screamed again, her throat raw, but her horse merely jittered and spun a futile circle. When she came around again, she saw Beatrice and her horse teeter on the fulcrum of the boar's back. She realized that Beatrice was going to be killed not by the boar but by her own horse when it toppled and crushed her. She could only watch with utter horror as Beatrice began to slip almost gracefully from the saddle, about to fall beneath her horse's great sagging belly. But there was no fear in Beatrice's hard, dark eyes. Only excitement.

Somehow Beatrice's collapsing marionette limbs jerked erect, as if the strings that controlled them had been drawn taut by some miraculous hand. She pulled herself back into the saddle and sat up straight, her posture so astonishingly correct that her horse might merely have stepped over a small brook. Her teeth flashed as she muscled the reins. The horse stumbled back to earth, and the boar squirmed free of its burden, pivoted, and began another attack.

Something like a single swift bird streaked through the bower, followed by a loud *thwack-thwack* and the almost supernatural appearance of two arrows in the vast, heaving side of the boar. A lancetip sparkled in the sunlight, followed by a giant figure on an equally giant white horse. The boar emitted a plaintive, squealing exhalation as Galeazz's lance pierced its chest. It quizzically shook its head, took several steps, and slumped to its knees. The boar's red eyes blinked, and blood spurted from its mouth.

Another horse and rider charged into the clearing: Gian, mounted on his own white stallion, Neptune. Five or six of Gian's greyhounds darted about among the horses' legs, yapping crazily. Gian's two-legged favorites came right behind, the hooded hunting falcons on their wrists screaming and flapping their wings. Galeazz already had assisted Beatrice from her horse. Grooms on foot sprinted to help Isabella and the Marquesa from their saddles; the two women rushed to Beatrice and smothered her in their arms. More horses and shouting riders crowded into the clearing, their many-colored silk caparisons and riding doublets a riotous complement to the clamor. Il Moro dismounted and soundly clasped his wife's shoulders, as if assuring himself that his valuable merchandise was still undamaged. Beatrice laughed, her teeth exposed almost like fangs. For a moment it seemed that the ear-splitting din of the dogs and horses was the sound of her laughter.

Il Moro stared at the glistening red patch of boar's blood. He appeared frozen, his fixed black eyes the still center of all this noise and bustle. Then his entire face realigned. The corners of his eyes twitched, and his jaw contracted and shifted, as though furtively racing through a medley of suppressed passions. An instant later his face was as blank and impassive as ever. The animal cacophony abruptly faded. Il Moro turned and addressed the company. "If ever we wanted for proof that the Duchesses of Milan and Bari have recklessly taunted Fortune—"

"I have jousted with Fortune," Beatrice announced in a high, metallic tone, "and Messer Galeazz has jousted with the boar, and both of us have won!"

"I have seen men twice your size killed by boars half the size of this one, my Duchess," Galeazz offered with a frown.

Beatrice grinned. "But isn't that why we hunt, to know the glories and dangers of war without having to burn our peasants' huts and rape their wives?"

"I have never seen anything like it," enthused Gian, striding jauntily to the center of the group, his profile rakish and his platinum hair swept back, the grand arbiter of the hunt. "The Duchess of Bari rode a horse that itself rode upon the back of a boar, and not only did she remain in the saddle; her riding posture was correct all the while."

"Oh, dear God," the Marquesa cried out. "Someone help me!"

The men turned. The Marquesa struggled to support the dead weight of the Duchess of Milan, who had collapsed, pale as a corpse, in her arms.

CHAPTER

17

Francesco padded toward his mother's bed at a confident, barefoot trot. "Bab-ba," he said, reaching up. The old women at court often remarked that he favored his father, with his fine platinum hair and brilliant lips. "Bab-ba sick."

"Bab-ba is fine, and she is happy her *bello fanciullo* is here," Beatrice said. She picked the little boy up and kissed him before placing him in Isabella's arms.

Isabella was propped up on pillows set against the sculpted plaster headboard; a gilded Sforza viper hovered over her head. She whispered in Francesco's ear, then loudly kissed his neck until he began to squirm and giggle.

"Are you feeling well enough to have supper with us?" Beatrice asked. She sat on the bed and put her hand to her cousin's forehead.

"I'm starving." Isabella appeared entirely recovered from her faint. Her high, wide cheekbones were bright red from the day's sun, her eyes like polished jade.

Beatrice got up at the knock on the door. "My sister wanted to look in on you," she explained.

"You frightened me right out of my linens, Your Highness,"

the Marquesa said, breezing to Isabella's bed and making a funny face at Francesco. "But whatever malady you are suffering, it certainly agrees with you."

The look that passed between Beatrice and Isabella wasn't subtle enough to elude the Marquesa. "What is going on with you two—" the Marquesa demanded, then arrived at the solution in mid-query. "Tell me you are not!" she blurted to Isabella. "Tell me you are not! I am furious with you. I positively am. You are simply making me ill with envy. God, Beatrice, how can you stand her?" The Marquesa's voice actually had an angry edge. "How many months is it?"

"I would guess a little more than three months," Isabella said, her eyes glazed with pride.

"Per mia fe." The Marquesa sighed. "I already would have directed my stonecarvers to erect a triumphal arch to my little *puttino*. Why are you keeping it a secret?"

"I don't want to suffer through Messer Ambrogio's lectures. All he can prescribe is 'bed rest, bed rest, bed rest.' That's the problem when all the physicians are old men. They think we are in no better health than they are. It is simply absurd how they presume that carrying a child is a mortal illness."

"I am so pleased to hear you say that, Your Highness. God knows I worry about someone as frail as my sister-in-law Elisabetta, but for a woman as strong as Your Highness or myself, it is the relentless nagging of the physicians and the *vecchie* that most seriously threatens our health. *Cacasangue*, if Beatrice ever gets pregnant, they will hear Polissena in London."

"You have never heard a *vecchia* caw until you've heard my mother-in-law lecture a pregnant woman," Isabella said. "Compared to the Duchess Mother, Polissena's admonitions are as lovely as Maestro Cristoforo's singing. The woman can scarcely get out of bed, but her wind could drive a carrack from Genoa to the tip of Africa."

The Marquesa laughed wickedly. Beatrice took a step back from the bed. "I want to lie down before supper," she said.

The Marquesa reached out and coaxed Francesco into her arms. "I don't believe you two. You speak with one voice, you have given this precious *puttino* two mothers, and I can see that when

one of you takes to bed, the other must lie down as well." The
Marquesa touched her tongue to the tip of Francesco's nose and
spoke to him. "Now I'm waiting for your silly mother to tell me
that silly Beatrice is going to sit beside her in the birthing chair."

The ubiquitous tricolor pages rushed in to clear the remnants of
the fifth course, which had consisted of capons in parsley sauce
with a petal garnish, roast eel in a yellow sauce, trout in silver
sauce, gelatins in the shape of the Sforza crest, and whole pheasants
encased in a meticulous reconstruction of the original plumage,
with little sapphires stuck in the eye sockets. Chased silver cups,
gold saltcellars in the shape of Roman gods, and knives and forks
with gold niello handles were deftly plucked from the white linen
tablecloth, which was itself swept away and replaced. In a second
flurry the pages brought in the dessert course: pastries, tarts, al-
monds and oranges encased in a crust of solidified gold syrup, and
myriad *confetti*—spun-sugar figures that included birds, mythological beasts, and an entire castle surrounded by knights and siege
equipment. A thick, sugared wine was poured into Murano glass
goblets enameled with the Sforza crest.

Il Moro nodded to the master of the ducal choir, who led his
contingent from the hall. The pages bustled out after the singers
and sealed the doors behind themselves. Of the sixty guests who
had dined this evening, Il Moro had invited only his wife, the
Duke and Duchess of Milan, the Marquesa, and Messer Galeazz
to stay for dessert.

"This letter arrived today from Rome. It has been written by
the new Papal Vice-Chancellor," Il Moro said, smiling tightly.
"My brother Ascanio." Galeazz clapped enthusiastically, joined
by Gian, prompting the three women to offer their own discreet
applause. "I want to share Ascanio's words with my closest
family." Il Moro read Ascanio's accounting of the extravagant
pledges Pope Alexander had made to him. In addition to Ascanio's
new office, which gave him supervision of all church properties,
the grateful Borgia Pope had presented to him a *palazzo* in Rome,
entirely furnished with a fortune in art and antiquities, and had

signed over to him a good-size town in the papal territory north of Rome.

Gian tossed down his dessert wine and smirked with pleasure throughout the recitation, as if he had himself earned these rewards; his uncle Cardinal Ascanio was his favorite relative.

Il Moro's fluid diction did not alter when he began this passage: " 'His Holiness then spoke to me of his great admiration for you, my brother, and stated that his inerrant policy would be to maintain the warm relationship that already exists between himself and the Duke of Bari. His Holiness told me that he considers Il Moro the greatest man in all Italy, and he wishes to consult with you on any matter of importance, whether or not the welfare of Milan is directly involved. He offered in closing that his only regret was that Your Highness could not share the papal throne with him.' "

Beatrice looked between Gian and Il Moro, the latter standing impassively above them, his nose sharp and hawkish, his complexion darkened by the sun; the former flushed with inebriation, bobbing his head with a fool's arrogance. Her husband had not once mentioned the Duke of Milan. He had not even offered the usual diplomatic pretense that all these encomiums had been offered in the name of their illustrious sovereign. The tension was like stinging nettles in her stomach. She silently begged her husband to say something about Gian.

As Il Moro set the parchment down, Galeazz applauded again and Gian slapped the tabletop, vehemently nodding, a sneer of besotted self-satisfaction distorting his features.

"The Pope is now my chaplain," Il Moro said. He raised his goblet and smiled recklessly at the apparent jest, but the terrifying depth of his eyes was the only truth on his face. "The German Emperor shall be my general, the Signory of Venice my stewards, and the King of France my courier."

Galeazz laughed as if he were merely humoring Il Moro, but Gian convulsed into high-pitched giggles, knocking his goblet over and staining the fresh white tablecloth. Isabella's eyes narrowed until she looked like a cat staring into a wind.

Chair legs screeched against the marble floor. Beatrice fled toward the doors, pounded for the page, and slipped out as soon as the massive leaves came ajar. A moment later, Isabella followed her.

"Give it to one of your serving girls," Isabella said. She tossed the *camora* Beatrice had worn to supper onto the floor. The dress had been soiled with Beatrice's vomit; she had reached a bed of marigolds in the Castello courtyard before disgorging all five courses of the evening's repast.

Isabella sat down on the bed. Beatrice was under the covers, her head propped on a satin pillow.

"It isn't your fault, darling."

"I thought things were better, Eesh. I thought he had decided to accept things as they are. Why can't he just leave you and Francesco alone?"

"He can't do anything now. Everyone knows that we must be united against the Frenchmen," Isabella said, stroking Beatrice's hair.

"I can't believe he would say what he did about Venice with my sister there."

"That was why he said it. He knows that it will go straight back to the Signory. He needs the Venetians to join his league against the French, but he must show them that now he feels powerful enough to insult them. He's playing a game."

Beatrice pursed her lips, for a moment looking grave and older. "Eesh, I swear I would tell you if I had the slightest hint that my husband was going to do something. . . . I would come to you the minute I suspected."

"I know, darling. That is the greatest comfort Francesco and I have." Isabella stroked Beatrice's cheek with her finger. "You know as well as anyone how I never had a real *amica* when I was growing up. I was always with the boys." She laughed fondly, remembering. "My brother Ferrantino was my best friend. I didn't have a sister, and my mother . . ." Isabella shook her head.

Beatrice understood the aborted sentence. Eesh had always hated her mother. She remembered one family supper when Eesh, her face as red as Sicilian wine, had screamed at her mother and burst into tears. But then her father's mistress had usually sat with them at family suppers; Eesh, who had always worshiped her father in spite of everything, seemed to blame her mother for her father's infidelity.

"Then I came here and Bona, *la vecchia meretrice cacapensieri*, became my mother-in-law." Isabella's upper lip curled. "I do love Bianca Maria, but that is pity more than friendship. I never in my life felt close enough to another woman to trust her." Isabella touched her forehead to Beatrice's. "But now I trust you."

"I love you too, Eesh."

"I suppose we should sleep." Isabella kissed Beatrice and stood up. "We must be rested if we're to jeopardize our health again tomorrow." She made a long, dour face. "Bed rest, bed rest," she clowned, imitating Messer Ambrogio; she convincingly mimicked the physician's long, self-important strides as she went to the door.

Beatrice started at the thud of the heavy door closing behind Isabella. She tried to hold on to the lingering warmth of her cousin's intimacy as long as she could. But the cold thing at her center began to grow, a palpable chill that made her clutch her arms tightly around her torso. She tried to contract all her muscles, drawing herself in so tightly that she would crush everything inside her. She strained, and her color deepened. Finally she gave up, with an explosive exhalation, almost a sob. She sat defeated for a long moment, then slid from the covers as raptly as a sleepwalker. She stood beside her bed and with dreamlike deliberation pulled her chemise over her head. At last she looked down at her belly. Her hands trembled. She put her fingers to her abdomen and pressed painfully hard, drawing in her breath, trying to force her belly back against her spine.

She had always presumed, and dreaded, that one day she would be as fat as her mother, that one morning she would awaken and find herself with a waist like a wine barrel. Instead her constant physical activity—the daily riding, dancing, and tennis—had stripped the layer of fat from her adolescent physique. Her arms were lean, almost sinuous, her thighs as hard as a wooden sculpture. But her belly had grown. She pressed it again, feeling the fibrous, expanding sheath. Day after day for the past month she had denied it, attacked it, riding more recklessly, dancing more frantically, trying to make the rebellious flesh contract.

Her breasts had grown too. She touched her fingers to her broadening nipples, then cupped the tender, aching flesh. A moment later she felt the pain in her womb as well. Nothing was right with her body. Her bowels had been bilious and obstructed for weeks now; she sometimes felt as if there were malicious hands working inside her, twisting and moving things about. She had to pass water three times as often as before. Whenever she and Eesh were out riding and Eesh had to go behind a tree and hike up her skirts, she did too. And of course she had missed three of her out-of-ordinaries, but that had been the norm even before. . . .

Beatrice retrieved her volume of Dante's *Purgatorio*. She sat on the bed and riffled urgently through the velvet-smooth kid pages. When she reached Canto XXV, her fingers slowed and traced carefully over the words. Dante, accompanied by the virtuous pagan poet Virgil and the Christian poet Statius, had just begun to climb the mountain of Purgatory, and Statius was giving the relentlessly curious Dante a scientific explanation of the origin of a human soul. According to Statius, a recently conceived child was not yet human but instead was a creature so primitive that it was half beast, half vegetable, "like a sea sponge." This fetal being might move and feel but had no higher purpose. Only when the fetal brain had been fully formed, some months into the pregnancy, would God look with favor on His creation and breathe into it a new, living soul capable of contemplating the wonder of its own existence.

She read the passage again and again, until her eyes ached from the flickering lamplight. A sea creature. Half beast, half weed. She could no longer deny it. She had known it, and had fought it, for too many agonizing days and nights. The thing was in her, a bestial, thorny, strangling growth. Had it been in her long enough to know itself, to contemplate its terrible purpose? That did not matter. This creature would never have a human soul. Conceived without love, fashioned from the blood of a man who threatened everything she did love, the thing would only become more monstrous. It would kill her, of course, then it would kill Eesh, and finally its monstrous tendrils would reach out and destroy little Francesco.

Beatrice returned the book to her cabinet and opened the

wooden storage chest at the end of her bed. The smell of the rose water sprinkled over the clothes was sickeningly sweet. Her hunting knife lay atop a stack of neatly folded chemises. She closed the chest and lay down on the bed. With her right hand she gripped the knife so that the gold, finial-like pommel projected from the bottom of her fist. She pounded the pommel into her bare abdomen. The first blow was tentative, but she pummeled herself again and again, her blows rising quickly in ferocity until her skin seared with pain and her bowels ached. Again and again, until she believed she would lose consciousness from the pain, that she would awaken to her victory and her husband's defeat . . .

Some thread of reason finally saw the futility of this and drained the vehemence from her arm. She gave up with a vicious explosion, burying the blade of the knife in her mattress. She held a pillow to her face and screamed until she imagined herself suffocating in her own superheated rage. And then she cried. She had been trying to destroy the thing for weeks now, she admitted to herself, but its brute resilience had defeated her. Soon it would have a soul, soon it would know its own purpose and begin to kill.

Beatrice lay on her face for a long while, her thoughts wheeling, an awful humming in her ears, like a dozen trombones endlessly playing the same discordant note. When she couldn't stand it any longer, she walked to the big arched window facing Pavia and cracked open the shutters. The city lay before her under a quarter moon. Scores of slender rectangular towers stood like trunks in a ghostly geometric forest. Torches flickered from the flat tops of some of the towers, probably as guides to travelers, since the original defensive function of the brick spires, each of which represented a different noble family, had long ago been subverted by the Dukes of Milan. Beatrice heard vague shouting from the vicinity of the university, but the noise, more spectral than real, seemed to emphasize the loneliness of the darkened city.

She brought her face away from the glass. Her own reflection stared back, a phantom wavering over the flaming beacons. Her eyes were black orbits with a spark of fire at their center.

It has to die, she told herself, even if I die with it.

CHAPTER

18

The kitchen of the Castello Visconteo in Pavia was an enormous two-story food factory, busy with dozens of cooks, serving maids, and butchers, as well as a continuous traffic in assorted smiths, liverymen, grooms, game wardens, clerks, and butlers pursuing between-meals favors, both culinary and sexual, from the kitchen maids. The walls of the kitchen were entirely covered to the coffered rafters with utensils and supplies: hundreds of majolica and embossed pewter plates set in rows on the upper shelves; the next tier of shelves filled with porcelain and glass ewers, candlesticks, and goblets; and beneath that oaken cupboards stocked with gleaming silver tableware, plates of eggs, flasks of wine, baskets of fruit, crates of clucking capons. The hooded fireplace was as big as a cottage; attendants pumped the massive leather bellows and cranked rows of gear-driven spits studded with sizzling carcasses. Long tables filled the center of the room, crowded with women slicing fruit, rolling pastry dough, or plucking capons. At a small table in a corner, two butlers meticulously folded white linen napkins with hundreds of tiny creases, transforming them into strikingly naturalistic peacocks.

The center of attention was Scappi, the butcher, a small man with bulging forearms and a rattling singsong voice. Scappi methodically took a capon from his assistant, swiftly cleaved its head off, and passed the kicking amputee to another assistant, who let the blood drain into a clay urn before turning the headless corpse over to the serving maids for plucking.

"A man went to a priest to confess his sins," Scappi said, his voice raised as if each person in the kitchen was listening to him; most of them were. "He confessed to the father that he had stolen from a man, but this man had in return stolen something more valuable from him. So the priest said to him, 'One sin balances the other. You are absolved.'

"So the man went on and told the priest how he had beaten a man with a club, but the man had struck him back. 'One sin balances the other,' said the priest. 'You are absolved.' This went on for some time, the man reciting his sins and how they were repaid in kind, the priest each time absolving him."

Scappi held up a struggling capon by the neck and flourished his cleaver. "So finally the man said, 'I have but one sin left, but it causes me the deepest shame, for it is a sin against you, Father.' The man was almost too ashamed even to speak of this offense, but the priest kept urging him to make a full confession. Finally the man submitted. 'Father,' he said, 'I have slept with your sister.' "

The cleaver thudded into the chopping block, and Scappi's voice crescendoed. "To this the priest replied, 'Don't be concerned, my son. As is the case with your previous sins, one balances the other. I have slept with your sister a half-dozen times. You are absolved.' "

The kitchen resounded with laughter, shrieks, catcalls, and follow-up jests about oversexed priests. Beatrice had heard the entire joke from the hall, and she waited until the laughter subsided, knowing that her entrance would immediately dampen the high spirits. She strolled as casually as she could through the open door that led to the dining hall. The heat, generated by the enormous fire and compounded by the sweltering climate, almost made her choke. Her presence quickly hushed the banter. All of the women curtsied, and the men dipped to one knee.

Beatrice whisked her hands the way she had seen her mother do countless times, meaning that everyone should ignore her and return to work. The conversation picked up, but cautiously. She wandered over to a group of kitchen maids cleaning fresh trout and pickling live eels in barrels of wine. There were five of them, ranging from adolescents to a stout woman her mother's age. Perspiration beaded their faces and soaked through their linen blouses. They curtsied again at her approach.

Peering into a bucket half full of sluggish black eels, Beatrice offered, "Ser Scappi is quite a wit."

The kitchen maids nodded respectfully and continued working, but Beatrice could tell they were impressed that she knew the name of even one kitchen worker. The oldest woman, her immense bosom straining against her muslin apron, glanced up as she slit the belly of a trout. She had a blunt nose and a distinct mustache.

"I don't know why everyone is so offended by the excesses of the priests," Beatrice said wryly. "You've heard, haven't you, how word of such scandals reached the Heavenly Father, who immediately dispatched an angel to investigate. The angel selected a priest known for his sinfulness—perhaps the very priest Ser Scappi has told us about—and alighted before him as he dined in his refectory, demanding that he offer proof of any good works he had performed that might compensate for his many transgressions. Well, this priest, being a clever man, told the angel, 'Come, I will show you the myriad acts of charity I have performed in this town.' And so he led the angel out into the streets and stopped among a group of gamblers tossing dice in the piazza. After the gamblers had greeted the priest familiarly, the priest informed them that the gentleman with him was an angel of the Lord, and could they tell said angel whether or not their priest was a charitable man? The gamblers immediately doffed their caps, and one of them said, 'Father, I can swear before God that no man has given us as many gold ducats as has yourself.' "

The stout kitchen maid snorted and nodded her head.

"So the priest led the angel to the town wine merchant, the town butcher, and the town cloth merchant, and each time he asked the same question and received the same answer: 'Father, no man has given us as many coppers and ducats as has yourself.' " Now all the maids were smirking and responding. "The angel kept a careful accounting of these myriad acts of charity, and when the priest had been throughout the town, the angel informed him that considerable as his charities were, they were still short of the penance required for his sins. And that being the case, the errant priest could expect no lessening in the severity of God's punishment.

"Rather than casting up his hands and begging to be spared the woes of Hell, the priest smiled and said, 'Ah, Magnificence, I have saved my most important work for last.' He quickly led the angel to the town whorehouse, where he found the woman who ran the establishment. The *meretrice* listened to the priest's inquiry, and then pointed to the immense *palazzo* in which her business was conducted. 'Not only do you provide the bread and eggs and capons to feed a dozen young women, Father, but you have built the roof over their heads.' And at this the angel was so impressed with the priest's compassion that he flew away immediately and left the priest to pursue his vocation as he had before."

The stout maid put her beefy hands on her hips and chortled with laughter. She winked at Beatrice. "Well, Your Highness, there must be a dozen such priests here in Pavia, because there are a dozen good whorehouses."

"Which is the biggest?" Beatrice asked. The woman looked at her curiously. "I overheard the Papal ambassador inquire of my husband," Beatrice explained with a smirk. The women laughed. Rome had an extraordinarily large prostitute population, in no small part due to the holy city's high concentration of clerics.

"The Saracen is the biggest," offered a younger woman, perhaps ten years older than Beatrice; her otherwise pleasant face was marred by a large purple birthmark covering her cheek and eye. "There are fights outside in the street every night. All the university students go there."

"I imagine an ambassador would prefer a more dignified establishment," Beatrice said idly. "I wonder where he might go if he didn't wish to be observed?"

The stout woman laughed. "Santa Margareta. The convent near San Teodoro. *Tutte meretrice.*"

Beatrice poked her finger in the eel bucket. She took the woman with the birthmark by the sleeve and told the stout woman, "Tell the overseer that the Duchess of Bari has taken this *signorina* from her work for a moment."

She led the startled maid to a small *guardaroba* next to the kitchen. She shut the door. The room smelled of flour. "I want to play a prank on someone," Beatrice said. "I will need to take your clothes. In exchange you may keep my *camora*."

The maid nodded, numb with astonishment. Beatrice's gold-embroidered *camora* was worth more than she could earn in a lifetime; it was also a dowry sufficient to buy her a decent husband.

"And I shall ask one other favor of you," Beatrice said, unlacing the bodice of her *camora*. "You must tell me how to find this convent of Santa Margareta."

The new Duomo of Pavia, under construction for four years, had already risen to the clerestory level, but the unadorned brick exterior was still caged within a framework of wooden scaffolding. Shirtless masons worked along the upper tier, filling the scorching late afternoon air with dust, shouts, and the chiming of trowels.

The piazza in front of the west facade of the church was dominated by an enormous bronze equestrian statue called the Regisole. Beatrice stood beneath the ancient statue, thought variously to be a Roman Emperor or a Goth King, and looked across the roofline to the south, an expanse of red tile peaks punctuated with brick chimneys constructed to resemble tiny houses. She located her next landmark, the cupola of the church of San Teodoro, three colonnaded octagonal tiers of steadily diminishing size, set one atop the other. Thus far she'd had no trouble finding her way. Pavia's main streets obeyed an orderly grid established by Roman engineers two centuries before the birth of Christ.

Exiting the piazza, Beatrice entered a narrow cobbled street. Several scrawny dogs slunk against the walls. The three- and four-story buildings were crowded together, presenting a single canyon of brick; intermittently, the street tunneled directly through annexes joining the buildings on either side. The shadowy brick vaults held unsavory surprises—a large black pig rooting in the garbage, a scurrying rat, an unshaven laborer urinating. The street began to twist and meander. In spite of the suffocating heat, Beatrice clutched the kitchen maid's threadbare wool shawl around her shoulders.

The street turned abruptly at a high brick wall. Beatrice realized she was already lost. "*Meretrice*," muttered a voice from a dark doorway. A white-haired old man nodded at her, a wineskin cradled in his arms. A bearded man, a huge carbuncle erupting from the side of his face, sat on a doorstep, sharing a piece of bread with two boys; next to him a woman, stripped to the waist, nursed an emaciated infant. Another small child, naked and filthy, clung to the woman's skirt. The woman looked up at Beatrice, her weary eyes terrifyingly vacant. Three boys darted past; the last of them hit Beatrice in the thigh with a stick. Tears welled, and for an overwhelming instant she wanted to be home. She had never been into a town alone.

She forced herself to turn the next corner and entered a dark, vaulted section of the street. What she saw seemed to rip her legs out from under her: a dead baby in a pile of rags. She wanted to run, but her legs wouldn't respond, and she had to look again. She gagged, her horror only partially relieved. The decomposing corpse was a dead monkey, a pet someone had skinned and discarded.

Blinking as she emerged into intense sunlight, she saw the landmark she had been told to look for: a stucco niche, topped with a little triangular pediment, that had apparently once held a relief sculpture of the Virgin; all that was left was the head of the small figure. Farther down the street were the paired, nail-studded wooden gates of a stable. Immediately across from the stable was the doorway, just as it had been described, a pointed brick arch framed with a single band of terra-cotta rosettes.

The large wooden door had a smaller inset but no viewing grate. Beatrice pounded and waited. Finally she heard a woman's voice. "What do you want?"

"I want to see the Mother."

No response. Beatrice waited, panic beginning to drum in her ears, until the smaller door opened. She hesitated before stepping inside.

The room was cool, musty smelling, so dark that she could detect nothing except another door just to her right.

"What do you want?" Though also disembodied, this voice was different from the first, so ancient and frail that it seemed like a spirit. "What do you want?"

Something moved on the wall to the left. Beatrice looked closer. A little wooden panel had been opened a crack, and the voice was seeping out from it.

"What do you want?"

"I want to see the Mother."

The panel revolved, becoming the back of a wooden turntable. Beatrice hadn't been able to obtain gold coins without arousing suspicion—all of her purchases were made with bills of credit— so she had brought some small pieces of jewelry. She placed the cloisonné earrings on the wooden ledge, and the turntable revolved back into the wall.

The door to her right opened. Light flooded in, revealing the barren, plastered antechamber. Beatrice entered the hall beyond. An incandescently verdant courtyard was visible through a window to the left; a sister in a long gray habit tended the flower beds. Ahead was the convent chapel. The open door allowed a glimpse of gold altar furnishings, a freshly varnished painting, and sprays of intensely colorful flowers.

Just past the window a dimly lit hallway beckoned. Beatrice walked by rows of nuns' cells, each with a single iron-grated window. At the end of the hall a woman waited. She was young and wore nothing except a silk chemise unlaced almost to her navel; her nipples pressed against the sheer fabric. Her lovely white skin and deeply colored, full lips, reminded Beatrice of a Botticelli Madonna.

The woman led Beatrice down another row of cells, but these smelled of perfume, and the iron grates were covered with damask curtains. A woman's laughter came from behind one of the doors. Another door opened, and a naked woman, fleshy breasts swaying, padded into the hallway and nonchalantly walked past; a man called to her from within the room, asking for wine. Beatrice was mildly alarmed at the realization that she was actually in a brothel, but the location of the business was unremarkable to her. Convents were dumping grounds for surplus daughters whose fathers were unwilling or unable to provide their dowries, and more than a few of the sisters in any convent would have carnal urges rather than the chaste devotion required of a bride of Christ. Some convents operated virtually openly as brothels. More common was a thriving side business such as this, which afforded all the sisters a more comfortable existence.

The woman in the chemise stopped and unlocked a door at the end of the long cloister. She gestured for Beatrice to go in. The room was lit by a sweet-smelling oil lamp suspended from a wall bracket. Sprays of flowers in porcelain vases had been set on the floor beneath a framed icon of the Holy Virgin, an ancient, Greek-style painting with a flat gold background. The only furnishing was a single stool placed beneath a wooden grate set into the opposite wall. The woman gestured for Beatrice to sit, then left the room and closed the door.

Someone coughed from behind the grate. "*I fiori*," intoned a strident voice. For a moment Beatrice was startled into thinking that Polissena was sitting behind the wall. "The flowers," the voice repeated.

Beatrice's mouth was leathery with fear. "They are beautiful," she said, her voice trembling.

"I am the Mother Abbess. What do you want?"

"I want to do something about a baby." A long while passed with no response. Beatrice reflexively pressed her hands to her belly. "I want to know how to get rid of a baby."

"Are you married?"

"Yes," Beatrice whispered.

"Then have the baby. Tell your husband it is his."

"No."

"Then go away and have the baby. Pay a family to take it. If it's a pretty baby someone might pay you."

"I cannot have this baby."

Another lengthy pause followed. "It's very dangerous. For every woman who expels her baby and lives, two die. And even if you live, you may become so ill that you will never leave your bed again. Do you understand that?" The old woman's voice seemed to echo from a cavern.

Beatrice hesitated. "Yes."

"We use rue and savin. They've been used since the time of Hippocrates and Pliny the Elder," the Mother Abbess said. "We grow them in our courtyard. That is so we know exactly how strong they are. But if the dose isn't sufficient, it merely weakens the woman; the baby gets bigger while she rests to try again, and so the next dose usually kills her before she can expel the baby. Your best chance is to take a strong dose the first time."

Silence. Beatrice listened to her thudding heart and heard a faint whispering from behind the grate. Wild thoughts swirled through her head; she saw Bianca kneeling beside her candle-framed bier.

Beatrice almost leapt off the stool in alarm when the door opened and the woman in the chemise entered. She handed Beatrice a small blue phial like those used for perfume.

The voice from behind the grate gave Beatrice another start. "Empty the entire phial into one cup of wine and take it immediately. The wine will keep you from vomiting it up. You will vomit later, of course, but by then the agent will already be at work."

Silence. The phial in Beatrice's hand was as cold as frozen iron, as heavy as an anvil. Her stomach roiled.

The Mother Abbess's voice was a dreary exhalation, a door closing, sealing all that was living behind. "May our sweet Lord forgive you and have mercy on your soul."

The woman in the chemise escorted Beatrice as far as the chapel but left her at the doorway, as if she was expected to pray. Beatrice wandered in, entranced by the prismatic light streaming through the stained-glass windows. The large three-panel altarpiece had been opened to reveal a nativity scene painted in the meticulously realistic modern style. Flowers heaped the altar, the scent suddenly fragrant and delicious.

Newly cut marble slabs patchworked the floor; the neatly incised inscriptions revealed that most of the bodies interred beneath them had been sisters of the convent. Beatrice wandered raptly over the crypts, a curious order restored to her universe. More than the existence of God, she believed in God's system of rewards and punishment, that vast, multilayered, spherical harmonium described in such vivid detail by Dante. As she watched the dazzling lights play over the names of the dead, she heard the music of those vast spheres, an immense cathedral organ playing notes of pure golden ether. She was not a murderer. If the soul of the monster had not been formed, she had no more sinned than had a Neapolitan fishseller displaying his basket of dead octopuses.

(She saw Giovanna's dead baby again. . . .) She did not wish to die, so she didn't see how she could be condemned to the Wood of Suicides, her body transformed into a tree endlessly ripped by screaming harpies. And if she did not destroy her husband's evil spawn, she could well be accused of treachery to her kin and spend eternity in the black, frozen lake of Cocytus, in the ninth and last circle of Hell. Perhaps for her far lesser betrayal she would be condemned to wait for centuries beneath the barren cliffs of antepurgatory. But someday, on some bitter, lonely dawn, she would be permitted to begin her climb to the highest sphere.

Beatrice knelt on the hard, cool floor and gratefully clasped her hands. Now she needed only a single, final absolution. No, not an absolution, merely a witness to her tragedy and ultimate triumph. And two days hence, that witness was expected to arrive.

"Father," she murmured, staring up into an ineffable light. But it was not the Lord of Paradise whom she addressed. "Father will be here on Thursday," she whispered to herself.

C H A P T E R

19

Vigevano, 5 August 1492

The Marquesa encouraged the skirt of her *camora* to lift in the powerful easterly gust. "This is one way of keeping cool," she told Beatrice. "As we are so high, I shouldn't think anyone can see up my dress. Do you remember the time we apprehended Diodato wandering beneath the grandstand at the joust, enjoying the view?"

Beatrice and the Marquesa stood on the observation platform just beneath the brass cupola of Maestro Bramante's tower, which commanded an unobstructed panorama of the city of Vigevano and the surrounding plains. The center of the city, which during medieval times had deteriorated from Roman order to a haphazard cluster of rusty-red Romanesque dwellings, had been completely razed and reconstructed in the preceding few years. Bramante's tower crowned a polygonal *castello*, also of his design, itself as large as many towns. The enormous courtyard of the *castello* already featured a neatly groomed labyrinth; a classically styled wooden pavilion, designed by Leonardo da Vinci, had been built at the center of the elaborate maze of hedges, flower beds, and gravel paths. But the central glory of the city was Bramante's stately re-creation of the old Roman Forum. The long rectangular piazza was framed with a three-story arcade incorporating Bramante's usual repertoire of elegantly simple classical motifs: rounded arches, columns with Ionic capitals, rows of oculi.

Il Moro's new order broke down at the outskirts of the city, where the red tile roofs were strewn in medieval disarray. But past the city walls, the impeccable geometry resumed. The system of canals and irrigation conduits was a silver grid extending for dozens of miles in every direction; scores of farm complexes and village church spires dotted the countryside like pieces on a vast verdant chessboard. To the south and east, the neat procession of croplands faded into a hazy distance. To the north and west, the great wall of the Alps established the horizon. The snow-capped rim glowed softly pink in the morning sun.

Beatrice felt the wind like a great suction, carrying her out over the landscape. But all she could see from her lofty perspective was the blue phial in the chest at the foot of her bed, waiting for her, an inevitable fate. For two days she had soared and plunged, from grandiose visions of martyrdom to intense, strangling fear. She did not question that she would do it, however. It would have to be at night, when she could be certain that everyone would be present in the *castello*. Then actually taking the fateful draught would be as simple as leaping from this tower, to fly in the wind.

"Beatrice! You must tell me you can see them!" The Marquesa pointed to the south, where the main road from Pavia paralleled a canal. "There they are! I'm absolutely certain it's them!" Pinpoints of sunlight glimmered on distant armor, winking through the faint cloud of dust stirred by the horses. "Beatrice, it *is* Father! He has brought *everyone!* Now, we must go down and have our horses saddled and ride out to meet them. No. What we will do is get our horses and wait for them in the Forum in a very stately fashion, as if we are greeting Caesar and his legions on their return from Gaul. No. I am too impatient to wait. . . ."

Accompanied by a half-dozen guards, the Marquesa and Beatrice intercepted their father's escort within sight of the city gates. Duke Ercole d'Este, mounted on a white stallion with gold-embossed leather harness, rode at the head of his contingent of armored guards, who in turn preceded the "everyone" to whom the Marquesa had referred, a contingent of at least two score actors, poets, singers, and musicians wearing a variety of colorful tunics and an eccentric collection of often-beplumed caps. Hundreds of grooms, pages, and dog handlers, proceeding among a swarm of greyhounds on leash, brought up the rear.

Beatrice believed that no man had ever looked more handsome on a horse than her father. Duke Ercole's powerful chest and shoulders stretched taut a tunic of pale yellow brocade embroidered with gold thread; his muscular legs were sheathed in maroon hose. The sheer planes of his face had a golden summer sheen, highlighted by the long silver hair flowing from beneath a velvet beret. His posture was so erect he seemed to be standing in his stirrups rather than sitting in the saddle.

As a little girl, Beatrice had never even had a notion of what a father actually looked like. Her porcine, bejowled grandfather Ferrante had doted on her in his jovial, casual fashion, as if to hear her laugh was his favorite entertainment, but he had evoked no more awe in her than the court buffoons like Diodato. And menacing, diabolical Uncle Alfonso had been the opposite; she could not remember him ever speaking to her directly, and had he, she probably would have screamed in terror and run off. Then she had returned home to discover this tall, forbidding, granite-faced stranger, so rarely glimpsed because he attended interminable Masses, both in the morning and at Vespers, day in and day out; when he wasn't in church, Ercole was organizing passion plays or collecting food for the poor or leading white-robed pilgrims through the streets. Beatrice had quickly learned that she could go to her window overlooking the courtyard and watch her father ride out to Mass every morning, his fine silver hair streaming from his velvet cap like moonlight frozen in the dawn. The ritual of watching him had become her own daily devotion. Women, she had been taught in Naples (though she would eventually be told differently by her Ferrarese sister), were the sore-kneed worshipers at the altar of love, and men merely the flat, gilded altarpiece images to whom they prayed, no more real or substantial than the cut-out, gold-silhouetted figures in an old-fashioned painting. So on those first moon-washed mornings it had been enough for her that Duke Ercole, straight in his saddle, with his singers riding behind him on their mules like the twelve apostles, had simply looked like a father.

"Father!" The Marquesa whacked her horse's rump and galloped to her father's side. She leaned over, threw her arms around him and kissed him, but he remained so erect and still in the saddle that she might have been embracing a painted equestrian statue. "Father! I cannot believe all of the treats you have brought us. You have brought *everyone.*" The Marquesa looked over the contingent of performers. "What are you going to do for us? Is it the *Cefalo* that Messer Niccolò has been working on?"

Ercole's lips carved a tight smile. "Plautus. *Cassina.* Maestro Matteo has translated. Are you well?"

"I am marvelous. I miss my husband, of course. Beatrice has been sick. Father, you look exceptionally well. I have never seen that cloth before. Have you heard that I am going to Genoa at the end of the month!"

Beatrice wiped away her tears. She told herself that when Father learned the truth of her husband's mad ambition, he would understand why she did it. He would weep for her, and as long as he lived the candles would blaze in the churches of Ferrara, in memory of her sacrifice.

She could not ride as closely alongside her father as her sister had, because her legs were swung to the side facing him. "My lord Father," she said, her voice so high and fragile that it sounded like the finest Murano glass fracturing.

Ercole offered her his grimacing smile. "Your sister says you haven't been well."

"I am fine, Father. I think I ate some undercooked venison."

"Well, you must be more careful. Your mother has given me letters for you." Ercole turned and looked to the rear of his column; two wagons loaded with vegetables had backed up behind the Ferrarese contingent. "We are holding up some traffic. Why don't you and your sister ride alongside me? We shall enter Vigevano with an impressive display."

Beatrice reined her horse about. He is proud of us, she thought, and the pain in her heart was suddenly so intense that she could not breathe.

Ercole d'Este limped slightly as he proceeded down the vast nave of the Certosa di Pavia, his lame foot the result of a wound incurred in battle more than thirty years previously; in winter he often had to use a cane. Oblique shafts of sunlight filtered through the small rosette-shaped windows; the ribbed vaults high overhead, painted deep blue and studded with countless gold stars, were a glimmering false heaven. As he passed the aisle chapels, each framed with an ornate arch and lit with massed candles, Ercole nodded as though personally greeting the enshrined images of the Virgin, various saints, and the crucified and infant Christ. At the fifth chapel Ercole paused to study one of the large paintings. Saint Sirus, identified by the inscription on his marble throne, sat in startlingly lifelike splendor, surrounded by four companion saints in similarly coruscating golden robes.

"Who is the *maestro?*" Ercole asked.

"Bergognone," Il Moro answered quickly, like an eager schoolboy. He placed his hands behind his back and rocked slightly on his heels. "I believe he is the most faithful to nature of all our painters. And faithful to God as well."

Ercole nodded again and resumed his progression down the nave. Il Moro, Messer Galeazz, and several other high-ranking Milanese officers of state trailed behind. The semicircular apse at the far end of the church was obscured by painters' scaffolding. Two craftsmen were working on the choir stalls, installing a decorative panel in the headboard behind one of the richly carved wooden seats. Il Moro directed the craftsmen to clear out and motioned to his retinue to follow them. He and Ercole stood alone beneath the immense hushed vaults.

Il Moro waited while Ercole raptly studied the workmanship of the choir stalls, crowned with elaborate arches and finials. The decorative panels were intarsia, mosaic pictures composed from a variety of inlaid woods; these were so expertly done that they appeared to be sepia-hued paintings. Ercole peered intently at several of the intarsia saints. Finally he turned back to Il Moro.

"A splendid choir." Ercole's eyes were not as dark or as opaque as Il Moro's, but they seemed even harder, as though sealed beneath diamond sheaths. "Do you think Naples will honor any agreement we reach?"

"Why wouldn't they? They are the principal object of the French desire."

"I do not trust this Borgia Pope you and your brother have

created. Have you considered that Naples might pursue an independent alliance with Rome? If Naples and Rome came to an agreement, Piero would join them." Piero de' Medici had inherited leadership of the Florentine ruling council when his father, Lorenzo, had died in April. Lorenzo de' Medici had been Il Moro's best friend, but his heir was a whining incompetent whose loyalty to all save his own self-interest was suspect. "Naples, Rome, and Florence could then create their own anti-French league, leaving Milan as Italy's offering to French martial ardor."

Il Moro motioned casually with his hand. "You are certainly correct about Piero. But Ferrante and Borgia will never come to an accommodation."

"But Ferrante's son and Borgia might find a common objective, regardless of their personal animosity. Satan in his pit does not require amiable companions."

"Ferrante is in good health," Il Moro said, lifting his hand again. "I do not think the Duke of Calabria will become the King of Naples for quite a few years."

"Fortune may decide otherwise. In the event of Ferrante's death, any agreement we have with Naples would be worthless."

"Of course. But in that event everything would change."

Il Moro's last statement, delivered with an offhand, gradually fading inflection, had the contrary effect of amplifying rather than muting his intentions. Had Ercole been a woman, this would have been a carnal invitation.

Ercole nodded stiffly. "Yes. In that event we would have a new equation to consider."

Il Moro took one step toward his father-in-law. His voice dropped. "In that event we might find it in our interest to encourage King Charles in his adventure."

The two men's eyes locked. Ercole's voice was a whisper. "What would you do about Orléans?"

"I could, with the proper inducement, enlist the German Emperor to distract the Duc d'Orléans. Of course I would have to offer the German Emperor a surety."

Ercole nodded. "Go on."

Il Moro's eyes fired, an eerie opalescence. "I would have to seal any agreement with the Emperor by allowing him to invest me as the Duke of Milan."

Ercole's blade-thin lips remained drawn, his eyes unblinking, his reaction measured only in the forced moment of silence before he said: "The people of Milan will not allow that until you can offer them a secured succession. The present Duke of Milan offers them an heir to the Sforza dynasty. You can currently offer them only the chaos that followed the death of Filippo Maria." Filippo Maria had been the last Visconti Duke of Milan, whose bastard daughter Bianca Maria had given her husband, Francesco Sforza, a legitimate right to the title only after a brutal siege of Milan. That Francesco Sforza had subsequently proved an enlightened, even a visionary ruler had only deepened Milanese fears of another rupture in their ruling dynasty.

Il Moro lifted his chin as if his manhood had been challenged. "I can assure you that Messer Ambrogio and I have been exerting ourselves mightily. His calculations have been most exacting, and I have followed his schedule rigidly. Were Beatrice more attentive to her own health, we might find conception easier."

Ercole's face shifted in minute contractions. It was hardly lost on him that his other legitimate daughter, the Marquesa, had failed to conceive in over two years of marriage and that Il Moro was with reasonable justification suggesting that Ercole had peddled defective merchandise. "Yes. Beatrice did not seem well when she rode out to greet me this morning. Perhaps she is taking too much exercise."

"Well, that is enough of that." Il Moro pursed his lips. "I am sending for Messer Ambrogio. I have repeatedly warned her of the dangers of immoderate activity and have been resolutely ignored. Perhaps you could speak with her. She certainly did not learn these habits in Ferrara, and we have done nothing to encourage them here in Milan." The obvious inference was that Naples was the source of the corruption.

Ercole lifted his left shoulder slightly, his version of a more demonstrative man's shrug. It was not unusual for a father to administer postnuptial discipline; many good marriages—not to mention alliances—had been saved by such intercession. Then his icy eyes lifted to the vaults high overhead, flecked with gilded plaster stars. "I envy an architect. Once he overcomes the resistance of brute stone, he can be assured that his creation will never mutate from his original vision. But we, as architects of the state, must fashion our constructions from human virtues and frailties, materials even more intractable but far less dependable."

Il Moro took his father-in-law's arm. His lips relaxed with subtle amiability. "That is why, my lord Father, the state is the ultimate work of art."

"Don't you keep her up all night with your gossip and whatnot." Polissena's ancient head bobbed furiously between the Marquesa, who stood beside her sister's bed, and Beatrice, who lay beneath the satin bedclothes, her head inclined forward by several plump silk pillows. "It is nothing less than a national scandal how the Duchesses of Milan and Bari go racing about whither they will on their horses every day, and that both of them have fallen ill is far more warning than our Lord will usually give such prodigal behavior. I've seen many a fair lady waste and perish before my eyes from far less strenuous pursuits." Polissena's head attacked the Marquesa exclusively. "And don't think you are exempt, Your Highness. You used to have the most beautiful milk-white skin, but since you have taken up your sister's pursuits, the sun has given you more color than a painted Roman prostitute. When your husband sees you again he will think he has married a *negre* from Libya."

The Marquesa turned to Beatrice. "Did you hear what happened when Polissena rode beneath the Regisole last week?" The Marquesa allowed herself a comic pause. "When Polissena came into view, this great bronze emperor, a fixture of countless centuries, was suddenly frightened into leaping from his horse and has not been seen since. Everyone is trying to make the best of it by remarking on how nicely the horse has been done, but I don't think the statue is the same without the emperor."

Beatrice smiled weakly; she had hardly heard the jest. She had vomited this afternoon and again this evening. She remembered what the mother abbess had told her about taking the abortifacient with wine to keep it from coming back up. How could she expect the abortifacient to work when she could not even keep her food down? The blue phial seemed to scream at her from her storage chest.

Polissena's head bobbed for a contemplative moment. "You'll be the next to take to bed, Your Highness, and don't think your sainted mother won't hear my views on the foolishness that has corrupted the health of both her girls. I already have composed letters to send back with your lord father." With that Polissena curtsied and stomped out of the room; the last that could be heard of her was a cawing command that the page shut the door.

"I want to know." The Marquesa stood over Beatrice, her hands on her hips, just like their mother. "I want to know immediately."

Beatrice flinched as if she had been struck, and her lips began to tremble. She was certain that she could never do it if Bel found out now.

"I don't care how long you cry. I intend to stay here until you tell me."

Tears welled in Beatrice's eyes, but she obstinately set her jaw and vowed to resist.

The Marquesa moderated her demand. "I know something is wrong, and I want to know what it is. *I* thought you have been behaving strangely ever since I got here, but for the last few days everyone has noticed." The Marquesa sat on the bed and took her sister's hand. "You know that if it is something to do with your husband, this is absolutely the best time to tell us. Father will talk to him. It's so obvious that your marriage is not that of Orpheus and Eurydice. Father is already concerned, but he thinks that your husband is trying very hard and you are the one who is being petulant. If your husband is doing something we don't know about, you *must* tell us."

Beatrice shook her head slightly.

"He *is* sleeping with you, isn't he? He has told father he is. Is he violent? Does he ask you to do unnatural things? In the name of God, Beatrice, you would not believe some of the stories I have heard recently, and from reliable sources. My husband says there is one member of the Signory in Venice who likes to dress like a woman, even plucks his eyebrows, then goes out and opportunes some sailor, brings him home, and requires not only his wife but also his *sons* . . . Well, when you're feeling better I shall tell you the rest of it. It's really quite remarkable."

Beatrice was lost somewhere behind her hazy eyes. The Marquesa snuggled next to her and put her arm around her. "What is it, baby?"

"I love you so much, Bel." She began to sob, clutching her sister in a desperate embrace, realizing that it was a farewell.

The Marquesa held her sister and rocked her and kissed her. "*Mia unica sorella*, my most special, special love," she murmured. Then suddenly she drew her head back as if she had discovered she were embracing an impostor. Her eyes were wide and keenly focused. She put her hand on Beatrice's breast and, before Beatrice could even react, moved the hand to her sister's belly. She leapt up. "No! I cannot believe I didn't see it before. . . ." The Marquesa had not seen it because she had never for a moment considered that it would happen to Beatrice before her. "Of course, of course, of course. *Per mia fe.* The sickness, the melancholy . . . Oh dear God, oh dear God! Maybe you didn't know? You must know! You really must know, and you have been hiding it from all of us! God, I'm so furious I cannot stand it! God, I'm going to have a little nephew! God, how will I ever hold my head up again when my little sister has had a baby before me?" The Marquesa fleetingly reflected that perhaps Beatrice would only have a daughter, that she could still be the first to give their father a grandson. She pounced back onto the bed and embraced her sister. "God, you're going to have a baby! I'm so envious I want to weep."

Beatrice cried enough for both herself and her sister. It was a while before the Marquesa realized that these were not tears of joy. "What in the name of God can be wrong now? Beatrice, I am the one who should be crying. I should be pounding the floor and ripping out my hair like the Franks mourning Rolando. I should be making an epic display of my grief. Really now, you are going to have to tell me."

Beatrice sniffled mightily and blurted, "I can't have a baby, Bel. If I have a son, my husband will use it to take Milan away from Eesh and Francesco. He isn't afraid of anyone anymore. You heard him the other night."

The Marquesa's round, slightly fleshy jaws tensed; she had that icily adamant Este look. Her voice matched her face. "Beatrice, look at me. This is for you alone to know. Even Eesh cannot know. I swore to my husband that I would never tell anyone, not even Father. But I am telling you. What you fear will never happen. The Signory of Venice has drafted a secret resolution that Venice will move to attack Milan with every force at her disposal if Il Moro attempts to become Duke of Milan. It is no longer an issue that might be debated or postponed. It will not matter if His Holiness wears the miter and the German Emperor watches while Gian willingly drapes the ducal mantle on your husband's shoulders. The Signory of Venice will never permit Il Moro to become Duke of Milan."

The Marquesa's revelation clanked through the elaborate construction of Beatrice's fear like a great engine of war, leveling the huge dark walls, allowing her a sudden dazzling glimpse of some brilliant empyrean horizon. She let the relief carry her like a warm, lulling tide. And then the fear her sister would never be able to vanquish reminded her of its cold embrace. Even if her baby could no longer harm Eesh and Francesco, it would still kill her.

"And that is assuming you do have a son." The Marquesa wiped her sister's wet cheeks with the cuff of her chemise. "You might have a daughter, you realize." The Marquesa shook her head wistfully. "At this point *I* would settle for a daughter. I really would." She glanced upward. "But, our Father in Heaven, if you heard that, remember that I would prefer a son. Beatrice! Do you know what! Father is coming to see you! I entirely forget in all this excitement! He said that when he returned from the Certosa, he was coming to see how you are!"

Beatrice was as stunned by this as she had been by any of the preceding shocks. The entire time she had lived in Ferrara, her father had never ventured the intimacy of visiting her in her rooms, except the one time she'd had a serious fever and there had been some concern for her life.

"You must tell Father tonight, you realize. I will not let him leave this room without your telling him. I'm going to sit right here with you until he comes. Then if you won't tell him, I will."

The Marquesa launched into an extraordinary litany of ribald gossip from Venice, Paris, Rome, Genoa, Florence. Beatrice heard nothing of it. Her morbid determination had given way to a melancholy both stirring and unbearably sad. Already the demon in her belly, the agent of her husband's obscene ambition, had vanished. In its place was a poor little thing that would come squalling into the world only to find itself alone. Suddenly she could feel the premonition of her death in childbirth far more strongly than ever, a palpable chill that chattered her teeth. She would ask Eesh and Bianca to look after her baby. She hoped it would be a little girl who would always remind them of her. . . .

The page knocked and announced the Duke of Ferrara. Ercole entered, smartly dressed in an embroidered tunic and a velvet beret. Beatrice's emotions wheeled: awe, shame that she had actually hoped to deprive him of his grandchild, sorrow that he would never see her hold the infant in her arms, the hope that when he held her baby he would think of her.

Ercole stood rigidly beside the bed, his face a magnificent creation in stone. He inclined his head slightly to gaze down at Beatrice. The diamond-hard eyes registered a mild curiosity. "Your husband is concerned about your health. He intends to send for his physician."

"Beatrice." The Marquesa began to squirm as if she had fleas in her *camora*. Her twitching lips could only momentarily resist. "Why don't you enlighten Father as to your condition?"

Ercole glanced quizzically at the Marquesa, who squirmed so violently she might have been goosed. "Bee-a-trice . . . Oh, Father, I can no longer stand it! Beatrice is going to have a baby! Father, Beatrice is going to have your grandson! Or at least your granddaughter. Father, I am so jealous that I should be the one in bed. I am dying with envy. I absolutely am. . . ."

Ercole remained implacable for an instant longer. And then the miracle occurred. It was as though his face, this icy Alpine massif, had been animated by a pink-flushed sunrise. Beatrice watched in wonder as the mountain came to her, bending almost in supplication. Her father sat beside her and took her in his powerful arms, and he kissed one cheek and then the other, again and again. There was a rushing weightlessness, as if she were leaving the earth entirely, speeding on toward Dante's incandescent Paradise. Her father held her away for a moment, his eyes unabashedly glistening with tears, and then kissed her on the lips, and at that moment she imagined that she had, like her poet, been granted a final, ineffable vision of the face of God.

"I am so proud of you," Ercole said. "I am so very, very proud. You must give your husband this news at once."

Her husband. For a glorious moment, Il Moro had not existed

in Beatrice's new universe. Her husband. "Father," Beatrice said, "I think it would be best if you told my husband. There is someone whom I must tell first."

"Duke Ercole. I am pleasantly surprised." Il Moro motioned for the chamberlain who had escorted Ercole into the room to bring some wine. "Messer Galeazz and I were examining Maestro Dondi's workmanship. You know he devoted sixteen years to this instrument."

Ercole strolled around the enormous clock, a brass-and-wood edifice that reached to Galeazz's chin. Galeazz had removed a brass plate and was studying the fantastic network of chinking cogs and whirring gears inside. This mechanism set in motion an elaborate crown of sculpted brass zodiacal symbols, celestial charts, and scored and painted spheres, all circling to the cadence of the universe.

Galeazz looked up at Ercole and nodded his head in a perfunctory bow; the minor slight was instinctive, habitual rather than intended. "This device records the position of the sun, stars, and planets as well as the time," Galeazz said, his tone so hushed and self-important that one might have assumed that he had set in motion both this miniature cosmos and its full-size counterpart.

Bending to study the almost lacelike filigree of clockworks, Ercole's head bobbed rhythmically in time to some music suggested by the ticking machinery. Finally he glanced up at Il Moro. "I have ascertained my daughter's malady." Ercole paused for an uncomfortably long moment. "She is carrying your child."

Galeazz snapped erect. "*Per cap de Dieu!* How splendid. *Stupendissimo!*"

Il Moro's sensual dark lips worked as he looked between the two men. "My mother was the wisest woman I have ever known. She had the motto *merito e tempore* engraved on the frontispiece of all her books. Do your best and be patient, and your efforts will be rewarded. I have patiently done as Messer Ambrogio has advised me, in spite of the many who criticized our method, and now I have my reward." He stepped forward and warmly clasped Ercole's hands.

The page entered with three glass goblets of wine on a silver tray; Galeazz quickly snatched his up. "Let us drink a toast to the mother," he said, "and offer a prayer for her health."

Il Moro and Ercole took their goblets. "Yes," Il Moro said, "let us drink to my Beatrice." He glanced briefly at Galeazz, his hawkish profile flashing, then offered Ercole a frank, open smile. "And let us pray for a son."

Beatrice found her cousin in Francesco's nursery, singing her little boy a Neapolitan lullaby. Beatrice waited until Isabella had finished the song and laid her son back in the cradle.

"He had a bad dream," Isabella whispered.

Beatrice leaned over the railing of the cradle and just touched her lips to Francesco's forehead.

"I'm glad you came," Isabella said when they had left the nursery. "Your sister and I have been discussing . . . we know something is troubling you. She wanted to talk to you first." Isabella glanced toward the window overlooking the vast, darkened courtyard. "Why don't we go for a walk in the labyrinth?"

Isabella took Beatrice's hand and led her through her rooms into a single-story arcade open to the central court. The labyrinth, a maze of flower beds and waist-high hedges, shone with the faint pearlescence of the quarter moon. Only a few years old, the labyrinth nevertheless appeared ancient and mysterious, an artifact of some supernal power that had long ago resided here. The duchesses found an entrance at the south end of the broad circle and began gyring inward along the gravel path. Isabella put her arm around Beatrice's shoulder, and Beatrice slipped hers around her cousin's waist. They wandered silently for a while, not worrying about their progress toward the center, steering around the abrupt corners or retracing their path when they encountered a dead end.

At length Isabella asked, "Are you still upset by what your husband said the other night? You know your sister has told me that the Signory of Venice would almost certainly oppose him if he tried to coerce Gian. She was very reassuring. I really enjoy having her here. It is simply remarkable the ways in which you and she are alike. And the ways in which you are different."

Beatrice pulled away and faced her cousin, all of the terrible will she had mustered to abort her child now directed to this seemingly far more difficult moment. Her heart screamed in her ears. "Eesh . . . Eesh . . . Eesh . . ." She imagined she was drowning, gasping for breath. "Oh, Eesh, I'm going to have a baby. . . ."

Isabella's bosom rose in a quick, breathtaking jerk. Then she became entirely still, as though suspended in time, herself an artifact of this ancient place. Her face appeared to pale, though perhaps the change was merely a quirk of the light. And then she stepped forward, so slowly that it seemed she was moving beneath a moonlit sea, advancing through the viscosity of time. With exquisite care she took Beatrice in her arms.

"I can see it now," Isabella murmured. "You changed so gradually that I never thought . . . I did wonder why you always went behind a tree when I did. But even that . . ." Her lips pressed against Beatrice's ear. "Darling, I won't lie and tell you that there wasn't a time when I would have feared this more than anything. But I can honestly tell you that now there is this . . . joy in knowing that you . . . that we can now share this . . . miracle. Darling, we are more than empty vessels for men's dreams. What we create in our bodies is the one true miracle in the world. And it is ours, and only we can share it. Soon I will not need to tell you that. Soon you will feel the new soul stirring inside you, and no one will ever again be able to convince you that it belongs to anyone else."

Beatrice's tears slicked her cheeks. She should have been convulsing with sobs, but she was so drained that the tremors passed through her like ripples on a pond. "I'm afraid, Eesh."

"No, no, darling, you mustn't be. You are so strong. You know you are. There's nothing for you to fear." Isabella suddenly clutched Beatrice powerfully, as if to prove to her cousin that her body could withstand the ordeal of childbirth. Beatrice responded with a fierce embrace. She was so close to Eesh, as close as she had ever been to another human being, their bellies and bosoms pressed as tightly as lovers'; she believed that she could hear Eesh's heart beating alongside hers. The passion Beatrice had never even imagined in her husband's arms shuddered through her, a sensation that she could see and feel and hear at once, surrounding her with pealing notes that burst into great rings of light. Her soul filled with a vast, choraling revelation: she had just conceived her baby. Not the furtive liaison that had planted her husband's seed, but a higher union, the endowment of a new human soul. Now her baby had been conceived in love. And now she could love her baby.

She clung to her cousin, the night expanding limitlessly into sound and light, her heart racing to the rhythm of four joined souls. And then something stirred in her womb, a single note both sharply discordant and more beautiful than every other magic sound. She pulled away from Isabella and pressed her tingling fingers to her belly. She looked up at Eesh, wondering, the entire universe hushed.

Isabella's eyes glittered in the weak moonlight. "Your baby moved," she whispered.

· PART ·

FOUR

CHAPTER

20

The French Alps, Near Grenoble, September 1492

His Most Christian Majesty Charles VIII peered down the muzzle of the massive siege cannon. Narrow shoulders hunched forward, humped nose jutting, and vaguely focused eyes bulging, the French King looked like the transfixed victim of a bronze serpent that was twice as long as he was tall and easily capable of swallowing him whole; the cannon's gaping bore could accommodate an iron ball about the size of Charles's disproportionately large head.

"I propose we harness it and bring it up the col," offered Louis Duc d'Orléans, the King's cousin. Louis's shifting gaze wandered rapidly over the team of three dozen horses drawn up in front of the cannon, then darted to a grass-covered ridge, framed by violet-tinted blue sky, just several hundred paces up the narrow, roughly graded road.

Charles stared for a moment at Louis, his slack mouth open. Then he fluttered his hand at the team of gunners. The uniformed men immediately set about harnessing the horses to the heavy wooden carriage—supported on two massive, iron-rimmed wheels—that cradled the gleaming bronze siege gun.

"Do you think it will work?" the King asked Louis.

Louis shrugged his athletic shoulders. A slight flicker of his lazy, lascivious mouth suggested that this was all sport regardless. Louis had a curious mien, always poised between a scowl and a smirk. His strong chin and straight, handsome nose were countered by a small forehead and narrow temples that seemed to have entrapped his alert, mischievous eyes, forcing them to flit about like a pair of caged birds.

"Do you think it will work?" Admiral Louis Malet de Graville, a stout, mid-sixtyish man, whose head swiveled on a collar of multiple chins, echoed the King's question in a whispered aside to Antonello di Sanseverino, the exiled Prince of Salerno and the most ubiquitous of the King's growing council of military advisers.

"It will go very nicely on the way up," Antonello answered. Tall and white-haired, he stood among the King's velvet-capped retinue like a bare-headed prophet. "However, I am convinced that His Majesty will decide in his wisdom to return to a four-wheeled design for the gun carriage. Not as maneuverable on flat terrain, but much safer in the mountains."

"Shouldn't you . . . speak now?" Admiral Graville offered. "We are moving precipitously as it is." As one of the most cautious voices in the King's council, Graville referred to Charles's entire Crusade as much as to the test of the new carriage design.

"His Most Christian Majesty's ardor is the keenest weapon we will take over the mountains. I see no need to dull that blade with unnecessary cautions." Antonello watched the King and Louis mount their horses. He signaled his page for his own horse, then turned back to Graville. "His Most Christian Majesty's ardor is certainly warranted by the latest news from Italy."

"Indeed." Admiral Graville inhaled importantly, his heavy chest straining against his embroidered doublet, as if he were preparing to devour Prince Antonello's latest intelligence. The opportunistic Admiral was anxious to detect any shift in the political winds that might require a more aggressive tack on his part.

"The Milanese league with Rome, Florence, and Naples is finished." Antonello hoisted himself onto his horse and settled his feet in the stirrups; his silver spurs twinkled in the bright sun. "Piero de Medici has defected and has persuaded King Ferrante of Naples to withdraw as well. Il Moro will soon realize that France is a more reliable ally than any of his Italian brethren. And then the mountains will be the only obstacle between here and Naples."

Graville mumbled his reply to himself; Prince Antonello had already ridden to the King's side. "And then perhaps Il Moro will pay for the three hundred additional ships we will need to ensure that Naples can be supplied once our army has taken it."

The thirty-six horses, whipped on by the gunners clinging to the carriage, moved the cannon up the steep incline at a surprising clip, easily pacing the King's advisers and the mounted Scots archers who served as His Most Christian Majesty's bodyguard. King Charles swept his white sable cap in a triumphant circle above his head. "*Montjoie! Montjoie!*" he shouted. "Our siege guns shall be able to advance as rapidly as our cavalry!" He turned to Antonello. "Is it true that the Italians must use oxen to draw their cannons?"

"Indeed it is, Your Majesty," Antonello replied. "They can move no faster than a funeral procession. If this were an Italian gun, it would still be back in Amboise."

Charles honked his nasal laugh and shouted *Montjoie!* again. The gun carriage passed through a tiny Alpine meadow sprinkled with late summer flowers and quickly crested the ridge. To the east, misty snowcaps towered along the horizon like a spectral wall. The looping descent carved through sheer rock facing. The carriage groaned with stress as the team of horses picked up speed. Charles, accompanied by two mounted Scots archers, trotted alongside the gun carriage as it began to whip through the curves. "*Montjoie!*" The King's white cap twirled against a backdrop of gray rock.

Iron wheel rims screeched. A chorus of whinnies came from the team drawing the cannon, and several of the horses stumbled. The gun carriage careened toward the King, and one of the gunners leapt off.

Wide-eyed, straight in the saddle, his head inches from the rock wall behind him, Charles watched the glimmering bronze monster bear down on him. An instant later sparks showered as the huge gun thudded against rock, once and then twice, the dull metallic sound punctuated by a pop much like the report of a small firearm. Carriage and cannon tumbled over twice, flinging off the gunners and bringing down the horses in a chaos of equine screams and kicking legs. The snout of the cannon rose into the air again and then, captured by its own mass, fell back onto the road and came to rest.

The gunners frantically began to cut the horses from their harness while the King's advisers and guards scrambled to the aid of their sovereign. Charles was still in the saddle, leaning to one side, staring down at the road. Directly beneath him lay a motionless gunner in a yellow doublet and black hose, entirely intact except for his head. A single eyeball stared from the mess like an ox eye peering from a lump of freshly butchered offal.

"I don't believe I have ever seen anything quite so . . . ," the King said, earnestly searching for words. "Quite so . . . His entire head."

Louis's relentless eyes scampered over the corpse, then leapt to the rock escarpment behind it. He pointed to a glistening crimson stain, which might have been made by a bloody sponge hurled against the rock wall. "He must have been caught against the rocks, whereupon his head was struck by the muzzle of the gun," Louis said abstractly.

"The poor dear man," Charles said.

"I'm sure Your Majesty will want to try an alternative design now," Prince Antonello offered. "Four wheels, with the rear set detachable to allow maneuverability where the terrain permits."

"We must see that this brave man's widow is not neglected," Charles said, gaping at the gunner's pulped head. "And we shall next try a four-wheel design."

"We do not have money enough to build ships," Admiral Graville whispered breathlessly to Prince Antonello. "Where will we find money enough to pension all the widows we will make when we cross the mountains?"

Prince Antonello glanced casually at Graville. "In Italy," he answered.

Milan, 7 January 1493

The pain, like talons clutching her belly, brought Beatrice from a half slumber. She drew her legs up and waited, fear buzzing in her head. Eesh and Polissena had warned her that she would have these cramps now; unless they recurred within a quarter hour or so, they did not mean that her labor was imminent. But to her this mock labor was already terrifying.

Nothing followed the first stabbing contraction. After a while Beatrice pulled the covers aside and went to the window. In the early evening darkness the forest seemed like an advancing bank of inky mist. The moat beneath her had a dull, phantom gleam. Swallows, visible only as a wraithlike motion in the gloom, flew past the window.

Confinement, Beatrice thought, wondering if whoever had named this prenatal ritual had considered the cruel irony of the term. Following the usual prescription, Messer Ambrogio had ordered her to her rooms, where she would stay—by the letter of his instructions, always in bed—until her baby was born. Eesh had said she intended to inquire of Messer Ambrogio exactly for what crime a woman was being punished when she was confined to her rooms for the month preceding and the month following childbirth. Better for a woman merely to fornicate as the devil commanded, Eesh had joked; as long as she didn't engage in God's business of procreation, she was free to come and go as she pleased. . . . But now that Eesh was also in confinement, Beatrice couldn't even see or talk to her.

The must of cold stone penetrated the scent of the pine logs in the fireplace. Beatrice's suite of rooms had been moved from the light and airy Ducal Court, where she had lived since her marriage, to the Rochetta, the more heavily fortified citadel of the Castello di Porta Giovia. The immensely thick stone walls held the winter chill like blocks of ice. She could feel the weight of this prison around her, as oppressive as a tomb. Even the shortened days had closed in on her, each long night enfolding her like a shroud.

She crawled back under the covers and waited. After perhaps an hour her sleeping baby awakened with a sharp kick. But to Beatrice this pain was an antidote to all the rest, a wound so tender and delicious that she imagined warm honey flowing through her veins. She placed her fingers on her abdomen and gently stroked the hard knot created by a tiny fist or foot. In a whispered communion, she talked to her baby: "I wish you could stay like this inside me forever."

CHAPTER

21

Extract of a letter of ELEONORA D'ESTE, Duchess of Ferrara, to ERCOLE D'ESTE, Duke of Ferrara. Milan, 16 January 1493

My most illustrious lord husband,

. . . I arrived here this afternoon and . . . was greeted with great generosity and ceremony, as well as many shouts of "Moro! Moro!" . . . Beatrice is not resting well in her confinement, which I attribute to her unwarranted anxieties now that the birth is imminent. I pray that her labor comes soon, because her constitution has been weakened by these apprehensions. But it is my faith that within a week all this will be behind her and that I shall hold our first grandson in my arms. . . .

Il Moro has disclosed to me that His Holiness has proposed a new league to include Rome, Milan, and Venice. Il Moro intimated that he would be willing to set aside his differences with Venice if you would accommodate yourself to do so as well, as he is most desirous of our participation in this league. I told him that only you can make this decision, but that I felt certain you would agree to take the proffered hand of an old enemy to prevent a new and far more aggressive power from establishing itself in Italy. . . .

Milan, 25 January 1493

"What do you feel? What do you feel?" The midwife's eyes were glassy with fear, and her shouts were only through some quirk of pitch audible at all through Beatrice's screams.

"I can't tell . . . ," answered the midwife's assistant, unheard by anyone, her adolescent features livid with distress. She was kneeling on Beatrice's bed; her arm, concealed almost to the shoulder by Beatrice's hiked-up chemise, disappeared between Beatrice's legs.

"Feel for the nose! Feel for hair!" the midwife shrieked. "Find the head! Find the head and bring the head down!"

Beatrice's head snapped up, the cords of her neck standing out against her blanched skin, her lips drawn away from yellowed teeth and pale purple gums in a death's-head grimace. Her eyes fixed for a moment of insane purpose on the midwife's assistant. She whipped her leg from the grip of one of Messer Ambrogio's assistants and flailed it against the girl's slender back before it was captured and again pinned to the bed.

"Do you have the head!"

The girl's head snapped up as vehemently as Beatrice's, her tear-glazed eyes almost as wild. Now the girl's shrill voice could be heard. "She keeps moving! She almost broke my arm!"

Messer Ambrogio shouted into the ear of Beatrice's mother. Eleonora nodded. With an urgent sweep of his red cloak, Messer Ambrogio went to the door. A moment later two burly pages followed him back in. He assigned them to relieve the men attempting to immobilize Beatrice's legs, then moved the two assistants to Beatrice's midsection and directed them to hold her pelvis as firmly as possible. Beatrice thrust up her hips in a last desperate bid for freedom, and her chemise fell back, revealing the girl's arm inserted into her vagina almost to the elbow.

Beatrice's head pounded against the mattress, and her seemingly continuous scream changed pitch, becoming an eerily inhuman growl. The midwife's assistant lurched back, convulsively withdrawing her blood-smeared arm from the birth canal.

"Did you turn it?" the midwife screamed at her.

"I think so," the girl said, her answer inaudible against Beatrice's long, bestial moan. The girl's eyes flooded with tears, and she began to cry, still unheard.

Messer Ambrogio ushered Eleonora into the antechamber, signaling the dour, tough-looking surgeon and the midwife and her assistant to follow. He closed the door. When he spoke, his voice hissed like an oracle, a calmly sinister accompaniment to the animal noises still coming from the bedchamber. "Was the version successful?" he asked the midwife, giving her a halfways glance.

The midwife clasped the shoulders of her youthful assistant and looked at her searchingly. The girl was perhaps thirteen. She was still sobbing. "I felt the head," she whimpered. "I . . . I moved it down."

"Would she know the difference between a head and a rump?" the surgeon asked Messer Ambrogio, not deigning to address even the midwife, much less her assistant. "I make it tantamount to treason to entrust the Duchess's health to a girl who is no doubt witnessing her first birth."

Angrily snatching up the girl's frail, bloodied arm, the midwife said, "The Duchess's womb is shut so tight I would have been lucky to get my thumb through. It is rare to find a girl with both an arm as slight as this and half the wits to follow instructions. And when they have done the version once, they do not want to do it again."

Eleonora addressed all of them, her green eyes sweeping purposefully. "Let us assume that the head is in position," she said, giving the girl a grateful nod. "What can we expect now?"

"*If* the version has been performed, we will see the birth progress normally," responded Messer Ambrogio, his whispered skepticism seconded by the surgeon's imperious scowl.

"If the version had been performed hours ago, as *I* urged, we might expect the birth to progress normally." The midwife curtsied apologetically to Eleonora. "But now I fear she is exhausted. She has been in labor for a night and a day. A very hard labor."

Eleonora's eyes did not flinch. "And if the birth does not progress normally?"

"Massage of the afflicted parts might be more effective now," Messer Ambrogio offered.

The midwife curtsied reflexively. "Herbs. Salves. But she is so fatigued, Your Highness. . . ."

"Then it is likely that these prescriptions will be no more successful now than they were last night and all this day." Eleonora turned to the surgeon. "I do not intend to let my daughter die with a child in her womb. Do you have the instruments necessary to remove the child?"

Messer Ambrogio's slack old lips drooped. He visibly paled. "We would have to consult with the Duke of Bari before—"

"The Duke of Bari did not lie in pain like that to bring *my* child into the world," Eleonora snapped, throwing out her hefty arm and menacingly pointing a thick finger toward the bedchamber. *"Do you have the tools?"*

The surgeon swallowed thickly and nodded yes.

"Then we will go back in and pray that our Lord bids this baby come into the world." Eleonora held the surgeon's grim gaze.

Beatrice saw them come back in. Not as separate individuals but as a single menacing presence, a many-headed demon of pain. Her own pain she already knew like the affliction of a lifetime, the hot acid that burned in every tiny vein, the stinging bile in her lungs and throat, the immense aching weight against her bowels, like a torrent of molten lead blocked up inside her. She had come to know this pain well enough to negotiate with it, to offer it something here for a moment of respite there, to be assured that when it finally killed her it would take her like an expert executioner, in a clean swift stroke. But this moving, multiarmed creature of pain could not be reasoned with; it would tear her apart bit by bit. It had already tried.

She watched it surround her, all eyes, the only thing she could see clearly now. The massages and smearing of salves and prodding and poking and endless getting in and out of the birthing chair had maddened her beyond imagining, but the memory of those torments had fallen away from her consciousness like a black flake drifting into a bottomless well. Now all she could remember was the version, a lightning bolt of clarity, every instant visible and distinct. The arm sliding inside her, each movement a separate knife thrust, deeper and deeper. And then the poisonous fingers wriggling in her belly, every touch a rushing tremor of agony that began in her bowels and exploded in her head in an obscene cacophony, a shrill demon's horn that blew daggers instead of notes. She vowed to herself that if they tried the version again, she would somehow get her head free and with her teeth tear out the monster's throat.

But the thing did not move on her again. After a long while Beatrice ignored its leering eyes and talked with her own pain, found it yet more reasonable, felt parts of herself begin to drift into that dark well beneath her, brilliant, tinsel-like bits of her soul sparking into oblivion. For a moment she saw Mama standing there, her eyes so green, and she thought to talk to her; perhaps she did. I am going home, Mama.

She imagined that each of her own eyes saw entirely differently. One slumbered, dreaming of a huge darkness lit by dolls in white lace dresses and saints in brilliant brocade robes. The glowing dolls and shimmering saints rushed past her like an army of lanterns, this way and that, banners flying. Her other eye could look down on the beast that still leered at her; this eye saw Mama standing inside the monster, not entirely part of it. I am coming home, Mama. I have a baby with me. I want you to see my baby.

And then the many-eyed creature stirred again. Mama roused it! Why, Mama? Why do you hurt me again? But she knew why Mama had brought the monster to life, and the pain of that truth was like the hand in her womb reaching up to rip out her heart. The dolls and saints streaked past and disappeared, and she watched the surgeon reach into his leather bag and take out the shiny metal things. She remembered in an instant where she had seen those tools before and what they would do and why the monster had come for her baby.

Beatrice engaged the surgeon in a slow combat, straining with every fiber of her strength, but she was only able to move her body to the ponderous beat of a *bassa danza*. He advanced on her, the hammer and spike and hook in his hands. With infinite effort she rose to meet him. Hands grasped at her arms, but she pulled away. She stood straight up and began to fade into a black whirl-wind. She put her hands on her knees and told them to bring the birthing chair. She squatted down. They all spoke to her at once, but she decided she would listen only to her own breathing. She already knew the simple terms of the agreement she had just ne-gotiated and merely wondered with whom she had dealt. Had it been Fortune? Or Mama?

Life passed in and out of her in strong, regular surges, with a sound like distant breakers. She imagined that she was in a ca-thedral, as ornate as the Duomo but a thousand times longer, a great tunnel with a single candle flickering at its end. She began to walk, telling herself she must save her strength. Now and again saints stared down at her from their niches, lifelike statues that bent and admonished her in muddy, droning voices before she blinked them away. Periodically the floor tilted up like the face of a mountain, and she had to use all her force to keep going before it leveled again. Afterward, each time she was weaker.

She walked so far. The altar was brighter now, and thousands of candles blazed around it. She no longer noticed the exhorting saints. She began to run, the huge gulps of air searing her lungs, her legs aching with fatigue. Running so fast. The infant rested on the altar, naked, swaddled only in pure light. The floor tilted up crazily, but somehow it was easy now, though she knew that when she reached the top she would fall back farther than she had come, fall all the way back. That no longer concerned her. The warmth of the candles was like the sun, and there was the baby, his eyes twinkling like gems. In a final effort that left her weight-less, free of pain, she reached out for him. He was so smooth, so perfect, his skin like a warm rose petal. The words "I love you" sparked from her fingertips, and she knew he was her baby and that it did not matter that she was rushing away now, falling back into the darkness. She heard her baby cry, saw the glinting golden notes of his first cries drift down after her, and the last thing she told herself was: I can go anywhere now.

Count Girolamo da Tuttavilla removed his spectacles and rubbed his eyes. He looked up at Il Moro. Milan's most experienced at-large envoy, the white-haired Tuttavilla was fifteen years Il Moro's senior; indeed, he had also served under Il Moro's father, Francesco Sforza. He was studying dispatches from Il Moro's extensive intelligence-gathering apparatus in Venice, the kind of network of merchants, envoys, bankers, and even courtesans that Il Moro had organized in all the great capitals of Europe. "You know the saying," Tuttavilla remarked, " 'We both know how many days to Saint Biagio's feast.' The Signory of Venice understand as well as we do that the French must not be permitted to cross the mountains. Certainly they intend to enter into the league His Holiness has proposed. The real question is to what extent they will support the league if more than words are required."

Il Moro sat back in his chair. The light in the room, cast by large glass globes suspended from the wall by brass sconces, was curiously steady in an age of candles and oil lamps, and it sharpened the regal lines of Il Moro's face. "That is my concern exactly. The Signory will hope that this display of Italian unity will persuade King Charles to stay home. But if the French army actually crosses the mountains . . ." Il Moro made a slight, disdainful motion of his head. "In that case I'm certain the Signory would send us their prayers."

"Then perhaps we should agree to enter into this league only on the condition that each member state publicly pledge to assist any member state attacked by the French. That would make the Venetians accountable and would certainly give caution to the hotheads in King Charles's retinue."

"The Signory will never agree to that," Il Moro offered. "Right now Venice fears Germany more than she does France. And as long as the French are in a position to counter the German threat to Venice, the Signory will never take such an aggressive position against the French. The Signory will try to pursue a more circumspect policy. Of course if the French and Germans were to settle their differences, Venetian policy might become more adventuresome."

"Is that possible?"

"Count Belgioioso informs me that King Charles has been trying to arrange a parlay with the German Emperor's son Maximilian. A peace between France and Germany would remove the most important obstacle to King Charles's Crusade. And that would be a most unhappy state of affairs." Il Moro traced his index finger over the little ruby bust of Caesar on his ring. "Well, for now I think that a vague alliance with Venice is better than no alliance at all. It is the first step. Then we can gradually increase the pressure on the Signory to put some teeth into our agreement." Il Moro stared thoughtfully for a moment. "It occurs to me that we should make the league as visible as possible. To confirm the league, I could send you to Venice at the head of a very large suite of ambassadors and ask Duke Ercole and His Holiness to do the same. I wish that Duke Ercole and I could personally go, but we have too many enemies among the Signory."

"Perhaps your wife? And Duke Ercole's wife. With very large suites of ladies. That would certainly underscore the importance we attach to this accord."

Il Moro nodded his satisfaction. He sat silently for a moment, then got up suddenly and walked over to one of the lamps. He peered at it and tapped the clear glass globe, which was filled with water; the wick burned in a glass cylinder set inside the globe. "Did you notice it while you were reading?"

Tuttavilla turned in his chair and studied the lamp. "Quite certainly. Where one might read by an oil lamp for two hours before becoming fatigued, with this the only limitation is the need for sleep." He brandished his thick, wire-rimmed spectacles. "Perhaps we are not yet able to restore sight to the blind, but our science has assuredly extended the usefulness of old men."

"Leonardo made it for me," Il Moro said, tapping the globe again. "He sends me a list of ten ideas, one of which might be useful. A most peculiar man. Always railing against the humanists, no doubt because he cannot read Latin. Yet there is something to be said for the quality of his vision, unencumbered by the past, focused fully on the future. Of course as soon as one of my scholars has translated a text from the Greek into the vernacular, Leonardo must have it." Il Moro smiled wistfully. "My father would have been amused by him. He would have pitted Leonardo against

Filarete—Filarete drawing his perfect cities shaped like stars, Leonardo imagining roads stacked one atop the other and carriages drawn only by some concoction of gears and springs. My father had a gift for seeing genius where other men could see only nuisance." Il Moro took his seat again, a subtle reminder of his smile remaining on his lips. He did not look at Tuttavilla.

Glancing up from under his black eyebrows, Tuttavilla studied Il Moro for a moment before he broke the silence. "You were always your father's favorite, though of course he could not openly declare it of a fourth son, so far from the succession. But we all knew it. Do you remember when you were fifteen or sixteen and you were out near Binasco on May Day? You got into that wrestling tournament with the country toughs, and you beat them all. When I told your father, he pounded his fist in that way of his and boomed, '*Stupendissimo*, Lodovico Maria!' Then he said to me, 'Do you know how he beat them, Messer Girlaomo? Not with his back, though it is strong enough. With his mind. With tricks and cunning, always a half-dozen moves ahead of his opponent. That is why he will be a stronger man than I. No one can defeat Lodovico Maria's mind.' " Tuttavilla smiled warmly and openly, without any suggestion of a flatterer's guile. "I'm sure that your father's soul is comforted in knowing that Milan enjoys your governance."

Il Moro looked up. His opaque black eyes suggested, though not unkindly, that Tuttavilla retreat from whatever border he was attempting to cross. Then he peered abstractedly into Leonardo's unwavering light. "The light of reason," he said with a slightly ironic edge. "We are asked to believe that this light will someday illuminate the entire world. And yet any learned painter can tell you that without darkness in contrast to light, the appearance of form and shape cannot be created. *Chiaroscuro*. Light and shade. The more brilliant the light, the more profound its absence must be. Look at the work of the Florentine painters. The boundary between light and dark is as sharp as a blade."

As if validating his hypothesis, Il Moro stared into the sharp, distinct shadows behind his secretaries' lecterns. At the knock on the door, his shoulders jerked lightly with surprise.

The messenger was Bernardino da Corte. Il Moro's chief of

security was an angular man with aquiline Milanese features and a swarthy, southern Mediterranean complexion. He dipped to his knee and clutched his cap to his breast. "Messer Ambrogio has bid me inform you that your wife has borne you a son, unflawed, with no unusual markings and in robust health."

Il Moro's face and voice conveyed nothing. "I have dictated to Messer Calco a complete agenda for the celebrations. You may tell him to proceed."

Unexpectedly, Bernardino did not rise, and his fingers tightened on his cap. "Your Highness. Messer Ambrogio begs to consult with you on a situation that has developed regarding the Duchess of Bari."

A strange reflection seemed to dart across Il Moro's eyes, as if Leonardo's lamp had suddenly flared and then died. "Where is Messer Ambrogio?" he asked evenly.

CHAPTER

22

It was a place of translucent light, a deep, clear sea. Once in a long while a curious floating statue, perhaps a tomb effigy, might glide past, brocade robes billowing as they propelled it along like a huge cuttlefish, its gemstone crust twinkling until it disappeared into the distance.

The pain brought her closer to the surface. Occasionally she could see the people on the shore; they appeared briefly like figures painted on tarot cards, then blew away when the clouds covered the sun. Once she saw Mama and told herself: Mama isn't dead. Why is Mama here?

The throbbing in her womb stripped away the gauzy layers of her dream. The light in the room steadied and brightened, turning everything hard and real. Her hands and feet were cold. She knew she was alive, and the panic that immediately gripped her was the worst pain of all: Did I dream my baby? She had to get up.

Mama was there, and for an instant her entire life was her hatred of Mama for keeping her from getting up. But she did not have the strength after that. When she opened her eyes again, she could hear her own voice through the whooshing in her ears. "Mama, where is my baby? Where is . . . ?"

Mama left. When she came back, the bundle of mulberry-colored velvet in her arms sparkled for an instant, struck by light streaming through the partially opened shutters. A glimpse of ruddy skin and fine black hair. Beatrice expected something magical when Mama set the baby next to her, the full chorus of the turning spheres, but there was nothing, only surprise at his coarse, pinched little features. *"Il suo fanciullo, mia fanciulla,"* Mama whispered to her. Your baby boy, my baby girl.

Beatrice touched her baby's cheek. He was so much softer than he looked; he felt as warm and velvety as she had imagined him. His lips puckered and his head wobbled toward her breast. Instinctively she fumbled at the laces of her chemise.

"No, baby," Mama said. "You are too weak. And it will be better if you don't start. If you do not take it up, you will not have to give it up."

Clutching at her chemise, Beatrice raged at Mama and her own cold, clumsy, lifeless fingers; was part of her still dead? And then her baby opened his eyes and looked at her. She heard only a single note, but it was the clearest, purest sound she would ever hear. His eyes were some indistinct color, the lenses of a strange omniscience that Beatrice immediately understood. He did not simply know her soul, hear her soul sing. He was her soul.

Perhaps Il Moro had been in the room for a short while before Beatrice realized that her husband was present; it never registered with her that this man was also her baby's father. He spoke animatedly to Mama—she did not know of what—and sat on the bed beside her. He kissed her and the baby, but the kisses had no more meaning than when Mariolo the *buffone*, in one of his clowning routines, would pucker and primp and pretend he was her lover.

"My son is becoming acquainted with his mother," Il Moro said.

Idiot, Beatrice thought. I do not need to become acquainted with my own flesh, my own soul. In a hundred years you could not know him as I know him now. For a moment she was dismayed that she could feel such anger while she held her baby in her arms, but then she realized that her anger had saved his life. And would always protect him.

Il Moro stood up again and spoke with Eleonora. Beatrice

continued her unblinking communion with her baby. I will never hurt you, she sang in silent oath, I will never let anyone hurt you. I will never let anyone do to you what Mama did to me.

"He's almost here, Your Highness. Almost here." The midwife stepped away from the birthing chair and murmured to her assistant, the same girl who had performed the version on Beatrice. "In three days you have managed to see one of the most difficult births I have observed in twenty-six years of attending, and now one of the easiest. And you would not imagine how much easier this birth has been for Her Highness than her first."

Isabella heard the midwife's remarks, and they stirred in her the sense of competition she had felt throughout her brief labor: competition with herself, to bring her baby out as quickly as possible, and the far more serious competition with Il Moro, to match his son with her own, to again bring the simple balance of numbers in her favor. As much as she hated to, she had to consider poisoners and plots and of course all the natural illnesses that took so many children in their first few years. This baby was her guarantee. Her first son, Francesco, would no longer have to assume alone the enormous burden of fate. And at the very least her second son would be a talisman, a symbol of Fortune's continued favor.

She could feel how close the baby was, and suddenly she did not want her moment to end. She gave herself to it again, rising slowly into the intense light, occasionally exerting herself to stay aloft but often simply gliding, making huge swoops through the glittering vault of her expectations. This is love, she told herself, the true making of love, the most exquisitely sexual moment of life, the highest validation of my power.

She soared amid her baby's cries. She watched them take him from her, head out first, bloodied yet perfect, already her image. He twisted; she shuddered once and pushed his torso out, without shame reveling in the surge of his flesh through hers. The umbilical twined across his legs like a blue Sforza viper. . . .

An alarm pulsed through her, bringing her crashing down. He is flawed, deformed! She was stunned, vacant, plunging through a sky that had lost the sun, everything drained from her. He is . . .

An instant later she understood what she had seen, even before she heard the witnesses murmur "daughter." Her son was not flawed, the bud of power she had expected to find between his legs somehow clipped in the womb. This son simply had never existed.

The witnesses dutifully exited the birth chamber. The midwife rinsed the little girl and showed her to the Duchess of Milan. "Your birth was so easy this time, Your Highness. I am certain you will have no difficulty nursing her now if you wish."

Isabella numbly shook her head. "You had better see that her wet nurse is ready for her."

Extract of a letter of TEODORA DEGLI ANGELI, lady-in-waiting to the Duchess of Ferrara, to ISABELLA D'ESTE DA GONZAGA, Marquesa of Mantua. Milan, 20 February 1493

. . . indeed for a time I feared for the well-being of Madame your mother, she spent so many hours kneeling on the cold floor of the Ducal Chapel beseeching Our Sweet Lord to deliver Madonna your sister, and certainly all of this has done nothing to relieve Madame your mother's stomach difficulties, of which you already know. But Madonna your sister has regained her health most marvelously, and now Madame your mother insists that Madonna your sister can look forward to nothing but the most salutary births in the future. Madonna your sister rests quietly most days (so altogether different from her demeanor as we know her), but she glows like the altar of the Duomo when her *bello puttino* is brought to her arms. . . .

The ambassadors, counts, cardinals, magistrates, and various and sundry dignitaries were invited in to view the gifts and decorations as soon as it was judged that Madonna your sister had recovered sufficiently. As you have requested, I have made every effort to be as detailed as possible and ascertain the value of the items described herein . . . a set of crystal flagons supported on gold bases in the shape of griffins, satyrs, and dolphins valued at 3,500 ducats apiece, a large chased gold urn of *all'antica* design in excess of 15,000 ducats. . . . The canopy of Madonna your sister's bed is crimson *velluto riccio sopra riccio* with . . . a fringe of little golden spheres which I am informed is valued at 8,000 ducats by itself . . . the cradle [has] four gilded columns [and] a canopy of blue *tabi* silk fringed and laced with gold, wherein your little nephew Ercole slumbers beneath cloth-of-gold valued at 150! ducats an arm-span. . . . Madame your mother is concerned that the display is excessive and will unnecessarily provoke the Duke and Duchess of Milan, since these oblations have exceeded even those which greeted the birth of the Duke of Milan's heir. Already, we hear, there have been comments to that effect from the Duchess of Milan's chambers. . . .

Madonna your sister will be freed from her rooms four days hence, as will the Duchess of Milan, the time having been determined by Messer Ambrogio da Rosate. (From all the regard paid this individual's pronouncements, Your Highness, you would think that Messer Ambrogio, not Madonna your sister, had actually given birth to *il bello puttino*.) . . .

CHAPTER

23

Milan, 24 February 1493

"He's been such a sweet little boy this morning, Your Highness." The wet nurse looked into the glassy, satiated eyes of four-week-old Ercole Sforza. The infant released her nipple with a wet pop, his lips vivid beneath a translucent coating of milk.

Beatrice took the swaddled bundle and held her son against her shoulder, his downy head cradled against her bare neck, his clean, moist scent more exquisite to her than the finest Milanese perfumes. She stroked his back, and when he erupted with a resonant belch, she and the wet nurse exchanged smiles. At first she had been jealous of her baby's wet nurse, who was two years older than she but seemed much younger because of her unsophisticated manner. But Beatrice had quickly warmed to her son's provider (whose own child had been stillborn the same day as Ercole's birth) and had already given her a fortune in cast-off gowns.

"If he spits up you will ruin your lovely *camora*, you will have to select a new one from your *guardaroba*, and we do not have time for that if you are to leave your rooms at Messer Ambrogio's designated hour." Eleonora advanced through the doorway, a formidable presence in glistening black satin highlighted by the enormous diamond brooch perched on her considerable bosom. "And even if you care nothing for Messer Ambrogio's schedules, you must not keep the Duchess of Milan waiting. You know that everyone will be watching you carefully for any suggestion that you are behaving in a fashion disrespectful of the Duchess of Milan and her daughter."

"Listen to your sainted mother." Polissena followed Eleonora into the room, her hooded head bobbing furious agreement. "You will be hard-pressed as it is simply to stay on your feet today, Your Highness, what with the *Te Deum* at Santa Maria delle Grazie this morning and the reception at Count Della Torre's *palazzo* this afternoon. And after the scare you put us through, your sainted mother and I are neither of us well enough at present to carry you off in our arms if you become fatigued, as we did when you were a babe."

Beatrice glanced at the ridiculous couple, her massive mother done up in mourning hues and her withered matron of honor nodding along after Mama like a skeletal dancer in a death masque. She turned away from them and squinted into the bright pewter morning haze visible through the windows of her baby's nursery. Mama always sounded so far away now; Beatrice imagined herself on a sunny windswept promontory, with Mama's voice so vague and distant that it surely belonged to another life. But of course Mama didn't understand that she was addressing a ghost, that the Beatrice whom Mama still admonished and advised had died the day her baby was born. Not because she had almost lost her life but because on that day she had finally found it. No one else could understand that her journey through darkness had begun the day she was born and had ended the day her baby was born.

Surrendering her baby to his wet nurse, Beatrice felt a stinging vestige of fear, almost like the pulling of scar tissue over a wound. In the first few days after Ercole's birth, each time she had given him up to his nurses she had experienced the utter terror that she would not see him again; she had yet to entirely convince herself that each parting was only temporary. When she came back into her *guardaroba*, her ladies-in-waiting greeted her with a flurry of dramatically deep curtsies. They proceeded to swarm about her with predatory ferocity, openly squabbling among one another for the honor of draping the Duchess of Bari in her white-sable-trimmed satin mantle or straightening the ribbons entwined around her single braid. Beatrice could hear the rustling of ambition in her ladies' silks and see the fear behind their obsequious smiles, and she hated their sudden attentiveness more than she had their two years of studied contempt. It was as if they expected her husband to declare himself Duke of Milan before the day was over.

Beatrice ignored her ladies and kissed Il Moro's illegitimate daughter Bianca, who waited shyly on the periphery of the fray, cheeks blazing against her pallor. Trailed by her glittering retinue, Beatrice took Bianca's hand and proceeded through her study and her all-too-familiar bedchamber, finally leaving her rooms for the Sala della Palla. There she was applauded by an expectant audience of the court fixtures, whose existence she had almost forgotten: fools and dwarfs, diplomats and clerics, bureaucrats and men-at-arms. She felt as if she were the victor in one of the great tournaments, and for an instant everything inside her constricted into a single icy anxiety: He has already done it. He has already used my baby to make himself Duke. Reason quickly discarded that scenario (most of all, he would not dare do it with Mama here), but the residue of fear heightened a curious exhilaration she had never felt before and could not pause to examine.

The Duchess of Milan and her retinue waited in the open portico of the Ducal Court. It was a smaller group than that attending Beatrice, largely limited to ladies-in-waiting. Isabella's ladies were as glossy as a freshly varnished painting in their silks, satins, face paints, and gum-arabic-slicked hair, awaiting the rounds of postpartum celebratory *feste* with the coiled insouciance of hunting leopards. But their cold blue eyes and perfunctory smiles made it clear that they had nothing to celebrate. The contrast with Beatrice's entourage was so evident that even Beatrice had to admit it to herself: It is thought that I have won and Eesh has lost.

She had never seen Isabella so richly dressed, her *camora* of green-and-gold-striped *appicciolato* velvet shot through with silver threads and crimson braid, her hair laced with tiny diamonds, her mantle of crimson velour wrapped loosely around her broad shoulders, leaving a ruby pendant exposed between her cleavage like a glistening dab of blood. Isabella smiled at Beatrice wanly, almost wearily, the tight corners of her eyes betraying her tension. Again Beatrice thought: What has he done that I know nothing of, that perhaps even Mama does not know?

Beatrice curtsied urgently, kissed her cousin on the cheek, and whispered, "I have missed you so much, Your Highness."

Isabella folded her in an embrace; Eesh's tense, powerful back felt almost like armor beneath her soft velvet dress. "The first month of confinement felt like a week," Isabella said in her usual flippant tone, "and the second month felt like two years. Next time I am pregnant I will insist that Messer Ambrogio be chained to his bed for the duration of my confinement. He will quickly agree that two or three days in bed is all that should be required to ensure a mother's health."

"I can't wait for you to see Ercole, Eesh. I never imagined I would love him so much. And I can't wait to see your daughter. Everyone says she is so beautiful."

"Gian has insisted we name her after his mother, so now she is cursed with the name Bona." Isabella pulled away from Beatrice and greeted Eleonora.

"Perhaps we should all move along to the carriages," Eleonora suggested. "We have a long day ahead."

Isabella nodded. She involuntarily caught Beatrice's eye again but looked quickly away.

Beatrice found Bianca and clutched her hand again, taking solace in her innocent warmth. Two concerns now churned inside her, the first unpleasant truths of her new life. Of course there was Eesh's obvious agitation and resentment, perhaps because of something Il Moro had done during their confinement, something Mama hadn't told her about. Or perhaps Eesh was piqued simply because Il Moro now had an heir. It was dismaying for Beatrice to think that she and Eesh would have to rebuild their trust, but she was certain that whatever the cause, the misunderstanding could be settled between them. But the second thing Beatrice realized troubled her far more deeply. The observation lay sharp and dangerous in her mind, like the memory of the baby she had once seen destroyed, and she had to force herself to confront it: Eesh does not love her little girl.

"I would wager my Bergognone altarpiece that she is two inches taller," commented the Contessa Della Torre. "I could tell as soon as they made their entrance. When a woman has a child at her age, she always shoots up a bit." The Contessa was the thirty-three-year-old wife of Count Della Torre, host of the first post-partum celebratory *festa*. She peered over one of her gilt saltcellars, a naked Diana posed provocatively with a tiny, intricately crafted bow. Her experienced eyes narrowed at Beatrice, seated at the head of the table along with Il Moro and the Duke and Duchess of Milan. The Contessa already considered herself one of Milanese society's consummate survivors, a hoary veteran next to the predominately teenage or early-twentyish women arrayed around her table, all cerused gloss and gleaming white cleavage, many of them the showpiece second, third, or even fourth wives of Milan's aging, silver-haired magnates, replacements for predecessors felled by childbirth, disease, and in some cases husband-administered poison (though more humane husbands might simply force an aging wife into a convent in order to make way for a younger replacement).

"She's wearing Flemish platform slippers, I am certain. It's that, and that she is so much thinner. Fashionably . . . drawn, I would say." Madonna Anna da Casate was the twenty-five-year-old second wife of Francesco da Casate, a member of Il Moro's inner circle of advisers. She directed her elegant Lombard nose at the Contessa's ear and leaned closer; still attractive enough to exploit her sexual assets, she shared with the Contessa a cynical intelligence that might ensure her usefulness long after a succession of mistresses and whores had usurped her from her husband's bed. "You do know that she almost died. I am told with absolute reliability that she was given the sacraments. I can only assume that all her riding has given her a remarkable constitution. She has never looked better."

"*Cara amica*, you really must learn never to waste flattery on anyone out of hearing."

"At least I had the good sense not to sneer every time Il Moro's little *forestiera* bride rode by. My father always told me, 'Offer a woman a kindness and she will quickly discard it. Give her a slight, and that she will keep forever.' " Madonna Anna's stiletto glance jabbed up and down the enormous banquet table, littered with gold plate, crystal goblets, silvered candies, and hundreds of pink spun-sugar *confetti* cherubs. The din of conversation among the four dozen seated dignitaries and their wives had a strained, anxious undertone. "Look at the Duchess of Bari's ladies now, scheming like thieves to gain her favor. *Sciocce.* Think of all the time they wasted trying to get Il Moro into their beds. They could have secured more influence by showing simple civility to the Duchess of Bari."

"Or by sleeping with Messer Galeazz."

"Oh, that would be rather *too* easy. Do you remember the theatrical last Carnival, that silly Greek thing they did at the Castello? I left at the first *intermedo* to go to the lavatory, and he followed me in."

"How gallant of our Captain General. Did he offer to conclude the liaison before the *intermedo* was finished?"

"Actually he remained standing throughout the second act. And I don't believe my feet ever touched the floor."

"*Per dio.* He *is* gallant." The Contessa focused for a moment on Bianca, who was cheerfully conversing with Eleonora. "I wonder when they will let him butcher Il Moro's little bastard."

"I wonder if now that Il Moro has provided for his succession, he will begin to pursue his pleasure."

"I trust you're not hoping that Galeazz will give him a recommendation on your behalf. Il Moro prefers more enduring romances. He was faithful the entire time he was with Cecilia Gallerani."

"A faithful lover in Milan? That would be almost as remarkable as a faithful husband. Why haven't the papal authorities in Rome been informed of this miracle?"

"In Rome the current notion of a miracle is finding a woman the Pope has not slept with." The Contessa paused and studied Il Moro, who was in turn studying his wife's fluid, almost musical hand gestures—Beatrice was speaking animatedly to the Duke of Milan—as if he were trying to decipher a sign language. "What is curious is that Il Moro has also been a faithful husband. Faithful to Messer Ambrogio's schedules, at least." Il Moro quickly looked away from Beatrice, almost as if he had caught himself daydreaming. "You know, that is the first time I have ever seen him more than glance at her. But as you say, she's never looked better."

"What I meant was, take away the jewels and the gowns, and you would have a pretty merchant's daughter. Still, she has a certain *leggiadria*, those . . . vivacious mannerisms that are at last charming now that they are balanced by a hint of maturity and a touch of pallor. Before her confinement she was simply a fidgety, rosy-cheeked brat. You can spend every morning washing with nettle juice or plastering your face with milk-soaked veal, but nothing endows one with an exquisite porcelain-white complexion like two months in bed." Madonna Anna was distracted from her critique by the kind of social nuance she had conditioned herself to observe: the Duchess of Milan, seated next to Il Moro, turned to him and gestured emphatically with her knife. "Do you think the Duchess of Milan is jealous?"

"Hardly . . ."

"Jealous of Il Moro, that is." Madonna Anna leaned forward eagerly, watching with rapt absorption as Isabella continued to speak to Il Moro, thrusting her gold-handled knife in precise, enumerative jabs. "Oh, quiet, everyone," Madonna Anna said in *sotto voce* frustration, drawing up her bare shoulders as if trying to get a better view. "I think we are going to have an exchange of opinions."

But whatever Isabella had to say she had already said. She abruptly stood up, her eyes feverish with anger, nodded at her host, and went quickly to the door. Her astonished ladies-in-waiting tittered among themselves and their escorts for a moment. Then they convulsively rose almost as one and followed her out.

Madonna Anna turned to the Contessa, plucked eyebrows lifted, glistening lips toying with a smirk. "Do you care to wager your Bergognone altarpiece as to when we will have a new Duke of Milan?"

Eleonora sent the serving girl and the lady-in-waiting out of the room and began to unlace the bodice of Beatrice's heavy brocade *camora*. "Such a lovely gown." She stroked the rows of tinselly, narrow silk *stringhe* ribbons that covered Beatrice's sleeves like the plumage of a tropical bird. "Everything is so different than when I was a girl. I remember when some of the *vecchie* accused me of impropriety because I wore a black dress with red sleeves. I suppose I am a *vecchia* now. I confess to you that I was shocked by the necklines of the *camore* we saw this evening. *Nostro Signore,* when some of those girls inhaled, you could see the tops of their nipples." Eleonora stroked the *stringhe* wistfully, seemingly as troubled by her own lost youth as by the excesses of the younger generation.

"Mama, what did he say?"

"I spoke with our ambassador first, and Messer Trotti informs me that there is nothing afoot save rumor," Eleonora said, looking Beatrice in the eyes, her fingers still plucking at the laces of her daughter's bodice. "Your husband is devoting all his efforts to preventing the French from coming over the mountains."

"But, Mama, he is trying to get the Signory of Venice to come to his side."

Eleonora sighed. "Since Piero de' Medici has persuaded my father to withdraw from the anti-French league, your husband has no choice. He must have a rapprochement with Venice. Even your father is agreed to that."

Beatrice was not convinced that her husband's rapprochement with Venice had anything to do with keeping the French out of Italy. Was it possible that her husband had already persuaded the Signory of Venice to withdraw their secret resolution to attack him if he attempted to become Duke of Milan?

"Mama, did you talk to him?"

"I very candidly expressed my concerns to your husband. He has assured me that he has no desire whatsoever to usurp his nephew, wishing only to maintain the peace that has brought all Italy, and most notably Milan, to such a state of prosperity."

"But, Mama, Eesh is right. She told me that they only rang the bells for three days when Francesco was born, and my husband had them ring the bells for six days to announce Ercole's birth. And there have been all sorts of other things, like the gifts and decorations. No one at the banquet today even cared about Eesh's little girl."

"Nonsense. All of the celebrations are for *both* your child and

Isabella's child." Eleonora sighed again. "Beatrice, I must tell you that I think your cousin is being unfair not only to your husband but to you as well. You and your husband are entitled to your joy over the birth of your son, and if Isabella cannot share that joy, then she is behaving shamefully when she asks you to share her envy. There is no disgrace in giving birth to a daughter. I have borne two girls, and I can assure you that you and your sister are as dear to me as your father's heirs."

"I know they didn't ring the bells for me when I was born."

"That simply is not true."

Beatrice shook her head slightly; an eyelid trembled. "Mama, I have been told that by people who were there. People who wouldn't lie to me."

Eleonora finished unlacing the bodice and fussily pulled the stiff, heavy dress over Beatrice's head. She laid it carefully on the bed and smoothed out the wrinkles before she responded. "Well, if they cared for you they should not have told you that. Your father's subjects were understandably dismayed that his first two children were girls. You are fortunate that you have not experienced the anxiety that results when the succession has not been provided for." Eleonora alluded to their grisly family history. Her husband, Duke Ercole, had fought a virtual civil war against his nephew Niccolò over the succession following the death of Ercole's older half-brother, Duke Borso d'Este; five years later, Niccolò had attempted the coup from which Eleonora and her three small children had narrowly escaped. For several years afterward the public executions of Niccolò's supporters had been a regular feature of Ferrara's civic life. Niccolò had finally been beheaded on a cold spring day, so clear and brilliant that Eleonora could still see the crazy flutter of his eyes at the moment the sword struck. Ercole had ordered Niccolò's head sewn back on for the lavish funeral and had raised Niccolò's nine bastards under his own roof.

Beatrice stood rigid, her chin set obstinately. She stared into the fireplace.

"Beatrice, I know how much you love your cousin, and God knows as her aunt I love her too. But she was always a difficult child, too much indulged by her father. I fear that if she enlists you in some kind of protest, the two of you will encourage exactly

what you hope to prevent. Fortune favored you when you protested against Cecilia Gallerani, thanks also to the certainty of your
cause and Messer Trotti's judicious intervention. But you are not
ready to involve yourself in this kind of thing. If you are truly a
friend to Isabella, you will advise to her the same caution that I
am advising to you."

Beatrice started at the laces of her thin silk chemise, her fingers
fumbling with suppressed emotion. Of course her husband was a
liar; of course Mama was too. But now the black stain of doubt
had spread to someone she thought she'd never have to question.
If Eesh couldn't love her own little girl, how could she love anyone else?

Il Moro looked out from one of the square open ports of the
rooftop defensive gallery that ran from the Ducal Court to the
immense round turret at the northwest corner of the Castello. Off
to his right Milan slept in predawn darkness, the only signs of life
a few lanterns and the steady upward drift of sparks and embers
from the forges along the Via degli Armorai. He snuggled his chin
into the collar of his fur cape and looked to the north, into the
featureless darkness of the ducal park. He waited with only an
occasional shuffling of his feet, as if testing his patience against
nature's. After perhaps an hour the sky lightened and the noises
of early morning penetrated the stillness. The Alps materialized,
first as distinct shadows, then as a mother-of-pearl mirage against
the horizon. Il Moro tilted his chin up and waited a while longer.
Within minutes the peaks began to flush a soft lustrous pink, giving
their angular, masculine ridges the subtlety of a woman's flesh.
After another few minutes the curiously erotic illusion vanished
and the snowcaps sparkled with hard, faceted brilliance. Il Moro
turned and walked back to the Ducal Court. Behind him, the
streets of Milan still lay in deep mauve shadows, but the city's
countless red tile roofs were fiery with the morning sun.

CHAPTER

24

Milan, 27 February 1493

"I beg your pardon, Your Highness," said the Marchesino Stanga, Milan's polished Minister of Public Works, as he bowed somewhat unsteadily to Beatrice. "I am afraid I must admit that the excellent Malavasia wine has emphasized the clumsiness of my footwork, when I had intended to impress you with my grace. I am so sorry."

"But, Marchesino, you have stepped on my foot with such grace," Beatrice replied. She held out her hand so that she and the Marchesino, who was both a contemporary and an acquaintance of her mother's, could rejoin the circle of paired dancers moving with varying degrees of proficiency around a hub of red-white-and-blue-liveried musicians. The Marchesino was far from the most unsteady of the revelers packed into the great hall of the Palazzo da Pusterla, one of Milan's grandest private residences. While many of the pairs still dipped and turned with deft assurance, more than a few others stumbled comically; the Duke of Milan, attempting an extravagant *fioretta* pirouette, had just fallen on his rear. Far more complex than the fairly simple *bassa danza* routines, however, were the physical and psychological maneuvers—also practiced with varying degrees of proficiency—through which dancers of both sexes communicated their availability for a wide variety of sexual activities.

Beatrice had herself consumed enough wine to enjoy the relaxed decorum and forget for a moment that Eesh had virtually ignored her for the last two days. She had even begun to consider, albeit with ambivalence, the notion of claiming some of the social rewards for her successful labor. On the one hand she felt she had finally escaped her bondage to all these people here in Milan, having fulfilled the essential obligation she had to them—and to her husband. But as keenly attuned as she was to the bitter irony of her miraculous transformation from unwanted *forestiera* bride to beloved mother of the wealthiest—and perhaps most powerful—scion in Europe, she could not escape a strange sense of finally belonging. Perhaps she was only the hub of a screeching wheel of flatterers and sycophants, but the urgency with which these people were now drawn to her, however self-serving their attraction, gave her a feeling of security, of having arrived at some fixed place for the first time in her life.

The sonorous, lilting *bassa danza* music ended, and the circle of dancers stopped turning. The court poet Gaspare Visconti appeared on the balustraded mezzanine overlooking the great hall. His first pronouncement merely brought silence among the crowd. Then, with a hand flourish, he said: "In honor of the Duke of Bari's son, an original *cantione alla piffarescha*, with the addition of *trombone*, by Maestro Franchino Gafori." The dancers applauded. An interlude followed as the musicians, joined by the trombone players and several vocalists, took a few last glances at the sheet of music.

Beatrice stood on her toes in anticipation; she intended to memorize every note so that she could hum and sing the tune to little Ercole when she returned to the Castello. Notes of joy already filled her buzzing head, and she realized that so many of the formalities of court, which had previously seemed merely foolish and hollow, would now have meaning because they would be for her little boy. . . .

"Walk out with me."

The voice entered Beatrice's reverie like a shout in a dream. With dread she turned. Eesh was at her side, her eyes catlike with ire.

"The first dedication should have been to the Duke of Milan's child. This is the last affront I will accept from Il Moro. I am leaving, and I want you to walk out with me. We must make it clear to him that his insidious assertion of his unlawful claims cannot continue."

"Eesh . . ." She thought for a desperate moment of Mama's warning about such protests, thought of offering that caution to Eesh, but realized that wasn't the reason she could not leave. "Eesh . . . ," she pleaded. "Eesh, this is for my little boy, his first song. It . . . it would be like walking out on my baby."

"Did you ever think that your little boy might cost my little boy everything that is rightfully his? He might even cost us our lives."

"Eesh, that isn't fair—" Beatrice stopped herself abruptly, suddenly outraged that Eesh could not see that Ercole was *her* little boy, the love of her new life, and not some sinister agent of Il Moro's ambition. The old competitive anger she had felt toward Eesh when she first came to Milan welled up again, so hot that it hurt. But that initial reflex was quickly replaced by something colder, more calculated, and to this she gave words. "You are wrong, Eesh. You are wrong to hate my little boy just because you cannot love your little girl."

Isabella jerked back as if she had been struck, her eyes stunned and watery. Her cheeks and forehead flushed. "He will use your little boy to turn you against me," she said, her tone no longer angry or resolved, only weary and sad.

The music began, the woodwinds and horns so gay and vibrant that they seemed ridiculous. Beatrice's anger had vanished. She had only the sickening sensation of plunging after her words, trying to capture them and take them back. She wanted to embrace Eesh, to say how sorry she was. But Isabella whipped her shoulders about and stalked through the crowd so quickly that hardly anyone noticed her departure.

The baby's cries were audible from the *guardaroba* adjoining the nursery. A page scurried to open the door to the nursery as the Duchess of Milan swept past. When the door was opened, the cries escaped with stinging intensity.

The wet nurse was rapidly rocking the heavy, gilded cradle. She stopped and curtsied rapidly to Isabella, then attempted to speak loudly over the din. "Your Highness—"

The butt of Isabella's hand caught the stocky wet nurse high on the jaw and sent her sprawling, arms and legs akimbo. The woman looked up, her irises pinpoints of terror, then quickly got to her feet and frantically curtsied several times. "Get out!" Isabella screamed at her. "The devil take you—get out!"

The wet nurse curtsied twice more and fled, closing the door behind her.

Isabella stood over the cradle for a moment, her eyes closed. She had a strangely pensive beauty in the aftermath of her rage. She bent as if to kiss the shrieking infant.

"Bitch!" Isabella screamed directly into her daughter's face. The infant writhed, struggling against her swaddling, her wine-red little features distorted inhumanly, and wailed even louder. "Bitch! Bitch!" Isabella was almost as livid as her daughter. "Bitch! Bitch! Bitch! Bitch!"

After a moment Isabella's own tears came, and she stood sobbing over the little girl, her shoulders heaving in a silent mime of her daughter's unabated fury.

Beatrice pulled Bianca's fur-trimmed mantle up around her ears, then took her gloved hand and cradled it in her lap. The torches mounted on the roof of the carriage cast a dim glow through the silk window drapes. The sounds of snorting horses, clip-clopping hooves, and revelers' laughter signaled a general exodus from the Palazzo da Pusterla. Beatrice settled into the thick cushions, assuming that the crush of carriages in the Piazza del Duomo would briefly delay their departure for the Castello.

"Toto," Bianca asked her, "have you ever known anyone who died?"

Beatrice found the abrupt question entirely logical; Bianca's mind worked much like her own. And she welcomed the distraction from her anger, both at herself and at Eesh. Eesh *had* been

wrong and unfeeling in the timing of her protest. But Beatrice
knew that she herself had been just as unfeeling to accuse Eesh of
not loving her daughter. . . . It occurred to her that no one she
loved had ever died. She remembered the Requiem Mass for Polissena's second husband, how she had forced herself to glance at
his face from twenty paces away, that brief glimpse of a pale,
waxy mask in the brilliant light of hundreds of memorial candles.
He had been less real than a marble bust. She could not even
imagine Father or Bel or Bianca like that. People you loved didn't
die. "Were you thinking about your mother?" she asked Bianca.
"You know that just because I have my own baby now doesn't
mean that you are no longer my most special *amica*."

Bianca squeezed Beatrice's hand tightly. The door on Bianca's
side of the carriage clicked and opened. "*Carissima*," a man murmured, then whispered something to Bianca. Beatrice knew the
voice, the sibilance, and she had to force herself not to clutch
Bianca's hand in panic.

"I'm going home in my father's carriage. He says there is a
surprise in it for me." Bianca giggled and kissed Beatrice. "I love
you, Toto," she said, then reached out and in a swish of brocade
and fur disappeared into the night.

Beatrice silently recited her fears to the hammering of her heart.
No wonder Eesh was so upset; he intends to do it tonight. . . .

The carriage swayed as Il Moro climbed in, his features dark
and sinister in the dim light. His smell came to her, a faintly
perfumed masculinity. He settled himself, leaned back, and rapped
on the door. The carriage lurched off.

"I was touched by Maestro Gafori's composition," Il Moro
said. "It was entirely a surprise to me."

Beatrice hated the calm assurance of his diction, so opposed
to the frantic rhythm inside her. She sat silently, her mother's tales
of internecine treachery screeching at her like angry raptors. Now
she even wished she had accepted the invitation to go home in
Mama's carriage.

"Are you angry with me because your cousin walked out this
evening?"

"I know what you are doing."

Il Moro shifted his weight before responding. "And what is
that?"

"You intend to make yourself Duke of Milan." Beatrice suddenly felt an enormous relief, and she wondered why she had never before thought to leap into the pit and shout her challenge right in Satan's filthy, evil face.

"You are my wife . . . ," Il Moro said abstractly, as if trying out the first words of a speech that he knew needed to be rewritten. She could feel his black eyes on her, pits of unfathomable darkness against the flickering gloom. The clip-clop of the horses' hooves seemed thunderous. When he started to speak again, his tone was more familiar. "Has your cousin told you she intends for her husband to claim his majority and remove me as his regent?"

This is absurd, Beatrice thought. She could not imagine Eesh even thinking of doing that. Perhaps Il Moro's ambitions needed reining in, but as the mule pulling the wagon of state, he was essential; to remove him would be as foolish as pulling down the city walls or dismantling the Castello. And Gian had little enough interest in his titular status as Duke of Milan, much less in assuming Il Moro's burden. She attempted a haughty, ridiculing laugh, which came out cracking with fear.

"Clearly you have given thought to my ambitions," Il Moro said. "Just as evidently, you have given no thought whatsoever to your cousin's motives."

"I understand that my cousin the Duchess of Milan wishes to protect the birthright of her husband and her son."

"You are really far too clever to understand so little." He paused as if silently lamenting her shortsightedness. "I would submit to you that I care more for my nephew Gian than does anyone else in Italy, including his wife and mother. I have at least protected the Duke of Milan from his enemies, amused him, and made him rich, and I can hardly be blamed if I have not made him useful. Your cousin makes too much of claiming for Gian what Gian himself has already discarded. Perhaps she actually wants for herself the power she accuses me of coveting."

"My cousin is aware of what functions her husband does and does not wish to perform. For herself, she wishes to ensure that when her son is of age, he will be able to inherit the title that is rightfully his."

Il Moro turned so forcefully that Beatrice believed he was about to pounce on her. "Your cousin's son does not even have Sforza blood in his veins."

He will try to turn you against me, she heard Eesh say. Then she heard herself laughing out loud, a harsh sound like tinny cymbals. Suddenly she was very much afraid of him; he was clearly a madman, his allegation so preposterously self-serving that a child could see through it. She forced the laugh for a few more seconds. Then, with as much contempt as she could muster, she asked, "If you know this remarkable fact, then why not use it to get what you want? Stand up in the Duomo in front of all the nobles and ambassadors, and accuse the Duchess of this treason with which you have just slandered her." Beatrice thought to herself: They would think *I* am mad if I accused him of this slander.

"I have not used what I know to be true, because my ambition is to secure peace and prosperity throughout Italy, not, as you assume, to become Duke of Milan. Your uncle Alfonso has already threatened once before to bring his army to the gates of Milan to defend his daughter's honor. I'm sure you know of that."

An annoyingly lucid note suddenly punctuated her husband's mad melody. She remembered Mama, Bel, everybody, even Father, talking about it. Gian had not been able to consummate his marriage to Eesh for almost a year; Alfonso had demanded the return of his daughter's dowry, and there had indeed been talk of war between Milan and Naples. When Eesh's pregnancy had conveniently defused the crisis, there had been gossip about that too.

Il Moro settled back slightly, velvet and fur rustling. "I am certain that you are clever enough to see why your cousin might have been compelled to find a father for her . . . ambition."

"Get out!" Beatrice's voice was piercing, as if played at the highest register of a flute. "If you do not get out, I will get out and walk and leave you to explain why the Duchess of Bari has leapt from her carriage in the middle of the night. I would believe Judas in the mouth of Satan before I believe a single word you say! Get out!"

Il Moro rapped on the door, and the carriage groaned to a halt. He waited until the coachman opened the door, then stepped to the ground. But after a pause he stuck his head back into the compartment. The coachman standing directly behind him held a torch, and for a moment Beatrice imagined that her husband was wearing a crown of flames.

"I can understand that you do not trust me," Il Moro whispered. "But before you can presume to cast the light of truth on my lies, you really must ask your cousin who is the father of her son."

CHAPTER

25

Extract of a letter of TEODORA DEGLI ANGELI, lady-in-waiting to the Duchess of Ferrara, to ISABELLA D'ESTE DA GONZAGA, Marquesa of Mantua. Vigevano, 1 March 1493

. . . yesterday the Duke of Bari transported all of us here to Vigevano for hunting and still more *feste*. This morning our occupation was a tour of Madonna your sister's *guardaroba*, which would require until Easter if one intended to see everything! You could visit all the shops on the Via Torino in Milan, Your Highness, and not find so many goods as you would on Madonna your sister's shelves. . . .

Madonna your sister has been out of sorts in recent days, and Madame your mother is worried that all the activity is too much for her. But the Duchess of Milan, who had a far easier delivery, is showing a similar distress, and I have not seen said Duchess so much as nod to Madonna your sister in two days. Thus I am of the opinion that all the conversation concerning what honors have been paid to which child has troubled the friendship of said duchesses. . . .

Vigevano, 2 March 1493

"Eesh!" Beatrice pounded her horse's rump with her riding crop; he sensed the weakness in her hands and chopped his gait in a halfhearted attempt to throw her. When her horse did not run smoothly, she could feel the pain inside, as if the organs were still bruised from her labor. She was vaguely conscious of a tree flashing past, the new buds like little emerald ornaments. "Eesh!" she shouted again.

The chase had begun as soon as Isabella had, as usual, separated herself from the main body of the hunting party. After two days of her cousin's icy disregard, Beatrice had realized that this hunt was her best opportunity to confront Eesh and obtain what she most desperately wanted: reconciliation.

She could see Isabella's crop flailing and flecks of lather flying as her white stallion crested a grassy rise. Isabella did not look back from the high point, and her head, crowned by a green velvet cap and a single peacock feather blown back like a wind vane, quickly dipped beneath the horizon.

Beatrice rode hard to the top of the rise. Isabella waited for her in a shallow, muddy depression stitched with brilliant threads of new spring grass. She wheeled her horse about and stood her ground like an armored knight, her head high, the now-erect feather in her velvet cap emphasizing her stature.

Beatrice slowed and tried to recover. Her heart pounded recklessly, and her vision was blurred. She could hear her rasping inhalations against the mushy, sucking sound of her horse's hooves in mud. "Eesh . . ." She gulped a breath. "Eesh. I'm sorry, Eesh. I want to make everything the way it was before."

Isabella's horse jittered, and she jerked hard on his embroidered halter.

"Eesh, what do you want me to do? I will do anything, Eesh. Eesh, he is trying to say horrible things about you."

Isabella's complicated mouth twitched with possibilities. Finally she said, "Thank God for that. There isn't anyone in Italy except for your husband's fool Mariolo who believes a single word he says. If I wanted to escape the Inquisition, I would pay Il Moro to accuse me of heresy."

"I hate him, Eesh. He says you want him to resign as regent so that Gian can rule Milan."

A gamekeeper's trumpet blared. Isabella looked up at Beatrice with a wry smile. "Now I see why your husband employs so many poets. He keeps them all busy writing these fables," she said with familiar, casual flippancy. "Of course if Gian could be convinced that I actually wanted him to rule Milan in Il Moro's stead, he would ride Neptune over the mountains and we would never see him again. *Gesù.*" She shook her head in mock astonishment, then smiled at Beatrice with her characteristic, girlishly dimpled innocence.

Isabella's smiles and banter were a song in Beatrice's soul. Things would never be the way they had been before. They would be better, their friendship now so much richer and deeper. She couldn't wait to show Eesh her little boy. . . . But she knew that first they had to deal with the nemesis who haunted their friendship.

"Eesh, we have to stop him somehow. He's mad. Eesh, that isn't everything; he's saying the most awful things."

"What kind of things?" Isabella's eyes narrowed.

On the periphery of Beatrice's vision a hunting falcon hurtled into a nearby stand of trees. An instant later a hare screamed, a sound too much like a human child shrieking in pain. She knew she had to tell Eesh; it was the only way to stop her husband. "Eesh, he is trying to say that Francesco isn't Gian's son. Can you imagine?"

For a moment Isabella's face seemed as waxy and still as that of a corpse. Then she smiled, a cold, brittle animation. Beatrice remembered a gold-haloed Virgin she had once seen in a church in Naples, painted in the old Greek style, so menacing in her archaic, stylized serenity that her unintentionally wicked smile had haunted a little girl's dreams for weeks afterward.

"If anyone else but you had repeated such an obscene slander, I would have them tried and executed for treason." Isabella raised her riding crop, loudly thwacked her horse's rump, and rode off.

Through a sparkling halo of sunlight and tears, Beatrice

watched her cousin disappear over the rise. She made no attempt to follow. She focused on details—the muddy water pooled in the depressions left by the horses' hooves, a hunting falcon spiraling high in the cobalt-blue sky, anything to keep the icy needles of intuition from rushing through her veins. Oh, dear God, she pleaded. Please don't let it be true.

Isabella rode directly back to the *castello* in Vigevano. Within an hour she had her children and their nurses loaded in carriages and on the road. She left instructions for her husband, organized a small contingent of guards, and rode south along the canal to Pavia. For much of the journey she drove her relay of horses at a furious gallop, leaving her guards pressed to keep up with her.

She arrived at the *castello* at Pavia at nightfall. She paced from room to room while the permanent serving staff hurriedly lit the lamps in the sconces and set the fires. Then she ordered them out.

She continued to walk about her rooms, the sense of confinement oppressive, the cold walls chasing her from one room to the next. So many thoughts flew through her mind, a thousand screaming blackbirds released from a cage all at once. "Bitch!" they cawed. That was what it was, the bitches. What the bitches were doing to her. The bitches: Fortune; Beatrice, whom she never should have trusted; her daughter, who should have been a son. Her mother, the primordial bitch. Her mother, that helpless, desiccated bitch. The crying, the fainting, the months she would vanish to some spa in Abruzzi so that she could "rest." The way she smelled when she came back, reeking of her Milanese perfumes. No wonder her father never slept with her mother.

Suddenly the screaming birds quieted. The stillness was awesome, the sound of all the engines of fate paused and waiting. Waiting on her. That was how strong she was. How strong she was in spite of all of them.

She shouted for a servant, desperate to do the thing while the wheel waited. When the door opened she quickly gave the orders, and in only a minute the servant returned with several blank vellum sheets and her pens and ink. Isabella placed the writing materials and a lamp on a little table beside her bed. She dipped her quill into the inkwell and held her breath and waited, listening, assuring herself that the silence of destiny had not yet been disturbed. Then in that stillness she scratched the salutation in rapid strokes: "My most beloved and illustrious lord Father . . ."

Beatrice whispered to Ercole's night nurse to lie down for a while, telling her that she would sit with her baby and get the wet nurse if he awakened. She put her candle on the table in the corner and stood over the cradle in the guttering light. Ercole looked most like her sister, Bel, she decided; he would have a fair complexion and sandy hair. She marveled at the precision and delicacy of his features, so tiny yet so perfect. In a world suddenly gone mad around her, this was all the reason she needed. "I believe in you," she whispered to her sleeping son. "And you will always be able to believe in me." He puckered and smacked as if he had heard. She thought of Dante's universe, where the light of divine love turned all the spheres, each sphere acting on the one beneath it, transmitting that light like a series of lenses. Whatever God was, she imagined that all His love was now focused on her baby.

The flutter of light and shadow made her pivot in alarm. Il Moro stood behind her, his black hair like a cowl, his face indistinct. She wanted to rush out, but she was afraid to leave her baby with him.

Il Moro went to the cradle and gazed at his son with his head bowed. He said nothing for what seemed a very long time. Then he whispered, "The spheres in their grades take love from the highest and do their work below."

The quote was from Dante's *Paradiso*. The coincidence frightened Beatrice, and more than ever she wanted to leave. But she had lost her legs.

He spoke in a soft, familiar whisper. "Your cousin has decided to leave us for the *castello* at Pavia. I tried to persuade Gian to stay on here, but rather than risk offending his wife, he intends to join her in the morning."

Beatrice hadn't known that Eesh had left. She felt bitter re-sentiment toward Eesh for widening the gulf of uncertainty that now separated them. But more than that she hated her husband for being the one to tell her.

"Have you had an opportunity to pose your cousin the question I put to you?"

Beatrice felt her legs return to life. She hated him most of all for destroying this moment with her baby. She took a last lingering look at Ercole and quickly walked out into the half-darkened *guardaroba*.

Il Moro caught up to her and grabbed her arm and turned her around.

She looked with disgust at his hand. "Has Messer Ambrogio given you instructions for tonight?" she said acidly. "I have already given you the son you need. If you try to come to my bed again I will give you a knife in the ribs."

He released her arm. "If you have asked your cousin the pertinent question, then you must know the truth—"

"I know that you are the most expert liar in Christendom." It isn't true, Beatrice angrily argued to her own gaping doubt. What I read in Eesh's face was not a confession. . . . "Tell me the name of the father."

"I have no desire to place the father in jeopardy, any more than I wish to threaten the peace by revealing the Duchess of Milan's treason."

His response startled her viscerally, like the sudden kick of a baby in the womb. If he were lying, she realized, he would blithely offer to produce his proof. "Then why tell me?" she asked, but just as quickly she answered her question. "I see." She nodded to signal her understanding. "But you have wasted this secret of yours. Because even if the Duchess of Milan's child was fathered by a savage from Guinea, I will never help you become Duke of Milan."

"You are such a passionate student of my ambition. Have your studies revealed a reason why I would want to make myself Duke of Milan?"

She realized that she had never gone beyond the simple conclusion that he wanted it because he wanted it, that he merely hoped to add the Duke of Milan's scepter to the rest of the baubles in his treasure vault. It infuriated her that in all her imaginary rehearsals of this confrontation, she had overlooked this essential point.

He turned away from her, his position altering the pitch of his voice in a way she'd never heard before. "You come from a family that has ruled in Ferrara for two hundred years. My father's father was born in a tiny village in the Romagna and on the day he died could not sign his own name. He was a shoemaker's apprentice who became the greatest *condottiere* of his time. He was christened Muzio Attendolo, but his strength, his *sforza*, gave our family its name. He fought in hundreds of battles, but he never forgot his humanity. He drowned trying to pull his page, a mere boy, from a flooded river.

"My father, who fought for the first time when he was twelve, was twenty-three years old when his father died and he took over his troops. He was everything his father was and much more. A legend more than a man. He never wore a helmet in battle, and they say that often when the soldiers who opposed him saw his face they gave up and laid down their weapons. He fought for most of his life. He was almost fifty years old when he fought to make himself Duke of Milan, and he fought for years after that against the Venetians to keep his state. In spite of all that, he had the wisdom to build. Castles, churches, Milan's first charity hospital. He hired the architect Filarete, one of the greatest minds of his generation. Half of what you see in Milan my father built."

When Il Moro spoke of his father his cadence had quickened to a crescendo of controlled passion, perhaps a subtle vehemence. Now his voice fell again. "I was my father's fourth son. I never expected to succeed him. But I never expected so much of what happened after my father died." An undertone of regret inflected this last statement, as simple and sad as a mourner's sob against the elaborate polyphony of a Requiem. "I never tried to be the warrior my father was, and even trying mightily I will never be half the man he was, even in those qualities that have nothing to do with war. But I will build this edifice of state my father has left us higher than even he could have dreamed, if only because of the strength of the foundation he erected. And I pray that our son will build higher still and see further than I ever dreamed."

He turned, his shoulders slumped like a brickmason's at the end of the day. "I am not a bad man, *cara sposa*. Perhaps, as you think, I am also not a terribly good man, but I am endeavoring to do good works, to make Milan prosper so that all of our people will prosper. I live in a world of men who do not respect good works nearly so much as they respect the capacity to reduce those works to dust. Men like your uncle Alfonso. The King of France and the Duke of Orleans. Ask your mother about the good works of the Signory of Venice. And as long as my nephew is Duke of Milan, we will be hostage to the intrigues of Naples and France and at the mercy of the Signory's whim. All Europe protests the danger of my ambition. But who protests the danger to Milan of a drunken, simple boy, the pawn of a dishonest wife who would escort her father's army to the gates of Milan to further her ambition? And even if you assume the best of Gian's wife, what of his vicious, idiot mother, who all but openly begs the French to deliver her son from the oppression of Il Moro?"

It was not his words that affected her but the timbre in which he recited them. The most expert liar in Christendom actually believed these things. Or was this in fact just part of his intricate game, a game in which all his previous lies had been presented as lies, so that the final, climactic lie could be disguised as truth?

"So you do intend to do it," she said. "Make yourself Duke of Milan."

He looked down and pulled at his ring. "I don't know," he answered, his diction weary, even slightly slurred. "And even if I could be certain that I want it, I am not certain that I could do it."

She was astounded that her husband had ever in his life doubted anything at all. The opacity that had always shielded him seemed to shimmer, giving a translucent glimpse of whatever lay beneath the hard casing of his soul.

But when he looked up, that brief opening might never have existed, an illusion of the uncertain light. "I have told you what I wanted you to know," he said with renewed assurance. "So good night, my wife." He bowed, turned, and stepped into the shadows.

· PART ·

FIVE

C H A P T E R

26

Naples, 28 March 1493

"We should summon all of the ambassadors and allow them to examine it." Alfonso, Duke of Calabria, sat on his huge, nervous war-horse, his own legs and torso so powerfully fleshed that he appeared to be part of the beast, a brutish centaur.

Ferrante of Aragon, the King of Naples, with one pudgy finger languidly stroked the breast of the hooded falcon perched on his wrist. "Where is the letter now?" he asked his son, edging him farther away from the brightly colored train of musicians and men-at-arms—already hovering at a respectful distance—who had accompanied them on their inspection of the city walls.

Alfonso looked up at a massive arch of new-cut stone wedged in between two enormous turrets, the most seaward gate of Naples's just-completed eastern wall. A team of stonemasons, perched on a large scaffold, struggled to install a marble decorative panel, still under canvas wrap, on the flat expanse of wall rising above the archway. Ferrante's eyes narrowed to glassy green slivers while his son leisurely observed the workmen. Finally Alfonso answered vaguely, "I have it locked away."

Ferrante released a bemused exhalation from his pinched nostrils, ridiculously small vents for his bloated face. "Good. I insist you keep it secured. When we have a better notion of what the French intend to do, we can discuss what use we may have for it."

With almost no discernible action of either his silver spurs or the gold-embroidered reins clutched in his beefy hands, Alfonso backed his horse beside his father's. His bulging neck, squeezed out of his high brocade collar, muscled his blockish head around. He looked Ferrante directly in the eyes. "When Il Moro brings Venice into his anti-French league, our opportunity will be gone. If we use the letter now as justification for a blockade of Genoa, the Signory of Venice will stay out of it. What the Signory fear most is that they and the rest of the Venetian nobility will be taxed to pay for a military undertaking. That is the critical failing, among many, of the republican form of government. It is ludicrous to assume that men will levy taxes on themselves."

Ferrante continued to stroke the falcon's breast, the action more repetitive now. "We do not even know if the allegations made by your daughter are supportable. You have encouraged her to find injury if Il Moro doesn't provide an escort of five hundred knights and hang silk awnings over the streets every time her husband and child ride to the Duomo. If your daughter's husband were more familiar to the people of Milan than to the boars and stags of Pavia, perhaps he would have more occasion to receive their acclaim. That *uccelliaccio* Gian Galeazzo cannot find his *cazzo* to piss with, much less wave it in Il Moro's face."

"My daughter has endured these indignities and worse for years without a protest. Any other duchess in Italy would have been shouting curses from her window like a Roman whore. Because she has kept her silence until now, the ambassadors will believe her claims. Which is why they must see the letter." Alfonso's squinty, heavy eyelids closed to menacing slits. "This is not a question of my daughter's honor regardless. It is an outrage against *our* blood."

"Yes. If we use the letter against Il Moro, the ambassadors will no doubt believe it, and Il Moro's new league will collapse. Isolated, his port of Genoa blockaded, he will make an easy prey for the French army. Do not forget that the French may be close to settling with the Germans, and that Louis Duc d'Orleans can reach the French King's ear even more easily than can that *impicatto* the Prince of Salerno. And then, having taken Milan, the French will not even have to borrow from Il Moro's treasury to finance their march south against us. But consider this: We continue to allow Il Moro and the Signory of Venice to sniff each other's assholes like dogs. The Venetians will agree that the French must be kept from crossing the mountains, thus sparing us that concern. But the Signory will never support any attempt by Il Moro to make himself Duke of Milan, also sparing us that concern." Suddenly Ferrante turned from his hooded falcon, his eyes as brilliant as the gems on his fat fingers. "We will be free to devote our treasury to defeating the most dangerous man in Europe, this Borgia Pope Il Moro has created. And when we invade Rome, then we will be able to use your daughter's letter to prevent Il Moro from rescuing the whore's afterbirth he has placed on the papal throne." Ferrante's face colored almost instantly, as if a purple pane of glass had been placed between him and the sun. He spoke through clenched teeth, his puffy jowls trembling. "I intend to embalm Rodrigo Borgia's corpse and bring it back to Naples. I want to stand him up in my bedroom and make him watch while his daughter sucks my *cazzo*."

Alfonso registered his amusement with a light heaving of his shoulders. "Well, His Holiness has already seen his daughter's head between his own legs."

Apparently contemplating his father's plan, Alfonso observed the stoneworkers for a moment, then turned and looked down the long expanse of wall to his right. A hundred paces away, some crude shelters of dried brush leaned against the immense stone wall, most likely erected by impoverished peasants hoping to beg from travelers entering the city. With a flurry of curses, Alfonso dispatched his men-at-arms, who galloped into the midst of the improvised dwellings and within a few seconds reduced them to the makings of a small bonfire. Out of the cloud of dust darted a few small, shrieking figures, so brown that they appeared to be frightened monkeys. Only after they had paused in their flight, standing unsteadily and bawling hysterically, could they be identified as scrawny, filthy, naked children.

Alfonso had already turned back to Ferrante. His white teeth gleamed. "When we embalm the Borgia Pope, we must be certain that his *cazzo* is still stiff enough for all the whores in Hell. Then I intend to bring Il Moro down here and stick his Pope's dead prick up his ass."

C H A P T E R

27

Extract of a letter of LEONARDO DA VINCI, engineer at the Court of Milan, to international traveler and raconteur BENEDETTO DEI. Milan, 4 April 1493

. . . that the Duchess of Bari survived has merely served to elevate the prestige of the magician Ambrogio da Rosate, to the result that divers officers of the court have mortgaged their health to every itinerant necromancer and alchemist who endeavors to relieve their purses. . . . Physicians are destroyers of life, my dear Benedetto, their remedies a plague that will ever be in want of a cure. . . .

. . . the ladies of her court, whose wantonness would bring scandal to a brothel, insist that the Duchess of Bari has refused her husband her bed since the birth of their child. I can reliably report that the Duchess of Bari does not accompany her husband on his inspections of the projects with which we are currently proceeding. But said Duchess has taken an interest in these endeavors for her own illumination and often sallies forth in the company of our friend Messer Galeazzo di Sanseverino for the purpose of giving consideration to our labors. Yesterday I was deputed to ride with them along the new canals we have built near

Val Seria, where they observed our success in allowing the cultivation of all varieties of grain, as well as rice and mulberry for silk production, this in land formerly as arid as a desert, said improvements by virtue of the many sluices and irrigation devices we have engineered. The Duchess of Bari asked innumerable questions of this work, and I was pleased to answer her, as she has a capable intellect and does not make noisome refrains of the most elementary inquiries. She has now made the acquaintance of a number of learned men here, and most are well pleased with her attentions and expectant that she will take notice of works of true merit and assist in their advancement at court, though of course the mediocrities are already grumbling. . . . Of the Duke and Duchess of Milan there is no word at all, for they have confined themselves to Pavia, where the Duke can find a readier abundance of wild game, his ardent and sole pursuit. . . .

Extract of a letter of ISABELLA D'ESTE DA GONZAGA, Marquesa of Mantua, to FRANCESCO GONZAGA, Marquis of Mantua and Captain General of the Armies of Venice. Mantua, 9 April 1493

My most illustrious lord husband,

Mama has written me that Il Moro and my sister have agreed to visit Ferrara in May, and she has presented me with the list of the company who are to attend them, which list I enclose for your inspection (though I had to find an extra ducat to pay the courier!). Can you believe it? I for my part cannot! I could pawn everything we own and still have neither half as many ladies in my suite nor half as many jewels on their persons, and I have no doubt that my sister can attire each of her ladies in a gown of cloth more costly than I myself can afford to wear. Would to God that we had their money, since we know so well how to spend it!

. . . Mama is going to Venice afterward, but she already has assured me that she will stay at Father's *palazzo* on the Grand Canal and will not require you to entertain her with any great ceremony! The ambassadors in Il Moro's company will also go on to Venice to confirm the new league, but Mama cannot persuade my sister to accompany her, which I consider a blessing since Venice would no doubt sink into the sea from the weight of my sister's retinue. . . .

Extract of a letter of ISABELLA D'ESTE DA GONZAGA to FRANCESCO GONZAGA. Mantua, 22 April 1493

. . . Can you believe it! Mama says that the league with Venice is of such pressing importance that Beatrice simply must represent her husband at the confirmation. Though I concur with Mama in her estimation of the importance of this league, I am simply undone at the thought of subjecting myself and my ladies to the endless comparisons that will no doubt be occasioned by the extravagance of Beatrice's retinue and the modesty of my suite. Nothing on earth can now persuade me to go to Venice at the same time as my sister! If Beatrice and Mama do not change their plans, I shall change mine. . . .

Decoded secret dispatch of COUNT CARLO BELGIOIOSO, Milanese ambassador to France, to LODOVICO SFORZA, "Il Moro," Duke of Bari and regent for the Duke of Milan. Original encrypted and marked "*cito! cito!*" (urgent! urgent!). Amboise, 27 April 1493

[Your] Highness: C. [King Charles is going] to Senlis to settle treaty with M. [Archduke Maximilian]—[there is] every expectation that agreement will be reached. C. talks of nothing but crossing mountains now. O. [Louis Duc d'Orléans] campaigning furiously for Milan as first objective. Situation could not be more dangerous [for us]. [I am going] To Senlis w/C.—will try to exert influence w/Germans to deter O. [My] Opinion [is] that French do not expect Venice to keep faith w/us. Opinion that we must immediately make offer required to bring M. to our side. —B.

C H A P T E R

28

Near Vigevano, 1 May 1493

Galeazzo di Sanseverino stood in his stirrups. His velvet cap grazed the leafy boughs shading the canalside horse path. "What is that?" he asked. A sound drifted across the plush green fields of grain. Perhaps it was a natural chorus, a distant swarm of locusts pursued by a flock of voracious birds.

"*Cacarelle*," Beatrice replied. The noxious buzzing always reminded her of her wedding night. "Also Jew's harp, drums, and at least two lutes."

Galeazz doffed his cap in comic homage to Beatrice's extraordinary ear. "A country band. Of course. It is May Day. One forgets because in Milan May Day is regarded as a country *festa* suited only for sweaty rustics."

"In Ferrara everyone gathered the May branches." May Day had been her favorite *festa*, and that she hardly remembered it this year gave her a pang of regret, though she also quickly noted with satisfaction how far behind she had left her unempowered girlhood. She decided to bring some branches home for Ercole and vowed that next year she would at least take him riding in the ducal park.

Galeazz pointed to a church spire some distance across the

248

irrigated fields, a centuries-old rectangular tower with a simple tile roof, the venerable Lombard design ubiquitous throughout the countryside surrounding Milan. "Why don't we attend their *festa?*"

"Yes!" Then Beatrice looked around with dismay at her two-dozen-strong contingent of men-at-arms and engineers. "We will spoil it as soon as the villagers see who we are."

"Then the two of us will attend *en masque.*" Galeazz began to unbutton his flashy brocade doublet. "You will have to remove your jewelry, and we will exchange saddle cloths with two of the men-at-arms. They will think I am a middling merchant who has spent too much on his wife's gown."

"You don't think someone will still recognize you?" Galeazz was a head taller than the average man and had won a half-dozen jousting tournaments in northern Italy, all of them attended by tens of thousands of spectators.

"They have always seen me in armor. To them Galeazzo di Sanseverino is twice the man I am and has an iron head."

Galeazz and Beatrice completed their preparations and sent their escort back to Vigevano. They headed off at a right angle to the canal, riding beside one of the main irrigation conduits. Hedges, rows of trees, and the grassy ridges of the irrigation ditches neatly squared the boundaries of the fields. Only once did they cross a natural stream, bordered with trees, its bed thick with cattails and vines. Periodically they saw in the distance prosperous farmhouses with colonnaded porches and brick stables stocked with hay; each farm's obligatory vineyard could be identified by the bristly rows of dead saplings used to train the vines. More frequently they passed the well-kept cottages of tenant farmers, with their raucous poultry yards and precise little herb gardens.

Eventually their path intersected a rutted dirt road lined with cypresses. The music blared. They passed a peasant in a wine-stained smock shuffling almost unconsciously down the road; he attempted to tip his hat to the travelers, realized that he didn't have a hat, and began furiously to curse some imaginary companion.

The village consisted of the church and a few shops arranged around a tiny piazza. A crowd of several hundred people, so dense and antic that it appeared to be engaged in pulling down the little cluster of buildings, packed the road, the piazza, and the shop arcades. Many were tenant farmers in their best colored hose and dyed wool tunics; the owners of the larger farms wore silk or damask doublets and tooled leather shoes. Gamblers, fortune-tellers, and traveling musicians worked the crowd, their gaudy multicolored hose and short jackets adding a rakish accent. The *vecchie* wore conservative wool dresses and old-fashioned white aprons, but many of the younger women were dressed like middle-rank Milanese prostitutes, with plunging damask bodices and cheap jewelry; most had put aside the ceremonial, newly cut May sprigs in favor of wineskins and flasks filled from the barrels set up around the piazza.

The new arrivals were welcomed by bellowing vendors offering spitted capons and pigeons, pastries arrayed on tables, melon slices, cheeses, pickled eels, baked trout, a healing oil said to cure burns and relieve gastric distress, and an aphrodisiac made of sparrows' brains. The wine had proved to be the most effective aphrodisiac, however. Young men and women, their faces wearing the brilliant flush of advanced inebriation, clutched one another so shamelessly that they might have been in bed with the lamps out instead of standing in a public square.

The farm boys openly eyed Beatrice as she walked among them, and she found their frank, besotted appraisal an appealing contrast to the sexual stealth practiced in Milan. She watched a rustically handsome young man wearing ridiculous, curled-toe French-style slippers wriggle his hand into the bodice of a big-boned girl about her own age, and she felt no surprise or shame at the stirring inside her. Ever since Beatrice had come under the sway of her older sister's adolescent sexuality at age twelve, her girl's dreams of romance had included increasingly graphic images of raw passion. And while marriage had destroyed that and every other aspect of her romantic yearnings, motherhood (and of course her liberation from Messer Ambrogio's schedule) had somehow relit the lamp of desire. She had a child and all that meant to her, yet her love for her baby made her acutely aware that something was still missing. She wanted a man. Someone to hold *her*. The love of a man would make her love for her baby complete.

Galeazz bought Beatrice a flask of wine, and soon she was buoyant in the late afternoon heat. Local dignitaries shouted speeches against the increasing din of the celebration. Most of the speakers began by toasting Il Moro as the architect of local prosperity and, having no need to observe the protocol of court, said nothing about the Duke of Milan. Beatrice observed this with far less surprise or chagrin than she would have felt only a few months previously. When she had first started visiting the various engineering and agricultural projects—usually in the company of Galeazz—she had imagined that she would expose the meagerness of the "good works" her husband had claimed to be so intent on accomplishing. But instead she had exposed her own ignorance of the vast transformation in the countryside around Milan, the irrigation and canal projects and the revitalization of scores of towns and villages—things she had never seen while riding in the ducal parks with Eesh.

When the speeches ended, the makeshift band attempted to construct a fast-paced dance at about the tempo of a *moresca*. Three professional lute players bravely established the melody, their practiced notes challenged by the flailing beat of a one-armed drummer and a corps of local boys with their *cacarelle*. The awful hum of the *cacarella* was produced by drawing a string through a hide membrane stretched over a pot, and the boys' arms jerked up and down frantically, as if they were trying to pound a harmony into their noisemakers.

Beatrice brought Galeazz into the whirling circle of dancers and found the thread of rhythm in the band's cacophony. She felt light and airy in a way she never had under her dance master's baton at home, suddenly free of heavy girlish legs and inhibitions. Her polished style soon drew attention, and for a while she captivated the crowd; they gathered around her, murmuring "*Che bellezza*" and exclaiming, "She dances like a goddess!" Eventually her worshipers were distracted by a particularly spirited slugfest between two young men. But by then, Beatrice had accepted what she never would have permitted herself to believe as a girl. I *am* beautiful. Especially when I dance.

Not so beautiful as Galeazz. She clutched his powerful, graceful hand and thought: If only he didn't belong to Bianca, whom I can never betray . . . Would she really risk it? She remembered one of the most vivid experiences of her childhood. Her father's father, Niccolò, who had died almost a half century before she was born, had sired so many bastards that he had inspired a local ditty: "*Di qua e di la del Po, tutti figli di Niccolò*"—On this and that side of the river Po, all are the children of Niccolò. As an old man, Niccolò had taken a young second wife, who had been more attracted to Niccolò's eldest son. Betrayed by a lady-in-waiting, the lovers had been confronted and condemned to a last night in the dungeon of the Este *castello;* the next morning a weeping Niccolò had manfully enforced his double standard and watched while his wife and his heir had their heads chopped off. One night Beatrice and her sister had gone down to the dungeon, then no longer in use; legend had it that if they were very quiet, they could still hear the doomed lovers' tears and whispers as they waited for that last dawn. Beatrice and her sister had stood there in the darkness, hands tightly clasped, trying not to disturb the baleful silence with even the sound of their own breathing. After a while they heard a hiss like distant surf. The ghostly whispers became sighs, racing in cold spirit gasps through the eerily animate shadows, and when she and Bel couldn't stand it any longer, they had run screaming out of love's dark underworld. . . . What about Eesh? Had Eesh really slept with someone else? If she had, Beatrice envied her.

Beatrice paused to empty half a flask of wine. Then she rejoined the whirling, chaotic dance, the colors softening in the dimming evening light, until motion itself seemed to become a pale golden hue. Free, she thought, freer than I ever have been. I have learned more in the past two months than I did in all my old life. She saw her baby's face, his first toothless smiles, just as she did a hundred times every day she was away from him. My baby is the center. But around him everything else whirled.

Eesh. Why hadn't she just gone to Pavia and settled with Eesh? Perhaps because she was afraid she would prove what she suspected in the depths of her soul, that she didn't really know Eesh any better than she did her husband, that just as her husband was capable of good works—if only to serve his own vanity and pride—Eesh was capable of the most terrible lies and deception. For a dizzying instant she could see Eesh and her husband spinning around her like a ring of dancers, proclaiming their own virtues, shouting their mutual accusations.

Eesh or her husband. Was that a choice she would one day have to make, to find the truth in their shouting circle of lies? Not

today. Today she could not choose, did not need to choose, because in her new world of spinning possibilities, truth was a blur.
A lover perhaps, a deception of her own. She swished her dress
and pirouetted in the twilight, the speed of her movement mul-
tiplied by the revolving circle of dancers, and imagined herself a
spinning star rushing through the heavens on the orbit of Fortune's
wheel.

CHAPTER

29

Naples, 14 May 1493

The two men found slight handholds in the joints between the huge gray stones at the seaward base of the Castel Nuovo. They looked back across the Bay of Naples, an inky void curtained by a fabric of stars. Surges of dark water slapped against the stone, lifting the men's bodies and forcing them to expend energy simply to rest. Strong swimmers, they had entered the water more than an hour previously, dropped from a tiny rowboat far out in the bay.

The swimmers turned their attention to the steeply angled stone face extending another ten arm-spans above them. The entire seafront of the enormous fortress-palace was surrounded by this skirt of stone. Above it the Castel Nuovo's towering facade rose to command a panoramic view of the Bay of Naples. Just past the line where the slope of the stone skirt merged with the sheer, vertical facade was a single small window, barred and shuttered.

"Now we'll find out what our gold has bought," one of the men whispered. "If that window isn't open . . ."

"It will be open," the other replied. "If we have been betrayed they will be waiting for us."

Both men fell silent, contemplating in the dark the certainty of prolonged torture and death if they were discovered. In tandem they cinched the knives strapped around their bare waists; they had made the swim in their breeches. Finally the first man whispered again. "Our father's soul will never know peace until we have done this."

They began slowly to make their way up the steep incline, finding precarious perches for fingers and toes on the slight ridges created by massive stones cut only slightly less than perfectly. The two men were brothers, one twenty-two, the other nineteen, the sons of one of the Neapolitan noblemen who had vanished on the night of Ferrante's infamous reconciliation banquet. The two young men did not need rumors of the Christmas Day massacre to incite their courage. Their mother had also been taken prisoner at Ferrante's banquet, and had later been released—raped, tortured, a sobbing corpse. All of the family's property and lands had been confiscated and the surviving members banished. Like many of the exiles who had not fled to France, these two young men had disappeared into the rugged countryside of southern Italy. What little of their jewels and gold they had been able to take with them had been spent buying spies and informants inside the Castel Nuovo. Their acquisitions included one of the Duke of Calabria's secretaries, who had informed them—for a staggering price—of the prize they had come to claim tonight.

The shutters had been unlatched. The brothers crossed themselves. The elder brother, who was called Giovann by his friends and family, slipped through the bars, pausing to survey what he could of the room. The metal of small firearms and pikes glimmered in the faint illumination from the starlight outside. Giovann dropped to the floor and waited. A moment later his brother's bare feet slapped the wooden floor beside him.

The opening to the passageway within the walls was where they had been told it would be. After prying the wood panel away, Giovann again went in first. The blackness was so complete that it seemed to have density, making the dank air even more difficult to breathe. Crouching, his head grazing the low stone ceiling and his elbows rubbing against the slimy walls, Giovann imagined encountering a dead end and returning to find the entrance bricked up. He wondered how many days he and his brother would live, scratching the walls like trapped rodents.

They had been told that the passageway would end at a large *guardaroba*. After spending some time forcing another panel, Giovann crawled into the storeroom. Still on his knees, he looked up, felt fear like a cold hand stroking his back, and tried to muffle his involuntary cry. The eyes, closely set and lit red by some faint, indirect light, floated just in front of his face, then flashed as he reached for his knife. His scalp seared and his cheek itched. Not until he felt the weight against him did Giovann realize that his assailant was not human, and only then did he vaguely remember something about leopards used to deter theft and control the rat population in Alfonso's *guardaroba*. He somehow got his knife free and frantically pounded it a half-dozen times into the supple, frighteningly powerful body. The leopard howled and stilled. Giovann scrambled up, his face and back fired with pain, his brother pushing behind him. The doorway exploded with light.

His brother collided with the first guard and sent the blazing wax taper flying against the wall. The second guard also carried a torch, and Giovann leapt at him and pounded his knife into his stomach. The guard called out *"Gesù! Gesù!"* and Giovann had to silence him with a slash across the windpipe. Then he wheeled on the guard struggling with his brother and savagely plunged the knife into his back. A deep groan followed, and the guard collapsed.

The only sound was the hissing and gurgling from the guard's severed windpipe. Giovann picked up a still-burning torch and went to help his sibling. As soon as the light revealed his brother's eyes, Giovann knew that he would leave the Castel Nuovo alone.

His brother pressed bloody fingers against the glistening bowels bulging from the slash across his abdomen. He shook his head. "I am a dead man," he said almost in wonder. "Sweet Jesus will take me out of here tonight."

Giovann stood motionless, holding the torch in one hand, his knife in the other.

"Get it," his brother whispered desperately. "Get it and go!"

Giovann knelt and tenderly kissed his brother, then pressed the knife to his throat.

His brother answered the implied question with a rapid nod. "For Mother and Father and Je—" He shuddered at the quick movement of the knife across his neck. Blood surged over his collarbone. He looked into Giovann's eyes and weakly smiled. He would not be alive when Alfonso's guards found him.

Giovann entered the adjacent *guardaroba*. He heard a shout from somewhere, seemingly far away. The *guardaroba* was a treasure trove that might have held his wonder for hours in different circumstances; he had glimpses of majolica vases and gold statues and stacks of diamond-studded dog collars. He was looking only for the silver box. Where was it? Gilded candlesticks shaped like satyrs. A set of niello-handled knives. Serving trays painted with lifelike little scenes. There. Four silver boxes, all of them floridly engraved. Two were too small to hold letters. The other two, large enough to contain small documents, were identical. A glimpse of nudes engraved on the lid of one. No time to look through them and find what he had come for. Take them both.

He clutched the boxes awkwardly under one arm, remembering that his brother still had the small waterproof pouch, briefly cursing himself for not bringing a larger pouch for this contingency.

Now the shouts came from the next room. Giovann hesitated. Then he ran directly toward the voices. The guards were taken entirely by surprise, and he bulled past them.

A long hallway with a window at one end. Shutters partially open. Running, the sound of his own bare feet pounding stone, the sound of leather soles slapping behind him. If the window opened onto the interior courtyard he was dead. He flung the shutter aside, climbed onto the ledge, gathered for the leap necessary to clear the stone skirting of the facade, then flew into the abyss. The rushing stars were brilliant and precise, as if he were moving through the heavens at exactly their speed.

When he hit he had a dreadful instant of thinking that he had leapt into the interior court. But water surged into his nostrils and his limbs began to uncoil against his yielding, liquid salvation. He came to the surface, gulped air, then began to swim underwater.

The salt water in his wounds was like burning oil. He continued to swim underwater, surfacing for air a dozen times before he paused and looked back at the Castel Nuovo. Some of the windows glowed with lights, and torches moved along the long concrete mole jutting into the harbor. But he knew they could send out a dozen boats and have little chance of finding him now. Only then did he realize that he had lost one of the silver boxes.

Trying to hold the remaining slippery prize out of the water, Giovann swam on, his mind juggling a hundred things. Images of his broken mother and his disemboweled brother, an effort to remember the last time he had seen his father, the beginnings of an observation about Fortune choosing among pairs: his brother was dead; he had lived; one silver box lay at the bottom of the Bay of Naples. Giovann treaded water and looked back again at the lit-up seaside facade of the Castel Nuovo, wondering if the silver box he still held contained the letter that would bring down the house of Aragon.

C H A P T E R

30

Extract of a letter of ELEONORA D'ESTE, Duchess of Ferrara, to ISABELLA D'ESTE DA GONZAGA, Marquesa of Mantua. Ferrara, 19 May 1493

. . . Your sister and her consort were greeted with shouts of "Moro! Moro!" which surprised me coming from our own people, but such is his popularity throughout Italy today. . . . Your sister wore a *camora* of crimson brocade embroidered in gold with that motif of the lighthouse tower at Genoa, which I know you girls regard as the latest *nove foze*. . . . Your sister looks exceptionally well, and her bearing and grace, which are so much improved, made me so proud that I fear I will have to confess! I truly feel that even though you and Beatrice no longer live under the same roof, it is those years with you as her model that have enabled her to acquire her present dignity and charm. . . . You would not believe the jewels and gowns your sister's ladies have been provided for their appearance in Venice. So as not to have my ladies come off second best, I have given all of them pearl rosaries and new *camore* of green *velluto allucciolato* contrasted with stripes of black satin. I am holding in reserve a quantity of jeweled pendants and brooches for my ladies, in the event that your sister is inspired

259

to provide her ladies with additional embellishments when she sees what I have done. . . . Your father has arranged a continuous week of entertainments, including three days of jousting and three nights of theatricals, innumerable *feste*, and a horse race, which your brother has entered. Today, however, will be a day of relaxation for your sister and her consort, as they have gone alone to the Palazzo Schifanoia, which Beatrice has always loved so. . . .

Ferrara, 20 May 1493

Standing in the main hall of the Palazzo Schifanoia, Beatrice remembered another homecoming, seven years earlier. Compared to the colossal Castel Nuovo in Naples, with its magical vistas of sapphire-blue sea and the vast, flowered city climbing the hills behind it, the Este *castello* in Ferrara had seemed a cramped medieval fortress looking out on a flat, colorless town and a malarial park only recently reclaimed from a swamp. But the Schifanoia, her family's pleasure house (the name meant "without cares") set among the cool woods just east of the city, had given her a different sense of her curiously alien heritage. As a ten-year-old she had wandered these sleek *all'antica* rooms filled with Roman statuary and French tapestries, and even then she had been impressed by the intangible sense of assurance the Palazzo Schifanoia had conveyed, a feeling of centuries of refinement rather than the house of Aragon's few frenetic decades of ostentation.

At that first homecoming nothing had impressed her like this main hall, called Salone dei Mesi, the Salon of the Months. It was named for the magnificent fresco cycle that entirely covered the walls, a breathtakingly illusionistic pageant of mythology, courtly extravagance, and everyday life, unfolding on an imaginary landscape of fantastically shaped hills, fairy castles, and ancient Roman ruins. Each month was represented by a god or goddess parading in triumphal procession through scenes of the season's labors and diversions. March's Minerva, her chariot drawn by white unicorns, presided over pruning farmers and a ducal hunting party charging through the countryside, teams of dogs yapping at the feet of the horses; rose-crowned Venus, seated on a floating throne drawn by swans, watched over an April garden party where trysting lovers were serenaded by musicians. As a girl, Beatrice had at first been embarrassed and later intrigued by the explicit eroticism of so many of the scenes: the Three Graces, entirely nude, in poses more prurient than classical; couples kissing and groping in the garden; and the culminating image of a man and woman embracing in bed, their clothes tossed on the floor in the disarray of hasty passion. She remembered how her sister had told her in rapt detail what was going on beneath the sheets.

Now she found the painted figures somewhat stiff and wooden compared to Leonardo's or even Bergognone's, the fashions quaintly out-of-date. But the rest was still vividly sensual. She glanced at Il Moro. He stood a few paces away, gravely studying the month of September, with its mythological vignette of one-eyed Cyclops forging armor on Vulcan's anvil. She wondered if he ever fantasized about someone, perhaps Cecilia, ever clutched a pillow in his arms and pretended it was his lover.

She did not think about him making love to her. Since their exchange in the *guardaroba* at Vigevano, he had conducted himself as if he took seriously her threat to welcome him with a knife in the ribs the next time he tried to visit her bedroom. His respect had made her less defensive, and she had found that she could relax around him, even tease and joke with him during their occasional suppers together. It was still remarkable to her how much easier it was to be the mother of Il Moro's son rather than simply to be Il Moro's wife.

But this excursion had threatened their fragile rapprochement; in Milan they could largely avoid one another, but here they were expected to function as a couple most of the time. So far there had been no friction, and they'd even had some lively conversations about literature, various people at court, and several of the engineering projects Beatrice had visited. She only hoped the truce would last until she left for Venice.

"Copiosità," Il Moro said, admiring the sheer abundance of the frescoed imagery. *"Grandezza."* He turned to Beatrice. "Shall we take a look at the garden before the mosquitoes come out?"

"The mosquitoes aren't so bad here at Schifanoia." For some reason the idea of visiting the garden gave her a sense of foreboding, but the reason was so indefinable that she swept it aside.

He offered her his arm as they descended the stairs. The gardens were behind the *palazzo*, several immaculately groomed acres of fruit trees, vine-covered pergolas, marble statues, and terraced flower beds laced with geometric gravel paths.

Everything appeared unchanged. They wandered by the small zoo, and Beatrice greeted the tiger and giraffe like old friends. They went inside the aviary, a pavilion of fine copper-wire netting erected over several towering trees. Beatrice immediately recognized the big African parrot, Almanzor, and called to him and tried to get him to say her name. It saddened her that he didn't remember. She saw a sulfurous flash of yellow but couldn't be certain if it was her pet canary, Gia, in whom she had confided so much. She had even thought of taking Gia to Milan, but how could she have expected him to be happy where she wasn't welcome?

"Beatrice!" belatedly squawked the parrot. Beatrice applauded gratefully. She decided that she would come back with her little boy to look for Gia.

They left the aviary and walked among the orderly gravel paths. Some things *had* changed: a grove of newly planted orange trees where there had once been beds of purple irises; a pair of new topiaries shaped like swans. But the rosebushes were exactly as she had left them. Gnarled and knobbed from decades of pruning, they wore blooms of a creamy, slightly pinkish white or a crimson so deep and rich that it turned dewdrops into little rubies. She had always admired these bushes, ancient and scarred yet perpetually the source of such exquisite new beauty.

Her anger came with astonishing suddenness and violence, as though in one beat her heart had pumped venom through her entire body. "I hated you so much," she said fiercely.

Il Moro looked at her, blinking rapidly with surprise.

She knew she had to say it all now, that the words would come as inevitably as blood from a wound. "When I came home from Naples it wasn't because Mama wanted me home but because I was already betrothed to you and it was time for me to prepare to become your bride. I used to walk in this garden and dream of you, that you were a gallant knight like the heroes of my books, on bended knee pleading for my perfumed glove to hold to your breast. I sat beneath that pergola and cried until my eyes were swollen shut the first time you postponed the wedding. The second time, I cut a rose from this bush and left my blood in exchange, a token of my wounded heart, certain that my knight would never come."

Beatrice paused, her mouth pinched with anger and her hands quaking. "We were here at Schifanoia that summer night you sent your emissary to withdraw the contract. Father's face: I will never forget my father's face. The next morning I could not bear even this garden. I walked on the paths by the Po and thought I would throw myself into the river. I thought my father was angry with *me* and that only by dying could I spare my family further humiliation." She paused again and stared into the past. "I came here the day before I finally left to come and live with you. There was snow on the ground, and they had to light fires to keep the birds and animals from dying. I told my canary, Gia, how much I hated you. It was all so foolish. Because here in this garden I never dreamed how much I would really come to hate you."

She had no more words. The pain was gone, the venom flushed from her limbs. She felt a strange exhilaration, like rushing along in a whistling wind.

"Do you think I didn't hate you?" Il Moro asked smoothly but with a strange, coldly squeaking undertone. A tic began beneath his right eye. "I loved Cecilia Gallerani more than I can believe I will ever again love a woman. Not the love you imagine from picture books and French romances, but a love that is nurtured and rooted so deeply in the soul that when it is removed everything is ripped out with it. When you took Cecilia away from me I mourned as I have not mourned since my mother died—". He broke off as if his final words had been some accidental, self-annihilating incantation. But then he dully repeated, "My mother . . ." before trailing off again. Now his eyes conveyed something unmistakable yet incongruous: fear. His cheek twitched wildly. But after a few seconds the tremor passed and he composed himself.

"In the ten years that I lived with Cecilia Gallerani I never made love to another woman," he said with a sadness that rang true. "Until your wedding night. When I entered you for the first time, I felt . . . violated."

"It was I who was violated, you will remember. And not only on our wedding night. I realize that our hurried liaisons at Messer Ambrogio's behest haven't made me an expert in the arts of love, but I am quite unable to see how it would be possible for *me* to have forced *you*."

"Your father forced me."

True, she told herself, that thought entering her suddenly vacant consciousness like the trilling of a single frightened bird in the silent wake of a storm. He believes this, he felt these things. He loved Cecilia, still loves her. Perhaps he wept for her, still weeps for her. Had Cecilia and Il Moro also been victims in this tragedy? Does he love our son, she abruptly wondered, in the way he loves Cecilia, not simply as a tool of his ambition? Suddenly she blushed furiously, ashamed that she had forced both herself and her husband to strip naked and stand staring at one another's pale, starved souls.

His powerful shoulders slumped. "I am sorry for this. For all of it. For what I have just said. I am sorry for you. I wish I could have been the gallant knight of your dreams. I am sorry for myself and for Cecilia. I am sorry that there will always be between you and me this unspannable, dark sea. . . ." He gestured feebly with both hands, like a sick man reaching out.

Beatrice could only think how extraordinary this was, that the garden at Schifanoia was still touched with magic. Perhaps the sea of which he had just spoken never could be crossed. But at last she had called across those darkened waters and discovered on the opposite shore another human soul.

Extract of a dispatch of COUNT CARLO BELGIOIOSO, Milanese ambassador to France, to LODOVICO SFORZA, "Il Moro," Duke of Bari and regent for the Duke of Milan. Marked "*cito! cito! cito!*" Milan, 22 May 1494

My most illustrious lord Duke of Bari,

I had intended to deliver to Your Majesty in person this account of the proceedings at Senlis, but having completed a journey of six hundred miles in seven days and not being certain that Your Highness is still in Ferrara, I have dispatched this by courier along with messengers to Toriaga and Mantua in the event that Your Highness can be found at those destinations. . . .

. . . His Most Christian Majesty Charles VIII and Maximilian Archduke of Austria have agreed to a treaty of peace between the nations of France and Germany. . . . The extent of the territories ceded by His Most Christian Majesty offers ample proof of the urgency with which he has sought this alliance. . . .

. . . immediately following the signing His Most Christian Majesty called me to a private audience and informed me that he has now determined to cross the mountains and intends to petition for the support of Your Highness in this endeavor. He was blithe to offer assurances that his cousin Louis Duc d'Orleans's claims to Milan would be put aside because of the surpassing value His Most Christian Majesty attaches to the friendship of Your Highness. His Most Christian Majesty is also most desirous that Messer Galeazzo di Sanseverino, whom he calls the foremost paladin of Christendom, be dispatched to France to advise him on the tactics required for an attack on Naples. . . .

. . . I am certain that I merely echo Your Highness's own judgment when I suggest that His Most Christian Majesty's assurances concerning Louis Duc d'Orleans should be regarded as bait for the French snare and nothing more. . . .

Ferrara, 24 May 1493

Ercole d'Este, Duke of Ferrara, passed Belgioioso's dispatch to his wife. With a gold-handled, two-prong fork he speared another piece of roast pheasant and chewed it deliberately; Eleonora had finished reading before he chased the morsel with a sip of wine and meticulously dabbed his lips with a linen napkin. Il Moro and Beatrice were seated to his right, the two couples alone at the center of the long table. Even the pages had been asked to leave.

Ercole prefaced his remarks by staring out the window overlooking the ducal park just north of the Este *castello*. Rows of lamps placed on stakes marked the future streets and major building sites of a vast new addition to Ferrara, already planned in precise detail before the first brick had been laid. The rows of lights sketched a flickering phantom city in the darkness.

"The German matter we discussed in Vigevano," Ercole said, turning to Il Moro and giving him a diamond-hard look, his lips so tight they appeared drawn with a single line. "This would be the time for it."

"I have done it." Il Moro offered this revelation with only a slight hesitation and utter neutrality. "Two weeks ago Count Belgioioso warned me that the Germans and French intended to settle their differences at Senlis. In response, ten days ago I wrote the German Emperor's son, Archduke Maximilian of Austria, and offered him the hand of our Duke's sister, Bianca Maria, along with a dowry of four hundred thousand ducats. I expect an answer by midsummer. By then Maximilian's father, who I am informed is gravely ill, most likely will be dead, and Maximilian will be the new Holy Roman Emperor."

Beatrice immediately imagined hapless Bianca Maria as an empress, presiding from an enormous glittering throne in some frosty hall in Innsbruck or Antwerp. At first she had believed that Belgioioso's urgent dispatch simply reported another abstract diplomatic maneuver, its contents of no more consequence than a dinner-table sonnet recited by a court poet. But the thought of sweet, foolish Bianca Maria packing her trousseau and disappearing over the mountains forced Beatrice to admit that this treaty signed at Senlis would change all their lives.

"And the investiture?" Eleonora asked Il Moro in a strident soprano. "Milan is an imperial fief, but no Sforza duke has ever asked the Emperor to formally invest him as Duke of Milan. The Elector Princes of Germany can hardly be expected to endorse the marriage of their next Emperor to the sister of a mere duke who has not even been legitimized by imperial investiture. Obviously you also have been clever enough to propose that when Maximilian becomes Emperor, he avail himself of the opportunity to invest the Duke of Milan."

Il Moro nodded, his features wooden.

"Then who is to be invested as Duke of Milan? Gian Galeazzo?" Eleonora did not blink during her pause. "Or you?"

Beatrice almost envied her husband's ability to stare back at her mother with the same unblinking calm. "I would be quite foolish to petition the German Emperor for *my* investiture," he said casually. "As you may know, the Signory of Venice has passed a secret resolution calling for an immediate invasion of our territories, and my assassination, should I even attempt to become Duke of Milan."

He knew, Beatrice thought. He has always known about the secret resolution. That is what he meant when he said he was not certain he could do it.

"In that event you will permit the Signory of Venice to destroy you in a more expedient fashion." Ercole spoke with the smug, elegant diction of a man tutored virtually from infancy. "The Signory will not have to spend a single ducat to be rid of Il Moro. Because when Alfonso of Aragon becomes King of Naples, he will do it for them."

Eleonora's eyes flashed irritably to her husband. "That danger does not exist at present. My father continues to enjoy—"

"Your father has had a very long life," Ercole said, interrupting. "Longer, one would think, than God would wish to suffer his impiety." Ercole's muscular jaws flexed. "Longer than the devil should have to wait for his soul."

"God will count my father's sins, not you, husband." Eleonora crossed herself. "As for my brother Alfonso, I believe that the states of Italy can restrain him when that time comes."

"The states of Italy will do nothing if Gian Galeazzo, after having been invested by the German Emperor, wishes to exercise his full dominion as Duke of Milan—as no doubt Gian Galeazzo's father-in-law will insist he do. Il Moro will be forced to resign as regent, and Milan will become a province of Naples."

Eleonora sat erect and turned menacingly to her husband. "You have spent too much time with your architects, drawing plans on paper of things that do not exist."

Ercole continued to look at Il Moro, his jaws clenching and pumping as he methodically worked at another piece of pheasant. Finally he dabbed his mouth and put down his napkin. "If *you* do not insist on receiving the investiture from the Emperor, you will not survive, your family will not survive, and Italy will not survive."

"Nonsense!" Eleonora hammered the table with her beefy fist. "Who is telling you these things? That sorcerer you are always closeted with, who tells you he can conjure the dead?"

Beatrice had the sense that she was tumbling down a flight of stairs. She was stunned by her father's apocalyptic forecast, but she was even more astonished by the realization that Father and Mama, who she always had assumed worshiped the common religion of a united Italy, disagreed so violently.

"You know that I share your concerns, my lord Father," Il Moro said, turning to Ercole. He calmly pressed the tips of his fingers together. "But my only concern at the moment is simply to keep the French out, and to that end I must devote my attention to the integrity of our alliance with Rome and Venice. The last thing we need at this juncture is an opportunistic defection that would convince the French that we lack the unity to oppose them."

Ercole gave his dry, grimacing smile. "If the Signory are faced with the choice of taxing themselves for the common defense of Italy or abandoning their allies, they will offer us to the French already basted and spitted." Ercole angrily snatched Belgioioso's dispatch from the tabletop. "Show this to the Signory. Tell them that if the French are allowed to conquer Milan, the Signory will awaken to find French soldiers pissing in the Grand Canal. The only thing that binds an alliance more strongly than greed is fear. Tell the Signory that if they do not commit publicly to our mutual defense, then we shall have no recourse but to make the King of France our ally and permit his army to cross the mountains."

"Madness," Eleonora muttered.

Beatrice glanced to the windows, wondering how this spring evening had become so sultry. The lights in the park seemed to flutter as if painted on a slowly spinning top. She felt bathed in heat and knew she had to leave the room or she would faint.

"My lord Father," she said, standing and awkwardly curtsying, "if I may be excused, I have need of some air."

The balcony, suspended three stories over the moat by a row of small stone buttresses, commanded a view of the ducal park to the north of Ferrara. Beatrice leaned against the marble balustrade.

Her father's city of lights shimmered in the still, cloying spring night. Terra Nova, the vast development was called. The New Land.

She focused on the purposeful rows of lamps, trying to make sense of what she had just heard at her father's table. She remembered what Dante had written about Fortune: From season to season and land to land, she changes her changes endlessly, and so she must be swift of her own necessity. Beatrice had the sense that she was racing after Fortune into some kind of Terra Nova, a new land where the lanterns of hope flickered dimly in a wilderness of uncertainty and fear.

Footsteps clicked on the stone walkway. She did not turn to look, but she knew it was her husband. He stopped at arm's length from her and silently looked out into the night.

"Your father will build it," Il Moro finally said. "I have seen the plans. Magnificent. What you see tonight in lights will still stand in stone a thousand years from now." He seemed satisfied with this assurance and became silent again.

Beatrice conjured the city, a monument to her father long after he had vanished from its streets. But strangely, she could not conceive of her father dying, could not even with her deepest intuition see herself condemned to mourn him.

"The light of reason," Il Moro said almost to himself. "Perhaps this is the light of reason, these lamps in the darkness." He paused as if struck by his own revelation. "And perhaps that light is also visible in the Ticino Valley, when the irrigation canals are lit by the sun and they become a grid of liquid silver as far as one can see." He turned to her. "That is what your father and I are building. We are sending the light of reason and peace and prosperity across all Europe. Not in the sudden dawn of a new sun, but one by one we are hanging the lamps of reason in a dark wood."

For a moment Beatrice let him lure her into that dark wood, guided only by the beacon of his words. He grasped her shoulders firmly but gently and turned her to face him directly. She wondered if he intended to kiss her. She wondered how she felt about that. . . .

"Your father and I want you personally to take Belgioioso's dispatch before the Signory and ask them for a declaration on mutual defense. You speak as well as any of our ambassadors, and as Duke Ercole's daughter and the wife of Il Moro, you will by your presence proclaim to all Italy the urgency with which we regard the situation. And of course as a new mother, you may even incline the Signory to regard you with sympathy. Certainly more sympathy than they will show Count Tuttavilla."

Liar. Or perhaps he was revealing only a fragment of the truth. "You want something else," she told him sullenly.

"Yes." Il Moro sounded abashed, surprised by his own candor. But his eyes advanced aggressively. "I want you to query the Signory on my behalf. I can assume that you are now aware that the Signory has passed a secret resolution calling for my—"

At the words "secret resolution," the truth rose from the gloom of that dark wood. Beatrice had an image of herself running madly out of Terra Nova, clutching her son's little hand, trying to out-race a merciless night. When she spoke, she was as breathless as if she had actually been running. "If you want me to appeal to the Signory to withdraw the secret resolution that prevents you from becoming Duke of Milan, you must know that I will never do it."

"No. I am not asking you to do that. I only want you to ask them under what circumstances they would consider with-drawing—"

"I am not some fool ambassador you can trick with word games."

"You heard nothing of what your father said?"

"My father sold me to you. I am certain you can also afford to purchase his words." Beatrice was surprised at how easily her anger came against her father; she was so used to blaming every-thing on Mama.

He gave her his infuriating "you don't understand at all" look. "Obviously you are unaware that I am the one who is holding all of this together. Your father is already preparing to send your brother to France to offer the French army free passage through Ferrara in the event that I cannot obtain from the Venetians a firm and public commitment to our mutual defense."

Beatrice laughed, her high, harsh notes leaping off into the night. "So you are the man upon whom Italy must depend for peace?"

Il Moro's eyes flared with real annoyance. He turned away from her and set his hands on the stone railing of the balcony. For some time he looked down into the oily black moat, his bangs shrouding his face.

"I have never slept beside you, so you could not know what I dream. I dream of blood. Not the sweet, wine-red blood of Christ that washes the world clean. I dream of the blood that congeals black and foul and crawls with flies. The blood I have seen." His hands clenched at the railing, the knuckles rising and cording. "I have with my own hand signed the death of a man whose only crime was his loyal service to our state, and stood and watched the blood pump from his neck. I have . . . I have witnessed things my brother did that I will not tell you because you would not forgive me if I did, things . . ." Il Moro gripped the railing so fiercely that his arms trembled. "I can still hear the screams. The screams of innocents who could not comprehend the evil . . . I smell it too. I smell a village after the mercenaries have visited it and ripped out the bowels of the plowboys. Blood and shit. They smell the same.

"The day I became my nephew's regent, I vowed that I would never bind the mortar of our state with blood, and I have suffered the wrath of many of the princes of Italy, including your grand-father and your father, for seeking a peace that no one else wanted. I do not need to prove my passion for peace to a girl who imagines that war is three days of jousting." He turned to her. "I can only tell you this. If my nephew continues to preside as Duke of Milan, we will certainly have war, because your uncle Alfonso will use your cousin Isabella's hatred of me to justify his aggression. And then everything I have built will be plundered and ruined."

But Eesh wouldn't do that, Beatrice told herself. Eesh hadn't really lied to *her*, even if Eesh had wounded her with doubts, even if Eesh had perhaps lied about something that had nothing to do with whether Gian should or shouldn't be Duke of Milan. Beatrice knew that her husband was the real liar; so were her father and mother. She had proof that *they* lied, scars on her heart. They would betray her, but Eesh never would. Love was the only truth that really mattered. And in spite of the months of doubts and separation, she realized that she still loved Eesh.

"If I were to assist you in becoming Duke of Milan, I would betray my cousin," she said with righteous fervor. "And I can never do that."

He took a step toward her, and she thought for a moment that he might erupt with rage and throw her off the balcony, a glorious martyrdom. But he simply looked down at her and said, "You are faithful. I respect that." He studied her carefully. "When I wedded you two years ago, you were a child. Now you are becoming a woman. An attractive and very clever woman. I do not know if you also wish to become wise. I know that at your age I did not. I have never fallen in love with a woman who was wise when I met her. It seems they acquired wisdom as a result of suffering me."

Beatrice did not understand his use of the word "love." He did not love her, did not intend to love her. . . .

He lifted a hand and brushed her cheek with his fingers. Without knowing why, she reached up and pressed his hand to her lips. He came closer and kissed her fingers. She looked into his eyes, then looked down. A moment later his lips whispered silently against hers. Something stirred in her, the tentative note of a lyre strung so tightly that she knew that if its extravagant melodies were ever played, she would never again be able to detect the subtle discord of his lies.

He pulled away. "You must be on the river early tomorrow. And I know you want to spend this time with our son. I will only ask that you deliver Belgioioso's dispatch to the Signory and petition them for a public declaration on mutual defense. That and nothing more." He touched her cheek again and turned away.

Beatrice watched him walk off, everything spinning in her mind, Fortune's machinery cranking out strange new permutations. She momentarily panicked at the thought of leaving her son for ten days, afraid that somehow she was doing to Ercole what Mama had done to her. Then she saw her husband pause in the doorway beneath the tower, taking a last look at the lights in the distance, and for the first time since her wedding day she felt the nervous, fluttering thrill of wondering what it would be like to make love to him.

Perhaps he was asleep, perhaps not, but he could hear the ghosts murmuring in the thick, sultry air. Only when they began to scream could he be certain he was awake.

Il Moro leapt from his bed and scrambled to the window as if seeking an escape. With quaking hands he drew aside the already partially open shutters. A few torches still burned out in Terra Nova, specks of light in the void.

The screams had stopped, but the horror of what he had heard was a continuous drone. The girl had screamed first, while Galeazzo Maria raped her, savaging her with unspeakable perversity. And then her father had screamed, the muffled, hysterical protest of a man already sealed in his coffin. These were sounds he had actually heard years ago, and would never forget. But the last scream he had never heard before. It was not a shrill register of fear and pain, but the terrifying, metaphysical keening of a soul flayed of all dignity, all hope. The scream of a woman who had looked up at the face of Satan and seen the grinning, insane visage of the first child she had carried in her womb.

Il Moro pressed his fingers to his shrieking temples and willed silence. He greeted the profound emptiness that followed with a convulsive, bitter sob.

"Forgive me, Mother," he whispered.

C H A P T E R

31

Extract of a letter of BEATRICE D'ESTE DA SFORZA, Duchess of Bari, to LODOVICO SFORZA, "Il Moro," Duke of Bari and regent for the Duke of Milan. Chioggia, 26 May 1493

. . . and as I have promised to send Your Highness a full and exacting report of my mission to Venice, I begin with particulars of my success at *scartino*, achieved during our voyage today . . . by the time we arrived here this afternoon I had won five hundred ducats from my ladies, who threw down their cards in disgust and proceeded to argue furiously among themselves as to whether my victories were due to my skill or the favor of Fortune. Truthfully, I won so many hands that I must ascribe my success to both, and I took this to portend well for the rest of my journey. . . .

Extract of a letter of BEATRICE D'ESTE DA SFORZA to LODOVICO SFORZA. Venice, 27 May 1493

. . . At the isle of S. Clemente, His Serenity Doge Agostino Barbarigio conducted us on board his *bucintoro*, which is a galley of enormous size with rows of oars like great wings and many gilt ornaments and crimson awnings. A hundred and thirty Venetian ladies were seated in rows behind the Doge in the forepart of the *bucintoro*, and the Doge bid myself, Madame my mother, Count Tuttavilla and the other ambassadors, and as many of our retinue as could be accommodated to be seated in front of them. We set out again, and after passing between the isles of La Giudecca and S. Giorgio we encountered galleys, barges, gondolas, and carracks in numbers so great that the city of Venice itself seemed merely an extension of this floating isle of ships of every type, some of them armed with rows of cannons, which boomed out salutes (at each of these Count Tuttavilla could be seen to cringe), and others decked out like gardens. Even the gondolas were most elaborately decorated with flowers and canopies of colored silk. . . . Among these vessels we encountered a large raft with figures of Neptune and Minerva seated beside an enormous mountain fashioned of painted wood and canvas, said mountain crowned with the Sforza viper and Venice's lion of Saint Mark. First Neptune began to dance and juggle balls to the music of drums and tambourines. . . . Next Minerva struck the mountain with her spear, and an olive tree shot up from within the mountain as if by magic, apparently through the agency of some mechanical device similar to those Maestro Leonardo has devised. Neptune then struck the mountain with his trident, and up came a live horse. Then personages of all sorts appeared from within the mountain, with open books in their hands, signifying that they were considering how to name the city to be founded on the mountain, the honor of which they finally adjudicated in favor of Minerva over Neptune. Minerva chose the name Athens, the birthplace of all learning. This, we were told, was to signify that great states are founded by means of peaceful arbitration. . . .

In addition to this brief theatrical presentation there were many floats carrying actors and figures representing the various guilds of Venice, all very ingenious and lovely to see. And so we entered the Grand Canal, where the Doge, who spoke to us in the most familiar and animated fashion despite his venerable age, took immense pleasure in pointing out to us all of the principal palaces, these having rows of window frames which resemble white lace in their exquisite patterns. Persian carpets hung from every balcony, and garlands adorned the columns of all the loggias. Everyone had come to the waterside to observe our procession, even the *negre* slaves, who perched on pilings outside the kitchen doors. The Doge indicated to us the many fine ladies who appeared at the windows and balconies in all their jewels, attended by poodles, monkeys, and peacocks. He also discreetly indicated to us the many courtesans, equally as finely attired as the ladies of the noble families. His Serenity was not ashamed to recognize these women, he said, because they contribute very many good works to the Republic as a result of the heavy taxes to which they submit—the tax on prostitution alone is sufficient to fit out the entire Venetian navy! After seeing all these sights, we arrived at my father's palace, where the Doge insisted on escorting us to our rooms, although Madame my mother and I begged him to spare his health. We found the palace all hung with tapestries and draperies in Sforza colors, and the beds covered in satins embroidered with the Sforza emblem. . . . This evening three gentlemen of the Signory came to call, at which time I requested an audience with that body. . . . I shall write again tomorrow if the audience has taken place. I commend myself to Your Highness. . . .

"If Your Highness will excuse me, I will post this letter to His Highness your husband and begin sorting through the messages you have received here. I'm certain that Your Highness must require some rest." Vincenzo Calmeta, Beatrice's new secretary, a handsome young poet with a polished yet sincere manner, held a sheaf of sealed notes and invitations in one hand and the letter Beatrice had just dictated in the other. He looked expectantly to her.

Beatrice gave Calmeta his leave, although she enjoyed his witty company and obvious devotion to her. And she was not ready for sleep despite the long, wearying day. She still had the sense of riding a pitching deck, but rather than making her queasy, the light, floating sensation heightened her buzzing exhilaration. She could close her eyes and relive it all: the riotously colored sea of ships, the ancient, almost Oriental city silhouetted against the dazzling blue sky, the thunder of cannons, the blare of trumpets, and the surprising choruses of "Moro!" Next to the day she first held Ercole, this had been the greatest day of her life. Venice, the most powerful city in the world. The center of the world. And today, she told herself, I was the center of the center of the world.

She reluctantly surrendered the triumphant images and picked up the packet of documents she had placed on the small table beside her bed. She hurried through them again, merely satisfying herself that she had already put to memory the points her husband had instructed her to emphasize when she presented Belgioioso's dispatch to the Signory. She had no ambivalence concerning her mission; everything her husband proposed was calculated to ensure the defense of Italy. Even the most skeptical eye could not find among his words an argument for his own ambitions.

She put the papers down at the knock on her door. Eleonora came in without being announced, hurriedly inspected the room, and retied one of the gold cords that gathered up the curtains of the bed canopy. Beatrice was soaring too high to be annoyed by her mother's fussing around like a chambermaid. Mama couldn't help it if she was so irrevocably earthbound.

"You must be very, very careful when you address the Signory tomorrow," Eleonora said when she finally directed her attention to Beatrice. "We are in a very delicate situation, so deliver your address exactly as your husband has instructed you. Would to God that your husband had not burdened you with this responsibility and instead allowed you to enjoy your first visit to Venice."

"Mama, Count Tuttavilla says that our reception this afternoon was the most extravagant seen in Venice for many years. I hardly think that the Venetians are in the habit of providing such a welcome for their enemies." And Beatrice already considered herself virtually an intimate of the Doge.

"Remember that the symbol of Venice is the Lion of Saint Mark," Eleonora said. "And the time to worry about the Lion of Saint Mark is not when it roars but when it invites you to place your head in its mouth."

"Mama—" Beatrice was grateful to be interrupted by another knock on her door. "Mama, I have to see who has come." She opened the door and readmitted Calmeta, who began to bow and make excuses when he saw Eleonora. Beatrice grabbed his sleeve. "No, no, Maestro Vincenzo," she said for her mother's benefit, "you know we have to finish the letter to my husband."

Calmeta was sensitive enough to have already discerned the

nature of Beatrice's relationship with her mother, so he understood why she needed to finish a letter he had already posted. He took up his writing tablet and made a pretense of preparing to receive dictation. Beatrice kissed her mother good night and closed the door behind her.

"Your Highness, I'm not certain what to make of this." Calmeta produced an unsealed note from beneath his writing tablet. "The author, who has not signed his name, says that he has a letter for your husband, and he suggests Your Highness as the agent to deliver it." Calmeta frowned quizzically. "Your Highness, he says that this letter he wishes you to pass on to your husband is from the Duchess of Milan." Beatrice's eyebrows shot up. "Our correspondent *incognito* says you must send someone you can trust to San Marco tomorrow morning, wearing this pin fastened to a red mantle, and have him wait near the icon of the Madonna in the west wing." Calmeta opened his right hand to reveal a cheap metal brooch enameled with, of all things, a French fleur-de-lis. "Does Your Highness think that this is some sort of French machination to disrupt our mission?"

Beatrice thought for a moment, her pounding heart seeming to hammer her still-at-sea legs back to earth. Of course Eesh would never write her husband—and then to deliver it in this circuitous fashion? But at least she was certain of one thing. "No, Vincenzo, this is not a French plot. Even the French are not so clumsy as to have tipped their hand in so obvious a fashion."

"Nor are they subtle enough to send us this brooch in the hope that we will discount their hand in the matter," Calmeta added with a wry smile.

"Whoever it is, I'm certain that this person is bent on making trouble for his own gain." Beatrice felt secure in her intuition that somehow this little intrigue boded a large trouble. If anyone but Eesh had been mentioned, she would have insisted on ignoring it entirely. She recalled the tactics she'd used to beat her ladies at *scartino;* a good player knew when to discard bad cards. . . . But was it possible that Eesh *was* behind this, that in some complex fashion she was engineering a reconciliation?

"Your Highness, I am willing to go to San Marco tomorrow, if only to satisfy your curiosity."

"No, Vincenzo." She took the note and pin and examined them. "I don't like this. This could be dangerous for you."

"Your Highness, I hardly think that I would be at risk in San Marco, save of losing my purse to a thief or surrendering both my purse and my virtue to a courtesan. I only regret that this mission could not be more dangerous, so that I could more energetically prove my devotion to Your Highness."

She realized that Vincenzo said this with all sincerity. Perhaps, she thought with a little thrill, he was even falling in love with her—in a chaste, knightly fashion. She didn't want him to go to San Marco, but if she forbade him she would extinguish the joy in his soft gray eyes. "I think it is very dangerous, Vincenzo, but I trust that you are also dedicated to sparing me the pain I would suffer should anything happen to you. You will be very careful."

The five vast Byzantine domes of the basilica of San Marco echoed with three levels of sound. Foremost was the sonorous chanting of the priests singing Matins from the massive gold-and-alabaster architecture of the high altar. A charming polyphony was added by the delicate trilling of the courtesans as they paraded throughout the nave. Their shoulder-length blond curls, gleaming cleavage, and concentric layers of pearl and gold necklaces were an appropriate addition to the extravagant fittings of the church; with its seven-century accumulation of glittering mosaics, swirling marble panels, gilt-and-enamel altarpieces, and Byzantine chandeliers and icons, San Marco looked like an enormous jewel box.

The third sound was a low resonant buzz provided by furtive conversations in a dozen different Italian dialects and foreign tongues. As much as San Marco was a bazaar of flesh, it was also an exchange for one of Venice's other leading commodities: secrets. Diplomats, agents, exiles, and assassins from all over Europe congregated here to barter information, lies, and lives.

Two men, disguised like most of their colleagues in the anonymity of Venetian-style black velvet capes and shoulder-length hair, had set up shop in the left arm of the huge Greek-cross basilica; this transept was virtually a cathedral unto itself, with its own soaring dome and richly decorated barrel-vaulted aisle chapels. A soft morning light filtered down from the windows ringing the dome, and one of the men inclined his head forward slightly, careful that his long hair draped and concealed the four livid parallel scars across his left cheek.

"Have you considered what you will do if no one comes?" asked the man with the scarred face.

"Giovann, you must understand that you are no longer hiding in a village in Apulia," answered his companion. "If I have learned nothing else here, it is that in Venice there is always another buyer."

"We shouldn't even be selling it. If someone comes we will make certain that they represent the Duchess of Bari and then be done with it. This letter has been purchased with blood and can only be sold in that coin," Giovann said bitterly.

"We have no assurance that Il Moro or the Signory will do anything with this letter, except perhaps to burn it," the second man whispered urgently. "But if we can interest Il Moro and the Signory in bidding against one another, *we* will at least profit enough to get to France and contribute to Prince Antonello's efforts."

"How do you intend to approach the Signory?" Giovann asked.

"I have already initiated a conversation with their representative," the second man whispered. "I suggested the nature of our merchandise, and we arranged to talk again after he had consulted with the Signory. Which will allow us to establish what Il Moro is willing to pay before we have to negotiate with the Signory. Now look for the red mantle."

A half hour passed. Giovann nudged his companion. "That priest there in the black cassock, near the icon of the Madonna. He isn't here to beg alms or attend Mass. He's been doing nothing but watch us."

A throng of maybe thirty people virtually obscured the jewel-framed Byzantine icon, the centerpiece of a small marble altar. The second man searched the crowd intently. He shook his head. "I don't see a priest."

"He's gone," Giovann said. "He saw us looking at him. I believe he is here to administer the Signory's sacraments. We were foolish to think that the Signory would pay for something they can so easily steal. We should leave now, immediately." His whisper was sibilant with alarm.

"There's someone with a red mantle near the—" The second man broke off, and his eyes popped wide with terror and pain. The priest stood behind him, one hand clutching his arm, the other fist shoved against his back. He gasped, "Go, Giovann . . ." Then nightmare quick, his eyes rolled and blood trickled down his chin and his body slumped in the priest's arms.

Giovann caught only the vaguest glimpse of the priest's acquiline Venetian features before he turned and started through the crowd. He fumbled inside his cape for his knife. He looked back and saw the priest knock down a courtesan, who fell with a shouted curse. Suddenly it occurred to him that it wasn't enough simply to escape; unless he killed the Signory's murderous hireling, within minutes his description would be circulating among Venice's notoriously efficient security force.

His mistake was stopping for the priest instead of slowing and allowing himself to be caught. After a moment he realized that and wheeled in alarm. The only indication that the priest had ever been there was the courtesan, who had gotten back on her feet. She plucked haughtily at the puffs of white silk chemise showing through the slitted foresleeves of her gown, muttering something about priests who sodomized little boys.

"Your Highness, you understand that you will address the six presiding officers of the Signory in the Sala del Collegio, not the entire body of the Signory in their Senate chamber." Count Girolamo da Tuttavilla, head of the Milanese embassy, lowered his heavy eyebrows. He wasn't quite sure that Beatrice was listening to his brief. "These men are elected from among the three hundred members of the Signory, who are in turn elected from the twelve hundred noblemen who share by birthright membership in the Maggior Consiglio. So when you address these six gentlemen, you will be addressing all Venice."

Beatrice nodded; she could excuse Count Tuttavilla for assuming she was distracted. She glanced at the crumbling marble fireplace in front of her, still bearing the scorch marks of the fire that ten years previously had ravaged the Doge's Palace, the seat of Venice's government. The exterior of the palace had been sumptuously reconstructed, but the penurious Signory had decided to hold off on refurbishing the interior. The walls had been hastily replastered and hung with draperies, while the serious business of repainting the murals and gilding the ceilings had been postponed indefinitely. The antechamber in which Beatrice and the Milanese envoys waited was small as well as plain, an anteroom one might find in the home of an average Milanese merchant. In her imagination, Beatrice had rehearsed an impassioned oration to hundreds of gallant gentlemen in a vast, splendid hall. Now she anticipated sitting cheek to jowl with a half-dozen functionaries in quarters that would most likely be no larger and certainly less splendid than one of her own closets.

"Your Highness should not take as an affront the duration of the delay," Tuttavilla added. "The more urgent and vital one's mission, the longer the Signory requires one to wait. If you had come to inquire about the price of an arm-span of cheap linen in the Merceria, they would have seen you a half hour ago."

The door to the outer hall opened slightly. Tuttavilla went to see who wanted in. He looked back at Beatrice. "Your secretary wishes to be admitted, Your Highness."

Beatrice had been so anxious about Calmeta's clandestine errand that she had ordered him to report to the Doge's Palace as soon as he returned from the adjacent basilica of San Marco. She hurried to the door and motioned Calmeta back outside, into the brightly sunlit room that served as a waiting area for the chambers of the Senate and the Council of Ten, the Venetian security apparatus.

Calmeta shook his head. "I wore the red mantle and the brooch, feeling quite unsuitably attired, and stood by the icon throughout most of Matins. No one approached me. It was a disappointingly salutary enterprise, Your Highness. Not even a courtesan threatened to handle me roughly. However, there was a disturbance of sorts just as I arrived. A man fainted and a lady took offense at a priest who had somehow interfered with her trade." Calmeta smiled winsomely and shrugged. "I suspect that

I have fallen victim to a prank that you were wise enough to advise me to avoid."

Tuttavilla appeared at the door and signaled to Beatrice. She thanked Calmeta for his valor regardless and hurried back into the fire-scarred antechamber. A page swung open the door to the Sala del Collegio. Tuttavilla nodded his encouragement, and Beatrice went on in.

The Sala del Collegio was longer than its antechamber and more brightly lit, but just as narrow and hastily decorated. The walls had been hung all around with crimson velvet drapes, and the floor was a fire-darkened and cracked marble *opus sectile*. A varnished oak dais at the far end of the room elevated a single wooden bench. Seven men sat on the bench side by side, separated from each other by flat armrests upholstered in purple satin. Along the wall to the right, two secretaries sat at an enclosed wooden writing lectern.

Beatrice had little time for orientation before she reached the shallow steps leading to the dais. She was almost close enough to shake the hands of the gentlemen, who stood politely but did not bow. She could arrive at only a general impression of the faces of the six members of the Signory, partly because she didn't dare study them individually, but also because the centuries of political and social exclusivity enjoyed by the Venetian nobility had bred men who looked—and thought—very much alike. This collective face was tautly powerful, shadowed with a smoothly shaven but heavy beard, and lined with creases as sharp as knife cuts. Tightly drawn lips, a sharp, prominent nose, and unyielding blue eyes completed a portrait of toughness, practicality, and indifference.

The only welcoming human presence was the aged Doge, who remained seated at the center of the bench, his watery eyes winking beneath drooping lids. His voluminous cape of silver-and-gold-embroidered white damask was a stark contrast to the other men's long, loose-sleeved robes of costly but plain-looking scarlet velour. The Doge's matching damask cap had a hornlike protuberance at the rear, and this combined with his flowing white hair and beard gave him the aspect of a kindly sorcerer captured in some distant land by a group of ruthless adventurers. Suddenly Beatrice realized that the Spartan decor conveyed exactly what the

Signory desired—that the visitor was negotiating with men whose only concern was the utterly efficient exercise of raw, expedient power.

The Doge motioned for Beatrice to take the seat to his right, which now made it impossible for her to look directly at any of the men, with the exception of the two secretaries; it occurred to her that this arrangement also suited the style of men who valued secrecy and discretion far more than diplomatic effusion. Fine; she could learn more by listening to them than by staring at their resolute, immobile faces.

The Doge welcomed her floridly, as if he was permitted (or perhaps condemned to) all the courtesies the Signory so obviously disdained. Beatrice overcame an initial moment of panic and then responded with the rhetorical skills that had been drilled into her almost as soon as she could talk. Fear had attended every one of her childhood Latin recitals—the first had been when she was four years old—and so she had learned not simply to speak well in front of an audience of her elders but to speak well with her heart pounding a distracting rhythm and her throat fighting every breath.

The pleasantries done with, Beatrice produced Belgioioso's dispatch. She was forced to sit in excruciating silence while each man read the document. But as the sheet of parchment passed from hand to hand she could feel the atmosphere charging around her, almost as if the coffered ceiling were steadily lowering and compressing the air.

When the parchment had reached the end of the bench, a voice to her left asked, "I see that the French King intends to ask your husband for assistance in his Italian adventure. How does your husband intend to reply to this request?"

Beatrice noted both smug authority and slyness in her unseen questioner's grating nasal voice. He intended to test her, perhaps lure her into some inadvertent confession of her husband's du-plicity. Suddenly she was eager to match words with this anon-ymous adversary. "My husband has done all within his power to oppose any French adventure in Italy. He sees no reason to alter that policy now that crossing the mountains has become a fixed objective of the French King."

"Indeed. One might suggest that this would in truth be an appropriate time for your husband to alter his policy," the nasal voice offered with a brisk annoyance that gave Beatrice a pang of fear. "The French will now tempt your husband with both promises and threats to abandon his Italian allies and enable the French enterprise."

So this was the game: the Signory would excuse their own lack of resolve by claiming that Il Moro had more incentive than the rest to defect from the alliance. Beatrice decided to move off this point by turning the accusation back on the accuser. "It is my husband's contention that not only Milan but also Venice will be subjected to the same promises and threats." Beatrice was too caught up in the moment to notice the combative pride with which she brandished the phrase "my husband." But here in this tiny room, elbow-to-elbow with the most powerful men in the world, she had begun to nurture the idea that Milan, her husband, and their baby had all become enfolded into one indivisible cause.

"Under our agreement as it now stands, the Signory has committed to an alliance of mutual friendship, calling for consultation on matters of mutual defense, with the states of Rome, Milan, Ferrara, and Mantua. Certainly your husband does not question the guarantee provided by the Signory's stated commitment?"

Beatrice controlled her elation, just as she did when looking at a winning hand in *scartino* or *buttino*. Her counterattack had driven the Signory directly into her trap. "My husband believes that the provision for 'consultation on matters of mutual defense' will not sufficiently discourage the King of France. My husband therefore proposes that Milan, Rome, Venice, Ferrara, and Mantua draft and publish a revised agreement calling for the immediate assistance of the entire league should any member state be attacked. My husband further proposes that the league issue a specific warning to the French King that any incursion into Italy by the French army will be regarded as a simultaneous attack on the entire league."

The silence of a tomb followed. After a moment someone seated to Beatrice's left whispered and hands motioned to her right, as if the gentlemen were also communicating with signs. The whispering became a generalized low-pitched sigh; Beatrice could hardly make out individual words, much less discern the direction of this unusual policy discussion. The Doge turned to her and smiled wanly.

After several minutes the room became silent again. The nasal voice addressed Beatrice. "Your husband will certainly understand that we wish to consult with His Holiness on this matter."

Beatrice wanted to shout, "My husband owns His Holiness!" Instead she snapped, "My husband already has the commitment of His Holiness on this. It is your commitment he wishes to secure."

The nasal voice sounded almost bored. "The Signory will make its own determination of His Holiness's wishes in this matter."

Beatrice could not believe that this man, whoever he was, imagined that she had not heard his icy subtext: The Signory will still be making this determination when Louis Duc d'Orléans marches into Milan.

The Doge smiled at her again, his hooded blue eyes only slits of color. Then he stood up, offering Beatrice his hand. When she got to her feet, the realization of what had just happened swiped at her knees and she thought she would collapse. Then the panic vanished, and a cold, brassy sound began to echo, more in her stomach than in her ears. You have lost this hand, it said. And in the game you are now playing, the cost of defeat is war.

Beatrice lay awake far into the night. She had opened the shutters so that she could hear the wonderful liquid murmur of the gondolas and rafts passing by; her first-floor bedroom looked directly over the canal, and occasionally she heard snatches of conversation and laughter so clearly that the boats might have been gliding by at the foot of her bed.

She mentally recited again and again every word of her conversation with the Signory. Count Tuttavilla had told her that the response of the Signory to the mutual defense appeal was much as he had expected, and she had done well to expose their dilatory policy. But while Mama hadn't said anything, she obviously regarded the audience as a mistake and a grievous failure—which she had communicated by nothing more than a lifted eyebrow and a certain acceleration of her speech in dismissing the matter.

On this point Beatrice agreed with Mama. She had expected so much more; she had even entertained visions of herself as Italy's foremost stateswoman, the acclaimed arbiter of unity and concord. Now she wanted every word back—to rephrase, to cast a wholly different emphasis, to match the frigid reserve of the Signory with her own implacable calm. Fortune had provided her with an opening, but she had lacked the skill to use it properly. She had charged in and tripped over her own feet.

Finally she slept, and dreamed, but not of diplomacy and hard-edged men. She was on the water, a river much like the Po at home in Ferrara, lying in one of the small gondola-like punts that she and her sister had often gone out in. The boat drifted along the bank, sometimes in bright sunlight, at other times in the shadows cast by the huge trees overhanging the river. The water was strewn with flower petals, and she trailed her hand through them. She wore a loose chemise, and the breeze lifted the sheer layer of fabric and stroked her skin. Then a man was with her, his fingers wandering where the breeze had gone, and every touch made her more fluid until she was like a warm river, teeming with sensation. . . .

Something fell on her and threw her into the water, and the brackish, suffocating smell rushed up her nostrils. She was drowning immediately, the water like gummy mud in her mouth, and she looked up and saw the white eyes leering out of the darkness, the dark skin. . . . Too real! She screamed, the sound muffled nightmarishly. Too real! And then: This is not a dream! And more calmly: I am dead. I will never see my baby again.

The thing that had her was a man. A young man. Perspiration glistened on his face, and his white shirt was open. His knees pinned her arms, and one hand clamped her mouth. She could still breathe through her nostrils. "Listen carefully, Your Highness," the young man whispered, his voice a tremolo of fear, fatigue, and purpose. "I have a letter written by the Duchess of Milan that I'm certain your husband will want to see."

Beatrice stopped struggling. The man reached into his shirt

and took out a folded parchment with a broken seal. "Do you recognize her hand?"

Beatrice could make out only a vague pattern of script. Then she saw the monogram beneath the signature. IX. Isabella. The flourish of the big letters was unmistakable.

"Your Highness, can I trust you not to scream if I permit you to light a lamp so that you can examine this letter?"

Beatrice motioned with her head, and he removed his hand. He quickly stepped back to the window, still holding the parchment. For a moment she hesitated, wondering if she *should* scream, certain that she heard Fortune's mocking laughter. Then she got up and lit the lamp, unmindful that she was wearing only a chemise.

"Who are you?" she asked. He had three or four recent scars on his left cheek, all in line, as if he had been mauled by a big cat. He was most likely in his early twenties.

"I am a man who will not leave Venice alive," he said numbly. "I have eluded the minions of the Signory all day, but I fear I have exhausted Fortune's generosity. I need you to deliver this letter to your husband." He handed the parchment to her at arm's length, as if frightened of her.

The intruder's disclosure that he was fleeing the Signory enhanced his pedigree considerably in Beatrice's eyes. Then she examined the broken seal and realized that if not Eesh's, this was an expert forgery. But the handwriting, tight and rapid-looking, left no doubt that the document was authentic. The letter was dated 2 March. It began, "My most beloved and illustrious lord Father . . ."

The rest of the letter seemed to bring back the pain of Beatrice's version, each sentence a malignant hand clutching inside her womb: "You wedded me to Gian Galeazzo on the understanding that in due course he would ascend the throne of his Visconti and Sforza ancestors. Now Gian Galeazzo is of age, has sired an heir, and should be expected to be given full dominion as Duke of Milan. Instead all power remains vested in Il Moro, who has assiduously labored to prevent Gian from assuming any of the duties or privileges of his birthright. . . . His wife behaves as if she is the Duchess of Milan, and the court regards her as such.

Everyone here assumes that Il Moro's son will succeed to the dukedom, and to that end all the honors of a royal heir were paid to said child at his birth, while we and our children have been treated with contempt, have scarcely been given the bare necessities of life, and have had to flee to the *castello* at Pavia because we fear for our lives. . . . If you have any fatherly compassion and if love of me and the thought of my tears can still move your soul, I implore you to bring your army to our assistance and deliver your daughter and son-in-law from their slavery by ending Il Moro's despicable regency and restoring to Gian Galeazzo the power which is rightfully his. . . . If you will not help us, I would rather die by my own hand than continue to bear the yoke of Il Moro and his wife. . . ."

Beatrice slowly began to slump as she read; when she finished she had to support herself with her hands on her knees. She wanted to be sick. The deeper wound, the brutal death of Eesh's love, had been as swift as an amputation, and she could not yet deal with it. She had an image of her uncle Alfonso, the dark-faced, scowling demon of her childhood, thundering toward Milan at the head of his army. Bring your army and deliver us . . . Everything Father and her husband had said was true. Everything Eesh had told her was a lie. . . . She stared at the letter again. She could not have been more horrified if this man had brought her Eesh's head on a tray. Finally she looked up and asked "Why?" with a victim's plaint. "Why have you done this?"

"I have done this for my father's soul. And my brother's. For my mother. I have done this to free my people." He no longer seemed afraid. "You have a son. Will you swear on the head of your son that your husband will see this letter?"

She nodded yes, unable to tell him that this letter would come as no surprise to her husband, that she was the one person in all the courts of Europe for whom this letter was a knife in the heart.

He watched her for a moment, and she had to meet his eyes. She wondered why and how Fortune had engineered this collision of spinning fates. Then, with no parting, not even a flicker of his gaze, he looked away and climbed through the window. She heard the thump of his feet as he stepped into his gondola and then the soft sigh of a hull parting the water.

The entire universe had changed, the spheres reeling in discord and confusion. And in this new universe there was only one fixed point, a hard crystal of terror, like a diamond that captured darkness instead of light. What would happen to her baby when Alfonso came?

Venice, 29 May 1493

"I must say I was surprised to receive your petition for this meeting." His Serenity Doge Agostino Barbarigio motioned Beatrice to the chair opposite his. "Though of course I am delighted for another opportunity to visit. I had simply thought you'd had quite enough of old men and their woes. A lovely young woman like Your Highness might better spend her time enjoying the beauties of our city. And in so doing contribute her own beauty to that of Venice."

Beatrice settled on the edge of her chair and accepted the Doge's compliment with a gracious nod. His Serenity's apartments were on the second floor of his palace, beneath the chambers of state on the third floor. He had situated his study—which was as sparingly adorned as the rest of the building—in an outer room, taking advantage of the brilliant morning light reflected off the crescent sweep of the Canale di San Marco and the lagoon beyond. The panorama included Venice's destructive might as well as the placid expanse of sea and sky; a forest of masts marked the location of the Arsenale, the immense naval yard where fully fitted galleys were turned out as rapidly as mold-stamped terra-cotta Madonnas at a pottery factory.

After an awkward pause the Doge spoke again. "The gentlemen of the Signory were most impressed with the elegance of your address. They all remarked upon how well you spoke and how clearly you presented your husband's position."

Yes, Beatrice thought, they were all impressed at how quickly I revealed my hand. Again she did not respond. This time Venice would squirm.

The Doge smiled and motioned with his white, wizened fingers. "I understand your disappointment at the rather ambiguous response you received from the gentlemen of the Signory. But let us wait and see. His Holiness will no doubt have his own views on the matter of mutual defense."

Beatrice sat back and gave the Doge a look that said: Don't bother repeating that fiction.

After yet more silence from his guest, the Doge cocked his hoary head curiously. "Why have you come, my daughter?"

"Allow me to be frank. I believe that Your Serenity, being the wisest of men, is more favorably disposed to my husband's concerns than are the gentlemen of the Signory."

The Doge nodded ponderously. "Certainly I place great value in the friendship of your husband." He smiled, showing his stained teeth. "You know, my daughter, it is often said that there are two qualities the Signory most values when electing their doge. The first is the wisdom of a venerable old age, and the second is an absence of personal ambition, a quality that so often blesses old age. I am certain that I at least satisfy my colleagues on the second quality. I do not try to persuade the Signory of anything to which they are not already inclined to be persuaded."

"And they cannot be persuaded that Venice shares the danger presented by the French."

The Doge smiled patiently. "My daughter, the French cannot cross the mountains without first having access to Il Moro's treasury. Without loans from your husband, the French King will not even be able to pay his army's way to Grenoble. And your husband hardly seems inclined to finance the destruction of his state. On the other hand, should he be so foolish, Venice can hardly expect to benefit from chaining itself to Milan's folly."

"My husband will have no choice but to finance the French adventure if he is threatened by attack from Naples."

"No such threat exists. And none will exist as long as Alfonso of Aragon's son-in-law remains Duke of Milan."

Beatrice had already decided that to offer Eesh's letter as proof of her husband's plight would merely force her to negotiate from a position of weakness—which she now knew to be fatal when dealing with the Signory. Instead she had decided to feign a position of strength, just as in a game of *scartino* she might pretend to hold the winning cards when she had nothing. Except that this was no longer a game.

"Alfonso will attack Milan when my husband makes himself Duke of Milan."

The Doge was as still as a dead man. His eyes were no longer animated but merely seemed reflections of the cerulean sea and sky outside his window. Finally he said, "The Signory would regard the usurpation of the Duke of Milan by your husband as an outrage of the most serious consequence."

"You are suggesting that you would enforce the secret resolution calling for Venetian intervention to prevent my husband from becoming Duke of Milan. But one wonders," Beatrice went on, "how effective the Signory's resolution would be if my husband were to be invested Duke of Milan by the German Emperor."

"Our agents do not report any such commitment on the part of the German Emperor," the Doge said blithely.

"I am sure your agents will soon become better informed." Beatrice had no trouble convincing herself that her husband's deal with the Germans was as good as done; even if it did not call for her husband's investiture, the Signory would have to suspect some secret clause. "And when the Emperor agrees to invest my husband as Duke of Milan, the Signory will have two choices. Either you can withdraw the secret resolution and allow my husband to use the mere threat of French intervention to force Alfonso to acquiesce, or you can enforce the secret resolution, thereby allying Venice with Alfonso of Aragon and ensuring that the French and very likely the Germans will enter Italy in my husband's defense."

The Doge folded his hands inside his white cape and settled his chin as if he were preparing to nap. After a moment he smiled and said, "It has been my pleasure to visit with you, my daughter. But now you must excuse an old man whose health does not permit a more lengthy interview."

Extract of a dispatch of COUNT GIROLAMO DA TUTTAVILLA, head of the Milanese embassy to Venice, to LODOVICO SFORZA, "Il Moro," Duke of Bari and regent for the Duke of Milan. Venice, 31 May 1493

. . . our last night here will see us at the banquet celebrating the league, to be conducted at the Doge's Palace, in the great hall of the Maggior Consiglio. As the extravagance and duration of this event will be in inverse proportion to the Signory's true commitment to her allies, I fear we must gird ourselves for an exhausting and interminable evening of festivities and food, certain to be exacerbated by the heat. . . .

The gondolas crowded the quay in front of the Doge's Palace; pages waited at the landing to escort the ladies and gentlemen from their boats. Beatrice almost slipped as she stepped from her gondola. She ascended the steps to the piazza with the disembodied dread with which she imagined a condemned man would climb an executioner's scaffold. The palace facade was a gaudy Gothic confection, lacy columns and trefoils of white Istrian stone contrasted with patterned brickwork of pink Verona marble. It reminded her of the ornate puppet-show stages in Naples, where marionette knights battled sinister Moors.

Inside the palace Beatrice climbed another flight of steps, then was ushered into the cathedral-size expanse of the Sala del Maggior Consiglio, the meeting place for the twelve hundred noblemen of the Maggior Consiglio, the governing body that elected the Signory. The heat in the huge hall was suffocating, and the light from the big windows overlooking the water disconcertingly bright. She would not look directly out over the rows of tables, but she already had an oblique sense of the splendid multitude: row after row of sober-hued men alternating with row after row of their wives or mistresses, all gold and pearls and puffs of white silk and ripe white breasts. She was certain that each one of them already knew of her pathetic attempt to coerce the Doge into withdrawing the secret resolution.

Even more than she was humiliated, Beatrice was frightened.

She wouldn't have behaved so recklessly if she hadn't been so desperate to save her baby. Even to revenge herself on Eesh she would have waited. But she had been so certain that the way to deal with the Signory was to threaten, to demand more than she wanted. She had convinced herself that if she portrayed her husband as ready to crush Alfonso, the Signory would offer to mediate between them. She'd envisioned some treaty that would warn Alfonso to stay away forever and let Eesh scream all she wanted until everyone knew she was crazy. But she had been wrong again. Now the Signory would probably support Alfonso, might even encourage him to attack. In two days she had gone from imagining herself Italy's savior to the certainty that she had destroyed Italy, her family, herself, and her baby.

Again she climbed, this time to the enormous dais at the far end of the hall. The red chalk underdrawing of a mural-in-progress covered the entire freshly plastered wall behind the dais like some Titan's sketch; it depicted Christ's celestial throne flanked by choirs of angels. Two long tables, already occupied by several hundred members of the Signory and their wives, had been set up on the dais, on either side of a raised theatrical stage. Beatrice was seated along with her mother, the gout-ridden Bishop of Como—the senior member of the Milanese delegation—and Count Tuttavilla, the senior diplomat. She focused on the silver, gold, and crystal tableware and tried not to look at anyone. She assumed (and dreaded) that the Doge would take the empty seat to her left. But to her surprise her dinner companion turned out to be the man who had shown her to her chair, a tall, imperious, steel-gray-haired man about her father's age.

"Your Highness, I am *nobilomo* Ser Constantino Privolo," her companion said after he had taken his seat.

Beatrice had to clutch her chair to keep from toppling off. Following her audience with the Signory she had conjured again and again that arrogant nasal voice, feeling it grate against her bones; she hadn't recognized the man's face tonight because she hadn't been able to see him clearly during her audience.

"His Serenity regrets that he cannot join us this evening," Ser Privolo went on. "His Serenity offers you his sincere apologies and hopes you will understand that his poor health has denied him this pleasure."

Beatrice felt the hot hollowness of utter defeat and humiliation. Of course it made sense. The Doge would not deal with her again, even as a formality. He had instead sent his executioner.

Dance music, played with woodwinds and lutes, stirred the stifling air; couples began to trickle onto the stage for brief turns of slow-paced *bassa danza*. Beatrice watched the deliberate circle of dancers for a while, her head spinning as if she were whirling a *moresca*. She fought the giddiness, but then her stomach fluttered with nausea and she knew she had to leave before she became sick at the table. She was so disoriented that it seemed someone else stood and issued her apologies.

She wasn't even certain who escorted her upstairs and down a hall to a small bedchamber overlooking the water. A wonderful sea breeze drifted through the windows. She lay on the bed, and her mother put a wet towel on her forehead.

"This is a very poorly presented *festa*," Eleonora said irritably. "They have too many people in the hall, and they have scheduled too many entertainments and have thus had to begin too early in the evening, while it is excessively hot. And when it becomes dark and they light the torches, it will still be as hot. The Venetians have no better manners than the Germans."

"Mama, go back in. I just need to be quiet and alone." Beatrice dreaded most of all what Mama would say when she found out. Mama had been right. She wasn't ready for this responsibility.

Beatrice pretended to be asleep, and after a while Mama left. Then the cool breeze began to calm her, and she did feel drowsy. She slept.

When she awoke the room was dark. She could hear the music from the banquet hall. She saw images of Ercole and ached to hold him. She thought of what this Ser Privolo was doing to her baby, and suddenly she was determined to go back and confront him. Or at least show him that she was not frightened of him and his lying Signory.

The hall was lit with hundreds of wax torches and was as hot as Mama had predicted. A procession of costumed actors portraying allegorical figures—Sforza serpents, Venetian lions, Justice enthroned on a gilded chariot—snaked among the tables. Beatrice slipped into her seat, drawing only a minimal flurry of attention.

Mama frowned at her as if she shouldn't have come back. Ser Privolo bowed and glanced at her diffidently.

On and on the actors came, moving around the hall before enacting their parts upon the stage, their entrances and exits sometimes marked by brilliant bursts of gunpowder. Giants with golden cornucopias, chimeras ridden by naked Moors beating tambourines and cymbals, Diana and Meleager enacting the death of the latter. Every now and then enormous golden balls, carried on sedan chairs as if they were Turkish sultans, exploded in puffs of smoke and spewed out still more actors, done up as serpents and lions.

At last trumpets announced the beginning of the banquet. The courses were brought by torchlight, the big silver platters proceeding around the hall as relentlessly as the costumed actors, round after round of bejeweled, befeathered, or gilded whole birds, pigs, stags, lambs, goats, and so many different sea creatures that it seemed the entire ocean had been plundered. The dessert courses featured a staggering variety of cakes along with an entire population of *confetti* figures, all of them intricately colored with dyes and gold syrup. These spun-sugar confections reproduced many of the allegorical figures that had appeared on stage, but there were also detailed depictions of real people—the Pope and his cardinals, the Doge, Il Moro, the Duke and Duchess of Milan, even Beatrice herself.

Like the main courses, the *confetti* were paraded by torchlight, on small silver trays. Beatrice was rapt now, dreamily watching the flickering light dance over the faces of real people and their tiny spun-sugar surrogates, as lifelike as elves. She imagined a table where she was being passed about like a *confetti* figure, destined to end up on some Titan's plate. Perhaps the Titan would look just like her, and she would devour herself.

Torches flared behind her, and she could feel the heat. Two *confetti* appeared on her plate. She was so amazed at the accuracy with which the features had been reproduced that for a moment she did not consider their symbolism. She had been served the figures of the Duke and Duchess of Milan. Gian and Eesh.

So the final allegory had been presented. She and her husband were being warned in the most humiliating fashion to accept Gian as Duke of Milan; the secret resolution would never be withdrawn. She was suddenly so furious that she trembled. She wanted to knock the *confetti* to the floor.

Ser Privolo hovered next to her ear, and she had a scarcely resistible urge to knock him to the floor as well. "Do you still want them?" he whispered.

She was stunned with simple confusion. What did he mean?

He turned to her with the tight essence of a smile and leaned so close that she could feel his breath on her ear. "The Signory has considered your husband's ultimatum, and we find that in present circumstances we must reject it. But of course circumstances are subject to change, and we have considered that as well. Understand that we cannot publish our decision. We did not even record it in the minutes of our meeting. But we give you in the name of the *Serenissima Repubblica* these conditions under which we will withdraw the secret resolution. Should Alfonso of Aragon succeed his father as King of Naples, or should King Ferrante permit Alfonso to send troops against Milan, we will not only accept but encourage the investiture of your husband as Duke of Milan."

"Could you believe the Bishop of Como, endlessly droning on like a *cacarella* about the heat and the pain in his legs and asking when the *festa* would end, and all the while shoveling his food like an army erecting battlements and washing it down with enough wine to float every ship in Venice? When we finally did get up, I saw him stuff his purse with gilded nuts and grab a fistful of candied fruit with each hand." Beatrice's high voice and shimmering laugh echoed like music across the water. The rest of her retinue, trailing behind her in a dozen gondolas, was by contrast wearily mute after the ordeal of the endless banquet.

When they arrived at the Este *palazzo*, the passengers were assisted from their gondolas directly onto the steps of the first-floor loggia. Beatrice waved aside the pages offering her assistance; she bounced up the steps, feeling so light that she wondered why she hadn't just skimmed across the water instead of taking the gondola home. A chorus of little angels seemed to sing in her head: *Vittoria! Vittoria!* The victory belongs to Beatrice, who has bested the mighty Signory and the terrible Alfonso and the traitor Eesh! She has saved Italy! She has saved her baby.

"Beatrice."

Beatrice turned to her mother, who had come ahead in another boat and stood in the loggia like a sentry, her hands on her hips. "Beatrice, I want you to have some food before you go to bed. You hardly ate at the banquet, and you took too much wine for an empty stomach. A table has been set in my balcony."

A spiral staircase led to the small third-story loggia adjacent to Eleonora's bedchamber. Beatrice dashed up the winding stairs like a child playing; Eleonora trudged heavily behind. The table was set simply, with silver bowls containing soup and Murano glass goblets half full of heavily watered wine. The narrow, high windows were unshuttered, and Beatrice could look down the canal to her right. Lanterns still burned in many of the loggias and balconies of the nearby buildings, outlining the patterns of delicate stone colonnades crowned with almost-Moorish carved trefoils.

Eleonora stirred her soup, then put her spoon down. "When we went to war with Venice, this house was confiscated by the Signory. After the peace was negotiated, the house was restored to us. I guess I could not believe that the war was really over until I had come here again. But Venice was never the same for me. Parts of this house have been standing here for five hundred years, yet even this house seemed changed after the war. I could never again bring myself to love even the one thing in Venice that was ours."

Beatrice wasn't accustomed to the weariness, almost frailty, in her mother's voice. She considered Mama as durable as the house itself.

"What did Ser Privolo promise you tonight?"

Beatrice heard her own spoon clatter into her bowl.

"I saw the business with the *confetti*. He might as well have made an address to the entire Maggior Consiglio."

In spite of herself, Beatrice was relieved that Mama knew. "Mama, I tricked the Signory." Somewhere deep inside her a voice pleaded: Mama, please be proud of me. And deeper still: Please love me.

Eleonora crossed herself. "*Nostro Signore,* you are as mad as your father. What in the name of God do you mean?"

"Mama, by telling them that my husband intends to be invested by the German Emperor, I got them to agree that he could become Duke of Milan if Alfonso does something. I asked for more than I wanted and got exactly what I wanted. I have secured peace for us, Mama."

Eleonora looked at her daughter with mixed horror and astonishment, her eyes piercing and her jaw slack. "What in the name of God would make you do something so utterly—"

"Mama, Eesh has asked Alfonso to attack us, and I have a letter that can prove it. I can show you Eesh's letter, Mama."

"Where is this letter?"

Beatrice dashed down the stairs to her bedroom. She removed the letter from her tooled silver document case and bounced back up the stairs, her heart pounding with joyous anticipation. Now Mama would see.

Eleonora examined the seal. She read quickly, shaking her head slightly. When she finished, she looked up at Beatrice. "I would expect this from your cousin. But what you have done is far more reckless and foolish. You have no idea what you are playing with. You may well have brought us to the threshold of war. I want your most solemn oath that you will never tell your husband what Ser Privolo told you tonight."

The word "foolish" was a slap so hard that Beatrice's lips trembled. And then she was just angry. "No, Mama, you are the fool. Because if Grandfather Ferrante dies, the only way we will avoid war is if my husband is allowed to become Duke of Milan."

Eleonora looked off into the distance. A black gondola glided by on the darkened water like a floating bier. "Peace is every man's wife," she said. "And war is every man's mistress. The *condottieri* like my brother love war so much because they do not have to live with its consequences. To them war is just a great hunt or tournament. They gallop across the countryside in their armor, gaily pursuing one another's armies, avoiding at all costs actually meeting in battle. If a town or city is too weak to oppose them, they sack and loot it or simply extort their expenses from the terrified citizens. And they burn and pillage every village in their path. In all the wars that have been fought in Italy since I have been alive, a hundred women and children have been murdered by soldiers for each soldier who met with some accident while avoiding battle."

"Mama, I really believe that my husband doesn't want war." And yet a doubt came up like a whisper from a deep well. Do I?

"Yes, I believe that is true. And your husband is even more dangerous than my brother. Your husband believes he can use the threat of war to wage his peace. He will threaten Naples with France and Venice with Germany and Florence with Rome and say it is all done in the name of peace. He thinks he can call the King of France across the mountains and then send him back as easily as if he were a *condottiere* with fifty footmen."

"Mama, the King of France will never have to come to Italy as long as Alfonso doesn't attack—"

"That is your husband's fantasy, to conquer my brother with threats, just as it is my brother's fantasy to conquer Milan with his army. The men who rule Italy live in castles of their fantasies, parading in their armor at jousts and ordering their architects to draw cities with the streets all in rows and romancing their mistresses with sonnets written by their poets." Eleonora bemusedly shook her head. "But you, my dear daughter, like even the simplest plowman's wife, are condemned to live in the real world. And you as well as any woman know the violence and suffering required to bring a single child into that world. Every moment of every day, somewhere a woman is waging a mortal struggle to create life. And every moment of every day we must struggle to nurture and protect that life we have created with *our* pain and *our* blood. At our breasts the lamb of peace must be suckled, for it will find nothing at a man's dry teat."

Eleonora crossed herself, her pudgy hand moving across her bosom with practiced grace. "Merciful God, Beatrice, what I have seen of war! I promise you I pray to the Virgin every day that my girls will never have to see such things." She crossed herself again. "And I thank God every day that I have not lost any of my babies. I remember when the Venetians besieged us. No food could come in. The water was quickly fouled. Then the plague broke out in the city. So many died that the bodies they carted to the Duomo each day filled the entire piazza. Day after day. They were all black from the disease. So many babies, all in rows, their little faces all black, like fallen statues of little *negre* angels. Each one of them once cradled in some woman's womb and fed at her breast. All dead, all that sweet milk and whispered love and gentle caresses turned to rot and decay. I would beg sweet Jesus to take me before I ever have to see anything like that again. I beg our sweet Lord to take me if my death can save one baby from that. That is all war is. Dead babies.''

Beatrice stared as if examining those rows of little black corpses. Then she shook her head violently. "You are a liar and a hypocrite, Mama. Yes, I know the pain and fear that it took to bring Ercole into the world, and I know that I would do it a thousand times again to hold him in my arms just once. And I would die for him, Mama. I almost did." Suddenly she stood up. "You left me in Naples, Mama. For eight years I didn't know what it was like to have a mother hold me in her arms. How can you love all these other women's babies and not love me, Mama?"

Eleonora shot out of her chair. "I will not listen to you tell me that. . . ." Then the conviction drained from her heavy, powerful face. She looked down at her soup, her thick jowls trembling with each little sideways motion of her head. She reached out and pressed her fingers against the tablecloth. Her arms were shaking. Finally she said, "I suppose I never wanted you to know how much your father despises my father. Of course after the other night I am sure you realize that. They have been rivals since your father was a boy." There was a terrible resignation in her voice, as if her words were marching her to her death. "I brought you children to Naples with me because your father's nephew Niccolò had just attempted to overthrow us. After we arrived, your father blamed my father for supporting Niccolò, and one thing led to another and it seemed we would have war yet again. Already I had seen too much war, and I had seen only the smallest fraction of what I have seen since then. So I agreed to return to Ferrara and negotiate a peace between my father and your father."

Eleonora stopped, and her dark swooping eyebrows twitched. "My *own father* forced me to leave one of my *own children* with him as a hostage to that peace." Eleonora's tone was so venomous that Beatrice understood instantly something she couldn't have imagined in her wildest conjecture: Mama hates her father.

Beatrice felt her mother's hate draw up her own, like two

spitting adders facing off. "So why did you choose me, Mama?"

"Of course your brother Alfonso had to come back. He is your father's heir. You were the second girl. . . ."

Beatrice was so stunned by the simple mathematics of her mother's choice that it was a moment before she realized that this wasn't the truth, either. Her scream exploded in the loggia and echoed down the canal. "Liar, Mama! Liar!"

Eleonora reached across the table, a pathetic, beseeching gesture, as if trying to escape her ponderous body. "You don't know how it hurt me, baby. It hurt as much as if you had been torn from my womb. In the name of God, baby, if you believe nothing else, believe that I loved you and have always loved you."

"I don't love you, Mama." Beatrice straightened triumphantly, seeming to tower next to her mother's defeated posture. "And I don't care if you ever loved me." She rushed past her mother in a whisper of taffeta and disappeared into the house.

Eleonora turned and raised her arm again, even more feebly, then let it drop. She stared out across the canal. Directly opposite was one of the newer churches in Venice, an *all'antica* design of radical geometric purity, its virtually unadorned facade as simple as a gravestone.

The images she had kept locked away for so long appeared in the darkness, a shadow mime against the blank wall of the church. Her father coming to her bed, a heavy, dark incubus reeking of wine. The blackened skeleton of a village and rows of fresh little mounds in the raw red earth of the Campania. Mass executions, processions of headless necks spurting blood . . . And then she examined her own guilt, a mental ledger kept in meticulous detail. Beatrice. God knew how much she loved Beatrice. But her first-born, Isabella, had always been the child every mother dreams of, so golden and gifted that it was as if an angel had been sent to earth. Even now she could feel the grief when Bel had gone away to Mantua to be married, the next day walking through her daughter's empty rooms as if walking through her tomb, the day after that ordering Bel's rooms sealed forever so that she would not have to see them empty again. God forgive her. In Naples she had never questioned which child she would leave behind. God forgive her, because in her heart she had thanked God that she had Beatrice to leave behind.

Eleonora struggled to her feet. She supported herself against the marble balustrade and challenged all the horrors she had conjured in the night. I cannot give you back your childhood, she silently confessed to Beatrice. I can only give you and Italy the peace for which your childhood was slaughtered. If I have to come back from the grave I will see that you and your baby have that peace. And perhaps then you will know that I loved you.

Beatrice came quickly awake in the darkened room and reminded herself that she was in Venice. A monkey jeered somewhere, followed by a dog barking, the sounds so distant that they seemed from another time. She could not hear anything moving on the canal outside her window.

Her dream was still vivid. She had been in the darkened nave of a cathedral, except this cathedral had been round like a wheel, its circumference as vast as a city wall. The cathedral had turned, and she had stayed at its center, watching the aisle chapels glide past, each illuminated for a moment by a brilliant pop of light, like fireworks going off. In that instant of light the contents of each chapel had materialized and disappeared. Strange things. Her grandfather on his bier, like something made of wax. Eesh dressed in black, sobbing, her face so sunken she might have been a corpse. One of Mama's dead babies, a statue of black-glazed terra-cotta with terrible ruby eyes. A painting of her uncle Alfonso, surrounded by pomegranate wreaths and kneeling saints, his face blue. Her baby, but another boy's name on the marble plaque beneath him. A nude madonna, her legs spread, her genitals painted red . . .

Around and around the cathedral had spun, faster and faster, the great wind of this motion rising in her ears, the images popping so fast that there was no longer an instant of darkness between them. Stop the wheel, the wind had soughed beneath its roar, stop the wheel. But she knew that if she did, the force that held her at the center would send her flying off into one of the aisle chapels, and there she would stay forever, frozen in some eternity, her place at the center taken by a new penitent watching her fate rush past.

She sat up. This night she had slept naked because of the heat. She pressed her hands to her breast and felt for her heart, her own touch arousing her, a delicious mingling of fear and desire. The fear was the terrible import of the secret she now held locked in her breast, known only to herself, Mama, and the Signory. But she did not have to unlock that secret. Not until she needed it to save her baby. Only then would she tell her husband. Perhaps Grandfather Ferrante would live forever; perhaps he would never allow Alfonso to do anything.

Her desire was more complicated. Power, that was part of it. Of course she had the power to avenge herself on Eesh. Whenever she wanted. But now she also had power over her husband. The power to give him the thing he held dearest. The power to raise him up or cast him down. The power to play the game of fate.

Beatrice lightly stroked her nipples, making them hard. She shuddered, and a tremor of excitement ran through her. "Touch me," she whispered to her imaginary lover. "Hold me. Listen to my heart and imagine that you understand its music, that your caresses have authored its every song. Because you will never hear the music of my secret heart. You will touch me never knowing that just beneath your fingers is the key you can never reach, the key that unlocks every fate. The silent choice of my secret heart."

◆ PART ◆

SIX

CHAPTER

33

Extract of a letter of the scholar Ponzone da Cremona to Isabella d'Este da Gonzaga, Marquesa of Mantua. Ferrara, June 1493

. . . I hear that a man named Colombo has recently discovered an island for the King of Spain, on which are found men of our size but with skin the hue of copper and noses like apes . . . they all go about naked, men as well as women. Twelve men and four women have been brought back to the King of Spain, but two of them fell ill of some disease the physicians cannot ascertain, and have died. . . . The rest have been given clothes. . . . They seem intelligent and are quite tame and gentle. No one can comprehend their language. . . .

Pavia, 1 June 1493

"Gian, let the grooms brush Neptune." Isabella sat up straight in the saddle, her shoulders heaving with each breath. Her face was livid with the late afternoon heat and the exertion of trying to keep up with her husband's riding pace.

Gian Galeazzo Sforza, Duke of Milan, dismounted and surrendered the reins of his favorite white stallion to the waiting groom. He stood in the shaded brick arcade and squinted out at his wife. With sudden inspiration, he stepped back into the glaring sun and helped her from her horse.

"It's so hot, Gian," Isabella whispered in her husband's ear. "The water in the pool will be so cool."

The pool at the Pavia *castello* was indoors, in the northern wing, facing the ducal park. A circular basin of white marble, its centerpiece was a fluted marble column crowned with four naked *putti;* each of the chubby carved infants held a curling, vinelike marble spout that spurted a steady stream of water back into the pool. Maestro Leonardo da Vinci had installed hot-water spigots for winter bathing, but in the summer the thick marble kept the water comfortably cool.

Isabella took an armful of towels from the pages and ordered them to lock the doors. She pulled her dress off before the locks even clicked and slipped out of her chemise while Gian was still bending over to unstrap his engraved silver spurs, worn directly over his riding hose.

"Just unlace your hose, Gian. Leave your spurs on."

Completely naked, her heavy breasts swaying, she came to him and led him down the marble steps that ringed the pool until he was knee-deep in the water.

"Doesn't that feel good on your feet, Gian? Sit down and let me take your doublet off."

Gian slowly settled, the water lapping into his crotch. Isabella dove off the steps, wriggled underwater for a moment, then rose like Venus coming out of the sea, hair slicked back and pale skin gleaming. She walked up the steps and straddled Gian's legs, then squatted on his thighs. Her nipples were tightly erect. She unlaced Gian's riding doublet and his shirt and peeled them off, then cupped a handful of water and trickled it onto his bare, hairless chest. Hands clasped behind his neck, she pulled closer, letting her nipples tease his skin. Her strong, elegant fingers played over his long blond hair and half-sneering, half-angelic face.

"*Gesù*, you are beautiful, Gian."

She pulled his hose down past his knees. He was already semi-erect, and when she stroked his scrotum he stiffened immediately and reached up for her. She congratulated herself on the success of her tactics: Gian relaxed from his ride, the element of surprise, from his horse to his wife so quickly that he hadn't time to panic. But then Gian had never been healthier and happier—a consequence of her curtailing his drinking binges and sending his more dissolute companions back to Milan.

"Kiss me first, Gian. The way I like it."

With dutiful tenderness he gave her slow caressing kisses. Isabella closed her eyes, temporarily masking their sharply erotic glitter, giving herself a look of girlish innocence.

She awakened again and guided him to her. Eyes wide, she lifted up, then relaxed and let him slide deeply inside her. His hands kneaded her breasts, and the initial startling pain subsided into thrilling stabs of pleasure. Should I tell him now? she asked herself, then decided that she felt too wonderful to threaten this moment.

His lithe body was supple and hard at once, a lover's body, she thought. "Good, good, Gian," she murmured. "You've gotten so good. So good to me." The light glowed above her, and in her passion she wrestled him off the steps into the pool. She thought fleetingly of Pygmalion, enamored of the statue he had carved, and wondered if she was starting to love Gian, the husband she was creating.

Gian stood chest-deep in the water, and she wrapped her legs around him. She was weightless now, her only link to the earth the pressure of his lips and the touch of him inside. There is a baby in there, she silently told her husband. Your baby, Gian, I am certain of it. This time it will be your son.

C H A P T E R

34

On the River Po, Near Pavia, 11 June 1493

The pilot stood next to Beatrice on the elevated stern of the galley. He pointed toward a wooden platform jutting into the river from the right bank. "Your Highness, that is the last ferry before Pavia. We will dock within an hour."

Beatrice shaded her eyes. A group of five or six horsemen had gathered in a clearing on the tree-lined riverbank, waiting to board the small, flat barge that would carry them across the water. As the galley came within shouting distance, one of the horsemen rode out onto the ferry. Even from a distance he was dashing, a dark-haired, dark-skinned man in a trim white-and-gold riding doublet, mounted on a beautiful white horse. The whites were unreal, brighter than the sun.

When Beatrice realized that this fantasy rider was her husband, her first thought was: Something is wrong. The last she had heard, Eesh and Gian were still in residence at the *castello* in Pavia; she could well imagine that hostilities had broken out between Milan and Naples, and her husband had been forced to come out and warn her. . . .

But her husband waved with such enthusiasm that she had no further theories to explain his welcome. "Pilot!" Il Moro shouted.

312

"I have come to abduct the beautiful Duchess of Bari! I warn you to surrender her, or we shall direct fire at you from our cannon hidden in the trees!"

The pilot laughed and steered the galley to a docking beside the ferry. He signaled the two remaining galleys and five barges carrying the rest of Beatrice's entourage and baggage to continue on to Pavia. Crewmen scrambled over the railing to tie up the boat.

"There is a certain little boy who is most anxious to see his mother!" Il Moro shouted up to Beatrice. She found it hard to believe that this was the same man who had dispatched her from the docks at Ferrara three weeks previously, much less the man who had greeted her with icy formality at the end of her cold, foreboding nuptial voyage two and a half years before. Perhaps he hadn't changed so much, though his face was thinner than she had ever remembered it and so darkened from the sun that his teeth gleamed like ivory; he looked fit, rested, and ten years younger than his age. But his eyes had changed entirely. Rather than the blank, obsidian stare she had become accustomed to, those eyes now had soft, almost velvet texture, a curiously erotic depth.

Il Moro shouted to his company of guards, and one of them led onto the ferry a big gray Barbary stallion, Beatrice's favorite horse from the Pavia stables. "You can imagine how my wife suffered in Venice, where the only horses are made of bronze, and to be considered a *cognoscente* of the equestrian arts one must simply know which end of the horse to face when one sits in the saddle," Il Moro announced to Beatrice's ladies-in-waiting, who crowded the railing. "So I have brought my wife the means to recover her skill at riding."

"Her Highness has not lost her skill at *scartino*," called out one of Beatrice's ladies. "On this journey she has won a thousand ducats going and now another thousand coming back! Anyone foolish enough to play cards with her will soon learn that Her Highness is Fortune's favorite."

Beatrice went into her cabin to find her riding gloves. And to remove Eesh's letter from her document case; after the unspeakable oath she had sworn to deliver it, she did not want to postpone a moment longer. When she emerged, Il Moro helped her over the railing, lifting her in a grand sweeping gesture. He kissed her on the lips, as he often did for public display, but this kiss was strangely private, with a sparking contact that unsettled her stomach. Was it possible he already knew about the Signory's decision? Had Ser Privolo also told Count Tuttavilla of the conditions under which Il Moro would be permitted to become Duke of Milan?

"We shall beat you to the *castello* by an hour!" Il Moro shouted to the pilot after he and Beatrice had mounted their horses. They rode off along the graded path beside the river. The guards followed behind, discreetly out of hearing.

After they had gone a short distance, Beatrice said, "I have a letter I promised to deliver to you. I presume it was stolen from a courier." She wondered what had happened to the young man with whom she had now kept faith.

She watched his face as he read. The corners of his mouth turned down slightly, as if he were mockingly reciting Isabella's rhetoric to himself. Finally he looked up, his expression neutral. "I hope you realize now that your cousin is hardly worthy of the loyalty you have shown her."

"Is she here?" Beatrice asked, not certain which answer she hoped to hear.

"No. Your cousin and Gian left Pavia two days before I arrived. She is determined to turn Gian against me, which is sad, because I am truly very fond of him. Fortunately we don't need to worry about Isabella's father"—he slapped the letter with his hand—"bringing his army to her assistance as long as your grandfather is alive. That I can assure you. And the news we have from Germany is very good. We can expect within a fortnight an official announcement of the betrothal of Bianca Maria and the Archduke Maximilian." He smiled, looking boyishly glamorous. "I don't believe we will hear the sound of guns in Italy this summer."

She marveled at his casual self-assurance; the last time she had seen him, the *oltramontani* barbarians had virtually been at the gates. "You're not alarmed at the refusal of the Signory to commit to our mutual defense?"

"Not when I will soon have the next German Emperor in my employ. I must tell you, Beatrice, that I would have been more concerned had the Signory blithely made a public pledge to defend us, a pledge they had no intention of fulfilling. That they vacillated shows that they take seriously their alliance with us. I am very proud of how well you did with them. You were direct, as I knew you would be. If I had given the task to Tuttavilla, he would still be phrasing the question. You immediately obtained an answer." He paused and dropped his gaze from her eyes to her torso, almost as if staring at her breasts. "I understand from Count Tuttavilla that you also arranged a private meeting with the Doge. Why?"

He doesn't know, she told herself. His tone was too genuinely suspicious. It delighted her that he seemed to wonder if he could entirely trust her. "I believed that the Doge was more sympathetic to our interests than was the majority in the Signory. I hoped that even if the Doge would not differ with his colleagues, the meeting itself might help divide the Signory."

"Just so." He quickly looked into her eyes again, sounding relieved by her explanation. "Beatrice, you are becoming a very clever diplomat. But then I always suspected that you had a very special gift." His smile was too glib, as if *he* was really the clever one and had engineered her entire dialogue with the Venetians. And yet there was something else to it, perhaps the sensual gleam of his teeth against his dark lips, that stimulated a distinct fluttering in her breast. For a moment she imagined him an ardent suitor from one of her girlhood romances, preparing to declare his love. Then she realized that in Venice even her fantasies had changed, that now she had more substantial dreams to chase, more complicated games to play. All her life she had waited for love. Now she would pursue her desire.

They rode on, splashed with the dappled light that filtered through the shade trees. Dragonflies hovered and darted in the sultry air. You really don't know, Beatrice inwardly told her husband. You think you are playing me to your own end, when I hold in my breast the secret that can raise you up or cast you down. You think you are going to seduce me, and you do not realize that I have already seduced you.

"This is the first volume of the works of Pliny, which Messer Minuziano intends to print in their entirety. He has also promised me Cicero and Tacitus." Il Moro offered the book, bound in red morocco leather polished to a sheen, to Count Girolamo da Tuttavilla.

Tuttavilla reverently fingered the pages of immaculate new vellum, the printed text so crisp and dark that it seemed engraved. Il Moro watched him, an expression of satisfaction working at the corners of his mouth. "I believe our presses are the equal of any in Europe," Il Moro said. "Were you aware that the grammar of Lascari my brother commissioned the year he died was the first book printed in Italy?"

Tuttavilla looked up, jarred from his reverie. "Your brother was a complicated man, wasn't he? What you said some months ago about *chiaroscuro*, the contrast between light and shadow, certainly applies to him."

Il Moro's relaxed mouth tightened; there was a slight tremor of his lower lip. "Yes." He paused for a moment. "Why do you suppose my wife arranged a private meeting with the Doge, without informing anyone in the ambassadorial mission?"

Tuttavilla made a small shrugging hand gesture. "My own opinion is that she is a very competitive young woman who felt that the Signory had gotten the better of her in their interview, and she hoped, in a manner of speaking, to swing her *palla* bat at another ball."

"She insists that after having determined that the Signory was opposed to a proclamation of mutual defense, she hoped that an unannounced meeting with the Doge might serve to foster suspicion among the Signory as to the firmness of their own policy."

Tuttavilla nodded. "So she told me. And indeed she may have been correct. In my informal conversations with members of the Signory during our farewell *festa*, I perceived a certain softening of their position."

"So you believe that Beatrice's interview with the Doge advanced the interests of our state."

"Indeed yes. As I wrote you, she conducted herself splendidly throughout our mission. She is a marvelous speaker, with a keen wit and a natural charm that is most compelling. There was not a Venetian I spoke to who failed to mention with all sincerity her delightful nature," Tuttavilla offered. "Though we have ample enough evidence of Her Highness's charms without requiring the Venetians to validate them."

Il Moro looked into some abstract middle distance between himself and Tuttavilla and nodded thoughtfully. "Yes," he said, "you are certainly correct about that."

Beatrice listened to the faint whisper of his breathing beside her, the only sound she had heard. The passion she had always dreamed of had been an exquisite inner music, a chorale of erotic angels. This had all been silent, an unspoken poetry of touch. His fingers and lips had roamed over her with the patience of a sculptor, reshaping and transforming her, polishing her skin with the luminescence of the night. Nothing in their previous sexual history had led her to imagine that his true expertise, which she had always believed to be the game of deceit, was actually this game of the senses.

She tried to reconstruct the events that had led to this, to analyze where she had lost control, but she realized that even her memory had changed in the last few hours, that just as her baby had forever altered her perception, so too had this night. After she had put Ercole to bed she had dined alone with her husband in his rooms. And at first they had seemed so evenly matched, the clever banter and innuendo, actually joking about the irony of seduction after more than two years of marriage and one child. She had been able to see more clearly what she desired, and she could even recognize the element of revenge in it. On Eesh, of course, by taking as her lover Eesh's mortal enemy. But also revenge on him. In making him want her like this, she would wrest back the power he had taken from her every time he had used her like a brood mare. And then perhaps he would find himself at the mercy of her power.

The first long kiss had seemed like a choreography of mutual desire, a dance to which she knew all the steps. But then she had become lost, swept off so quickly that she'd scarcely had time to acknowledge that in all but the most technical sense she had been a virgin until this night. The only assurance left to her had been knowing that in her heart she held a secret that he needed more than he needed her. Don't tell him, she had pleaded with herself as she drowned in her own senses, don't ever tell him. But in the end she had not even been certain what it was she must never tell him.

He shifted his body, and the moonlight shimmered over his flesh. His fingers traced lightly over her ribcage, a lightning strike inducing an instant of near paralysis. God, she heard herself say. Every pore was an exposed nerve. Her hair tingled, and she felt as if it were floating around her.

"I want to make love to you again, *amore*."

Love. The word was an alarm deep in her soul. "Wait," she told him, sitting up and clutching his hands. "Wait." She looked into his hot black eyes. "Don't tell me that. Don't tell me that you love me until you love me more than you loved Cecilia. Don't tell me until you can call me *anima mia*, your own soul, until I am everything to you, until you would give up everything for me. You cannot say you love me until you would walk into Hell like Orpheus to bring me back."

He folded her hands tightly in his. "I cannot tell you that now," he whispered. "I cannot promise you I will ever be able to tell you that."

She kissed his hands. "That is all I ask. The truth. I don't care if you cannot say it now or if you can ever say it. I only care that in this one thing you respect the truth." She looked into his eyes to seal an unspoken agreement, then settled back onto the cool silk sheets and anticipated his touch.

Extract of a letter of LEONARDO DA VINCI, engineer at the Court of Milan, to international traveler and raconteur BENEDETTO DEI. Milan, 1 September 1493

. . . I offer you this brief inventory without recourse to further consideration or opinion, as you will understand how pressed we are to complete to our satisfaction and that of others the afore-mentioned endeavors:

Word received here that German Emperor Frederick died 19 August. To be succeeded by son Maximilian, Archduke of Austria. Great rejoicing here—as of 10 July Duke of Milan's sister betrothed to Maximilian. Wedding by proxy in our Duomo in November and the bride to be conveyed to Germany thereafter.

News of said betrothal occasions great relief among the more prudent gentlemen of France, who cannot finance and do not wish to sanction their King's adventure and are now afforded compelling cause to discourage him.

The Duke of Bari in ardent pursuit of the woman to whom he has been married for near three years. Always to her rooms— he has the hollow-eyed look of a man recently wedded to a much younger woman.

The Duchess of Bari has become Milan's new muse, the projects under her aegis too many and variegated to mention—hence the haste with which we write. The poets proclaim Milan the New Athens.

The Duke and Duchess of Milan not seen at all—she is said to be with child.

Rumor that Duke of Bari will be invested as Duke of Milan when new German Emperor takes his Milanese bride. If so, why make present Duke's sister an empress?

My assistant, the boy Salai, has stolen from me again. . . .

CHAPTER

35

Ferrara, 11 October 1493

Her children were in the next room, and she could not open the door to get to them. Screams came from the courtyard, vague as if issuing from within a stone crypt. She turned and said, "I'm not finished."

The light, white like sunlit snow, led her to another room. When she went in she could not recognize the woman's face at first; it floated in the light. The woman was dressed in glowing white brocade and sat in a white satin chair.

"Mother?" It was her mother, and the joy and anger were stunning, like emerging from absolute darkness into the most intense sunlight. "Mama, you're alive." She reached out and touched her mother's face. "Oh, Mama." Then she turned and looked back. "Mama, I can't stay here. I'm not finished. I have so much to do."

Her mother drew her back, and she was ten years old again, the year her mother died. She rested her head on her mother's airy thigh.

"Eleonora, *mia fanciulla*," her mother said, stroking her hair, her glowing hands lifting it like sticky gossamer. "Look at me, *fanciulla*."

Eleonora looked into her mother's eyes and realized that Mama knew everything. "Mama, why did Father hurt me after you left?"

Her mother shushed her, and the anger came back. "Let me go. I'm not finished, Mama."

"We never finish," her mother said. "That is the tragedy of life. But that is why our lives never end. Did you leave them your dream?"

Suddenly she struggled furiously, the panic like an immense weight on her chest. They were in danger. She hadn't told them. . . .

"Yes, you did. You left them your dream. That is the only substantial thing you can leave behind, a creature of air, unclasp-able, to lead your children to their own dreams."

Now the weight was gone, and her own words were white light. "Mama, don't ever leave me again."

Her mother took her in her arms.

Milan, 11 October 1493

> *"As starlings in wide and shrieking files*
> *Are driven by winter's icy tempest*
> *So were tossed these sad damned souls . . ."*

Ser Antonio Grifo, Milan's foremost Dante scholar, paused in his reading and looked up to see if the Duke or Duchess of Bari wished to comment.

"These are the souls of carnal sinners," Beatrice said, with a sly glance at her husband. Il Moro sat beside her on the cushioned bench, opposite Ser Antonio's chair. "In life they abandoned will to lust, and so are condemned to be blown hither and thither as rapidly as birds in a whirlwind. By this device the poet emphasizes that when we choose to surrender our will in this life, so in the next we shall have neither will nor choice."

"Or perhaps," Il Moro said dryly, "the lovers are still swept along by the tempest of their lust and are condemned eternally to repeat their sin."

Beatrice let out a high-pitched laugh, and Ser Antonio looked down to hide his own amusement. "Go on, Ser Antonio," Beatrice said drolly. "We shall ask Francesca da Rimini and her lover if my husband's interpretation is correct."

Ser Antonio began to read again. His practiced voice gave Dante's vivid images a harrowing realism; the black whirlwind of tormented souls almost seemed to wail just outside the window of Beatrice's bedroom. In the narrative, two of the storm-tossed sinners were permitted to pause from their eternal flight and identify themselves to the poet. They were Francesca da Rimini and her husband's brother Paolo, both murdered by the jealous husband and now inseparable in their eternal woe. Ser Antonio's voice shifted to a beautiful, lilting tenor as he voiced Francesca's lament:

> *"Love, which cannot pardon the beloved,*
> *So strongly possessed me with delight*
> *That even now we share our first embrace.*
>
> *"Our love has led us two to one death . . ."*

"You see, they embrace one another still," Il Moro said. "And surely with all the turning and whirling through the air, they are able to vary this embrace and enjoy various *invenzione*."

Beatrice blushed and laughed, thinking of her husband's own amorous *invenzione*. "Read on, Ser Antonio," she said. "My husband will soon see that the lovers' position is not enjoyable at all."

Again Ser Antonio took on Francesca's voice. She answered with a heart-piercing preface Dante's request that she tell how she came to this place: " 'No sorrow is greater in this eternal woe than to remember in pain that moment of happiness. . . .' "

Beatrice nodded smugly, and Ser Antonio went on to finish the tale. Innocently amusing themselves with a French romance based on the legend of King Arthur, Francesca and Paolo had come across the passage where Lancelot kissed Guinevere. They impulsively exchanged their own kiss, and then, as Francesca recalled with graphic allusion, "that day we read no more." Ser Antonio somberly concluded the canto in Dante's narrative voice:

" 'And while the one spirit told me thus, the other wept so that out of pity I fainted as if dead. And as falls a lifeless corpse, so fell I.' "

Beatrice's eyes glistened, and Il Moro took her hand. "This day we read no more," he said. "*Mille grazie,* Ser Antonio. When you read, I feel we are arm in arm with Dante and Virgil, swatting the embers from our hair."

When Ser Antonio had left the room, Il Moro pulled up Beatrice's heavy damask skirt and put his hand on her thigh. "Shall we pretend you are Francesca da Rimini?"

"Then you will have to pretend you are not my husband."

Il Moro swept her up and carried her to her bed. He dumped her unceremoniously but then lay down beside her and tenderly caressed her and removed her clothes. They made love in a complex orchestration of passion and practice, at times athletic and abandoned, at times with exquisite deliberation. But each respite was followed by a more fevered pitch, their breathing becoming rasping and frantic.

"No! Stop!"

Il Moro instantly pulled away. "Did I hurt you? How . . . ?"

Beatrice lay back and clutched her arms around her torso. "I don't know. . . . No. It wasn't . . . it wasn't you. It felt inside me, but it wasn't. A moment of such cold . . . I have never felt anything like it."

"I should remind you that as husband and wife we are not committing a carnal sin," Il Moro said lightly. "But perhaps we should confine our evening readings of Dante to the *Paradiso.*"

She smiled weakly. "I'm still cold from it."

He pulled the feather quilt up over them, and she fell asleep in his arms.

Extract of a letter of ERCOLE D'ESTE, Duke of Ferrara, to BEATRICE D'ESTE DA SFORZA, Duchess of Bari. Ferrara, 12 October 1493

My beloved daughter,

. . . having been informed by your most illustrious lady mother that this condition had further weakened her, I returned from Belriguardo on the night of 8 October to discover that her gastric distress had now spread to the lungs, where it occasioned a pleurisy and most grievous cough. . . . On the evening of 11 October Our Lord God summoned his angelic host to convey your most illustrious lady mother to His Heavenly Throne. We can only be comforted in the knowledge that at the Highest Tribunal our Lord God will bestow on your most illustrious lady mother the rewards her exemplary virtues have most certainly earned. . . . Her last words were for you children. . . . I know that this news, unexpected as it is, will cause you the most abject sorrow, but your mother would doubtless concur in my wish that you conduct yourself with a dignity and dominion over your emotions that will credit both the Este name and your most illustrious lady mother's blessed memory. . . .

Letter of Isabella d'Aragona da Sforza, Duchess of Milan, to Beatrice d'Este da Sforza, Duchess of Bari. Pavia, 17 October 1493

Your most illustrious Highness,

We have received the news here of the most untimely and undeserved death of Madame your mother, my own most illustrious lady aunt. Perhaps it will be of little consolation to you to know that I loved her more than my own mother, but she was a woman of uncommon strength, virtue, and compassion, and Italy can ill spare her to this terrible caprice that has taken her from us. I know that my own grief can only be the smallest fraction of the pain you feel, and I pray that the healing hands of Time will soon find you and soothe and heal you.

Isabella d'Aragona da Sforza, Duchess of Milan

With my own hand

Milan, 25 October 1493

"*Carissima*," Il Moro whispered. "I can see nothing, *carissima*."

After a moment the room materialized in the light of a single candle, a wavering hallucination of light and shadow racing across darkness. The walls as well as the windows were draped in black and indigo satin. Beatrice's bed looked like a catafalque; it was covered with a black bedspread, the four columns and the canopy wrapped in black crepe. The motionless figure stretched out on the bed was attired entirely in black.

Il Moro sat beside his wife. "*Carissima*, you must come out of here. Come only for a quarter of an hour. We'll go up to the gallery and watch the sun set." He could not caress her hair because it was tucked away beneath a black silk cap, so he stroked her chilly, dry cheek. "Oh, *carissima*, you have to come out of here. You have to eat."

"I have eaten." Beatrice sounded like a *vecchia* on her deathbed.

"Let me open the curtains. There is still an hour of light left." Beatrice shook her head drowsily. "Very well, *carissima*, but you must talk to me. You must permit someone other than our son to console you. Little Ercole loves you, but he cannot understand your grief."

Beatrice turned on her side, away from the small candle on the table beside her bed. She said nothing for a long while. Finally she looked up at her husband, the candle reflected in the corners of her eyes.

"I told her I didn't love her. That was the last thing I ever told her. Our last night in Venice. I wouldn't talk to her for the rest of our trip."

Il Moro lay down beside her and held her tightly. "Oh, *fanciulla*, I didn't know that. Oh, *carissima*. Now I understand."

"You can't. No one can."

Il Moro sat up on the edge of the bed, his back to her, his head and shoulders slumped. He pressed his palms to his forehead. "Perhaps I can." His voice was so strange that Beatrice turned toward him. "I have never told you how my mother died. I have never admitted it to anyone. My mother. Do you know that I wrote her once a week from the time I was five years old until . . . In Latin. Whether I was home with her or away. Every night until I was twelve years old she came into my rooms and selected the clothes I would wear the next day. When I fancied myself as too much of a young man for that, she simply talked to me every evening. Politics. Literature. Even women. She was the truest friend I ever had. She never said anything about my father's mistresses, and there were many, because she did not want us to think any less of him. He died in another woman's arms, and still she admonished herself at his bier for not having been a more obedient wife. We had to force her to bury his body. Bianca Maria Visconti da Sforza." Il Moro shook his head in wonder, saying the name as if he had invoked the Holy Virgin.

"My mother was the first to see the monster my brother had become. She tried to reason with him, to save him. He began with little things: withholding her household allowance, forcing her to smaller rooms, selling off her jewels and books. Then he accused her of infidelity to my father, of worse crimes. None of it true, of course, but lies that hurt her more terribly than any truth. He knew everyone's weakness. That was why he excelled at torture. Finally he exiled her to a small house in Cremona. Away from everyone who loved her, with only one servant, a stranger. A week later she died. None of us were there. My brother would not permit it. The physicians could find no cause for her death. At the time, I told myself she died of grief. And yet she was a woman of such strength and faith, it did not seem possible." Il Moro's right arm trembled violently. He did not speak until it had stopped shaking a moment later. "Later, I . . . discovered what killed her. How . . . he . . ." Il Moro's cheek twitched so wildly that it drew his mouth up into a grimace.

When he managed to speak again his voice quivered. "I never said a word to my brother about what he had done to my mother. The day I buried her I greeted him with a clasp and a kiss. He murdered her as certainly as if he had put poison in her cup. And I said nothing. I choked on my grief and my honor and said nothing. Until he finally exiled me, I could not permit myself to love a woman because I feared . . ." His arm shook again. "I feared . . . what he might do to her." He let out a hideous, grunting laugh. "The only woman I made love to in that time was my brother's mistress. For some sick purpose of his own he forced us . . . He watched us. Only after he was dead could I admit to myself that I had permitted him to defile and destroy the one woman I loved. My mother. Only when the fear of him was gone could I know the shame."

He sat motionless for a long while and then turned back to Beatrice. "Whatever guilt you feel, however you think you may have tormented your mother's soul and however painful this wound to your own soul, you cannot know the remorse that still haunts me after twenty-five years."

Beatrice flew out of the bed and ripped the satin drapes from the big arched window. Daylight exploded into the room. She stood there in black, suddenly illuminated, clutching the drapes. "You don't see anything!" Her scream was deafening. "No one sees anything!" Il Moro recovered and started toward her. "I still hate her! I hate her more than I ever hated her!" Now Il Moro had her in his arms, but she struggled wildly. "I hate her, I hate her, I hate her!"

She froze in a final paroxysm of fury, her mouth wide and nothing coming out. Then a retching, moaning sob came up from her chest, and she jerked convulsively. She shuddered again and began to sob hysterically. Il Moro hugged her and rocked her.

One thought spun through Beatrice's grief like a shrieking soul caught up in Hell's whirlwind of the damned: She had no right to leave me. Mama had no right to leave me again.

C H A P T E R

36

Milan, 30 November 1493

Bona of Savoy, Duchess Mother of Milan, slapped away the hands
of her daughter's matron of honor. Her gnarled fingers pecking
like little birds, Bona herself adjusted the pearl-and-diamond-
studded aigrette that crowned the bride's cascade of golden hair.
"Just so. Just so," Duchess Bona said in a chirpy singsong. She
smiled, her rotted teeth seemingly drawn in black chalk against
the stark white layer of ceruse that caked her oval face. "Everything must be just so for Her Most Serene Highness the Empress
of the Holy Roman Empire."

Bianca Maria Sforza, who within hours would indeed exchange
her aigrette for the crown of the Holy Roman Empress, stood
motionless, her sublime dark eyes wide and dreamy. Her tall,
elegant figure graced a gown of imperial crimson satin, liberally
sprinkled with precious gems and embroidered all over with imperial eagles in thick gold thread. Her enormous winglike sleeves
reached to the ground, and her train was three times as long as
she was tall. She resembled a gorgeous, mythical bird about to be
sacrificed on the high altar of transalpine diplomacy.

"No one has ever seen anything like it," Bona chirped on to

no one in particular, though she was surrounded by a dozen ladies-in-waiting. "There is no state that has not sent an ambassador, including that of Russia, and there isn't a house in the city that hasn't been decorated especially for this occasion. The Marchesino Stanga informs me that Her Most Serene Highness's trousseau is valued at two hundred thousand ducats and will be the glory of all Europe. We are displaying it here in the Castello before she leaves, and of course it will be unpacked again when she arrives in Innsbruck. The Germans will know then the quality of the lady whom Lord God has given them as their Empress."

"And don't forget, Duchess Mother, that Bianca Maria's husband will soon be the most favorably endowed man in Europe." Isabella pushed aside the ladies-in-waiting crowded around the future Empress. "He will have our Bianca Maria's beauty and virginity, his father's crown, the King of France's friendship, and Il Moro's purse. He will have been constructed from nothing through the generosity of Fortune and my father's enemies."

Bona turned on her daughter-in-law like a white-faced owl defending her nest. "Who cares about your *impicatti* in Naples. They are nothing. You are nothing. *Niente*." The black scar of her smile showed again. *"Niente, niente, niente,"* she sang, the words a gleeful ditty.

"Even you will have the wits to care when I tell you what I have heard." Isabella glanced at Bianca Maria, whose fixed eyes had begun to roam slightly but who seemed otherwise as yet undisturbed by the discord. "Come with me into the *guardaroba*."

Duchess Bona accompanied Isabella into the adjacent *guardaroba* with a series of cawing "hah"'s, as if she would soon expose her daughter-in-law's madness for all the world to see.

The two women faced each other in the narrow space left between the rolled Persian carpets and the stacks of fine linens, a fraction of the treasure trove that Bianca Maria would bring to her new home. Three gilt-framed mirrors, also part of the trousseau, leaned against a pile of tooled and gilded leather saddles and gold saddle cloths. The mirrors reflected multiple images of Bona and Isabella, the former in her widow's black silk, the latter in a *camora* of ducal crimson. Isabella's profile showed clearly the swell of her pregnancy, though she was remarkably slim for a woman in her seventh month.

"It is inconceivable to me that you haven't heard, or that if you have heard you are so unconcerned," Isabella said.

Bona blinked several times.

"Every ambassador present is convinced that Il Moro intends to use this opportunity to force the Emperor to invest him as Duke of Milan. The rumor is so thick on the streets that you could walk from here to the Duomo and never touch the pavement. Surely you do not think that Il Moro is paying the Emperor four hundred thousand ducats simply to see your daughter well married."

Bona smiled at one of her reflected images. "*Sciocce, sciocce, sciocce.* All of you, fools. Even Il Moro has finally made a fool of himself. He has made my daughter an Empress. Can he think that Bianca Maria's husband will permit him to steal Gian's throne? Never, never, never. Only an *uccelliaccia* like you would believe it possible."

"It will be possible because the Frenchmen and Il Moro want it. Because they both want war in Italy."

"My nephew King Charles has already sworn to me that he will never permit Il Moro to become Duke of Milan." Bona turned to one of the mirrors and fluffed the dyed brown curls that framed her thick, pouchy neck. "You don't understand at all, do you, *uccelliacca.* I am the most important woman in Europe. No one in all the world, the Sultan of Turkey included, would dare risk giving me offense. My nephew is the King of France, my son is the Duke of Milan, and my daughter is the Empress of Germany—"

"Your son will no longer be Duke of Milan if you permit Il Moro to trade your daughter for your son's title. And your nephew will permit Il Moro to make himself King of Heaven if only Il Moro will finance a French campaign against Naples. And having conquered Naples, then your dear nephew will turn back and snatch up Milan *and* Germany and leave you as nothing more than an old crone in an empty bed."

Bona whipped around. "The only threat to my son is the *puttana* who sleeps in his bed and in that of any other man she pleases. If you are thinking of making some kind of protest today, I warn you that I will personally summon the might of France and Germany to destroy your grandfather and father. And when

Naples is finished, I will have you sent to a convent, where the stinking priests and their lice can satisfy your filthy lust."

Isabella brought her face so close to her mother-in-law's that she could smell the decay of her teeth. "When my father enters Milan, I will take you up to the tower of the Castello, make you squat on the spire, and let you spin up there like a weathercock."

Bona smiled stupidly, then burst into tears as abruptly and inexplicably as an infant.

Isabella's face sagged with amazement. She stood motionless, watching the tears roll off her mother-in-law's mask of white lead paint. After a moment she raised her hand and slowly reached for Bona's shoulder. But when she had almost touched her, she dropped her hand and in a rustle of silk left the *guardaroba*.

A collective tolling of bells throughout the city announced the hour of ten o'clock in the morning. The triumphal car that would carry the bride to the Duomo waited at the foot of the drawbridge connecting the Ducal Court with the Piazza d'Armi, the large outer court of the Castello di Porta Giovia.

Beatrice followed her ladies-in-waiting down the stairs to the right of the gate. She marveled at the car, an enormous, silk-draped, enameled and gilded portable throne drawn by four snow-white horses, then searched for her husband among the escort. He was standing next to Gian, smiling and gesturing, obviously sharing a joke with his nephew. She felt a delightful queasiness at how handsome her husband looked, but she didn't pause to catch his eye. She was waiting for the Duchess of Milan.

She had not even set eyes on her cousin for nine months. In some ways it might well have been a lifetime since Eesh rode off that day at Vigevano, yet at times it seemed only yesterday that they held each other in the labyrinth, four hearts beating as one. Four hearts. If Eesh's baby had been a boy and hers a girl, perhaps that perfectly symmetrical love would still exist. But love was not an architect's grid. Love was her baby. Her son. And her husband. She still couldn't dare tell him, but it was true.

But even if her love for Eesh was dead, she had to admit to

herself that she could not live with the idea of Eesh as her enemy. Perhaps—no, likely—Eesh's letter to her father had been an impulsive act, later regretted, to be hidden away just as Beatrice had kept secret the Signory's capitulation on her husband's investiture. The other letter, Eesh's condolences on Mama's death, that was the real Eesh. Perhaps Eesh was far more flawed than Beatrice could have imagined when she had loved her, but Eesh was still fundamentally good. Probably Eesh had even accepted her little girl and loved her as much as she did her son, perhaps even more. . . .

A glimpse of beige-and-silver taffeta skirts appeared at the top of the steps descending from the second floor of the ducal apartments; the covered landing still concealed the women's faces. Beatrice's heartbeat began a sudden, surprising acceleration. As the women came down the steps, the brilliant painted faces began to drop into view, lips like blood against white ceruse. Then the hem of a ducal crimson skirt, a swollen belly, and finally Eesh. The Eesh she had once loved, stunningly beautiful in her pregnancy, the chin still slightly tucked, the vaguely Oriental, muted green eyes. As if nothing had ever happened. But Isabella looked straight ahead and quickly disappeared behind the triumphal car.

A commotion at the exit to the opposite wing of the ducal apartments announced the tedious disgorgement of the bride's escort, two hundred courtiers in long silver and gold brocade tunics. Finally Bianca Maria emerged. Three noblemen in ceremonial armor walked behind her, two of them holding up her enormous sleeves, the third carrying her train. Her back slightly arched into an elegant curve, her head completely motionless, Bianca Maria glided along like a statue on wheels, her posture remaining impeccable even as she climbed the narrow steps to her portable throne.

Beatrice prepared to ascend to her seat on Bianca Maria's left; the Duchess of Milan would sit to the bride's right. She gathered up her skirts and focused on the steps. The car swayed slightly; for all its opulence, it was just a shell of wood and fabric. She reached the top and carefully eased into her cushioned perch. Then she looked to her right. Her vision was completely blocked by the high, scrolled arm of Bianca Maria's throne. She would not even be able to see Eesh until they got to the Duomo.

"Toto."

Beatrice looked up. The future Empress, trying surreptitiously to glance downward without moving her head, swiveled her eyes with comic determination.

"Toto," Bianca Maria whispered urgently, "my mother is going to let me get a monkey to take to Germany. Help me think of a name for him before we get to the Duomo."

The bridal procession was so long that the head had passed beneath the huge central tower at the far end of the Piazza d'Armi before the tail had even left the Ducal Court. Upon leaving the Castello, the vast, splendid serpent crawled beneath a red-white-and-blue canvas awning, supported on rows of white wooden columns wreathed in ivy, that extended all the way from the gate of the Castello to the steps of the Duomo, running for most of its length down the Via degli Armorai. Huge crowds, not just armorers but tradesmen and merchants and laborers as well, stood in the shop and factory porches and cheered Milan's latest conquest by marriage.

Inside the Duomo enormous draperies covered the walls, the sheen of candlelight on brocade alternating with the sunlit, transparent polychrome of the towering stained-glass windows. The high altar was heaped with silver vases, chandeliers, gold-framed icons, reliquaries, jeweled censers, and thousands of wax candles. In the center of the church, beneath the unfinished dome, stood an immense Roman-style triumphal arch crowned with Maestro Leonardo's colossal, three-story-high plaster statue of Francesco Sforza on horseback, intended to be the wonder of the world when finally cast in bronze. The scent of perfume and incense was so strong that at first it was difficult to breathe; the music of the choir, trumpets, flutes, and organ drifted sonorously through this fragrant medium.

The service proceeded with the magisterial splendor of a dream. After the singing of the Mass had been concluded, the wedding ceremony and coronation began. Beatrice played her part with the awe of a spectator, accompanying Bianca Maria to the high altar along with her husband, the Duke and Duchess of Milan, the German ambassadors, and the Emperor's proxy, the Bishop of Brixen, a slender eminence virtually consumed by his vestments and dome-shaped bishop's crown. Isabella never even glanced at Beatrice; she seemed as self-absorbed as Bianca Maria.

Finally the Bishop of Brixen took up the imperial crown, two intersecting gold arches, studded with rubies, pearls, and diamonds, topped with a globe and cross. He carefully placed the crown on Bianca Maria's marvelously motionless head. At that moment bells and trumpets resounded inside the church, followed by the massive percussion of cannons fired outside.

The cannonades continued at intervals as the entire wedding party proceeded laboriously out of the church. Beneath the steps of the Duomo a corps of gentlemen in fur-trimmed satin capes formed up to escort Bianca Maria to her horse. Beatrice and Isabella were expected to follow behind, but there was some problem in erecting the white damask baldachino that was to be carried like a big umbrella over the bride and her horse. Suddenly Beatrice found herself stranded at the top of the steps, shoulder-to-shoulder with her cousin. She couldn't help herself and turned her head.

Eesh was so near, so familiar: the sharp dimple at the corner of her mouth, the reddish flare of her hair and the long, straight slope of her nose; the elegant, powerful neck, pale and lightly pulsing, so close; the smell of her, balsam and a faint hint of lemon. And yet she seemed unreachable, behind some perfectly transparent yet infinitely thick glass. Beatrice had the strange feeling that if she tried to touch Eesh, everything would shatter; even the stars would explode and fall to earth like glitter.

And she wondered if silence wasn't preferable to anything they might say. Then, almost impulsively: "Thank you for your letter about my mother."

Isabella tensed as if flinching from the cannons. But the guns were temporarily silent. "I'm sorry," she said stiffly. She did not turn her head. "About your mother."

With sudden spite, Beatrice wanted to say: I read your letter to your father. Then Eesh turned and looked at her. Isabella's eyes had a brilliant, crystal clarity, the bloom of pregnancy. Her full, innocent lips trembled as if considering words. But after a long pause she said nothing. The cannons boomed again and her shoulders tightened reflexively and she turned away.

The cape-clad gentlemen successfully raised the baldachino

over Bianca Maria. Two Milanese noblemen stepped forward to assist Beatrice and Isabella to their horses.

The two duchesses rode back to the Castello without looking at one another again.

Il Moro propped his son on the broad stone window ledge overlooking the city. Little Ercole, dressed for the wedding in a blue-and-gold satin jacket and matching cap, his legs still swaddled, milled his arms in excitement and looked back at his father with a smile and a stream of ba-bas and trills.

"I don't like him there," Beatrice said. They were at the highest observation level of the Castello's central tower. Milan, lit with tens of thousands of torches, was a huge wheel of light beneath them.

"Your mama is the most recklessly courageous woman I have ever known," Il Moro told his son playfully. "Every time she gets on a horse I fear for her life, but she is afraid to let her big boy sit here in his father's arms. Your mama is silly." Ercole responded with a fine sentence of babble. Il Moro answered him in the same incomprehensible tongue.

By ducal fiat Ercole was allowed to remain on his perch while his father pointed out the principal sights of the torchlit city. Suddenly a clarion of every bell from every tower rang the hour, and Ercole screamed in concert and pumped his arms. After the clarion died away, the city was almost supernaturally quiet. Then several pops like small mortars firing sounded from somewhere out in the wheel of light. A moment later a huge whoosh, like some great door closing, swept across the city.

The black sky filled with sparking pinpoints of light and then exploded into multicolored brilliance. Fusillade after fusillade of fireworks thundered skyward and fell back to earth in dense showers of sparks. Beatrice had never seen anything like it; her father's fireworks displays had not used in an entire night a hundredth of what burst over Milan every few seconds.

Ercole sat captivated for a moment, awe stilling his little arms. Then without warning he began to cry. His flushed face, lit by

the incandescent sky, glowed an eerie red. He screamed hysterically, and Il Moro immediately pulled the little boy away from
the open window and tried to comfort him. Ercole continued to
writhe and howl even when Beatrice held him. Only when his
wet nurse interceded did he pause to hiccup and paw at his nurse's
breast.

"He wants to go down," Beatrice told the wet nurse. "I'm
certain he will sleep after he has fed."

Ercole, his nurse, and Il Moro's two guards vanished into the
staircase, leaving Beatrice and Il Moro alone. The storm of light
continued. Beatrice glanced at her husband. He was totally absorbed, his eyes sparking with all the colors of the exploding
rainbow. A sequence of booms like rolling thunder announced the
final salvo, and the sky glowed so intensely that she drew back
from the window ledge with an almost physical fear.

In profound silence the sky darkened, and a last fine veil of
sparks settled and dissolved against the tile roofs of Milan. All
over the city, the torchlights began to go out. Beatrice imagined
she could hear Fortune whispering in her ear, cautioning her.

Beatrice put her arm around her husband's waist. She wondered if he would answer her question. "I was asked at least a
dozen times today, ever so discreetly, what you intend to do about
the investiture. The rumors are flying. Did you arrange anything
with the German ambassadors?"

Il Moro continued to stare out over the city, studying the fading
pattern of lights. Beatrice accepted his silence; she realized she
already had whatever truth she needed from him. But there was
a moment of the old pain, and a tinge of fear.

She was surprised when he spoke. "The new Emperor does
not wish to invest anyone as Duke of Milan until he has settled
the usual internal disputes that follow a succession. We do not
even intend to discuss the matter until next spring, much less when
this investiture will take place and who will be invested."

"Do you still want it?"

"Of course. But if the Venetians will not permit it . . . ." He
shrugged and pulled back from the window ledge. For a panicky
moment Beatrice thought he would turn and question her again
about her meeting with the Doge. Even as she realized that she
had fallen in love with him, she was determined more than ever

to keep her secret, the last defense for her naked heart, the one power she could always wield over him. But he said nothing.

"Wouldn't it be better in that case to deny all the rumors?" she asked. "Why antagonize Naples and give the French a pretext for attacking Milan?"

He turned and smiled. "Because I want to antagonize Naples. I want to frighten King Ferrante into entering into a binding treaty of peace with us and put an end to this nonsense about Alfonso marching on Milan and Gian assuming full ducal authority. When that is done we will not have to worry about the French or Naples. At least as long as Ferrante lives."

"And that will satisfy your ambition?"

Il Moro looked out over the darkened city. "Ambition," he said vaguely, as if he wasn't certain what the word meant. "Ambition. I should tell you about my ambition." He paused again, seemingly lost in thought. "Twice in my life I have found myself at an impasse from which I thought no ambition could ever lead me. The first time was when my brother exiled me from Milan. I believe now that in some grotesque fashion he loved me and didn't want to kill me, as he inevitably would have had I stayed. I wandered between all the courts of Italy, to France, to Spain, to Germany. Always the same welcome for the fourth son of Francesco Sforza: the women with desire hot in their eyes, the men with cold smirking contempt for a vagabond with no destination. Years with no purpose, my strongest years wasted on drink and games and meaningless embraces. And then Fortune contrived to make me my nephew's regent. I won't lie to you and say that Cecilia wasn't a part of that rebirth, and that when she . . . left I did not think that my life had once again ended. She was my strength. Cecilia wanted me to be Duke of Milan more than I ever wanted it for myself." He smiled faintly, fondly.

"I am forty-one years old. I have learned that something happens to a man at this time in his life. Perhaps the circle of people and possibilities around him is greater than ever. And yet he has never been more isolated, never felt more confined by what he has made of his life. Loneliness is what he fears, even more than he fears death and failure. He is terrified that he will reach out in the dark and no one will be there. I don't mean just a body. That he can buy. He wants to touch another soul. Without that, his ambition is meaningless. He is a fool building a tower to reach God, when God is only someone beside him in the night who truly knows his soul."

He faced her directly. "I never thought I could love again after Cecilia left. Even when you and I became lovers."

Beatrice felt completely empty, as if whatever he said next would occupy her entire soul.

"I know the conditions you demand for love. Perhaps I can never be the lover of whom you have always dreamed. But I want to try. I want to try to love you in that way. I imagine you charging headlong through the darkened labyrinth of my life, finding pathways I have never tried before, leading me to some center I have never been able to find. You and Ercole. You will be the last and best of all my lives. You are my ambition."

Perhaps once she had imagined a joy as explosive as the fireworks, the music of the spheres bursting into ever-expanding, all-encompassing circles of light. But this was quiet, like wandering into a huge, hushed cathedral, waiting for the dawn that would reveal its unimaginable splendor.

She put her arms around him, and he looked into her eyes in a way that made her knees weaken. When he kissed her the wheel of possibilities whirled, and she said to whatever fate she had empowered, Stop. Stop the wheel. This is my choice.

As if he had heard that command, he simply held her, no longer needing to speak to her or caress her, the city below them so dark and silent that they might have been the only two people in the world.

Extract of a dispatch of ANTONIO STANGA, Milanese ambassador to Naples, to LODOVICO SFORZA, "Il Moro," Duke of Bari and regent for the Duke of Milan. Naples, 1 January 1494

. . . After some discussions of the points you instructed me to raise, His Majesty King Ferrante of Naples suggested that as proof of his determination to arrive at a settlement guaranteeing peace he would willingly journey to Milan to negotiate such an agreement. To that end, and to expedite his progress when he receives your reply, he has already begun to assemble his ships for the voyage to Genoa. . . . King Ferrante burns with the spirit of accommodation . . . and the cause of Italian unity has entered this new year with the brightest prospect we have seen in many long and fearful months. . . .

Extract of a letter of ISABELLA D'ESTE DA GONZAGA, Marquesa of Mantua, to BEATRICE D'ESTE DA SFORZA, Duchess of Bari. 1 January 1494

Your most illustrious Highness and my only sister,

You will have heard that I have given birth to a daughter— born 31 December—and that both she and I are doing well, although I am sorry not to have a son. But this is Fortune's determination, and so I have determined to love her with all my heart. . . . As you also may have heard, we have named her Eleonora after our mother of blessed memory. It is a bitter joy to know that Mama is not here to hold her, and yet strange to tell, I have felt throughout that Mama is here. . . .

CHAPTER

37

Naples, 2 February 1494

The high altar of the church of San Domenico Maggiore was a dense constellation of candles. The strong light blanched the faces of the gray and black-clad mourners, making the living look like corpses. But the puffy face visible on the bier at the foot of the altar had a curiously lifelike, rosy tint, accented by the black crepe draped over both the body and the catafalque. The mourners closest to the altar correctly assumed that the corpse was in fact a wax effigy and that the mortal remains of His Majesty King Ferrante of Naples had already been interred. But these mourners were too close to the new power in Naples to allow their blank, light-washed faces even the merest hint of speculation or suspicion as to why the old King had been so hastily put to rest.

The Requiem Mass droned on. The principal mourner, the soon-to-be-crowned King Alfonso II of Naples, frequently swiveled his burly head to receive whispered messages from a relay of several aides; the messengers came and went through a shadowed aisle chapel closed for new construction. Finally Alfonso himself strode heavily off into the aisle chapel. Two men-at-arms in silvery steel breastplates escorted him to a small room adjacent to the

340

chapel, used by the painters to store their pigments, plaster, and tools.

A tall, athletic-looking man, perhaps in his mid-thirties, stood illuminated by a single lamp. Dressed in expensive riding clothes, he had a youthful face with experienced, self-confident eyes. He fluidly removed his velvet hat, revealing a fashionable blond coif.

Alfonso waved the guards out. When the door had been closed behind him he stared at the man for a moment. "The man who murdered my father," he said, his deep, mysterious whisper penetrating the hollow moan of the Requiem choir.

The man's eyes lost their glitter.

Alfonso took a step forward. His massive face, framed by a black cowl, seemed disembodied, a creature powerful enough to intimidate this man without the assistance of limbs. "Do you realize how much discoloration there was? We had to bury him within hours."

Only the distant lament of the priests occupied the silence that followed. There was no trace of confidence in the man's voice when he finally spoke. "I . . . Your Highness . . . Your Highness will remember that I . . . When a predictable result is desired, there can be that effect."

"You are about to suffer an effect," Alfonso whispered. "Given that there already is suspicion about my father's illness, I can hardly allow you to . . ." Alfonso paused and raised his open hands like a saint delivering a benediction. "To remain in Naples."

The man appeared to age ten years in an instant, his face suddenly shadowed and drawn with fear.

"However, you could be useful to me elsewhere."

The man nodded warily.

Alfonso's congenitally squinty eyes narrowed to glinting slits. "Milan," he whispered at the threshold of hearing. "Now I need you to go to Milan."

Vigevano, 10 February 1494

The big stone fireplace had been heaped with enough logs to last all evening, and the heat and glare radiated across the room. Little

Ercole drooled open-mouthed at the spectacle for a moment and then tried to run toward the fireplace. Beatrice caught him up and pulled him into her lap so that he faced her. He flipped his head back to watch the fire.

She tried to find her grandfather in her son's face and realized that she couldn't really remember Ferrante, at least when she tried. It was more surprising to her to realize that she hadn't seen her grandfather for eight years than to realize that he was dead. He had last written her when Ercole was born: nothing that had seemed personal at all, merely a diplomatic obligation. Yet there had been a time when he was all she had of a father. Suddenly the image of him popped into her mind's eye, laughing, his cheeks puffed out and his eyes squinted, a big, sumptuously dressed clown. He'd wander from place to place at the dinner table, always plucking morsels from his guests' plates, often eating his entire meal that way. To a little girl that had seemed so funny. Now she could see the sinister undertone, that Ferrante's strange eating habits had been intended to convey the warning that whatever he gave he could just as easily and capriciously take away. And the things she had heard about him since coming to Milan: even if nine of ten were lies, it made her shudder to think that she had lived in the house of Aragon.

But the most terrible thing her grandfather had done was simply to die, to leave the void only his son could fill. She could always see Alfonso, a memory made indelible by fright, his angry red eyes seemingly oozing out through his slitted lids. Now the secret key she had obtained in Venice was like a hot blade in her breast. She would have to tell her husband that the Signory had given him a free hand if Alfonso should become King of Naples. And yet she knew that when she did, the wheel would spin again, and when it finally stopped, her husband might no longer be with her. She realized that she would rather lie to him than lose him.

Ercole popped up on her knee, babbled some request, and set his chin. That was it, the upward cant of his dumpling chin, just like Ferrante. That was her grandfather's legacy to her son. They were blood, all of them. They would settle among themselves, as a family. She would talk to Eesh when the opportunity presented itself. There was time. Alfonso couldn't mount a military campaign in winter anyway.

An image came to her of her mother, as clearly as if she were still alive, and something lifted from Beatrice's heart, the weight of her anger. She could understand the resentment that had inflamed her grief, that Mama had died before offering some final, incontestable evidence that she had loved her. But Mama hadn't died simply to spite her, to abandon her again; Beatrice knew that. Of course she could never forgive Mama for leaving her in Naples, but it was possible to despise that Mama while still loving the Mama who had tried to make up for it, who had in her clumsy, overbearing fashion tried to love her. That Mama she would always love. And now she could finally forgive herself for loving her.

Mama, and now her grandfather, so quickly gone, vanished into elusive memory. She remembered a line from Petrarch's sonnets: "Vicious Death, how quick you were to fling / Into gray dust the fruit of long age." Fortune is swift enough, Beatrice told herself; I do not need to hasten her step.

Ercole grabbed her fur collar and pulled himself up so that he could gaze right at her. For the last few months she had observed that her son had begun to look less like her sister and more like her, but now she imagined that she saw the living image of herself as an infant, as if she were peering into some magic mirror where her mother still held her in her arms, before the trip to Naples, before everything changed.

Little Ercole stood in her lap, his head cocked with curiosity, wondering why his mother had suddenly started to cry.

Extract of a dispatch of COUNT CARLO BELGIOIOSO, Milanese ambassador to France, to LODOVICO SFORZA, "Il Moro," Duke of Bari and regent for the Duke of Milan. Amboise, 22 February 1494

. . . the King and his Council are more divided than ever upon the issue of the Italian adventure. With each day that passes, His Most Christian Majesty becomes more vehement and resolute in his determination to proceed. He has expelled the Neapolitan ambassadors, and I was informed yesterday that in several weeks the court will be transferred to Lyons so as to be in closer proximity to the mountain passes. In addition I have learned that the King intends to send to Asti a small advance guard commanded by Bernard Stuart d'Aubigny as soon as weather permits. The King has additionally ordered Briconnet to prepare a schedule of taxes and sundry levies to exact the expenses of the campaign from his people. Those among the King's Council who oppose the King's enterprise (and it is my observation that this faction grows daily) expect that the refusal of the towns and municipalities to yield these revenues will present an insurmountable obstacle to the said enterprise, a fiscal mountain that no amount of determination on the King's part can enable him to climb. The King will then realize that only Your Highness is capable of financing his campaign, and he will renew his entreaties. . . . When I spoke with the King yesterday he was sorely disappointed that Your Highness has again refused to dispatch Messer Galeazzo di Sanseverino to counsel with him concerning his invasion plans, saying to me, "Truly! Is not Alfonso the sworn enemy of Il Moro? Why then will Il Moro not join with me against our common foe?" Thus, once again he requested me to petition Your Highness for the dispatch of Messer Galeazz to France, saying, "Seigneur Galeazzo is the foremost paladin of Christendom. If he were to ride with us, it should signify to all the world that our Christian enterprise enjoys the good offices of Lord God in heaven and Il Moro on earth." This can be taken to mean, Your Highness, that such a gesture would signify to the King's increasingly skeptical Councillors that you intend to make available to his campaign the considerable resources of our treasury. . . . In short, Your Highness, the King is now quite unable to cross the mountains unless you permit it. . . .

C H A P T E R

38

Pavia, 16 March 1494

Isabella's third labor was not nearly as hard as her first or quite so easy as her second, but the euphoria that had attended both was absent. She was detached, finding the whole procedure mechanical and uninteresting. To distract herself, she thought much of her home and childhood. Everything she remembered of Naples was brilliant, painted in fresh pigments. Everything after Naples seemed dull, a series of sepia sketches.

The head came out. The baby's face was blue. A perfect little baby dyed Sforza blue. The midwife immediately began to pull even as Isabella's panic contracted her muscles and seized the tiny body. "Let him come, Your Highness," the midwife admonished, her voice breaking with fear. "You must let him come!"

Isabella held her breath and pushed the shoulders free. She looked down and saw the umbilical like a hangman's noose around her baby's neck. Some instinct told her to let him go, give him up, or he would die.

The midwife's assistant quickly freed the baby from its umbilical, and pandemonium broke loose as the physician, surgeon, and midwife began to argue over whether to sever the cord and how to revive the limp, apparently lifeless infant. Isabella closed her eyes and pushed again, and the baby slipped free of her. The midwife produced her own knife and slit the cord and took the baby in her arms. She turned away from Isabella and pounded the baby's tiny blue back and then began to knead its chest.

Isabella stared at the cut umbilical that protruded from her vagina, seemingly draining her of her own life. I am not part of any of this, she thought. For some reason she found her powerlessness comforting.

She had already begun to deliver the placenta when she heard her baby come to life. He coughed, then cried fitfully, almost delicately. The happiness lifted her gently, like a swell in a warm sea. "Give him to me," she said.

The midwife turned. The baby was still pale, but the pallor was miraculous compared to the unearthly hue minutes before. Isabella reached out and felt the cool wet body and wanted only to give her baby her warmth. When she brought the baby to her breast she realized that it was a girl.

Nothing happened. Isabella continued to float in that eddy of well-being, not even asking herself why she wasn't disappointed in her baby's gender. "She's beautiful," she whispered, looking up gratefully at the midwife. "My beautiful little girl."

Milan, 18 March 1494

The old dungeons beneath the Castello had a distinct brackish smell, much like that of the sea. The reason was simple: the dungeons were below the level of the moat, so water always seeped in, and they were now used to store salt. Galeazzo di Sanseverino rubbed the chill from his muscular arms and complained that he had not brought a cloak. "Where is the woman?" he irritably asked Bernardino da Corte, the assistant castellan of Porta Giovia.

"I've sent for her." In torchlight Messer Bernardino's dark complexion and sharp features were diabolically suitable for a denizen of this place. Galeazz looked more like an angel harrowing Hell.

"Who is she?" Galeazz asked.

"A kitchen maid. She works here in the Castello."

"Well, that much of it makes sense. What if he doesn't confess?"

"If he doesn't confess, we will tie her up in his place and let every horse groom and pantryman in the Castello have at her."

A door boomed shut and a torch flared in the darkened hall. The kitchen maid, wearing a wool shawl and an expression of wooden fright, was escorted by a single guard. Bernardino opened another door and motioned to the others to go inside.

A man had been tied naked to the wheel-shaped rack. His feet, hands, and genitals were purple with cold. The kitchen maid flinched at the sight of him.

"Do you know this woman?" Bernardino asked, his voice echoing against the damp, moldy walls.

The man tilted his head up; he was an athletic-looking blond in his mid-thirties, composed despite his predicament. "Yes," he said matter-of-factly. "I would guess she's the reason for my trouble. As I told you, I'm a *procuratore* from Rome, here to buy some gold plate for a client. Milanese goldwork, that's what everyone who can afford it wants. I met her at the church of Sant'Eustorgio and decided to take her back to the inn where I am staying, the Saracen. I paid her for her work and tried to send her on her way, and she screamed and made a row and threatened to make trouble for me. Finally the innkeeper helped me throw her out. Is she someone's wife?"

The kitchen maid snorted disdainfully. She looked at Bernardino and Galeazz. "It's as I said. Why would a merchant with a thousand ducats sewn into the lining of his cloak go to Sant'Eustorgio to meet a kitchen maid?"

Bernardino looked off into a corner and pursed his thin, angry lips. "If he is what you say he is, why would he lie so ineptly?"

The kitchen maid tilted her chin up. "I gave you the poison powder he gave me."

"That means nothing," Bernardino said. "Anyone can obtain poison. Perhaps you are what he says, just a spurned woman looking for revenge."

The kitchen maid spit dramatically on the floor. "*Sciocca.* I should have taken what *he* offered me. He gave me five ducats just for putting the packet of poison in my wallet and agreeing to think about the rest of his offer."

Galeazz stared at the woman. "You took the money? Where is it?"

The woman eyed Galeazz suspiciously. "Right next to the warmest place on my body. You want to look for it?"

Galeazz's blue eyes were like ice. "Get it."

The woman put her hand inside her skirt and pulled out a worn cloth wallet tied to her waist with a string.

Galeazz grabbed the wallet and counted out the thick gold coins. "Five ducats. That's all he gave you?"

The woman nodded.

Galeazz's hand darted from his side, just flicking against the kitchen maid's face but making a sharp smack. The woman collapsed instantly, and her head struck the floor with a heavy thud. "Get that treasonous bitch out of here!" Galeazz snapped. The guard hastily dragged the unconscious woman out the door.

The man on the rack looked up again, his eyes suddenly keen with self-assurance. "You see, as I told you, I paid her for her work. Several nights' worth. Certainly she is a cow, but her stamina is remarkable."

Galeazz turned to Bernardino. "Don't let him die until he has confessed." The man's eyes became as big and white as two eggs. "That cow is telling the truth, and you are lying," Galeazz told him. "The first time you told us you spent only one night with her. For five ducats you could've had a first-class courtesan for a week. She isn't worth a ducat for a lifetime of humps."

The man determinedly retold his tale while Bernardino dragged a bag of salt from the corner of the room, pulled a knife from his belt, and slit the burlap. Bernardino spread the grainy crushed rock salt on the floor in front of the wheel, threw the empty bag aside, and crunched across the salt to the rack. He pumped a wooden lever and ratcheted the wheel up until it was almost horizontal, then leaned over the man's face. "Shut your mouth now. I have only one question I wish you to answer. Who sent you?"

"As I told you, I am a *procuratore* from Rome. I—"

Bernardino walked around the wheel to the man's feet. With the point of his knife he appeared to trace an outline of the left foot, as fluidly as a *maestro* drawing with a pen. The man howled and pounded his head back against the wheel. Blood streamed off his heel and spattered over the layer of salt on the floor.

Bernardino circled back around to the man's head. The man stopped screaming and grimaced with determination.

"I've cut all the way around," Bernardino said. "Now with one pull I can skin your foot like a rabbit. I'll cook the raw meat with a torch until the fat runs, and then make you walk on salt until you answer my question. If you are still reticent, I will skin, cook, and salt your remaining foot. That failing, I will skin your hands and leave you down here with no water and enough rats and salt to last the rest of your life. Who sent you?"

"This is how I believe the step is done *alla Turca*," Beatrice said. She stretched her arms straight over her head and clapped her hands as she twirled. "The costumes should have lots of *stringhe* and bits of mirror like the Scythians you did for my wedding joust, Maestro Leonardo. The effect when the Turkish dancers spin will be quite dazzling, don't you think?"

Leonardo da Vinci nodded vaguely and made another notation in his sketchbook.

"The guests at our Oriental masque will imagine themselves transported to the court of the Sultan at Constantinople," the poet Gaspare Visconti enthusiastically offered.

"I believe our masque is already quite dazzling as danced by Her Highness," drawled Leonardo's "assistant," a young man called Salai, who performed no discernible function and was rumored to be Leonardo's sexual pet, though anyone who knew Leonardo well understood that he abhorred physical contact and merely enjoyed browsing at pretty faces and physiques. Salai was about Beatrice's age, with blond Milanese coloring and a pale fuzz on his cheeks and upper lip. His features were striking, but only because the Grecian beauty of his straight nose and broad, intelligent forehead was countered by sullen eyes and a snarling upper lip. A thin strip of Rheims linen shirt peeked above the lace-trimmed collar of his expensive green velvet doublet; his shapely legs were sheathed in pink hose, and silver buckles sparkled atop his rose-colored brocade slippers.

Gaspare Visconti and Beatrice's secretary, Vincenzo Calmeta, looked at Salai with open disapproval; his comment was almost suggestive and presumed a familiarity with the Duchess he in no way enjoyed. Salai apparently took the reproving glances as a challenge, because he approached Beatrice with a pretentiously languid, hips-forward walk.

"Your Highness is quite the most splendid woman in all Italy," Salai said in his lazy, drawn-out diction. "You are grace, you are elegance, you have quite the finest jewels and the most extravagant gowns of any woman who has ever lived. One can see why these Milanese women bray after you like hounds at a hunt, quite furious with envy."

At this inelegant metaphor even Leonardo's head popped up. Leonardo had flowing gray hair and a long gray beard, but his high, unlined, baby-pink forehead and large, wondering gray eyes gave his face an incongruously youthful, feminine aspect.

Beatrice smiled at Salai, who stood with a hand propped defiantly on his hip. "Thank you, Ser Salai, for envisioning me as a vixen pursued by a pack of snarling bitches," she said, shooting a wry glance at Calmeta.

Salai stood his ground for a moment and then gave up the game to prowl Beatrice's study, affectedly nodding at the rows of leather or damask-bound books like a scholar contemplating his research.

Beatrice and the three artists began to gossip about the Turkish Sultan's exiled brother, who resided in Rome; the Sultan paid the Pope an enormous fee to keep his brother in a state of luxurious confinement, thus eliminating a potential rival at home. The Sultan's brother was noted for his prodigious appetites.

They didn't even notice the liveried page when he entered the room and made his first announcement. The young man cleared his throat and again said, "The Duke of Bari wishes to see his wife alone."

The artists looked to Beatrice. "We will have time to finish after supper," she told them. The men bowed and departed, Salai pausing to flourish with his arm like a *buffone* miming a courtier.

A moment after Salai had languorously exited, Il Moro came in. He appeared ill, a green tinge to his pale skin, his forehead misted with perspiration. His eyes were shattered, the look of a man gone quietly mad.

"Ercole," Beatrice said as she rushed to him. "Oh, dear God."

Il Moro shook his head. Beatrice spun through a catalogue of the remaining possibilities: Father, Bel, Bianca . . .

"He sent someone to kill our little boy. To poison our little boy and me—"

Beatrice grabbed her husband's shoulders and actually shook him. Her voice was so shrill that he winced. "Who did? Alfonso? Was it Alfonso? Our baby—where is our baby!"

Il Moro spoke as if in a trance. "Ercole is in his nursery. Nothing happened. Messer Bernardino caught the man—"

"Who sent him? Alfonso?" Beatrice's face was bright red.

Il Moro nodded. "I myself heard the confession, before . . ." Il Moro looked away, his forehead now beaded with sweat. He swallowed so thickly that it appeared he might vomit. "Alfonso sent a man here to poison us. He tried to bribe a kitchen maid to poison our food."

Beatrice saw a whirling image of little Ercole as still and black as the babies Mama had warned her about. She wanted Alfonso instantly dead, his fat scowling head rolling off a scaffold, his neck squirting blood. Eesh. This was what Eesh wanted her father to do, to free her from "the yoke of Il Moro and his wife." If only Eesh were here she would strangle her with her own hands. . . .

Her husband took her in his arms and pressed her head to his chest. "Everything I have tried to hold together is coming apart," he said.

Strangely, Il Moro's weary, desperate tone settled her. All the spinning images of catastrophe fluttered and winked out. She felt no emotion whatsoever, only a dead, cold purpose. She extricated herself from her husband's embrace.

"I have to know something," she asked him. The question seemed to be written in her mind; she was not even consciously thinking anymore. "You told me that Francesco is not Gian's baby. Who is the real father of the Duchess of Milan's child?"

Il Moro had to sit on the bed. His head lolled like a drunk's. Perspiration ran down his cheeks.

"I must know. I must know for certain if she lied to me about her son."

Il Moro looked up helplessly, then looked down again.

"If you cannot tell me, then there can be no trust between us."

When he spoke, his voice was small and hollow: "Galeazz."

"Dear God." For a moment she felt a curious outrage that Galeazz had betrayed Bianca. Then Beatrice realized that Galeazz had in fact betrayed *her*, that Milan's shining knight was a tarnished fraud.

Il Moro looked up at her. He was entirely defeated, his eyes dull and foggy. "You see why I cannot make an issue of the boy's legitimacy. Even now. Everything is undone."

Her thoughts were clear and astringent again. "No. Everything remains to be done. When I was in Venice, the Signory agreed that if Alfonso ever became King of Naples, they would withdraw the secret resolution and permit your investiture as Duke of Milan."

Il Moro sat benumbed for a moment. "How? How can you be sure?"

"Ser Constantino Privolo himself told me in the name of the *Serenissima Repubblica*." She waited for the obvious question, but when it did not come she asked it for him. "Do you want to know why I didn't tell you until now?"

He looked up at her and shook his head weakly. "No. I think I understand your reasons. I want to know how you did it."

"I told the Doge that you had concluded negotiations with the German Emperor and that you intended to receive the investiture regardless of the Signory's objections."

He took this in without immediate response, then offered a slight, abstracted smile. "I can't do it. If I declare that I intend to receive the investiture, I will have to bring the French over the mountains."

She seemed to be standing beside herself, watching a person who looked like her go to her husband and clutch his head with both hands like a *condottiere* steeling a young soldier before his first battle. "Now is the time to do it."

"The Emperor will make no public agreement until—"

"I don't mean that. Now is the time to send Galeazz to France and bring the French army over the mountains and have done with Alfonso. Otherwise we must simply wait for Alfonso to send a more skilled assassin."

"And we escort to our doorstep the Duke of Orleans, who may well be a more profound menace."

"No. Once you ask the German Emperor to deliver the investiture you have already purchased from him, the Emperor will have to indemnify your title against Orleans. King Charles will not risk war with Germany simply to acquire another title for Louis Duc d'Orléans."

Il Moro stood up quickly, the hard obsidian gleam returning to his eyes. "You are reckless, irresponsible, probably mad." Again the abstracted smile. "But you are also the most remarkable woman I have ever known. Yes. Of course. I will have Galeazz make it very clear to King Charles that the Emperor has agreed to secure Milan and that we must have a waiver of Orleans's claim to Milan before we will finance the French campaign against Naples."

Il Moro thought for a moment after he had stopped talking, as though waiting for a translation of his own words. "Yes. Everything is in place. It all works now." He embraced Beatrice, clutching her tightly. "This is the moment. This is the moment that Fortune has given to me."

Pavia, 22 March 1494

"Messer Antonio de Gennaro, His Majesty your father's ambassador to Milan, Your Highness." The chamberlain bowed and withdrew.

Isabella was in her little girls' nursery. Her new baby slept in her cradle beneath a down coverlet, while fourteen-month-old Bona pushed a beautifully carved and painted wheeled donkey across the carpet. Antonio de Gennaro entered with big, heavy-footed strides, still in his riding clothes, his face livid from the cold wind. He dipped to his knee. "Your Highness, you must pardon me. I have information of utmost urgency for His Highness."

Isabella motioned to the nurses, and they bowed and scurried off into the antechamber. Her eye on little Bona, Isabella said, "His Highness is out after stags. I will give him a complete accounting of your information." She looked up directly at the ambassador.

"Of course. I had assumed that since Your Highness has given birth so recently and is still in confinement—"

"We do not observe confinements here," Isabella said. "I have already sent my physician back to the university whence he came. He is fully qualified to treat whatever maladies his aged texts may suffer, and I am only too happy to return him to that endeavor."

"Pardon me again, Your Highness." The ambassador cleared his throat and got to the point. "Galeazzo di Sanseverino is preparing to leave Milan with a large traveling company. His reported destination is Asti, but I have every reason to believe that he intends to meet with the French King in Lyons. If so, we can assume that Il Moro has decided to assist the French in their attack on Naples."

"But you are not yet certain."

"Your Highness, the Duke of Bari's secretary has officially protested to me that a man allegedly in the employ of your father has confessed to a plot to poison the Duke of Bari and his son. Of course I was denied an opportunity to question or even to see the alleged assassin. This 'plot' is clearly an invention of the Duke of Bari, intended to serve as the scantest pretext for the dispatch of Galeazzo di Sanseverino to France and any subsequent hostilities."

"Do you believe that my husband and I are in danger?"

The ambassador furrowed his ruddy brow. "I suspect we are all now in danger. I would advise you not to leave Pavia until you have received instructions from your father."

Isabella pressed her hands together at her waist and straightened her shoulders. "Thank you for telling me, Messer Antonio."

Milan, 24 March 1494

"Refuse her."

The unctuous chamberlain stood by the door, transfixed by Beatrice's curt command, his mouth seemingly arrested between syllables. "Ah," he finally said. One of Beatrice's ladies-in-waiting emitted a ladylike gasp.

The chamberlain made a little leap of alarm as the Duchess of Milan elbowed past, as broad-shouldered as an armored knight in her big white sable *cioppa*.

"You cannot refuse me," Isabella told Beatrice. "I am the Duchess of Milan." Her eyes swept the half-dozen ladies-in-waiting who had gathered in Beatrice's rooms to hear a recitation of verse. "Get out." Beatrice's ladies performed anxious, hopping curtsies and scampered out the door. "Get out and close the door," Isabella commanded the chamberlain. The chamberlain continued to mouth inchoately but bowed and pulled the door shut behind him.

Beatrice stared at her cousin. The two women were about two paces apart. Beatrice's face was white, blank, punctuated by eyes like black beads. Then her face flushed. She pounced forward and her arm swung in a frantic marionette arc and the back of her hand cracked into Isabella's face. Isabella wobbled and then fell so hard that her feet left the floor.

Shaking her head, her satin headband loose and her hair disordered, Isabella sat up. Blood trickled from her nose onto her pale lips and chin.

"I read your letter, bitch!" Beatrice screamed at the top of her register. "You are the reason your father sent that man to poison my baby! Your lies tried to kill my baby! If you try to get up I will kill you!"

Isabella dabbed at her nose. "You are listening to your husband's lies. My father wouldn't do that." She stared at the blood on her white leather glove. "I came to ask you not to send Galeazz to France. If you invite the French in, we will all be ruined."

Beatrice's forced laughter sounded like a shriek. "If we do not bring the French in, your father will kill us."

"No." Isabella shook her head. "I just wrote that letter to my father to frighten Il Moro into giving Gian more say in things. I knew our grandfather wouldn't let my father attack Milan. But even with Grandfather gone we can all still arrive at an agreement. Gian would have a greater role in governing, but your husband could still be his regent. I just want things better than they are for Gian and Francesco and me. I don't want war. If we have war, there will be nothing left for my little boy or your little boy."

"Who is the father of your little boy?"

Isabella's stunned wide eyes narrowed, the corners as sharp as blades. "I don't want to hear that slander again."

Beatrice's voice quavered with fury. "Before I offer to negotiate over what will or will not fall as your son's inheritance, I want to know who Francesco's father is."

"Gian. Of course Gian is his father."

"Liar."

Isabella sprang up from the floor, seized Beatrice by the shoulders, and sent her sprawling backward. They wrestled for a moment before Isabella emerged on top. She straddled Beatrice and pinned her arms to the floor.

"Listen to me," Isabella said, leaning over Beatrice. "I don't care who you or your husband believe is Francesco's father. It is indisputable who Gian's father was. Galeazzo Maria Sforza was the Duke of Milan. Gian is his rightful heir. I am begging you not to listen to your husband's self-serving lies. I am begging you not to send Galeazz to France. I am begging you to stop this before it can no longer be stopped."

Beatrice grimaced up at her cousin. "The father of your little boy is going to France to save the life of my little boy."

Isabella's face went so white that she looked like an alabaster bust splashed with red glaze. She let go of Beatrice's arms and stood up. She stepped back from her still-supine cousin and with angry, self-absorbed motions stripped off her blood-stained gloves. She rolled them up and tossed them on the floor.

"I have done what I have done," Isabella said, showing Beatrice her bare palms almost like a saint displaying the stigmata. "But there is no blood on my hands. When the Frenchmen cross the mountains, your own blood will be on your own hands. The entire world will be stained with your blood."

CHAPTER

39

Lyons, 8 April 1494

"Monseigneur Galeazz has presented me with his lance!" His Most Christian Majesty Charles VIII, King of France, Jerusalem, and the Two Sicilies (he had expanded his title in anticipation of his Crusade), with some difficulty brandished the enormous, iron-tipped jousting lance. The shaft, almost as thick as a bower branch, extended virtually across the entire length of the King's antechamber. Galeazz, standing beside the King in the sweat-stained padded doublet he had worn beneath his jousting armor, looked around at the assortment of royal advisers and cronies playing cards at two tables in the center of the room. To their sour Gallic indifference he offered a smug, sardonic smile.

"Montjoie! Montjoie!" Charles crowed, awkwardly sweeping the wooden shaft just above his advisers' heads. "You all saw Galeazz ride in the lists today! Ten men unhorsed, and never for an instant did our brave paladin's feet leave his stirrups, so steadfast and straight was he! Ten bold knights felled with this very lance! Rise up, O fair and noble warriors of God! Roland has returned to ride among us, to lead us forth against the paynim horde! *Montjoie! Montjoie!"*

Louis Duc d'Orléans, slouched at one of the tables in an unlaced doublet, deigned to glance balefully at Galeazz. Next to Louis sat another of Charles's most influential advisers, Guillaume Briconnet, the Bishop of Saint Malo. Judging from the dark, narrow-eyed cast of his bearded face, Briconnet was no happier than Louis to hear yet another panegyric to the "foremost paladin of Christendom."

Antonello di Sanseverino, the Prince of Salerno, rose from his chair, nimbly avoiding the sweep of the ponderous lance shaft. He gracefully plucked his cap from his head and bowed. "Indeed, Your Majesty, if my nephew can be compared to mighty Roland, it is only because in Your Majesty he has found a mighty Charlemagne, a Charles the Great who will lead him forth on the Holy Crusade to which he has now dedicated his heart and soul."

Briconnet leaned next to Louis's ear and whispered, "Perhaps you had better warn His Majesty that Il Moro is the Charlemagne who has sent forth Monseigneur Galeazz."

Louis's restless, caged eyes roamed the room, as if tallying the sentiments of the other advisers. The King had not stopped talking about the wondrous Galeazz since the arrival of the Milanese embassy. For the last three days virtually every royal sentence had begun: "Did you see how Monseigneur Galeazz . . ."

"Bravely Roland goes and thrusts up his lance, high in the sky he lifts his lancehead far!" Charles jammed the lance into the coffered ceiling, bringing a shower of gold-painted stucco down on the heads of his advisers. The King gaped at the damaged ceiling for a moment, then announced in his whining, nasal voice, "I wish to introduce our Christian champion to my companions. Where are the pictures?"

The Gentleman of the King's Bedchamber hurriedly produced a damask-bound portfolio fitted with gold corners and clasps. The sound of the locks popping could be heard in the sullen silence of the room. Apparently this was a signal for the King's advisers to return noisily to their gambling.

Charles leafed through the portfolio of sketches. They were detailed drawings of various nude women in a remarkable repertoire of sexual positions. Each time the King turned over a leaf he looked up at Galeazz and his receding lower jaw dropped slightly, as if he were awaiting the miracle of the great Roland's response.

Galeazz examined the drawings with sincere interest. He whispered something to the King, who honked furiously with laughter.

"Would you like her?" Charles asked.

Galeazz nodded. After some additional research, he produced another drawing that interested him, to Charles's obvious excitement. The King picked a drawing for himself, then returned the portfolio and the selected leaves to the Gentleman of the Bedchamber.

Charles and Galeazz conferred in French for several minutes. The King's advisers rowdily played on. Finally the Gentleman of the Bedchamber returned, escorting three gorgeous young women dressed in Italian-style gowns so low-cut that they revealed delicate little mauve crescents of areolas. An anticipatory smile crept across Galeazz's Olympian features, and Charles regarded his hero with impish glee. The Gentleman of the King's Bedchamber opened the door to that bedchamber, and the King extended his arm and ushered Galeazz and the three women inside.

Briconnet glowered as he watched the King's exit. When the door to the King's bedchamber had been shut, he looked at Louis Duc d'Orléans and shook his head with disgust.

Louis shrugged his lithe, athletic shoulders, his usual carefree smirk restored. "This all sits well enough with me. I seem to recall, my good Bishop, that Roland and his men were slaughtered defending their Charlemagne's rear."

Extract of a dispatch of COUNT CARLO BELGIOIOSO, Milanese ambassador to France, to LODOVICO SFORZA, "Il Moro," Duke of Bari and regent for the Duke of Milan. Lyons, 11 April 1494

. . . in addition to these honors, Messer Galeazz was enrolled in the fraternity of Saint Michel, the King's own knightly order. At the ceremony His Most Christian Majesty informed me with tears in his eyes that Messer Galeazz has convinced him of the absolute necessity of maintaining cordial relations with Your Highness if his enterprise in Italy is to succeed. . . . His Most Christian Majesty went on to say that the good will of Your Highness and his "foremost paladin" is of such paramount importance to His Most Christian Majesty that he offers Your Highness his oath that he will never allow the territorial claims of his cousin Louis Duc d'Orleans to impinge on the sacred bond that now unites Milan and France. His Most Christian Majesty vows to look to Your Highness for guidance in all things. . . . If I had not witnessed with my own eyes the success of Messer Galeazz's mission I should not have believed it. . . .

Extract of a dispatch of ANTONIO STANGA, Milanese ambassador to Naples, to LODOVICO SFORZA, "Il Moro," Duke of Bari and regent for the Duke of Milan. Naples, 11 May 1494

. . . King Alfonso summoned me to his table, and leaving me standing like a meat carver, he reminded me in front of all his household that the visit of Messer Galeazzo di Sanseverino to Lyons was responsible for the French King's determination to pursue his adventure against Naples. King Alfonso next instructed me to tell you, Your Highness, that you will be the first to regret the day the French set foot in Italy. After subjecting me to this humiliation, King Alfonso ordered me expelled from his court and his territories, and issued his formal proclamation of war against the state of Milan. . . .

PART

SEVEN

C H A P T E R

40

**Extract of a letter of international traveler and raconteur
BENEDETTO DEI to LEONARDO DA VINCI, military engineer
at the Court of Milan. Asti, 10 September 1494**

My dear Leonardo,

I arrived here a day after the entry of the French King and his
army into Asti subsequent to their oft-delayed crossing of the
mountains. Upon making inquiries, I ascertained to my surprise
and regret that your lord the Duke of Bari had not brought you
here with him to study the French ordnance, which is a pity as
there is much here to interest you—I am led to understand that
your ongoing projects in Milan and Vigevano detain you. In spite
of his dilatory progress, King Charles was greeted with news of
the first great victory of the war. On 5 September French warships
and marine infantry under the command of the King's cousin Louis
Duc d'Orleans turned away a force of several thousand men and
a dozen ships dispatched by the King of Naples for the purpose
of taking Genoa. . . .

In the course of my conversations I have discovered the cause
of the French King's difficulties in passing over the mountains. It
was not the deficiencies of the French gun carriages but rather His

Most Christian Majesty's reluctance to abandon the pleasures of a young woman with whom he became acquainted during his residence in Lyons. I am told that this woman, formerly a courtesan of some standing in Naples, fortuitously lodged herself with the King's fortune-teller in Vienne (this being a town near Lyons) and by this clever device made her charms known to His Most Christian Majesty. Warned by her associates not to satiate the King's lust in one sitting, this sublimely beautiful and professionally skilled young woman so starved His Most Christian Majesty's affections that when he was finally permitted to dine at her table (in a manner of speaking) he found his appetite sufficiently ravenous that it could not be sated for many weeks. Thus His Most Christian Majesty refused to leave Vienne until 22 August. . . . Once under way, the French army moved with admirable efficiency, departing Grenoble 29 August. . . . As explicated above, I did not see the entry of their army into Asti, a spectacle which astonished one and all, though just to see their tents surrounding the city is marvel enough. . . . I did have occasion to inspect their siege cannons and can offer you these particulars. . . . Unlike Italian guns, which employ balls made of stone, these are provided with balls of iron, which weigh considerably more, and these balls and a great sufficiency of charges are transported on the gun carriages, so that the rate of fire is vigorous indeed. . . . Their bombardiers claim that they can reduce the walls of the Castel Nuovo to dust in two days, though you know what braggarts the French are. . . .

The number of pilgrims to this new shrine of Asti is already worthy of note. In addition to your own lord Il Moro, we have seen his father-in-law, the Duke of Ferrara, and any number of cardinals. . . . Il Moro commands the ear of the King and promises to make His Most Christian Majesty greater even than Charlemagne and to assist him in conquering the Turk at Constantinople if only His Most Christian Majesty will expedite the passage of the French army out of northern Italy. As little faith as your lord Il Moro places in French pledges of friendship while their army is quartered four days' march from Milan, that paucity of trust is shared by many in the French camp, who suspect that Il Moro intends to turn on them once they have done with Naples. . . .

. . . The French army will parade again tomorrow, in honor

of the arrival of the Duchess of Bari and what is said to be a contingent of Milanese ladies so formidable that the King may suffer a fatal apoplexy at the mere sight of them, thus bringing to an unexpected conclusion the most audacious military enterprise of our times. . . .

Asti, 11 September 1494

Eighty Milanese ladies of distinction, all of whom had vied viciously for the honor of greeting the French King, rode behind the Duchess of Bari into the center of Asti, proceeding up the main avenue, a concourse of medieval shop arcades punctuated randomly with ancient Roman colonnades. The arcades were jammed with spectators, who gaped at the Milanese ladies as if they had never seen women before. Certainly few of them had ever seen women like these, faces painted as vividly as polychrome statues, diamonds and pearls flashing in the glaring sunlight like hundreds of little lamps, plump gleaming breasts so exposed by plunging bodices that at first glance they seemed naked to their high waists.

Beatrice rode with her straightest posture ("Ride tall," she heard Mama say), conscious that she represented not simply her husband and her family but all Italy. She wore a *camora* of green silk velour with contrasting gold stripes, the yoke studded with diamonds, pearls, and rubies; the white linen of her chemise puffed out of the patterned slits in her sleeves. Her hair had been pulled back into a single long braid wrapped with silk ribbons, and she wore a pearl-laced hair net beneath a rakishly tilted French-style velvet riding cap. She looked into the entranced, even stunned eyes of the spectators and experienced a thrilling yet vaguely frightening communion with them, a premonition that when these people were old and dying they would still recall the Duchess of Bari riding into Asti at the head of her ladies.

Beatrice led her retinue to the west side of the cobbled piazza in front of the cathedral, directly opposite a grandstand already filled with a dazzling assembly of brocade-and-damask-clad nobility (spotted liberally with red-robed cardinals and white-robed lesser clerics), who had made the pilgrimage to Asti from all over northern and central Italy. Beatrice stayed in the saddle, and her ladies-in-waiting, also still mounted, arrayed themselves in a file to her right, as if they were part of the spectacle about to unfold. In a sense they were, combatants in the confrontation of Italian sophistication with the brute power of France.

The chattering crowd was suddenly blasted into silence by a thunderous, rattling percussion. A minute or so later, dozens of boys entered the piazza at the north end, red-faced from the baking late summer heat, pounding a furious tattoo on the barrel-like drums strapped to their waists. Once the drummers had passed, the music was provided by the endless tramp of the infantrymen's leather boots against the cobblestones. On and on they went for more than an hour: tens of thousands of Swiss and German mercenaries in perfect military order, marching forests of long, ax-headed spears called halberds; corps of arquebusiers shouldering the ponderous portable firearms; thousands of Gascon arbalesters armed with heavy wood-and-iron crossbows. With their banners and plumed hats and multicolored doublets, the foot soldiers seemed more like prosperous tradesmen than merchants of mayhem, their battalions summoned to build a new Italy rather than destroy the old. Whatever lingering anxiety Beatrice might have felt about her instrumental role in bringing these men to Italy vanished with their every purposeful stride.

The sound changed to a long, steady rumble. At the north end of the piazza, sunlight glittered on polished steel. The French knights hesitated for effect before beginning their promenade. Then they came on at a proud canter, rank after rank, mounted on huge war horses, fully sheathed in steel from head to toe, iron-tipped lances pointed straight up, helmets crowned with feathered plumes. The concussion of their passage was so powerful that when Beatrice closed her eyes she could feel them go by. She wondered if the baby who had just begun to kick in her womb could also feel them.

After a quarter of an hour a reedy whine rose above the roar of the passing cavalry. A corps of flutists appeared, then more knights, armed with iron maces, and finally hundreds of mounted arbalesters in silken doublets embroidered with fleurs-de-lis, formed in a tight cordon around a cloth-of-gold baldachino that rose above the horsemen like an enormous gold mushroom cap. Beneath this canopy, mounted on a black horse, rode his Most Christian Majesty Charles VIII, King of France, Jerusalem, and the Two Sicilies. King Charles wore a flat, round white sable hat embroidered with gold fleurs-de-lis, and a doublet of gold silk over his steel breastplate. He propped a battle lance on his thigh, striking the pose most commonly used for equestrian statues of famous *condottieri*. Beatrice's first thought was that the French King was not nearly so ugly or small in stature as she had heard.

The King and his bodyguards dismounted in the middle of the piazza, and Beatrice signaled the Milanese pages to assist herself and her ladies from their horses. Once on the ground, she could not see the King among the circle of approaching archers and knights, hot sweating men who brought their own pungency to the prevailing odor of horse sweat and manure. Then the body-guards stepped aside to reveal His Most Christian Majesty.

Only by the white sable cap could Beatrice be certain that this was the man she had seen at a distance moments earlier. Unhorsed he was not as tall as she was; his armored legs looked like little metal stumps. He was ugly indeed, his face dominated by an absurdly oversized nose and lips. But what she found truly re-markable was the animation of the King's features, or rather the lack of it. His huge eyes seemed incapable of focusing, his slack lips incapable of speaking; his head wobbled as if attached to his shoulders by a string. He gasped at the sight of Beatrice's ladies-in-waiting.

Charles swept his hat from his head and held it before him with trembling hands. Beatrice curtsied deeply. A French inter-preter made the introductions, and Beatrice took the King's hand. The little monster attacked her, pressing his clammy lips to each cheek. He quickly moved down the entire rank of her ladies, kissing each cheek along the way. While he did so, Beatrice was introduced to another armored Frenchman, wearing a sable cap much like the King's, a man of medium height who seemed to possess almost everything the King lacked: rakish features, a smile that hinted at intellect and radiated sensuality, and a firm handshake that communicated a vibrant physical energy. Only when she heard the name, Louis Duc d'Orléans, did she try to look into his eyes. They held hers for a moment, then with absolutely no embarrassment slid across her bare shoulders and down the exposed tops of her breasts before moving on to the ladies nearest her.

The King returned, mesmerized by the welcoming kisses. He stammered for a moment before he could deliver his message to his interpreter, and Beatrice felt sorry for him. He seemed utterly overwhelmed by the might he commanded.

"His Most Christian Majesty begs you to remain in this heat a short while longer, as he is most desirous to show you his artillery," the interpreter said. Beatrice nodded and smiled at the King, who actually blushed in response. She marveled that this hideous little man was winning her with all the qualities he was deficient in.

Charles stood timidly beside Beatrice while his guards cleared the piazza; the Duke of Orleans, as First Prince of the Blood, took his place next to the King like a faithful alter ego. From the north end of the piazza came another steady rumbling.

The big siege cannons burst into the piazza with heart-stopping suddenness. Mounted on four-wheeled carriages loaded with iron projectiles the size of a man's head, drawn by thundering teams of thirty-six horses, they swept by at a fast canter, dozens of them, war machines so daunting that their mere display might conquer Naples. Yet the cannons themselves were strangely lovely, with sleek, tapering contours in brightly polished bronze; the carriages drew them across the cobbles so evenly and quickly that they seemed to be marvelous golden dolphins gliding past.

The big guns appeared and disappeared with such speed that Beatrice felt light and exhilarated and certain she had just seen one of the great marvels of her day. As the rumble of the siege cannons faded, smaller, cast-iron fieldpieces mounted on two-wheeled carriages continued to roll by. Beatrice turned to her left and looked up the street that fed the piazza, wondering if this river of French arms stretched all the way back to Lyons.

Louis Duc d'Orléans leaned forward, and his rapid glance intercepted her gaze. He nodded slightly to confirm her attention. Then his eyes leisurely caressed her exposed flesh, the expression on his easy, handsome mouth so openly licentious that those lips might have been touching her breasts. At first Beatrice was amused. But after a moment she recognized the ambition in the hard edge of Louis's jaw. And then she saw something even more disturbing, a love of danger in his restless eyes that seemed eerily like her own, an aspect of herself she could not confront in her own mirror but was forced to recognize when she saw it on another face. She looked away. The guns rattled past. In some distant recess of her consciousness, Mama murmured a warning, words she would not allow herself to hear.

Extract of a letter of BONA OF SAVOY, Duchess Mother of Milan, to His Most Christian Majesty CHARLES VIII, King of France, Jerusalem, and the Two Sicilies. Pavia, 13 September 1494

My dearest nephew and your most illustrious and most Christian Majesty,

I pray to the Holy Mother that this reaches Your Majesty, as I am certain that Il Moro stops all my couriers. By all the love I still cherish for your mother of blessed memory, I have sworn to regard Your Majesty as my own son, and so I will risk whatever I must to warn Your Majesty of the great danger that Il Moro presents to you. Your Majesty cannot trust him. He has made my daughter Empress of the Germans only to obtain for himself the title my son holds as Duke of Milan. I know this is so because a priest who has gone to Germany with my daughter has reported to me that Il Moro has requested that the German Emperor should grant him investiture as Duke of Milan whenever Your Majesty has dealt with the scoundrels from Naples. He will use Your Majesty thusly and then turn upon you when he has achieved what he wants. I am comforted by Your Majesty's promises to ensure the title my son now holds. But Gian Galeazzo has been ill for two weeks, and I am certain that Il Moro is trying to poison him, which has been done to prevent Gian Galeazzo from welcoming his most beloved cousin as he would have wished. If your beloved mother's soul is to have any peace, Your Majesty must come to Pavia, where my son and I have taken refuge, and you must extend Your Majesty's mighty arms around us to shield us from the perfidy of the tyrant who wishes to deceive us and Your Glorious Majesty. . . . Again I invoke your mother's name and pray that

as she watches from her heavenly seat she will witness Your Most
Christian Majesty's bold succor of a widowed mother and her son
whose lives are now in peril. . . .

**Extract of a letter of international traveler and raconteur
BENEDETTO DEI to LEONARDO DA VINCI, military engineer
at the Court of Milan. Asti, 6 October 1494**

My dear Leonardo,

He goes forth! The Great Charlemagne goes forth on his Crusade! The fever that has confined His Most Christian Majesty to
bed for these two weeks (during which his entire enterprise was
in doubt) finally broke two days ago. His Most Christian Majesty
departed for Casale today, with the main body of the army marching directly to Piacenza. The King's Councillors insist that the
affliction from which His Most Christian Majesty most miraculously recovered was smallpox. Others tell me that the French
have brought with them a new disease said to be transmitted by
coitus and that the King suffered an attack of this affliction, which
is called the *mal francese*. God save us if this is so, for our women
will forever be a source of pestilence even when the French are
long departed.

Your lord Il Moro will no doubt be troubled to learn that Louis
Duc d'Orleans has taken to his sickbed just as the King has
left his. Louis has been struck down by a fever which does not
appear in any fashion to endanger his life but is sufficiently severe
that it will necessitate his prolonged residence in Asti, in the
company of fifteen thousand elite troops. Indeed, most of the
King's Councillors are now of the conviction that the Great
Crusade need venture no farther than Milan to achieve its glorious
ends. . . .

Vigevano, 9 October 1494

The Marchesino Stanga, Milan's Minister of Public Works, halted
his exit for an afterthought. "Your Highness," he told Il Moro,

"you are aware that we are maintaining a reserve to cover our loans to the French in the event of their default?"

Il Moro waved his minister out. "Yes, yes, Marchesino. But when I have extended the canal to the Sestia, we will recover more than the cost of the work in additional revenues from the new farms. I will have Messer Calco send you the necessary documents as soon as we have received all of the requests for concessions and have arrived at a tax rate."

The Marchesino bowed again and departed; a second later Galeazzo di Sanseverino's artificially handsome face peered around the heavy marble doorframe. Il Moro flipped his fingers and Galeazz came in. He was followed by Il Moro's security chief, the slender, dark-complected Bernardino da Corte.

Il Moro briefly lifted his hands from the arms of his chair. "His Most Christian Majesty has not been sufficiently delayed by his recent illness. Now that Messer Ambrogio has effected his cure, the King is adamant about going to Pavia. We can expect him here in Vigevano in two days and at Pavia two days after that."

"Where is he now, Your Highness?" Galeazz asked.

"Casale."

"That is a half day's ride for me. I could go there tomorrow and try to dissuade him."

Il Moro shook his head. "The King has it fixed in his mind that he must at least offer this courtesy to his mother's sister and his cousin. It is a question of his honor, so I am told. And as you know, Galeazz, when the King has an *idée fixe* concerning his honor, any amount of persuasion is wasted."

Galeazz stared at the floor. "I'm very concerned about this. According to the information I have from the French camp, had the King remained in bed a week longer, the French army would now be marching on Milan. And the continued presence of Louis Duc d'Orléans and his army in Asti is in my opinion tantamount to a hostile act. Your Highness, forgive me for having to say this, but right now the only man in the French camp who trusts you is the King. But if the King goes to Pavia . . . Your Highness, I presume you know that the Duchess Mother is spreading the rumor that you are poisoning her son."

"Of course. It is the same poison that Gian was administered when he was twelve and just starting to drink seriously, and again when he was eighteen, when his idyllic existence was interrupted by the arrival of his wife. He became deathly ill both times. Moderation in the consumption of wine is the only antidote Gian requires."

"Your Highness, the simple fact of the Duke of Milan's illness, combined with the Duchess Mother's slander, will be sufficient pretext for Louis Duc d'Orleans to turn this entire enterprise against us. He will argue to the King that with the fall rains imminent, why should they go south when the richest spoil is already at their feet, along with a just cause to excuse their treachery? And of course when you are out of the way, Your Highness, the Duke of Milan will no doubt succumb to the lingering effects of the poison you gave him."

Il Moro nodded soberly and pressed the tips of his fingers together.

"It is a most serious situation, Your Highness." Suddenly Galeazz turned to Bernardino, who stood as stiffly as a page. "Messer Bernardino has an interesting thought, Your Highness. I have asked him to repeat it to you in the same spirit in which you have so often solicited my more . . . aggressive outlook on certain policies. I have assured him that you will not judge him or accuse him on what he presents as mere theory and nothing more."

"Certainly. Go on, Messer Bernardino." Il Moro continued to study his steepled fingers.

Bernardino licked his lips. "Your Highness . . . ah, Your Highness. If you are to be damned by rumors concerning the Duke of Milan's health, perhaps your only defense against these rumors is to make them true."

Il Moro did not even blink; his steeple of fingers did not waver at all. The heavy silence was broken only by the slight friction of one of Messer Bernardino's leather soles against the marble floor.

Finally Il Moro spoke in a very soft, even voice. "What you suggest reflects a certain political astuteness, Messer Bernardino. But of course it is out of the question. Our Duke is my nephew. I am not capable of such infamy. I could not even consider it." He looked up at Galeazz, his eyes both vulnerable and intense, as if he were making a confession to a lover. "I am simply not capable of such a thing."

CHAPTER

41

Pavia, 14 October 1494

The physician, a middle-aged man perspiring under the burden of his heavy velvet cloak, watched in horror as the chamberlain brought a silver dish containing a single blushingly ripe pear to the bedside of the Duke of Milan. "Your Highness, I would not encourage him to consume fruit or vegetable as yet—"

"Sorceror!" snapped Bona of Savoy, Duchess Mother of Milan. "How can he reverse the effects of the poison if he hasn't the strength to expel it?"

Gian Galeazzo's eyes were luminous with fever, and the blue veins at his temples appeared to have been painted on his vellum-pale skin. He weakly lifted his arm to receive the offering.

"Your Highness," the physician was finally prompted to say, "we believe that this is a gastric affliction that can only be exacerbated—"

"The Duchess Mother is right, Messer Cussano. Let my husband eat." The Duchess of Milan's entrance lacked the usual brisk, crackling sense of command. Almost shyly, she approached Gian's bed and smiled benevolently over him. She stood directly opposite the Duchess Mother.

Bona nodded earnestly at Isabella. "You see, Messer Cussano, we are all in agreement. My son's wife and I have had our differences, to be certain, but on this we agree. His Highness should have more fruit. His Highness's cousin the Most Christian King of France has come here to see him today. He will need his strength."

The physician mopped his brow with a dirty linen handkerchief. He bowed and followed after the chamberlain, who had bustled off for more pears.

"The King and his company arrived a quarter hour ago," Isabella said. "They are coming right up. I was informed that His Most Christian Majesty is most anxious to see Gian and inquire about his health."

Bona beamed her black smile at her son. "Of course the Most Christian King is coming right up. Gian is His Majesty's favorite cousin." Suddenly the Duchess Mother's smile vanished. She looked up at Isabella, her perfectly round face twitching with ambivalence. Finally she said rather mildly, "Of course you cannot stay."

"Gian is my husband, Duchess Mother," Isabella said equally temperately. "I certainly intend to regard His Most Christian Majesty with the utmost civility. I believe that when His Most Christian Majesty realizes that Il Moro is his real enemy, His Most Christian Majesty will be more favorably disposed to the house of Aragon."

Bona contemplated this, sucking at her teeth. "Very well. But if my nephew the Most Christian King asks that you leave, I will insist that you do so."

"Thank you, Duchess Mother."

Gian had time to eat a pear before the chamberlain announced His Most Christian Majesty. Bona kissed her son's damp, translucent forehead. "Your deliverance is at hand," she whispered. "God has sent us an avenging angel."

The royal entourage arrived to the arrogant jingling of spurs and the rattling of scabbards. Wearing riding hose and doublets, swords hung on their hips, the Frenchmen looked road weary and overheated, their stubbly faces ruddy with sunburn. The King, no better dressed than his comrades, by size and appearance easily mistaken for a court dwarf, would have been entirely overlooked if Il Moro had not entered at his side. Wearing a clean white-and-

gold brocade tunic, his posture impeccable in contrast to the careless Gallic slouches of the King and his advisers, Il Moro made
the Frenchmen look like country bumpkins.

Bona had never imagined that Il Moro would have the effrontery to attend this private conclave between the Duke of Milan
and the King of France. Her lips contracted to a perfect circle. She
forgot to curtsy, and Charles came forward on his own initiative,
his sable hat in hand. "My dear Aunt. Aunt, it is I—your nephew
Charles *le Roi.*"

Bona stepped stiffly forward and awkwardly exchanged kisses
with her nephew. She took his arm and urgently led him to the
bedside.

"Oh, my poor dear cousin," the King said on viewing Gian,
his jaw slack with genuine distress. "You poor dear boy. You
really are ailing so."

Gian gave his cousin the pathetic, endearing smile of an eager-
to-please sick child. Isabella, who had morosely lowered her chin
and eyes at the entry of the French party, now began to sob quietly.

"My son's assassin is in this room," Bona said in vehement
French. Her eyes contracted and aimed directly at Il Moro.

Everyone looked between the Duchess Mother and Il Moro.
Some of Charles's advisers began to whisper. Il Moro's expression
of implacable courtesy and reserve did not change.

"He thinks that his being here will silence me," Bona went
on, spitting rapid French at her nephew. "The entire world knows
that he has poisoned my son. You will all soon enough know that
he has obtained the papers of investiture from the German Emperor. When he has made himself Duke he will turn on you. He
will betray you as he has betrayed his own blood. Be done with
him. Do not leave Pavia until you are done with him. In your
mother's name, put him in chains and lock him in the darkness
forever."

Isabella sobbed audibly. Angry muttering came from the
King's entourage.

Guillaume Briconnet, the King's principal adviser, his face red-
der than anyone's, suddenly barked in French, "Everything she
says about Il Moro is true. Your Majesty, if you do not seize him
now, I fear that you will not leave here alive."

Charles stood absolutely dumbfounded. All around him, hands

went to the hilts of swords. The King had only to give the order—and if he didn't, it was obvious that Briconnet would. Il Moro's right hand twitched just once, but violently, like a speared fish.

"No," Isabella blurted out tearfully. "No, that isn't so." She spoke in Italian, and the King's interpreter translated with hushed, gasping urgency. "What the Duchess Mother says about Il Moro poisoning my husband is not true. No one man is poisoning him. Everyone is poisoning him. Gian has a nervous constitution, and this discord, this coming and going of great armies, has so unsettled him that his stomach refuses all food. . . ." Isabella rubbed her sleeve across her runny nose. "The antidote to my husband's poison is peace. If we but had peace . . . My husband must not be the first martyr of this war."

Bona's entire body trembled with rage at her daughter-in-law's defection. Even Il Moro's face showed something, a rapid inward calculation: Isabella had finally given him a problem in the mathematics of deceit that he could not quickly solve. As the translation was delivered, the puzzled Frenchmen shook their heads.

King Charles looked between Bona, Isabella, and Il Moro, his huge head bobbing. It seemed that in a moment his head might start spinning from confusion.

In a desperate lurching motion, Isabella threw herself to the floor at the King's feet. She grasped Charles's spindly ankles and kissed his enormous scalloped slippers. "I beg you to spare my father!" she wailed hysterically. "O good and brave King, please spare my father! For the love of all that is just and good, treat kindly with my father, whose intention it has never been to anger you!"

"She is mad!" Bona crowed, grinning with black glee, convinced that the outburst would discredit everything else Isabella had said. Il Moro watched the spectacle impassively. He was no longer confused.

The interpreter sputtered Isabella's words into Charles's ear. The King looked down; Isabella's henna-tinted hair draped his feet like the plumage of some beautiful slain bird. He vainly reached to lift her up. "Oh, dear," he said. "Dear, dear." He gestured for the interpreter to kneel beside Isabella.

"You must tell this beautiful and brave woman that my honor

will not allow me to abandon my quest," Charles said. "Not to mention the great amount of money my treasury and others have advanced us for our Crusade. But assure her that I consider herself and her little boy commended to my care, and that when her father yields to me, I shall tell him what a faithful daughter he has sired. She has my word as a Christian cavalier that her father shall be treated fairly in defeat."

Isabella again kissed the King's goose-foot slippers, her shoulders heaving, the sobbing motion punctuated by strange whimpers. None of the Frenchmen could have guessed that she was laughing.

Extract of a letter of His Most Christian Majesty CHARLES VIII, King of France, Jerusalem, and the Two Sicilies, to his brother-in-law PIERRE DE BEAUJEU, Duc du Bourbon. Pavia, 15 October 1494

. . . We dine here in the most remarkable fashion . . . my table was set with cups of crystal and cutlery of gold, and a napkin folded to resemble a pheasant, and when I had opened this, a live bird flew forth. . . . Each course was brought by boys in uniform, who removed the table linen so that a clean one might be found beneath. So myriad were these foods that I cannot describe them fully . . . and indeed many of them glittered with sauces of gold and silver. . . . Between each course they have an entertainment, wherein scenes are enacted from tales of yore, or some to comedic purpose, and always with the accompaniment of music. The costumes are the most extraordinary I have ever seen, for they are in all manner of forms, that of devils and saints and ancient gods. Women also participate in these entertainments, wearing these costumes as well, and where they wish to create the impression that they are as naked as Eve, they do so in hose of the sheerest weight, and tinted like flesh, so that indeed one is most convinced. . . . And so the banquet proceeds far into the night, with one not knowing which to await more eagerly, the next serving or the entertainment that will follow. . . .

. . . As splendidly as Il Moro amuses me, all about me caution that I cannot trust him and that I must be done with him before I can continue my Crusade. . . . I am confused and wish that you and my dear sister were here to assist my council . . . but [I] reside in my faith that God will show me my way. . . .

Il Moro's fingers traced across Beatrice's swelling abdomen. They were both naked, lying atop the silk covers. Well past midnight, the air was still warm, heavy, clinging.

"I feel as if the Frenchmen have been here for a month," Beatrice said in a brittle voice. "Even their speech is offensive. Mooing and growling and trilling like a barnyard. It is remarkable to me that so many lovely tales have been written in that hideous language."

"Be grateful that Messer Niccolò reduced the number of *intermedi* in tonight's theatrical. He had originally scheduled seven. In the name of God, we would still be down in the courtyard entertaining them. As it was, I thought the King would never permit the dancers portraying the Three Graces to leave the stage. That one *intermedo* lasted almost as long as the entire third act."

"I believe the dancers had your interest as well. They might as well have been naked." Beatrice looked down at her swollen middle. "Certainly a more graceful sight than this."

Il Moro's hand flowed over the contour of his wife's belly. "You have no idea how beautiful this curve is."

She pensively studied his caress. "I'm sad that your hands never touched Ercole while he was in my womb."

"I thought we had crossed that dark sea."

She took his hand. "We have. It is something else. It is this season, the summer that will not end, the Frenchmen who will not leave. . . . It's as if this bad air seems to whisper terrible things. . . . I don't know. I don't want to hear them. Dear God, Lodovico. I know you're trying to make light of it, but you were in real danger yesterday. We all were. God knows where we might be right now if—"

"*Carissima*, that was just Briconnet crowing like a *gallo*." Il Moro smiled at the pun; the Italian word for a Frenchman, *gallo*, also meant "rooster."

Beatrice stared abstractedly into the darkness. "Serafino has collected reports of the things people have seen all over Italy. In Apulia three suns appeared at night, in the midst of the most tremendous thunder and lightning. In Arezzo clouds in the shape of armed men on enormous horses passed through the sky for days on end, with a thunder like drums and trumpets. Statues sweating blood in a dozen churches. Monstrous births everywhere. Of all the portents of disaster known throughout history, only a comet is lacking."

"Well, no doubt the peasant women responsible for these *invenzione* will soon see dozens of comets."

"You believe in the stars."

"That is science, calculated with great precision by learned men. Your father is certainly no fool, and he believes. So did your mother. But these portents you are talking about are created by the confluence of rumor, country wives, and too much wine."

"I believe the things I feel in my soul. The stars are somewhere else, cold and indifferent."

Il Moro propped himself on an elbow. "I will not say that the stars rule us. But they guide us just as they do a sailor at sea. The vast and complex movement of the heavens reflects the complex movement of our own fates. There are times when the alignment of the celestial bodies bodes well, and times when those aspects bode ill. The same can be said for the alignment of earthly affairs. If we choose the moment when that alignment favors us, Fortune will favor us."

"Perhaps Fortune chooses for us. She chooses any moment she pleases, and fools us into thinking that it is the moment we have chosen."

"Perhaps. But if we act wisely, Fortune will choose wisely."

"I don't believe that the Frenchmen are going to leave. The rains will come before the advance guard of their army reaches Florence. The main body of the army will winter here. And Louis Duc d'Orleans has no intention of leaving Asti."

Il Moro stroked Beatrice's belly again. "No, *carissima*. Not only do I believe that the King is going to leave . . ." He sat up with sudden animation. "I had wanted to save this until the Frenchmen were gone, but this time seems most appropriate." He paused, and his eyes gleamed in the moonlight. "*Amore*, today I received something from the Emperor of Germany. The authorizing papers for my investiture as Duke of Milan. It is done. He only asks that I delay their publication until December, which suits me entirely because no one must know of this until the French are well south of here."

Beatrice silently recited the title. Duke of Milan. Lodovico Maria Sforza, Duke of Milan. And then she thought: Duchess of Milan. Beatrice d'Este da Sforza, Duchess of Milan.

"Everything is aligned for us, *carissima*. Everything. Florence will blood the French before they even reach Naples, and then Naples and France will blunt their swords against each other. By next summer the French will count themselves fortunate if they are permitted to go back over the mountains. And then three great powers will remain in Europe: ourselves, Germany, and Venice. Germany and Venice are rivals, whereas we are now allied to both. We will be the arbiters of everything. Everything."

He took her face in his hands. "*Carissima*, I thought this dream was gone, vanished while I looked on as helplessly as a man watching ashes blow away in the wind. Now I dare to hold it in my hands again, resurrected, whole. I do not mean to pain you when I say that this is the fulfillment of the dream that Cecilia for so long held for me. Because I never could have achieved it without you. Not because you have given me a son. But because you have restored my soul. You have given me the courage to confront my own doubts. To defeat my greatest enemy. Your love has set in motion the entire mechanism of my fate. You are my Fortune, *amore*, you are my stars. There is no other lady who rules my destiny. Only you." He kissed her softly. "Only you."

Duchess of Milan, Queen of Europe . . . She had already begun to assemble vague, fantastic images for this dream, the pageants and the palaces, watching her son crowned Emperor of the mythical realm of Everything. . . . And then a fear punched at her stomach, a pain too sharp to be a fetal kick. There was one fundamental, primal obstacle to that dream. Eesh. She would have to snatch her dream right out of Eesh's hands. And she hadn't even had the courage to stand in the same room as Eesh. She had lived in terror since she'd been told four days before that she would have to go on to Pavia with her husband and the French King.

She had come from Vigevano in a carriage, arriving several hours after the King and her husband, because she'd dreaded that Eesh would be waiting at the *castello* gate to greet the visitors. She had then constructed elaborate defenses, commissioning her servants and ladies to seek out intelligence about Eesh's movements; if Eesh was expected to attend a supper or theatrical, Beatrice intended to use her pregnancy as an excuse to stay in her rooms. But so far Eesh had remained either in her own rooms or in her husband's sickroom. The relief Beatrice felt at each reprieve merely heightened her fears of an eventual encounter. Every time her chamberlain appeared in her rooms to announce someone, Beatrice imagined Eesh charging in behind him like a horned demon.

Beatrice looked up at the ceiling, briefly noting that this was the same coffered ceiling she had stared at on her wedding night. "Why do you suppose Isabella didn't take advantage of the opportunity to turn the French against you? If she had joined Bona in accusing you of poisoning Gian . . ." Beatrice shook her head, the speculation too frightening for words.

"She is certainly clever enough to realize that the French have no more respect for her husband's title than they do for her father's throne. She needs the French army to move south as urgently as we do. So she very deftly eliminated the best pretext for the French to stay in the north. And of course she was also able to humiliate her mother-in-law. As to her begging for her father, that was done only well enough to convince the Frenchmen. But it certainly distracted them from any further discussion of Gian's illness. All in all a superb performance. And one that served us quite well."

"That's what troubles me."

"I thought the same at the time, *carissima*. But I don't think her gift is a Trojan horse. Your cousin is clever, but she is no Ulysses."

This time the sensation in Beatrice's womb was her baby's kick, a much gentler pain than her abstract fear but even more disturbing. You are wrong about Eesh, she silently told her husband. And you are wrong about Fortune too. She still rules our lives. You may achieve everything you have dreamed of and yet find that I am not there to share it with you. Because this time Fortune might decide to let my baby kill me.

Certosa di Pavia, 16 October 1494

"Remarkable." King Charles's mouth fell open at something he had noticed in one of the small chapels tucked into the aisle on the right side of the nave. With the spontaneity of a child, he veered off to examine it, Il Moro and Galeazzo di Sanseverino following behind like indulgent parents. Il Moro had been heartened that the King had requested Galeazz as his interpreter on this sightseeing excursion; he presumed that Charles wanted a serious, confidential discussion. A conversation that would most likely reveal whether or not the King actually intended to lead his army out of northern Italy.

The King stopped before the object of his interest, a towering candlelit painting, one of several panels in which the donors of the chapel knelt beside various saints.

"Remarkable," the King repeated with even greater emphasis. He gaped with astonishment.

The painting depicted Saint Peter standing stoically and grimly in his bishop's robes, his skull split directly down the middle by a huge cleaver still buried to the depth of a palm's width; fresh blood streamed from the wound. The improbable scene was painted with such uncanny realism that one could almost hear the gruesome whack.

"Extraordinary. It truly is. I would believe that the saint is present before us. I truly would. Look at the blood. Each drop. Is it real blood which through some magic stays wet? It must be real." Told that the blood was also a product of the painter's art, Charles asked the name of the master. Bergognone, Il Moro answered.

Charles studied the painting for several minutes, pausing to feel his skull as if verifying the fine points of anatomy. Finally he turned to Galeazz but glanced shyly at Il Moro. "This Seigneur Bergognone," he said. "Is he as expert as this in the drawing of the unclothed female body?"

Il Moro listened to the translation, then nodded warily.

"I wonder if Seigneur Bergognone might consider rendering some pictures of my companions. I would like to have pictures so real that I could fool myself into embracing them." The King honked furious amusement, his hunched back heaving. "I would like that indeed."

"Your Majesty," Il Moro said smoothly, "I would like nothing more than for Maestro Bergognone to attend to your companions as you wish. But I have sent him to Rome to paint my brother's portrait."

Charles's huge eyes were virtually grief-stricken.

"Your Majesty, if you were to go south, I could arrange for Maestro Bergognone to meet you in Florence."

Charles appeared not to hear, and Il Moro gave Galeazz a meaningful glance. "Your Majesty," Il Moro said, "we would be only too glad to lodge you here in Pavia for the entire winter. But think of the additional cost in wages for your troops. You must move south now if you are to be in Naples before the rains."

Charles hung his head and did not look at either man. "Everyone is telling me not to leave," he mumbled. "Truly. They say I must not turn my back on you."

"Why, Your Majesty? The Duke of Milan's own wife has testified that I am not engaged in anything untoward."

"They say that you have negotiated with the Emperor to become Duke of Milan and that when the Emperor has invested you, you will turn against me. That is what I am told. Truly."

"I can offer Your Majesty my holiest oath that there is no truth whatsoever to that slander. I swear it in this holy place."

Charles looked back into the cavernous nave as if expecting verification from a higher power. Galeazz caught Il Moro's eye, pursed his lips gravely, and shook his head.

Il Moro studied the macabre painting for a moment. Then he fixed his eyes firmly on the King. "If Your Majesty will not have my pledges, then let me offer you this surety. You will not have to turn your back on me. I will go south with you. I will personally escort you to the gates of Naples. I will make myself hostage to my own promises."

Galeazz's eyebrows lifted with surprise, and he gave the translation haltingly.

The King's apparently autonomous head snapped to attention. "You would? You would indeed? Oh, that is very much to my liking. Very much so. That will answer all of them and enable me to continue my Christian enterprise." The King impulsively stepped forward and embraced his host. "Onward to Jerusalem," he said brightly.

Pavia, 17 October 1494

The hastily arranged farewell banquet for the French King and his entourage had lasted until after midnight, despite the company's scheduled departure for Piacenza early the next morning. For the three bathers in the *castello*'s indoor pool, the festivities continued on toward dawn.

Lit to a pale, marblelike sheen in moonlight amply supplied by two banks of big second-story windows, the three figures composed an interesting sculptural counterpoint to the tall, fluted column, crowned with three naked *putti*, in the center of the pool. The central support of this new sculptural group was a man of Herculean stature, the pulsing muscles of his back more complex than anything ever carved in marble or cast in bronze. A naked nymph, no taller than a child, her short but well-shaped limbs trembling with a passion a sculptor could only imply, wrapped her legs around Hercules' hips and her arms around his back. A second naked nymph, taller than the other and as sinuous as a snake, rode on Hercules' shoulders, facing him, her legs splayed down his back, her groin pressed to his face. Hercules held her aloft, his hands beneath her armpits and his thumbs pressed against her significant breasts. Her hair, loose and glistening, fell down her back as she closed her eyes and turned her face to the vaulted ceiling.

Without losing its basic configuration, the sculpture grappled, grunted, whimpered, gasped, and made a few shrill cries. The tall nymph's pelvic motion shifted from a steady undulation to arrhythmic spasms. *"Gesù!"* she screamed with terrifying vehemence. *"Gesù!"* Her body stiffened, and she wrapped her arms around Hercules' head.

"Caterina." The voice came from the vicinity of the door,

which had been locked. The tall nymph shook her mop of wet hair as if clearing her head.

The moonlight revealed a third woman, taller than the other two, with long legs and full breasts. She was as naked as the rest except for a sequined black velvet mask she held to her face like a carnival masquer. The mask created a strange effect in the dull light, the metal sequins occasionally twinkling like stars in the black void of the masquer's face.

"I waited until you finished, Caterina." The full-face mask gave the masquer's voice a hollow, ghostly echo. "Lucrezia will have to resume her work at another time."

The tall nymph commanded Hercules to set her down, and the other unwrapped herself from his trunk. The two women said nothing as they climbed the steps and moved in silvery flashes to the door. Intrigued, Hercules also remained silent as the masquer walked with shameless grace to the steps. She stopped at the marble rim of the pool. She lowered her mask.

The Herculean figure stood an arm's width away from her, his glistening erection pointing to his navel, a line of archaic simplicity against the fluid, Hellenistic curves of his body. When he recognized the masquer's face, his head moved from side to side in tiny, stunned motions, like a man observing a distant catastrophe.

"I matched that pair for you," the masquer said. "I know that short women are ordinarily not to your taste, but you must agree that Lucrezia was a perfect fit. And Caterina loves tongue." She sauntered down the steps.

Moving very slowly, almost as if he were indeed a statue gradually discovering life in his limbs, Hercules placed his hands beneath her buttocks and lifted her onto his priapic shaft. She wriggled to adjust herself and then seized the ends of his hair, forcing him to look into her eyes.

"I have dreamed of this," he said in a trancelike cadence. "Every day and every night, with every other woman, for four years I have dreamed of this. You coming to me."

"Coming to you," replied the Duchess of Milan in a hot, growling whisper. "I have come back to you, Galeazz."

Bernardino da Corte visually inventoried the shelves of Il Moro's *guardaroba* as the porters emptied it of the tooled saddles and silver dinner service His Highness intended to take on the journey south; with all the Frenchmen about, Il Moro's chief of security was concerned about theft. Satisfied that the packing was proceeding without incident, Bernardino opened one of the window shutters and observed that the night had lightened into the dull silver of dawn. He ordered the porters to open the remaining windows and snuffed his candle lantern. For a moment he stared out at Pavia's thicket of brick towers.

He turned when he heard someone dismiss the porters. Galeazzo di Sanseverino came toward him with his bounding, curiously light stride. His blond hair was damp and his skin as rosy as a berouged woman's. His blue eyes had a frightening cast, a strange icy whiteness, as if glazed with frost.

The last porter out shut the door behind the two men.

Galeazz looked down into Bernardino's dark, expectant face. "Now," he whispered. "Do it."

The tip of Bernardino's tongue rapidly traced a nervous circuit of his lips. "Has His Highness authorized—"

In a lightning motion Galeazz's hand went to Bernardino's throat, his fingers flexing slightly and cradling Bernardino's swarthy chin. "You accuse yourself of treason by even mentioning his name in connection with this," Galeazz hissed.

Bernardino stared back, his eyes glittered with fear.

"Do it," Galeazz whispered. "Not because His Highness has asked it, not even because our lives depend on it." Suddenly Galeazz bent forward and kissed Bernardino on the lips, tenderly, almost romantically. "Do it for me."

Beatrice gingerly lifted her twenty-month-old son from his cradle. Little Ercole contorted his face and made several frog kicks but continued to sleep with his head against his mother's shoulder. Beatrice carried him into her husband's bedchamber, where his servants were just finishing lacing up his riding doublet. Il Moro motioned the servants out.

"He's going to be so sad when he realizes that Baba isn't coming back right away," Beatrice said.

Il Moro took his sleeping son in his arms. "Within a month the French will realize that they are going to get no farther than Florence before spring. And by then His Majesty will be only too happy to allow me to return home to arrange the additional loans required to pay his troops."

Beatrice looked down, her face offering a vestige of her once familiar adolescent pout.

"*Carissima*, you know that it was the only thing I could do. We are so much safer with the French on the move again."

"Louis Duc d'Orleans will still be in Asti."

"Well, I am much less concerned about Louis Duc d'Orleans in Asti than I am with the idea of Orleans in Asti *and* Charles in Pavia."

"I . . . I have seen things." She paused, waiting for him to ask, but he said nothing. "Blackbirds. Yesterday. One on each tower of the *castello*."

"Well, we have a great many blackbirds. *Carissima*, you have been my courage throughout all this. Be brave now. Everything favors us."

Beatrice began to cry, quaking, childish sobs. Ercole awakened with a start and added a harsh, cracking protest of his own. Il Moro called for one of his servants and asked him to take the boy to his nurse. He held his wife in his arms and stroked her cheek and hair.

"*Carissima*, I don't understand this. You would not hesitate for a moment to go yourself."

"I would rather go myself. I would rather . . ." She pressed her cheek to his chest and stared out the window. The sun lay molten on the treetops, and the eastward walls of the city's rectangular towers were a fiery pink. "I have everything I have ever wanted. Right now. Everything I have ever dreamed of. Perhaps that is what frightens me." And yet to herself a deeper voice whispered: No, you want more. Much more. And that is what frightens you.

"I love you."

She looked up at him warily. "You don't need to say that."

"I love you in every way that it is possible for me to love, with all I know of my own soul. What I do not know of that soul you will help me understand. That is my faith. That is the faith that will bring me home. So let us say goodbye now, *amore*. I want brave faces for the Frenchmen."

She clung to him, her eyes closed, feeling as if some huge motion of fate's machinery had just begun to carry him away from her.

Finally Il Moro gently unwrapped himself from his wife's frantic embrace. Together they went into the nursery, where Ercole was nursing. Il Moro waited until the feeding had ended. Then he took his son and kissed him and sang him a ditty about Scaramella, a scarecrow who became a soldier. Ercole laughed and shrieked. Beatrice could not watch her husband give her son a last kiss, believing that if she saw it she might somehow endow this farewell with the force of dreadful prophecy.

Then they walked out onto the second-story loggia with its rows of elaborate Venetian-style Gothic arches overlooking the gardens and pavilions in the central court. Beatrice took her husband's arm as they descended the narrow brick stairwell at the main entrance to the *castello*; built to discourage armed attack, for a moment the chutelike enclosure seemed to Beatrice as dank and inescapable as a tomb.

The French King waited outside the *castello* walls, at the foot of the drawbridge spanning the sun-silvered moat. His Most Christian Majesty appeared only too eager to leave this place of inertia and doubts concerning his glorious Crusade. Most of his troops had already gone ahead to Piacenza, two days' march to the southeast. But the King's flutists, drummers, Scottish crossbowmen, and armored household guard waited in ranks. The file of musicians and warriors extended across the drawbridge and through the park in front of the *castello*, finally disappearing into the cobbled streets of the red-brick city.

The King stood beside his black horse, chatting with Galeazzo di Sanseverino. Charles removed his cap with an elaborate flourish, and Il Moro responded by removing his beret; Beatrice curtsied. She looked quickly for Eesh and was both relieved and annoyed at her relief when she did not see her.

The farewells were florid and insincere, with the King kissing every lady in sight. Beatrice was grateful that her husband had given her a last moment of intimacy upstairs. She kissed him perfunctorily on both cheeks, only for an instant meeting his eyes.

Finally, with everyone ready to mount, Bianca, dressed in expensive black silk, bustled up to her husband, Galeazz. Standing on the toes of her wooden-soled black velvet slippers, she kissed him on each cheek. Then she hurried back to Beatrice's side and took her hand. The drums rattled and the pipes shrilled and Il Moro's trumpeters sounded a fanfare. Brandishing his white fur cap with the gold fleurs-de-lis, His Most Christian Majesty resumed his pilgrimage.

Bianca tightly clutched Beatrice's hand while the procession disappeared into the streets of Pavia. "I recited prayers this morning for my father and Galeazz," Bianca said meekly, as if uncertain that this amounted to much. "Do you expect that they are in great danger?"

Beatrice drew herself up against the leaden premonition in her heart. "No. I don't expect that they are."

"Toto, when do you expect that I will go to live with Galeazz? It is quite absurd to contemplate that I have been married for five years at present, and still . . ." Bianca's pale cheeks flooded with color. "And still the marriage has not been consummated. It is really becoming a matter of embarrassment to me."

Beatrice looked at Bianca and saw herself at fourteen—the self-important diction, Bianca as awkwardly frail and emaciated as Beatrice had been pudgy and overactive. "I would want you to have a few years yet, *carissima amica*. I didn't feel comfortable being married until I was very much older than you are now."

"I know. Toto, Caterina da Borromeo told me that Galeazz will split me in two. I told her that such an occurrence was most absurd even to contemplate, but she said that when a man is hard he can be bigger than any baby's head."

"Caterina is a liar."

"I know."

Beatrice studied Bianca's brilliant cheeks and questing, deep-socketed eyes. She realized that she needed to spend more time with her, and that sense of responsibility served as a catharsis for her fears. She put her arm around Bianca's impossibly slender waist and steered her back through the vaulted entrance to the *castello.* The gardens in the courtyard glistened with dew, and she felt a renewal of her hope.

Then her eye was drawn to the sharply pointed stone merlons atop the third story of the *castello*'s inner facade. A half-dozen crows sunned themselves on these stone perches, their fat, glistening black bodies like the obsidian finials of an enormous crypt. She looked quickly down, but on the second-story loggia she caught a glimpse of a woman standing in the still shadowed arcade, her black dress partially concealed by one of the white marble columns. Beatrice could not really distinguish the features of the woman's face, but some essence of an expression was visible through the veiled light. She knew it with an instinct that traced along her spine like the cold edge of a knife: Eesh, chin slightly tucked, smiling.

C H A P T E R

42

Dispatch of BERNARDINO DA CORTE, assistant castellan of Porta Giovia, to LODOVICO SFORZA, "Il Moro," Duke of Bari and regent for the Duke of Milan. Marked "*cito! cito! cito!*" Pavia, 20 October 1494

Your most illustrious Highness,

I must convey to you the most unfortunate news concerning your beloved nephew, our most illustrious Duke of Milan. After showing much improvement, His Highness prevailed upon his wife and mother to allow him a large quantity of wine, to the great consternation of his physicians. The sudden decline in His Highness's health subsequent to this indulgence has caused the most profound alarm here, and His Highness's physicians believe that only through Divine Mercy can it now be reversed. Your Highness must be advised that by the time this reaches you the Duke of Milan may already be dead. I wish it were not for me to dispatch these woeful tidings, but as always I am your faithful servant.

Piacenza, 20 October 1494

Galeazzo di Sanseverino led Il Moro out onto the balcony overlooking the garden. They had been lodged in one of the best villas
in Piacenza, a cavernous late-medieval structure that had been
renovated and provided with a marvelous new garden. The topiaries, shaped like lions, rams, and dolphins, sent out long, distorted shadows in the late afternoon light. Galeazz spread his map
on the marble railing of the balustrade. The map was a rough
sketch of the principal roads between Piacenza and Florence, with
x's marking the location of the fortresses that controlled those
routes.

"Now that they have decided to take the route through Florence and Rome, they must cross the Apennines and advance along
the coast here," Galeazz said, tracing a line that proceeded south
from Piacenza to the coast, then looped back inland to Florence.
"That means they must take the Florentine fortress at Sarzana"—
he pointed to an x on the coast about halfway between Piacenza
and Florence—"or expose their supply lines to continual harass-
ment. Because of the height of the promontory on which the
fortress is perched, their cannons will not be effective. By itself,
the fortress at Sarzana is capable of delaying the French advance
until the rains begin."

Il Moro studied the map silently, and Galeazz stared out into
the garden. Suddenly Il Moro turned around, as if he had sensed
an attacker. A moment later his chamberlain, elegant in tricolor
Sforza livery, appeared on the balcony, escorting a courier in riding
clothes the uniform reddish-brown of the local roads; even the
courier's face was caked with sienna-hued dust.

The courier fell heavily to his knee in front of Il Moro. "Your
Highness, I was directed to deliver this to you with my own hand.
You will forgive me."

Il Moro waited until the chamberlain and the courier had
bowed and exited. He impassively broke the messy, obviously

hasty wax seal. Galeazz watched him intently while he read. Il Moro revealed nothing and quickly handed the note to Galeazz.

Il Moro's unblinking black eyes now fixed on Galeazz; it seemed that Galeazz required an unusually long time to digest Bernardino da Corte's brief dispatch.

Galeazz's hand trembled slightly as he returned the dispatch to Il Moro. "What will you do?" he asked, his voice fractionally higher than usual.

"Of course I must return to Pavia immediately. The King will understand."

Galeazz folded his hands together. "Your Highness, you do not know what to expect in Pavia. I would like to come with you in the event . . ." He shrugged his powerful shoulders.

Il Moro studied Galeazz for a long moment before replying. "Yes." He nodded coolly. "Yes, of course. We do not know what we will find."

Pavia, 20 October 1494

Beatrice ran into the horses in the hall just outside the Duke of Milan's sickroom. The scene was unreal, hellish: the wavering torchlight in the narrow passage, the harsh rattling of the horses' hooves on the pavement, the flared nostrils and glaring eyes of the frightened beasts. Beatrice wondered for a moment if she was inhabiting a nightmare. But she could understand why the Duke of Milan wanted to see his horses. She was not at all certain why he had sent for her.

Gian's kindly chamberlain, Messer Dionigi, showed Beatrice into the sickroom. The miasma of the perfumed, smoking censers only partially masked the stench of medicines and vomit, churning the anxiety in her stomach. Only with great will could she force herself not to bend over and retch. Eesh stood beside the bed, utterly composed, wearing her sinister, menacing-madonna suggestion of a smile. Bona sat on the opposite side of the bed, her shoulders clenched, her round eyes zeroed to tiny points of malice.

Four physicians in long velvet cloaks, droning on *sotto voce*, stood in the background like the chorus in a Greek tragedy.

At first glance Gian seemed surprisingly well, his head propped up on a pillow, his lank platinum hair framing his face. The feverish intensity of his irises and the pink tint that suffused his translucent skin gave him a luster of vitality. But Gian had lost too much weight to sustain the illusion. When Beatrice looked into the shadowed hollows of his cheeks and eyes, she saw the head of death.

Gian held up his hand to her. For a moment she had the utterly terrifying, utterly irrational fear that he would drag her into the underworld with him. Almost to spite that fear she took his hand; it was cool, with the dry, fine texture of the best goatskin parchment.

"Dear Beatrice," Gian whispered. "Everyone is so worried about me."

Beatrice squeezed his hand. "Yes, we all are, Gian. We so much want you to get well."

"Beatrice, you know what everyone is saying. . . ." Gian's eyes rolled toward his mother. "Uncle Lodovico still cares for me, doesn't he? And Uncle Ascanio too. I have had letters from Uncle Ascanio all about the hunts they have had in Rome."

Beatrice's throat knotted. "Yes, Gian," she whispered. "You know your uncle Lodovico loves you very much. He always has. So do I."

"That makes me so very happy. My physicians say I am improved, you know."

The shadows seemed to vanish from Gian's face. Beatrice could see only an angelic whiteness and light, as if Gian, stripped of his unwanted ducal trappings and his opportunistic favorites and the corruption of wine, had finally been revealed in all his innocence, an innocence as shocking as the revelation of his father's pure evil might have been to one of his victims. Gian the lamb . . . He must not become the first innocent to die. Beatrice clutched his hand, willing her own life into him. Please live, Gian. We all need you. You are the innocent who guards us against the terrible things in all our souls.

Beatrice only vaguely heard the clicking and whimpering in the hall. Gian's greyhounds, at least a dozen of them, burst into the room, spinning and bounding crazily, their long snouts reaching for their master's outstretched arms. Gian invited them up on the bed, and they surrounded him, licking and prodding. Gian rubbed their heads and began calling them by name, beaming, the sick child surrounded by his favorite toys.

"I will look in on you tomorrow morning," Beatrice said, happy to leave Gian to the creatures he most truly loved and could understand.

Beatrice had reached the hall when a bony hand clutched her arm like a claw. She turned to Bona's beady little pupils.

"This treason will be proved, and you and your husband will pay like those who killed his father. You will be hanged and gutted and quartered, and the birds will peck out your eyes on top of the tower. Murderer. Murdering filth. Your day of judgment is at hand."

"Go back to Gian, Duchess Mother." Isabella's voice was so soothing, so controlled, that even Beatrice was reassured by it. Isabella stood behind her mother-in-law, her hand lightly under Bona's elbow. "Gian asked for you, Duchess Mother."

Bona glared a moment longer at Beatrice, her frail body quaking with fury. Then her claw grip vanished, and she whisked around and vanished like a shadow.

Isabella cocked her head slightly in a patronizing fashion, her smile frozen on her face. She held her hands at her waist. "The Duchess Mother doesn't know that you and your husband are already finished."

"I don't want to fight." Remembering their last encounter, Beatrice meant this in a physical as well as verbal sense. "I hope Gian rests well."

Isabella's smile became hideously artificial. "And I hope you rest well too, Beatrice." She took a step forward. "I hope you rest well knowing this. Tomorrow Gian intends to sign papers abdicating as Duke of Milan, citing his delicate constitution. Gian will designate his son Francesco as the new Duke of Milan. I will be named as my son's regent. Of course your husband's position as Gian's regent will no longer exist. And since your husband will no longer be needed here, and as my father has already seized your little Duchy of Bari, I wonder where you will go."

Beatrice felt everything rush out of her, leaving nothing but a membrane of nerves filled with cold air. That was why Eesh wanted everyone on the way south, that was why Eesh was giving Gian wine and feeding him fruit. She had to tell her husband. . . . Suddenly Beatrice realized she was alone to face this monster. The monster who in one mighty swipe had shattered her mythical realm of Everything. Then her fear and despair contracted to a single icy center: My baby. Will Eesh hurt my baby?

"Rest well, little girl." Eesh's smile was unforced now, perfectly serene.

"You will have to be approved by the Council of Nobles. I will go before them and testify that Francesco is not Gian's son."

"And as you will be able to produce no witnesses to corroborate your slander, I will have you taken out and beheaded for treason."

"Galeazz will—"

"Galeazz? Where is Galeazz? He is away with your husband and the Frenchmen. And even if he were here, would he sacrifice his own head for you and your husband? And who would believe him? Perhaps Galeazz is the liar. Have you considered that?"

Beatrice felt as powerless as she had when Eesh had pinned her to the floor. She couldn't say anything, she couldn't move. Shadows danced at the periphery of her vision, and she struggled to keep from fainting. She focused so hard on holding back that flickering corona of darkness that she did not hear Isabella cheerfully bid her good night and recognized only the vague, dreamlike motion as Isabella returned to her husband's sickroom.

There was not enough to keep Beatrice busy that night. She hurriedly packed her most valuable jewels and papers and made certain that little Ercole's nurses would be ready to travel in the morning. At first light she intended to go to Vigevano, away from Eesh's people. Once she was certain her baby was safe, she would dispatch couriers she could trust to Piacenza, informing her husband of the situation.

But after her simple preparations were completed, she had nothing left to relieve her anxiety. Her husband had been so wrong. The stars were not aligned. The stars were falling from the sky. In her mind's eye she saw the shower of fireworks after Bianca Maria's wedding. Fortune's warning. She had heard it then, but she had not really understood and in her own haste had forgotten it later. Then she realized that it had already been too late, even on the night of Bianca Maria's wedding. The moment to choose had been in Venice. Mama had been right. For an aching instant she wanted to go back, to hold Mama in her arms and beg her to make everything right again.

Finally Beatrice went into her baby's nursery and sat beside him as he slept, thinking that he would somehow absolve her. But all she could think, over and over again, was: I have done this. To myself, to my husband, and to our baby. I have done this.

Two hours before dawn Beatrice was startled by a whisper in her ear. "Your Highness." She turned and saw the sturdy face of Ercole's nurse. "Your Highness. The Duke of Milan . . ." The nurse trailed off in a way that drew a line of ice from the nape of Beatrice's neck to the tip of her coccyx.

"Stay with Ercole," Beatrice said. "Lock the doors behind me and admit no one except me."

She raced out into the darkened loggia. Immediately she noticed the torches in the lower arcades and in the stables at the north end of the courtyard. Scores of people, the Duchess of Milan's people, were moving about. She hesitated, wondering if she should flee now. But she had to know what had happened to Gian. If some accusation was to be invented later, she wanted to be able to offer her own witness in her husband's defense.

The hallway next to Gian's sickroom was empty and utterly silent. Had Gian already been taken to Milan to appear before the Council of Nobles? Had they lured her here to finish with her? Would they later say she had come to poison Gian?

But she could hear nothing. With real dread and a bit of girlishly morbid fascination, she tiptoed forward. She slid against the wall and peered as stealthily as she could around the thick stone molding.

Two things: Gian's pasty face, and a woman in black, seated, head bowed. The woman was Bona.

Beatrice crept past the molding and stood in the doorway, ready to run if Bona called out. But Bona merely stared at something cradled in her hands. A portrait miniature. Beatrice tiptoed two steps farther in. Suddenly Bona looked up, and her eyes instantly froze Beatrice's heart. Just as quickly Bona's eyes failed to recognize her and returned to the little round painting.

Beatrice looked at Gian. She prayed for his delicately purple eyelids to quiver, to open. His skin appeared to be little more than a white, waxy film stretched over his bones. His lips were as pale as his skin, except for a curious indigo coloring where they met, like a thick line of ink drawn across his face. She shuddered with the memory of a snatch of court gossip she had heard a few years previously: someone had mentioned a poison figuratively said to seal lips, its only trace a black discoloration visible on the lips for an hour or so after death.

Then an even more profound realization struck her. This is a dead man. A man who held my hand and spoke to me just hours ago. With that a thousand images of death came screaming down from the shadowed ceiling coffers and corners of the room: murdered Christs and slaughtered saints and Mama's black babies, diving down at her in their terrible flocking splendor and vanishing into Gian's lifeless face. All the death that had surrounded her for her entire life in religious ritual and art now had a human face. Gian the dead man. The first dead man she had ever really seen. And then, with a pain so awful that she had to clutch her heart, she saw the truth that Gian's waxy face had just revealed to her. Mama is dead. Mama is really dead. For the first time she allowed herself to see her mother as a corpse like this, rotting in the earth, not some distant presence with whom she would one day be reunited, like the almost mythical Mama she had dreamed of as a girl in Naples. Mama no longer existed.

Something made her touch Gian's face. He was not as cold as she had thought he would be. "Oh, Gian," she said. "I'm so sorry." Then everything collapsed inside her, and she began to cry. "Oh, Mama," she said, gasping for breath. "Oh, Mama."

Bona finally looked up, her round face soft and quizzical. She blinked several times and then held up the portrait medallion, a tiny image of the late Duke Galeazzo Maria Sforza. "This is my husband, the Duke of Milan," Bona said with black-toothed, smiling pride. "My daughter is the Empress of Germany. My son . . . My son . . ." Bona's smile turned into a grimace, and she, too, began to cry.

Il Moro found his wife just after dawn, still standing beside Gian's corpse, Bona still seated opposite her, in a silent communion of grief and regret. He and Galeazz were so fouled with road dust that Beatrice didn't recognize them at first. Only when he spoke did his wife fall into his arms.

"Give her some wine, half water," Bona said, looking up, then looking down just as quickly. Il Moro stood over Gian for a moment, shook his head sadly, and turned away. He guided Beatrice into the hallway and shut the door on Bona. He put his still-gloved hands firmly on Beatrice's shoulders.

"When did Gian die?"

She looked up numbly at her husband. He really did look like a Moor now, his face as dark as a *moresca* mask. "Several hours ago. He was poisoned. I saw it." She described the sign. She could immediately tell from her husband's eyes that he'd had nothing to do with it. Then, a moment later, something flickered across his vision, something not as readily on the surface of his consciousness as a willful conspiracy. But she dismissed it, realizing that he had many things on his mind now, things she could not even begin to think of.

"Your Highness." Galeazz was questioning her now. "Where is the Duchess of Milan?"

The question was as shocking as its almost simultaneous answer. She hadn't even thought that Eesh wasn't here to grieve beside her husband's deathbed. "Milan," Beatrice blurted out. "She has gone to Milan to appear before the Council of Nobles and submit Francesco as the new Duke of Milan. She intends to serve as his regent."

Il Moro swallowed thickly. "I must go to Milan," he said almost absently.

"If you will excuse me, Your Highness," Galeazz said, "I wish you would stay here long enough to organize as many men as possible to serve as your guard, and at least rest long enough to wash your face. Let me go ahead to Milan. Again pardon me, but I am a much faster rider than Your Highness." He paused, glancing nervously at Beatrice. "And I am the only one who can question Francesco's right to the succession."

Il Moro turned to Galeazz and looked at him for a significant moment. "You know what that could mean, Galeazz," he said very softly.

Galeazz nodded. "I am no longer in the employ of the Duke of Milan," he said in a grave whisper. "Now my allegiances are those of the heart."

CHAPTER

43

Milan, 21 October 1494

At midmorning Il Moro entered the Castello di Porta Giovia from the ducal park to the north of the city; he decided against bringing his guards in and left them hidden in the trees. The guards at the Castello drawbridge told him that the Duchess of Milan had summoned Milan's Council of Nobles and that at least a hundred gentlemen had already been admitted to the Sala della Palla in the Rochetta; the last had arrived only minutes before, and still more were expected.

The entrance to the Rochetta was just to the right of the gatehouse. Il Moro with great difficulty climbed the stairs to the mezzanine overlooking the Sala della Palla; cramps knifed his thighs, the consequence of riding all night and morning at a courier's brutal pace. The guards at the door to the mezzanine were surprised to see him but admitted him without challenge.

The noblemen milled about the floor of the Sala della Palla, their monogrammed velvet caps giving a deceptive suggestion of unanimity to the clustered factions. The hum of these anxious caucuses rose into the vaults. At the far end of the mezzanine, shielded from the audience below by a purple brocade curtain, stood Galeazz and the Duchess of Milan.

Il Moro crossed the mezzanine quickly, but he was noticed by a few of the noblemen. A buzz of speculation swept through the crowd.

Isabella was dressed entirely in black. Her veil was pulled back, however, and the satin bodice of her *camora* revealed her shoulders and cleavage; she looked more like a fashionable Neapolitan courtesan than a grieving widow. Galeazz appeared tired and worried and made little squeezing motions with his huge hands. Il Moro did not try to catch his eye.

Il Moro removed his cap before addressing Isabella; she regarded him with a strange detachment, her long straight nose at a slightly oblique angle to him. "Your Highness, my profoundest condolences on the loss you have suffered. All of us—"

"We can well imagine how sorry you are, Signor Lodovico," Isabella interjected with a dismissive, airy wave of her hand. Suddenly Il Moro had the undivided attention of her malice-sharpened eyes. "In five minutes you will be nothing. A man without a state, without a home. Grieve for yourself, Signor Lodovico."

"Perhaps you are the one who is to be disenfranchised," Il Moro said with a dull, menacing cadence. "No bastard has ever been crowned Duke of Milan."

Isabella smiled slowly but fully, her lips parting to reveal her perfect teeth. She inclined her head slightly to Galeazz. "Tell him, Captain General. Tell him how you have offered me a full confession of your treasonous slander. Tell him how I have mercifully pardoned you." Her voice lowered. "Tell him what you intend to tell the Council on my behalf."

Il Moro wavered like a man struck squarely on the chin. His eyes darted to Galeazz.

"Tell him."

Galeazz looked down. "I intend . . ." His neck corded, and he spit the words out. "I intend to tell the Council that I am the father of the Duchess of Milan's bastard son and that I will submit to any interrogation necessary to verify my claim and invalidate the unlawful succession of Francesco Sforza." He stared vehemently at Isabella, his chiseled jaw set like that of a god pronouncing vengeance against some ancient crime.

The smile remained carved on Isabella's face, but her eyes blanked.

"No," Il Moro said. He looked directly at Galeazz. "Your sacrifice will accomplish nothing. Even if your word were accepted against the Duchess of Milan's denials, a state founded on that accusation could never endure. She has always known I would never use it. It is over for us."

"Your Highness, I must." Galeazz's voice was high and plaintive. "My honor demands it. I have done things of which I am ashamed. . . ."

"Your honor is not at issue, Galeazz," Il Moro said in a low voice. "The survival of our state is the matter at hand."

The life returned to Isabella's eyes, reanimating her fixed smile. "Your 'honor,' " she told Galeazz mockingly. "What you mean is your vanity. Did you really believe that you were necessary to my success? You were to be my pet soldier, paraded in front of the Council like a leopard on a leash. You were always expendable." She turned to Il Moro. "Make your nomination, Signor Lodovico."

Il Moro went directly to the balustrade. When he called for order, his voice was quickly recognized and the crowd hushed and looked up. Like the Signory of Venice, the Milanese nobles were largely of a type, with sharp, aquiline features, hard blue eyes, the indolent mouths and arrogant chins of ancient Roman patricians.

"I have the sad duty of informing you that the rumors you most likely have heard are true. Early this morning in Pavia our beloved and illustrious Duke Gian Galeazzo departed this life. I myself viewed the body." A brief buzz of affirmation escaped from the crowd. "I cannot at this time offer my nephew a worthy eulogy, and so I will honor him in the most meaningful way possible by making this simple appeal. I petition this esteemed Council to immediately acclaim Gian Galeazzo's lawful son, Francesco, as his successor. He will be Francesco II, Duke of Milan."

The buzzing now became furious. Someone shouted to be heard, and shortly the rest of the conversations subsided. The man who had taken the floor was Count Antonio Landriano, who was considered a somewhat neutral observer, because although he held the office of Treasurer, thanks to Il Moro's patronage, he had also placed his second wife, Giulia, among the Duchess of Milan's ladies-in-waiting.

"Your Highness, are we to assume that you will continue to

serve as regent to the Duke of Milan?" Count Landriano asked in his high but mellifluous voice.

"I intend to resign so that the new Duke's counselors can make an unprejudiced decision as to who will serve as his regent," Il Moro declared, to a rising clamor. "I am certain that Francesco's mother could perform quite capably as his regent."

The hall erupted, and Count Landriano had to shout to regain the floor. "Your Highness, esteemed peers," he said, turning to each side and nodding to his colleagues. "I need not tell you that a foreign army mightier than any ever assembled is now in Italy and that we are now at war with another powerful Italian state. Thus we have entered a new and dangerous season, such as we have not seen in many years. Why in this perilous time must we place our welfare in the hands of a child not yet five years old and his mother? I can remember the last time Milan was ruled by the Duke of Milan's mother, and so can many of you. Our policy was dictated by a meat carver." Derisive laughter followed. "Your Highness, esteemed peers, I must with all respect say that I reject this nomination and urge this esteemed Council to do the same." The hall resonated with shouts of agreement.

Once again Count Landriano prevailed to make himself heard. "I would ask instead that the man who has governed us so wisely these many years as the Duke of Milan's faithful regent now come forward to take possession of the ducal scepter he has so selflessly wielded on behalf of his lamented nephew. Your Highness, I petition you to accept our acclamation as Duke of Milan!"

Il Moro's hands flew up against the cries of agreement. "No, no," he shouted in protest until he could be heard. "For me to do so would be against all laws of God and man! By law our late Duke's son must be designated his successor. To deny him his birthright would make us infamous throughout Europe. Our state could not stand on such a dishonest pretext!"

Now the chorus lost its general sense of accord, many shouting against Il Moro's self-denial, others wondering what was to be done, only a few suggesting that they go ahead and accept Francesco as their duke. Finally another respected voice claimed the floor. Andrea Cagnola, a lawyer said to own every judge in northern Italy, spoke in a hoarse, retiring voice that demanded the close attention of his listeners.

"Your Highness, esteemed peers. The issue of legality is more complex than we have considered. It might be argued that neither the late Duke nor his father, nor even his esteemed grandfather, was indeed legitimate, because they were never invested by the German Emperor. Thus it might be argued that a determination of the legality of the succession can be made only by the German Emperor. However, if Il Moro were to obtain the papers of investiture from the Emperor, we could in good conscience, with the full sanction of God and the community of nations, acclaim Il Moro as the only legitimate Duke of Milan."

"The Emperor has not agreed to invest Il Moro!" shouted a dissenter. "And the late Duke's sister is now the Empress. Can we expect that the Emperor will place her status in question?" Arguments broke out. Il Moro shook his head vehemently and waved his arms.

Count Landriano took over again. "Let us propose this compromise. I believe that most of us agree that the issue of legality can be decided only by the German Emperor at his convenience, and indeed this is the prudent course for the future stability of our state. But it is equally vital to the welfare of our state that we immediately place the burden of our present peril on capable shoulders." Landriano paused and allowed an eerie silence to settle within the huge hall. "I petition the Council to grant to Il Moro the simple title of Duke, with no designation as to what he is to be duke of. We cannot wait for the lawyers and ambassadors to settle this."

Landriano's compromise clearly struck the right chord. The shouts rose into a regular chant of "Duca! Duca! Moro! Moro!" Il Moro did not try to silence the acclaim.

Isabella rushed from behind the curtains, trailing her long black sleeves and hem. She alighted beside Il Moro, and her hands clutched the balustrade like talons. At first her screams could not be heard over the acclamations of her rival. Then all other sound fell away dramatically, and her voice shrilled through the great hall. "Traitors! All of you traitors! You will be hanged and quartered and all your properties forfeited! Traitors! Guards! Arrest the traitors!"

At first the Council listened in stunned silence. Then, as the unfortunate widow's hysterical diatribe continued, a steady buzz of renewed concurrence rose against her hollow screams, the esteemed Councillors having received ample proof of the wisdom of their judgment.

Vigevano, 21 October 1494

Beatrice's secretary, Vincenzo Calmeta, found her walking in the labyrinth late in the afternoon. He stood on tiptoe and peered over the neatly planed hedge that separated them. She was just on the other side, but the path to her was likely to be circuitous. "Your Highness!" he called out. "I have such important news that I do not think you will want to wait until I have found my way to the other side of this hedge. Unlike Theseus, I have no string to guide me."

Beatrice was almost too numb with tension and fatigue to be encouraged by Calmeta's bantering tone. After her husband had left for Milan early in the morning, she had brought her children and the most trusted members of her household to Vigevano. They had arrived an hour before, and since then she had paced the seemingly endless gravel paths of the labyrinth, wondering and worrying about what was happening in Milan. But when she spotted her secretary comically straining to peer over the flat top of the hedge, she had to laugh. "Go ahead, Vincenzo! Think of all the tormented lovers who have found themselves this close yet unable to achieve their desire."

"Indeed, Your Highness. Contrary to the ancient myth, many a virgin has been pursued into this labyrinth and emerged unscathed. Your Highness, I really have the most wonderful news from Milan. Your husband has been acclaimed Duke by the Council of Nobles. He tried to refuse this honor, but the Council insisted that in these uncertain times your husband must accept full authority over all matters of state. Your husband rode through the streets of Milan at midday, and all the people came out to shout his name. From what I am told, it was a reception worthy of a Caesar. Your husband will style himself Duke, and he has said that he will not accept the title of Duke of Milan until the German Emperor has adjudicated the succession. That is all I know at this time, Your Highness. But if Your Highness will excuse me, I will try to find the path back to civilization and see if any new couriers have arrived."

"God bless you, Vincenzo." Beatrice fought to control her voice, the sobs of relief already choking her. My husband is safe. My baby is safe. For a long while she stood and blinked at her tears, content with that single theme. My husband and my baby are safe.

Finally she began to walk along the graded gravel path that led to the labyrinth's center, the dimensions of her victory expanding with each step. Eesh was shattered, all her plots and schemes utterly defeated, not by questions of her baby's paternity but by the simple desire of the people of Milan to perpetuate the just and able rule of Il Moro. And of course everyone would soon learn that the Emperor intended to make her husband the first truly legitimate Duke of Milan in three generations. And of course everything else her husband had foreseen would happen. The French would be delayed by the Florentines, and then Naples and France would blunt their swords against one another, and in the new Europe all men would turn to Il Moro and seek his just and able counsel and guidance. . . . The imaginary realm of Everything rose again from the ashes, to heights of glittering magnificence she had never before imagined.

She was surprised to find herself in a cul-de-sac; she had been certain she knew this labyrinth so well. A little lizard scurried among the leaves, and a bird sang three high notes. She turned, suddenly feeling out of place in time, as if she had left her real self several steps behind. Then she remembered being here with Eesh, exactly here, holding her, four hearts beating in concert. She had loved Eesh. Really loved her. She had an eerie sense that they were all still there, that somehow the engines of time had stopped that night, that none of this had happened and she still loved Eesh. . . .

No! She ran, fleeing to her new life, the life she had chosen, the sound of the gravel crunching beneath her slippers huge and ominous, as if a thousand feet were tramping in pursuit.

Another unexpected wall of hedge stopped her. She turned

frantically to face her pursuers. She saw Gian's face, an image so vivid in her mind that it might have been floating just in front of her. Gian, his sunken eyes pleading with her, his lips a sealed line of black. Poisoned. Who poisoned him? The question echoed to the rhythm of her pounding heart. Not her husband. Not Eesh: Eesh needed Gian alive so that he could abdicate. The French? But why would they? No one? Everyone?

She closed her eyes and shook her head, trying to escape the question in Gian's spectral eyes. "I can't help you anymore, Gian," she whispered. "I'm sorry. You're dead. You are the slaughtered lamb, the sacrifice to peace. Fortune asked for you. Perhaps Fortune even murdered you. But we have all dipped our fingers in your blood, and none of us will ever be innocent again."

Pavia, 22 October 1494

Isabella awoke in her own bed, the images of the previous day a nightmare that could not remain behind in sleep. The windows were shuttered, and she wasn't certain what time of day it was. She remembered that she had been forced to drink a strong sedative and had gone to sleep in Milan. Before dawn she had been driven back to Pavia, still only semiconscious. With sudden clarity she realized she had one last opportunity to stop them.

She did not even bother to dress; she dashed into her husband's sickroom in her chemise. The room was dark, the windows shuttered. Black damask had been hung all along the walls. The canopied bed looked like a bier, with drawn curtains of black crepe. Isabella threw the bed curtains aside. The bed was empty, covered with black cloth.

"Where is Gian!" she screamed. "Where have they taken Gian!" She screamed at the empty bed as if expecting it to answer: "Where have you taken him!"

Isabella whipped around. Duchess Bona stood in the doorway in her usual widow's black, a hideous grin on her round face. "Gian has gone riding," Bona said in a cheery voice. "He has two new horses."

"Where did they take him!"

Bona blinked. Her lady-in-waiting Giovanna da Maino, also dressed in black, appeared behind her. "Your Highness, your husband's body has been removed to Milan."

"By whose order!"

"By order of the Council. To lie in state in the Duomo."

"By order of the traitors who poisoned him!" Isabella screamed. "By order of his murderers! Now we can never prove it! They are burying their crime, and we will never prove it!"

Isabella's livid face twitched with fury. Her body shook with two quick spasms. Then her face relaxed, and her head bobbed forward, and she seemed to gag. She fell to her knees. Giovanna rushed to help her, but Isabella flailed with her arm, beating away the assistance. The gags turned into horrifying sobs, like a man with his throat cut gasping for breath. Isabella pounded her palms against the floor again and again. Her sobs became more high-pitched, a continuous keening.

Finally she looked up, her face so distorted and purpled that she appeared to have been beaten. She stared at Bona. "I never wanted him to die," she said in a hoarse whisper. "I wanted him to be happy. I really did. I never even told him goodbye." Her head fell and her body convulsed with sobs.

"You really mustn't cry. Gian will be back this afternoon." Bona took a careful step forward and stood over Isabella. Slowly she reached out and placed her hand on her daughter-in-law's head. Then she tenderly began to stroke Isabella's hair.

Bona looked at Giovanna and smiled warmly. "She really mustn't cry, you know. Gian has gone riding. His father gave him two horses yesterday."

CHAPTER

44

Extract of a dispatch of the Venetian diplomat MARINO SANUTO to the SIGNORY OF VENICE. Milan, 23 October 1494

. . . whatever this man does prospers, and that which he dreams of by night comes true by day. We now see Il Moro regarded as the wisest and most successful man in Italy, and esteemed and revered throughout the world. All men fear him, because Fortune favors him in everything he undertakes. . . .

Sarzana, 31 October 1494

His Most Christian Majesty Charles VIII dined in his silk campaign pavilion, at a table set up on a Persian carpet. He leapt from his seat when Il Moro was announced. "Monseigneur Lodovico, you have returned to guide our Crusade!" He extended his arms and gave Il Moro an eager hug. "But then Monseigneur Galeazz assured me you would."

Il Moro glanced at Galeazz, who had been sent south a week

previously to allay French suspicions. Galeazz had rejoined the
French army at Fivizzano, a small Florentine fortified town that
had quickly fallen. But now the French army was encamped before
the reputedly impregnable fortress at Sarzana, preparing for a pro-
tracted siege.

Galeazz stood over the King's shoulder, his lips pursed and his
eyes straining to communicate. He looked as agitated as he had
at Isabella's side in the Sala della Palla. The King's ever-present
advisers crowded around the new arrival, their usual attitude of
slouching flippancy replaced by a sneering swagger.

Galeazz bent to Il Moro's ear, as if translating the King's greeting. "His Majesty is very happy because he is holding three balls
in his hand," he said in soft, extremely rapid Italian.

Il Moro set his inscrutable face. The three balls was the symbol
of Florence's ruling house of Medici. Apparently the Florentines
had suffered some disastrous reversal.

"Your Majesty must tell me what conquests he has made while
I have been occupied with the tragic events in Milan," Il Moro
said. His eyes coolly swept the King's entourage during the
translation.

"*Montjoie*, Monseigneur Lodovico! *Montjoie!* We have per-
suaded the good King of Medici to join us in our Christian venture.
He came to us yesterday under safe-conduct with Monseigneur
Briconnet and has given us what we must have for our campaign!
Montjoie! We shall parade our army through Florence, welcomed
as comrades."

Galeazz hurriedly translated: "Piero de' Medici came here yesterday and all but threw himself at the King's feet. He has surrendered Sarzana and given the French army free passage through
Florentine territories. He has promised loans as well. The French
were stupefied by Piero's largess. He gave them things they never
would have thought to ask for. You should hear them ridicule his
cowardice. I am humiliated to be an Italian."

Il Moro smiled indulgently at the King, an expression not
lost on the arrogant royal entourage. "Well done, Your Majesty.
But do not allow the Florentines to use these concessions to lure
you away from their greatest prize, the city of Pisa. It is their
seaport, and it will be essential to your resupply of Naples. The
Pisans have long chafed under Florentine rule, and I believe that

if Your Majesty were to go to Pisa and meet with the noblemen of that city, Your Majesty would be welcomed as their
deliverer."

King Charles's jaw dropped, and he wheezed contemplatively.
"Of course. One of the objects of our quest is to liberate the people
of Italy wherever they suffer the oppression of tyrants. Certainly
I must deliver these good folk of Pisa."

The King abruptly turned to his advisers. "Peeee-zuh," he
announced.

The King's entourage began to gesture in spirited debate of
this new objective. Il Moro made a perfunctory exit and drew
Galeazz outside the King's pavilion. They stood in the dust, looking up at the massive brick fortress on the rocky promontory
behind them, framed by a Tuscan sky so blue it seemed to
pulsate.

Il Moro gave a delicate, sardonic smile. "Once I made the
mistake of overestimating Piero de' Medici as a friend. Now I
have made the mistake of overestimating him as an enemy."

"He lost his nerve," Galeazz said. "Perhaps you don't know
what happened at Fivizzano. They broke down the walls and
stormed it in a quarter hour. Then the King sent the Swiss in, and
they slaughtered the garrison and half the townspeople before they
were pulled back. I didn't need to go in. I could hear it. I could
smell it."

Il Moro's right eyelid fluttered. He turned slightly. "Fortune
is a slippery bitch."

Galeazz pursed his lips. "What will you do?"

"Well, the liberation of Pisa may distract His Most Christian
Majesty for a week or two. Perhaps by then we will have the
rains." Il Moro squinted dubiously into the cloudless sky. Heavy
autumn rains were usual; this had been the driest fall in memory.
"The Florentine people may not accept Piero's concessions on their
behalf. He is unpopular enough as it is. There could still be trouble
here."

"And if not?"

"Yes. I must begin preparing for that." Il Moro jutted his chin
and looked out over the silk and canvas roofs of the huge French
camp. Brightly colored pennons fluttered from the crowns of the
tents. "It is never too soon to prepare for the worst."

Extract of a dispatch of the Venetian diplomat MARINO SAN-UTO to the SIGNORY OF VENICE. Sarzana, 3 November 1494

. . . I do not know whether to make good or ill of this and will leave it to the collective wisdom of the Signory to divine the meaning in what I report. This morning Il Moro departed for Milan. I do not know what argument Il Moro made to the Most Christian King to persuade him to acquiesce in this defection. I do know that Il Moro agreed to leave Galeazzo di Sanseverino in attendance on the King and rendered His Majesty an immediate cash payment of 30,000 ducats. However, in exchange for this payment, Il Moro obtained the papers of investiture for the Duchy of Genoa, formerly granted to his late nephew. In Milan the week last, the people were saying, "God and Moro alone foreknow whither these winds of war will blow." I would submit to you that now even God does not know what Il Moro's intentions are. . . .

CHAPTER

45

Milan, 2 December 1494

Il Moro and Beatrice looked up into the nearly finished dome of the church of Santa Maria delle Grazie. Two painters worked from scaffolding high above, their light provided by a ring of round windows encircling the drum of the dome. The artists were painting a second, illusionistic ring of oculi, as believable as the real ones.

"They will be done in two weeks, Your Highness," offered the architect, Maestro Donato Bramante, a rugged-looking man with a high forehead and furiously intelligent, deep-socketed eyes. "That is assuming we continue to have dry weather."

"Dry weather," Il Moro said absently.

"Leonardo says we will pump the Ticino River dry by January if we don't have rains before then," Bramante added.

"What is the name of the Florentine priest who says that God has sent the Frenchmen to purify the Church?" Beatrice asked.

"Fra Girolamo Savonarola," Il Moro answered.

"Perhaps Fra Savonarola is right," Beatrice said. "God has sent the French, and he is giving them perfect marching weather."

"The Florentines are certain enough that God has sent them Savonarola," Bramante commented sarcastically. "He has engaged quite a following in recent months. He decries everything modern as a 'vanity,' be it a painting by Fra Angelico, whose Madonnas he likens to prostitutes, or a printed volume of 'pagan' poetry by Virgil. Savonarola's disciples are urged to surrender these vanities, which they burn in the piazza in huge bonfires. You know, Your Highness, since you are sending Caradasso to Rome to acquire antiquities, perhaps you can have him spend some time in Florence. He could offer to relieve Fra Savonarola's penitents of their vanities without the labor of carting them to the piazza."

Il Moro laughed and then began to discuss seriously with Bramante the kinds of Roman statues he was hoping to add to his collection. Suddenly Bramante looked up at the painters working in his dome and began shouting curses at them in his usual uninhibited style.

"I'm going to have to go up there and take the paintbrush myself," Bramante said. He scrambled up the towering, creaking scaffolding.

Bramante's sudden ascent left Il Moro and Beatrice standing alone directly in front of the black onyx railing of the high altar. Il Moro looked down at the marble pavement and tapped it with the tip of his velvet slipper, his expression absorbed and enigmatic, thoughts moving across his face as subtly as faint variations in the light coming from high above. He remained silent for some time.

"Here," he finally said very softly, still looking at the floor. "Here is where we are going to be buried. Side by side. Looking up into the light."

Beatrice took her husband's arm. She imagined her bones beneath that floor and wondered what she would see when she was dead. What did Mama and Gian see now? A sunlit dome or the black underside of a marble slab, screaming souls or singing angels? Anything? But she could not deal with that now. She could only tell herself that her husband wanted to sleep beside her forever. She moved closer to him, letting the touch of his body deny his vision of death.

"Dispatches came this morning from Florence," Il Moro said. "His Most Christian Majesty marched out of Florence two days ago. The Florentine Senate agreed to a treaty of friendship with the French, offered them free passage, and paid them 120,000 ducats to be on their way. In return the French agreed to let the Florentines banish Piero de' Medici. Now that Piero is finished,

Fra Savonarola has suggested that the Florentines allow Christ to rule them. One wonders how many ducats His Most Christian Majesty would demand to free Florence from Christ's tyranny." He shook his head. "Not at all the sort of campaign I had hoped for. And still no rain."

Il Moro looked back up into the brightly lit dome. He squinted and turned his head from side to side. "I want to bring your cousin back to Milan."

"You mean so that you can keep her under closer watch?" They had already discussed the possibility that Isabella might flee to Asti and in her desperation appeal to Louis Duc d'Orleans to restore her son's birthright.

"No. The King's position isn't as yet so secure that he can permit Louis Duc d'Orleans to go after his own prizes. That will come after the King has conquered Naples."

"Then why bring her here?"

"We need her." He paused and looked up again. Bramante was painting, gesturing at his assistants, and cursing, all at the same time. "We need her friendship."

Beatrice bemusedly cocked her dark eyebrows. "I'm certain there is logic to this. I simply fail to see it."

"Duchess Bona has partially recovered her wits, such as they were," Il Moro said. "Enough so that she has dispatched letters to her daughter in Germany, making the usual allegations about Gian's death."

Beatrice felt the visceral tinge she had whenever the subject of Gian's death came up. But she no longer believed that Gian had been poisoned. Her husband had ordered Gian's body examined in Milan by a half-dozen physicians and even several ambassadors, and no sign of poison had been found. Probably what she had seen on that terrible dawn had been only a quirk of the light. And even if somehow Gian *had* been poisoned, her husband clearly hadn't had anything to do with it. He had made every effort to investigate.

"Apparently the Emperor has seen some of Bona's accusatory letters," Il Moro went on. "Today I received a letter from the Bishop of Brixen on behalf of the Emperor, asking me to assure him that nothing untoward took place in Pavia. I can protest my innocence until the Day of Judgment, and I will never entirely be believed. But my claims would have immediate credibility if your cousin Isabella were to corroborate them."

"What possible reason would she have to help you in that way?"

"I sent Galeazzo Pusterla to Pavia, simply to look in on Isabella now and then and keep me informed as to her state of mind. He reports that Isabella has been making conciliatory overtures toward us."

"With her usual sincerity. Obviously she hasn't abandoned her ambitions."

"Her present ambition, I believe, is to save her father."

"And she would expect us—" Beatrice broke off. A flush spread over her shoulders. "Dear God, Lodovico, are you now so frightened of the French that you would even consider reconciling yourself to Alfonso?" Her face glowed, and she spit her words with rapid, sibilant fury. "*Cacasangue*, he is the man who tried to poison you and my son. In the name of God, you cannot mean this. We can never be safe as long as he lives." Her eyes filled with angry tears.

"I would offer Alfonso support only as needed to prevent his complete collapse. Obviously he has urged his daughter to make overtures to us, which shows how desperate *he* is. If Alfonso can simply last the winter, the French will run out of money. Then we could arrange a negotiated settlement in which Alfonso would be forced to take an oath to the French King, which would corrupt his authority. Alfonso's people would rise up against him as soon as the French left. What now seems a bitter medicine would soon rid Italy of two plagues."

"So we would use Isabella to convey these assurances of assistance to her father." She paused, and the tears welled up again. "That is obscene."

Il Moro's voice remained quiet, but his cadence slowed to a suggestion of restrained anger. "Was it obscene when you told the Signory of Venice that the Emperor had agreed to my investiture, when in fact he had not? That was the moment when you of your own volition decided to play this game. Now that you don't like the cards you are holding, you find the rules of play objectionable. Fine. I will not insist that you remain at the table. Simply do not interfere with those of us who have no choice but to continue to play."

Beatrice heard a ringing in her ears. Her husband had not spoken to her in such a hostile, patronizing tone for years. But what stung her most was the implication that the game had now surpassed her level of skill.

Beatrice's eyes suddenly had that diamond-hard Este gleam. "What do you want me to do?"

Il Moro spread his hands in his "very little" gesture. "When your cousin comes here, I simply want you to welcome her and talk to her. With civility, nothing more or less. You do not have to offer her undying friendship."

Milan, 6 December 1494

A half hour after passing through Milan's southern gate, Beatrice ordered her carriage parked just off the gravel path that ran beside the canal from Pavia. She pulled aside the window drapes and watched the barges drift past in the late afternoon twilight, decks loaded with livestock, bags of grain, and barrels full of wine, cheeses, and oil.

The early darkness was the only sign of approaching winter; the air was dry and pleasantly cool. Warning lanterns began to appear on the barges. A few transport wagons crunched by on the cart path, hurrying against the night.

When the date had been set for Isabella's return to the Castello, Beatrice had decided to meet her cousin here, outside the city, before stone walls and formalities prevented all but the most superficial contact. Her agenda for this meeting was curiously ill-defined, however. On the surface she was pursuing her husband's diplomatic objectives, to which she had reconciled herself. But she also was haunted by the terrifying ferocity of Eesh's ambition and the threat that ambition might still pose to her husband and son and unborn child. So perhaps she intended an element of maternal confrontation, a warning to Isabella to leave her family alone. And perhaps she was pursuing something even deeper and more profound. Something articulated only by whispers in her mind that did not make sense, fragmentary, middle-of-the-night thoughts that now seemed to awaken her at every hour.

The night settled like a velvety fog. The solitary lanterns on the barges drifted by in the darkness. Beatrice watched one light wink into view far to the south and then followed it until it disappeared in the direction of Milan. When she finally lost sight of the lantern, her feeling of sadness was suddenly so profound that she had to fight the urge to sob. She could imagine everything, her life and everyone she loved, passing by like that tiny, flickering point of illumination.

She had begun to follow another lantern, when one of her coachmen called out to someone on the road. The muffled reply from the other carriage indicated that the meeting was at hand. Beatrice waited until a coachman came down to open the door; he helped her to the ground. She was light-headed and breathless, and the air seemed cold. For a moment she distinctly saw Eesh and herself on a balcony high above the Bay of Naples, and then the shattering snowball of her beautiful doll's porcelain head.

The gentlemen in charge of each lady's small contingent of guards met and conferred. Paolo Bilia, one of Gian's chamberlains, came over to verify that Beatrice was who her escort had said she was. He went back to Isabella's carriage and knocked on the door. When the door squeaked opened he stuck his head in. A moment later he waved for Beatrice to come over. When she came close she could see the black mourning streamers tied to the gilded finials of Isabella's carriage. Paolo assisted her into the cabin.

The darkened interior was vaguely lit by the guards' torches. All she could see was a white face and an indistinct black-clad form. Almost as soon as she had settled herself into the cushioned seat opposite Isabella, the coachmen shouted and the carriage lurched off. "Your Highness," she said, her voice immediately striking herself as far too loud and fearful.

Isabella said nothing in reply. She turned her head to the side. That movement in the weak light gave a sudden definition to the indistinct pallor of her features, almost like a swimmer's face emerging from a muddy river.

Something pulled in Beatrice's chest. She could not believe it. Eesh was nothing. Her face was so gaunt that her eyes and cheeks were grayish hollows, her nose seemingly a sharp blade of white bone. Her hair had thinned dramatically. She might have been a corpse, except that her skeletal features lacked the serenity of death.

Now Beatrice's agenda became clearer to her: she had come to absolve her guilt. A guilt she could not define; she didn't believe that she or her husband had done anything wrong. And yet she felt the need to apologize, if only because Fortune had rewarded her at Isabella's expense. "Eesh . . . You have to believe I didn't want this to happen to you," she said almost desperately. "I didn't want any of this."

Isabella gave a small, hideously dry laugh, a sound like an old hinge. "I warned you, you know. I warned you before all this started."

"You started this as much as I did, Eesh. You started it when you wrote to your father."

"I was forced to. Once you had a son, it was the only thing I could do."

"No, Eesh. Even then there was still time to stop him." Her words, the abstract reference to her husband as "him," shocked her; she felt as if she had uttered some obscene heresy. That was another Beatrice speaking, she realized, the Beatrice still lost in the labyrinth with Eesh. The Beatrice she had chosen to leave behind. And as she looked back at that Beatrice, her guilt came into sudden sharp focus. She wasn't sorry for Eesh, or even for Gian. The best choice she had ever made was to embrace "him" and his dreams, to give her husband her heart and soul. To say she didn't want any of this was a profound lie. Perhaps she hadn't wanted Gian to die, but she wanted everything else, everything that had happened because Gian died. That was what awakened her at night.

Isabella slumped against the cushions. Her movements did not have even the languid grace of exhaustion but exhibited a desperate, jerky nervousness. "Fortune started this," she said. "Fortune played us against one another. The contest was inevitable. And I have lost. I have lost!" She offered a death's-head smile and settled back again, her next words infinitely weary. "So it really doesn't matter anymore, Toto. I am finished."

For a moment Beatrice wondered if the whole display, the use of her pet name Toto, wasn't another masquerade. She forced herself to search Eesh's shadowed, ravaged face. But there was no guile there. There was hardly even life.

"Toto, you know why I have come back to Milan, don't you?"

"Yes." No matter what, Beatrice vowed she would always hate Eesh's father.

They sat silently for a while in the gently rocking carriage. Then Isabella said, "A construction of lies. That is all the world is now. A construction built by the Signory and the Frenchmen and your husband and His Holiness. My father too. I know that. And us. We helped them build it. Perhaps we are even more guilty than all of them. Lying is a craft they were bred to practice." She sniffed sarcastically. "Lying is their native tongue. But you and I once shared the truth. We truly loved one another. Once we did."

Now another truth stared back at Beatrice. Eesh's grief was genuine. And so once was her love.

"You don't know what it's like, Toto. In here. In the darkness. It is so dark that often I cannot breathe. Sometimes the air is like an atmosphere made of blades. If I even open my mouth to breathe, my lungs are sliced to ribbons. I want to help my children, but I cannot move. My children need me, but I cannot . . ."

The authenticity of Eesh's need and remorse overwhelmed Beatrice. She could hear the ugly clicking of the metallic, deadly air Eesh was trying to breathe. She could feel the pain in her own throat. Tears came to her eyes. "I will make certain your children are safe and cared for while they are in Milan, Eesh. I promise you that."

Isabella's torso snapped forward, and she reached so vehemently that Beatrice jerked back with racing alarm, certain that Eesh was trying to claw the baby out of her womb. But Isabella merely clutched at Beatrice's hands, still clasped protectively over her pregnant belly.

Isabella's hands were so cold and bony that they seemed carved of stone. Her eyes pleaded from within her hollowed skull. "Toto, don't let them take Francesco from me. Please don't let them take my little boy. Please don't let them take my babies." Her shoulders heaved, and she began to cry.

After a moment, without even thinking why, Beatrice crossed over to Isabella's bench and sat beside her. Arms locked around one another, the two duchesses cried in the darkness all the way back to Milan.

C H A P T E R

46

**Extract of a letter of international traveler and raconteur
BENEDETTO DEI to LEONARDO DA VINCI, military engineer
at the Court of Milan. Rome, 1 January 1495**

. . . once again we have been treated to the spectacle of the French
army marching unopposed into an Italian capital. Yesterday His
Most Christian Majesty entered Rome in triumphant procession.
. . . His Holiness has taken refuge in the Vatican. Fortunately His
Holiness's lovely mistress, Madonna Giulia Farnese, is at hand to
offer His Holiness the deepest spiritual succor. Only last week,
while returning from a wedding in Acquapendente, the said lady
was taken captive by elements of the French advance guard. These
French warriors, being under the command of gentlemen,
promptly released the fair Giulia subsequent to His Holiness's
astonishingly swift payment of a considerable ransom. Now, of
course, His Most Christian Majesty is in a position to ransom the
entire City of Rome and all her occupants. . . .

Extract of a letter of ISABELLA D'ESTE DA GONZAGA, Marquesa of Mantua, to FRANCESCO GONZAGA, Marquis of Mantua and Captain General of the Armies of Venice. Milan, 20 January 1495

My most illustrious and desperately missed lord husband,

I arrived here yesterday, having spent an extra day at Pavia at Messer Ambrogio's request, as the eighteenth was not considered a propitious date for my entry into Milan. Fortunately I was still in advance of my sister's child, which they expect within the week. I spent the evening with her at her bedside and amused her as best I could, but she is most apprehensive, and certainly she is justified to be so after the difficulty of her first birth. . . . This morning I visited the widowed Duchess Isabella in her rooms in the Castello. Her room is all hung in black, with only enough light admitted to see one's hand in front of one's face, and just enough air to prevent suffocation. She wears a cloak of black cloth so cheap that even an honest monk would disdain it, and a veil that entirely covers her face. They say she takes her meals more regularly now, but to see her you would not know it. I felt such compassion at her lamentable state that I could not keep from crying. After I offered her my sympathies and made condolences in your name, she sent for her children, the sight of whom merely made me weep more copiously. The girl is too young to understand her loss, and the boy looks well, but he complained to me that he is weary of wearing black. . . .

You would not recognize Milan! They have cleaned and widened so many of the streets and built new *piazze* and gardens and parks, and it seems that every building is new or has been restored to a former glory. And you would guess that the city has passed an ordinance requiring every woman who wishes to appear in public to adorn herself with at least ten thousand ducats' worth of precious gems! The carriages rumble by all day and night, conveying these *belle donne* from one *festa* to the next—and no doubt from the arms of one lover to the next!

I supped the evening last with Il Moro in his rooms, and he showed me the dispatches from Rome confirming that His Holiness has offered the French free passage through his territories and has agreed to sanction His Most Christian Majesty's coronation as King of Naples. His Holiness has in addition made a cardinal of Briconnet, which does not please Il Moro at all. . . . Il Moro also submitted to me reports from his agents in Naples regarding the fitness of King Alfonso. It seems that Alfonso is much concerned lately with the piety he has disregarded all his life, and cannot spend enough time washing the feet of paupers and weeping over their misfortunes! When I had finished reading these papers I asked Il Moro what changes of policy he intended in response to this unhappy state of affairs. He was full of reproach for the Signory of Venice, avowing he had warned them that a firmly committed league was required to keep the French out and that he saw no reason to enter into such a league now that the French had virtually conquered Italy with a piece of chalk—this being the chalk with which they mark the houses for the billeting of their troops. He says that he is now obliged to counter the French very cautiously, because, to use his words, "Should the King of France win the Kingdom of Naples and then learn that I alone have shown displeasure at his success, would that be to my advantage?" Thus he insists that the key to turning the French back is to persuade Spain to invade France along the Pyrenees. . . . You should advise the Signory to keep their ambassadors in close attendance on Il Moro, and hope that events will soon persuade him to closer cooperation in ridding Italy of this menace. . . .

Il Moro has yet to receive the papers of investiture from the German Emperor. They say that this is because the Prince Electors of Germany have been troubled by the accusations regarding the unfortunate Duke of Milan's demise. Il Moro says he is not concerned about the delay, but for my part I do not think these papers can arrive soon enough, as Milan without a Duke of Milan is a most unsettled state of affairs at a most unsettling time. Even the Signory will have to agree that there is no alternative to Il Moro now, save the nefarious Louis Duc d'Orléans, who is still in Asti and regularly sends forth messengers to proclaim that *he* is the rightful Duke of Milan. . . .

Naples, 23 January 1495

When he awoke, Alfonso of Aragon, the King of Naples, first thought that the thunder of a terrible storm had disturbed his sleep, a storm not unlike the Christmas Day tempest three years earlier. Then he realized that he could hear the French cannons. They were still more than two hundred miles away, but he could hear them. His silk sheets were wet with perspiration. He had to get up. He put on the coarse monk's robe he wore when he washed the feet of his paupers, and he took up his silver pail. Holding a single candle, he crept silently out of his bedchamber and walked around the loggia of the inner court until he reached his late father's sealed rooms. He unlocked the doors and locked them again behind him. He lit a polished bronze lamp shaped like a female griffin, with big woman's breasts.

Most of his father's belongings had been stored, and the rooms were empty. Alfonso went down a flight of stairs to a series of subterranean storage rooms. He stopped before a metal-studded wooden door and examined his key ring for the appropriate key. The lock ratcheted noisily. He paused before he opened the door, making certain that he still had his pail and sponge. He briefly wondered why he had not considered coming here before. It was so obvious now that this was what he had to do.

The room was about the size of a *guardaroba*, with a musty, camphorlike smell. The walls were bare stone, windowless. Two long rows of what appeared to be statues stood several paces apart, facing each other. This had been Ferrante's private collection, but Alfonso had helped assemble it.

Holding his lamp high, Alfonso walked between the two rows of standing figures. They were dressed in real clothes, expensive tunics of embroidered silk and damask such as a nobleman might wear. As Alfonso passed, the light glinted in glass eyes. Alfonso stopped and thrust his lamp into the face of one of the figures. The glass eyes glared; the shrinking, desiccated facial skin had pulled away from the sockets. The withered lips had parted slightly to reveal real teeth. This was one of the older pieces in the collection, a nobleman Ferrante had executed and embalmed forty years previously. He was not keeping well.

Alfonso looked for someone newer, someone he knew. He

found a man who had been in the collection less than ten years, the vellum-white pallor of a long final imprisonment now yellowed by embalming and lamplight but the skin still seemingly elastic, the lips full and proud. A line of neat stitches circled the neck; for aesthetic reasons, the head had been sewn back in place after being severed by the executioner's ax.

"Don Marino," Alfonso whispered. He fell to his knees at Don Marino's feet. Realizing that he would topple the mummy if he tried to remove Don Marino's velvet slippers, Alfonso symbolically sponged water over them. He began to weep, his squinty eyes compressed to bleeding slits, his massive round face contorted with grief.

After much weeping and wringing of the sponge, Alfonso stood up, his cheeks glistening with tears. "Forgive me, Don Marino," he whimpered.

"France."

Alfonso had expected Don Marino to speak; he had not expected this reply. But he knew he had heard it, as clearly as he had heard the cannons that had roused him from his sleep. He had even seen Don Marino's lips move. "What?" he demanded.

"France."

Alfonso swung the pail in a savage arc, and Don Marino's tentatively attached head went flying into the shadows. It cracked against stone and rolled across the floor, rattling like a dry gourd. Then blessed silence. The silence of forgiveness.

"France."

Alfonso whipped his mighty head around.

"France. France."

He could not tell who had said it. He lunged several steps this way and that, thrusting the lamp in the dead faces.

"France. France. France."

They were all saying it—he could see all their lips moving— and he lashed out frantically with his pail, sending heads flying and corpses toppling, but even the disembodied heads continued the chorus of "France, France, France." He hurled his pail into the wall and ran for the door.

Alfonso's powerful legs pounded up the stairs. Out in the loggia, he found he could breathe again and he could no longer hear the traitors. But the French cannons had got closer, so close that their salvos shook the walls.

He ran to his secretary's rooms and pounded the door. When the startled man appeared, Alfonso ordered him to dress and bring writing materials and meet him in his stepmother's rooms.

His stepmother's servants were up, and he stormed past them, flinging open the double doors to her bedchamber. The lamps in the sconces were lit, and a big fire provided additional light and a stifling heat. His father's widow, Giovanna, a second wife who was in her mid-thirties, lay on white silk sheets, entirely naked, her face concealed by two big slabs of milk-soaked veal. She was a fleshy woman with a disproportionately slender neck and a prominent nose that jutted from between the two pieces of meat. Two female servants continued to sponge her skin with sweet-smelling water, doing nothing to cover their mistress.

"What do you want, darling?" Giovanna asked in Spanish.

"Witness this."

"Witness what? Are you going to do something naughty? I thought you had done everything naughty there was to do."

"Cover her," Alfonso barked at the servants. "I have a secretary coming."

Giovanna peeled the veal slabs off her face and tilted her head up. She motioned with her head, and the servants patted her face dry and wrapped her in a white silk robe.

Suddenly Alfonso's huge shoulders jerked with alarm. He looked at his stepmother. "Didn't you hear them?" he asked frantically. "The guns. The guns are all around us. You know that when they breach the walls they put everyone—man, woman, and child—to the sword. They are not men—they are beasts!"

The secretary arrived. Giovanna, her pale, unadorned face composed and curiously elegant, watched the scene with the worldliness of a woman who had already seen too much.

"Witness this, Mother," Alfonso repeated. His shoulders jerked at another imaginary salvo, and he convulsively turned his head to the secretary. He motioned rapidly with his powerful hands, indicating the usual formal introduction. Then he spoke, much more loudly than his usual near whisper, as if he were competing with the sound of the French cannons. "I have with God's guidance determined to abdicate my throne in favor of my son and heir, Ferrantino, so that I may leave this kingdom and make my peace with God before—" Suddenly he screamed, "Do they not have the simple courtesy to stop their firing until this business is done? They are dogs!"

But even after Alfonso had finished dictating his message of abdication, he could not make the French cannons fall silent.

C H A P T E R

47

Milan, 5 February 1495

"You are luckier than Satan."

Blond curls framing a radiant smile, the Marquesa entered Beatrice's bedchamber, carrying in her arms one-day-old Sforza Francesco Sforza—named after Il Moro's late brother Sforza, from whom Il Moro had inherited the Duchy of Bari. The newborn's two-year-old brother, Ercole, wearing a little blue tunic and matching hose, clutched a ride on the Marquesa's skirt, grinning and shrieking, *"Cia Mama! Cia Mama!"*

The Marquesa sat on the bed and placed the satin-wrapped bundle in Beatrice's arms. "Consider all the women, myself included, who have fruitlessly labored for years in hopes of a son. It wasn't enough for you simply to have this darling little boy" —she scooped Ercole off the floor—"who I am going to take with me when I leave. Now you have the most perfect little *putto* I have ever seen. Look at him!" Sforza's huge indigo irises peered out from his puffy, ruddy little face. "Look at how he looks at us! I have never seen a newborn do that!" She leaned closer to the infant. "I am your aunt Bel, the most beautiful sight you will ever see." Sforza stared at her steadily, and Ercole sputtered, "Pputto! Ppputto! Spputto Spporspuh!"

"I am ill with envy," the Marquesa added, looking skyward as if seeking redress for this inequitable distribution of sons. Then she soberly studied Beatrice, brushing her sister's cheek with her fingers. "Your color is really good, baby. You know the bleeding has to have stopped. If it hadn't, you would have bled much more during the night." For a terrifying quarter of an hour after delivering the placenta, Beatrice had bled heavily. Somehow it had stopped. Beatrice had been more affected by the fright than by the actual loss of blood.

"I just . . ." Beatrice worked her teeth over her lower lip. "The first time I was too tired to be afraid. This time I could think. I thought of everything: everyone I love whom I wouldn't see again, my children growing up without me. Never making love to my husband again. I was so frightened, Bel. It was as if my soul was spilling out of me. Just lying there and watching it."

"Your midwife said you did much better this time. Your next one will be over faster than a *meretrice* can find a customer in the Vatican."

Beatrice smiled weakly and continued to bite her lip.

"Isn't that good news about Uncle Alfonso!" the Marquesa said brightly. "Your husband says that Alfonso's abdication will make it so much easier to provide support for Naples now. Can you imagine? Three Kings of Naples in the space of one year. I don't remember our cousin Ferrantino terribly well. Did you like him when you were there?"

Ferrantino was two years older than Eesh, but for most of the time Beatrice had been in Naples, he had been shorter than his sister. Ferrantino and Eesh had been inseparable companions in mischief, but Ferrantino had always been fairly quiet and gentle; he had never taunted or teased Beatrice unless it was something Eesh made him do. He had always been so slender compared to his father, with big rabbity teeth. "He was a nice boy, Bel. Maybe he will bring an end to all the terrible things that have happened in Naples."

The Marquesa nodded and crossed herself, one of her mother's mannerisms she had adopted after her death. "You know, baby, I think so often about Mama, how she always talked about this peaceful and united Italy of hers. It was more than a faith with her. It was her dream, really, and I place dreams ahead of faith, because dreams can never be corrupted. Otherwise they would no longer be dreams. Of course I always thought that Mama's dream was so silly and impossible." She smiled wistfully. "But now I think that despite the Frenchmen, or really because of them, someday we will have that peace."

Beatrice wondered why she never could discuss Mama with her sister; the subject had already foundered a dozen times during Bel's visit. Perhaps because she was afraid that Bel would learn about the ambivalence of her feelings toward Mama. Or perhaps because she had always known that Bel had been Mama's favorite.

"It is time for the two young gentlemen to return to their nurseries and for the Duchess to put her lights out and go to sleep . . . ," Polissena interrupted from the doorway.

The Marquesa did not turn at the sound of Polissena's voice but instead continued to look at Beatrice, bobbing her head and miming Polissena's speech to extraordinary comic effect. Beatrice burst into laughter so abruptly that her womb seared, but she couldn't help herself and laughed so hard that tears spilled down her cheeks.

". . . And what the Marquesa chooses to do is between herself, Our Lord, and the devil," Polissena continued, her head bobbing fiercely, "as she has disregarded every advisement concerning her health that those of us with long experience have offered her."

The Marquesa finally turned for her counterattack. "Polissena, your experience is so long that—" Suddenly Polissena gasped and shuddered, and the Marquesa broke off.

"*Nostro Signore,*" Polissena said, crossing herself. "When Your Highness turned around just now I thought I saw your sainted mother sitting there. Your mother fifteen years ago. The most beautiful woman I have ever seen. Just then Your Highness was the image of your sainted mother. Dear God, I thought I had seen a ghost." Polissena offered a final baby-buzzard glare of defiance—apparently to her own emotions—and then began to cry.

The Marquesa looked at Beatrice helplessly, then got up and went to Polissena. Her eyes glistening with tears, she gingerly wrapped her arms around Polissena's frail, stiff torso. "I miss her too, Polissena. I miss her too."

Milan, 27 February 1495

"*Per mia fe.* I always wondered how it was done." The Marquesa walked around the base of the ancient Roman statue. Carved in luminous white marble, the sculpture depicted Zeus, transformed into a swan, making love to Leda, the all-too-human wife of the King of Sparta. The considerably larger-than-life-size swan gripped the life-size Leda's plump white buttocks with his webbed feet and folded his wings around her naked back. "Entirely convincing," the Marquesa added. "*Per dio,* Beatrice, you can virtually hear them grunting with passion. Or perhaps she is whimpering and he is honking. Anyway, such *vivacità*. It's new, isn't it?"

"My husband had it shipped from Rome a few weeks ago," Beatrice said. The statue was one of dozens arrayed across the lawn bordering the artificial lake. Acres of the surrounding ducal park had been transformed into formal gardens—geometric patterns of trees, hedges, and flower beds, all interlaced with gravel paths. Nearby was what appeared to be a complex of immense Greek temples: Il Moro's menagerie, the late Duke of Milan's stables, and Galeazzo di Sanseverino's new stables. The winter that had never really arrived had left the foliage a brilliant green; only the relative paucity of flowers betrayed the season. In lieu of nature's most extravagant hues, the park was sprinkled with hundreds of Milanese courtiers and their ladies in their best riding clothes. Most of them had dismounted, leaving their horses with their pages. They walked in pairs or clustered around the various musical entertainments: *alta* bands, consisting of two woodwinds and a *trombone*, playing lively dance harmonies, and lone lutenists singing lengthy comic or romantic narratives.

The Marquesa took her sister's hand and headed for a heroic nude statue of a Roman emperor. As she walked she looked off to the north end of the lake, where a long table covered with white brocade and laden with fruits and pastries had been set up on the lawn; several dozen ladies and gentlemen roamed in the vicinity, conversing, picking at the food, and listening to the music.

"Beatrice, can you believe that half these people could even get out of bed this morning?" The *festa* the previous evening, a masked ball at a private home, had gone on until the early hours of the morning. "It is those carnival masks. Once people are suitably disguised they will do anything. Do you have any idea who that woman was who paraded her bare breasts for the better part of the evening? I can assure you that if I ever see those breasts again I will recognize them immediately. And I swear to you that if you'd had the temerity to look under one of the tablecloths you would've imagined you were in a brothel. *Signor mio caro*, I saw an entire table shaking and squirming like some kind of great beast. And then this set of bare buttocks suddenly popped up from under the tablecloth, and one of the masked gentlemen walked up to them, unlaced his codpiece, and went to work without even bothering to see if they belonged to a man or a woman. I presume he intended to assume the latter and make the necessary adjustment if it turned out to be the former."

"It got worse after we left, I am reliably told. Some of the theatrical dancers stayed and continued to perform, quite without costumes, of course."

"Of course," the Marquesa added, cocking at a jaunty angle the flat, almost saucer-shaped velvet riding cap that crowned her impressive blond mane. She plucked at a puff of white silk showing through the slitted black satin sleeves of her *camora*. Finally she looked up and asked, "Well, aren't you going to provide the details? What you have told me so far is like saying, 'The painting depicts a mythological subject.' You know I am not satisfied unless I have every available detail. I am dedicated to the finest distinctions and nuances."

"Bel, you don't want to know."

"I do."

"Bel, they brought horses inside—"

"*Nostro Signore!*" The Marquesa crossed herself. "You're right. I don't want to know." The Marchesa squinted off toward the table at the north end of the lake. "There is your husband. Very shapely legs. He looks splendid in riding costume."

"He's with the King of Spain's representative."

The Marquesa pointed to a pair of far-from-dashing gentlemen who stood a dozen or so paces upslope from Il Moro and the

Spanish ambassador. The two men, one solidly built and fortyish, the other portly and bald, looked equally ill at ease in their poorly fitted riding hose and doublets. "And there are your husband's faithful shadows, the Venetian ambassadors. I've never seen anyone from Venice who made a good appearance in riding costume. Your husband would certainly make those two more comfortable by sending them back to Venice with an agreement to form a new league."

"My husband believes that the crisis has yet to sufficiently engage the Signory's attention. He says that Venice merely offers to assault the French with pledges, while the King of Spain has already sent dozens of ships to Sicily to harass the invaders. My husband is right, Bel. Isn't it rather unlikely that the French will leave Italy simply because the Signory of Venice chooses to anathematize them?"

"Of course. *My* husband is trying to persuade the Signory to finance an army of fifty thousand men to throw the French out. But the Signory tell him that they see no need to undertake that kind of expense as long as the armies of Naples still have the prospect of success."

"One hopes the Signory's optimism will be justified," Beatrice said. "I don't know. I have seen the French army."

"Our cousin Isabella is encouraged by her brother's prospects," the Marquesa said. "She has had letters from him. You know, when she first heard about her father's abdication I thought that would be the end of her. But she has been doing much better in the last few weeks. She's very fond of Ferrantino, and I think perhaps a little relieved that she no longer has to defend her father." The Marquesa paused. "You should look in on her."

"No, Bel." Beatrice turned almost vehemently to face her sister. "It's too hard. I have tried. We've both tried. Too much has happened. I can never love her again, and I don't want to hate her anymore. It's just better if we are dead to one another. To everyone else we can still be alive. But for her I died the day Ercole was born. For me she died the night in Venice when I read her letter. We have even grieved for each other. I think that's what happened the night she came back to Milan. It took me a while to understand why we had nothing to say after sharing that. Now I do. The dead don't speak."

Beatrice looked down and fussed at her skirts. "Has she asked . . . about me?"

"She asked when you will become Duchess of Milan."

"What did you tell her?"

"What you told me. That you have received assurances from the Emperor and that it will be done as soon as the Emperor's ambassadors arrive. Probably before the end of May."

"She will hate me for that. But by all that is just, my husband should be Duke of Milan."

"She seems resigned to it. Perhaps that will even things between the two of you and you can forgive one another." The Marquesa shaded her eyes and looked across the lake. The water shimmered silvery under the oblique winter sun. "That was Mama's greatest virtue, I think. She could forgive anything. Even Father's nephew Niccolò, who for God's sake tried to kill her."

There was someone Mama couldn't forgive, Beatrice thought. I heard it in her voice that night in Venice.

The Marquesa put her arm around Beatrice's waist. "I want to tell you something, baby. You must realize that I will deny this if tortured by the Inquisition, and if questioned on the matter at the throne of Jesus I will say I never said it. But on the day you become Duchess of Milan, I am going to be so proud of you. Of course I am also going to be furiously, insanely, hysterically jealous—and I don't care who knows that. But against every aspect of my nature, I'm going to be so proud. My only sister the Duchess of Milan. I will kill myself!"

The sisters embraced. Beatrice closed her eyes; the memories of girlhood swirled around her like a swarm of iridescent butterflies. When she finally blinked into the sunlight, she saw a man racing across the lawn from the direction of the Castello, wearing the red-white-and-blue uniform of her husband's household. He was within fifty paces when she identified him as one of the official messengers who ordinarily ran important papers from her husband's office to the various departments spread throughout the Castello.

The messenger in turn recognized Beatrice. He abruptly arrested his headlong flight and skidded to his knee in the grass in front of her. "Your Highness, I beg your pardon," he said, gasping, his youthful face bright red. "Where is His Highness?"

Beatrice pointed to her husband, still standing beside the Spanish ambassador, still watched by his faithful Venetian shadows. The messenger sprinted off before she could ask him anything.

"Well, I'm not going to stand here waiting," the Marquesa said. "It has to be something important!" She gathered up her skirts and dashed off in pursuit. Beatrice pulled up her own hems and charged along behind.

Beatrice was still over a hundred paces away when the messenger reached her husband. The messenger fell to his knee, then quickly rose and cupped his hand to her husband's ear. For a few seconds Il Moro remained motionless, the embroidered golden *M*'s on his white tunic vivid in the sun. Then, in a quick gesture, he placed his hand on the edge of the table beside him, as if surreptitiously steadying himself. He said something to the Spanish ambassador, who nodded several times rapidly. Then he turned and began to walk up the slight slope toward the two Venetian ambassadors.

The Marquesa reached Il Moro before he got to the Venetians. She stayed a step behind, and he did not seem to notice her. Beatrice caught them just as the ambassadors dipped to their knees. Her husband's dark eyes remained fixed on the Venetian envoys. He addressed the balding senior diplomat.

"Magnificent Ambassador," Il Moro said, his tone so vibrant and purposeful that Beatrice was certain he was announcing some triumph. "Naples has fallen. The people have thrown open the gates and invited the French into the city. King Ferrantino has fled to Sicily."

Beatrice could see the waxy face of the Venetian ambassador, his greenish-blue eyes dull with shock, the deep creases framing his nose twitching with alarm. Then everything began to spin. How would it matter if she and Eesh forgave each other, when Fortune would never forgive them? Her husband was saying something else, and she tried to hear through the whooshing rush of blood in her ears.

"This is not an occasion for despair, gentlemen," Il Moro said, reaching up to brush at his bangs, the ruby cameo on his ring flashing. "This is the time for all Italy to unite."

Milan, 11 March 1495

Beatrice rode with her sister to the Darsena docks, just outside the Porta Ticinese, the city's southern gate. These were the same docks at which she had disembarked to begin her life in Milan, a series of wooden quays arranged around a shallow, muddy lagoon at the head of the perfectly straight Naviglio Sforzesca, the main canal to Pavia. The Marquesa was traveling in a small galley accompanied by two barges. Her suite had only slightly disrupted the usual commercial bustle on the quays, a continuous clamor of shouting porters, rumbling wagons, and the variegated protests of the livestock coming in from the country.

The Marquesa pressed little Ercole's cheek to hers and kissed him a half-dozen times before handing him to Beatrice's nurse. Tears made two long straight tracks down her rosy face. She clutched Beatrice and said, "They already have the mooring ropes off. Everything is ready. I'm just going to go. I'm just going to go right now. I'm going to go and sit in my cabin and not look back. I can't do this any longer, baby. I just have to go. I love you so much."

"God, I love you, Bel," Beatrice said, squeezing her sister as tightly as a wrestler, tears spilling onto her own cheeks. "I can't believe I'm going to wake up tomorrow and you aren't going to be here. I knew this day would come, but now that it has happened, it's like a . . ." She stopped because she didn't want to say the word "death," but that was the way she felt. She ached with this loss, far beyond any parting they'd ever had before.

The Marquesa pried herself partially out of her sister's desperate embrace. "I'm almost certain Francesco and I will be back when your husband is invested as Duke of Milan. We really want to be here for that. I'll be back before you know I am gone."

No, you won't, Beatrice told herself with dead certainty. Because the investiture will never happen. Nothing has happened as it should. Louis Duc d'Orleans will be the next Duke of Milan.

The Marquesa understood the renewed fervor of her sister's embrace and said, "It's going to be all right, baby. All the ambassadors are meeting in Venice right now. There's going to be a new league, and the Frenchmen will be gone so fast they won't have time to put on their ridiculous goose-feet shoes. Someday you will tell your grandsons stories about how the horrid little King of France kissed you on both cheeks.''

As if mocking the little French King, the Marquesa gave her sister a lavish complement of kisses. Then she pulled away and held Beatrice's hands. ''It really will be all right. You don't know how it warms my heart to see how wonderfully everything has turned out for you here, baby. A rich, handsome husband who adores you and two precious little sons. You know, Mama always thought that I was the lucky one. But you're the lucky one. Now remember to write me a full description of the clavichord Maestro Lorenzo is making for you as soon as it is delivered.'' She kissed Beatrice one last time and then ran down the quay to her galley. Like a dancer she extended her arms for her pages, and they helped her onto the deck. She waved once and then, true to her word, disappeared into the small cabin.

The crewmen pushed off from the quay, oars dipped into the brackish water, and the galley led the two barges into the canal. Beatrice was startled by the speed with which the little flotilla moved away. The boats seemed to get smaller so quickly, the canal to narrow and lengthen. The day was bright and sunny, but she sensed a darkening, not just thin clouds veiling the sun but a thick, threatening pall. Everything continued to be distorted, her vision narrowing and lengthening, as though she were looking into a painting with flawed, exaggerated perspective. She wished she could faint, so that she could wake up and this would be over. But this wasn't like a faint. The darkness settling around her was a huge, palpable shadow, a descending cloud of cold soot.

Suddenly the cold pierced deep inside her, like the icy ripping of her soul she had felt the night Mama died. She knew what it was even before she said it to herself: You are never going to see your sister again.

She could hardly breathe, but still she knew she had to get to her horse. She ran and shouted to her startled page, and he helped her into the saddle. She pounded her horse's flank with her crop and was off so fast her guards didn't have a chance to respond. The crush of dockside traffic gave her something to focus on, and she frantically maneuvered among the ox-drawn wagons.

The exertion of riding somehow enabled her to breathe again. Her vision lightened. She began to feel relieved and foolish. The

boats were not so far away as she had thought; a moment previously she'd vowed she would ride to Pavia if necessary. Now
she saw an arched wooden bridge a few hundred paces farther
down the canal and realized that would be close enough.

When she reached the base of the narrow bridge her sense of
dread had vanished. This was a game now. She expertly guided
her horse up the planked slope and paused at the crest. Her sister's
galley had glided under the bridge just moments before and was
still close enough that if she'd had a rock she could have hit a
crewman on the deck. "Bel! Bel!" She waved, and the crewmen
looked and pointed. "Bel!" she shouted again. One of the crewmen
went to the cabin.

The wait seemed long, the game becoming serious again.
Please, Bel, she silently pleaded. Her horse began to jitter and
prance, and suddenly she was aware of how easily he could leap
over the wooden balustrade. Please, Bel. I have to win this. I have
to beat Fortune at this one silly game. If I can just see you, everything will change.

And then her sister came out, her hair like spun gold in the
sun, her crimson *camora* as brilliant as a ruby. The Marquesa waved
and blew kisses, and then they both waved and blew kisses for
many minutes, until Bel was nothing more than a fading red speck
in the distance.

C H A P T E R

48

Extract of a dispatch of PHILIPPE DE COMMINES, Lord of Argenton, Councillor to His Most Christian Majesty Charles VIII and Ambassador Plenipotentiary to the Republic of Venice, to GUILLAUME BRICONNET, Cardinal of Saint Malo and Chief Superintendent of Finances for the Kingdom of France. Venice, 2 April 1495

. . . and as His Most Christian Majesty has disregarded all of my previous warnings concerning the great diplomatic conclave that has been taking place here, I have deemed it appropriate to risk dispatching this news to you in addition to those letters that I have already had conveyed by courier to His Most Christian Majesty as well as the Duc d'Orleans. As you indeed know, His Most Christian Majesty, because of his youth, must rely on the prudent counsel of his advisers. . . .

Yesterday morning the Signory sent for me at an earlier hour than usual. I was shown into the great salon with almost all the members of the Signory present, and no sooner had I taken my seat than the Doge informed me that in the name of the Holy Trinity the Serene Republic of Venice had entered into an alliance with Our Holy Father the Pope, the Emperor of the Germans, the King of Spain, and the State of Milan. When I asked the reason for this league, the Doge answered that it was intended to defend Italy and preserve the sovereign territories of the member states. I retorted that it seemed that these states had joined in league to prevent His Most Christian Majesty from returning to France. To this the Doge responded, "Far from that. Every one will offer him free passage, the Signory foremost, and we will even supply victuals for your King's return journey. And if he does not care to risk the journey by land, we will provide him thirty-five galleys to carry him off by sea." In the Italian fashion, this assistance was offered in all earnestness, though from the insolent spirits of the men seated before me I could discern a yet more devious intent. . . . Upon leaving this council I encountered the Neapolitan ambassador, attired in a fine new gown and very gay, and indeed he had reason to be so. . . . That evening I went out in my boat and was rowed past the houses of all the ambassadors of the league, where there was great banqueting . . . there were extraordinary fireworks upon the turrets, steeples, and chimneys of the ambassadors' houses, and multitudes of bonfires were lighted, and throughout the city cannon fired. The entire city glowed as if our Lord had cast down the fires of the Last Days, and I prayed for the safe return of our King. . . .

. . . I have also warned the Duc d'Orléans that he can expect to be attacked at Asti by the armies of Milan, and I have written the Duc du Bourbon that he must send reinforcements to Asti immediately. . . .

. . . you cannot emphasize strongly enough to His Most Christian Majesty how urgent it is that he depart for France immediately. The fury of the entire world is about to come against us . . .

Extract of a dispatch of GALEAZZO DI SANSEVERINO, Captain General of the Armies of Milan, to LODOVICO SFORZA, "Il Moro," Duke of Bari. Annona, 19 April 1495

. . . by afternoon the troops under my command had driven the forces of Louis Duc d'Orléans back into the city of Asti. I have learned from some captive French soldiers that Orleans does not have sufficient forces at hand to attempt to break out of Asti, although we do not currently have enough men to effect a blockade of the entire city. . . .

Extract of a letter of international traveler and raconteur BENEDETTO DEI to LEONARDO DA VINCI, military engineer at the Court of Milan. Rome, 20 May 1495

. . . We are told by traders and diplomats just returned from Naples that His Most Christian Majesty, welcomed only three months ago as a deliverer from the Aragonese tyrant, will depart for France this day or the next, with the populace biting their thumbs to his face and spitting at his feet. I am of the opinion that His Most Christian Majesty went there with the most earnest intentions of bringing Christian justice to that benighted land, but unfortunately he was distracted by the wealth and luxury of *bella Napoli* and did not impose order on his troops, who have inspired the hatred of the entire city with their drunkenness and moral license. We are told that the French take their lodgings in whatever houses suit their fancy, seating themselves at the table attired in clothes purloined from the *guardaroba*, commanding the occupants to serve them their best foods and wines, and then selling the rest of the stores—and should the women of the household escape with only the loss of their jewelry and other valuables they are deemed lucky. In an effort to inspire order among this mob he commands, the King hanged six of his own troops, but shortly after this act of penance, His Most Christian Majesty was introduced to a daughter of the Duchess of Melfi, said Duchess contriving to retrieve some lands confiscated by the invaders. The Duchess of Melfi's daughter is a comely young woman with a reputation as an equestrienne of unusual proficiency, and after displaying her remarkable command of an extremely mettlesome courser in the presence of His Most Christian Majesty, "la Melfi," as she is known, apparently demonstrated to His Majesty her facility in a different sort of riding (this done bareback) and has thus become the King's constant companion. . . .

. . . the armies of the League of Venice, which are under the command of the Marquis of Mantua, are said to number forty thousand men. The mission of the League armies, as we understand it here, is to block the French King's retreat from Naples

and destroy the French army so that it can never enter Italy again
. . . we hear that Orléans has been reinforced in Asti. . . . Perhaps you can confirm what we have heard here, that a suite of
imperial ambassadors has been dispatched to Milan and that as
soon as they arrive, your lord Il Moro will be invested as the Duke
of Milan. . . .

C H A P T E R

49

Milan, 25 May 1495

"Your Highness."

Had there been even a note of sarcasm or bitterness in Eesh's greeting, Beatrice wouldn't have been so chilled by the tone of her cousin's voice. But this was the most haunting sound she had ever heard, a voice inflected with nothing, words without life. The voice of the dead.

Beatrice looked around the room. The bed, chairs, and walls were still draped in black. Eesh had pulled aside the black velvet curtains to let in the morning light, but the illumination seemed to harden rather than lessen the darkness, as if coating the room with glossy black lacquer.

Eesh's face had filled out again, but she was shockingly, spectrally pale. Beatrice returned her curtsy and forced herself to look into her eyes. The color of Eesh's irises confirmed what she had heard in Eesh's voice. Instead of the opalescent depths of the Bay of Naples, Beatrice imagined a dull film of scum over a shallow stagnant pond. The color of decay. Even as her flesh revivified, Eesh was rotting inside. Suddenly Beatrice realized that Eesh was no longer mourning the death of their love or Gian or even the fall of Naples. Perhaps she never had been. She was mourning for herself.

Isabella gestured for Beatrice to sit on the bed beside her. Beatrice sat half an arm's length away.

"You know that the investiture is tomorrow," Beatrice said. The ceremony had been put together so hurriedly that the exact date had not been set until two days previously. Beatrice regretted that none of her family would get word in time to attend. But she just wanted it to be over.

After an uncomfortable pause Isabella said, "Did you come for my blessing?"

Beatrice really didn't know why she had come. Perhaps to ask for forgiveness. Perhaps to forgive. Perhaps merely to look her rival in the eyes before she plucked them out. She only knew that she could not become Duchess of Milan without doing this.

Finally Beatrice offered, "I came to tell you that I never wanted this for myself. But I must be honest with you and tell you I wanted this investiture for my husband. For my sons and our people."

"I think you want it more than he does," Isabella said in a dry monotone. "Life for you has become an endless circle of desire and deception, acquisition and apology. I have stepped off that wheel, and you are still spinning. You can't see it. We do not know our own souls. That is the only truth to life. We do not even know our own souls."

I do, Beatrice thought. My soul is with my husband and my little boys.

Then Eesh said, very softly, without emotion, without accusation, "I think you came here because you believe that someone poisoned Gian."

Gian wasn't poisoned, Beatrice told herself, the argument she had waged a hundred times in the still of sleepless nights. What I saw was not what I thought I saw. What I saw was death, nothing more. Natural death. A thing terrible enough. Gian's body was examined in Milan, and not a trace of poison was found.

"I think Galeazz did it," Isabella said, her voice remaining quiet and flat. "He did it because I told him how Gian planned to abdicate in favor of Francesco. He murdered my husband to punish me. And to prove his love for your husband."

The fluttering thump of her heart gave Beatrice a terrifying queasiness, as if something alive and autonomous were struggling to escape her breast. "Eesh, even if Gian was poisoned by God knows who, I know my husband had nothing to do with it." I *know* that, she angrily told herself. My soul knows that.

"Then your conscience can be clear. You are fortunate." There was no sarcasm in this. Perhaps an inflection of sincere envy. "I never wanted him to die, you know. I tried to make him sick by letting him eat the fruit and giving him wine. I just wanted him to surrender his title to Francesco. Then he would have gotten better. He would've been so much happier once he was no longer Duke. I never wanted him to die."

"None of us did."

"Someone did."

"If you would like, I will insist on an investigation."

Isabella slightly raised her pale, limp hand, then let it drop back on her thigh. "The question requires no answer now. Not for me."

There was a faint stirring of an emotion in Eesh's voice that was not exactly malice. A cruel mischief, as mindless as a child's. What Eesh meant was: The answer does still matter to you.

The blackness around Beatrice was no longer a glossy lacquer; it had become viscous and sticky, a foul pitch she never would be able to remove if she stayed any longer. "Can I provide anything for you and the children?" she asked. "Anything that is in my power to give."

"We have everything that is in your power to give. We are grateful."

Beatrice made a quick farewell and hurried into the courtyard. She deeply inhaled the sweet air, scented with the blooms of spring. Bees buzzed around the flower beds and topiaries.

Back in her room, the corners of Isabella's subtle lips twitched with the merest suggestion of a smile, and for an instant her irises glimmered. Then the expression vanished, and she lowered her blank, unfeeling eyes.

❖ ❖ ❖

Il Moro graciously requested his wife's ladies-in-waiting to leave the room. As they curtsied and rustled out, several of the younger women glanced back at him surreptitiously, despite their constant presence at court still awed by the sight of the man said to hold the fate of the world in his hands.

If Beatrice could have had one image of her husband to hold in her heart forever, this was it. He had dressed for the morning's ceremony of investiture with dramatic simplicity. His *vestito*, a trim-fitting tunic of purple damask, was daringly modern, certain to make a telling contrast to the billowing medieval robes of the clerics and ambassadors. The fabric was embroidered all over with tiny gold motifs, ranging from imperial eagles to mulberry leaves. A thin band of cloth-of-gold hemmed his high collar, leaving exposed a narrow width of white Rheims linen shirt. He held in his hands an indigo velvet cap, a grape-size diamond dangling from the *M* embroidered on the side. Illuminated by the morning light that streamed through the big arched windows, Il Moro was the embodiment of Europe's new dawn.

His staff-straight posture was the only vestige of the bullying arrogance Beatrice remembered from the early days of their marriage. Otherwise he carried himself with relaxed grace, the bearing of a man who understood his power and accomplishments and had no need to flaunt them. His neatly singed black bangs were slightly mussed, an endearingly casual touch. His smile, intimate and a bit mischievous, rippled through her in a warm wave of sensuality and love.

He paused and looked at her, shaking his head slightly with wonder and delight. Beatrice wore a gold-and-purple-striped velour *camora* with circlets of white silk puffs at each shoulder. Her hair, parted down the middle, fell loosely to her shoulders, where it was gathered into a waist-length, ribbon-wrapped braid. A net woven of gold braid and pearl strands fell like a transparent kerchief from the crown of her head to the nape of her neck; a band of gold satin, studded with rubies and pearl pendants, wrapped around her forehead. She wore a three-tiered diamond choker with a pendant composed of an enormous violet-hued ruby surrounded by diamonds; a longer necklace of white and black pearls fell down across her shoulders and hung beneath her breasts. Beatrice knew she had presented herself in all the splendor her husband's treasury could provide, but looking into his eyes she could have believed that even in her chemise she was the most beautiful woman in the world.

He made no comment or attempt to embrace her, but simply said, "Take off your choker." His eyes gleamed.

Beatrice worked for a while with the clasp and finally removed the heavy ornament. Her husband fidgeted with his hat, and she realized that he had concealed something inside it. He pulled out another dazzling diamond choker, set with fewer gems than the one she had worn but with much finer, more elegantly cut stones. The heart-shaped pendant spelled out the motto "merito et tempore" in letters composed of small diamonds against a background of tiny rubies. As reverently as if he were handling a holy relic, Il Moro fastened the choker around her neck.

He put his hands on her shoulders and stood back and looked at her. "The last person to wear this necklace was my mother," he whispered, his voice trembling with significance. "She always believed that patience was the highest virtue." He closed his eyes. "I would give my soul for my mother to be here today. To see the happiness you have brought me."

She held out her arms to him, and he embraced her tightly. His voice was husky with emotion. "Today I will become the first Sforza ever invested as Duke of Milan. Our son will be the second. God, *amore*, soon everything I have ever dreamed of will be realized. And now, looking back, I cannot believe there was ever a time when you were not part of that dream. I know I lived before I loved you, but I cannot remember it. You are my only life. The only life I have ever had. I begin with you."

This was the music Beatrice had always imagined, the vast choir of angels and the great singing of the spheres. And yet there was a discordant note she could not ignore, a thin screeching doubt that disturbed the entire magnificent orchestration.

With his acute sensitivity to touch, his uncanny knowledge of a lover's body, Il Moro felt the faint stirring of his wife's apprehension. "Don't worry, *carissima*," he said. "The French are finished."

The wail of doubt was now all Beatrice could hear. There was nothing she could do except say it. "I talked to my cousin yesterday. She believes that Galeazz poisoned Gian."

Beatrice felt her husband's reaction, a slight tightening of his back. He still held her, his words hot against her ear. *"Carissima,* I had Gian's body examined for just this reason, to allay any doubts or accusations. Even your cousin's doctor from Naples was there, and he could find no traces of poison. I am satisfied."

"But is it possible Galeazz could have done it? Thinking he was protecting us. He knew what Isabella's plans were."

He hesitated, nothing more. Then he said, "Galeazz left with me five days before Gian died. It isn't possible."

Of course. Galeazz hadn't even been there. Why hadn't she thought of that as soon as Eesh mentioned Galeazz's name? Had her guilt really become that irrational? Yes, she realized. Despite all her efforts to defeat it with reason. But now that she could see so clearly that her guilt was a delusion, perhaps she could finally see beyond it. She was suddenly buoyant with relief.

He pulled away and looked at her soberly. "I think we should allow poor Gian to rest in peace. Now, *amore,* I have something very important to tell you. Today I intend to draft papers designating you as regent in the event of my death or incapacitating illness."

Her first reaction was an enormous pride, that from all his trusted counselors her husband had chosen her. This was beyond what was required by his love, indeed had nothing to do with love and everything to do with respect. Then she thought of the grim eventuality he had referred to, the dark subtext of his praise. And in an instant she understood what all her absurd doubts about Gian's death actually disguised, a truth that percolated through her consciousness like a cold, cleansing rain.

You are afraid of this, Beatrice admitted to herself. You are afraid because today you have everything *you* have ever dreamed of.

And now you have everything to lose.

The second investiture Beatrice had ever attended, like the first, took place just in front of the Duomo. The temporary porch of richly carved wooden columns and embroidered awnings was even more lavish than that erected for Gian's investiture as Duke of

Genoa. The French fleur-de-lis had been replaced by the black imperial eagle of the Holy Roman Empire. A select group of ambassadors and officers of state were seated on the porch. They listened while the imperial envoy, the Bishop of Brixen, read the list of properties and privileges attached to the title of Duke of Milan.

Beatrice knelt with a small group of her ladies at the top of the steps. Her stepdaughter, Bianca, was at her side, and they exchanged fond, proud smiles throughout the long ceremony. Finally the recitation of privileges was finished, and the jewel-encrusted ducal sword and scabbard were draped over Il Moro's shoulders and the gold ducal scepter was laid across his arm. Then the new Duke of Milan came to the steps to receive the acclamation of the huge crowd gathered in the Piazza del Duomo.

Il Moro extended his hand to his kneeling wife. Beatrice looked up at him with surprise—this hadn't been included in her instructions. He mouthed *"Amore"* to her and motioned with his fingers for her to rise. A subtle, wry twist of his lips seemed to say: We can do whatever we want now. She stood up, entirely at ease with this improvised protocol, feeling almost that she was alone with her husband, sharing a moment of intimacy that would have been hard for anyone else to imagine. When he took her hand, the first instant of contact was stunningly sexual. After that she could not even feel his hand; there was no distinction between her flesh and his.

Beatrice looked out over the Piazza del Duomo. She had a moment of supernatural clarity, a feeling that she could distinctly see every face of the hundred thousand before her, see each emblem on the flags flying from the surrounding rooftops, count each pomegranate that flecked the ivy wreaths hanging from the balconies and loggias. Huge banks of thunderclouds piled up to the north, towering behind the *palazzi* like some fantastic celestial architecture. The chorus of "Moro! Moro!" began, joined by "Duca! Duca!," the two rallying cries no longer in competition. The acclamations exploded with astonishing force, as if warning the French that their mighty cannons were nothing next to the power of Il Moro, who could make his enemies vanish with a wave of his hand.

Listening to her own music, the massive chords of a pipe organ driven by light rather than air, Beatrice saw among the dignitaries standing just beneath her her sister's husband, Francesco Gonzaga, the Captain General of the Armies of the League of Venice, who had coincidentally been in Milan for consultations. Francesco's inelegant yet curiously charismatic face—he was bearded, with squashed, almost impish features and intense dark eyes—reminded her of the faces she did not see. Bel and Father. She vowed she would not conjure Gian, because she had at last put him in his grave. And Eesh. She was done grieving for Eesh. It had been Eesh's choice to live with what Fortune had given her, or to bury herself with regrets for what was no longer possible. Eesh had chosen to die.

At that moment Beatrice realized the meaninglessness of her own regrets and fears, saw how urgent it was that she accept the magnificent gift Fortune had offered her. She looked into the sun. It had just begun to slip behind the advancing storm, sending spectacular shafts glinting around the ragged edge of the thunderclouds. She immediately recalled an image from the first canto of the *Paradiso*, when Beatrice and Dante had stared into the brilliant sun above the heights of Purgatory and in an instant had been transported to the golden vastness of Paradise.

The earthbound Beatrice called up one final face among the missing. I wish you were here, Mama, she silently told that ghostly yet indelible image, at first with a feeling of anger and then with a terribly bitter regret and loneliness. And then it was all gone, all pain and regret, everything that bound her to earth. She clutched her husband's hand tightly and let the music of his fame lift them into the limitless sky.

PART

EIGHT

CHAPTER
50

Vigevano, 14 June 1495

The sun played hide-and-seek among the clouds. The dry winter had been followed by a wet spring, and the patchwork of irrigated fields in the Ticino River Valley lay under flat, shallow sheets of water; here and there the elusive sun lit the exposed tips of the grain sprouts and rice shoots, creating swatches of shimmering green brocade. The network of irrigation ditches and canals, swollen with the runoff, crisscrossed the landscape in a thick silver grid.

Il Moro stood in his stirrups and looked out over the valley. "It would be interesting to build one of Leonardo's cities and see what kind of revenues it produced," he idly told his riding companion, the Marchesino Stanga, Milan's Minister of Public Works.

"Currently, Your Highness, we could use several dozen new cities to replenish our treasury," the Marchesino said dryly. "We have paid the French handsomely to come over the mountains, and now we are paying the Germans and the Venetians handsomely to send them home."

Il Moro smiled in grudging appreciation of the Marchesino's wit.

"In all seriousness, Your Highness, I suggest that the schedule of projects you have given me be substantially reduced. The same men who insisted that you assume the title of Duke are beginning to complain about their taxes."

"Well, if they made me Duke to reduce their taxes, we shall no doubt see them become still more vociferous. And I might remind them that *they* merely made me Duke, while the Emperor has made me Duke of Milan." The sun came out again, and Il Moro paused and shaded his eyes. "However, let us review the list again this evening and see what we can eliminate. The only thing I insist on seeing to completion is the painting in Beatrice's rooms here. I want the frescoes finished while she is still in Milan." He squinted up at the sun. "My wife insisted that I come here to relax, and here I am on my horse in the heat of the day. I'm going back to the *castello* to bathe and sleep."

Il Moro did just that, and he was annoyed to be awakened from a deep slumber by the knock on his door. He cracked open the shutters and saw that it was still early evening. Putting on a loose *turca* of scarlet silk, he went to the door.

The Marchesino Stanga came into the room and closed the door behind him. The Marchesino usually looked younger than his thirty-eight years; now he seemed to have aged fifteen years in one afternoon. His forehead was glazed with perspiration, and the color he had acquired on his afternoon ride looked like the flush of a fever on a sick man's pallor.

"Three couriers have come from Novara in the last quarter of an hour," the Marchesino said, his Adam's apple struggling. "I questioned each of them separately to make certain that their information was not manufactured."

Il Moro nodded.

"Your Highness, Louis Duc d'Orléans is in Novara. The Caccia and Tornielli families conspired with him to open the gates and admit his army." Novara was a satellite city east of Milan, only three hours away for a fast courier riding a relay of horses; it was also only about two hours north of Vigevano. The Caccias and the Torniellis were Novara's most powerful noble families. They had long protested their taxes and the diversion of some of the local water supply to the projects near Vigevano.

"I assume Orleans escaped from Asti with a small company of a few hundred men," Il Moro said calmly.

The Marchesino's Adam's apple bobbed again before he could speak. "Your Highness, the average of the three couriers' estimates is twenty thousand men."

"That simply isn't possible, Marchesino." Il Moro's voice was soothing, as if he were trying to placate a madman. "How could that many men have gotten into Asti right under Galeazz's nose, much less march undetected to Novara."

"Your Highness, Messer Galeazzo has been complaining for weeks now of his need for reinforcements from Venice. He has spread his men all over the Piedmont, chasing down the companies of French infantry and cavalry that have infiltrated across the Alps. For ten days he has had scarcely enough men near Asti to post a watch on the city gates."

From Novara an army of twenty thousand men could be at the gates of Milan by the next morning. Il Moro was quiet for a moment, then asked, "You are entirely convinced that these reports are credible? I think we should dispatch several reliable men to Novara to confirm them."

"Your Highness, I don't think we have time to wait for confirmation. Orleans is said to have five thousand cavalry. They could raid Vigevano before dark. If they have already left, they could be here within an hour. Even less."

Il Moro spread his hands and smiled. "Certainly you are correct, Marchesino. It is best to be prudent. We will send couriers to Milan. I will instruct my wife and my castellan to maintain vigilance there. As to our departure from Vigevano, I think it best that we wait until morning and see how matters stand. Assuming that there are Frenchmen on the road, we are better off here than wandering about the countryside. Would you ask my secretary to come to my room in a half hour? I would like to get dressed and consider our strategy before I send my instructions to Milan. And perhaps by then we will have further news from Novara."

Mollified by Il Moro's considered course of action, the Marchesino bowed and left. Il Moro stood beside the door for a moment, completely still, his head cocked just slightly as if listening for something. He went to the window and firmly closed the shutter he had partially opened minutes before. Then he lay down on his bed again, staring up into the fuzzy darkness.

The vision that came to him was not a dream, because although it proceeded with the inexorable narrative of a dream, it lacked the fluid logic and quirky perspective. This was real. Twenty-five years had done nothing to alter it. And dreams didn't smell, dreams weren't cold. He was in the dungeons beneath the Rochetta, below the level of the moat, a place of perpetual damp and cold. Beside him stood his brother Galeazzo Maria, the Duke of Milan. In a final instant of contact with the present, Il Moro marveled that his brother was alive. Then he lost himself in the utter lucidity of the vision. He was there. His brother had never died.

Il Moro looked at his brother and saw his own face in some hideous distorting mirror. Galeazzo Maria was at once more angelic-looking and more diabolic. His huge hawklike nose was almost a deformity, a cruel, menacing beak, yet his small, deeply colored mouth had an effeminate sweetness. His big, sensitive, terrifying eyes combined both the delicacy and the fury of the rest of his face.

The cold air reeked of decay. Light from their torches raced through the long, damp hall. They passed rows of black oak doors. Il Moro had never been down here before. He knew that occasionally a local nobleman or even one of his brother's officers of state had come here and not reappeared. Perhaps one every six months. Never so many that the accompanying charges of treason seemed invented, the work of a persecuted mind. With youthful cynicism Il Moro attributed the disappearances to the usual business of court. Courts were dangerous places. The less substantial rumors, of what took place down here, he did not believe at all.

Galeazzo Maria paused before a door with a brass Sforza viper nailed to it. As he unlocked it he glanced sideways at Il Moro, his lips twisted into a smirk. He pushed the door open. Il Moro stepped back involuntarily when he realized that there were people in the cell. He wanted to run. Then his brother turned and looked at him, and he had to go in.

A large, lumpishly powerful man and a small, slender woman hung side by side from the wall, their bound hands raised straight over their heads and tied to iron rings; on second look Il Moro realized that the ropes had been adjusted so that the prisoners could just stand on tiptoe. They had black hoods over their heads. The man wore soiled wool breeches and the women a torn but expensive linen chemise. A third prisoner, naked, sat bound to a chair placed against the opposite wall. He also wore a hood, but his slack skin and sagging breasts evidenced that he was not as young as the other two. Beside his chair was a massive wooden coffin, the lid removed and leaning against it.

"Good," Galeazzo Maria said. "Everything is here." Il Moro had never heard this tone in his brother's voice. Even as a child Galeazzo Maria had not spoken like a child; his diction had always been deliberate and polished, his childhood Latin orations famous for their precocious gravity. Now he sounded like a gleeful little boy. Il Moro felt a prickly nausea and a slight loss of control over his legs. He still tried to convince himself that this was some nasty prank.

Galeazzo Maria whipped the hood off the woman first, and Il Moro could see from her eyes that it was no prank. Even with a wooden gag shoved in her mouth she appeared young, probably no older than fourteen or fifteen, with very refined, aquiline Lombard features. Local nobility. He looked away from her pleading, racing, desperate eyes. The hood came off the man next to her, and his scarred, thuggish face marked him as the kind of man who belonged in a dungeon. Moving with languid grace, Galeazzo Maria removed the third hood. Il Moro knew the blanched face beneath the wispy crown of gray hair. Tommaseo Visconti, a distant relation to the Viscontis who had once ruled Milan. Il Moro glanced back at the girl. Now he knew her too. She was Visconti's daughter; he didn't know her given name.

"Signor Tommaseo and his lovely daughter," Galeazzo Maria said. He had a long hunting knife in his hand, and he pointed it at the big man. "A convicted murderer and rapist. He calls himself Il Lupo." Galeazzo Maria sneered as if the name offended his taste. He went over to Il Lupo and with the point of his knife cut the hide cord that held the wooden gag in place. Il Lupo worked his brutish jaws and spit the gag out. Galeazzo Maria reached up and cut the bindings that held his hands. Il Lupo slumped over and rubbed his wrists and then raised up, glaring at Galeazzo Maria. Il Moro was suddenly frightened for his brother and himself. In a lazy, effeminate gesture, Galeazzo Maria twirled the knife before Il Lupo's nose. The tiny, piggish eyes of the criminal locked onto Galeazzo Maria's. Il Lupo saw something that frightened even him, and he backed away.

"You're a rapist," Galeazzo Maria told Il Lupo in his boyish voice. "So rape her."

The father bucked against his heavy chair, and the girl's eyes searched the room frantically. Il Moro told himself that his brother was only teaching the father a lesson. It wouldn't happen. When the girl's wild eyes found his, he shook his head at her in an attempt to communicate this conviction.

Il Lupo walked over, studied the girl for a moment, then ripped her chemise down the front. With several savage pulls he ripped it entirely off. He clutched at his breeches and tore them and stepped out of them and immediately pressed himself against the girl's stretched-out form.

Il Moro waited a moment for his brother to stop it. He watched with rising panic while the huge thug enfolded the writhing girl, and finally he had to step forward. It was just a step; he didn't know exactly how he would stop this.

His brother seized his arm with a shockingly powerful grip. He looked in his brother's eyes and with absolute certainty knew that if he took another step his brother's knife would be in his throat. He could taste the steel, the blood. The room seemed to whirl once. Il Lupo pumped his hips and grunted, and the father's chair bucked again.

Galeazzo Maria stepped slowly toward Il Lupo. He held the knife in both hands and he lifted it with a triumphal, ecstatic fury and brought it down into Il Lupo's back with a tremendous thud. Blood spurted when he ripped the blade out. Il Lupo whirled around, his eyes red, his penis still half erect. He took one stumbling step, theatrically threw both arms out, and fell on his face, his body hitting the stone floor with a wet slapping sound.

Thank God, Il Moro thought. It's over. Thank God. Now let them go. He wanted to cover the girl, but he was still afraid to move. Her eyes were closed now.

Galeazzo Maria flipped the corpse over and stared at it, his chest heaving. Then he reached down and pulled up Il Lupo's penis and testicles and savagely sliced them off. He held the bloody organs like an offering in front of the girl and waited. When she opened her eyes he ripped her gag out and pulled it down around her neck. He grasped her jaw and with some unbelievable strength in his elegant little hand held her mouth open while he threatened to sodomize her with the amputated penis. Il Moro stood trembling, his stomach cramping and his head pounding.

Apparently satisfied just listening to the girl's horrified screams, Galeazzo Maria threw his head back with manic glee and let go of her jaw. He turned his back on her and tossed the limp genitals onto Il Lupo's chest.

Il Moro's legs felt so weak that he couldn't see how he still stood. God, it has to be over, he told himself. His brother was laughing hysterically, a high-pitched boyish laugh.

Galeazzo Maria cut the father out of the chair and jerked him to his feet. At knifepoint he forced him to lie in the coffin. He turned to Il Moro. "I need you to help me lift the lid, Lodovico."

For some reason this seemed relatively benign, a lesser form of cruelty. It was ending. Surely this was only a mock burial, Signor Tommaseo's final humiliation. Almost gratefully, Il Moro helped his brother lift the heavy lid. They began to slide it into place.

"Wait," Galeazzo Maria said. He reached into the coffin and cut the cord that held the gag. The man made some awful noises, but he couldn't spit the wooden gag out. "He'll get it out soon enough," Galeazzo Maria said. "Then we'll be able to hear him scream."

Galeazzo Maria handed Il Moro a large shipwright's mallet and a dozen heavy steel pegs. "The nail holes are already drilled. Nail him in."

The truth came to Il Moro in an icy epiphany. Signor Tommaseo isn't going to get out, he told himself. And I can't kill a defenseless, most likely innocent man. I can die, but I can't kill a man like this. Then he realized that his brother had just given him a weapon. He dropped the nails on the floor. The metallic little clinking sound was eerie, like bells echoing from some ancient time. He grasped the handle of the mallet with both hands and looked up at Galeazzo Maria. His brother was smiling at him.

Il Moro raised the heavy mallet.

Galeazzo Maria erupted into madcap boy's laughter. He sprang from side to side like a clumsy marionette, mocking his brother's grim resolution. After what seemed like several minutes of this bizarre performance, Il Moro all the time watching him as if he were a bobbing adder, Galeazzo Maria wiped away genuine tears of mirth.

"You see, you see, Lodovico, this performance wasn't for Signor Tommaseo. It was for you." Galeazzo Maria spread his arms as if waiting for an embrace. "You see how much I love you, Lodovico, that I would have them suffer for you. But you, Lodovico, you don't love me as you should. You're much too clever. Perhaps that's why you were always the Duke's favorite. And Mother's pet." Galeazzo Maria dropped his arms and his manic grin faded. "Whereas Mother never really understood me." Something moved over his face, an ineffable expression that crawled at the base of Il Moro's neck. "She never understood me until the day I brought her down here."

Il Moro listened to the rising, reason-assaulting drone that followed his brother's last words. He told himself that this was only his brother's perverse invention, intended to drive him mad, maddening in its mere suggestion. Even Galeazzo Maria wasn't capable of such an obscenity. And yet Il Moro knew that his mother's sudden death in Cremona—just a week after Galeazzo Maria had exiled her—had never been satisfactorily explained, that it was not in her character to perish simply from the agony of isolation. Even the death of her husband had not broken her.

"Trust me, Lodovico. She was here." Galeazzo Maria cocked his head wryly. "Rest assured I never harmed her. I merely invited her to watch me at work."

The most terrible revelation of all stood before him. It was true. His mother had such strength, such implacable faith, that Galeazzo Maria could have flayed her on the wheel and she would not have cried out. But to be forced to watch her own son brutalize innocents like these . . . That was the instrument that had ripped out her soul, the torture that had so quickly extinguished her will to live.

"You see, this is such an education for you," Galeazzo Maria said, smiling at the horrified recognition on his brother's face. "Before we are finished, you will be very much more clever than you were when you walked into this room. To that end, I must now insist. You either nail Signor Tommaseo into his coffin or get in it yourself. And in that case I will include the girl to keep you company. I made certain that there was room for all three of you."

Galeazzo Maria lunged forward, the knife flashing, catching Il Moro entirely by surprise. Il Moro's cheek itched, and he touched his fingers to it and felt the hot wetness. His feet were ice cold, frozen to the floor.

"Do you know what I taught Mother in this room, Lodovico?" Galeazzo Maria stared for a moment at his knife. "That she no longer wanted to live. However, I believe that you will learn quite the opposite: That above all else, you want to live." Galeazzo Maria lunged again and the point of the knife stung Il Moro's lip and he tasted blood.

"Nail him in," Galeazzo Maria said in an awful whisper.

Il Moro forced his benumbed hands to grip the heavy mallet. Dizzy with shock, nauseated by the ferric scent of his own blood, he willed one last challenge, for the peace of his mother's soul. He stepped forward.

"Yes. Come closer." Galeazzo Maria's expression was composed, strangely sincere. "Look into my eyes. If you think you have the courage to kill me, then you can look into my eyes before you do it. You will recognize yourself, Lodovico. You are more like me than you can ever allow yourself to admit."

Il Moro looked into his brother's eyes, the last time he would ever be able to do it. What he saw was nothing like the savage cruelty and menace that had so thoroughly shocked him just minutes earlier. The dilated pupils were utterly without focus or animation. They were simply little round windows into oblivion, an unfathomable black pit completely and terrifyingly void of light and reason. And he knew in that instant he would be afraid of what he saw there for the rest of his life.

Letting the mallet fall to his side, Il Moro knelt and scooped the nails off the floor. He convinced himself that he could go ahead and do this and then come down later and rescue the man. Or certainly it was still a prank, no more real than the absurd lies Galeazzo Maria had just told him about forcing their mother to come down here. Sick, ugly, perverted, but still a prank. He began to pound the nails through the lid of the coffin, telling himself these things. But he knew that something had irrevocably fractured deep inside him. With each blow of the mallet he could feel his soul shattering, a soul that would never be whole again. He could spend the rest of his life atoning for these blows, building his citadels to light and reason, and yet he would never come close enough to the sun to escape the terrible darkness behind his brother's eyes.

Signor Tommaseo did start to scream, when he heard Galeazzo Maria begin to rape his daughter. But then something strange happened to the horrible vision. Il Moro became conscious that time had circled back on itself, that he was reliving this memory with the full power to alter it, that at last he had an opportunity to atone, to do now what he could not do then.

Finishing with the girl, Galeazzo Maria turned away. But this time Il Moro could see that the girl was Beatrice. Beatrice who had made him whole again, who had purified him and would lead him to the light. Il Moro clutched the mallet with all his force, and this time he vowed to bash his brother's skull to pulp.

He couldn't move. His arm simply couldn't move. It wasn't that his courage had failed again. Something was wrong with his arm.

Galeazzo Maria's face was now as white and gaunt as the face of Gian's corpse. His tunic was covered with blood and ripped by his assassins' knives. "You killed my boy," he said in an unreal, spectral voice.

Il Moro tried to deny the accusation, to explain himself, but he couldn't talk. Somehow his waking memory had become a nightmare in which he couldn't talk and couldn't move.

"You killed my boy," Galeazzo Maria repeated, starting to laugh. "Not with your hands but with your eyes. Remember how you pleaded with your eyes? You're very clever, Lodovico, so you must remember. They killed him for you. Didn't I tell you that you are more like me than you can ever admit?"

Il Moro tried to scream with such force that he felt as if a knife had been plunged into his throat. His temple exploded with pain, and black snow filled the air. And still he could not move, could not make a single sound.

CHAPTER

51

Milan, 15 June 1495

"That's you," Beatrice told Ercole as he sat in her lap. She pointed to the detailed, hand-painted illustration in his Book of Hours. The artist had portrayed Ercole as an older boy, about five or six years old, with long, curly blond hair. He was standing between two voluptuous, virtually identical blond women dressed in classical Roman togas, gesturing to the woman on his left. "This woman is Virtue," Beatrice said, "and the other is Vice. You are choosing to follow Virtue."

"Virtù," Ercole said happily, pointing to the woman his little image had selected.

"Good, Ercole. I hope you will always be able to tell the difference," she told him wistfully. "When you get older, sometimes it is almost impossible to tell one from the other."

Beatrice wondered for the thousandth time what was happening. Several messengers had arrived the previous evening from Novara, each of them independently reporting that Louis Duc d'Orleans had taken the city. Rumors had swept through Milan during the night. But if Novara had fallen, why hadn't couriers arrived from Vigevano, carrying official news of the catastrophe and orders to defend the Castello? As virtually the entire upper tier of the government was with her husband in Vigevano, leaving only lower-level functionaries in Milan, Beatrice had decided that the worst thing she could do would be to set off a false alarm in the leaderless city. So she had resisted requests to post additional guards or seal the Castello gates—defensive measures that might well have inspired panic. The absence of further word from Novara or Vigevano during the long night seemed to confirm the prudence of her wait-and-see approach. However, at first light she had sent a courier to Vigevano to find out what, if anything, they had heard there.

At midmorning Beatrice was visiting with her dressmakers in their sunlit little factory overlooking the Piazza d'Armi when her chamberlain found her and made a surprising announcement: Her husband had returned from Vigevano. Now she knew that something had indeed happened, but she was relieved to know that the head of state was where he belonged in a crisis.

She hurried to her husband's rooms in the Rochetta. The Castello's inner sanctuary was as quiet as it had been during her husband's absence, the massive stone walls a cool refuge from the summer heat. Her heart skipped when she saw the guards at the carved wooden doors to her husband's antechamber, five men in steel helmets and breastplates, armed with Swiss-style halberds. At her approach one of the guards cracked the door and whispered inside. After a moment he swung the door open and bowed to Beatrice.

The Marchesino Stanga waited behind the door. The windows in her husband's rooms were shuttered, but even in the dull light Beatrice was shocked at how tired the Marchesino looked. His eyes were dark circles. "Your Highness . . ." His voice cracked.

Beatrice immediately surmised that the French had killed her husband. His closest advisers had brought his body back. Of course they had to keep it secret, because pandemonium would break loose in the city, leaving Milan defenseless against Orleans. This was all very clear to her, and she was amazed at how calm she was. "Where is he, Marchesino?"

The Marchesino led her into the darkened bedroom. When she saw the vague shape on the bed, her lungs constricted and she vainly tried to argue with her own conjecture. She felt just as she had when she'd read the letter about Mama. Empty, unable to think, able to think too much. She looked at the dimly silhouetted tassels of his bed canopy, and she thought to herself that they had already draped his bed in mourning cloth.

Taking another step forward, Beatrice couldn't avoid looking at him. Light glanced from his eyes. She was furious that they hadn't closed his eyes.

His eyes moved.

She virtually leapt back with alarm, her heart screaming. "He's alive," she snapped at the Marchesino, as if he had tricked her. She rushed to her husband's side. His head remained motionless, but his eyes turned to her. He weakly raised his left hand and she took it. She remembered standing beside Gian's bed and taking his hand. But she did not feel death in her husband's grip.

"Lodovico," she whispered. His eyes were fixed on her, his mouth open. A horrible wheezing came from his throat. The dark, pouchy skin beneath his right eye twitched wildly.

"Dear God," she said, turning to the Marchesino. "Is he wounded? Who is treating his wounds? He can't breathe. Where is Messer Ambrogio? He can't breathe—"

"Your Highness, he can breathe," the Marchesino said, putting his hands on her shoulders. "He has been like this since yesterday evening, when I brought him the reports about the surrender of Novara. He is trying to speak. But he cannot make the sounds. He cannot move his right hand, either."

Beatrice pulled the covers aside to disprove this preposterous claim. But her husband's right hand and arm were as limp as a sleeping child's.

"Messer Ambrogio has been in attendance on your husband all night. He suggests that His Highness has suffered an attack of apoplexy, and that as His Highness is otherwise in good health, and as his attack does not appear severe, he will recover all his faculties. Perhaps within a few weeks."

Dear God. She knew that her husband had once been so sick that he had almost died and that Messer Ambrogio had made his reputation by nursing him back to health. But that was before she had known him. Thereafter, except for an occasional fever, he had never been ill. This was so unexpected.

"Your Highness, he is in no danger. Messer Ambrogio suggests that you visit him regularly but do not encourage him to exert himself by attempting to speak. Your Highness, could you come with me into the antechamber?"

Beatrice squeezed her husband's hand and told him to rest and not to worry, that she was coming back shortly. But by the time she reached the antechamber she understood the real nature of the crisis.

"So it is true about the surrender of Novara," she told the Marchesino in a low voice.

He nodded. "Your Highness, Louis Duc d'Orleans has twenty thousand men a day's fast march from the gates of Milan. Some of his cavalry have already ridden through villages only an hour from here. The main force could be here by nightfall."

"And my husband will not be able to appear before his people to exhort them to defend the city." Beatrice remembered the story of her father lying near death, with the Venetian army camped in the ducal park just outside Ferrara, a tale she had heard more often than the *Pater Noster*. It had always sounded so unreal.

Beatrice noticed that the Marchesino was staring at her, waiting for her to dictate some course of action. Suddenly it occurred to her that none of her husband's advisers had been picked for their leadership ability. They had been selected because they were capable and informed in their limited areas of expertise. Now she was the regent, as her husband had specified in the event of his incapacitation. She was expected to lead.

"Who knows that my husband is . . . ill?"

"Your Highness, we arrived here in just two carriages. That was to avoid drawing attention to our party. When we carried your husband into his rooms, we kept a shroud over him to conceal his identity. We have been here for a half hour. Just minutes ago I received a note from Count Landriano indicating that he and the rest of the Council of Nobles have confirmed by their own means that Novara belongs to Orleans. The Council wishes to dispel the rumors that the Duke of Milan is dead or a prisoner of the French. Count Landriano insists that His Highness personally address the Council of Nobles in the Sala della Palla this afternoon. He maintains that this is the only way to prevent widespread panic in the city. If the people cannot be assured of your husband's leadership in this crisis, he warns, we will see Milan become a mob clamoring for immediate capitulation to the French at even the appearance of their army before the city gates. Of course what he means is that unless your husband is able to rally the city against the French, the Council of Nobles will greet Louis Duc d'Orléans with garlands and welcoming speeches."

Beatrice shook her head angrily. This was so much in the fickle Milanese character, always scampering eagerly behind Fortune's favorite, even more eagerly recasting their allegiances at the merest rumor of Fortune's scorn. Did they imagine that the French would loot and rape with less vehemence if the city surrendered without a fight?

"So we must assume that by nightfall the entire city will be demanding to see my husband."

When the Marchesino simply swallowed and nodded, Beatrice pursed her lips and stared at the floor. What she needed was a miracle. The miraculous recovery of her husband. Or perhaps Galeazz would be able to get sufficient forces to Novara to contain Orleans before Milan erupted with panic. But there had been no word of Galeazz's whereabouts; she was not certain that he even knew of the crisis. Her mind began to wander desperately in search of a solution. She recalled the smirking scrutiny of Louis Duc d'Orléans in Asti and wondered if he intended to make her one of the spoils of his conquest. She heard Polissena's ancient voice, rattling on about the war with Venice. But now she was interested. In that crisis rumors had swept Ferrara that her father was dead, and the frightened city had been on the verge of surrender to the Venetian mercenaries camped in the park. What had Mama done? She had brought the leading nobles to her husband's bedside to prove that he was still alive. And then she had stood on the garden wall and addressed the entire populace. She had challenged them to defend their city as she intended to, alone if necessary. . . .

"Very well, Marchesino," Beatrice said, looking directly at him. "We will prepare to defend the Castello against the French, and in my husband's name we will send word to every precinct of the city, calling on the people to assemble their weapons and stores in anticipation of an assault and siege. I want you, in my husband's name, to summon the Council of Nobles to the Castello, the appointed time to be nine o'clock this evening. At the very least my husband can persuade the Council that he is not dead and that his recovery can be expected. It will fall to me to persuade the people of Milan that in the meanwhile, I am capable of leading them against the French.''

Isabella learned about the crisis just minutes after Beatrice left her husband's bedchamber. She was in her son's room, part of her suite in the Ducal Court opposite the Rochetta, helping four-and-a-half-year-old Francesco with his Latin lessons; Francesco had been taking daily tutoring in Latin since shortly before his fourth birthday. Isabella's *vecchia*, Lucia, who seemed to pull secrets out of the Castello walls, came into the room and announced, "Il Moro is deathly ill. And it is true that Orleans is in Novara.''

An hour later, Lucia came back and told Isabella about the call to arms and the meeting of the Council of Nobles scheduled for nine o'clock in the evening. Isabella understood immediately that the Council of Nobles hoped to negotiate with the French, and that they probably would end up panicking and unconditionally surrender the city when the French army arrived. Beatrice, she realized, was making a desperate attempt to delay the inevitable.

Only a few minutes later, Isabella's older daughter, Bona, came running for her mother, one of her porcelain dolls in her arms. The child and the doll were dressed exactly alike, in little mock-Moorish dresses covered with tinsel-like *stringhe* and elaborate taffeta ruffles. "Stanzie fell,'' Bona said with a pout, holding up her doll for additional comforting. "Mama, when are the bad men coming here?''

With that Isabella made her decision. For the first time in almost eight months she could think with her old clarity and boldness. She was going to Germany. She could pack her valuables and take the children and a small household and be on the road while it was still light. They wouldn't get far before dark, but if they went north toward Lake Como, they would at least be able to spend the night safely in a village well outside the city walls; the French would be too busy with Milan to bother with the surrounding countryside. Once they got to Germany, Bianca Maria would give them refuge at her court. And perhaps the Emperor would eventually liberate Milan from the French and install Francesco as the new Duke. . . .

But she really didn't care about that. Wasn't it enough just to get out of Milan, where she had known nothing but sorrow and misfortune? She had always been the *forestiera* here. Now she was perfectly happy to leave Milan's fate to the Milanese. And to Beatrice. It occurred to her with no great satisfaction—or sadness—that Beatrice had been Duchess of Milan for less than three weeks. She called Lucia and gave her instructions on what to start packing.

She enjoyed the activity of preparing for her journey, feeling as if she had been napping for eight months and had suddenly awakened fresh and invigorated. If the Emperor should liberate all of Italy, she might even be able to get more than just Milan for Francesco. . . . She rummaged purposefully through her *guardaroba*, decisively and without lingering sentiment deciding what she would take and what she would leave. All of her wedding gifts would be left behind. She found several piles of white satin that had been used to drape her nuptial chamber and wished she had time to burn these things. Perhaps the French would.

By late afternoon she had almost finished with the packing. She was surprised that she wasn't at all fatigued. She was watching her pages carry a storage chest out of her bedchamber when Lucia came in again, her toothless gums working with agitation.

"Count Landriano has come to see you, Your Highness."

Isabella laughed. "Has he come to remove his daughter from her service as one of my ladies-in-waiting? I would think he has more pressing matters to concern himself with. But send him in." Isabella had hardly forgotten how Count Landriano had ridiculed the notion of her regency before the entire Council of Nobles. To see his distress would be a nice farewell.

She watched as Count Landriano advanced with the casual, almost lazy gait of a Milanese courtier artfully disguising his urgency. He wore a black steel breastplate and had a sword strapped around his hip.

"Count Landriano," Isabella said with husky-voiced sarcasm. "I'm surprised you aren't in full armor. It is indeed, as you recently said, 'a dangerous season.' I'm certain that the people of Milan are grateful to you for providing them a duke with such *sforza* in the face of this adversity." She smiled wryly at the pun on Il Moro's family name and its meaning, strength. "Certainly my little boy couldn't have responded with such resolution on hearing that his incompetent Captain General has let the French into Novara."

"How well informed is Your Highness as to Il Moro's condition?" Landriano asked in his piping, earnest voice.

"I know that he is in no condition to assume the burden you so confidently placed on his shoulders."

"Just so. Your Highness, I couldn't help but notice that you are packing for a journey."

"How astute. I'm going to Abbiategrasso."

Landriano shifted uncomfortably at Isabella's flippant belligerence; Abbiategrasso was halfway between Milan and Novara, hardly the direction any sane person would choose to travel. "Your Highness, may I address you in all candor?"

"You may. The question is whether you can."

"Your Highness, I will admit that I egregiously overestimated the capabilities of Il Moro. But you will recall that *I* only urged him to assume the title of Duke. The Emperor has made Il Moro Duke of Milan. But the Emperor is not here to defend his feudatory, and thanks to the Emperor's intemperate meddling in Italian affairs, Milan is now a headless state."

"The Duchess of Milan now heads the state."

"Your Highness, most of us who sit on the Council of Nobles do not believe that the Duchess of Milan is a suitable choice to lead us against the French. In all sincerity, Your Highness, we believe that you, acting in the name of your son, have the qualities required in this crisis."

Isabella immediately perceived the scheme behind Landriano's almost sarcastic "sincerity." She had never felt so clearheaded. "*Cacapensieri*," she snapped, curling her lip. "You think that I have the qualities required to go to the French and hysterically beg them not to burn the houses of Milan's noble families. Do you think Louis Duc d'Orléans would allow my boy to remain Duke of Milan, even if the Council of Nobles had the power to give him the title?"

Now it was Landriano's turn for a smug, patrician smile. "Your Highness, you are aware that the Venetians have an army of forty thousand men in the field. The Emperor is sending thirty thousand men over the mountains. Yes, Louis Duc d'Orléans will conquer Milan before these forces can rescue us. But we believe that if we do not resist, the French will treat us fairly. Certainly you and your children will not be harmed, particularly if your son has been designated Duke. The French have been very generous to heads of state who have capitulated to them without a fight. It is only when opposed that they are dangerous."

"I have already seen to it that my children will be safe."

"Of course, Your Highness. But let us just assume, for the sake of argument, that you permit the Council to designate your son as Duke of Milan. The French march in and confine you and your son to the Castello with all the privileges that you are currently enjoying." Landriano shrugged theatrically. "And then, when in a matter of days, weeks at the most, the forces of the League chase Louis Duc d'Orleans out of Milan, your son will still be Duke of Milan."

"My son will not have been invested by the Emperor."

"Do you think that the Emperor will refuse the opportunity to make another profit on the same title he sold Il Moro?"

"And of course the Council will designate me as my son's regent."

"Of course."

Isabella's eyes were like polished jade. "I will give you my answer when the Council meets at nine o'clock this evening, Count Landriano."

"Your Highness." Vincenzo Calmeta whispered in her ear. Beatrice's secretary had come into her husband's bedchamber so quietly that she had not even heard him. She turned. Her eyes were adjusted to the dim light, and she could clearly see Calmeta's gray, anxious face. "How is he, Your Highness?"

Beatrice shook her head and fought the jagged constriction in her throat. She had vowed to herself that she wouldn't cry until this was over. If she appeared weak, everything would be lost. But her husband was worse. Far worse. His breathing was an ominous, light rattle, and his eyes no longer recognized her. They were alive, perhaps awake, but what they saw she could only imagine. He had retreated to some place on the border between life and death. Now only he could decide in which direction he would journey.

"Messer Ambrogio bled him an hour ago," Beatrice said. "Perhaps that will bring him back. But I must assume that it is no longer advisable to allow the Council of Nobles to see him."

Calmeta nodded agreement. "Your Highness," he whispered. "I just returned from riding to the Duomo and back. If you will come into the antechamber I will tell what I have seen and heard."

Beatrice lit a lamp in the antechamber, one of Leonardo's flickerless, water-filled glass globes. The long summer twilight had finally conceded to night. In a few minutes she would have to meet with the Council of Nobles.

Calmeta's jaw was set with youthful determination, but there was something tragic written on his face, almost like a fine, dark veil that lay over his high forehead and soft poet's eyes. "Your Highness . . ." He stopped and shook his head slightly, incredulously. "Your Highness, it no longer matters whether or not the French attack tonight. We will have blood in the streets of Milan regardless." Calmeta gestured helplessly with his hands. "Madness. Madness out there. There are rumors that your husband is dead or a prisoner of the French, rumors that he and the Emperor will arrive within hours with a hundred thousand men. The city has split into two irreconcilable factions. The armorers, tradesmen, and laborers want to resist the French, and they are calling on your husband to lead them. The merchants and nobility insist that your husband is dead. They want to open the city to the French in the hopes of preserving their property, and they are organizing an army of *bravi* and thugs to oppose the tradesmen and laborers. Your Highness, the entire city is armed. I have seen a dozen men dead in the streets already. There are fires along the Via Torino. And the night has only begun."

Now Beatrice understood that Fortune had given her everything in the way a drunken duke might seat his *buffone* in his place at the head of the table, so that everyone could laugh at the clown briefly transformed into a prince. The Bitch of Fate was an overwhelming opponent, mean and capricious when merely left alone, incalculably furious and vindictive when challenged. All Beatrice wanted to do now was to bring her children up here and take

them into her husband's darkened bedchamber and spend the final
hours together with her family. That was all that was left of her
mythical realm of Everything, all she could hope to preserve. And
then she had an irrational thought that to her was entirely compelling in its logic, so much so that it swept her mind clear of
everything except fear. *I can't let Mama see me give up. Whatever
happens, I can't let Mama see me be afraid.*

The Duchess of Milan entered the Sala della Palla from the double
doors on the ground floor. She had come alone, feeling that if she
brought along any of her husband's advisers she would merely
offer proof of the argument the Council obviously intended to
present—that she was incapable of governing on her own. The
surly pages at the doors did not wear red-white-and-blue Sforza
colors. Apparently they were the Council members' hirelings.

The Sala della Palla was inadequately lit by wax tapers hurriedly
pressed into the sconces along the walls. Some tennis rackets and
balls had been left on the floor. No more than twenty men were
assembled in the center of the vast, empty hall. The lighting was
too poor to enable her to recognize any of the faces. The quiet
sibilance of their discussion drifted into the vaults high overhead
like prayers in a cathedral. Even that noise fell away when she
started across the floor. The wooden soles of her slippers clattered
awkwardly.

Her initial encouragement at the small size of the group quickly
vanished. She remembered what Vincenzo had just told her about
the nobility organizing an army to oppose the anti-French faction.
Obviously most of the Council's members were preparing to fight
their fellow citizens so that they could surrender to a foreign invader. The Council had simply sent a small embassy to announce
the change in government. Suddenly she hated everything about
them. She wished she had a knife.

For an instant she wondered who the woman was. Then of
course she knew. There was something unmistakable about Eesh's
posture, even in semidarkness. She wore a black dress with a high
collar and her usual black headband.

Each man respectfully dipped to one knee. She could smell

their perfume. She recognized some faces. Landriano, of course. He was a weather vane. Which way would he point tomorrow? Count Borromeo, father of Isabella's lady-in-waiting Caterina. He was a vicious opportunist with a hatchet-sharp nose and puckered, fishlike lips.

Isabella curtsied and Beatrice curtsied in return. For a moment she was transfixed by Eesh's face. Eesh was pale, but her eyes glittered in the candlelight. Her lips were brilliant, rich with color. She was so perfectly composed. There was no trace of anger, no sense of triumph. Just those pure, white, indescribably beautiful features. Beatrice thought, This is how Dante's Beatrice looked when he found her waiting for him in the Earthly Paradise, ten years after her death. Purified, resurrected, beautiful beyond any memory.

Count Landriano began to speak, his voice fluty and his eyes wavering in the candlelight. "Your Highness, the Council is deeply saddened by your husband's terrible affliction. You can be assured that countless candles are burning in our churches and chapels this evening in supplication for his eventual recovery. However, Your Highness, your husband is presently in no condition to defend his state, the state that he alone has governed for the past ten years. In the absence of his peerless guidance, we can hardly expect our citizens to resist the most formidable army Milan has faced since the Lombards battered our gates a thousand years ago. Therefore, the Council has determined that the people of Milan will be best served if we negotiate with the French rather than take arms against them."

"You are talking about capitulation, not negotiation."

"We are counseling prudence in the absence of the forceful leadership we had expected your husband to provide. The French have already established that they treat fairly with those who do not oppose them."

"Then apparently you have an curious affliction of your hearing, Count Landriano. It obviously strikes you whenever the atrocities committed by the French in Naples are discussed. There is no one in Italy, with the exception perhaps of the hermits of Saint Jerome, who does not know how the people of Naples have suffered. Particularly the women and children."

Count Landriano's face constricted, as if he had encountered a disagreeable odor. "Your Highness, there are always claims of these atrocities. That you choose to believe them underscores the correctness of the decision we have had to make. Your Highness, your clearly stated disregard for the French makes you a poor choice to negotiate with Louis Duc d'Orléans for the safety of the city. We rather think that by designating the son of the late Duke of Milan as our Duke during this time of crisis, we will present to the French a more . . . moderate posture."

"So we will have two Dukes of Milan. My husband, the Duke invested by the German Emperor, and Francesco, Duke of Milan by order of the Council of Nobles. Of course when Louis Duc d'Orléans arrives, the question will be moot. Orleans already considers himself the Duke of Milan, and once he is in possession of Milan's treasury, I believe he will be able to purchase his title from the Emperor."

"I don't believe that the armies of the League will permit Louis Duc d'Orléans to make that purchase," Isabella suddenly offered.

Beatrice turned to face her cousin. Now she understood the deal in its entirety. When the armies of the League finally forced Orleans out, Isabella intended to purchase the investiture of her son as Duke of Milan. "So you will be the buyer," she told her cousin.

Isabella stepped forward, her expression still composed, almost beatific. "You must know that I don't want this for myself. I want it for my son. For our people."

There was no sarcasm in her tone, just a sad, strangely sensual resignation. And yet of course it was a lie. Beatrice wondered if she had sounded just as insincere when she had said the same things to Eesh just weeks ago: "I never wanted this for myself. . . ." Of course she had. Of course they both had. Beatrice was seized with an impulse to knock Eesh to the floor and settle this between them once and for all. But she was equally restrained by the curious feeling that somehow it would be wrong to disturb Eesh's beauty, that beneath Eesh's deceit and terrible ambition was something pure and exquisite that should not be destroyed.

"Fortune is a bitch," Isabella told Beatrice with a slight, careless tilt of her head. "Tonight she is my bitch."

Beatrice turned back to Count Landriano. "Does the Council intend to make me their prisoner?"

Landriano seemed truly shocked, even indignant. "Indeed no. You belong with your husband. Your Highness must understand that the Council has only the greatest personal affection for you and your husband. We deeply regret—"

One of the men who had been guarding the door charged pell-mell across the Sala della Palla like a tennis player in full pursuit of a ball. Dispensing with all formalities, the guard shouted, "The Castello is under attack!"

Everyone looked to the big arched windows overlooking the moat. If the French were coming by way of Novara, they would first assault this northwest face of the Castello. Several of the Council members slowly walked a few steps toward the windows, crouching as if preparing to flatten themselves when crossbow bolts and cannonballs came flying out of the darkness.

The forest was dimly visible in the last hint of twilight. Nothing stirred in that dark wood.

The guard watched for a moment, his mouth open. Then he shouted once again. "Not the French! The Castello is under attack from within the city!"

The Council members and their guards rushed through the court-yard of the Rochetta and crossed the narrow drawbridge that allowed direct access from the Rochetta to the Piazza d'Armi. Beatrice and Isabella, suddenly forgotten in the panic, followed. The huge central court was dotted with flaming torches held by scurrying guards; lights also moved along the defensive galleries high atop the surrounding wings of the Castello. As they crossed the Piazza d'Armi, Beatrice saw clusters of Castello guards pushing artillery pieces mounted on two-wheeled carriages—long, pipelike culverins and short, blunt-snouted mortars and bombards.

The arched gateway directly beneath the soaring central tower glowed with torchlight; the portcullis had been lowered and the drawbridge was already up, raised quickly by huge, counter-weighted wooden beams. Beatrice could hear the roar of the city, a vast, discordant, ghostly chorus. It was as if the terrible city of Dis, the citadel of the damned, lay beyond that gate.

She followed the Councillors up the narrow, zigzagging staircase that led to the spired turret atop the central tower. The Councillors pushed open the door at the third-story landing and went out onto the open terrace. The main shaft of the tower rose into the darkness behind them. Before them was a high brick wall notched with rectangular crenellations so that crossbows and artillery could be fired from protected positions.

The noise was visceral now as Beatrice slowly walked to one of the crenellations, a cold fluid inside her, and she had to force herself to get close enough to look out. The great wheel of Milan lay before her in the night. She drew in and held a breath, for a moment captivated by the spectacle. The piazza in front of the Castello was a phosphorescent lake, teeming with thousands of blazing torches. The Via degli Armorai, the central street leading into the piazza, was a river of torchlights. So were many of the other main streets of the city. Scattered in the darkness surrounding these rivers of light were hundreds of huge, boiling orange flares marking burning houses and *palazzi*.

The shouting rose beneath her, and Beatrice looked down. There must have been fifteen thousand men in the piazza below, many armored with steel breastplates and helmets; some wore entire suits of armor. Most carried a torch in one hand and a pike or sword in the other. They shouted improvised battle cries as they swarmed like belligerent fireflies toward the head of the street that ran from Sant'Ambrogio to the Castello, trying to block a phalanx of armed men attempting to push into the piazza.

Beatrice watched the skirmish with sudden, knifing horror. The attackers surged into the defenders, pikes and swords thrusting, torches hurled onto the heads of the enemy or swung as flaming clubs. The torches quickly began to dim, and the conflict compressed into a dark, ugly, writhing mass. Suddenly the attackers retreated back into the street and the men in the piazza rushed forward, jabbing with torches and pikes. At least a dozen men lay on the cobblestones in the wake of the retreat. Dark slicks of blood glimmered beside them.

Dead men, Beatrice thought. In the winking of an eye she had increased twelvefold her catalogue of corpses. Dead men like Gian. Men who once had felt a woman's warmth in the night, who now hadn't even a hand to clutch. Their blood still hot, everything else black and cold. This is war, Beatrice thought, sickened and feverish with horror and shame. *This is what Mama meant. The war has finally come home to Milan. The war I started.* In a dreadful instant she saw the entire piazza dark, covered with black corpses. *When would the babies start dying?*

"Moro!"

Beatrice wasn't certain what she heard at first. But then the victory chant became unmistakable.

"Moro! Moro! Moro!"

The men defending the piazza began to move wagons to all the entrances, tipping them over to barricade the streets. All the streets except the Via degli Armorai. Now Beatrice understood. These men were armorers, wearing their inventory to defend their city. They obviously hoped that Il Moro would appear to lead them against the French; apparently they had discounted the rumors of his illness or demise. Their attackers, the men surging up the streets, were the hirelings of the Council of Nobles, whose intention, of course, was to take the piazza and eliminate any threat to an orderly surrender when the French appeared.

The Councillors high above the piazza were gravely alarmed by the demonstration in favor of Il Moro. They crowded at one of the crenellations, pointing to the piazza, gesturing and shouting to one another. Beatrice felt completely vacant. She knew that there was something she should do to stop this carnage. But whatever she did in this life Fortune twisted and made a mockery of. So she would do nothing. Almost in a trance, she watched the Councillors discuss their strategy. She drew closer, with some morbid, detached curiosity, wanting to hear. *Let them choose,* she dreamily instructed herself. *Let them game with Fortune.*

It all seemed fascinating and meaningless, like a strange puppet show. Count Borromeo, chopping with his hand, his hatchet nose snapping forward, his puckered mouth spitting vehemently: "Get the artillery up here, and we will blow them to offal in five minutes! Get the bombards and mortars up here!" Count Landriano, horrified, but nodding agreement. The guards, running to execute the order. Eesh, watching.

As if an angel's hand had passed in front of her face, Beatrice realized what she had to do. She walked over to Isabella. Eesh's face was as serene as the moon, her eyes impossible to read.

"Eesh, if you will agree to resist the French, I will support you."

Now Isabella blinked. "I don't think so, Toto," she said with unreal calm. "I don't need your support, and I don't believe that it is possible to resist the French."

"Yes, you do, Eesh. You do need my support. You need me to tell these armorers that my husband is too ill to govern them and that he has sanctioned Francesco as the new Duke, as he had originally intended after Gian died. Because if I don't tell them that, these armorers will fight the Council's men, and Milan will be burned to cinders before the French even get here. You and Francesco will rule over a city of embers and corpses. Thousands of these men out here will be dead. Thousands of women and children trampled in the streets and burned in their homes. Thousands of dead babies."

Isabella looked out toward the city. Her profile was marvelous, as firm and elegant as an antique Roman bust. She turned back to Beatrice but said nothing.

"Eesh, no one has fought the French yet. Florence, Rome, Naples—they just gave up and opened the gates. And all the big guns are with the King's army. Orleans probably doesn't have siege guns in Novara. They expect we will surrender without a fight. If we go to the walls we can hold them off for weeks at least. Eesh, if we don't fight the French we will fight each other. The armorers are not going to be persuaded to put down their arms and submit to the French. They would not do it even if my husband appeared and told them to."

Isabella nodded very slowly. "Come with me." She put her hand under Beatrice's elbow and led her to the side of Count Landriano, who appeared clammy and distracted; he nervously watched Count Borromeo bark orders at the guards. Isabella waited imperiously until she had Landriano's full attention.

"Her Highness has no wish to see bloodshed in the streets of Milan," Isabella said. "She has decided to tell the armorers that her husband can no longer continue in his duties and that he endorses my son, Francesco, as Duke. I believe that will put an end to this disagreeable business."

Count Landriano was visibly relieved. He smiled gratefully at Beatrice. "I think Your Highness is making a very noble gesture.

Very noble indeed. I would, however, suggest that you make your announcement quickly, before Count Borromeo has his artillery in place."

Beatrice looked at Isabella; her eyes were dark, faintly silvered, the Bay of Naples in moonlight. Her chin was tucked down slightly. Beatrice realized that she had loved Eesh and hated Eesh and had never known her at all. But it was far too late now to ask if she could trust her.

She took a torch from one of the guards. The Councillors were all looking at her now. Even Count Borromeo had suspended his campaign.

The guard helped her climb up into the notchlike crenellation. She straightened up slowly. She was standing on a brick ledge somewhat more than an arm-span wide and almost as long. Advancing closer to the edge, she could see the moat directly beneath her, black water shimmering with reflected torchlight. She placed her left hand on the thick stone wall beside her, steadying herself. With her right hand she waved the torch over her head. The burning pitch spit sparks at her.

The armorers had been watching the Castello for any sign of an announcement, and they quickly saw her signal. But it was some time before the noise level fell in the piazza. And even then a haunting chorus of anger and chaos came from the outlying streets, a distant dirge. A voice inside her said to someone else: I'm not afraid, I'm not giving up. I'm doing what is right. My husband's title and my son's inheritance are not worth a thousand dead babies. They are not worth one dead baby.

"I am the Duchess of Milan!" The force of her shout gave her a moment of vertigo. It was so quiet in the aftermath that she could hear something else now, the dull whoosh of the fires burning throughout the city. "My husband cannot appear before you because he is seriously ill!" A low, angry rumble began, and she waved the torch frantically to signal that she had more to say.

The crowd became silent again. Beatrice closed her eyes and blinked at her welling tears. She had not had time to think how hard this would be. She had never imagined that there would be a time when she could not force herself to speak. But now it was almost as though a hand were clutching her throat.

Eesh was beside her, seemingly materialized like a dark spirit.

She lightly touched Beatrice's arm. A strange contact, almost soothing, encouraging. But of course she would. I have to say it, Beatrice told herself, in that moment identifying a hundred things about herself she had never known, among them how desperately she loved being Duchess of Milan.

Somehow she forced the first word out, telling herself that each moment of hesitation might bring about the deaths of innocent people. "Accordingly—"

Suddenly Eesh clutched her arm, a tight, startling grip, strong enough to seize her bodily, to hurl her into the darkness. Why now? Beatrice asked with the leisurely clarity that precedes catastrophe; why not wait until I have endorsed her son before she pushes me off? Then she realized she could shove her torch right in Eesh's face. . . .

But Eesh was pulling her back. Away from the edge. Eesh moved in front of her, and all she could see was her cousin's broad shoulders and long, dark hair, the subtle red tint fiery in the torchlight.

Isabella stood there for what seemed a long while, entirely still, almost as if she were debating whether to leap. Then her shoulders heaved and she shouted, "I have just come from the Duke of Milan's sickbed!" Her voice was astonishingly powerful, the words seeming to ring off the black dome of the sky. "His condition is much improved! He will recover fully within days and lead us to victory over the French! Accordingly, I ask that every citizen of Milan who has taken up arms tonight in hope of making my son their duke now abandon that cause! To those who would use my son to effect a disgraceful surrender to the invader, let me say I will put a knife into my breast and my son's breast before I will permit that to happen! We must be of one body and one soul to resist the French! And we must resist the French!"

Mysteriously, Beatrice listened to these words without surprise, with a serene feeling that she had heard them before. This was Eesh, here in these few shouted sentences, all of her complexities and contradictions. The lies and the truths, the histrionics and the heartfelt sentiment, the stealth and the sincerity. And ultimately, the goodness. Standing on that ledge, Eesh had discovered the truth of her own soul.

Eesh turned to her, and now Beatrice experienced the shock

she should have felt at Eesh's words. She had expected the beatific smile of a saint, a supernatural glow, a glimpse of God's face. Instead there was a terror in Eesh's eyes, a fear of some unspeakable torment, as if she had thrown herself off the tower and some malignant deity had suspended her an instant before her dreams ended against the pavement. And then Beatrice realized that as hard as it had been for her to think of surrendering her dreams moments earlier, it must have been a thousand times harder for Eesh actually to do it.

Beatrice took Isabella in her arms. Eesh was limp, dead again, the rest of her life thrown into those few words of self-definition.

The armorers in the piazza responded with a rising clamor of confusion. An armorer in a brightly polished steel breastplate, standing just beneath the tower on the grassy slope beside the moat, shouted to be heard. The crowd noise subsided, and soon only the eerily whooshing fires were audible. Beatrice watched with relief as the phalanxes of armed men in the streets pulled back and dwindled. Milanese would not fight Milanese tonight.

"That is all very well, Your Highnesses!" the man in the breastplate shouted up to the duchesses. "But who will lead us against the French tonight?"

"My husband has designated me as regent in his absence!" Beatrice shouted. "I will lead you against the French!"

There was a moment of silence. Then whistles and hoots of derision, followed by the harsh tremolo of massed laughter. Beatrice felt as if their torches were burning her face. The people of Ferrara hadn't laughed at Mama. Was Mama laughing too?

The armorers' spokesman again shouted to be heard. "All very well, Your Highness. But how do you intend to do that!"

Again the laughter.

Beatrice turned to Isabella and told her, "I'm going down there." She scrambled off the stone perch and helped Eesh down. The Councillors watched them as they had the entire drama, incredulously, powerless to intervene in front of the entire city. These were men who always did their business in private. Count Landriano's mouth was open.

Beatrice steadied Isabella. "Are you all right, Eesh? I have to go down there."

Isabella nodded. "Toto, I can't go down there with you. I just can't. I'm too tired. I am so tired now."

"I know, Eesh." Beatrice hugged Isabella again and kissed her cold, smooth face. "What you just did is more courageous than anything I will ever be able to do in my life. Thank you, Eesh. I know it is so little to say. You have saved us all." She turned to a guard. "See that Her Highness is taken to her rooms. And do not send for Messer Ambrogio. Find her *vecchia*, Lucia, to look after her."

Count Borromeo presented himself in front of Beatrice. "Your Highness, you must not go down there. I warn you that I have my artillery in place and intend—"

Beatrice thrust her face up at Count Borromeo so forcefully that he stepped back. "*You* do not warn the regent for the state of Milan. I warn *you*, Count Borromeo, that if you do not go back to your *palazzo* and stay there until my husband recovers, I will have you hanged for treason and stick your head up there!" She pointed to the brass spire far above them.

Count Borromeo meekly allowed Count Landriano to take him aside. No one else tried to prevent Beatrice from descending the steps to the gatehouse.

"Lower the footbridge," Beatrice told the guards on duty in the gatehouse. The footbridge was just to the right of the main drawbridge; it was so narrow that two men would have difficulty walking across it abreast. The timber hoists squealed and the chains rattled as the bridge came down. Beatrice opened a door in the gatehouse wall, entered a short brick passageway, and turned a corner. Through a small arched gateway she could see the torches in the piazza.

The bridge had no railing, and she again experienced a momentary vertigo as she glanced down at the water. She looked up at the men waiting for her across the moat. The torchlight gave a sheen to armor, to unshaven faces slick with sweat, to hard sinewy forearms.

The armorers' spokesman stood at the end of the bridge as if challenging her even to step into the piazza. She decided that he would have to throw her into the moat to stop her. She was within two steps. He had a tough, almost terra-cotta-colored face, seemingly fired to a glazed hardness by the heat of the forges. She did not slow her step.

The armorer stepped back. He had never seen a duchess this close; she was like some strange new species that had suddenly turned out to be more aggressive than he had expected.

Having reached the pavement, Beatrice reasoned that she had just begun a dialogue with these gentlemen. "You want to know how I intend to lead you against the French?" she shouted, her voice carrying throughout the piazza. "I do not intend to lead you against the French! I intend to go alone to the west gate and wait for the French! I am a fair shot with a light bow! Perhaps I could borrow one from one of you! But should any man here wish to join me in the sport of shooting Frenchmen, I will be glad to wager my skill against his!"

The armorers laughed, but just grudgingly. Beatrice realized that the moment was slipping away. She turned to the west and began to walk through the crowd. The men towered over her, their pikes crossing above her head like a lethal bower. At first they moved back to let her pass, but as she reached the outskirts of the piazza there was some shoving, and she was jostled a bit. Some of them had been wounded slightly: a cut eye, a split lip, an arm bandaged with a bloody rag. She was almost to the street. More men shoved just in front of her, some of them swigging from wineskins. Then the crowd cleared out.

A dead man lay on the pavement no more than a step away, trampled and tossed like a rag, his head and a leg at crazy angles. Next to his battered head was a pool of blood like a purple, crusted pudding.

Beatrice's stomach heaved and her legs swayed. You can't faint! she screamed at herself. If you faint, everything is finished! Then a rush of strength came almost like a hand at her back, and she walked past the corpse.

She entered the street that led to the city's west gate. The Councillors' army that had filled the street minutes before had vanished. A wagon smoldered in front of a shuttered shop arcade. Another dead man lay sprawled on his back, a dog lapping at his bloody face. She forced herself to walk on. Then she heard the noise behind her, a rattling of armor and the slapping of soft leather soles against cobblestones. She did not look back but squared her shoulders the way her mother would have done and quickened her pace.

When Beatrice reached the blocky brick towers of the Pusterla di Sant'Ambrogio, Milan's westernmost gate, she finally turned around. An army jammed the street behind her, backed up as far as she could see. The armorers had all followed her.

Beatrice stood atop one of the towers flanking the double arches of the Pusterla di Sant'Ambrogio gate. Three large bombards had been hoisted to the flat terrace atop the tower, massive iron snouts pointing west. Neat pyramids of spherical stone projectiles stood beside each gun. Twenty or so armorers leaned against the notched brick parapet, looking to the west, waiting for some sign of the French.

Beatrice had seen only demons out there, the vague, shadowy horsemen that periodically dashed through the darkness. She knew that these hallucinations were due to fatigue; it was only an hour or so before dawn, and she'd had no sleep after the longest, most tumultuous day of her life. But her anxious vigil was also haunted by more substantial uncertainties. She had sent three riders to Novara in the course of the night, each with instructions to come back as soon as he had sighted the French army on the road. And if the messengers did not encounter the French on the road, they had been instructed to enter Novara and find out if the French army was preparing to march on Milan. The first messenger had left almost seven hours before. Enough time to enter Novara and come back. Perhaps he had been captured. Perhaps all three messengers had been captured hours earlier by a French army waiting right out there in the darkness, preparing to attack at first light.

All along the immense brick escarpment of the city wall armorers leaned against the parapets, pikes in their arms, crossbows rested atop the merlons. But the defense wasn't as formidable as it appeared. The wall was centuries old, and the city had long ago outgrown it; tiled rooftops spread out to the west a considerable distance beyond the Pusterla di Sant'Ambrogio gate. Even Il Moro's new ducal chapel, Santa Maria delle Grazie, had been built outside the city walls, its dome another phantom shape in the darkness several streets away. To facilitate passage between the suburbs and the inner city, the wall had been knocked down or pierced with unfortified gates in dozens of places. Wealth had been considered Milan's best defense against invasion. Now Milan's only defense might be the pretense that the city was defended.

Beatrice had also sent a steady stream of messengers back and forth between the Castello. They reported that her husband had improved substantially; Messer Ambrogio attributed the miracle to a tonic mixed with finely ground pearls. Whatever the cause, that was one burden mercifully lightened. The messengers also told her that Isabella was sleeping. Again she saw Eesh turning back from the precipice, the face of a woman who had just torn out her own heart. Was that the price Eesh had paid to redeem her innocence? Beatrice wondered what price she would have to pay to redeem her own.

Some armorers shouted and pointed to the darkened street extending west from the wall. Everyone hushed. The sound was a massive clattering, hoofbeats on cobblestones. Weary bodies tensed and weapons rattled. A single torch came out of the darkness, moving toward them. No one relaxed. The messengers had been told to carry a light if they returned while it was still dark, so that they wouldn't be shot.

The rider halted his heavily lathered horse directly beneath the tower. "Your Highness!" he shouted up to Beatrice, his voice quavering with fatigue. "I left Novara three hours ago. The French army has learned from their own patrols that Milan is defended, so they have stopped their advance and are taking over virtually every house in Novara to quarter their troops. That would confirm what I heard as rumor, that they now intend to wait in Novara until the King himself can bring his army north to reinforce them!"

Incredible, Beatrice thought. Orleans was a smirking fool. Tonight he'd had Milan for the plucking. But the armies of the League would be here to defend Milan long before the French King arrived weeks from now—if he ever did. For a moment Beatrice enjoyed the sheer exhilaration of winning, of beating Louis Duc d'Orléans with nothing more than a ruse and a boast. Then she saw the sobering cost of her victory. For the men lying dead in the streets of Milan, this had been no game.

The news from Novara spread up and down the walls and backward to the Castello, a rising chorus of shouts and cheers and exuberant profanity. Within minutes a great buzzing storm of celebration rose above the city. Then the armorers nearest to Beatrice began to chant her name. "Beatrice! Beatrice! Duchessa! Duchessa!" The chant soon spread throughout the city. "Beatrice! Duchessa!" Again and again, the rolling thunder of adulation and respect.

Beatrice listened, too stunned and tired to be truly moved, dimly thinking that she would always remember this moment. Suddenly she could hear Polissena telling tales of war again, but this time about her instead of Mama, and she started to laugh out loud, almost screaming with hysterical release, conjuring an absurd image of Polissena growing eternally older and more wizened but never dying, outliving them all, telling their great-grandchildren for the thousandth time how the Duchess of Milan stood on the city walls and kept the French in Novara. . . .

Her cathartic laughter was abruptly halted by a feeling so strange that her neck tingled. She was alone again, despite the continuing refrains of her name, as alone as she'd been when she first started to walk to this gate, but now there was a great peace and freedom in her loneliness. And then she saw Mama. Not a vision of some corporeal or even spectral Mama, but a more profound inner image, an understanding so complete that at that moment they might have been sharing the same soul. For the first time in her life she could see Mama without prejudice or resentment, so clearly, so wholly, her flaws and all her far more considerable virtues. Now she could see why Mama had had to leave her in Naples, how Mama had put aside the interests of her own child to save thousands of children. And she could feel the pain and guilt Mama had suffered because of it. She could experience the depth of Mama's love for her, for the first time see how proud Mama had been of her. She could even feel how proud of her Mama would have been tonight.

Mama, I understand, she responded inwardly. I finally understand everything you did. I forgive you, Mama; can you ever forgive me? But the answer was so obvious. "Oh, God, Mama, I love you so, so much," she murmured. "But you always knew. Now I know you did."

It slowly faded, this intimacy Beatrice had never shared with her mother while she had been alive. Their reunion had been as passionate as a homecoming after a long absence, to be followed by the more gentle comfort of knowing that Mama would always be with her, would never leave her again.

Beatrice looked out into the gray genesis of dawn. In the distance she could vaguely see the steeples of the nearest village churches. "I know your dream, Mama," she whispered into the ongoing din of celebration. "I know it isn't finished. As much as anyone, I am responsible for starting this war. And now I must find some way to end it."

C H A P T E R

52

Extract of a letter of Francesco Gonzaga, Marquis of Mantua and Captain General of the Armies of the League of Venice, to Isabella d'Este da Gonzaga, Marquesa of Mantua. Fornovo, 5 July 1495

. . . We have encamped upon the right side of the Taro River, on a slope that affords our defense. This morning the French established their camp upon the left bank, and to continue their retreat to the north they must now cross the river and encounter the armies of the League. Thus I find myself on the eve of battle in command of the greatest army Italy has ever seen. My mission, as God wills it, is not merely to resist the French but to exterminate them. . . .

Fornovo, 6 July 1495

Rodolfo Gonzaga leaned next to the ear of his nephew Francesco Gonzaga and shouted against the roar of the rain: "There is no crossing!"

492

The two men stood in their stirrups and looked out across the Taro River. At this time of year the Taro was usually little more than a brook meandering through a rock-strewn wash on its journey from the Apennine Mountains to the Po River. But on this morning the Taro was a gray torrent several hundred paces across, its turbid surface roiling from the rain that swept across it in great, undulating curtains.

Francesco Gonzaga, Captain General of the Armies of the League of Venice, pushed up the visor of his helmet and glared into the stinging deluge. With his pugnacious lips and flaring nostrils, he looked like something half-man, half-beast. "Fortune is a woman!" he shouted. "She gives herself to the man who snatches her by the hair! We're going across!"

Francesco raised his arm to signal the elemental force at his back, ten thousand elite shock troops. Almost a thousand of them represented the cream of Italian nobility, sheathed like the Marquis and his uncle from head to toe in beautifully tooled suits of armor. The knights were supported by light cavalry armed with crossbows, and an enormous body of footmen, vaunted Greek mercenaries called stradiots, their ranks bristling with pikes three times as long as an average man's height.

Rodolfo Gonzaga put his spurs to his horse. The big white Barbary stallion, bred in Francesco's stables—considered the best in Italy—stepped off a shallow embankment into water almost to its belly. The cold torrent rushed into Rodolfo's iron-plated shoes. He thought of the countless battles he'd been in; never in weather like this. Rodolfo had inherited the town of Castiglione from his mother, Barbara of Brandenburg, who had come from Germany to marry Lodovico III Gonzaga, the grandfather of the current Marquis of Mantua. Not content with the modest income from his property, Rodolfo had always made his living as a *condottiere*. It was the most glorious life he could imagine. The battles were great pageants, the armies meeting and acknowledging one another like opponents in a joust, then wheeling across the countryside in intricate, chesslike maneuvers, a contest of wits and horsemanship that was inevitably decided when one side found itself overmatched and simply retired from the field. In a lifetime of campaigns, Rodolfo could count on the fingers of one hand the men he had actually seen die in combat. Of course he'd seen the corpses of many noncombatants, but these he attributed to renegade mercenary infantry, peasant soldiers robbing and raping their fellow rustics. These deaths did nothing to tarnish what his nephew Francesco had so aptly described as "a gentlemen's game of skill."

Now the greatest game of skill ever played in Italy was about to take place, and Rodolfo was to be denied the sheer visual spectacle of it by this untimely deluge. Rodolfo had even counseled against the attack, suggesting that they at least wait until they could see. But Francesco had pointed out that the French gunners would be unable to keep their powder dry in these rains. The battle would thus be won with intellect and invention, not the brute force of mindless machines.

The water surged up to his horse's flanks, and the mighty current sucked at Rodolfo's legs, trying to pull them from his stirrups. He dug his spurs in hard, keeping his legs in position and his horse moving. There were no distinct sounds to the huge movement of men at his back, only the vast rattling of rain, river, and steel.

The water got no deeper or swifter even in the center of the torrent. The worst obstacle to the crossing was the left bank, a steep incline covered with tangled, thorny vines. After making the ascent, Rodolfo looked back briefly. The pikes of the stradiots covered the river like a bed of giant, prickly reeds.

They rode along the rocky slope at the base of the low hills—invisible in the rain—that crowded the valley of the Taro into a rubble-strewn strip ranging from a quarter to three quarters of a mile in width, widening as they rode north. They skirted a tiny village, a forlorn cluster of farmhouses and barns illuminated in a sharp yellow burst of lightning. Thunder rolled through the valley, followed by another pulse of light, this time brighter, almost white. For an instant they could see directly ahead almost the entire configuration of the French army—the glinting little figures of the French knights, the brown, huddled shapes of the pack mules and baggage wagons.

"Some of their heavy cavalry have come back to defend the baggage train!" Francesco shouted. "When we are done with them, the entire army's rear will be as naked as a whore's ass!" Francesco had sent a third of his forces to make a diversionary attack on the vanguard of the French army, while his main shock force would gut the slogging underbelly of baggage carts, supply wagons, and camp followers. Once the French realized that they were caught in the Italian pincers, they would quickly surrender.

The lightning came every few seconds now, each flash presenting a closer, clearer image of the French knights. Their formation was disordered, offering no coherent line of defense. A group of archers clustered around one of the knights, a small man wearing a tunic of white silk over his armor. In the next flash of lightning the gold crosses embroidered on his tunic had a magical phosphorescence.

"*Cacasangue!*" Francesco shouted. "The King has come back to guard his baggage train! This will be over in one minute!"

For Rodolfo the rest came too quickly for thought or fear. Visor locked down and lance couched against his breastplate, no fumbling: he had done it a thousand times at jousts. The narrowed horizon through the slit in his visor. The slowly gathering charge. The crossbowmen kneeling, firing one salvo, the glint of a bolt caught by lightning, no time for them to reload. Gold crosses, closer, closer. Then a French knight blocking the gold. Leaning forward, feet into the stirrups. The numbing shock in his hand and forearm and armpit. The lance broken, dropped, sword out. Everything a reaction. Francesco to his left, hammering with his sword, only one man between him and the gold crosses. Turning to the dull thudding blows on his back.

Down. How? No memory of the fall. Just the shock of being on the ground. Everything crazy above, rapid glimpses of steel and horses' bellies and silk saddle cloths in a brilliant fusillade of lightning. Blood. A shadow passing over him and then the pain in his leg, shooting straight to the top of his head, then gone, leaving a curiously bearable throbbing.

Everything slowed down. The battle had swept past him. Rodolfo's visor had been knocked loose, and he could see off to his left. The still, dark belly of a war-horse rose up over his legs. He realized that the horse that had fallen on him was dead. He tried to move his leg, and the pain shot into his head again. He would have to wait for someone to help him. He could see dozens of men and horses, all down like him. His world was strangely horizontal. God, the tales he would tell and hear tonight.

The pounding on his armor startled him, and he moved his leg, to predictable effect. But it was hail. He looked up. The lightning flashed and the thickly descending hailstones had an eerie, snowlike, soft whiteness. He closed his eyes, and the hailstones rattled around him, a few striking his face hard. He could see the lightning going on and off through his eyelids.

The hail stopped. When he opened his eyes and looked off to the left he saw the men, dull images in the rain. Standing. No armor or breastplates. They looked like peasants from the village. He shouted. These louts could help him. As they came toward him, he could hear them speak. French. For some reason this did not alarm him. They were merely wagon drivers from the French baggage train.

Their shapes came over him, three or four. In the glare of the lightning he saw the crude mattock-like axes they carried, and he thought to himself: What fools to think they can fight with those. The lightning flashed again, and when it was gone he could see his life with amazing narrative clarity, just like the fresco that Andrea Mantegna had painted all around the walls of his father's bedchamber in Mantua, the entire Gonzaga family and court portrayed so true to life, in such detail, that to see himself on that wall for the first time had been frightening. That was what he could see now after every brilliant burst of lightning, these perfectly detailed pictures of his life, his father and mother and both his wives and the son each had given him, in a thousand vignettes, as if he were running past a fresco of enormous length. It was a magnificent pageant. Forty-four years. He had been present at every great battle and joust and wedding, he had been to France and Germany and Venice and Naples. . . .

Didn't the fools know they shouldn't move his leg! Something black darted over his face, and lightning exploded right above him in a huge white halo of numbing pain. Then miraculously the pictures came rushing back, and he saw the one he most cherished, his second wife, Caterina, dancing at his nephew Francesco's wedding to Isabella d'Este. Caterina dancing, her beauty still fresh, her hands light and floating in the air, the delicious whiteness of her breasts, softly trembling as she turned . . . An instant later the lightning and pain shattered the image, and he fought to bring it back against the exploding light, and finally he did. The last thing he ever saw was Caterina dancing at Isabella d'Este's wedding.

Extract of a letter of international traveler and raconteur BENEDETTO DEI to LEONARDO DA VINCI, military engineer at the Court of Milan. Asti, 15 August 1495

. . . I was admitted to the French camp here by virtue of my many friendships in all the capitals of Europe . . . after talking with the French commanders and men, I can now offer the most complete accounting of the Battle of Fornovo likely to be circulated in Italy for many years. . . . The lords of Italy can claim victory only in that they ended the day in possession of the French baggage train, a considerable booty indeed. But despite what we have been told, the great number of those slain that day were Italians. I can reliably report that the French losses in combat were only in the several hundreds, and as you know, it has been acknowledged that the Italian dead numbered four thousand, of whom three hundred and fifty were men of noble birth, among them the Marquis of Mantua's uncle Rodolfo and his cousin Giovanni Maria. . . . The Marquis's attack indeed was within a whisker of success, and had not the King himself fought so courageously (His Most Christian Majesty has been described to me as entirely unlike himself the morning of the battle, his eyes clear with purpose and his tongue quick with resolution), he should have been killed at once. . . . The opportunity was lost when the stradiots went off in pursuit of the baggage train, leaving the Italian knights without the support of their infantry. At that point, had the Marquis of Mantua not responded with fierce valor, the enterprise would have been utterly lost on our side. . . . Most of our dead were killed on the ground after they had been unhorsed, by French mule drivers armed with axes. . . . The entire battle lasted less than an hour, and most of those killed fell in the first few minutes. Thus in one quarter of an hour more Italian knights were slain than had perished by hostile arms in the preceding two hundred years.

The French suffered far more in their retreat to Asti than they did in the battle, and thousands of them perished from disease and want of sustenance. . . . His Most Christian Majesty has been unable to summon reinforcements to relieve the siege of Novara, in which the armies of the League are presently engaged. It is said that Louis Duc d'Orléans and his men are starving inside the walls, having put away no stores for this eventuality, while we hear that within the League encampment our Italian commanders have little to do but quarrel among themselves. Perhaps you can tell me if it is true that the Duchess of Milan was called upon to settle a dispute between Galeazzo di Sanseverino and the Marquis of Mantua? I understand that said Duchess and your lord Il Moro visited the camp at Novara on 3 August. I am also told that your lord Il Moro shows no ill effects of the malady that struck him down earlier this summer. Is that so? Once again all look to him to resolve the crisis. As for King Charles, he shows little inclination to leave Italy or, conversely, to relieve his cousin in Novara. His Most Christian Majesty spends his time in Chieri, near Turin, where he has found the healing hands of a young woman of noble birth named Anna Solieri. . . . You might also be interested to know that among the effects confiscated from the King's baggage was a portfolio of sketches of various women to whom His Most Christian Majesty has made love, all rendered in the nude and in positions of such invention that they may be considered the singular French contribution to the culture of Italy. Perhaps we should regret that His Most Christian Majesty did not have an opportunity to meet you, my dear Leonardo. Think what use he would have made of your talent. . . .

C H A P T E R

53

Extract of a letter of PHILIPPE DE COMMINES, **Lord of Argenton and Councillor to His Most Christian Majesty Charles VIII, to** PIERRE DE BEAUJEU, **Duc du Bourbon. Vercelli, 27 September 1495**

. . . Much has happened since my letter of 15 September detailing our first meeting with the Italian representatives. . . . Three days ago Il Moro himself arrived here to conduct peace negotiations on behalf of the League. . . . We go to his villa at Cameriano, not far from here . . . and are escorted into his chambers. We sit in two rows of chairs facing one another. On their side are the ambassadors of Germany, Venice, Spain, and Ferrara, the Marquis of Mantua, and the Duke and Duchess of Milan. On their side no one speaks but Il Moro. However, since it is not our custom to speak with the sedateness of temper with which these Italians do, sometimes two or three of us will speak at a time, at which Il Moro always interrupts, saying, "Please. One at a time, gentlemen." Il Moro remains absolutely inflexible on the matter of the territorial concessions His Most Christian Majesty has insisted upon, but he made quick assent to our suggestion that the garrison at Novara be allowed to leave the city. We adjourned for the day to conduct this merciful enterprise, though I wish God had spared me what I saw. No one who was not present can conceive of the pitiable condition of the men who marched out. They had no horses left, having eaten all of them, and of the five thousand who marched out, perhaps six hundred were capable of drawing a sword in their defense. They were so feeble that they collapsed frequently on the road (Novara is six French leagues or ten Italian miles from Vercelli), and the Italians were forced to carry many of them. I myself saved fifty of them . . . by lodging them in a garden and giving them warm broth, so that only one died, though four more of my pitiful little group perished before we reached Vercelli. . . . But no sooner had Louis Duc d'Orléans had a few days to rest and refresh himself (he having been permitted to leave Novara three days in advance of the garrison) than he once again endeavored to whip into a fury those around His Most Christian Majesty who are opposed to peace. In this enterprise Orleans has been most improvidently assisted by the arrival here today of upwards of ten thousand Swiss mercenaries, though even with this reinforcement we are still outnumbered two to one by the armies of the League. (The voices of war are already shouting, "Yes! And we were at a three-to-one disadvantage at Fornovo!") I cannot emphasize how grave the situation is for those of us who believe that this war can never be won. . . . My remaining hope is that Il Moro will be sufficiently concerned by this turn of events that he will make the concessions that His Most Christian Majesty declares we cannot leave Italy without, lest we also leave our honor behind. . . .

Cameriano, 28 September 1495

"I didn't know if you were sleeping." Il Moro stepped into the doorway of Beatrice's bedchamber. "I saw the lamps."

"I'm not ready to sleep yet. I just wanted to close my eyes." She removed the documents from her lap; she had propped her pillows against the headboard so that she could read in bed. "I had to reread the minutes of today's session. I want to make certain that we can turn the Lord of Argenton's exact words right back at him. Do you want to see them?"

He shook his head. In the uncertain light by the doorway he looked old and weary.

"I forgot." She smiled fondly. "You remember every word as it was spoken. Would to God that I had your memory. Then *I* would rule the world."

Il Moro remained standing in the doorway. He was still wearing the same tunic he had worn to the negotiating session in the afternoon, which was unlike him, since he usually changed his hose and tunic before supper. He seemed almost frightened at the prospect of entering his wife's bedchamber.

"Why don't you come in and sit," she said, nodding at the folding stool, styled after a Roman Emperor's camp chair, that stood by the shuttered window. It was unusual enough that he had come to her bedchamber; she was not going to scare him off by suggesting he sit on the bed.

He had not slept with her since his "illness"—as everyone now referred to his collapse. (And he did not speak of it at all.) She knew that he wasn't frightened of the physical intimacy, that perhaps he still needed and wanted it even more than she did. He was afraid of the emotional intimacy. He was afraid she would ask him what had happened that afternoon in Vigevano. She could see it in his eyes, eyes that were no longer capable of opacity but held locked in their swirling dark depths a vision no man could confront. That day in Vigevano her husband had stood in the bitter gloom of the last circle of Hell and had stared up at the monstrous face of Satan.

Il Moro walked across the room, his step measured, his footfall almost inaudible. He pulled the chair close enough to the bed that she could more clearly see his face in the lamplight. He had gained weight since the "illness," and silver gleamed in his dark hair. For his public appearances he wore a mask of composure and authority, putting all his effort into maintaining the illusion. At night he was like this, exhausted, aging, his sharp features sagging with doubt.

He sat with his head down, hands clasped between his knees, a hunched, nervous posture. "What can we do?" he asked. "Our Charlemagne insists that Genoa is his fief. Unfortunately I encouraged him in that delusion by purchasing the papers of investiture from him. Now that he realizes he is going to leave Italy without the territories he has mortgaged his state to acquire, he has gotten it into his head that his honor requires him to claim Genoa for his countrymen."

"He doesn't want Genoa," Beatrice said. "He wants to be able to garrison troops in the citadel at Genoa and use the dockyards for the fitting of his ships. He thinks that if he can supply the few French fortresses still holding out in the south, he will be able to get Naples back."

"Of course. But does it matter whether he is willing to continue the war because he wants the revenues of Genoa or because he wants the citadel and the dockyards? This is a man whose honor has compelled him to march an army halfway down the continent and back again, at the cost of a million ducats and thousands of lives, with as yet no more profit than a half-dozen Neapolitan fortresses, which will all be lost before next spring. What is simple reason next to this man's extravagant honor? Now he has ten thousand Swiss mercenaries to advance his latest folly. And another ten thousand on the way."

"There are fifty thousand soldiers of the League camped at Novara who are prepared to reason with King Charles."

Il Moro looked up. His face was all hollows and shadows. "Fifty thousand men," he said wearily. "Half of whom are suffering from dysentery, half of whom probably wouldn't fight because the Signory doesn't pay them on time. They don't know whether they are commanded by Galeazz, who is a splendid jouster and my dear son-in-law, so I will say nothing about his abilities as a general, or by the Marquis of Mantua, whose courage I admire but whose mindless abandon cost us dearly at Fornovo."

Beatrice loved the deprecating remark about Galeazz. Obviously her husband was abandoning one of *his* most annoying follies—that Galeazz was anything more than a peacock in armor. She looked at him sitting beside her, shaking his head slightly, his elegant lips shaped into a bemused smile. She realized that she cared for this man far more than the dashing Il Moro with whom she'd fallen in love. This new Il Moro had pierced his own private vanity, even if the public version was still intact. She wished she could somehow make him realize that she loved him now more than ever, that when she watched him like this she ached with longing for him. But of course they could never talk about who he had become. That would be touching too closely on the "illness."

"I don't know if I have the strength to go through another day of negotiations." Il Moro lowered his head again. His voice was muffled with fatigue. "I really don't. I am of a mind just to give the King back his papers to Genoa and be done with it. Get them out of Italy. If that is the price I must pay so that no more blood will be spilled, then so be it. Just get them out."

"Lodovico. Lodovico." Waiting until he looked up, she resisted her urge to hold out her hand to him. "We don't have to give up to get them out. I'm certain of that." Beatrice paused and calculated. "Tomorrow when they start making their threats, let me speak."

He nodded without hesitation. "Fine. Of all of us, you are certainly the most fearless. I'm afraid that my particular virtue is the ability to make promises I do not intend to keep."

"That is exactly what we will need. I will respond to their threats. And you will make promises we do not intend to keep."

Immediately grasping the plan his wife had sketched, Il Moro gave her a weary but hopeful smile. He got up and stood beside the bed. Beatrice felt a catch in her chest.

He reached out and very softly stroked her cheek. "You are my treasure. You are everything to me. Without you I would be lost. Utterly lost." He bent over and gave her a whisper-light kiss.

She was reminded of the kiss he gave her on the balcony in Ferrara, their first romantic kiss. Except that this time she wanted him so badly she couldn't breathe. Stay, she silently pleaded. Please. I won't ask anything of you.

He stood up again. "I really must go to my bed," he said awkwardly; even the difficulty of his excuse touched her. "I fatigue so much more easily. Ever since . . ." He gestured aimlessly with his hand. "Sleep well, *anima mia.*"

A beginning, she told herself; it was the first time he had even alluded to the "illness" in her presence. Then she realized what else he had said. *Anima mia,* she thought as she watched him walk into the darkness. My soul. He called me his own soul.

Cameriano, 29 September 1495

The air crackled with the displeasure of powerful men. Beatrice looked at the face directly across the long, narrow table. Cardinal Briconnet, the French Minister of Finance, had already erupted during the first day of negotiations, standing red-faced to demand the cession of half of Milan's territories before the French would send one man back across the mountains; he had called Il Moro a "traitor." Today Briconnet's swarthy color was every bit as inflamed with rage, as red as his cardinal's robe. His nostrils flared and contracted, like a bellows.

Briconnet didn't concern Beatrice. She studied Philippe de Commines, the Lord of Argenton, sitting next to Briconnet. A tall, fair-skinned, good-looking man perhaps ten years older than her husband, Commines had a polish and sophistication rare among the French courtiers. He was also the peacemaker among the French delegation. When Commines had been shown in this morning, however, he had seemed frustrated, with a deep undertone of sadness. Beatrice guessed that he had been requested to deliver an ultimatum. And as the morning had droned on, with the unyielding issue of Genoa—Commines and her husband had just gone through the daily ritual of the King's request and Il Moro's refusal—it had become obvious that the ultimatum would concern the cession of the King's "fief."

Briconnet muttered something in French to the man next to him—de Ganay, a black-robed lawyer who presided over the French Parlement; he had come with the army to help govern the short-lived Italian empire. Beatrice's brother-in-law, the Marquis of Mantua, gave Briconnet a stare of such feral fury that it seemed he might leap across the table and take the Cardinal's throat in his mouth. Briconnet glared back.

"His Most Christian Majesty desires peace above all else," Commines told Il Moro in passable Italian after briefly consulting with the French secretaries. "So he has agreed to place his properties in your trust. You may continue to govern Genoa in His Most Christian Majesty's name. But you must surrender the citadel of Genoa and allow His Most Christian Majesty to use the dockyards at his convenience."

Beatrice resisted making a show of her alarm and surprise.

This was what she feared most, that Charles would scale down his demands just enough to give her weary, frightened husband an excuse to give in. But the French King's concession was nothing of the sort. This deal would give him what he most wanted, the ability to wage war from Genoa.

Il Moro hesitated. Beatrice could feel his quivering will, a palpable vibration. Then he said, "I am not going to surrender the citadel. Make this clear to His Most Christian Majesty, Monseigneur d'Argenton. If His Most Christian Majesty desires peace, then I am willing to work with him to that end. If he wants to continue this war, then I can accommodate him to that end as well."

Commines's fair complexion colored. For the first time in almost two weeks of negotiations he wore an expression of anger. He clenched his fist. "Then the twenty thousand Swiss mercenaries who have joined our camp will make that accommodation most uncomfortable for you, Your Highness."

"Indeed."

Everyone except Il Moro turned in astonishment at the clear, high music of Beatrice's voice. The Frenchmen might have just heard a dog talk.

Beatrice aimed her vivid black eyes directly at Commines. "These twenty thousand Swiss you refer to, Monseigneur d'Argenton. They are subjects of His Most Christian Majesty?"

Commines looked at her as if he had been forced to humor a fractious child. "Of course not."

"Of course not. They are here because they are mercenary soldiers. The Swiss live in a poor country. They have come in such numbers because there is famine at home and they need the money to feed their families. They do not yet know that His Most Christian Majesty cannot afford to pay them."

Commines's face reddened again. "They know that they will be paid from the treasury of Milan."

"They will fight for your promises? These Swiss are simple mountain folk, *monseigneur*. They are not Florentine bankers who trade in promissory notes. You build the most marvelous cannons in Paris, Monseigneur d'Argenton. In Milan we build printing presses. By tomorrow afternoon I can have five thousand printed broadsheets circulating in the Swiss camp, warning them that the

King of France does not have the funds to pay for their services. By the next morning you will be the ones fighting these twenty thousand Swiss."

Commines suddenly had the vacant, bewildered look of a ship-wreck survivor. Cardinal Briconnet leapt to his feet, pointing at Beatrice, shouting in French. She made out a few words; he was saying, Why should they listen to anything a woman said?

Il Moro started to rise to challenge Briconnet, and Beatrice held him back with a firm hand on his thigh. But the Marquis of Mantua popped up from his seat and shouted at Briconnet, "That is my sister, *cacapensieri!* If you persist in insulting her I will gladly negotiate with you in the courtyard—"

"Francesco!" Beatrice snapped. "Thank you. But sit down." She turned to Briconnet and said pleasantly, "Would you be so good as to sit with us, Your Reverence."

Finding no support for his position, Briconnet sheepishly took his seat.

"Now, Monseigneur d'Argenton. You must convince His Most Christian Majesty that the citadel will remain ours. As to your use of the docks, perhaps that is an issue my husband is willing to negotiate."

Beatrice turned to her husband. Il Moro nodded approval, the infinitesimal twist of his lips—certainly detectable only to her—telling her that he understood. This was the promise he did not intend to keep.

"Thank you, Your Highness." Commines sighed with open French emotionalism. "You have given me something I can take back to my King."

Extract of a letter of PHILIPPE DE COMMINES, Lord of Argenton and Councillor to His Most Christian Majesty Charles VIII, to PIERRE DE BEAUJEU, Duc du Bourbon. Vercelli, 9 October 1495

. . . and so His Most Christian Majesty affixed his signature and seal to the articles of peace. . . . In the end it was our want of money that compelled us to accept this peace that few of us desired and most of us do not believe will last. . . . Louis Duc d'Orléans was obliged to renounce forever his claim to Milan, while in exchange Il Moro paid our expenses so that we might cross the mountains again. . . . We leave behind the bones of our country-men and take with us only the certainty that the afflictions we have suffered are an acknowledgment of the power of God. If any man has profited from this enterprise, it is Il Moro, who now governs all Italy. We must watch that he does not become the governor of all Europe. . . .

CHAPTER

54

Vigevano, 18 November 1495

Setting her clavichord on the table near the glowing fireplace, Beatrice pulled up a bench so that she and Bianca could sit side by side. She opened the leather-bound book of songs that her sister had just sent her. The rows of bars, notes, and lyrics were embellished with ornate lettering and beautiful miniature paintings of birds. In the lamplight, the jewel-bright little birds flickered as if they were about to spread their wings. Rain rattled against the windows.

Beatrice leafed through the pages until she found what she wanted. "My sister says this *frottola* is all the fashion in Mantua," she told Bianca. "Here, you hold the music, and I will try to play it." She put her hands on the narrow keyboard attached to what resembled a lyre set on its side—a sensuously scrolling, open wooden frame, strung with precise rows of the finest German gut. She struck several clear, wonderfully resonant notes, a sound so rich that it might have been made by an organ.

Beatrice practiced the lively melody several times. Then she began to sing in her high, lyrical voice:

"Good day, Good evening,
I believed it was still early.
But the day passes, the hours flee,
And how quickly night has come."

Beatrice paused to say, "Now we sing the refrain":

"Good day, Good evening,
I believed it was still early."

"Now we must increase the tempo."

"Therefore, Lady, while you can,
Don't let time slip through your arms.
Take the measure of each day,
If you never fish, you will never catch.
As quickly as fire ignites the tinder,
So embrace your desire now."

"That's so true, Toto," Bianca said with a practiced sigh. "I am fifteen years old. I feel I will wake up tomorrow and find that I am a *vecchia.*" As if underscoring Bianca's melodramatic lament, the rain came down harder and the wind moaned.

"You are almost a year younger than I was when I got married," Beatrice said, a gentle reminder that Bianca, who had celebrated her birthday only a month previously, would have to wait a while before she could move in with Galeazz. Then she reminded herself: I am twenty-one years old. If I live as long as Mama, I have already lived more than half my life. Suddenly Bianca didn't seem so girlishly impatient.

"Toto, is there a way you can keep from getting pregnant? Caterina da Borromeo says that there is a book in Arabic in the library at Pavia that tells a hundred different ways, and that it hasn't been translated because if it were, within three generations there would be no one left in Italy."

Nothing Bianca said surprised her. "There is only one way

that really works, *carissima figlia*. The method that is practiced by children, pious nuns, and the dead. And now that I think of it, there is also the method practiced by Caterina. But for everything else they tell you, there are a dozen women with fat bellies to tell you otherwise. Don't worry, you won't get pregnant right away."

Beatrice glanced sideways at her stepdaughter. Bianca on the threshold of womanhood was gorgeous, her natural color more vivid than the typical Milanese lady's ceruse and rouge, her small features perfectly shaped. But she was as fragile as eggshell-thin porcelain; it mildly frightened Beatrice to think of her in Galeazz's powerful arms. But it simply terrified Beatrice to think of Bianca having Galeazz's baby.

"You almost died with Ercole, didn't you? They didn't want me to know then, but I've heard about it since."

Beatrice felt the vertigo of that black, silent descent. It hadn't frightened her then. But now it did. "I don't think I was that close to dying, baby. I really don't. You know how the *vecchie* exaggerate. And by the time the story started among my ladies, well, by then I had not only received the stigmata and died, but three days later I was resurrected."

"I think it must have been terribly frightening. Toto, you know my mother died having me. I dream about my mother sometimes. Once she warned me not to have a baby."

Beatrice felt that icy finger along her spine. She took Bianca's hand. "I will promise you this, baby. Whenever and wherever you have your baby, I will be there with you. That is my pledge. The solemn oath of the Beatrice and Bianca League."

Bianca put her arms around Beatrice. "Toto, I will always be sorry that my mother died. But you are the best mother I ever could've had."

In some ways, Beatrice realized, she was even closer to Bianca than she was to her own little boys. So much of raising little princes was letting them go, sending them off to lessons and instruction in the manly arts. Bianca was much more an extension of herself.

"This time we will both sing," Beatrice said, plinking the keys of her clavichord. They joined in on the little ditty, but after the second refrain a light baritone broke into their harmony.

"Father!" Bianca said with an adolescent squeal.

Il Moro bent to kiss his wife and daughter. His face was relaxed, his eyes sparkled in a way they hadn't since the "illness." Then he stood and sang out, " 'Whoever would be merry, let them! / Of tomorrow none are certain!' That is the refrain from my friend Lorenzo de' Medici's 'Song of Bacchus.' May God rest his soul. When I think of how Lorenzo loved life, and love, and then to hear what is going on now with this Fra Girolamo Savonarola proclaiming Christ the King of Florence. They are allowed to sing nothing but hymns in Florence these days, and children are taught to break into houses to confiscate paintings and poems and musical instruments. Of all the forms of government, government by priests is the worst." He shook his head. "Well, this is not an occasion for melancholy. Today I received news from Lyons. His Most Christian Majesty has returned whence he started on his Crusade. It is over. It is finally, irrevocably over."

Beatrice shared her husband's relief; for weeks she, too, had worried that the hotheaded, impetuous French would change their minds before they made their final descent to impecunious reality. Kisses were exchanged all around. Then, with a knowing look at her father and his wife, Bianca demurely suggested that she was fatigued and intended to retire. Beatrice caught the sly gleam in Bianca's eye and realized that her baby was already developing a woman's instincts.

When Bianca had left, Il Moro lowered his head. His voice had a charming tentativeness. "Would I be presuming too much if I asked to spend the night in your rooms?"

"You would be presuming to know my fondest desire."

He looked up. "Before we . . . I want to say something now that should have been said many weeks ago. I am ashamed that I have never even acknowledged your courage and initiative, much less thanked you for what you did when I was . . . when I could do nothing. When I lay helpless. You saved us. You saved everything. And I did not even have the courage to thank you."

This was it, his expiation, his full confession, all she had ever wanted or needed. They would never have to speak of the "illness" again. In reply she simply took his hand and led him to her bed.

They held each other for a long while before they began to

make love, kissing softly, whispering, and caressing. He was softer, a bit paunchy, as if his body had yielded along with his will. And yet she found that this heightened her passion; it was as though she was now physically embracing the gentler inner spirit she had always loved, the part of him that was not the vaunted Il Moro, master of all Europe.

Everything was slow, dreamlike, exquisite. This was how she had so long ago imagined her wedding night, the way it had been when they first became lovers. His tempo rose and fell lyrically, so familiar to her again, a cherished poetry of caresses.

But as he rose to his climax something went wrong. He hardened all over, clutching her so tightly that she entirely lost the rhythm, pumping into her so furiously that it hurt. It was almost like the first time he had tried to make a son, that terrible night.

"Lodovico," she whispered, trying to break through his rage. "Lodovico. Lodovico, you're hurting me!"

He emerged as if from a trance. "God help me," he gasped. His entire body was still rigid, but he no longer pressed against her. He was withdrawing, pulling the anger back into his depths. "God help me, I never want to hurt you," he whispered harshly, staring past her into the fire-tinted shadows. "I have already done so much to shame myself in your eyes. I will lose your love. That is what frightens me. That is what I am clinging to. If I lost your love I couldn't live. I simply couldn't go on."

"Oh, darling, you could never lose my love. I promise you there is nothing you could do that would ever make me stop loving you."

She had imagined that her unconditional declaration would bring him back, draw him close in the way that they had been only minutes before. But he remained hard, distant, locked inside his shell.

Beatrice listened to the rain patter against the windows. In a sudden, awful vision her dead men paraded by, white-faced Gian and the corpses lying akimbo in black pools of blood on the streets of Milan. And then the dead she'd not seen but only been told of: the women and children thrown off the battlements of Fivizzano by the Swiss, the knights lying in the rain at Fornovo, their faces hacked to pulp, the walking skeletons dying in the ditches along the road from Novara to Vercelli.

She held her husband, vainly trying to embrace the soul she could no longer touch. The war isn't over, she told herself, trying not to sob. It will never be over.

· PART ·

NINE

C H A P T E R

55

Extract of a letter of LEONARDO DA VINCI, engineer at the Court of Milan, to international traveler and raconteur BENEDETTO DEI. Milan, 10 August 1496

. . . upon hearing that the French King was once again making intemperate comments concerning his intentions to return to Italy and pursue the conquests he failed to achieve in his previous sojourn here, my lord Il Moro determined that he must persuade the Emperor Maximilian to take a more active involvement in Italian affairs, as a guarantor of the peace against the aggressive intentions of the French King. To this end the Duke and Duchess of Milan embarked on a journey from Milan to the Abbey of Mals, which lies at the base of the prodigious massifs that separate this country from that of Germany. As one of those selected to join Their Highnesses' suite, I can offer you the full particulars of this embassy. . . . We took leave of Milan on 5 July, journeying the length of Lake Como before taking the road east that passes through Bormio, all the while entertained by the magnificent and overawing presence of the great mountains to our north, a constant and daunting reminder of mankind's insignificance against the achievements of nature. . . . In the course of our journey I was able to make many observations concerning the motion of air over these great massifs and the attendant storms caused by the compression and condensation of clouds. . . .

. . . we reached the Abbey of Mals, finding the said abbey a Benedictine establishment of ancient and noble construction, admirable in its simplicity of form . . . the Emperor came to greet the Duke and Duchess on 20 July, and then closeted with both Their Highnesses for a considerable duration of time—the Duke of Milan conducts no business of any import unless the Duchess of Milan is also present. . . . As a result of this embassy, in which I was pleased to participate, the Emperor has agreed to come to Milan in September to advance discussions intended to ensure peace, concord, and stability. . . .

. . . thereupon I returned to my labors on the fresco depicting the Last Supper of Our Lord for the refectory of Santa Maria delle Grazie. The Dominican friars who will dine beneath this glorious representation have become exceedingly vexed at my careful habits of work, and thus their Prior complained to my lord Il Moro that considering the great amount of money His Highness has advanced toward the completion this prodigy (indeed it is no great amount, my dear Benedetto), why had I not begun work on the head of Judas? When His Highness posited the Prior's noisome question to me, I told His Highness that I have already devoted the better portion of a year to traversing at great risk to my person the streets of the most scurrilous and disreputable quarter of Milan, seeking in vain the face of a heinous criminal who might provide me with the features suitable to the most villainous man who ever walked this earth. However, I informed His Highness, if the Prior was indeed so impatient, I could with no trouble employ the said Prior's own likeness for the head of Judas, as his character and appearance are perfectly suited to the task, and indeed I had not done so already only out of concern for the Prior's feelings. His Highness was most amused with this. . . .

Vigevano, 15 August 1496

From the grassy crest of the gradual slope, Il Moro and Galeazzo di Sanseverino could see back to the town of Vigevano, a circle of red tile roofs dominated by the tower of the Castello Sforzesca. Before them stretched a largely flat expanse of wooded parkland, the horizon bounded by the cool, mist-purple wall of the Alps. The countryside glistened beneath the midmorning sun.

Galeazz breathed rhythmically from the brisk ride. He looked over at Il Moro, tanned and taut-looking, his thick chest rising only slightly. "I don't remember that you've ever ridden this well," Galeazz said genuinely.

"Perhaps you are slowing down." Il Moro gave Galeazz a brilliant smile.

"Just the same, you've never looked better in the saddle. And that perception has nothing to do with the decline in my abilities."

Il Moro indeed hadn't looked better in many years. The trip to Austria had invigorated him, and he had gone on a riding regimen since his return. He'd also dyed his hair to eliminate the traces of gray. Only the tight lines around his eyes betrayed his age and experience.

"There are my wife's ladies, quite without her supervision," Il Moro said, pointing to the flat meadow just below them.

"How is Her Highness?" Galeazz asked.

"Messer Ambrogio examined her after she called him early this morning. He insisted she stay in bed. That of course means nothing. What is surprising is that Beatrice decided to take his advice."

"I hope she is well."

"She thought she was bleeding. But she has had two successful births. This one will be no different. I think as she gets older she is only becoming more prudent, not less robust."

Il Moro looked down at the cluster of a dozen or so young women, surrounded by game wardens and pages. The ladies were all mounted sidesaddle, wearing heavy damask skirts that billowed around them as if they were sitting on immense cushions. But the bodices of their *camore* were so tight that their torsos might have been painted with silk. They carried light silk parasols to preserve the delicate pallor of their liberally exposed shoulders, breasts, and backs. Every so often they lowered the parasols—particularly at the approach of a gentleman—allowing their jewels to sparkle in the sun.

"I suggest we have some sport with them," Il Moro said.

"Your Highness, you do realize that I am taking your daughter—my wife—into my home in less than a month?" Galeazz said, pretending to be nonplussed.

"I'm not suggesting that we select a brace or two and trot them off into the woods. We will engage them in an innocent flirtation. Remember, Galeazz, flirtation is like flattery. Both are meaningless yet essential to the functioning of any court. We must do our part."

The ladies were busy admiring a hunting cheetah with a diamond-studded collar. They were far too accomplished to make a fuss over the two most desirable men in Italy. Instead they delivered curt little nodding bows accompanied by grudging, bored smiles.

"Who owns the cheetah?" Galeazz asked.

The owner gave Galeazz a slight affirmative nod. She wore her blond hair in ringlets, a Venetian fashion. Her blue eyes were tinted violet. She had a small waist and full breasts traced with faint veins. "If you will send your beaters into that wood, you can see him run," she said. Galeazz noticed a subtle carnal buzz in her clear, resonant voice.

Galloping across the meadow, Galeazz shouted for the game wardens to organize a beating party. Within a short time men on foot could be seen entering the woods, armed with wooden staffs.

Il Moro rode to the side of the cheetah's owner. She introduced herself as Madonna Dorotea, one of the new additions to the Duchess of Milan's corps of attendants, another bauble for a court that had become increasingly extravagant following the war.

"My husband gave me this cheetah," Madonna Dorotea said. In the Milanese liturgy of seduction, such an immediate reference to the husband wasn't intended to deter an advance but instead established at the outset that the husband was amenable to his wife's taking a lover.

"They're quite a splendid sight in full pursuit," Il Moro said. "It's a pity that they so quickly tire. The chase is over within seconds. That's why I prefer falcons. They can glide for an hour, then plunge with sudden fury. Perhaps it's more exciting. Not knowing when they will select their prey. But then I must confess that I am not an avid huntsman. My wife is quite the better of me at this sport."

Madonna Dorotea snapped her head up slightly. Had he mentioned his wife to signal his availability? She had set her sights on Messer Galeazz and had never even considered the notoriously faithful Duke of Milan. Still, there were rumors that Il Moro had not slept with his wife for months—and had done so only infrequently before her pregnancy. She decided that she had nothing to lose by encouraging him.

"If Your Highness will forgive me, I think it is unfortunate that as hard as you work, you are so reluctant to provide yourself with recreation."

He shrugged his shoulders and gave her a subtle smile. "Well, I am enjoying myself today. Perhaps I will become an enthusiast. Ah, madonna, look. They have flushed some hares." Ears streaming back, the rabbits streaked across the grass. "But I presume you are waiting for larger game."

"He can take down a buck," Madonna Dorotea said. She motioned to the handler holding the cheetah's leash to remove it. More hares darted across the meadow, fleeing the phalanx of beaters thrashing their way through the woods.

Two does popped out of the line of trees. The cheetah strained at the hands on his collar. Then a small stag bounded out. "Wait!" Madonna Dorotea commanded the handlers, giving the stag a lead. "Now!"

The kill was not pretty. Racing after the stag with astonishing speed, the cheetah swatted its hindquarters, slowing it, then ran it down on the second pass. The cheetah was ripping out the stag's throat by the time a handler raced up with a bowl of fresh pig's blood to entice it away from its kill. The spectators arrived to find the cheetah greedily lapping blood and the stag still twitching.

Madonna Dorotea was hardly winded from the gallop. Her face and shoulders had a fresh, vivid flush. She looked astutely at Il Moro, who had not even directed a glance toward the cheetah or its victim. "I can see that this demonstration has not kindled your enthusiasm," she said.

"Perhaps not." Il Moro smiled. "But as I told you, I prefer a more leisurely pursuit." He nodded politely and turned away from Madonna Dorotea and her blood-spattered pet. As he did, he noticed that one of the ladies had dismounted and was bent over with her hands on her knees. Suddenly she convulsed and vomited into the grass.

"*Per Dio*," Madonna Dorotea muttered disgustedly.

Il Moro swung off his horse and went to help, putting his hands on the young woman's shoulders to steady her. She retched once more, then spit to clear her mouth. He pulled a linen handkerchief from his doublet and helped her wipe her face. She straightened up and looked at him and shook her head miserably.

"You're very kind," she said. Then she realized who had come to her assistance. "I'm terribly embarrassed, Your Highness," she said in a voice that was incongruously self-possessed. "This is my first week in your wife's suite, and already I have humiliated myself. I'm afraid I don't have the stomach for this sport. I hate to see anything killed."

Il Moro handed her the handkerchief, and she dabbed at her mouth. She was slightly taller than Beatrice, small-busted, with a straight nose that was too long and thick and a mouth that seemed too small. Her eyes were large and wide-set.

"I will share a secret with you," Il Moro said. "I would like nothing more than to put my hands on my knees and join you in your critique of this form of recreation."

She smiled weakly, and her face changed entirely, though it was impossible to say how.

"If you like, I will have you driven back to the *castello* in a chariot. I don't think you should ride."

She nodded. "Thank you so much, Your Highness. You are truly very kind."

"I'm afraid I don't have a name with which to properly address you," Il Moro said earnestly.

"I'm sorry, Your Highness. I am Lucrezia Crivelli."

"Well, Madonna Lucrezia, let me find someone to accompany you back to the *castello*. And please don't feel obliged to return the handkerchief."

"Your Highness, if this is an inconvenient time . . . ," offered the Marchesino Stanga.

"No, Marchesino." Beatrice motioned the Minister of Public Works to a chair set at an angle to hers. The room she now used as an office allowed a view of the sun-drenched labyrinth and the templelike, gleaming white pavilion at its center.

"I was concerned because it isn't like Your Highness to miss a hunt."

"I didn't have a good night, so I spent the morning in bed. And now I have an opportunity to read the diplomatic dispatches." In fact the night had been terrifying. Beatrice had been awakened by pains, and when she lit her lamp she'd found a few spots of blood on her sheets. She had been certain she was about to lose the baby. But after the morning passed without incident she de- cided to resume her preparations for the Emperor's visit. She was entirely at ease with her knowledge of Italian politics, but the new league against the French now included Germany, Spain, and En- gland in addition to all the major Italian states except Florence. So she was poring over the dispatches, wanting to be apprised of any situation in the rest of Europe that the Emperor might intro- duce into their discussions—particularly since her policy would be at odds with her husband's. Il Moro was intent on employing the Emperor's army to liberate Pisa from the Florentines, which he believed would not only punish Florence for rebuffing the League but prove to the French that the Emperor was serious about his commitment to his Italian allies. Beatrice believed that the last thing Italy needed was another "liberator" marching across the mountains. She was convinced that a stay-at-home German army, poised to march into Paris should the French army embark on another Italian campaign, would be the most effective deterrent to French aggression.

"Your Highness, I must observe that seeing you with these dispatches, I am reminded of your mother, may God keep her soul. She devoted so much of herself to the business of state. I don't see how your father makes do without her."

Beatrice smiled warmly, flattered to be compared to Mama. She had never appreciated it when she was growing up, but in retrospect she could see that Mama had virtually run Ferrara, shut up in her rooms with all the tedious administrative work while

Father led his singers from church to church. And added to that, Mama had entirely supervised the household and the education of her children. Now Beatrice could understand the sheer physical energy required for such a regimen, not to mention her mother's intellectual drive. But that admiration also inspired a certain fear. Mama was dead, this great edifice of a woman taken as suddenly and vehemently as a sickly infant. Mama's death was proof that the living were all just wanderers in a labyrinth, never certain when their path would come to an end.

"Your Highness, I would like to speak frankly."

"I consider you an old friend, Marchesino."

"Thank you, Your Highness." The Marchesino clasped his hands together tensely and leaned forward. "Your Highness, last week His Highness your husband brought me a new agenda of public works projects. Quite an extensive agenda. After estimating the cost of these projects, I went to the treasury to ascertain if these moneys were available, because, frankly, I did not think they would be. And indeed I was correct. But I had not imagined the extent of the deficiency. Your Highness, by the time the Christmas *feste* are over, we will have nothing."

That simply isn't possible, Beatrice thought. The state produces enormous revenues. I know the figures. That is the one thing we will never have to worry about in Milan. Our supply of revenues is inexhaustible.

"I don't see how that could be, Marchesino."

The Marchesino proceeded to enumerate the expenses of the last two years: the defaulted loans to France, the payments to Germany, the cost of military operations, the costs of diplomacy with all its attendant pomp and extravagance. "Your Highness, we have raised taxes three times this year. Have you noticed that when your husband rides through the streets, you no longer hear so many shouts of 'Moro'?"

"But we are taxing the big agricultural concessions, the armorers, the banks, the most affluent merchants—the people who have benefited the most from our state expenditures. And from our prosperity."

"Exactly. They are always the most ungrateful. And because we have made them so powerful, they have the means to make their displeasure known. I'm sure you understand the danger there.

Your Highness, we cannot tax our way out of this. We must undertake the necessary economies. Immediately."

"Have you brought this to my husband's attention?"

The Marchesino sat back and closed his eyes. "Many times, Your Highness; so many times that he will no longer hear me on this."

Yes, I understand that, Beatrice thought. Just as he refuses to hear me on the Pisa issue.

"Your Highness, I have come to you with considerable reluctance. But I think if you will review the figures you will see that the situation requires your intervention. I think you are the only one of us who can convince His Highness of the seriousness of the situation. This is like a rot, Your Highness. We can continue to assure ourselves that we see no signs of decay, until one day the entire structure collapses."

"Thank you, Marchesino," Beatrice said, feeling a twinge of pain. "I wish my husband were surrounded by more men like you. It takes a very good friend indeed to tell us something we don't want to hear."

When the door had been closed behind the Marchesino, Beatrice pulled her legs up and wrapped her arms around her knees, hoping that the brief pain would not recur. She realized that the Marchesino's revelation shouldn't have surprised her. Like a rot. Like her marriage. As partners in the business of state, she and her husband had drawn closer since the war—at least until the Pisa issue arose. But as intimate partners they had become steadily estranged since the French had left Italy the previous autumn.

There were as yet few outward signs of the decay. By all appearances, her husband had reached his apotheosis. He was, as he had predicted, the arbiter of all Europe, the idol of the ambassadors who came to him in an endless pilgrimage, the favorite subject of adoring poets ("In the heavens, one God; on earth, one Moro," was a typically modest paean), the cynosure of the almost daily *feste* that celebrated Milan's Golden Age. But the rot was there. Beneath this splendid, dashing exterior was a man whose doubts had become more obsessive, who could hardly step out of his rooms without consulting his wife or his astrologer. Yet as desperately as her husband solicited her advice, he often obstinately rejected it; as much as he needed her, he seemed to resent that

need. Their lovemaking had become torturous, the distance between them growing with each struggle for intimacy, every attempt to reach him somehow pushing him away. Gradually the
pain of trying had become greater than the pain of not trying.
The night on which her baby had been conceived had been the
first time they had made love in six weeks—and they had not
made love in the months since. She was disquieted by the unlikely
happenstance of her baby's conception, and in her darker moments
saw Fortune's malice at work. But now that the baby had become
more physically present inside her, she could feel the love growing,
replacing the love that was dying. She prayed that this baby would
be a girl. Especially with Bianca leaving her in just a few weeks.
A daughter, her own little girl.

Beatrice looked out into the labyrinth, its geometry etched in
the hard summer light, and saw the path before her. Without peace
no other dream had meaning. She was determined to persuade the
Emperor to bring peace to Italy, not another war. When the Emperor had left, then she would deal with this dreadful fiscal rot
the Marchesino had exposed. She would bring her little girl into
the world. And then, perhaps, she would try to see if there was
anything left of the dream that had once been her marriage.

Il Moro motioned to his chamberlain to leave him alone with his
guest. He shook her hand quickly and politely. Though he had
dined alone in his rooms, he was dressed fashionably enough for
a *festa*, in a high-collared blue silk tunic embroidered all over with
meticulous little representations of compasses, clocks, astrolabes,
and various other scientific instruments. A chain of heavy gold
links draped his collarbones.

"Madonna Lucrezia," Il Moro said. "I'm afraid that my chamberlain has become addled with the heat. I asked him to go and
inquire as to your health, not summon you hither to offer proof
that you are well. I'm terribly sorry."

She nodded slightly. "I must have misunderstood." In fact she
knew she hadn't misunderstood, and she was certain that the chamberlain wasn't any more addled than she was. She marvelled at
the ease and conviction with which Il Moro lied.

Madonna Lucrezia was dressed for supper, in a *camora* with a relatively conservative bodice of red and black satin shot through with gold thread; white silk puffs tied with gold satin *stringhe* ringed her upper arms. Her skirt was a light black taffeta. Madonna Lucrezia's features might have been assembled by an artist trying to prove that by combining flaws with beauty, he could create a greater beauty. The upper lip was thin, priggish, the lower lip poutingly erotic. Her masculine nose was ill-matched to her delicate round chin, but its sharp angles worked in mysterious concert with her wide, wondering eyes.

After a moment Madonna Lucrezia said, "I should apologize. This is most awkward."

"It needn't be."

Her face seemed to contract, the harsh lines indicating disapproval.

"I was looking at some new things," he said casually, undeterred by her expression. "Since you have come all this way, perhaps you would like to see them."

She hesitated and then merely nodded warily. Yet in a strange way her eyes were open to anything. Staying back a pace, she followed him through his study into the *guardaroba*.

He lit a lamp. The light revealed rows and rows of silver and majolica plates in wooden presses, credenzas full of rare antiquities. He went to a shelf cluttered with an assortment of small marble and bronze sculptures, some of them ancient Roman or Byzantine fragments, others, like a shiny gold saltcellar depicting a satyr ravishing a nymph, representing the astonishing realism of the contemporary *maestri*.

"I just received these from my *procuratori* in Rome and Venice," Il Moro said. He picked up a marble bust of a heroically handsome man, slightly worn by time. "I believe that this is Apollo. It really is of much finer quality than the small antique busts one usually finds. He has that sweet sadness that one finds so often in the larger portraits. It is as if these gods sense that their moment has ended, that a new age will hurl their proud statues into the dust. But perhaps they also knew that after centuries of darkness, our *maestri* would resurrect them."

She reached out and put her hand on his arm. "Your Highness, this is all very interesting. You intend to describe these objects to

me with great sensitivity, beginning with the sacred and progressing toward the profane. I will be expected to counter your
rising innuendo with a certain practiced coyness." She picked up
the little golden nymph and satyr. "By the time you begin to
rhapsodize about this, you expect that I will be in such a state of
arousal that I will lift my skirts and show you that I'm not wearing
any underlinens."

He smiled with complete aplomb. "I'm afraid that as generously as I have patronized the art of seduction at my court, I am
not at all practiced in it. I must say I admire the devastating precision of your critique."

She smiled. "I hope I haven't affronted you. God knows that
my husband and my brother, who not a week ago commanded
me to seduce you in pursuit of their ambitions, would consider
this moment the fulfillment of all *their* desires. I simply didn't want
Your Highness to waste his valuable time."

He seemed as relieved as Madonna Lucrezia that his halfhearted
seduction had failed. "Well, I do not consider this time wasted.
You are very charming. Even if you *are* wearing underlinens."

"I'm not." Her face changed so entirely that she might have
been possessed. Now her eyes were predatory.

She took the step between them and looked up into his fascinated face. With one hand she drew up her light silk skirt well
past her thighs. With her other hand she placed his hand on her
bare bottom.

When he pulled her against him, she whispered in his ear. "As
I told Your Highness, I simply did not want you to waste your
time."

CHAPTER

56

Vigevano, 29 August 1496

Ercole Sforza, the three-and-a-half-year-old Count of Pavia and heir to the Duke of Milan, walked purposefully to his mother's chair. He wore a tunic of beige-and-black satin, white hose, and brown velvet slippers. His small features might have been stamped out of the same mold as Beatrice's, but he had set them with a precociously masculine self-possession, something of his father's dark intensity. He was now very much a little man.

"His Highness isn't going to Latin today," Ercole said calmly and distinctly.

Beatrice arranged her son's unkempt, delicately curled hair. "Really? Who decided this for His Highness?"

Ercole stared defiantly. "His Highness decided."

"Well, this isn't something that His Highness decides. His Highness's mother decides."

Ercole stared a moment longer. Then he screamed shrilly, "I don't want to go to Latin!"

Beatrice shrugged. "I don't hear when you scream like that. You are going to Latin because that's how you will learn to make your mother understand what you want without screaming at her.

Who knows? If you do very well with your lessons, you might be able to convince your mother that you don't need to study Latin any longer."

Ercole turned to settle his malevolent gaze on his nineteen-month-old brother, Sforza Francesco, who already had his father's sturdy jawline and close-set dark eyes. The implication in Ercole's menacing stare was obvious: If he had to spend the next two hours with his Latin tutor while his little brother got to play with his mother and her guest, then his little brother was going to pay later.

Beatrice looked up at the boys' nurse. "Anna, you had better take Sforza and put him to bed. It's time for his nap. And ask His Highness which he would rather do: go to bed like his *baby* brother, or go to his Latin tutor."

After Beatrice had kissed the boys goodbye, Anna took each by a hand and led them off to their respective fates. "His Highness is going to Latin," Ercole pronounced on his way out.

Beatrice smiled wryly at the guest sitting opposite her. The guest, Isabella of Aragon, responded with a brief flicker of amusement. Isabella resembled a Spanish widow in her high-collared black silk dress, her hair veiled in black lace. Her eyes were the color of unpolished jade now, with a latent richness beneath their dull surface. But her skin remained morbidly pale and her once statuesque neck thin and corded. She did not appear so much weary as frangible, as if she would shatter at the wrong word.

It seemed Eesh would always be a casualty of the war. Her heroic self-denial, which as much as any single act had saved Italy from the French, had utterly drained her; for months afterward Eesh had suffered a paralyzing, wasting melancholy, withdrawing even more than she had after Gian's death. The good news of that fall, that Eesh's brother Ferrantino had reconquered Naples, might have revived her, but it soon had been followed by word of her father's death in a monastery in Sicily. Eesh had begun to recover this summer, however, and she and Beatrice had talked occasionally, always with excruciating circumspection, carefully avoiding the powerful currents of longing, shame, and recrimination that swirled around them. Then, just three weeks before, the news had come from Naples that Ferrantino had died suddenly of a fever. Eesh had plunged into the depths again, shutting herself up in her rooms, talking darkly of a curse on the house of Aragon. Beatrice had considered going to Milan to console her cousin, but there was too much to be done in preparation for the Emperor's visit. So she had decided to at least make the gesture of inviting Eesh to Vigevano.

"Bona has started Latin," Isabella said, her voice dry and brittle. "Her tutor is Messer Niccolò. He says she's doing better than Francesco did. God, do you know that this is the first time I've been away from my children since . . . It's strange. I thought they would forbid me to leave them. They hardly noticed. Even the baby. Only then did I realize how little time I really spend with them. How much of them has been given to other women. And now their tutors."

Beatrice smiled with wistful sympathy. "I feel the same way. I've gotten so involved with . . . other things"—Beatrice realized that it would be cruel to say she had gotten so involved with state business, a role Eesh once coveted for herself—"that I don't see the boys for two or three days at a time. Almost a month when we went to Germany. And now that Ercole has started his lessons . . ." Beatrice sighed. "It really makes me sad, Eesh. I keep thinking of what Mama once told me about loving our children. She said it was the most powerful passion there is, but to fulfill it you so often have to deny it. I didn't understand her at the time. But then I don't think I ever really knew my mother until after she was gone."

Beatrice looked down at her thickening midsection; some of her increased girth was due to the baby, most of it was the weight she had put on the preceding winter. "I know it's a strange thing to say, but I feel that I have become so close to Mama since she died. To her spirit. I know she's inside this baby. I really do. That's why I want so badly for this baby to be a girl."

Isabella seemed to retreat into her wrapping of black lace and Spanish silk. Beatrice realized that with all her painstaking effort to avoid the forbidden subjects—the war, Gian, Eesh's father, Il Moro, Galeazz, the mere use of the title "Duchess of Milan"—she had cut too close to an old wound. Eesh's mother.

"Anyway, I know I'm getting fat like Mama," Beatrice added, hoping that this trivial conclusion would put aside the painful subject.

"When do you expect the Emperor?" Isabella asked, accepting the offering.

"Within three or four days."

Isabella stared out the window overlooking the labyrinth. Beatrice wondered if she was remembering the night they held each other there. That moment when all their fates were suspended.

"So you are going to tell the Emperor that it would be a mistake for him to get involved in this Pisa business."

Beatrice was triply astonished—that Eesh knew about her opposition to the Pisa campaign, that Eesh at all cared, and that she had the strength to bring up a political matter of any kind. The careful protocol of their reconciliation had been completely discarded.

"We hear things," Isabella said, flipping her hand casually. "After all, the Empress is my sister-in-law. I can't believe that your husband is so foolish as to want to bring another *oltramontani* army into Italy. Of course I can't believe that the Emperor would be so foolish as to march into Italy with Il Moro as his sponsor," she added, almost taunting Beatrice now. "Your husband is the most faithless man since Judas. It isn't that he lies to his enemies to achieve his ends. We've all done that. But he keeps faith with no one. Friend, enemy, or lover." Isabella emphasized the last word. The dramatic silence that followed was also part of her syntax.

Beatrice looked away. "Does everyone in Milan know?"

"He has slept with her every night for the past two weeks. Right here in this *castello*, as I understand. Her brother, a whoring priest, has already gotten a benefice. In Milan they are talking of nothing else."

Beatrice felt the same cold hollowness she had the first time she'd heard the rumor about Lucrezia Crivelli. One of her ladies had "reluctantly" told her, no doubt in an attempt to curry favor. Beatrice had known immediately that it was most likely true. Her husband had once said that he needed to reach out in the night and touch someone who knew his soul. Now he needed someone who did not know his soul, someone who would not be able to share the agony of his inner struggle. Someone who might possibly save him from knowing himself. And of course when she had next seen him after hearing the rumor, just the blankness of his expression had been her confirmation. She didn't think he intended to lie to her; if she had asked about Lucrezia Crivelli he probably would have told her. But she hadn't asked. And after that they had simply avoided one another's eyes.

"I can't believe that after all you have done for him he can humiliate you like this," Isabella said sharply. "You have the power now to destroy him. *You* do. You don't even need your father anymore. You could put that bitch in a convent tomorrow and make him hang his prick on a peg for the rest of his life."

"Do you think I haven't thought of that? God, Eesh, do you realize how easily I could end it? I would simply have to tell my husband that if he does not place that whore in the most miserable, lice-crawling brothel in Germany, I intend to stay with my sister in Mantua until he does. That would be enough. I am not exaggerating, Eesh. He may not need me in his bed, but he could not function without me at his side."

"Then you must do it. Today. Even if you never want him to touch you again, you must do it for your children." There was a note of almost hysterical urgency in Isabella's voice, as if she were the wounded party.

Beatrice sat back heavily. "I have rehearsed that ultimatum a thousand times, I believe. A dozen times I have called for my chamberlain to announce me to my husband so that I could deliver it, then sent my chamberlain away with some other task." She shook her head sadly. "I cannot do it. I cannot do it to him. I think I understand his pain."

"His pain? You understand *his* pain?" Isabella was almost shrieking. "I can't believe you. That is the kind of thing I imagine my mother saying. The kind of weak, mewling self-sacrifice that drove my father away from her. From us. From all of us. She let my father's mistress sit in her place at supper just as though she were our mother. I had to sit there and watch that bitch Trusia Gazzella with her hand on my father's cock while my mother cried in her rooms. Yes, I'm sure my mother understood his pain just as she understood her own pain. She was always away at some spa, her servants sponging hot water over her pain, rubbing unguents into her pain. Who understood our pain, the pain of children whose mother might as well have been dead?"

Beatrice struggled for memories of Eesh's mother; for a long time she had thought that Trusia Gazzella *was* Eesh's mother. All she could bring back were quick glimpses of a beautiful sylph, more spectral than real, with an aura of quiet sadness.

"She killed herself, Toto. No one has ever admitted it, but I know that's what happened because she talked to me about it. She would tell me how she wanted to kill herself but couldn't because of us. She told me that. She killed herself right after I went off to be married, so that the news would reach me in the middle of my wedding *feste*. That's how much she cared for me. In one week I learned that I had a dead mother and a husband with a dead prick."

Beatrice reflexively crossed herself. She could see Eesh so much more clearly now. Her memories of Eesh's mother also sharpened. The cloying scent of too much Milanese perfume. As though by masking the must of the crypt she could fool the living. And the weeping. Beatrice suddenly remembered standing near a doorway, hearing the strange, murmuring sobs, wondering what made grown people cry.

"I'm sorry, Eesh. I never knew. I guess I should know by now that you can love people with all your soul and never truly know them."

Isabella lifted her quaking hands and looked at them as if they had suffered some terrible scarring. "She made me like this. Like her. Weak. Where every day is a struggle just to live. To keep repeating the lie of life."

"No, Eesh. You are stronger than any of us." Beatrice realized that she was about to cross the most forbidden threshold. "I couldn't have done what you did."

Isabella sniffed sarcastically, her black-wreathed head jerking. "You think you know what I did that night, and you have no idea. I wanted my son to be Duke of Milan so badly that I would have given my soul. And yet when I stood there beside you, my dream once again close enough to touch, only needing to let you speak . . ." She shook her head, a self-incriminating gesture. "I refused it because I knew that if it was taken from me again, I wouldn't have the strength to escape the darkness. Not again. I would waste and die. I didn't have the courage to risk that. I gave it up to save myself. Only after I had saved this vessel"—she held up her hands again—"did I understand that I had cast down my soul from that height. In an instant I could see myself lying in the piazza, dead. By my own hand, like my mother. What walked away that night was a corpse of no value to anyone. Like my mother."

"I don't believe that, Eesh. You said yourself that we don't know our own souls. I believe that you did it because you wanted to save our people. Because of the goodness in you. The love in you. The love that still has value, that is more valuable than anything." She looked searchingly at Isabella. "Perhaps some of that love came from your mother. From a time when she was strong enough to love you the way she wanted. Perhaps someday you will forgive her. Perhaps your soul already has."

"I envy you, Toto. You still live in a palace of dreams. You believe that you can still love a husband who has betrayed you. You think that you can win promises of peace from men whose only language is lies. You believe in forgiving the people who have only hurt you." She smiled slightly, sardonically. "You even believe that Fortune will someday forgive us for what we did."

Beatrice closed her eyes and leaned back. Her face was plumper than it had been even in her adolescence, yet shadowed with fatigue, a prophecy of what she might look like fifteen years thence. "I think you are also wrong about me, Eesh. Perhaps I do believe in peace, and even that my husband will love me again. I do want to forgive, and to be forgiven. I want you to forgive me. But I don't think Fortune will ever forgive us for what we've done."

CHAPTER

57

Vigevano, 5 September 1496

Beatrice had not realized how she would react when she saw her husband and Lucrezia Crivelli together for the first time—and not even close together; merely within the same field of view. Lucrezia had ridden to the hunt with Beatrice and her ladies; Il Moro arrived with the Emperor and a company of several dozen courtiers and diplomats. When the two parties converged and mixed, Lucrezia and Il Moro rode within a half-dozen paces of each other. Of course Beatrice had imagined them making love in countless different ways, but to finally see them both at once—fully clothed, mounted on their horses, not even glancing at one another— almost stopped her heart.

The anger that followed was so visceral that her horse felt it and jittered nervously. She had an almost irresistible urge to deliver her ultimatum now, in front of the entire court, to watch her white-faced husband send Lucrezia off to a German whorehouse on a mangy mule while the ambassadors looked on with gaping mouths. Then even that response seemed too considered, and some vestige of the little Ferrarese bride she had been a lifetime ago urged her to spit in their faces.

She found herself still sitting in the saddle a moment later, her hands quivering on the reins, thankful that her rage had subsided as quickly as it had come. She inhaled, set her shoulders, and responded like a proper Milanese for whom adultery was no more remarkable than a handclasp.

She received her husband's kiss on her cheek, as she had accepted all of his politically necessary displays of affection since the Emperor had arrived. Lucrezia, who in recent weeks she had seen almost as frequently as she had her husband, was still extended the same superficial politeness she offered all her ladies. Beatrice had no desire to engage a born-and-bred Milanese bitch in a contest of cold, indifferent stares.

The Emperor Maximilian rode to Beatrice's side, greeting her with a tip of his simple black woolen cap. A tall man with a small, thin face, a hawkish nose, tight mouth, and sad, expressive eyes, the Emperor was thirty-seven years old, but his hair had already turned a pale silver. Having recently vowed not to wear colors until he had led a crusade to the Holy Land, he wore a black velvet doublet, white shirt, and black hose.

"Since Duchess Beatrice is the finest horsewoman in Europe, I intend to stay by her side," the Emperor said in very adequate Italian.

"I'm certain my husband won't mind giving me up and accompanying one of my ladies," Beatrice said loudly enough for all to hear. Immediately she regretted the remark, though it wasn't entirely gratuitous. She had been looking for an opportunity to separate her husband and the Emperor.

A few titters could be heard among the group of ladies. Beatrice didn't dare glance at Lucrezia, though she doubted she had affected her stony composure. And she didn't even need to see her husband's face. With the same unbidden will that had allowed her to walk past the dead bodies in the streets of Milan, she put them behind her.

"Let's not wait here for the beaters to flush the game," Beatrice told the Emperor. "There are some good boar in the woods." She lifted her crop and galloped off without looking back. She already understood the Emperor well enough to know that he would follow. There was so much of the child in him; he was impetuous, romantic, eccentrically independent. And he clearly hated the confining ritual of court.

The smooth, fast gallop gave her less fear for her baby than the slow, jarring trot in the company of her ladies. And it was a risk she would have to take. She recognized a familiar path at the treeline, reined her horse, and entered a grove of towering oaks. The path cut through an undergrowth of ivy and blackberry bushes; she felt the light, cool mist of the shading trees on her face.

"You have the most magnificent park in Europe," the Emperor called out behind her. "I will come back when your boys are of age to hunt. I should like to take them."

Beatrice smiled fondly. Ambassadors from all the Italian states had descended on Vigevano, clamoring for audiences with the Emperor. But he had put them off, instead spending an inordinate amount of time with Beatrice's sons. And he talked a great deal of his own family. His first wife, Margaret of Burgundy, had given him two sons and a daughter in the first three years of their marriage. The second son died two weeks after his birth. Two years later, Margaret, pregnant again, had been killed in a riding accident. Their marriage had lasted only four years, but clearly Maximilian still loved her. He talked of Margaret as if she were still alive, and never even said the name of Bianca Maria, his present wife, occasionally referring to her abstractly as "the Empress."

On the other hand, the Emperor had turned the legacy of his love into a dynastic vise capable of crushing France. His first son, Philip, was married to the daughter of Ferdinand and Isabella, the King and Queen of Spain. His daughter was betrothed to King Ferdinand's heir. A concerted Spanish-German attack would end forever the threat posed by the restive French army, but Maximilian couldn't afford such an ambitious campaign. So, not unlike many impoverished Italian princes, the Emperor had hired himself out as *condottiere* to the Signory of Venice and the Duke of Milan. Maximilian had come to Italy not to prepare for the final destruction of Charles VIII's war machine but to soldier-for-hire in pursuit of an objective that Beatrice considered dubious even from the Milanese and Venetian perspective.

The path broadened into a small bowered clearing. Patches of sunlight glimmered like golden tesserae in the leafy canopy overhead. The Emperor came alongside Beatrice. "I hope I have not brought discord to your house," he said earnestly. "I have the greatest affection for you and your husband."

"You have not brought this discord."

"But you do not agree with your husband on my Pisa campaign."

"May I be honest with Your Majesty?"

The Emperor nodded with boyish enthusiasm.

"I understand that Pisa is an imperial fief and that you feel a responsibility to its people," Beatrice offered. "I understand that my husband and the Signory believe that your presence in Italy will discourage the French from mounting another Italian campaign. But even if you succeed in this venture, the results will be temporary. You will have to garrison Pisa against the Florentines, who will try to recapture it. Who will pay for that? The Signory will not, and my husband cannot. And if your campaign does not succeed as quickly as you expect and you require additional troops, again I ask, who will pay?"

"I will be welcomed into Pisa," the Emperor said, more wondering at his own stature than boasting of it.

"Perhaps. But your success will not discourage the French from waiting until you must inevitably leave. And when the French cross the mountains again, then who will pay you to come back and save Italy? The last war has taken everything we have, Your Majesty. Rather than waste the few ducats we have left on the transient conquest of Pisa, we would all be better served if that money were spent building a German army capable at any moment of marching into Paris."

"This war in Pisa is not big enough for you? You want me to attack France?"

"No. I want you to convince France that she cannot steal her prosperity from Italy. That instead of spending every *livre* on cannons and crossbows she must devote her revenues to putting new lands under cultivation and building mills and factories and universities. You would not have to attack France to eventually convince the French that their monstrous army, which can only be fed by conquest, is a luxury they can no longer afford."

"And when the French have become peaceful, that will leave the English free to adventure in Europe. I will be honest with you and say I do not like this English King Henry in our League."

"Then we will prove to the English that they cannot make war on the Continent. And then they, too, will have to find the way of prosperity and peace."

The Emperor had the rapt, distant look of a daydreaming boy. At length he said, "Duchess Beatrice, you are very brave, very noble. I hope that one day your boys will have your peace. Or maybe their boys. But there are two things I am certain I will never be able to do while I live. Bring my Margaret back. And bring peace to Europe." He turned his head quickly, listening. "I hear dogs. Come, let us go back to the hunt."

Vigevano, 7 September 1496

"You will be able to make do with one dining table, if it is long enough," Beatrice told Bianca. Galeazzo di Sanseverino's new *palazzo* was on the eastern edge of town, and the big arched windows of the second-story dining hall overlooked the verdant ducal park, affording a sweeping view of the Alps. At present, the big room was entirely empty except for several large stacks of folded damask drapes.

In two days Bianca was moving into Galeazz's home, the consummation of a six-year-old marriage. In little more than a week the onslaught of social obligations would begin, when she hosted a suite of Venetian ambassadors, arriving to consult with the Emperor on the now-inevitable Pisa campaign.

Beatrice walked over to the stacks of fabric and pulled up a length of red damask embroidered with blue Sforza vipers. "What we will do is drape the side windows with this and do the center windows with the gold drapes with the imperial crest. That should be your principal motif, so we must make certain that we also have *confetti* in the shape of imperial eagles."

Bianca's fragile, hollow cheeks had filled out in the past few months, but not so much that they detracted from the delicacy of her finely pointed nose and small mouth. Her wondering eyes had narrowed slightly, their feverish innocence replaced by the earthier anticipation of a young bride. She wore her brown hair parted down the middle, with a long Milanese-style braid, but she had also adopted one of the latest *nove foze*, a lock of hair wrapped beneath the chin. "Toto," she asked, "has the Emperor decided to go to Pisa?"

"I'm afraid he has."

Bianca bit her lower lip. "Why has my father brought the Emperor into Italy to pursue another campaign? It is a betrayal of what my father has always said he believes."

"Your father thinks that what he is doing will prove to the French that the Emperor is serious about his guarantees for the security of Italy. He hopes that this little war will prevent a big war."

"But you don't agree with him."

"No. No, I don't."

"I hate him," Bianca said, her face flushed bright red.

"No, baby, I don't ever want to turn you against your father. We just disagree—"

"That's not the reason." Bianca's voice broke. "I hate him because of what he is doing to you. I know about Lucrezia Crivelli. Everybody in the *castello* does. He isn't even trying to keep it a secret. I will never stop hating him for this, Toto."

Beatrice rushed to Bianca and embraced her, feeling her hot tears against her cheek. "Don't hate him, baby. Please don't. For my sake don't hate him."

Bianca sobbed harshly into Beatrice's ear. Finally she blurted out, "Toto, please don't let it change things for us. Please don't stop loving me because of him."

"Oh, baby, nothing could ever change what is between us. I will always love you. Nothing, nothing, will ever come between us. Death could not separate us."

Bianca sobbed with grateful relief. Beatrice took a handkerchief from her sleeve and wiped Bianca's nose and sat down with her on the stack of embroidered drapes.

"I loved you before I ever loved your father," Beatrice said.

Bianca sniffled. "Do you still love him?"

"Yes. Yes, I do. I will always love him."

"What's wrong with him? Why is he doing this to you?"

Beatrice gazed out the window for a moment, watching a bank of clouds march across the horizon. Then she said, "You know the first line from the *Inferno*."

Bianca recited the line almost automatically. " 'Midway through our life's journey, I found myself in a dark wood, having lost the straight path.' "

"I think your father is lost in that dark wood right now. Perhaps he believes that Lucrezia Crivelli will help him find his way."

"Do all husbands eventually become lost in this dark wood, Toto?"

"I would imagine that sooner or later we all find ourselves there. And we all must find our way into the light again. Dante had to descend into Hell and climb Purgatory before he found his way. Let us hope your father's journey will not be so difficult."

"Toto, you know how you told me about the romances you read as a girl, how you dreamed of gallant knights who would whisper magic words in your ear and give you kisses as soft as starlight?" Bianca looked to Beatrice for confirmation. "I never had to read those books. I always had Galeazz. He was my knight, but he was real. I was ten years old the first time I sat in the grandstand at a joust and listened to him dedicate his victories to me. You've seen all my dresses made from the cloth-of-gold he won as prizes in the tournaments, my *guardaroba* full of the gifts he has sent me. At a thousand suppers I stared at his face and thought to myself, He is mine. My Galeazz. My knight. Every time he kisses me on the cheeks I dream of what it will be like when he holds me in his arms and kisses my lips. He is my dream, Toto, my living dream. I love him so much.

"Am I going to be made a fool, Toto? All of your ladies tell me I am. And when I see what happens to marriages here, I believe that they are right. I am no longer a girl. It *is* foolish for me to have a girl's dreams."

Beatrice put her arm around Bianca maternally. "Galeazz probably won't be much like the knight you imagined him to be. You are likely to find marriage difficult at first. You might even find it miserable. You know I did. But I believe that someday you will find a love with Galeazz that will be much more profound, much more magical, than anything you ever could've dreamed of as a girl. I honestly believe that."

"And then he will go off into a dark wood and break my heart."

"I can't promise you that that won't happen, baby. I would

give anything if I could. But I don't think any love we have is ever lost or ever diminished." Beatrice paused, reflecting on her own life. "I think perhaps if it is really a true and noble love, it can only grow. I look at my Mama and see how her love for my father grew into a love for her children and then into a love for every woman's child. You will have your own children, and I know for myself that with each child your love grows. Your dreams are no longer so much for yourself as they are for them. Mama dreamed of peace for her children. She did not live to see that. Now I have her dream, and perhaps I will never live to see it. But if my children can dream it, and their children, and if each generation refuses to give up that dream, someday it will be real. So you ask me if you are foolish to hold on to your dreams. No; no, baby, you're not. We are only fools when we no longer have dreams."

C H A P T E R

58

Extract of a letter of LEONARDO DA VINCI, engineer at the Court of Milan, to international traveler and raconteur BENEDETTO DEI. Milan, 15 November 1496

. . . I can tell you without risk of contradiction that there is no love for Il Moro here. The tax levies have been increased yet again, and he has made such public demonstration of his lust for his mistress that no one here will speak his name without spitting. It is widely regarded that the treasury is exhausted, but you would not know it to see the schedule of *feste* for the Christmas celebrations. (I have often reflected, my dear Benedetto, that the true miracle of this Holy Season is the magnitude of the industry given birth by a poor carpenter from Galilee.) I myself have not received a ducat toward my salary in the past two months, yet Il Moro has imperiously summoned me from my labors on my fresco of the Last Supper at Santa Maria delle Grazie (this after all the calumny that I will never finish it) and commanded me to render a portrait of his paramour, one Lucrezia Crivelli. I have drawn her a half-dozen times already, and as I am unpersuaded of her carnal attractions, I can find no feature to which I can ascribe the qualities of beauty. . . . If not for the good will everyone holds toward the

Duchess of Milan, we should already have seen the mobs clamoring in the streets. In all this unseemly unfair the said Duchess has held her head high, and there is no one here who can claim with any veracity to have heard her disparage, in word or deed, her husband or even the woman with whom he so shamelessly consorts. . . .

Milan, 22 November 1496

"Your Highness, His Highness your husband."

Her husband hadn't called on Beatrice in her rooms since the night her baby was conceived—a baby now due in less than three months. Their separate lives had become a routine that grew less painful every day, partly because she was finally letting herself settle into it, but also, paradoxically, because as her baby's term progressed she could see an end to it. She was his wife and the mother of his children. Lucrezia was a flickering passion in his dark wood, no more enduring than a single candle. When the baby was born he would come back.

He came in right after the chamberlain. All she saw was his terrible face: The same quiet madness she'd seen when he came to tell her about Alfonso's attempt to poison him and their son; the same terror in his eyes she'd seen when he lay paralyzed with the "illness." And something new, something still more terrible.

He advanced unsteadily. She just stared at him, silently begging him not to speak. She didn't want to know. She saw in her mind something glistening and cold, like a dome of ice over her, an astringent but painless refuge for her soul. If he spoke, her icy sanctuary would shatter, and in would rush the terrible thing on his face.

He stopped, too far away even for her to touch him. His lips quivered. He was speaking, but the sound seemed to follow much later, as if his words were slowly boring through the ice that separated them, emerging spent, just at the threshold of hearing. "She's . . . dead. Dead."

Beatrice heard a high whistling sound. Of course, someone is dead, she thought. Someone I don't care about but he does. Like Lucrezia. Dear God, yes . . .

"My daughter. Bianca."

Silently: That is the sickest, cruelest, most hateful lie. Bianca couldn't . . . Oh, dear God, no . . . Marriage kills as many girls as childbirth, especially the frail girls.

"I . . ." His hands fluttered as he attempted to gesture but then fell lifeless to his sides.

For some reason the ice dome hadn't shattered. It only whistled where his words had entered. But now she couldn't breathe the cold air. She could breathe only if she screamed.

"Liar!" She lunged forward and hit him so hard that his head lolled and his knees sagged. The expression on his face never changed. "Liar!"

"I wish by all that is holy that this time I were," he whispered into the shrill silence. "In Vigevano. A fever. Galeazz didn't think it was serious, and then—"

"Galeazz didn't think!" she screamed, her face livid and her hands clenched like claws. "Galeazz killed her! He killed her! I want him hanged! If I ever see his face again I will kill him myself!"

Il Moro seemed to take this threat seriously, and he managed to get his hands up for a brief expository gesture. "He is near death with grief. I know the pain that this must bring you. . . ."

She didn't hear anything else. He talked for an eternity, his hands making pathetic little circling motions at his sides. She was just your bastard, you bastard, she silently told him, as his lips quivered on. She was my baby. She was my girl. She was my best *amica*.

Now he had his hands on her shoulders. She knew that if she didn't listen, his lips would never stop moving. She let his words in: ". . . Do you want me to stay with you?"

She felt the great surge of grief rising inside her and just wanted him to leave. She shook her head.

"I . . ." Again the helpless hands.

She couldn't speak. She just made a pushing motion with her hands, pushing him out. His expression changed slightly, and he turned too quickly to leave. As he walked out she could hear his heavy footfall much more clearly than she had his words. In the dimming light she had a final, dull realization, that by sending him away she had lessened his pain.

Il Moro returned to his mistress's suite of rooms on the second floor of the Rochetta, the rooms formerly used by Duchess Bona (who had been moved out of the Castello, to a *palazzo* on the Piazza del Duomo).

Lucrezia Crivelli took him in her arms as soon as he crossed the threshold.

"I told my wife," he said. "I had to be the one to tell her. She loved Bianca like her own. . . ."

"Of course you had to be with her. Perhaps it would be better if you stayed with her for a while."

He shook his head. Tears tracked down his cheeks.

Lucrezia undressed him and put him to bed. She propped him up on pillows and gave him a goblet of wine. She was silent throughout, her fingers consoling him with light touches and gentle, spontaneous caresses. Finally she stripped to her chemise and snuffed the lamp.

Il Moro felt the terror of sudden darkness, a violent tremor welling inside him. Then Lucrezia's body pressed against his and he marveled at the narcotic effect of her flesh. In the beginning he had believed that this liaison was never intended, that a mere caprice had resulted in the accidental betrayal of his wife. And even after the dalliance had begun in earnest, he had insisted to himself that he had never intended to make it public; that had been the result of a vicious gossip campaign orchestrated by the same ladies-in-waiting whose subtle advances he had spurned for years.

But now, his defenses reduced by grief, he admitted to himself the desperate need this passion had fulfilled. Beatrice possessed a courage he could never have, an unrelenting reminder of his own moral cowardice. She had become strong enough to unmask his most profound self-deceptions, to enter him and harrow the darkest vaults of his soul. He could argue that he had abandoned her out of love, an Orpheus who had realized he could only lead his wife deeper into Hades, but that too was a mask. It was simply less painful for him to deny Beatrice his love than to allow himself to suffer the loss of her love. And so he had found Lucrezia, whose infinitely mutable face wore as many masks as his own. He could love Lucrezia without pain, because she would never demand the truth that would force him to betray her.

"Lodovico," she whispered. "Give me your hand."

She placed his cold hand on her belly.

"Lodovico, nothing can ever bring Bianca back. She was unique. We must accept what time she had with us as Fortune's gift." She pressed his hand tightly. "And we must begin again. We must take the love she left us and go on. You are touching the child of our love, Lodovico. I am going to have your baby."

Extract of a dispatch of FRANCESCO FOSCARI, Venetian ambassador to Milan, to the SIGNORY OF VENICE. Milan, 11 December 1496

. . . hearing that the Emperor had left Pisa and gone to Pavia, I immediately made my way there but for many days was refused an audience. . . . None of my entreaties could persuade His Imperial Majesty to remain in Italy and complete the enterprise on which he so recently embarked. When I told His Imperial Majesty that the Signory could not be held responsible for the storm that destroyed our fleet at Pisa, he replied, be that as it may, he had no inclination to fight God and man at the same time. Indeed, I believe that the true enemy of this enterprise is Il Moro, who in his overweening arrogance assumes that he can employ the German Emperor as his *condottiere* and force the Signory of Venice to serve as paymaster, leaving to himself only the task of accepting the prize. . . .

Thus His Imperial Majesty began his journey back across the mountains. His enterprise, pursued at such great cost, has effected no result and leaves the affairs of Italy in still greater confusion than he found them. . . .

C H A P T E R

59

Milan, 2 January 1497

The refectory next to the church of Santa Maria delle Grazie was deserted except for the solitary presence of Leonardo da Vinci, who stood on the scaffolding at the far end of the small dining hall. Dressed in a long green velvet *vestito*, he stared at the anguished face of Saint Philip. He frequently worked like this, contemplating his almost finished *Last Supper* for days at a time, without lifting a brush. Then he might come in one morning and paint furiously until evening, without pausing to eat or drink.

He did not turn when Beatrice entered. She walked past the tables already set up for the friars' supper. On the far wall Christ and His twelve apostles dined in what appeared an extension of the room, suffused with the soft, mystic light streaming through three illusionistic windows that opened onto a vivid imaginary landscape. Leonardo's treatment of the subject was unconventional; instead of the usual rendition of Christ handing Judas a sop of bread, identifying him as the traitor, Leonardo had chosen the moment only slightly earlier when Christ said to all His disciples, "One of you shall betray me." In Leonardo's version Judas recoiled in horror, his face the only one shadowed from the radiance that bathed the rest of the figures. But all the apostles reacted with similar vehemence, a fury of denial, gesturing broadly and protesting, "You don't mean me, Master? Surely not I!" To Beatrice, Leonardo's message was obvious: at that moment each apostle had realized that he was capable of betraying Christ.

Beatrice took up a position almost directly behind Leonardo, staring at the painting as stoically as the artist himself. There was nothing mythical about the faces Leonardo had painted; all of his apostles—even his Christ—had been modeled from people the artist knew or had observed. Leonardo had created a parable of their time: the good men disclaiming "Surely not I," no less horrified by their own secret guilt than Judas was by the certainty of his. Beatrice looked at the face of Christ, supposedly drawn from the young Cardinal of Mortara but with an unformed innocence wholly lacking in the Cardinal's worldly prettiness. Nothing has changed, Beatrice thought, not in the fourteen and a half centuries since Christ gave his body and blood. The good men still protest that evil is not among them, the evil men claim their reward, and the innocents die.

She turned and walked out. The slanting late afternoon sun cast a sheen over the small, cobbled piazza in front of the church. She stood for a moment in the light. She had prayed in Santa Maria delle Grazie every day since Bianca's death. But she debated going in today simply because she didn't think she would have the strength to leave. She recalled what Eesh had once told her about the terrible exhaustion of despair, the unbearable effort required to sustain the lie of life. The lie of life. Beatrice decided to go in, if only because she didn't care if she ever left.

The altar, directly beneath the dome, was lit with dozens of memorial candles; a softer light fell from the windows high above. The first time Beatrice had seen the new, cleanly engraved slab right in front of the altar, the torment had been unimaginable: Bianca was in there beneath it, and she knew she would never hold her again. And somehow Mama had been in there too. But after visiting Bianca every day for the past six weeks, she now found the huge, pinkish-gray slab curiously reassuring. It was Bianca's fortress, guarding her from a world of pain and darkness. Bianca was untouchable now. No one would ever hurt her again.

Beatrice knelt on the wooden platform just beyond Bianca's slab, resting her arms on the black onyx altar railing. At the altar table a white-robed priest labored over Mass, chanting and genuflecting with dreary efficiency. She glanced up at the round windows circling the dome above her, a ring of softly glowing suns. That was where Bianca had gone. Into the light. She was pure and innocent, and she had flown at once into the Supreme Light, to bask beneath the ineffable face of God. Bianca was happy and loved. Those she had left behind grieved for themselves, because they were still falling into darkness.

The lie of life. Beatrice thought of the hypocrites in Dante's eighth circle of Hell, condemned to trudge through eternity in massive leaden cassocks. But in truth all the living wore the crushing cloak of lies, simply because they went on living. They promised their children peace when they could give them only wars, they promised each other love when they could offer only betrayal. The future had once promised Beatrice hope, but now she could see only the inevitability of her despair. The Emperor had abandoned Italy in disgust, and now the French were openly recruiting mercenaries for a new Italian campaign in the spring, an invasion with the sole objective of conquering Milan. Lucrezia was having his baby. Beatrice had confirmed that rumor just this morning. Now even her boys brought her sorrow. They would grow up like Eesh, watching their father love another woman. And soon she would have to lie to them, or otherwise tell them the truth: that in this journey into darkness good men suffer the woes of damnation and evil men prosper.

She looked up again at the glowing ring of windows far above her. Go, said a forbidden yet shockingly familiar voice. Fly up there. Take your little girl away from this. The voice became a tantalizing aria, an angelic siren song, luring her from her pain. The light began to draw her up like a luminous cyclone, lifting her out of her leaden shell. Her limbs became weightless, free, ready to fly. Let go, she pleaded to the last vestiges of her earthbound body. I am ready. Let me go.

But she could not fly. The light dimmed, and the weight settled back around her. It was not the burden of life's lies that bound her to earth, but a desire to fall all the way to the dark center of evil, to see at the end the only truth life allowed. To look into the face of Satan and see if it was her own.

"In a week I must go into confinement," Beatrice called out above the frantic melody of a *moresca*. "Until then we will have a *festa* every night! I have sent for everyone! Tonight we will bury our cares and grief!"

Beatrice's lady-in-waiting Dorotea nodded eager agreement, her violet-tinted blue eyes as hungry as her pet cheetah's. Eyes that mirrored the mood of the entire court for the past few weeks. The mourning over the universally beloved Bianca had been replaced by a foreboding. The empty treasury and the new French ambitions were common knowledge. If Fortune intended to turn against them, they could no longer deter or postpone her wrath. They could only respond with vicious self-indulgence.

Once again their Duchess would lead them in their time of peril. Beatrice had brought more than a dozen musicians into her rooms. Lutes, woodwinds, *trombone*, clavichord, even two Spanish-style guitars—the ensemble designed to inflame eager passions rather than soothe tortured spirits. The best wines had been taken from the cellars, the finest Murano glass goblets would shatter on the floor. To make the anticipated sexual melee yet more interesting, some of the *buffone* had been dressed like women. Dwarfs raced through the rooms. The aggressive laughter of the tautly strung women competed with the spinning melody of the music.

By half-past seven the rooms were so crowded with courtiers and ladies that it seemed there wasn't air left to breathe, only the intoxicating ether of abandon. Spinning circles of dancers formed, broke apart, and re-formed. Pearl-studded satin headbands went askew, plump breasts trembled in plunging bodices, hands roamed openly over bare flesh. Clusters of laughing ladies wagered on who would be first to make love in front of everyone, with whom and how, and when. The first goblet was thrown against the floor.

"You know who is missing!" Beatrice shouted to Dorotea. She pulled her lady away from the papal ambassador, a tall, horse-faced man who had become notorious for switching identities with his chamberlain just before the consummation of an affair with a necessarily besotted paramour; apparently the ambassador preferred to hide in a chest at the foot of the bed and listen. Beatrice put her lips to Dorotea's ear and whispered. Dorotea laughed wickedly and ran out through the antechamber.

A half hour later someone observed that Beatrice was nowhere to be found. "Where is our Duchess?" another reveler yelled drunkenly. "Our muse!" But there were other attractions, and the dancers whirled on.

A few minutes afterward the entrance of the evening occurred. Galeazzo di Sanseverino moved through the crush, the men stepping respectfully aside, the women pressing closer. "Galeazzzz," the ladies hissed like snakes, shameless participants in a lottery. Galeazz's features were as Apollonian as ever, but he had dyed his hair black, and there was a slight darkening around his eyes, a hint of mortality. He glanced nervously about the room. He had taken a risk in coming here, but then he was fond of this kind of risk.

After a few perfunctory exchanges Galeazz excused himself and went to the lavatory adjacent to Beatrice's bedroom. He shut the door quickly behind him. A scented taper burned in a little brass urn on the privy seat, casting enough light to illuminate the shadowy form of his paramour. Her back was to him. He waited.

The woman turned. "Galeazz," she said.

Galeazz jumped as if he'd heard a corpse speak.

"I knew you would come, even at the risk of seeing me. Haven't you made love to a different woman in every lavatory in this *castello?*"

"Your Highness . . . ," Galeazz said plaintively.

Beatrice stepped forward until her swollen belly almost touched him. "I'm sorry to disappoint you. You were expecting Madonna Dorotea. Why don't you fuck me instead? Haven't I heard that you like to get pregnant women on their knees and see if you can make their babies kick?"

Galeazz said nothing. The muffled music and laughter went on outside.

Suddenly Beatrice pounded on his chest, a massive, thudding blow that pushed him back a step. "She was my baby," she hissed through clenched teeth. "She was my girl. You killed her, you bastard!" She pounded his chest again. "You could have loved her, and instead you killed her!"

"No one—"

"No one suffered more than you. I know. My husband assured me of that. But then my husband never could see behind the shining armor of your hypocrisy." She gave a nasty laugh. "Perhaps he could only see the reflection of his own vanity. Perhaps that is all any of us saw. Who else have you killed, Galeazz?"

Galeazz stepped back toward the door, "Your Highness, I think—"

Beatrice lunged at him and pressed her hunting knife to his throat. He stiffened with pain as the point penetrated the soft skin beneath his jaw, but he made no effort to resist.

"I want to know who killed Gian. Who did it and who ordered it."

He said nothing, and she jabbed the point of the knife in again. "You can tell me here, or you can tell me down below. In the dungeons. I will have you strapped to the wheel and your feet roasted until you tell me. And if you think my husband will be able to save you, you are wrong. He isn't even here tonight. He has bought his whore a *palazzo* in town, for her convenience when she goes shopping. They are sleeping there tonight."

"Bernardino da Corte poisoned him," Galeazz said in a strangled voice. "I ordered it. I ordered it because Isabella told me what she intended to do. She thought she could convince me to support her. I knew then that the only way to stop Gian from abdicating was to kill him."

"Did my husband know?"

"He didn't order it. I ordered it."

"Did he know?"

"No."

"Was it ever discussed?"

Galeazz hesitated. "Yes. But your husband said he would never permit it."

She felt the truth then, a cold trickling inside her. "But you knew that he wanted it. If he'd had the courage he would have ordered it. You knew that. And when it was done he knew that you had done it."

"He never asked," Galeazz protested. "I swear he never did."

"My husband never asked because he was afraid you would tell him the truth. Because then he would have had to face his own guilt." Because then my husband would have had to look up at the face of Satan and recognize his own. Then Beatrice asked herself, Was my denial any less vehement than his? I suspected and too easily accepted any reason to dismiss my suspicions.

She lowered the knife, then let it drop to the floor. A moment before, she'd believed that she could kill Galeazz. Now she could not even hate him. She had an image of all of them sitting at a table like the apostles in Leonardo's *Last Supper:* herself and her husband, Eesh, Galeazz and Bernardino, King Charles and Orleans, Bona, Alfonso and Ferrante, Ser Privolo and the Doge. The face of Christ was Gian's. Perhaps dark-faced Bernardino had been Gian's Judas, but they had all schemed for Gian's betrayal in one way or another, had all been capable of his murder. She knew the protest they'd all recited, because she had said it to herself a thousand times. Surely not I. Surely, Master, I am not capable of such a thing. But they had all poisoned Gian, they had all slaughtered the thousands of other innocents who had perished in the war. And they had all poisoned their own souls.

She pushed Galeazz aside and opened the door. The renewed blare of the music heralded her arrival in some harsh new realm. Everything was wrong: the colors too garish, the mouths of the revelers distorted, their laughs like arrows in her womb. She wanted to scream to everyone to get out, but she was afraid to be alone with herself.

Beatrice joined a spinning circle of dancers, finding escape in her old refuge of motion. She shouted for the musicians to increase the tempo, trying to blur the excruciating colors. She remembered the May Day when she and Galeazz had danced on the whirling rim of fate, with every choice possible, every destiny a brilliant shooting star. Now the circle had closed, and all the stars had fallen from the sky. Every choice had been Fortune's deceit, Fortune's fraud. There was nothing left to do but spin, waiting for the darkness, waiting for the end.

A deep, stinging pain pierced her womb and she lost control of her feet, falling, tumbling off the spinning wheel. When she finally stopped she was on the floor, watching a frantic mosaic of hose-clad legs and swishing velvet skirts. The music lost its rhythm and then piece by piece stopped, the clavichord the last instrument to fall silent, a sad plinking of isolated notes. Men shouted, some women screamed. They came to her, bending down to show her their horrible faces. Why? she thought. Why?

She felt the warm gush between her legs. At first she imagined she had wet herself, and that was why they all looked so horrified. Then she knew. Dear God, she pleaded as the room began to spin. My little girl. Please, God, not my baby girl.

CHAPTER

60

The outer doors to the Duchess of Milan's rooms were blocked by four guards armed with bladed pikes. When they refused to step aside and let her pass, Isabella confronted the young officer who commanded them. "Her Highness has sent for me."

The young man removed his cap. "Ah, that may be so, Your Highness, but Messer Ambrogio has instructed me that no one is to be admitted except the Duke of Milan when he arrives."

"Then let me in to talk with Messer Ambrogio."

The young man pulled at his cap. "Ah, Your Highness—"

"Very well. I will return in five minutes with my own men, and then you will have to decide if you wish to shed blood simply to avoid obeying the Duchess of Milan's request."

The young man pulled at his cap a moment longer. "Ah, then, I will see if Messer Ambrogio will admit you."

Isabella nodded, and the young man unlocked the doors. As he started to slip inside, Isabella shoved past him and darted into the darkened antechamber. Behind her the officer softly called, "Ah, Your Highness . . ."

The bedchamber was stifling. Everything on the bed was tinted by the fire in the hearth: the embroidered white coverlet, the white pillows that propped Beatrice's head, her white chemise, the plasterlike hand that lay at her side. And her face. Eyes closed, a white marble bust, the blind witness to a final, apocalyptic conflagration.

Isabella approached the bedside, hoping that somehow this wasn't Beatrice, that this was some cruel jest. Something moved beside her, and she threw up her hands in terror. Messer Ambrogio stepped from the racing shadows.

"She's dead," Isabella said.

Messer Ambrogio seemed curiously relieved to see her. He shook his head. "Not dead," he intoned in his eerie, soughing voice. "But beyond the help of man. Only God can heal her now."

"What about her baby?"

"Born dead." Messer Ambrogio wrung his hands nervously. "I don't know why they cannot find the Duke of Milan. If you will stay with her, I will go see." Without waiting for a reply, he wrapped himself in his cape and walked off.

Very quietly Isabella sat down on the bed beside her cousin and took her hand. It was shockingly cold, as cold as dead stone. Beatrice's arm was limp. After a moment her eyelids fluttered and opened. Her eyes were dull, but they caught the glow of the fire.

"Eesh," she whispered. Her lips formed a slight smile, and only then did Isabella notice their ghastly pale lavender hue. "I told you my baby would kill me. But I never knew I would kill my baby."

"You didn't kill your baby. And your baby isn't going to kill you."

Beatrice again smiled slightly. "Lift the covers. Look."

Isabella lifted the covers and shuddered with horror at the same moment that Beatrice shivered violently, apparently from cold. Beatrice's chemise had been pulled up to her hips. What appeared to be her entire, fully ripened uterus lay in a bloody pulp between her legs. Isabella forced herself to look again. Only then did she realize that the obscene thing wasn't flesh but a bundle of blood-soaked rags.

"Oh, God, Toto. What have they done to you? Oh, God. I have to change these." Isabella removed the sopping rags and threw them onto the floor. She looked around frantically and then pulled up her own skirts and ripped big swatches of cloth from her chemise. She packed the improvised dressing between Beatrice's legs.

"God, Toto. I'm going to send for a real physician. And my midwife. We have to do something."

Beatrice shook her head with sudden animation. "No, Eesh. They can't . . . I just want them to leave me alone. I've been bleeding since the baby came. He didn't cry. A little boy. A beautiful little boy. But he couldn't cry. When I started bleeding I knew it wouldn't stop. Not this time. The priests have been here. I didn't want them here when . . ." She turned her head in agony. "It's so sad . . . knowing. I'll never see my little boys again."

"You will. I'll get them."

Beatrice shook her head. "No, Eesh. Please don't. Please . . . I want them so much. But don't leave them this memory." Beatrice closed her eyes, and her face twitched and convulsed. Then her eyes shot open and she looked at Eesh with a final fury. "Eesh. You were right. It's all a lie. Life . . . is a lie. Love . . . is a lie. I had to tell you before . . . You were right. Now I know your pain."

Isabella sat silently for a moment. Then she wrapped her blood-smeared fingers around Beatrice's cold hand. "No. It wasn't all a lie, Toto. I loved you. I truly did. I don't regret that love, Toto." The corners of Isabella's mouth moved subtly, as if forming a perplexing, bittersweet revelation. "Because I loved you, I finally learned how to love my little girls. I do love them, Toto. In a way I never thought I could." She leaned over Beatrice's blanched face. "That is the legacy of our love. A love that will endure after we are all gone."

Beatrice closed her eyes. "Eesh. Forgive me."

"I have," Isabella whispered. She hesitated. "Can *you* forgive *me?*"

"Yes." Beatrice attempted a smile. "Forgive her too, Eesh. Your mother."

Isabella said nothing.

"Eesh. Can you . . . bring me . . . my baby?"

It was a moment before Isabella realized what she meant. "Oh, Toto, I don't think you should."

"Please, Eesh. I never held him."

Isabella squeezed Beatrice's hand and got up. When she turned she thought Messer Ambrogio had come back in. But the man in the doorway was Il Moro. Isabella looked back to Beatrice. Il Moro walked slowly and silently to the end of the bed.

"Lodovico," Beatrice half whispered, half mouthed.

"Do you want him to leave?" Isabella asked.

Beatrice shook her head. Isabella and Il Moro looked at one another for a moment. Then Isabella turned and went out.

Il Moro fell to his knees beside his wife's bed. He clutched desperately for her hand. Then he pressed his face into the covers and sobbed.

Finally Beatrice whispered again, "Lodovico."

When he lifted his head, Il Moro's face was violently contorted, as if all the emotions he had suppressed for so many years had been allowed a single hideous expression. "God, I would give my soul to undo what I have done! You were my only love. My one love. God, I was coming back. I promise you I was coming back! I am back!" He gasped for air. "I have pledged to end the liaison tonight. I will never see her again. She was a trinket, a bauble, and to my eternal shame I put aside my true treasure for her. All that has ended. Oh, merciful God, I cannot live without you. Oh, merciful God. My one true love. Oh, merciful God." Finally his head fell, and he cried into the covers again.

When he had quieted she spoke to him, her voice drawing on some final, deeply hidden resource. "Lodovico. No more lies. Only the truth. However painful."

He raised his head.

"You knew Galeazz had Gian poisoned."

He could not look at her. He stared at the fire and whispered his answer. "Yes."

She closed her eyes and didn't move; only the pressure of her hand indicated that she was still alive. Finally she marshaled her voice again. "Was any of it real? Did you ever . . . love me?"

He intently studied their clasped hands, his eyes dark and still. "There was a time when you were my own soul," he said softly. "And I could not live with that." He looked at her, his features struggling for control and dignity. "Beatrice showed our poet the face of God. But only after Dante had the courage to climb out of Hell. I never had that courage. I was afraid to let you take me to the light. I was afraid that if you saw me in the light you could no longer love me."

"I still . . . ," she said with difficulty, "love you."

"I know," he said, leaning forward. "I know, *amore*." His lips brushed against hers.

Il Moro held his wife's hand until Isabella came back. The baby was wrapped in white linen, so tiny that he seemed scarcely more than a bandaged hand. Isabella placed him on Beatrice's breast. His face was perfect, white and peaceful, a little alabaster angel.

"I . . . have to . . . hold him."

Il Moro was too inert with grief to release Beatrice's hand. "Let her go, Lodovico," Isabella said gently. She arranged the little body in the crook of Beatrice's free arm.

Beatrice tried to look at her third son, her eyelids fluttering as she slipped toward a timeless sleep. "I'm taking him . . . with me," she whispered, her words the faintest exhalations. "To see . . . the face . . . of . . . God."

They lay there together, madonna and child, while the flames in the fireplace diminished to glowing embers. For almost an hour Isabella and Il Moro knelt by them silently, knowing the truth but refusing to move, waiting for some miracle.

Finally it came. The dying fire cast a rosy flush across the two dead faces, and for a moment they might have been alive.

Extract of a letter of the Venetian diplomat MARINO SANUTO to the SIGNORY OF VENICE. Milan, 3 February 1497

. . . I have never before witnessed such an expression of spontaneous grief by an entire people. A city that knew nothing but pleasure has put aside all pursuits save mourning. Remarkable indeed is the widespread conviction here that the Duchess of Milan's death signifies that Fortune, who looked with such favor on the Milanese and their Duke, has now turned away. . . .

For the two weeks following his wife's death Il Moro confined himself to a single shuttered room, refusing to admit the light of day into his presence, or even his children, much less his ministers and the ambassadors who desired to convey the condolences of their lords. He emerged on 17 January, but he has commanded his ministers to speak of naught save the business of state, and never to mention the Duchess of Milan's name in his presence, or make any allusion that might remind him of his recent bereavement. . . . He has shaved his head and wears a cloak of poor black fustian like a monk. . . . The greatest portion of his time is spent at Mass in the church where his wife is buried beside the tomb of his daughter. . . . His grief is beyond understanding. . . .

C H A P T E R

61

Extract of a dispatch of COUNT CARLO BELGIOIOSO, Milanese ambassador to France, to LODOVICO SFORZA, "Il Moro," Duke of Milan. Amboise, 8 April 1498

. . . His Most Christian Majesty's poor health prevented him from taking part in these tennis matches, but as His Majesty was desirous of observing them, he took himself and his Queen to the gallery overlooking the courts. The doorway to this gallery is quite low, and King Charles, who ordinarily has little to fear of such hazards, neglected to lower his head. His forehead struck the stone lintel in such a fashion that the noise was quite audible, but after picking himself up he went on in and observed the matches, talking as if nothing had taken place. An hour later, however, he quite suddenly pitched over backward and lay there, unable to speak. . . . The physicians were summoned but could effect nothing. . . . Shortly after dark he gave up his soul. . . .

. . . I fear we are more likely to lament the ill fortune that so recently deprived King Charles's little son of his life. I know of no challenge that will be presented (and legally there is none) to the succession of the First Prince of the Blood, Louis Duc d'Orléans. I am already informed by those who fear Louis's ambitions that he has declared that his first act as King Louis XII will be the conquest of the Duchy of Milan. . . .

Extract of a letter of the artist LEONARDO DA VINCI to international traveler and raconteur BENEDETTO DEI. Florence, 20 April 1500

. . . after fleeing to Como to elude the French, I have finally come here, my peregrinations having in the interim taken me to Mantua, Venice, and Rome. I live like so many in Italy of late, without the sure knowledge of what the next day will bring. . . . Two days ago a prodigious number of my fellow exiles came from Milan, to say that Il Moro has after great exertions to preserve his state and freedom finally been made captive by his enemies. . . . It is remarkable to reflect, my dear Benedetto, that this man who kept faith with no one was finally undone by the treachery of so many: his former allies Pope Alexander and the Signory of Venice, who conspired to divide his territories with the French; his castellan Bernardino da Corte, who so infamously surrendered the Castello to the invader, when it might have resisted for better than a year, so efficacious and ingenious were the bastions I had erected for its defense; and lastly the Swiss mercenaries whom he had employed for his protection, who sold him to his enemies for 30,000 ducats. Thus has Il Moro been deprived of his liberty, his state, and his fortune, and not one of his projects has been brought to completion. . . . Among the others who have suffered is the former Duchess Isabella, whose little son was taken captive by the French, to prevent him from making a claim to the throne of Milan. Il Moro's two sons have had better fortune, as they have received sanctuary from the German Emperor. . . . I say and believe that when Il Moro brought the French over the mountains, he created a breach through which the sea of Italy's woes now pours in endless and unceasing torrent. The lords of Italy endeavored to build an arrogant and grandiose edifice of their ambitions, but it could not last, for it aspired to the heavens on a foundation of lies. O earth! They should have left for their posterity a monument of true nobility and endurance if they had but sought less with more worthy means, for a small truth is always better than a great lie. . . .

Extract of a dispatch of BENEDETTO TREVISIANO, Venetian ambassador to France, to the SIGNORY OF VENICE. Lyons, 2 May 1500

Today, before two o'clock, Il Moro was brought into town accompanied by his guard. . . . He looked around him with no expression at all, as though he had determined to reveal none of his feelings despite the catastrophe Fortune had visited upon him. But he was very pale and appeared ill . . . and his arms and whole body were shaking. . . .

. . . he will be well guarded during the coming week, until the iron cage which will be his dwelling day and night is made ready. . . .

All men in high places should heed the miserable fate of this lord, whom many held to be the greatest man in the world. When Fortune sets you atop her wheel, she may at any moment bring you to the ground, and then the closer you have been to heaven, the greater and more sudden will be your fall. . . .

Loches, France, 17 May 1508

The Captain of Archers ducked his head beneath the roughly cut stone doorway. He entered a cell carved into the solid rock at the base of the Château of Loches; the only opening in the massive walls was a deep, narrow slot bored through the stone. The tiny window admitted enough light to reveal the features of the corpse. It lay on a small pallet set against the wall, the body covered with a linen shroud, the chalky face surrounded by long, almost translucently white hair. The dead man's humped nose was sharp, Caesar-like, the cheeks and eyes sunken and shadowed.

"Were you here when he died, *Père?*" the Captain asked the priest who stood by the body.

"Yes," the priest said. He seemed to regard the dead man with respect. "I gave him the Holy Sacraments."

"I doubt that will help him much, *Père.* They will dance in Hell tonight when Il Moro comes home. We have orders to take the body." The Captain looked around the cell. The gray rock walls were covered with painted Sforza emblems and scratched graffiti in Latin and Italian. He stepped beside the corpse and examined two lines of text painstakingly incised in the wall just above the bed, almost at eye level for someone lying on the small straw mattress. "What does it say, *Père?* Is it sorcery?"

The priest shook his head. The unlettered soldiers of France might consider Il Moro a devil, but the priest had found him gentle and charming, beyond a doubt the most learned man in Loches, perhaps the most learned man in France. The priest had come to this cell as often as he could, to read from Il Moro's one book, the *Divina Commedia,* and discuss its complex meanings.

"Those are the words of Dante," the priest explained. "An Italian poet. From his great epic. 'No sorrow is greater in this eternal woe than to remember in pain our moment of happiness.' "

The Captain rubbed his stubbled chin. "*Père,* you saw him die. Did he summon devils to take him to his father, Satan?"

"He called only one name at the end." The priest looked down and smiled wistfully at Il Moro's pale death mask. "The name of the woman who showed his poet the way to God: Beatrice."

$E\ P\ I\ L\ O\ G\ U\ E$

Bari, 9 February 1524

The two girls were about twelve years old; both had the heavy eyebrows and dark coloring of southern Italy, which gave a subtle sensuality to fresh adolescent features. They were the daughters of widowed serving women in the Duchess of Bari's household, and their faces had yet to be molded by an inevitable fate. But their mothers would be unable to provide them dowries, and so their choices were sadly limited: to be rudely used in marriage to some impoverished peasant who would take them for free, to be rudely used in some rough convent that would waive the dowry usually required by Christ (about a fifth of that demanded by a more corporeal husband), or to be rudely used as cheap prostitutes. In less than fifteen years they would be old women.

Both girls wore freshly washed linen smocks. There was something irrepressibly hopeful in their guileless carriage: the stiff, dignified backs, the fidgety, excited movements of their slender arms. The Duchess of Bari's lady-in-waiting smoothed back the taller girl's long dark hair, then stood back and appraised the pair.

"Well, that is as good as we are going to get," the lady said matter-of-factly, without spite or condescension. "Now, you both know how to curtsy to the Duchess. You don't have to say anything unless the Duchess asks you a question. And you must be very quiet and listen to the Duchess very carefully. The Duchess is not in good health, and we mustn't tax her strength. Very well, now, I'm sending you in."

The page opened the double doors to the Duchess of Bari's rooms, and the lady-in-waiting shooed the girls in with gentle pats on the shoulders. When the doors had been closed again, the lady turned to the Duchess's elderly chamberlain. "Messer Dionigi," she said, "I would have more hope for our Duchess's recovery if she would call for a physician instead of her servants' children."

Messer Dionigi smiled, his eyes squinting amid the surrounding wrinkles and folds. "The Duchess has always had an aversion to physicians."

The girls entered the Duchess of Bari's bedchamber, their eyes wide with wonder. They had never seen such a bed, a massive, canopied structure with bronze finials and embroidered crimson drapes and a gold-and-white satin bedspread. The Duchess was much less impressive, a gaunt-looking, gray-haired woman propped up by big tasseled velvet pillows. A down coverlet had been pulled up to her chin.

The girls came shyly to the end of the bed and made deep, touchingly awkward curtsies.

"You girls come over here." The Duchess's voice was a hoarse whisper, but with an underlying forcefulness. "I'm tired of all the *vecchie* who are in here all day and night. I want to see some girls with life ahead of them before I die. *Al nome d'Iddio*, don't look at me pop-eyed like that. The worms aren't going to eat me while you're standing there. I'll die when I've settled my affairs. By then I'll be good and ready. *Gesù*, I've had enough of life. What I haven't lived to see! Do you girls know who I am?"

The girls shifted uncomfortably. "You're the Duchess of Bari, Your Highness," the taller girl tentatively ventured.

"Come over here and I will tell you."

The girls filed to the side of the Duchess's bed.

"I wasn't always the Duchess of Bari. I became Duchess of Bari because a man named Il Moro left me Bari in his will. But once I was the Duchess of Milan. Back when I was a girl, that was better than being the Queen of France. There's never been anything like Milan when I was the Duchess. 'Paradise on earth,' all the travelers said. And it was. Before the French destroyed everything. Yes, there was a time when no foreign army would dare cross the mountains into Italy. Now the Frenchmen come every three or four years. And if they don't start a war, the Venetians or the Germans or His Holiness will."

The Duchess looked at the girls. They were respectfully attentive, but these abstract events had no resonance for them. "We're fortunate to be down here in Bari, away from everything," she told them. "Away from the fighting. Until you've seen a war, you imagine that it is very romantic and heroic. Like a joust. But in a war people you love die. My husband died. My father and brother died." She shook her head slightly. "I had a son. He wasn't ten years old when the French took him away from me. Back to France. He died there. He fell from his horse while he was hunting." She closed her eyes. Her voice was almost inaudible. "I hadn't seen him in twelve years."

The Duchess looked up. Her jade-green eyes were vivid against her pale face. "I had two daughters. My baby died when she was still a little girl. Fever." The Duchess paused, and her eyes shadowed with pain. "My daughter Bona is married to the King of Poland. That's a considerable distance from here. She's been gone six years.

"So now you know who I am. I am a lonely old woman who talks too much about people who are far away or no longer alive. But then that is my prerogative as a *vecchia*. It is also my privilege to ask young ladies like yourselves to grant me a last favor. Can I ask you to do that?"

The girls nodded gravely.

"Here is my problem. I have a not inconsiderable amount of property and little family to leave it to. I'm not going to send everything to my daughter in Poland, because between here and there I would just be giving it to mercenaries or bandits. That's the kind of world it is now. You can't even trust the Florentine banks. But if I leave my money here, as sure as the two of you are standing there, the priests will find a way to get it. So I require girls like you to help me save my money from the priests."

The girls nodded gravely again.

The Duchess looked off into the garden courtyard visible

through the narrow, Gothic-arched window. The colors of the tropical foliage, set aflame by the southern sun, seemed too intense for any earthly garden. She looked back at the girls. "I'm going to establish dowries for each of you, so you can have decent husbands."

Two pairs of eyes popped wide, and two jaws dropped.

"Don't think you won't have an obligation to me," the Duchess fairly barked. "You will have to choose wisely. If I learn that one of you has married some *ribaldo* who spends all your money on *meretrice* or some *pappatore* who loses all of it playing cards, I will come screaming out of my grave. Do you understand?"

"May we thank you, Your Highness?" the taller girl asked.

"When I am finished explaining your obligation. There's something else I expect you to do for me. I assume your marriages will be blessed with children. And I hope that each of you will have at least one girl. In addition to all your sons, of course. So what each of you must do is give your first girl the name I tell you." The Duchess nodded to the shorter girl. "Now, you. What is your name?"

"Giovanna, Your Highness."

"Giovanna. You must name your girl Beatrice. That is a very special name. Beatrice was Dante's love. It is also the name of my cousin and my *amica*, who died many years ago. She was once the Duchess of Bari, just as I am now, and she was also once the Duchess of Milan, just as I was. A very strange coincidence, isn't it? As if Fortune made us mirrors of one another." The Duchess's gaze turned inward. "We looked into those mirrors and saw the best of ourselves, and the worst. Mirrors of truth. I suppose Beatrice taught me that we could see the people we love in that unforgiving glass and still love them. And still forgive them." The Duchess waved her hand and refocused her attention on Giovanna. "Anyway, Beatrice is a very fine name, and your daughter will be proud to have it."

The Duchess nodded to the other girl.

"Leonora, Your Highness."

"Leonora." The Duchess paused and seemed to have trouble swallowing. Impulsively, Leonora stepped forward and took the Duchess's hand.

"Leonora. You must name your girl Ippolita." The Duchess

sat up and looked into the garden, no longer seeing the sunny colors, looking at something much farther away. For a moment she seemed infinitely weary. When she finally spoke, her voice was hoarser and very low. "Ippolita was a sad, gentle woman who . . . suffered a great deal. But she tried as best she could . . . to love. And to be loved." The Duchess blinked at her tears and pressed Leonora's hand tightly. "Ippolita," she whispered. Then she lay back and closed her eyes, and all the weariness left her face. "Ippolita was my mother's name."

A F T E R W O R D

When the French came over the Alps in the last decade of the fifteenth century, they also crossed a great divide on the landscape of history. Although sixteenth-century Italy enjoyed a final cultural florescence, the political power of the Italian city-states declined catastrophically following the French invasions, and for the next 350 years Italy lay at the mercy of a succession of transalpine invaders. France, rebuilt on the plunder of Italy, became the dominant power on the European continent for more than four centuries, as well as the principal check on the New World ambitions of Spain and England. As late as the eve of World War II, the French army remained the most vaunted military force in the world; the huge guns of the Maginot line, so swiftly outflanked by German tanks in May 1940, completed the circle of destiny begun by French cannons in 1494. The French cultural legacy, founded on the wholesale theft of Italian art, architecture, and cuisine, has proved even more enduring than the French tradition of conquest.

Isabella of Aragon died at Bari on February 11, 1524. Galeazzo di Sanseverino became the *Grand Écuyer* of France and was killed in battle in 1525 while shielding the French King with his own body. Leonardo da Vinci, who spent the last years of his life working for King Francis I of France, is today the most universally recognized Renaissance man. Beatrice's sister, Isabella d'Este, the Marquesa of Mantua, who lived to age sixty-four and saw her eldest son crowned Duke of Mantua by the Holy Roman Emperor, has entered history as the *prima donna* of the Renaissance, the patron of Michelangelo, Raphael, and Leonardo. Perhaps if Beatrice d'Este had lived even half as long as her sister, she might have given Fortune's wheel another spin, and today's world might be a very different place. But perhaps Beatrice's favorite poet, Dante, settled all such arguments when he warned that Fortune's purpose is always hidden, and no mortal hand can stay her eternal cycle of change.

GLOSSARY

Al nome d'Iddio In the name of God!

al'nuovo New; original; "the latest."

all'antica Literally, "in the style of the ancients"—i.e., the Greeks and Romans. The rebirth of classical civilization gave the Renaissance its name, so anything from architecture to typefaces done in the *all'antica* style was considered, paradoxically, the height of fifteenth-century modernity.

alla Turca In the Turkish style. Despite constant threats by Christian sovereigns to wrest Constantinople from the Turks (who had conquered the city in 1453) and subjugate the vast Ottoman Empire, Turkish-style masked balls and decorative motifs were as popular with the fashionably well-to-do in Renaissance Italy as *chinoiserie* was in France and England in the late eighteenth century.

allucciolati Loops of gold or silver thread woven into velvet to produce a rich sparkling effect.

amante Lover; mistress.

amatissima Beloved; dearest.

amica/amico Girlfriend/boyfriend.

amore Love; my love.

anima Soul. *Anima mia,* "my soul," was a profound endearment.

appicciolato A striped or floral-patterned silk damask.

bassa danza A slow, ceremonious dance popular in courts throughout Europe. Performed by a large circle of couples, often revolving around a group of musicians.

belle donne Lovely ladies.

bellezza Beauty.

bellissima Exquisitely beautiful.

bello Handsome.

braccio (pl. braccia) Arm-span or arm's length. The most commonly used Renaissance-era yardstick, measuring about 24 inches.

bravo (pl. bravi) A professional or semiprofessional thug, usually in the employ of a more respectable citizen.

buffone Court jester; clown.

buttino A game played with tarot cards.

cacapensieri Shit-head; shit-for-brains.

cacarella A noisemaker fashioned from a piece of hide stretched over the mouth of a pot. A string was drawn through a small hole in the leather to produce a crude droning hum.

cacasangue Holy shit!

cacastecchi Shit-ass.

camora Originally a simple, tight-fitting dress worn directly over a chemise by women of all classes, by the late fifteenth century the *camora* had become a sumptuous, daringly formal gown that revealed ample expanses of the shoulders and breasts.

cantione alla piffarescha A song written for *piffari*, large, oboe-like woodwinds.

Cara esposa My dear wife.

carissima My dearest.

carrozza Carriage. In an age when even the wealthiest citizens often traveled on muleback, the carriage—particularly the relatively spacious and stable four-wheeled variety—represented the ultimate in luxury transport. Visitors to Milan frequently commented on the astonishing number of carriages rumbling through the city's streets.

castello Castle or fortified palace.

cazzo Penis; prick.

che chiacchiera What nonsense; what horseshit.

chiaroscuro Light and shade. By using *chiaroscuro* to shade and highlight the human figure and other solid forms, Renaissance painters were able to produce startlingly realistic illusions of three-dimensionality, a revolutionary contrast to the flat, two-dimensional shapes characteristic of medieval painting.

cioppa A rich overgown or coat with long, full sleeves, often lined with fur.

cognoscenti "Those who know." The most sophisticated taste-makers and connoisseurs.

condottiere Mercenary commander. Mercenaries fought Italy's wars, and command of a mercenary army offered considerable social mobility; in two generations, the Sforza, whose family name signified their military successes, went from shoemaking to a ducal dynasty.

confetti Spun sugar figurines similar to modern cake decorations, but done with extraordinary complexity and artistry.

copiosità Abundance. In reference to a work of art, this term expressed admiration for the richness of invention.

d'arriere (French) From the rear, from behind.

dolcezza Sweetness. With an implication of shallowness, lack of sophistication or grandeur.

en masque (French) In disguise.

étalage (French) Display; show.

fanciullo/a Little boy/girl. Affectionate.

favola (pl. favole) Tall tale; whopper.

festa (pl. feste) General term for any elaborately staged celebratory party, banquet, or entertainment.

figlia Daughter.

fioretta In dance, a pirouette in which the steps trace the shape of a flower.

forestiera Stranger; foreigner. Often a pejorative, suggesting untrustworthiness or a disreputable character. In fifteenth-century Italy, a *forestiera* would usually be from another Italian state, not a visitor from across the mountains (*oltramontano*—see entry below).

frottola A short, lively secular song.

Gesù Jesus.

grandezza Grandeur. In reference to a work of art, this term would suggest high-minded themes—mythological or religious—presented with lavish formality.

grazia Grace; gracefulness.

grossa Fat; obese.

guardaroba A large, room-size closet, often furnished with credenzas and armoires and used for both the storage and display of expensive clothing, jewelry, and other luxury items.

impicatto (pl. impicatti) Literally, hanged man. In the fifteenth century, hanging was reserved for common criminals or unusually despicable traitors (beheading was the most dignified form of execution), making *impicatto* a particularly biting insult.

intarsia A mosaic created with different types of wood veneers.

intermedo An entertainment provided between the acts of a play. Often more elaborately staged than the play—with singing, dancing, and instrumental music—*intermedi* were integrated with drama in the early 1600s, creating the first operas.

invenzione Literally, invention; fabrication. An important concept in the Renaissance, which was characterized by striving for the new and original. Artists of all types were constantly challenged by their patrons to come up with distinctive *invenzione*, ranging from a new decorative pattern for a dress to a visionary plan for an entire city. This passion for the new was a profound departure from the medieval penchant for the tried-and-true.

leggiadria Charm.

livre (French) A gold coin, the basic medium of exchange in France. Roughly equivalent to the Italian ducat.

maestro Master. Often used as a formal, respectful address for the most accomplished craftsmen and artists.

majolica (English; Italian **maiolica**) Fired earthenware elaborately decorated with opaque glazes, often in detail approaching that of a painting.

meretrice Prostitute.

Monseigneur (French) The form of address for a high-ranking nobleman.

Montjoie! (French) The traditional French battle cry. Derived from the medieval custom of erecting a cairn—a "mound of joy"—at the site of a victory.

moresca A fast-paced, whirling, Moorish-style dance.

niente Nothing; "zip."

Nobilomo Nobleman. This utilitarian term was the only formal title or address used by Venetian nobility, who prided themselves on the egalitarianism—at least among their own class—fostered by Venice's republican form of government.

Nonno Grandfather (affectionate).

Nostro Signore Dear Lord!

nove foze The new styles; the new things (also *cose nuove*); the latest *invenzione* (see entry above).

oltramontani People from "over the mountains"—i.e., the other side of the Alps. Strongly pejorative; the Germans and French were considered impoverished, uncultured, and ill-mannered.

palazzo A large house or mansion. The ruling family of an Italian state usually lived in a fortified *castello*, while lesser nobility and wealthy commoners occupied *palazzi* (except in Venice, where the Doge lived in his *Palazzo* and the canalside homes of the nobility were designated as *Ca*).

palio A festive horse race run through the streets of a town. In Renaissance times the most famous *palio* took place in Ferrara on Saint George's Day in April. Today a semiannual *palio* still draws thousands of visitors to Siena.

palla A unisex court game played with a ball and bat. The object may have been to drive the ball through a ring.

pappatore Guzzler; "tit-sucker." A man who lives off his woman.

Per cap de Dieu (French) By God's robe!

Per mia fe By my faith.

procuratore (pl. procuratori) An "agent" employed by wealthy patrons to seek out and acquire art, books, musical instruments, and luxury items.

puttana Whore, slut.

putto (pl. putti) Little boy. In art and architecture, the cherubs often used as ornamental flourishes or structural devices.

puttino Baby boy.

regola Rule; order. Used in art criticism, this term signified the quality of precise measurement and proportion, valued by Renaissance thinkers in their search for scientific principles and the underlying order of things.

ribaldo Rascal.

riccio sopra riccio A velvet in which loops of gold woven into the plush silk pile are longer than the pile, giving an exceptionally rich effect.

scartino A game played with tarot cards. A favorite with gamblers.

sciocca Idiot.

Serenissima Repubblica Venice, "the Most Serene Republic." By habitually referring to their state with this elegant formal title, the Venetians emphasized that the republic itself was supreme, not the men who temporarily governed it. In marked contrast to the rest of Italy, where the state was subject to the whim of its individual overlord.

sforza Strength; force.

sgraffito Pottery with incised decoration.

Signor mio caro My dear Lord.

simmetria Not necessarily strict symmetry, but the quality of all the parts of a building or painting relating very clearly to one another, presenting an easily distinguishable pattern. The value placed on *simmetria* reflected the Renaissance desire to clarify, order, and reshape the world.

sorella Sister.

stringhe Narrow decorative ribbons attached to the sleeves or bodice of a dress.

stupendissimo Truly remarkable; astonishing.

Tenez! (French) Look here! The announcement traditionally made at the moment a tennis ball was put into play—hence the origin of the term "tennis."

turca A loose-fitting dressing gown.

uccelliaccia Idiot; birdbrain.

unica Only; unique; only one. Given the Renaissance emphasis on individuality, the designation *unica* was highly flattering.

vecchia/o Old woman/man. Rarely used respectfully, and often a mild pejorative. The Renaissance was a rapidly evolving youth culture, and the elderly too often represented outmoded ideas and repressive, old-fashioned morality.

velluto controtagliato A velvet with the pattern created by shaving the silk pile.

vestito A long, very formal tunic or overgown.

vivacità Liveliness.

The Ruling Houses of ITALY & FRANCE in 1491

FERRARA
The House of ◆ Este ◆

FRANCE
The House of ◆ Valois ◆

Azzo VI d'Este
MARQUIS OF FERRARA
FIRST ESTE RULER OF FERRARA
(1170–1212)

Louis XI
(B.1423)
KING OF FRANCE
(1461–1483)
m.
Charlotte of Savoy [1]
(B.1440–D.1483)

Ercole I
(B.1431)
DUKE OF FERRARA
(1471–)
m.
Eleonora of Aragon
(1473)

Anne de Beaujeu
(B.1461)
REGENT FOR THE
KING OF FRANCE
(1483–)
m.
Pierre de Beaujeu

Charles VIII
(B.1470)
KING OF
FRANCE
(1483–)

Isabella d'Este
(B.1474)
MARQUESA
OF MANTUA
m.
Francesco Gonzaga
MARQUIS OF MANTUA
CAPTAIN GENERAL OF
THE ARMIES OF VENICE
(1489)

Beatrice d'Este
(B.1475)
DUCHESS
OF BARI
m.
Lodovico Sforza
DUKE
OF BARI
(1491)

Alfonso d'Este
(B.1476)

Ferrante d'Este
(B.1477)

Ippolito d'Este
(B.1479)

Sigismondo d'Este
(B.1480)

---

1. Charlotte of Savoy was the sister of Bona of Savoy,
mother of the Duke of Milan; hence the Duke of Milan
and the King of France were first cousins.